April 6, 2010

A Pennsylvania Trilogy

To Nancy,
We trust you will enjoy reading the book as much as John & I enjoyed working on it together.
God blessings in your life and in your work.
John M. Eddinger (in spirit)
Carol Eddinger

A PENNSYLVANIA TRILOGY

BOOK ONE
ABE'S QUEST

BOOK TWO
ABE'S RETURN

BOOK THREE
NEW VENTURES

John M. Eddinger

iUniverse, Inc.
New York Lincoln Shanghai

A Pennsylvania Trilogy
BOOK ONE ABE'S QUEST BOOK TWO ABE'S RETURN BOOK THREE NEW VENTURES

iUniverse books may be ordered through booksellers or by contacting:

iUniverse
2021 Pine Lake Road, Suite 100
Lincoln, NE 68512
www.iuniverse.com
1-800-Authors (1-800-288-4677)

Because of the dynamic nature of the Internet, any Web addresses or links contained in this book may have changed since publication and may no longer be valid.

This is a work of fiction. All of the characters, names, incidents, organizations, and dialogue in this novel are either the products of the author's imagination or are used fictitiously.

ISBN: 978-0-595-45668-0 (pbk)
ISBN: 978-0-595-69627-7 (cloth)
ISBN: 978-0-595-89970-8 (ebk)

Printed in the United States of America

To my beloved wife Carol,
with whom all things are possible.

Acknowledgements

I owe my gratitude to a number of people. To my wife Carol who has shared equally in this entire effort. To the kindness, efforts and guidance from Rachel and Dr. Carl Spease, Claude and Louise Swartzbaugh and Sheldon K. Hoover. To the Brownstone Masonic Lodge, Hershey and the Harrisburg Consistory, Ancient Accepted Scottish Rite for their education and dedication to the principles of Freemasonry.

ABE'S QUEST

CHAPTER 1

▼

ARRIVAL

Abraham John Carlson was born in a ramshackle cabin on the outskirts of the Fort Mojave Indian Reservation, straddling the Colorado River in western Arizona. He lay in his mother's loving arms for just a little over an hour before she passed away—the rigors of childbirth had claimed another. His father, the Right Reverend Johann Carlson, reared him; as a circuit preacher, he would ride his black horse across the Reservation, wild-eyed son tucked behind, and soiled Geneva bands extending from his collar, to extol the Calvinist message. Abraham came right out of the Old Testament; John for John Calvin and the message was of a stern God. The Reverend went to be with the Lord when the boy was barely ten years old and thenceforth he was known simply as Abe.

There was something a little odd, perhaps a touch of eccentricity, about the mid-sized, graying man as he stepped out of his 1973 Jeep Commando in the rear parking lot of the Warwick Hotel, known to locals as simply The Wick, in Hummelstown, Pennsylvania; signs up and down the street proudly announced the town's establishment in 1762. Perhaps it was the vehicle itself, still in good, but not pristine condition, with the only amenities being an AM radio and a cigarette lighter, which no longer worked, but still plugged a hole in the dashboard. People did not see many of these big older workhorses these days, having survived hundreds of thousands of miles on the odometer. That was a matter for history in this case because somewhere in the 1990s, on its fourth complete turnover, the odometer simply died and refused repair. The man's Stetson, boots, slightly bowed legs, plus the Arizona license plates revealed at a glance his probable origins. The boots were not the pointed toes, higher heeled riding variety, but the squared toes, lower heeled walking sort. The weathered face and premature wrinkles belied his age, but served as confirmation. He had the look of someone in his late sixties, when in reality he had just turned fifty-one. Every farmer knew the look of a man, who spent years working hard in the out-of-doors, spare framed and taut muscled. As usual, he was traveling light—just a medium sized duffle and a laptop computer. The crunch of the gravel as he strode across the parking lot in the bright July sunshine was the only herald of the arrival of Abe Carlson, tracker, hunting guide, part-time ranch hand, some-time placer miner and occasional world traveler to Central Pennsylvania.

It promised to be a hot day, which he didn't mind, but he knew the humidity was going to take some getting used to. Like many reared in the dry southwest climate, he habitually wore long sleeved shirts and a wide brimmed hat year-round to prevent developing those unsightly little skin cancers which, if gone unchecked, could lead to a rather ugly and painful demise. He made a mental note to pick up a couple of new shirts more suited to this humid climate. Ninety-five degrees Fahrenheit was one thing in Arizona, but quite another in Pennsylvania.

As Carlson gazed up at the side of the three-story building from the alley, he was glad he had done his homework. No records seemed to exist for exactly when it was built, but in 1800 it was known as the Cross Keys Hotel, a regular carriage stop on the turnpike running between Philadelphia and Harrisburg. The name changed quite often as ownership passed to different hands over the years—one owner was the town's last Civil War veteran, another a major league pitcher for three different teams over his career, and yet another the son of a great hockey player for the local Hershey team. Its current incarnation was due to Warwick M. Siler, who seemed rather fond of his own first name and dubbed the establishment The New Warwick, though rumor had it that he probably had a sense of humor and wanted to distinguish his modest hotel from the more famous Warwick Hotels in Philadelphia and New York.

Following several people entering The Wick by a side door up a short flight of concrete steps, and removing his hat automatically as he passed through the entry, Carlson found himself, as expected, entering a large dark room with a "U" shaped bar wedded with a cherry bar backed by three French bevel plate mirrors, circa 1895. The people in front of him veered left toward the dining rooms which appeared to take up the entire first floor, along with the bar area and what looked like the kitchen tucked behind. He saw only three patrons on barstools, locals having a late lunch and a beer while watching CNN news, with its crawl across the bottom of the screen, on a television mounted near the ceiling. He took the first stool he came to and placed his hat, brim-up, on the empty place beside him.

"What can I get you?" asked the young woman bartender in a hometown friendly voice. As she whisked a napkin and menu in front of him in one fluid motion, he could tell she was experienced

"Just coffee, black, please," Carlson answered.

"Comin' up," she replied.

While waiting, he surveyed the room. There were two large dining rooms on his left and through the doorway to the second he could see a glassed-in porch further on. Wedged between the two dining areas lay a narrow door, with etched glass noting the name of the hotel in reverse letters, presumably leading to the front lobby.

"Excuse me," he asked the bartender when she returned with his coffee, "Is that the way to the Front Desk?" nodding toward that door.

"Afraid not," she said, spreading her fingers with both palms on the bar, "you're looking at the Front Desk right here." That sounded odd to Carlson, but he imagined that in a building this old, there might not be much of a lobby area and the halls would be long and narrow.

"I sent you an e-mail two days ago to book a room," he said in way of explanation. "I haven't received a reply."

"Oh, so you're the man," she answered. "We had a thunderstorm that knocked out our computer just after we received your request and it won't be back up until sometime tonight."

She then launched into a lengthy explanation about hotel policy. The first floor was dining and the bar area with kitchen. The second floor was reserved for office space and rooms used for local civic association meetings. Only the third floor accommodated guests. They had only six or eight guest rooms, depending on how you arranged things, with a shared bath and shower at either end of the main hall. Due to some problems with younger couples trashing their rooms in recent years, the owners had adopted a rather loose policy of simply renting the entire floor, such as it was, to families, for a week at a time.

The plumbing had been updated recently, but the furniture was vintage—a collection of pieces of differing age and style; beds of wood, brass or metal; wardrobes freestanding, some antique. Each room was named after various flowers, the names of which were painted on little ovals attached to its door.

"Sorry," he said when she had finished her explanation. "I hadn't realized you didn't take in singles. I shouldn't be in town for much more than a week and rather looked forward to staying in such a historic building."

"You might say we're now more of a bed and breakfast than a hotel," she refined the term. Central Pennsylvania was peppered with these and many more were opening up every month; they were mostly converted large Victorian homes or big farmhouses left on homestead plots after the usable acreage had been sold to other more successful farmers or to developers.

"Well, thank you anyway," he said, placing two dollars on the bar.

"You know, you don't look like you're too rowdy a man," she said with a smile and a glint in her eye. "Let me talk to the boss. That is, unless you have something against possible ghosts?"

"Where I've been in my life young lady," he replied with the hint of a smile turning up the edges of his mouth, "I've had the company of more ghosts, spirits and haunts than you probably have people in this town. And I have yet to meet one I couldn't get along with on a very personal basis. In fact, some of my longest and deepest discussions have been with just such entities."

She surveyed the room to find the three men at the bar had left. Reaching under the counter, she brought out a coffee urn and refilled Carlson's cup.

"Refills are on the house," she stated. "Make yourself comfortable and I'll be back in a few minutes."

As he waited her return, Carlson mused over some of the spirit experiences he encountered around the globe. There was the Lady In Blue of Arizona and Spain legend; the trio of long dead diamond miners in South Africa who had no idea they had died nearly one hundred years before; the Mad Monk and his brothers roaming the fields of Glastonbury, England; the Dancing Medicine Men in full regalia he watched through a long night in Montana; the line of emaciated children trudging up and down in the snow at Donner Pass in California; the Phantom Bell Ringer in a small village in Northern Italy; and the Lost British Regiment marching back and forth endlessly across the East Indian plain. These and many more were instances of his personal experience. And he had met many other people on this side of the veil who were willing to talk even more. For some humans, the contact between the two worlds—one we know as *real*, the other we *think* might be there—is a frequent event. How they handle the contact is another matter entirely.

"Good news," she said upon her return. "We have this one cubby hole of a room tucked up in a corner in the rafters. The ceiling slants at quite an angle and it was used for storage in the past. It's been turned into a small bedroom for children—they think it's a great adventure to have their own room while on vacation. It makes them more equal to the bigger kids in the family. That was the idea to begin with, at least. We all do a variety of chores around here and whenever I have to make up that room, I get the willies just putting the key in the door. And most of our guests won't use the room. The children don't seem to mind, but the adults have complained of a creepy feeling when passing the door in the middle of the night."

"I don't take up much room—slept on a shelf-of-a-bunk in an old freighter for a month once," he said. "Also, I don't get the willies very easily, or even a creepy feeling, and then it's just usually when I'm reading about the current state of political affairs."

This brought a bright smile in return. "I'll get the key and show you the room."

Carlson paid an inordinately modest fee for the room a week in advance and discovered the bartender-jack-of-all-trades was named Rachel, R.J. to her friends, and the way she pronounced it fell upon the ear for some odd reason very Victorian. When she addressed him as Mister Carlson, he asked to be called "Abe," more in keeping with casual family atmosphere the hotel exuded and the less formal Western manners.

The narrow hallway leading to the entrance, so restricted that two people passing in opposite directions had to turn sideways to get by, had small dark green and white tiled patterned floor reminiscent of a by-gone era. The steep, equally narrow flights of stairs twisted sharply at the landings. The Violet Room, as noted on the door medallion, was as midget-sized as described, not much more than a standard walk-in closet, only more cramped by the slant of the ceiling. It did have a large window in the short wall overlooking the roof of the sun porch dining area and the garden. Yet it served his purpose as a little-noted base of operations, with his primary focus on the town of Hershey a couple of miles away. He could well have afforded more plush accommodations at the Hershey Lodge or any national chain, of which there were many, but The Wick more suited his unobtrusive style.

Having stashed his duffle and laptop in his room, Carlson spent the remainder of the afternoon and into early evening by exploring Main Street around the town square. His first stop was across the street from the hotel, Rhoads Pharmacy and Gift Shop. The title was an understatement. It did contain a full-sized pharmacy/drug store in the rear of this large building, but more impressive was the larger front section, presenting collectibles galore—even a broad room full of themed villages, a circus, an amusement park or two and a railroad here and there. Walking along the street he saw churches, restaurants and a variety of small businesses. On one corner of the square was the Buse Funeral Home, with Bowser's Furniture beside. Another corner held Jo-Jo's Pizza, with a Chinese eatery along side. A third corner was an art gallery and the fourth The Main-Frame Professional Services.

One of his last stops was a rather highly titled Hummelstown News Agency—in reality a modest newsstand vending newspapers, a wall of magazines, snacks and sodas, plus a small range of tobacco products. As was his habit, he picked up a *New York Times* and assorted local papers from the East Indian proprietor and retired to a sidewalk bench to scan the news important to Central Pennsylvanians.

His last stop was two doors down, Bill Maloney Men's Shop, to buy a half-dozen shirts and a Virginia Gentleman's hat more in keeping with the east coast. The only western style hat he had seen in town was of straw on an older Latino sitting on a bench awaiting the bus. The one item of apparel he strongly refused to change was his boots. They were as comfortable as slippers and he had always walked much more than he had ridden a horse.

Toward dusk, Carlson returned to The Wick, had a light meal at the bar and headed for his room. The family that rented the rest of the floor looked sufficiently tired as they trudged up the stairs before him. By the balloons the children carried and the messages on their shirts, Carlson surmised that it had been one long day at Hershey Amusement Park. He merely nodded a greeting to the adults as he entered his room and closed the door.

As the light began to fade and the room shrouded in shadow, Abe Carlson sat on the side of his bed and pondered his reasons for coming here, or rather, as he began to think of it, his quest. As the Right Reverend, which is how his son always thought of his father—the only person to continually refer to him with the full "Abraham" and a man he dearly loved—was thrown from his horse one dark night and cleanly broke his neck, young Abe bolted out of a deep sleep, bathed in sweat. He knew the instant the accident occurred, even though it was over fifteen miles away. But then, he always felt he remembered being cradled in his mother's arms for her last hour on earth, feeling her pure unconditional love through to her last breath, even though his father, who had delivered him, had never mentioned it.

With no known relatives, the ten year old had been taken in and cared for by the childless Johnson family. The Johnsons had also gathered together his father's few possessions, mostly books and papers, which they put away for safe-keeping.

On his eighteenth birthday, Abe was presented with his legacy. They had never been read out of respect for the fallen Reverend.

Eight years later Carlson was working on a ranch in Montana. One freezing winter's night, sitting by the potbellied stove in the bunkhouse to keep the howling blizzard at bay, he picked up one of his father's older and more tattered Bibles and discovered a letter on thin onionskin paper tucked between two pages in Revelations.

The stationery was from the Bindnagle Evangelical Lutheran Church, Palmyra, Pennsylvania, addressed to his father in Arizona and dated June 12, 1933. At first all he could decipher was the writer's signature, Rev. L. W. Kleinfelter. The rest was in German, and by the calligraphy-style lettering he suspected it was what some had referred to as High or Old German. It was not until the spring thaw that he was able to purchase a German-to-English Dictionary that began a yearlong effort at translation. Some of the words used were so ancient that they are not found in modern translation.

The story as it emerged became confusing, complicated and complex by turns. Apparently, his father had a brother, or more correctly a half-brother named Sheldon C. Slate, an occasional attendant at the Bindnagle Church. Abe's uncle, or half-uncle if there were such a thing—Abe did not know—was also a member of the Masonic Temple, Brownstone Lodge in Hershey. What happened to this uncle was unclear, but he had "committed a Morgan," or "done like Morgan," the translation was not clear, and had disappeared.

Carlson kept the letter and the books safely secured for years as he traveled around the world. He had never considered that he may have any living relatives, but like many after they turn fifty, and in an age of renewed interest in genealogy, he wanted answers to two questions: What happened to Slate and were there any other Slates in his line still living in Pennsylvania? Much to his surprise, he found a sudden yearning for cousins. His father had never mentioned his east coast roots to most people, but had told the son of growing up on a farm and had taught him how to plant a vegetable garden, as much as one could in the arid climate. Most of all, he wanted to discover whatever traces of family history which may remain in the mountains and valleys of this sprawling state. The western states had broad vistas, but these were mostly flat, seemingly empty acres—that was until the settlers encountered the mighty wall of the Rockies. Pennsylvania held its own vistas, but there were so many convolutions to the topography, you most often had to climb to a higher elevation to get a better lay of the land. He had been used to long stretches of straight highway, but here every road went up and down and wound around, with the only straight stretches occurring in the valley floors.

CHAPTER 2

▼

THE LETTER

An early riser from habit, Carlson was washed and clean-shaven as he stepped onto the sidewalk in front of The Wick to see the first glimmers of sun just under the horizon, giving the nearly empty street a quiet peacefulness as the residents began to stir for their daily labors. As he sat on a bench to take in the ambiance of this setting—as he did most mornings of his life—he thought of the countless risings in a wide range of cultures he had observed over the years and the common characteristics of slow moving humanity to close the gap between deep slumber and wakefulness. For town dwellers stirring with the rising sun, unlike farmers tending livestock in the wee hours of darkness, this usually entailed a stretch, a yawn, perhaps a scratch or two as he watched people emerging gingerly from their houses. Many were small business people heading to open their shops to prepare for the day's customers. Others were going to jobs near and far, whatever their employment might be. The normality lent its own comfort by its gift of implied stability.

An elderly man in a short-sleeved white cotton shirt, surprisingly bright red Bermuda shorts, over the calf white socks and blue running shoes, and a tall-crested, wide-brimmed straw hat, ambled on his cane over to the bench and took a seat. By the look of his color scheme, Carlson thought the man probably wanted to carry the July Fourth patriotic theme through the end of the month.

"Morning," the man said, tipping his hat and reaching for a handshake from Carlson. "You new in town or just one of our beloved tourists here to soak up the great Pennsylvania Dutch culture, support the local economy and return home with tales of our quaintness and cleanliness?"

Carlson had noted the man's firm grip and keen eyes through his wire-rimmed glasses and shocks of pure white hair flowing over his ears. "Abe Carlson," he introduced himself, letting his hand drop. "I'm not exactly a tourist, just looking for some possible roots."

"Isaac Porr," the man replied. "So you're one of those genealogy buffs. We've had our share of folks looking for their ancestors in the last twenty years or so. This area was rightly settled in the 1700s, before the Revolutionary War, and plenty of people since that time have availed themselves the opportunity to seek their fortunes hither and yon."

"That's about it, in a way," Carlson said. "I take it that you have local roots?"

"Tenth generation born and bred," he replied. "I've retired to the family farm a few miles east, but owned a fix-it shop here in town for forty-five years. It wasn't much of a business in its last years—planned obsolescence, I suppose, or not being able to get spare parts, or even the fact that it didn't pay to get things fixed. It was cheaper to just buy a new toaster, iron or what-have-you. Anyway, it was a good living for Apolonia, my dear wife, and me. We live comfortably on the family farm, but sometimes I get the itch to come in to town and watch it awaken as I used to do. That may not seem like much excitement to city folks, but it's what serves around here. And Apolonia makes sure I get a good breakfast, two cups of coffee, farewell peck on the cheek and a kindly admonition to be home for lunch. I've always thought that woman understands and loves me more than I feel entitled to. But, I spoil her right back as best I can, so we come out about even."

"So the sidewalks are pretty much rolled up after dark?" Carlson asked.

"Well, not exactly," he corrected. "There are a few bars scattered around and restaurants that serve into the evening hours. Then there are the V.F.W and American Legion Halls, and some church activities on certain nights throughout the year, but mostly people just gather with neighbors on the front porch or in the parlor for libation and conversation. Of course, this being Central Pennsylvania, there is always plenty to eat at such gatherings. Everyone pitches in with a dish or two of favorite recipes, usually handed down through families, or borrowed from a friend. And it's not just the women. You'd be surprised at the number of men who compete with secret blends of spices for sausage, or venison, or even the proper ingredients and measures that make a shoo fly pie the legend it has become. Plus, say what you will about today's microbrewery products, home-made beer and ale from Old World German stills made on the farm or in the cellar are without peer."

The conversation strayed over a range of local issues, farming, seasonal variations, the Amish and Mennonite populations and even local and national politics. Carlson found Porr to be well informed, up-to-date and articulate. Finally talk turned to religion.

"What can you tell me about the Bindnagle Evangelical Lutheran Church over in Palmyra?" Carlson asked.

"Strange you should be asking me about that particular church," he replied with more than a bit of hesitation, which soon turned into a wry grin. "The Porrs have a history there."

"I trust I haven't treaded on an inappropriate subject," Carlson said apologetically.

"No, no, it's not exactly that," Porr said. "I haven't given much thought to that church in many years. You see, there was a family connection generations ago. Our parents wouldn't address the subject under any circumstances, but we younger cousins gossiped about it, trying to uncover the skeleton in the family closet—nearly every family has at least one, don't you think? Anyway, about twenty years ago, a man who had an ancestor who reneged on his original promise to financially support the building in 1803 or so, and as an act of apparent atonement, wrote a pamphlet on the history of the church and congregations over the years. In that pamphlet, the author mentioned that just before the Civil War, my ancestor, the Reverend W.S. Porr, Pastor for years 1859 and 1861, was for various reasons expelled from the Synod. This being a very old, German church, it has to the rear of the pulpit a painting of Christ and three mottoes: "*Bete und Arbeite*" (Pray and work), *Liebe deine Nachsten*" (Love your Neighbor) and "*Liebe Gott uber Alles*" (Love God Over All). Speculation among the various cousins led to the belief that Reverend Porr must have confused the last two mottoes. At least, it was a family scandal that brought much shame. We've been Methodists ever since. I remember my grandfather had a favorite saying about our religious affiliation, along the lines of 'we Porrs aren't big enough sinners to be Lutherans.'"

This pleasant talk eventually ended with Porr announcing his intent to stroll along Main Street to visit some friends and offering easy directions to the Bindnagle Church. Carlson already had a map firmly imprinted in his mind, but graciously accepted the proffered advice.

Carlson took a circuitous route to Palmyra, taking a leisurely drive through small towns, lush open fields covered in ripening crops, hills and dales of sylvan trees and watercourses big and small. He always enjoyed the abundant greenery found in the east. The arid southwest of his youth and the upper plains states had their own topographical features to admire, but the lower northeast farmland is rich and abundant with well managed and maintained fields, hardworking men and women whom he had always found friendly and helpful. It was refreshing to see acre upon acre of corn, soybeans, hay and a host of crops, broken by orchards, dairy farms, Amish and Mennonite communities and every small hamlet or cross-roads seemed to have a church of some denomination. This reminded him of parts of Nebraska, Kansas or Missouri, only packed more tightly together in between hills and mountains. In some ways, this seemed to be a distinct new cul-ture of old Europe. The midwest and northwest had been settled in large part by easterners traveling westward and devastating the Native American lands and population. Arizona, on the other hand, had been settled from the west coast, with a great influx from California, as the failed remnants of the Gold Rush sought their fortunes over the Sierra Nevada. Arizona did not become a state until 1912, several centuries after the east coast had established colonies.

Carlson had, for as far back as he could remember, a great appreciation for his upbringing, with never any regrets. In his younger years and throughout most of his life, he had gone to school, played with and learned from the Native Ameri-can tribes. Although mostly a self-contained quiet man, some interpreted this as stoicism, an indifference to pain or pleasure. These people misjudged what they thought was an impassive nature. In truth, he was particularly sensitive to pain and pleasure and his Indian friends and acquaintances showed him how to face pain, not try to bury it, and to enjoy the simplest pleasures without having to resort to extreme measures for gratification. More importantly, he was able to master the art of facing the world boldly and openly, accepting the vagaries of nature and civilization without judgment, gaining the knowledge to deal with life in all its wondrous facets, while recognizing the God in all things and all beings. He was never as sure as the Calvinism practiced by his father concerning the existence of good and evil—even the Reverend professed doubt at times—but he did take great comfort in many parts of the Bible, including the passage about God creating the world and when finished pronouncing that all He created was good.

"In my considered opinion," the Reverend had told him, "there are probably as many roads to God as there are people. The most important point is a belief in a Supreme Being, by whatever name you recognize, living life to the betterment of your fellow man, and a desire to be at one with Him in the end. You will dis-cover that most religions have some very clear form of 'do unto others,' will not be in conflict with many other basic tenants of our religion, and find it just as difficult as we do to get the idea across, much less put it into daily practice. Broadly speaking, very little tolerance has ever been practiced in this world as a whole, but there will always be those keeping the faith that it can be done."

Rounding one last curve on a two-lane road, Carlson pulled into the sloping parking lot nestled below the hilltop Bindnagle Evangelical Lutheran Church. Though still before noon, the heat and humidity had become oppressive and as he stepped from his Jeep, he noted the sweat sticking his shirt to the back of the seat, drops of moisture slowly absorbed into his loose collar. The morning newspaper had forecast temperatures approaching one hundred degrees and that prediction appeared correct. The vehicle had no air conditioning, or refrigeration as the old timers in Arizona had called it, and as long as you kept moving, the so-called two-forty-five system—two windows down, forty-five miles per hour—kept the air moving, which served just as well in a drier desert climate or in the higher elevations. High humidity was another matter all together.

Just standing on church property, surveying the setting, he could sense the solid strength that kept this congregation going for over two hundred years, like a steel core of rectitude even the Reverend would have admired. He also felt turmoil, the battering elements which could have torn it asunder, both physical and philosophical; yet, here it stood, weathered but proudly erect. The church itself was an impressive structure, two-storied rectangular brick, larger than anticipated, with the traditional steeple above the front entrance, sitting parallel to the parking lot and overlooking a field of vintage gravestones. Most churches he had encountered buried their dead to one side or to the rear, so this arrangement gave the impression of standing as sentinel over the remains of the many generations who had worshiped within its walls, now gone to meet their Maker. Another oddity was that in the side wall facing the parking lot was another doorway that looked as if it were the true, most-used entrance. Behind and to one side stood a more modern, one story building he assumed was a social gathering place with perhaps small office space. Not far to the right stood a modest two-story house with a separate garage, storage room above. On the grade beyond, he caught a glimpse through the trees of a fair-sized creek ambling through the countryside.

Just then a tall, lanky, but well muscled man in his mid-thirties appeared from around one corner of the house. He was dressed for the weather in cut-off shorts, tee shirt and sturdy work boots, as if he had been working the grounds. "Hello and welcome," the man called out. "Can I help you with anything or are you taking the tour of official designated buildings on the National Historic Register? As you can see by the plaque over there we have earned such designation."

"Abe Carlson," he replied, walking forward and shaking the man's hand. "I've come with a rather strange request. I'm looking for some information on a letter sent by the Pastor of this church in June, 1933."

"Tom Rogers," he introduced himself. "There are no strange requests here. You wouldn't believe some of the questions we've fielded just since I've been here. I'm the caretaker and Sexton. My day job is a construction supervisor, but we live here rent-free. There is quite a bit of upkeep on a place as old as this, but it's worth the effort and things sort of even out. My wife and I have college degrees, but decided our spiritual mission in life was to care for our church and wanted our children reared in the life of the church, as we were."

He paused and turned to look off in the distance as if trying to pry some information from the depths of his memory. "As for 1933," he said at last, "that's well before my recollection, but the old-time thrifty Lutherans kept everything, and I do mean everything. Perhaps we can root something out for you. Our congregation is small, just fifty or so families at the present time, but membership fluctuates. Besides, it seems that just when our finances are stretched pretty thin, one of the members passes on and leaves us a nice bequest. We do tend to want our religion straight up, with no foolishness, so many members want to preserve the old ways. Bequests are an avenue to that preservation. Would you like to see the church? We take great pride in showing people around."

"That would be much appreciated," Carlson said. It had begun to dawn on him why this very friendly part of the state stood out. In the west and southwest, people were apt to use few words to convey an idea or comment on a particular situation, passing only enough information to serve. Here, on the other hand, his experience with Isaac Porr and now Tom Rogers seemed to prove these people were not so much talkative as embroidering information, giving the context of the message, not just bare facts. And, although this could take some getting used to, he rather embraced the prospect.

As Rogers retrieved the key from the caretaker's residence, Carlson wandered around and, as expected, saw the Sexton move toward the side of the church, confirming his supposition of which door was used as the main entry.

The first thing Carlson noticed was the ancient door escutcheon, explained moments later by Rogers. "It's the original," he said. "The congregation dates back to 1775, but this building dates from 1803. This lock was selected for a Pennsylvania German Life exhibit at the Philadelphia Museum of Art a few year ago. John Rohrer from over in Lebanon made it and inscribed his name and the year on the back."

Stepping into the darker interior of the church, the tracker was immediately impressed by the seeming volume of open space, high stiff-backed, narrow-seated pews running along three walls, with a gallery above. The interior was designed in the form of a Greek cross, with an impressive wineglass pulpit towering from the far wall, accessed by a very narrow and steep staircase. The heat and humidity were nearly as stifling as the outside.

"The pew seats are very narrow and can't be that comfortable during an extended service," Carlson observed. "And I've never been in a church with such a variable paint scheme."

"As to the pews," Rogers explained, "we tend not to make things too comfortable; people might doze off and miss the message. Aside from which, we do so much standing for hymn-singing and sin-professing that it doesn't make much difference. And we like our sermons short and to the point. The paint you see has an interesting history, like everything else tied to this church has had since its inception."

As the sexton told the tale, it was, indeed, interesting as well as believable. For its first eighty-two years of existence the interior was painted plain, reposing in this quiet dignity. That was to change remarkably in 1885 at the hands of a young John Cardell, native of Sweden. As the tale unfolds, Cardell was walking his girl in their native Sweden when another young man approached, hurling abusive insults to the girl. A fight ensued and John so severely beat the young man that he died. He was a criminal fugitive when he arrived in America, trying to avoid punishment. Wandering through this part of Pennsylvania, he stopped at a farm, asking for food or employment. In exchange for food, he painted the farmer's kitchen, to the delight of the farmer's wife.

The church heard about this fine work and gave him the job of painting the interior. He commenced painting the walls and stand-alone Doric type columns in a style he had seen in his native country, Swedish marble. So *faux* Swedish marble made quite an impression on the congregation. The ceiling was painted with old-world style medallions in the center and four corners.

"And so it stands today," Rogers said. "The irony is that his fame spread quickly; however, on his very next job, he fell from a scaffold and died. We still say a prayer for him now and then, with the hope that perhaps his last finished labor of painting God's house got him some credit to balance his former misdeeds. We're all sinners, but we do beg the Father's forgiveness for our transgressions. There's a chance, perhaps, Cardell did too."

The sounding board above the wineglass pulpit featured a painting of Saint John the Evangelist. At each side of the top of the sounding board were painted flames of fire, symbolic of the Pentecostal tongues of fire. Behind the pulpit was the picture of Christ, as well as the three German quotes mentioned by Isaac Porr.

"We have two organs," Rogers explained as the two men strolled over toward one side. "The little one was purchased in 1883 from an organ factory in town. It carried a five-year warranty, bellows and all. We had it motorized in 1960. After more than one hundred and twenty years, it's still in use, but the warranty having expired still troubles some of more frugal members."

"Are those what I think they are, collection sacks?" asked Carlson, pointing to two long poles hanging from two of the interior columns.

"They certainly are," Rogers confirmed. "They are called *klingel-seck,* or bell-bags on eight foot poles to take up the offerings. Now, I can see you're sweating through your shirt. Come over to the social hall, where we have a small air conditioner, and I'll show you more of our treasures. We'll also see if we can scare up some information on that letter."

Inside the modest social hall, Rogers immediately went to a refrigerator, took out a pitcher of water and secured two glasses. "A little cooler in here, don't you think?" asked Rogers, filling both glasses and handing one to his visitor. "One of our few modern amenities."

"Have you thought of air conditioning in the church?" Carlson's replied.

"Certainly, on more than one occasion," Rogers answered, taking a mouthful of water, holding it there for a full thirty seconds before swallowing. "Summers we have only one very early service, due to the heat. We're a pretty hardheaded bunch of Germans here. The older folks don't want to see much change—'If it was good enough for my father and mother, it's good enough for me and that should be good enough for you too.' The only concession we've made in that direction was installing a couple of ceiling fans. Even at that, some people scrunch their faces when we turn them on.

"But, it has been that way forever. There is a chronicle going back to 1836, in the years when there were no services during the winter because of the cold, where some of the members prevailed upon the church to buy two cast iron coal stoves, though two elderly ladies were dead set against anything differing from their parents' time. The first Sunday after the stoves were purchased and installed, these ladies appeared with hand fans, vigorously fanning them during the entire service. At the close of the service, they swooped in on the Pastor, complaining how uncomfortable they were, couldn't stand it, wouldn't stand it, and something had to be done. After he allowed them to rant and rave until blue in the face, the Pastor abruptly ending the session by calmly remarking that 'Yes, well, ladies, there is no fire in the stoves this morning.' I think it's a human trait as we get older to resist change, maybe because we see the end coming near and if things change, it will hasten our demise."

Rogers led Carlson over to a massive safe standing against a wall in the corner that was several feet taller than he. As he rotated the combination, the Sexton remarked: "Big one, isn't it? Anyone wanting to steal this monster would have to tear down the building first, and then have a mighty large crane to even attempt moving it."

As the huge door swung outward, Carlson could see an added safety measure. The various shelves were fronted with sliding glass panels with additional locks, like you would see in a jeweler's display case. The shelves were stacked with very large, thick, vintage Bibles, beautifully bound and printed in elaborate High German. He noted an altar cloth initialed HBN under the date of 1754, which was the year of consecration of the first log church built on land donated by Hans Bindnagle, the forerunner of the larger current brick structure. He also spotted a rare communion set with a tankard bearing the date 1745. There were several stacks of square-looking, originally white, now browning papers.

"Those are continentals," Rogers said, following his gaze. "You know, as in 'it's not worth a continental.' During the Revolutionary War, the Continental Congress authorized the printing of a huge amount of those to pay the soldiers, but there was no money in the Treasury to back up those notes, so they were worthless."

"Interesting," Carlson said in response. "I've read about them in history books, but I've never actually seen one. I have seen a few authentic Confederate bills from the Civil War, but at least they were backed by cotton futures or something like that."

"Not only that," Rogers said, "but we have eighteen more Revolutionary War veterans, some even heroes, planted out front in the cemetery. One hero, John Palm, was the founder of Palmyra and served as a surgeon in the Continental Army. We also have a memorial out there to his three wives. He outlived two, but met his demise about a decade before the third."

As Rogers closed the safe and walked over to a bank of filing cabinets, Carlson mentioned the pamphlet Isaac Porr had spoken of and told him about the reason his cousins thought their ancestor might have been fired.

"Oh, I'll send you home with a couple of copies," Rogers said, scanning the files with nimble fingers. "And they're probably right about the firing. We've had more than a few scoundrels come in and out of this church, some even running away with the otherwise faithful wives of the flock. You'd think we could pick

Pastors better. We actually interview for the job as we can. We put them up front for three or four sermons just to try the mettle of their message. If we like what we hear, they're in. If not, they're out the door and we're on to the next candidate. When membership dwindles down to our current fifty or so families, we can't be as choosy, but the number of members fluctuates on a repeating cycle, so when we're more robust, we'll attract some of the better ones."

His fingers stopped scanning and Rogers pulled a file, licked his index finger and paced through the onionskin papers until he found the letter. "Here it is," he declared. "Yes, the Reverend L.W. Kleinfelter was one of our longest serving Pastors, for thirty years beginning in 1930, and one of our best for his strict adherence to the Word. If he couldn't turn a sinner back on the straight-and-narrow, man or woman, then they were surely lost forever. He was also meticulous, like making this longhand copy with some notes attached. I'm not familiar with all this Old German, but there are people around who still use it at home. Would you like me to check if I can find an interpreter from among our flock?"

"Not just now," Carlson said. "But I would appreciate a copy of the appended notes. This is just the beginning of my search and I have a few more stops before I can start to piece everything together, if that's possible. I do thank you wholeheartedly for all your assistance and the lessons in history."

After making the requested copy, Rogers walked Carlson back to his Jeep, pointing out along the way another feature that made the church so different. In the front of the building, the bricks were laid in the form of the Flemish cross, while at the rear and either side of the structure the bricks were laid differently. Carlson thought Rogers would have made a great tour guide anywhere he had chosen to live.

"May God be with you, Abe, wherever your destiny lies," Rogers said in farewell. "I trust you will be able to find the answers to your questions. Don't be a stranger. Come to one of our services while you're in the area."

"Thanks, Tom," Carlson replied, "I just may take you up on that last invitation and when I get some answers, I'll certainly let you know."

Rogers stood in front of his beloved church and watched Carlson drive out of the parking lot, returning his wave as he pulled on the main road. The thermometer on the side of the church registered one hundred one degrees.

The local newspapers had reported that the area was experiencing well above normal temperatures and relief could come any day now.

CHAPTER 3

▼

THE FELLOWS

Although Carlson entered Freemasonry at age twenty-one, he had not set foot in a lodge for over twenty-five years, but always kept his dues up-to-date and remained a member in good standing. Still, he hoped he could remember enough of the rituals and passwords to gain the assistance of Brownstone Lodge in his search for his long-lost relative. He also knew that the covert knowledge surrounding Masonry was passed on through oral tradition, so that the practices in Arizona might be quite different from those of the much older lodges along the Atlantic Coast. He found the Masonic Temple easily at a major intersection in Hershey, home of Brownstone Lodge, Free and Accepted Masons, and noted the building was dedicated in 1956. As he eased into the large parking lot to the rear of the building, he observed a car wash being conducted by a group of high school students, with enthusiastic horse-play, spraying each other to keep cool in the oppressive heat while earning money to support some worthy program.

Approaching the large double steel doors on the back of the brick lodge, Carlson saw a kind-looking healthily-built man in shorts and a casual shirt emerge from within and turn to lock the entry, then quickly turn back as he spied the stranger out of the corner of his eye.

"May I be of some assistance?" the man asked him in a neutral voice.

"I certainly hope so," Carlson replied. "I'm Abe Carlson from Arizona and a Master Mason. I'm looking for some information on an uncle I never knew I had until relatively recent times. All I know from one letter I have is that he once attended the Bindnagle Evangelical Lutheran Church in Palmyra and was said to have been a member of this Lodge in the 1930s."

"Well, Mister Carlson," the man said, "I'm Jack Hanover, but my friends call me Bud. I just dropped off some papers. Some of the Fellows will be here tonight to practice for the September stated meeting, but we're pretty much closed during July and August."

"Please, it's Abe," Carlson replied. "And since you called me Mister, I take it my examination has begun?"

"You're pretty quick, Abe. It's from years of habit and as a Past Master of the Lodge. I never use the appellation of Brother until another Brother I know introduces you as such, thereby confirming he has personally attended lodge with you, or you pass due and diligent examination. But that isn't necessary here unless you actually wanted to attend a lodge meeting. Why don't you come in out of the heat and I'll see what assistance we may provide."

Hanover lead them into a cool darkened alcove, with steps leading to the second floor, through a large room obviously used for social gatherings, a pass-through kitchen area to one side, and up a half-flight of stairs to a small room on the left which served as a library and meeting room. Hanover occupied the seat at the end of the table, Carlson to one side.

"This is the letter I referred to," said Carlson, handing over the protective envelope.

"To which you referred," he countered. "You know that we are obliged to kindly admonish our Brothers when they err. Besides, I'm a retired English teacher. I'm even so brave as to occasionally correct my wife," he smiled. "And I do pay the consequences on those adventurous outings."

"I stand corrected," Carlson replied with a smile of his own. "I did have proper schooling—my father was a preacher who did not want me to grow up talking like a ranch hand."

Hanover spent a full five quiet minutes reading and re-reading the letter before placing it on the table and looking across the room in contemplation.

"I haven't seen this much Old German in my lifetime," he finally said. "We have a few of the older members of the Lodge who still use it on occasion, particularly when they don't want the other Fellows to know what they're talking about. I get the gist from some of the words I can identify, but I certainly hope the reference to the 'Morgan' business is not what I believe it to be. This letter is dated 1933, so we'll have to examine some old records to see what we can find. Have you been to Bindnagle yet?"

"That was my first stop," Carlson replied, then gave Hanover a lengthy report on his experience.

"Yes, that is a grand old church," Hanover said when Carlson finished, "and that is a fine young Tom Rogers. I was a friend of his father and mother—fine folks who reared several bright and respectful children. It is just like that bedrock family to have a son who would devote himself so unselfishly to the church. And, they are a real hardheaded bunch. Once Tom made his decision, there would have been no deviation. The church is the better for it and the citizens of the community also benefit."

Carlson caught a quick glimpse of a very tall, white-haired man amble by the doorway, leaving the impression of a large head and very big hands. The tracker would have taken the man to be a farmer.

"Brother Will," Hanover called out, "could you spare a few moments of your most valuable time?"

The man entered, immaculately attired in sharply creased white pants, and highly buffed white shoes, pale blue socks and shirt.

"So, Brother Bud, is your dog suffering from mange again?" he asked light heartedly. "I cannot imagine how your lovely wife ever has such patience with your slovenliness."

"Abe Carlson, meet Brother Will Youst," Hanover said as the two men shook hands. "Brother Will is a general surgeon, a doctor of some distinction, and a man who knows fully well that I don't own a dog. It is a continuing jest resulting from the fact that the beautiful Rebecca Hanover chose my name over his. He has never married, claiming he could not find a woman quite as lovely."

"I've been blessed with the heart of a poet," Youst replied, hanging his head in false remorse.

"The preliminaries now over," Hanover said, "how is your High German these days Will? Abe has brought us a letter that concerns the Lodge."

"The language may be dying out in some parts, but in my household, of an evening, we still read the old classics in the original German. In my youth, I thought it was the language of love, but apparently Rebecca was of a different opinion."

After reading the letter twice in a matter of one minute, Youst agreed this could be a serious matter for the Lodge.

"Slate, Sheldon C. Slate," he said, soberly taking a seat. "I am aware of a few scattered families named Slader, with a 'd,' but spelled with a 't' is another matter altogether. Sheldon is common enough to pass through generations in this area for a first name. Do you know what the middle initial reflects?"

"Not a clue," Carlson replied. "This is the only document in my possession that even mentions him. He was apparently my father's never mentioned half-brother."

"I am troubled by the allusion to Morgan," Youst said.

"Yes," said Carlson. "The closest I can come through my less than stellar translation is 'committed a Morgan' or 'done like Morgan.'"

"You've gotten close, but it is more grave than that, I'm afraid. A truer translation is that he was 'Morganized,' which means either he was a false Mason, a rogue of sorts, threatening to reveal Masonic secrets to the uninitiated, spirited away to a fate unknown, or someone else kidnapped him and blamed it on Freemasonry. Brother Bud, has Mr. Carlson undergone due examination? If not, we would be wise to do so now before treading into these waters, lest some unintended information slip."

Carlson having consented to the examination, Hanover gathered two more Past Masters of the Lodge who were about their business on the second floor, conducted a fifteen minute test of the tracker's Masonic knowledge and credentials, and all were satisfied with his proficiency. "Now Brother Abe," Hanover asked at last, "how much do you know about the Morgan incident?"

"Nothing," came the reply, "but I suspect it might have something to do with the occasional Anti-Freemasonry flare-ups of the past. I did not delve very deeply into our history after I was first raised. I concentrated on going through the Chairs—became Junior Warden—and attended to the business of our Blue Lodge. I also spent some time visiting tribal Masonic Lodges and participating in the tribal Ritualistic Clan rites to which I was invited."

"I never gave much thought to the possibility of regular Indian Freemasonry," Youst said. "You'll have to tell us about it sometime, but let us get down to the Morgan affair. I'll try to keep the story as brief as possible and I think the shortest piece on the subject is on that bookshelf just to your left."

Youst went to the intended bookshelf and pulled out Volume Two of *Mackey's Revised Encyclopedia of Freemasonry*, Seventh Printing, 1956, the same year as the establishment of this building.

William Morgan was a Virginian, born in 1774 and lived in Lexington, Kentucky and Richmond, Virginia, a stonemason by trade. He moved briefly to Canada in 1821, then on to Rochester, New York in 1823. Three years later he took up residence in nearby village of Batavia, New York. There were no known records of his having been initiated into Freemasonry, other than his claim to having received a Royal Arch Degree at Le Roy, New York in August of 1825, but he was denied admission to the local Lodge and Chapter in Batavia.

Lodges usually have very good reason for denying admission, yet nothing was cited in the records for Morgan's case. When a second Chapter was proposed for Batavia, his name was on the petition to the Grand Lodge of New York, but strong objection being made, a second petition was advanced without his signature. Morgan became bitter and threatened revenge. He teamed with David Miller, the local newspaper printer claiming to have received his Entered Apprentice Degree, or First Degree, in Albany. They concocted a scheme to publish a malicious Anti-Freemasonry tome, revealing all the so-called dark secrets of the Craft. Some upset villagers set fire to Miller's print shop, but no serious damage was done. As a result, four hotheaded Masons were indicted and another three sent to the County Jail.

Morgan soon was arrested twice for failure to pay debts. Two months later, a third arrest for petit larceny landed him in jail in Canandaigua, the county seat. Released by the magistrate, he was immediately rearrested on a claim of less than three dollars to the keeper of a tavern. The next day a man named Lotos Lawson appeared and secured his release.

After this point, the story splits into two separate avenues. The first is that Morgan was kidnapped, forced into a coach, and driven across the country to the mouth of the Niagara River and into Canada. The second is that he left voluntarily, accepting the sum of five-hundred-dollars to vacate the area.

Unfortunately, another version emerged, spread by Anti-Masonic forces, with the Masons taking him by force and providing a violent death by drowning. The incident is credited with having created a wave of opposition to the Craft, which soon became a political party, the Anti-Masonic Party of the United States, which sought to throw out any officeholder who claimed Masonic affiliation. These foes nearly ended the political climb of Martin Van Buren, a Freemason, in the election of 1830.

With no proof of abduction or a body, a case still came before a court in this highly charged atmosphere. Four Masons were convicted and sentenced to varying prison terms on the abduction charge alone. There was a furor against Freemasonry in the region for many years, the number of Lodges dwindled, membership diminished and some families grew so bitter that fathers were arrayed against sons, brother against brother, churches were disrupted, poisoning community fellowship. As Mackey ended his article: "[B]oth in politics and business, home and market place, the venom of the ulcer spread far and deep. Public disavowal of any further connection with Freemasonry was made by thousands."

New York Freemasonry suffered quite a blow and other states were affected to varying degrees. It was to be another three decades, with the nation on the verge of civil war for the Free and Accepted Masons to recover.

"What were the consequences here in Pennsylvania?" Carlson asked. "And was it just a coincidence that nearly one-hundred years later a similar incident occurs and there was no public outcry?"

"As to your first question, I quite frankly don't know," Hanover responded, "but I would assume there had to be some. I'll have to do some research. I'm a little rusty on that score. I do suspect, however, that the stability of the spread of Freemasonry in Pennsylvania and our particular practice of the Craft, while not so different than in other states, probably provided some protection. Your second question is interesting. I don't ever remember any of the Fellows mentioning such an incident.

"We were a young lodge in 1933, having been constituted October 1, 1910, as we say: 'On the same night as the Earth passed through the tail of Halley's Comet, thirteen Master Masons met to form a Masonic Lodge in Hummelstown, Pennsylvania.' The first stated meeting was on October 8. Until this Temple was erected, we used to meet in the old Hummelstown Bank on the square, next door to Bowser's Furniture."

"Old Doc Straussburger might know something," Youst interrupted. "He was just a kid at the time, but smart as a whip. He always knew everyone and their business even at that age. He always claims he could beat any little old lady in town when it came to being nosey, but to his lasting credit, he just wanted the information for his own knowledge, not to dispense gossip. And it helped later, when he became a doctor, treating the generations and knowing personal relationships, with families and the community as a whole. He would not have missed something like that."

"One other thing," Carlson interjected. "Tom from the Bindnagle Church found these notes attached to the original copy of the letter," pulling a piece of paper out of his breast pocket. "It appears to be a list of names and places."

Youst scanned the notes and handed them over to Hanover for his perusal.

"So much for your two month 'off from labor' period," said Hanover. "It looks like some of us have some digging to do. I'll start in the morning with the Lodge records. Will, how about seeing if Doc is in town. He usually visits his sister up in Lewistown this time every year, but try anyhow. Why don't we all meet back here within the week, in the morning before it gets too hot? We'll give you our phone numbers, Abe, and we'll call on your mobile phone if anything important comes up before then."

With that, the group retired to their individual chores.

CHAPTER 4

▼

THE BRETHREN

Carlson had planned his next stop to be the Dauphin County Courthouse in Harrisburg to search for records on Carlson or the Slate family, but delayed that trip until after the more finely tuned local search of the Lodge records could be completed. He thought that to be a shorter path to the information he was seeking. This turned out to be a wise decision because as he headed back to The Wick, a late afternoon thunderstorm of fierce proportions opened the skies with shattering booms and sheets of lightening, rain coming in walls against the flat windshield of his Jeep, wind threatening to peel the canvas top right off the vehicle and making driving difficult as it pushed mightily against its square sides. The storm would last far into the night and cause widespread local flooding, with the Susquehanna and Juniata Rivers rising for days afterwards.

Most of the evening was spent in his cramped room, with only the slanted roof and sturdy walls and window separating him from the elements, as hail played an occasional tattoo on all surfaces and driving rain made seeing beyond the glass pane itself an impossibility. It was not until just before two o'clock in the morning that the storm suddenly abated and fizzled out in a surprising few minutes. That was when the so-called "ghost" made its presence known.

Carlson possessed a remarkable innate ability to go into deep meditation, so deep that he became unaware of any outside sounds or light. Some would classify this as a trance state, but this was not the case at all. Carlson had learned over years of practice to instead focus squarely on his inner-self, reaching beyond his natural breathing and heartbeat, opening the way to the God-force at his core and let it manifest itself in whatever form it chose. He had schooled in this technique with various shamans and spiritual women of the Native American tribes and a few holy men and women he had visited abroad. He found it natural that both sexes developed this state in tandem. In fact, it was probably the abrupt cessation of the storm, with the changes in temperature and barometric pressure that brought him out of his meditation with his senses acutely attuned to his surroundings. At various times in his experience, such an awakening brought a sense of being a part of the life in the flora and fauna around him, not just observing the surface colors and textures of a leaf, for example, but actually experiencing the pulse of life surging through the depths of its tissues.

Above his head and to the left, where wall met ceiling, he sensed a presence just out of his peripheral vision, as if seeing something out of the corner of his eye, knowing it would vanish if he looked head-on. There was also that sense of plant-self connection, only this took the form of feeling the emotions of another human being, setting up a means of communication, much as chemical reactions in a synapse of a nervous system passing information up and down the line. After a few moments, this settled into a steady flow of information.

Carlson sensed the presence of three entities, the strongest being a boy of perhaps twelve years of age, and then two other younger girls who just barely registered. They were waiting for something or somebody, not with fear or stress, but with calm confidence. They had died in their sleep in this room of some high-fever disease and did not know it. They were patiently awaiting the summons of their parents. One word seemed to be impressed on the young boy's consciousness: "householders." As the sun began to stream through the window, the entities slowly faded into the background until they finally disappeared.

Out on his early morning stroll, in blessedly cooler temperatures and storm-cleansed air, Carlson once again encountered retired-fix-it-man Isaac Porr sitting on a bench and taking in the sights. "Good morning, Mister Porr," he said in greeting, "isn't it nice to have such a break in the weather?"

"Always," Porr replied, "and please, it's Isaac. My father has been 'Mister Porr' all my life and he's still alive in a nursing home, although I doubt he realizes it to this day. I don't inherit the title until he's gone."

"Then please call me 'Abe.' My father is long passed, but I assure you I don't qualify to be called 'Reverend'—he was a man-of-the-cloth."

"It seems every family has one or two of those somewhere," Porr replied, with a smile. "I suppose it's just human nature. It sort of makes up for the transgressions of the rest of the brood."

They chatted on about the weather, the town and a little politics when Carlson finally asked: "What can you tell me about the term 'householders?"

"Householders?" Porr replied with a question. "I haven't heard that term used in years. It goes pretty far back in local history. It had something to do with the Cloister over in Ephrata, east of here. You have probably seen the road signs."

"Yes," Mason said. "I understand it was a type of religious community in a great age of experimental communal living."

"That's correct. It was a breakaway sect from mainstream religion. The founder had some strong opinions that didn't sit well with the traditionalists. One included observing the Sabbath on Saturday, rather than Sunday, because that's the way he read the Bible. He also held celibacy in high regard, with separate living quarters for men and women. Self-sufficiency was a high priority. The farmers in the area who belonged to the congregation, but rejected the celibacy idea to rear big families, were known as 'householders.' See that attractive woman just emerging from the silver Mercedes half way down the block? That's Veronica Steinmann, Professor of Law at Dickinson, in Carlisle. We're related somehow and I've known her since she was a girl in pigtails. She's a member of the Church of the Brethren, which grew from its Cloister roots.

"Hey, Ronnie, could you spare us a few minutes?"

Carlson looked up the street to discover one of the finest looking women he had ever seen walking toward them, giving a short wave of recognition. Veronica Steinmann was a vision of grace, covering the half block in long strides. She wore a perfectly tailored pin-striped charcoal suit, hemline just below the knee, medium high-heels, delicate blue silk blouse rolled at the neck. A black lizard purse, which matched her shoes, was slung from the right shoulder and perfectly manicured nails with clear polish. Yet, most stunning of all were her hazel eyes, ash brown hair framing the face, delicate jaw line and beautiful opaque skin that promised never to show age. What little makeup she wore was perfectly placed. To Carlson, this woman was every inch a thoroughbred, though he did not think any woman would like being compared to a horse. Make it professional then, he thought, and a very lovely one at that.

"Ronnie, meet Abe Carlson," Porr said by way of introduction. "He's visiting our fair realm in search of his roots and was just asking me about 'householders.' That's your branch of the family as I recall. By the way, I can't ever seem to remember just how we are related."

"Something like third cousins twice removed," she replied, eyes analyzing Carlson. "We're a very inbred bunch around here, Abe," offering her hand to be shaken. "As they say, scratch a German in this county and you've touched family. I'm Ronnie Steinmann."

Carlson shook her firm hand, noticing the long slender fingers enveloping his rough square palms and the absence of a wedding ring. "May I call you Veronica?" he asked. "It seems more fitting to a woman of your appearance."

"Ah, chivalry is alive and well in this world after all, Isaac," she responded. "Do you always begin flirting with women you've just met, Abe, or are you just being polite?"

"Just minding my manners," he replied reddening slightly. "And I always try to tell the truth."

"Oh my," Steinmann observed with a gleaming smile, "a man who can actually blush. I didn't think such a creature existed in this day and age."

"Pay her no mind, Abe," Porr interrupted. "She's been tripping up the male of the species since seventh grade with that wicked tongue of hers. Uncommon beauty does that to some girls. They just like to see us squirm. My dear wife was the same until I overwhelmed her with my charm in the third grade. She simply could not resist. It's a habit Ronnie never grew out of. I think it's a defensive move. She's still scaring them off left and right."

"I expect it's more of a sense of humor," Carlson replied, reading her natural delivery. "Intelligence often brings with it a sharp wit."

"I'm getting to like you already, Abe," she said. "A woman can never have too many compliments. What do you two say to an offer of a cup of coffee and a Danish at Bill's Café? My treat."

"I'd be obliged," said Carlson, revealing his western upbringing. "And I would like to ask you the favor of enlightening me on Ephrata and things of that nature."

Over the first coffee refill, Steinmann revealed the history of the Cloister. Its charismatic founder, Conrad Beissel, was orphaned at a young age in his native Germany. He became a baker by trade and joined the Pietists, a movement to reform the established, state supported Protestant churches. The established Church found Beissel in conflict with the law and following a personal religious awakening in 1715, he was banished from his homeland. He immigrated to Pennsylvania in 1720, spending a year in Germantown, outside Philadelphia, than to Conestoga, present day Lancaster where he was affiliated with the Brethren, an Anabaptist group who advocated baptism only after reaching the age of maturity. He was a church leader for several years, but his radical ideas soon forced him out. In 1732 he left and sought the life of a hermit along Cocalico Creek in northern Lancaster County.

This charismatic hermit attracted a small group of devotes, which grew to eighty celibate men and women and two hundred family members, known as "householders." His theology was a mix of mysticism, Sabbath worship, the ascetic life and the encouragement of celibacy. At its peak in the 1740s and 1750s, about three hundred members worked and worshiped at the Cloister. The community became known for its music and Germanic calligraphy, with a publishing center, paper mill, printing press and bindery.

There was plenty of internal discord within the community and upon Beissel's death in 1768 the new leader, Peter Miller, rejected the monastic way of life, discouraged celibacy and took the church in a different direction. The celibates remained, but eventually died out. By 1814 the last remaining married members formed a new church, which changed names several times before settling on the title Church of the Brethren. Steinmann had descended from the line of householders.

"What about epidemics like the flu?" Carlson asked. "Wouldn't it be passed along fairly quickly, particularly among the celibates where men lived in one building and the women in another?"

"That's a bit of an odd question," Steinmann replied. "Yet, I can probably help you out. I come from a long line of diary keepers—both men and women. They liked to record the weather, state of the crops, things going on in the community in general, plus personal family items. Several passed down in my family do mention several outbreaks over the years, hitting hardest among the celibates, crammed in together as they were. The householders were mostly farmers living and working outside the compound, therefore less at risk. If the illness became too widespread, these farm folk would pack the children off to relatives out of the area or to rented rooms in the small towns dotting the countryside until the danger had passed. In fact one of the ironies of my own family's history is a great, great, great ancestor on my mother's side, that's the Kellers, bundled up her three children and found a room in town. Unbeknownst to her, the children had already been exposed and on her way back to Ephrata to gather more clothing she became dreadfully ill. She died that night. When her husband went to fetch the children home, he was to discover all three had succumbed the same night."

"A young boy, with two younger sisters?" asked Carlson.

"Well," she hesitated and gave Carlson a questioning look, "yes. Ages twelve, eight and six respectively. How would you know?"

"If she brought them here to Hummelstown," he said cautiously, "I may have an answer. I don't know how you feel about the world of spirit, but I've had some experience. I did mean it when I said I always strive for the truth. Now let me tell you what happened last night."

Carlson reported his experience in a straightforward, matter-of-fact way, neither embellishing nor leaving anything out.

"Are you psychic?" Porr asked when he had finished.

"Everyone is, to one extent or another," Carlson said. "But, no, not in the usual meaning of the term. In my case, I think the word is 'intuitive.' I've spent many years among the various western tribes, participating in their rituals and ceremonies, even being initiated into several clans. The Indians take an intuitive approach in matters of the spirit, though they wouldn't put it quite that way. The Indian clears his thoughts and quietly awaits the information to come, in whatever form. When that information does arrive, only then does he evaluate, accept or reject, based on his own experience and the traditions of his people."

"I took a few electives in college," Steinmann said. "Some were in parapsychology, which I chose out of curiosity. At the time I thought it might come in handy after law school, ferreting out the demons in some felon or something. Who knows what goes through the mind at that age? Today, I'd be happy just to be able to ferret out the demons in some of my more unruly students."

"Come now, Ronnie," Porr broke in, "the way I hear it, you are a virtual tyrant in the classroom, keeping your students in line by the age-old threat of failure." Then turning to Carlson he asked: "Aren't such entities referred to as Earth-bound Spirits?"

"Some might call them that," Carlson responded. "I rather think that's not the whole truth. I don't believe a spirit, or soul, or whatever you call your spark of life, can be prevented from progressing to the afterlife. I think of the entities as being some form of imprint left behind in the space they departed. At times, people report ghosts at a place of tragic death, like murder or accidental death, like a car going over a cliff, or even in peaceful sleep. One theory is that, in most instances, these imprints do not know they have died. To remove the so-called haunts, all you have to do is make them aware the spirit has progressed and wish them well. I've heard the term 'turning them toward the light.' I rather like that."

"Okay, folks," Porr said at last as he stood, "I'll leave you two young people to your own devices. I have to be getting home. Apolonia will think I'm up to some mischief with the ladies about town. I was quite a draw in my day, you know."

"Right, Isaac," Steinmann interjected, with a sneer. "You forget I know you too well. First of all, anyone who had won the hand of your lovely bride, then went astray would have to be out of his mind. Besides, if she were to hear of such nonsense, you'd be on a quick trip to the other side yourself. Everyone knows for a fact that you put her on a pedestal and worship the ground she walks on."

"You are absolutely right," Porr corrected. "I will not contest your analysis, but bow to the righteousness of your statement." With that, he left the café.

Carlson and Steinmann spent another hour over coffee, giving each other their histories. She was a natural conversationalist and he was warming up to a newfound friend. He wondered if perhaps this might lead to something in the future, but then remembered he was only here for a few days.

Still, he could not resist asking her to dinner.

"Not tonight, I'm afraid," she answered as she watched the color drain from his face. "I'll tell you what, though. You get busy tonight to exorcise those of my family who are long passed, freeing them from whatever keeps them here. Even if unsuccessful, I would like to buy you dinner tomorrow for your efforts. I'll pick you up, say seven o'clock. Coat and tie required."

Carlson could not believe his luck and quickly accepted. They exchanged cell phone numbers in case circumstances changed. As soon as her car disappeared up the street, he made a second visit to Maloney's Men's Shop for a new suit, tailored on the spot. He had not felt this way since he first discovered puppy love at age sixteen, when Sara Christina Magnuson, sitting on the other side of his homeroom, absolutely captivated his young heart.

CHAPTER 5

▼

MASONS

Carlson spent his entire day roaming the grounds of the Ephrata Cloister to get a feel for what life must have been like for the three entities in his room. Many of the original buildings in the compound had been restored or rebuilt and the Cloister was now open to tours through the Visitor Center.

He found the unique European style buildings simple and sparsely furnished, but certainly utile. Conrad Beissel's house was between the large Saron (Sisters' House) and where the Bethania (Brothers' House) once stood. Cocalico Creek and spring running through the property provided fresh water and a place of baptism for newly arriving members. Each building had its own very necessary purpose, from the Bake House, to the Weaver's House, the Carpenter's House, the Printing Office and Press, and the ever-important Saal (Meeting House). Of particular interest on either side of the property are two burial grounds—God's Acres, where Beissel and other early members of the group are interred, and Mount Zion Cemetery, which contains a mass grave from when the site served as a hospital during the Revolutionary War in the winter of 1777-78.

Carlson saw what was a typical community for its time; a major difference to children of a householder's family, compared to the other children in the surrounding communities, was their attendance at the Meeting House on Saturday, the original Biblical Sabbath, rather than Sunday. Of course, the many white monastic robes favored by most celibate members would make them stand out to outsiders. But, the Church of the Brethren, which grew out of this religious community—once shed of several quirks of its founder after his death—continued to be solidly mainstream Protestant. It was Anabaptist, reserving baptism until reaching the age of reason, non-violent and non-resistant, based on the Bible and strongly dedicated to separation of church and state.

As he stopped to pick up a pamphlet at the Visitor Center on his way out, Carlson overheard a conversation between a man obviously on his own genealogy search and the clerk behind the counter.

"Yes," the man said with some relish, "we had a couple of generations of rogues in my family who passed through here circa 1750. Father and son claimed to be Doctors of Physic. They practiced augury and divination, were into the 'Spirits Game,' dowsed for ore with a divining rod, saw ghosts of the recently departed, had visions through trance. They also claimed to be Freemasons, having the 'key to Solomon,' whatever that was supposed to mean. Some of my neighbors in the Shenandoah Valley, where our family ended up, are Freemasons and they assure me that those two didn't have a clue about the Craft. Besides, they doubted the Masons would let such crackpots in to begin with. The standards for character are much higher than that."

As Carlson walked out to the parking lot, all he could think of was how little the world had changed since 1750 and how many other such people migrated westward with the tide of settlers.

As he reached for the door handle of his Jeep, the cell phone in his breast pocket rang a lyrical tune. He flipped it open and held it to his ear.

"Abe Carlson," he answered.

"Ronnie, here," came the reply as Carlson's spirits flagged fearing his hopes of tomorrow's dinner was about to be canceled.

"Yes, Veronica," he said in as pleasant a voice as possible. "Nice to hear from you so soon."

"I've had a change of plans," she continued. "How would you like to make a day of it tomorrow? I have to go up to Reedsville, in the Big Valley, to pick up a piece of furniture from a great woodworker. I thought you might be interested in seeing some fine workmanship and the tidy farms throughout the valley. There are many Amish farms of every variety and quite a few Mennonites. Besides, the views are spectacular."

"I'd be delighted to go along," Carlson sighed in relief. "Would you like me to drive? I have quite a bit of room in the back of my vehicle and if the furniture isn't too cumbersome, I can probably haul it better than you."

"Thanks, but no thanks," she replied. "It's simply a rocker I'm buying for my sister, Gloria, and there is sufficient room in my back seat. My sister is a real L.A.

girl, but misses something from home. I thought I'd surprise her with the best. I'll pick you up at your hotel around eight."

"I will anxiously await your arrival," Carlson said with sincerity.

"Don't you go all cavalier on me now, Abe," Steinmann warned. "Polite is fine, but gallant may be going a bit far. Although, now that I think about it, gallantry does look pretty good on you. See you around eight."

Hanging up before he could reply, Carlson had a very pleasant ride back to his hotel. The sun seemed more gentle, the trees and grass more green and the crops along the way somehow riper on his ride back than when he had driven out.

It was early evening when he passed through Hershey and decided to stop at the Lodge, hoping someone would be about their business. With luck, the door was unlocked and he found Bud Hanover catching up on some paperwork in the library.

"May I intrude?" Carlson asked, rapping quietly on the open door.

"No intrusion at all, Abe," Hanover replied. "I'm still working on the records, but it's getting a little complicated. What can I do for you?"

"May I have access to some of the volumes here?" Carlson asked. "I have a few thoughts rolling around in the back of my mind and want to delve deeper into Masonic history and practice."

"Be our guest then," Hanover said, waving a hand toward the shelves. "We're not the largest library, but we have very good coverage of basic Masonic lore and history, with special emphasis on Pennsylvania, of course."

Carlson began with *Mackey's Revised Encyclopedia*, re-reading the section on the Morgan affair to see if he could pick up any other leads, then browsing through the rest of the volume. He suddenly stopped to read two items entitled "Tolerance Lodge" and "Tolerance," wondering why the Lodge entry would come before the term.

Under the first item, he learned that when the initiation of Jews was forbidden in the Prussian Lodges, two members, "in the spirit of toleration," organized a Jewish one and aptly named it Tolerance Lodge. Unfortunately, the Masonic authorities never recognized this Lodge.

Under the second item he read: "The grand characteristic of Freemasonry is its *toleration* in religion and politics." So no specific religion was barred, as long as the person believed in a Supreme Being, and no political subjects were broached in the Lodge, so as not to upset the brotherly harmony.

Looking up, he saw Hanover closing one file and reaching for another.

"Don't mean to interrupt you Bud," he said. "There seems to be something missing here with Mackey's entries on tolerance."

"So you noticed that too," Hanover replied in appreciation. "The question has been debated throughout the Craft for many years. Mackey put together his encyclopedia quite a number of years ago, as did Gould in his *History of Freemasonry,* with its many volumes. They wrote with information available in their time. More has surfaced over the years and both massive works have been revised, appended and corrected with each new discovery. Hence the word 'revised' in the title by Mackey. This edition is the work of H. L. Haywood, a prodigious Masonic scholar, and if you look up the same item in the third volume supplement, you may find your answer."

Carlson opened the third volume to "Toleration and Freemasonry." Haywood's argument is that tolerance has never been a principle in Freemasonry because the Craft teaches neither tolerance nor intolerance—it is completely absent. "[F]or while a man might be proud to tolerate something or somebody, the recipient of the tolerance is humiliated. It is presupposed that there is something questionable, bad, disgusting, contemptible; if it is tolerated it is because it is endured, or put up with …" And should any form of tolerance be adopted, it would surely make way for unwanted innovations that could alter the pure traditions of Freemasonry.

"So it's the evolution of language, Bud?" Carlson concluded rather than asked.

"Exactly," Hanover replied, delighted that Carlson could make the connection. "How the word 'tolerance' was used, then abused over the centuries, brought us to a point where what began as a beautiful expression ended up with an ugly connotation."

"I would suppose this acceptance of differences without judgment is one of the things that appealed to the Indians who willingly joined Freemasonry, because it fit the general outlines of their own system of clans," Carlson said at length.

"Before you go much further in that direction," Hanover interrupted, "I'd like to ask a question, without any intended rancor whatsoever. You are obviously an educated man, yet you seem insensitive to the nuances of 'Native American' in lieu of 'Indian.' Why is that, if I may ask?"

"Because most Indians rather scoff at the relatively recent use of 'Native American' as politically correct nomenclature," Carlson smiled in reply. "They do not perceive it as providing any new dignity to the People; they have their own deeply ingrained dignity and sense of self that no new term could possibly convey. Plus, they are acutely aware they were here first long before there was an 'America.' 'Indian' is pretty much a neutral term. Those who were not indigenous to this land have provided plenty of pejorative terms that cause offense, of course, but in the long run it makes little difference. You see, the many different tribes I've come in contact with over the years have a separate and distinct impression of their place in the world. When referring to their personal selves, you will find these people claim they are 'Navaho,' or 'Apache,' or 'Mojave' or any other designation. Beyond that, it is the 'Navaho People' or the 'Navaho Nation,' or simply the 'People.' And when speaking of all Indians, it's the 'Indian Nations' in the plural."

"Thank you for the insight," Hanover remarked. "So what about this natural affinity of Indians toward Freemasonry?"

"It's really very straightforward," Carlson explained. "Since the very beginning of the colonies, European Masons—mostly in the British military at first—witnessed many rights and ceremonies among the native population that were strikingly similar to Masonic degrees. These Europeans discovered a Clan Lodge system, with initiation rituals, secret signs of recognition, etc. Most importantly, each clan had a specific goal in aiding the progress, safety and development of the People, preserving ancient custom and upholding the general ethos of the tribe. And, like Freemasonry, these clans were not secret societies, but societies with a few secrets. Although most of my Masonic history centers on the Indians, I do recall that it was your own Pennsylvanian Benjamin Franklin, a Mason through and through, who once put it something like: 'The secret of Freemasonry is that there is no secret.'"

"You are absolutely correct, Abe," Hanover concurred. "Now tell me more about Indian Freemasons."

"Allow me to first state that there was no Freemasonry as we know it among the Indians," Abe answered, "despite similarities in signs of recognition, passing on of specifics by oral tradition and a number of other things. But we of European stock did pass Freemasonry directly to the tribes."

As Carlson sketched the background of the times, he explained what later became known as the 'Indian telegraph,' an ancient web of communication which passed along information from east to west, and north to south, by word of mouth. It may take several years for this information to reach the outer fringes of Canada or South America, but the American middle was well informed. Long before American excursions westward, the western and plains Indians knew about the French in Canada, Dutch and English on the Atlantic Coast, and Spanish forays into the American southeast, Mexico and South America. They knew much about the good, the bad and the ugly things the newcomers brought with them and imposed at any cost on the native population.

The first authentically recorded American Indian to become a Master Mason was of the Iroquois Confederation, a Mohawk Chief named *Thayendanega,* known by his adopted name of Joseph Brant. There were many Military Masonic Lodges among the British and Brant had sided with the English during the Revolutionary War. He was taken to London and initiated in April 1776, returned to America and was a member of Lodges in Hamilton, Canada, and in Mohawk Village—there becoming its first Master of the Lodge. A highly literate man, he translated, among other works, the Gospel of Saint Mark into the Mohawk language.

A contemporary of Brant, the famous Seneca orator, Red Jacket, was claimed to be a Mason, but if so, probably only the first degree of Entered Apprentice. The list of others is extensive, with Indian Masons fighting on both sides in the war.

Among the more noted tribes, the Delaware, Ojibwa, and Shabbornee, the Pottawatomi who saved Chicago settlers from the fearsome Sauk Chief, Black Hawk. The Seneca Chief, General Eli S. Parker entered the Civil War as a private and ended up as aide-de-camp and Secretary to General Grant. Cherokee, Chickasaw, Sioux and Dakota Nations all became early participants in the Craft as the practice moved westward.

"Where I was reared in Arizona, many of the members of the Masonic Lodges and the tribal Clans are interchangeable," Carlson concluded. "We see no conflict and the transition back and forth is seamless."

"I seem to recall from Pennsylvania history during the Revolutionary War the name Red Jacket of the Seneca," Hanover said. "There also were some incidents involving General Sullivan's attempt to take the British Fort Niagara along Lake Ontario, starting from three points, one in Albany and two somewhere in Pennsylvania. General George Washington ordered the expedition, but that's about all I remember, except I don't think it was successful."

"The western tribes still know every detail," Carlson countered with some bitterness creeping into his voice. "From the Indian point of view, it was a huge black eye for the colonists and a shame on Washington personally. As explorers and settlers pushed west, the Indians were already suspicious of the so-called 'Great White Father,' and all I can say about the Lewis and Clark expedition ordered by President Jefferson is that it was a true miracle they made it back with their lives. But that's a story for another day. I've got to be going, Bud. Thanks for the information and discussion. I'll be awaiting your call."

As he drove back to the Warwick Hotel, Carlson contemplated his angst at the mention of the Sullivan Expedition. Perhaps he had long been too close to the tribes to not absorb their view on many matters, but decided in the end that it was his better nature and compassion for humanity, rather than prejudice that had prevailed. He also reminded himself that if any of us were perfect, we would not be here. In his travels through parts of Asia, he had grasped the notion of reincarnation, that we had to live many lifetimes to attain a state of perfection, resolve all our karma, before attaining a final place with God. Besides, from his reading of the classics, he had always admired Plato's imagery of the spirit, descending into a valley, crossing its floor where the memory was erased, then climbing the opposite side to be reborn again. It also lent credence to the idea of the collective memory of humankind, the interconnectedness of every living thing if you included the genetic instinct ascribed to animals and plants. He had never been so egotistical to think that in God's creations only man held the exclusive connection to the Creator. It may be far beyond his current abilities to understand, but he always kept himself open to all possibilities.

After a quick meal at the bar of the hotel, he discovered the family sharing his floor had departed, so he luxuriated in a long hot bath to regain his even composure and prepare himself for the last task of the day.

The sun had relinquished its hold on the clear sky some time before and moonlight was streaming obliquely through the window when he eased himself into a deep, releasing meditation. All the mundane thoughts of the day were put aside and he gradually calmed his inner self to the point of perfect reception. With no sense of elapsed time, the entities near the ceiling were felt—minutely at first, then growing in essence. Carlson concentrated on the facts he knew about the householders, the possible identity of the children, then merely envisioned "turning them toward the light."

With a final nod of acknowledgement, the traces of the children slowly pivoted, joined hands and rose through the roof.

CHAPTER 6

▼

AMISH

Abe Carlson had been sitting on a bench on Main Street reading the morning newspaper and sipping coffee for one-half hour when Veronica Steinmann pulled her Mercedes up to the curb promptly at eight, as promised. A slight refreshing breeze was stirring and weather reports promised a mostly sunny day.

As he approached the passenger door, Carlson was pleased he had chosen rightly in wearing jeans and a casual shirt. Steinmann wore denim and comfortable shoes, with a lime-colored summer shell and sheer weight cotton cardigan to match. Her perfect length ash brown hair complimented the look—casual, but smart. Carlson did not think there was anything this woman could don that would not be stylish.

"Did you bring breakfast?" Steinmann asked, noticing the bag as he slid into the seat.

"Coffee, black and an apple Danish," was Carlson's reply. "I noticed how you ordered and it was easy to remember because I usually drink my coffee the same way, unless it is so bad that I need to cut it with milk and disguise the bitterness with a dab of sugar."

"Very thoughtful and appreciated," she replied. "Any luck with your roommates, the ghosts, or spirits, or whatever they are?"

"Yes," he replied modestly. "I believe they've gone on to wherever they're headed, but I can't but believe The Warwick won't be a little less for the loss."

"A little less charming," she commented. "Yet, thank you for your assistance. I'll rest a little easier knowing for sure there is some family finality to the situation. Now, what do you say, ready for a sightseeing tour of our fair Central Pennsylvania?"

"Ready and willing," he replied. "Lay on Macduff."

"Ah, a reader of Shakespeare too," she smiled. "And correctly quoted. Most people I know, even most academics, manage to mangle the phrase to 'Lead on Macduff.' It seems there is a lot to discover about you, Abe. Perhaps you will reveal more of yourself today. You could be interesting."

"Actually, it was a very bad attempt at gallows humor," he sheepishly admitted. "The rest of the phrase is 'And damn'd be him that first cries, Hold enough!' They were MacBeth's last words before Macduff killed him in combat."

"What a wry sense of humor you have, Mr. Carlson," she replied with a wisp of a smile. "I assure you I will inflict no bodily harm—just show you some beautiful country."

The trip led up the Susquehanna River, and then followed the Juniata, winding through beautiful hills and mountain gaps, spectacular views of striking greenery, lush hillsides choked with trees and shrubbery, many miles of mountain ridges too steep for development, with small pockets of civilization scratching out a living in between. Carlson knew this must be quite a sight as the leaves turned in the autumn and a still-formidable landscape in the bare winter months. He had heard Westerners belittle the Allegheny Mountains as hardly a bump in the landscape compared to the mighty Rockies, but then most of these comments were from the Phoenix area where a mere mound of rock peeking up from the desert floor was given the venerable name of Camelback Mountain. To him, the complex interlacing of ridges as the roadway probed the gaps, was an exercise in appreciation for man's ingenuity toward settlement, development and expansion. He could only guess at the abundance of wildlife to be found in these mountains and the plethora of fish in the rivers, streams and creeks. Little wonder the original inhabitants thrived for so many generations. And as always, he was impressed to see the big white clouds drifting with the winds across the deep blue sky. For much of the year in the southwest you could wait for months just to see one cloud.

Carlson gave her a brief description of his visit to Ephrata and the impression he had about the community, its complex balance of religious and secular interests, plus his understanding of the evolution into the Church of the Brethren.

"I can't dispute any of your observations," she said when he had finished. "Remember that William Penn invited people of all faiths to join in the development of his lands. Thus many branches of Protestants, each in the process of evolving under various labels, thrived, grew and split into many sects under the same banner, but with differences both small and large."

"How was it with your family," he asked.

"Well, to start with," she began, "you have to look at the social divisions with the Ephrata community. It was more than simply celibates on the one hand and householders on the other. On the householder side, what were once thought of as farmers with families also included artisans, merchants and specialized professions. To some extent, by the way, there was a similar breakdown with the celibate class.

"My family, the Kellers, were mostly farmers who entered into marriage with various artisans, merchants and builders. One such union was with a Steinmann, which reflected a name change for the original Steinmetz. Steinmetz is German for stonemason and the Steinmann generations carried on the traditions of that profession. But over time, any particular Steinmann would revert to general farming and a Keller might become a mechanic or a shoemaker or banker or whatever profession was in need. You will see this reflected in the Church itself. You may have noticed there seems to be profusion of churches with Brethren in the title—off shoots that bear a remarkable resemblance to the main Church, but with slight differences in practice or ritual."

"That old human tendency to inject complexity where simplicity would better serve," he observed.

"There is, perhaps, no better example than some of the people you will see in Big Valley, where we're headed," she continued. "Let me give you a few observations on the Plain People, the Amish. They are a big draw for tourists throughout Central Pennsylvania and many other states. The first thing a tourist may say is that they are quaint. What do you think, Abe?"

"They may be the Plain People, but hardly the Simple People as far as I can see," he answered. "From what little I have seen of the neat well-managed farms, some being tilled by horse-drawn equipment, buggies on the road pulled by well-tended horses, carpenters at work and plain dressed women hard at work about other tasks, I'd say I've been looking at a highly complex, deeply religious, fiercely family devoted people living in a tight knit community. As for quaintness, I take some umbrage at the attitude that implies. Tourists traveling through my part of the country may think it a 'quaint' experience to stop at a roadside stand to buy Navaho blankets, jewelry and trinkets, as with the vendors of other tribes, and see what they perceive as the 'stoic reserve of the Indian countenance.' More often than not, the Indian is having the last laugh as he or she entices the more obnoxious buyers into purchasing the cheapest junk at the highest prices by inventing, on-the-spot, some outlandish Indian tradition connected to the item. I once witnessed a so-called 'stiff deer hide fetish purse' being pawned off on a sweating four-hundred-pound women in brightly colored tent dress who had been belittling the barefoot children as 'poor waifs of the desert.' In actuality, that purse was the…. Oh, sorry, Veronica. That tale does not need to be told in polite company," he ended shyly.

"Oh, goodness, Abe," she purred a soft grin teasingly, "thank you for protecting my virtue, but I've been around farms all my life. I get the idea and think it a very befitting transaction. I must say your description of the Amish is very insightful."

She painted the Amish society with a broad brush, explaining the range of differences in terms of conservative and liberal. Her understanding was that on the most conservative end were Old Order Amish, people living most closely under the old ways of the 1700s, no machinery other than that which could be made by hand, absence of electricity, plainness of dress, thought and religious practice, strict moral code, and most responsible for the survival of so-called Pennsylvania Dutch, Old German with new words and phrases that had crept into the language to suit the American environment. On the most liberal end were the Mennonites, living with all the modern conveniences, telephones and televisions in the home, driving cars, trucks and machinery, in some cases discarding the very plainest clothing for some variation on the theme. The Mennonites were historically the older of the two. The so-called Old Order Amish actually broke away to pursue what they perceived to be a purer form of Christianity, going back to the simpler forms of the early Christian Church. The great bulk of the Amish are found somewhere in between, but certainly on the conservative side, comparatively. But that was merely to put the subject in context, she emphasized. The complexities involved were too deep to be unraveled easily.

The Amish are Anabaptist, reserving baptism until reaching the age of reason, non-violent and non-reactive (turn the other cheek), espousing the separation of church and state, standing bedrock on the Bible, recognizing the realities of the harsh Old Testament, but relying heavily on the redemptive qualities of the New, with particular emphasis on Jesus and his teachings being the fulfillment of the Old. Most importantly is his or her personal relationship directly with God. The slight differences between the diverse Amish groups are minor and none will criticize the other or judge which is best. One group may practice baptism by a slight sprinkling on the head in the home. Another may prefer full emersion. Buggies may have different coloring such as White Top, Black Top, Yellow Top, and be open or closed to the elements. What some may deem "showiness" others see only as personal preference. Besides, the Elders, the Bishops are most always men of experience and even temper who referee minor disputes and apply common sense to some hair-splitting decisions, all for the good of the community. If there is any judging to do, they leave it to God.

As she turned off at the Reedsville exit, Steinmann suggested an early lunch at a local restaurant she frequented when in the area.

"Does this mean I miss out on the dinner offer?" Carlson asked lightly.

"Of course not," she replied. "In fact, since you present yourself as such a gentleman, I'm going to allow you to pick up the check. I may be a fully liberated woman, but I don't take it to extremes. On the more serious side," she suddenly digressed, "I imagine you are aware of the recent tragedy at the Amish School?"

"Can there be anyone in the world who hasn't?" he countered. "I was just stepping off the train from Glastonbury early one morning at the Victoria Station in London when the headlines shouted and the television news blared. For a full two weeks that was always the lead story. Five innocent girls slaughtered for no reason other than a madman found them conveniently vulnerable. I was greatly disappointed in the media coverage, to put it mildly. All that boasting of respecting the privacy requested by the Amish, while showing graphic visuals such as pictures taken from a helicopter of grieving relatives carrying a wooden casket toward an open grave. I found that inexcusable."

"As much as I agree with you," she said, "I think the Amish gave the entire world a lesson in pure Christianity. The immediate Amish reaction was to forgive the killer in their hearts, ask people to pray for him as much as for the slain and injured girls, and invited his widow to be the only outsider to attend their burial—something she could not bring herself to do. Then, seventy-two Amish attended his burial as an act of forgiveness and reconciliation. Now, how about that as an example for living with your fellow man?"

"I wasn't aware of most of that," he confessed.

"And it gets even better," she said, turning into the restaurant parking lot and shutting off the engine. "There was an outpouring of prayers and money from across the globe. They received the first, thankfully, and the second, only grudgingly; to be set-aside for the rehabilitation of the injured and the future needs of the community. I purchased some cheese at an Amish stall at the local market I frequent and a mention naturally arose about the tragedy. The Amish woman behind the counter said her reaction was to feel ashamed. At first I thought she may be referring to such self-sufficient people accepting outside financial assistance, but that wasn't the case. She said they were ashamed because when other such tragedies happened at schools in the outside world, they had not thought to send even prayers. For her personally, that would not happen again."

"That's rather profound," was all he could think to quietly comment.

"Okay, Sport," she said perking up her mood. "Now that's off my chest, what do you say about treating a girl to lunch?"

Carlson found the Honey Creek Inn to be a locally popular eatery, with a broad menu, open from five-thirty in the morning until three in the afternoon, sumptuous breakfast combination available all day. As with most places of this type, it had its own legend printed on the front of the menu. "During the days of Indian Chief Logan, friend of the white man, and 'Captain Jack,' famous Indian fighter and for whom Jacks Mountains are named, there lived a man known as 'Honey Jim' Alexander, who built his house near the mouth of the cavern. He earned his living by tilling the soil, but was best known for his 99 hives of bees." As luck would have it, one day when "Honey Jim" moved his hives down the hill near an unnamed creek to collect honey from the blossoms, heavy rains and a flash flood washed all away. From that moment on, it has been called Honey Creek.

Carlson ordered a simple breakfast of eggs, hash browns, whole-wheat toast and coffee. He was a bit surprised when Steinmann ordered the same, plus a side of corned beef hash and French toast, and then requested fresh orange sections to start. She noted his surprised hesitation.

"I'm a Pennsylvania German," she said in way of explanation. "As such, I have a great appreciation for good food and am blessed with a high rate of metabolism. Besides, people around here appreciate being appreciated and my not going away hungry."

"It's just that you look so slim and trim," he observed. "I doubt you have an ounce of body fat."

"I thank you for the compliment," she admitted. "I may not work it all off doing farm chores, but I do walk all over campus, take the stairs instead of elevators, stand giving lectures and pace around the classroom, and hike when I can. And I have my own secret weapon."

"Fresh fruit or vegetables?" he asked.

"You are observant," she said with a look of conviction. "It's called 'The Enzyme Diet.' I got it from a beloved Aunt who was a nurse. The idea is to eat a little fruit—a little apple, some orange, a few slices of tomato, whatever—just before the meal. It kicks on the fat burning system up front, so you don't take in as many calories, or something along those lines. In any event, I find it certainly helps me, particularly with fried foods."

"Well, you certainly are a testament to good health," he smiled as the dishes were laid before them.

The conversation turned to the portion of the Big Valley Steinmann knew well, from Milroy, Reedsville, Belleville and Allensville. The Scotch-Irish, German and Swiss who immigrated found fertile land for farming. The overwhelming majority of the population attended at least one of the over thirty established churches: no less than six Mennonite, several Lutheran, Presbyterian, Methodist, and Brethren in Christ, among others. The Old Order Amish held services in their homes on a rotating basis. One common characteristic of every group was the capacity for hard work, both as farmers, and artisans, builders, shopkeepers, tradesmen, whatever—not from some religious notion that "idle hands are the Devil's workshop," but for the sheer joy of work, sense of accomplishment and contribution to the family and community. This trait is very pronounced among the Amish, though most people are not aware they pay taxes, including local school taxes, although their children go to Amish schools through eighth grade; they do not accept Social Security because they take care of their own disabled and elderly, but pay the Social Security tax when working for non-Amish employers; they contribute quilts, hand made furniture and other items for auction to support local fire companies, police and other community safety and support groups; and they have an almost non-existent crime rate.

"One aspect of Amish life little understood outside of their world, and I suspect even inside of it at times," Steinmann said at length, "is the strict avoidance of being proud, displaying pride or even seeming to, which is considered to be a serious selfish act. Each individual wants to fit right in with each neighbor, not judging himself or herself to be any better than anyone else and firm in the knowledge that there will always be someone who does whatever you do just as well. It is a different look at true humility which serves the Amish community well."

"From what I have observed among many peoples," Carlson said, "and what I hear of the Amish, I would think that individuals who attain a certain distinction for an action or producing a particularly fine product would understand: 'This is not my talent, but God's work done through me. It is a manifestation of God, who granted me this gift to serve His purpose. This is not false humility. This is the simple truth.' At least that's the way I see it."

"Abe, you simply amaze me," she answered. "That's exactly what I've been searching for—a clear explanation. You'd make a perfect Amish man. You know horses and the out-of-doors, also you think like an Elder or Bishop. Just do me a favor. If you do decide to join, don't ask me to come with you. I need my curling iron and my electric toothbrush too badly. And I haven't worn a bonnet since I was a baby."

"Too bad," he replied with a twinkle in his eye. "I think you'd look cute in a bonnet."

CHAPTER 7

▼

WOODWORKERS

As they headed west on the two-lane road nearly centered in the valley, Carlson witnessed some of the best farming he had ever seen stretching out on both sides and framed by the backdrop of two parallel mountain ranges to the north and south. Every acre of usable land seemed to be planted with a variety of crops or to provide pasturage for dairy cows or Angus cattle. Some farms were fully mechanized; others tended by horse-drawn equipment, and there were scattered one-horse buggies on the roads or parked in front of stores. Remembering the legend of the Honey Creek Inn, he could only wonder at the origins of two other sites along the way, Tea Creek and Coffee Run. The many signs and billboards offered just about any service required in a farming community, with Yoder and Peachey being very common names.

"There are a lot of Peacheys in the valley," Steinmann explained. "They span from the Amish, through the Mennonites and the general population at large."

"So I've noticed," Carlson replied. "And there also seems to be plenty of Yoders, at least one with a sense of humor."

"Why do you say that?" she asked.

"Because I just figured out the name of a road we passed," he said. "I've been watching the names of the lanes leading to the farms and couldn't quite understand one named 'Redoy,' a word I've never heard before. Then it occurred to me that was Yoder spelled backward. I thought it might be some sort of inside joke among the family or neighbors."

"My, you are observant," she said with interest. "I've passed this way many times over the years and have never noticed it. I'll have to be careful with you, make sure you don't start picking up on my little secrets."

"Not much of a chance that will happen," he said smiling. "I've always found women to be very mysterious, so much so that I try not to pry—might find out some very scary things best left undisturbed."

"Then you are wiser than most men," she commented with a nod of her head. "Now let me tell you about the rocking chair."

Steinmann explained there were two brothers, both fine woodworkers living a short distance apart, one in Belleville, and the other in Allensville. They were Daniel and Joseph Peachey. Daniel specialized in handmade mission style and other heirloom furniture. He once made a handcrafted cherry console table that was presented to President George W. Bush during his visit to Penn State to speak at a Future Farmers of America convention. It was a replica of a piece made by a Scottish cabinetmaker circa 1760, a blend of both Queen Anne and Chippendale styles and given to the FFA Chapter at Crawford High School in Crawford, Texas, the high school near the President's ranch. It was to be put on prominent display in the lobby of that school. Former Secretary of Agriculture Sam Hayes was a good friend of Daniel's, who had made several pieces of furniture for him over the years. It was Hayes who commissioned the table as a gift to the President.

His brother, Joseph, specialized in reproduction Windsor chairs and highboys, but had done a massive Ark Synagogue carving. The carving, which framed the housing for the Torah Scrolls, was modeled after one seen in Israel and commissioned for a Synagogue in Brooklyn, New York. The work was seventeen feet high, seventeen feet wide and three to four feet deep, covered with an intricate hand-carved motif of grapes and grape leaves. It was so large that it was done in precise sections, shipped and assembled in New York. Joseph's creations were so in demand that he had a waiting list of up to two years for some pieces, but continued to produce a regular line of chairs and smaller tables. The rocker Steinmann had ordered promised to be some of the finest workmanship available because Joseph Peachey would never let a piece out of his workshop that was not up to his rigorously strict requirements.

Steinmann reached into her pocket and handed Carlson a business card for Joseph E. Peachy II, with the address of his workplace, The Wood Lathe Shop. "This says open Monday-Friday & Saturday by chance," he commented.

"I thought you'd notice that," she replied. "Do you think that's odd?"

"Not at all. I simply wish some of the businesses in Arizona, particularly on the Reservation, were that courteous," he said with a sigh. "My experience has been that 'by chance' applied to every day of the week, with special seasons making matters worse."

"I know what you mean," she confirmed. "Here in Pennsylvania, when the first day of hunting season arrives, schools are canceled because of lack of attendance."

"On the Reservation, it might be a nice day, or an itch to go fishing or hunting, or the simple urge to go over to so-and-so's to see what they are doing. Some people wake up in the morning devising such diversions."

Steinmann slowed, made a right turn, then wound around several lanes until pulling up to the front of Peachey's workshop, a two story barn-like affair built into a rise, with a second floor entrance level, the lower level falling off behind. The inside consisted mainly of two large open spaces, the first a room full of lathes of differing sizes and workbenches, the second with chairs and smaller tables lining the walls, along with a few pieces obviously left for repair. At a small, worn and cluttered desk sat a medium-sized man with strong looking hands sketching a motif that would later be hand-carved into some piece of furniture. Although neat and tidy, clean tools all in their orderly places along the walls, the rooms had the inevitable wood shavings and sawdust in small piles, with wood particles floating in the air.

"Hello, Mr. Peachey," Steinmann hailed as she approached. "I received the notice that the rocker is finished."

"Yes, Miss Steinmann," he answered, rising and shaking hands with them both. Carlson noticed his finely sculpted face and the kind, starkly blue eyes, made all the more prominent by the clear whiteness of the surrounding tissue. The man's grip was firm, but gentle, with the obvious strength necessary to his profession.

"There it is over there," she said to Carlson pointing across the room. "Come have a look at real workmanship."

The beauty of the piece could be seen from ten feet away, but as Carlson ran his hand over the back, sides and seat, the quality of the finish actually amazed him. All wood, light-colored cherry that would deepen into a mellow patina over time, with precisely honed joints and seemingly fine-tuned balance, reminded him of a true work of art.

"I like to make useful things," Peachey explained. "My neighbors expect I will make them to the best of my God-given abilities and they will last through generations. I do what I can, realizing that others may do much better."

"He's not being modest," Steinmann said with a slight smile and a twinkle in her eye. "I've known Mr. Peachey for years and I've found that he is probably the most naturally humble individual I have ever encountered. It is God's gift and his work is merely a demonstration of that fact. Will you show Abe the pictures of your ark synagogue carving, please?"

Peachey produced a series of pictures, spreading them across a table. This was indeed a fine piece of work on a large scale, but what impressed Carlson was how appropriate that God's gift should adorn a House of God, no matter the specific religion. The Old Testament religion and the New Testament woodworker were joined in homage to the same Divinity.

The new rocker tucked safely in the back seat and covered with a quilt, Steinmann took Carlson on a roundabout tour of the valley. She started on Front Mountain Road to the south, and then crossed over to Back Mountain Road to the north. Everywhere he looked, Carlson saw the undisputable evidence as to the fertility of the soil, whether planted or used for graze, and the ridges framing the valley lush with trees. He wondered how the first settlers must have felt upon their discovery and what their dealings were with the native civilization they were soon inevitably to replace.

"You seem a little quiet, Abe," Steinmann said. "Just awed by the scenery so unlike the southwest, or lost in thought?"

"Awed, yes," he replied. "But I was thinking more about the history of this part of the country and how the Indians were brutalized and eventually forced from the area—not all, of course, but the vast majority. News of every major incident passed quickly across the continent in all directions."

"I'm familiar with some of that history," she said, "particularly the Five Nations. I once taught a seminar on Seneca property rights and sovereignty issues involving a case wending through the higher courts. It didn't take me long to discover that the body of so-called Indian Law is a chimera. It should be more focused on Treaty Law, but then we all know how various treaties were ignored in the days of Manifest Destiny."

"Actually, I was thinking about the Revolutionary War period," he said quietly. "One major event in particular stands out. Are you familiar with the Sullivan Expedition?"

"I do recall an expedition of General Sullivan from the history books, but can't recall the details," she admitted. "I do seem to remember it was botched somewhere along the line and they never got to where they had intended. Care to enlighten me?"

Carlson related the story, not with anger, but with sadness, just as an ageless Mojave had related it to him years ago.

The Iroquois Confederation was originally comprised of five separate nations: Seneca, Cayuga, Onondaga, Oneida and Mohawk. This so-called Five Nations of the Confederacy later joined in 1724 by the more southern Tuscarora to become the Six Nations. The Confederacy's domain spanned a vast area from western New York to northern Pennsylvania. The Indians had fiercely discouraged encroachment of settlers into their territory with two raids—what the colonists called "massacres"—in 1778, one in July at Wyoming, Pennsylvania and in November at Cherry Valley, New York. On the eve of the Sullivan Expedition of 1779, the Colonials knew little about the area and what maps did exist were grossly inaccurate.

When war had broken out, the British offered persuasive words and elaborate gifts to entice the Iroquois Nations to its service, while the Colonies urged neutrality. Oneida friendship with the colonists prevented a solid pro-British front, but some members of other tribes succumbed. Some Oneida would later become guides to the Sullivan Expedition.

Indian farms and orchards in the Finger Lakes and Genesee Valley of New York were the breadbasket for most of the British armed forces, along with food sources throughout northern Pennsylvania. While Indian women tended the crops, their warrior husbands were out fighting with their Tory allies. Worse yet, the British had established a strong Fort Niagara, which is present day Niagara Falls. A major British invasion was in the works that would divide the Colonies in half.

"Excuse me, Abe," Steinmann interrupted. "I don't want to go on this expedition unfortified. One of my vices is ice cream, particularly on a nice July afternoon. What do you say we stop up ahead and indulge ourselves?"

"Certainly," Carlson replied. "I have to caution you, though, I'm pretty much a plain vanilla guy. If I get really daring, I let them add a few cherry bits."

Sitting in the shade on a picnic table, Carlson enjoyed his plain vanilla ice cream while Steinmann indulged in two scoops with such exotic names that he could not begin to unravel their probable contents.

"So, I guess this is where the Father of Our Country comes in, huh?" she said encouraging him to continue his saga.

"It certainly is," he replied. "General George Washington, Commander-in-Chief of the Colonial Army, saw the threat as so dire that he sent a full third of his forces to: 'Lay waste all the settlements around, so that the country may not only be overrun, but destroyed.' The capture of the British Fort Niagara would be the ultimate goal. Major General John Sullivan was just the man to get the job done."

The planned expedition was straightforward. General Sullivan would leave Easton, Pennsylvania with the main army of 3,500 men, 214 boats, 1,200 pack-horses and an estimated 1,000 cattle. He would proceed to the Susquehanna River, and then follow the river northward to Tioga Point, just south of the New York border. There he would be joined by General James Clinton from Schenectady, New York, traveling south and west down the Susquehanna, with 1,500 men and 212 boats, picking up another 200 men along the way. They would proceed through New York's Finger Lakes region and then to Fort Niagara, picking up another 650 men under Colonel Daniel Broadhead heading north from Fort Pitt, Pennsylvania.

As Sullivan and Clinton traveled north, they discovered an ambush not very far into New York at Newtown. Deploying Colonial forces to the flank and rear, the ambush failed.

Now the devastation began, as the systematic destruction of the Indian towns and fields all along the way was pursued in earnest. The Indians lived in log cabins much like the Colonials. One practice was to fill these cabins with corn and other goods, then set fire to the entire building. They also cut down fruit trees and Indians as the opportunity afforded. The largest Indian town to be destroyed was named the Genesee Castle, which had 128 houses. An estimated 20,000 bushels of corn was burned in the course of its destruction.

At this point winter was approaching and Sullivan decided not to go on to attack Fort Niagara. He was not equipped for colder weather and the Fort Pitt contingent under Colonel Broadhead had not arrived. Sullivan later learned that Broadhead's troops had devastated many acres of crops, but could not proceed because most of his men were literally barefoot. Sullivan also doubted his tired and poorly equipped army could successfully storm the heavily fortified and armed Fort Niagara.

Including more Indian towns obliterated on the return trip, a total of 41 had been wiped out of existence.

"It was hard winters for the Indians for some years to come," Carlson concluded. "Most were innocents having nothing to do with the British. Many children and old people were to starve and rebuilding towns would take time. After the devastation, Indians called Washington 'The Town Destroyer' and Sullivan 'The Corn Cutter.' Many more neutral warriors took up the Tory cause."

"And I take it that was just the beginning of the end?" she asked in low tones.

"It was for these people," he answered. "Such is the march of history, probably the same all over the world. The Peoples eventually were pushed out and moved either to Canada or to Ohio, or ended up in the Indian Territory, now known as Oklahoma. I have a Mohawk friend up in Canada who told me last year that his forefathers should have built a Great Wall of China twelve miles inland from the Atlantic Ocean and cancelled all visas. He figured the newcomers, thus contained, would devastate the land in short order, then just die out. Anyone coming after would see their bones and wisely decide to go elsewhere."

"Your friend has a very dry sense of humor," she said.

"I'm not sure he has any sense of humor at all," he replied. "I think he was telling me exactly how he felt about the subject."

"Don't I recall correctly that several important Indians fought at the side of the British during the war?" she asked.

"Oh, yes," he confirmed. "One of the ironies about the Sullivan Expedition is that the Mohawk Chief, *Thayendanega,* who adopted the name of Joseph Brant, fought on the British side. He was so articulate and learned that he became the first documented Indian to be raised to the degree of Master Mason in London about 1776. He once saved the life of Colonial Colonel McKinistry who had been captured and was about to be put to death. Brant recognized McKinistry's Masonic brotherhood when he gave a special sign and had him released and transported to a safe Masonic Lodge in Canada, from whence he eventually returned to Colonial hands.

"During the Sullivan Expedition three years later, Brant again saved the lives of Lieutenant Boyd and Sergeant Parker under the same circumstances, but it was not to last. When Brant was called away, a British officer named Butler grew frustrated in his failed attempts to gain information about the Colonial Army from the two captured men and turned them over to the Indians, who harshly tortured them to death."

The return drive back to Hummelstown was just as beautiful as restful. The conversation drifted to more mundane matters, swapping minor details about their pasts and the present, but not venturing into the unspoken taboo subject beyond tomorrow.

CHAPTER 8

▼

BEGINNINGS

Carlson had never owned a suit in other than western cut, with bolo tie, but decided upon reflection in the mirror that his perfectly tailored gray pinstripe, light blue dress shirt and maroon geometric tie, Windsor knotted, looked pretty good. He had even put a high buff to his boots and brushed his Virginia Gentleman's hat. With one last comb through his graying hair, he decided to leave the hat for the evening. Glancing at his watch, he realized he had time to spare and headed for the bar.

"You look real spiffy tonight, Abe," R.J. said from behind the bar. "Who's the lucky lady?"

"I'm the lucky guy, R.J.," he responded. "How about a cup of coffee?"

As she served his coffee, Carlson surveyed the room and found he was probably the most dressed man in the place—which made him a bit uncomfortable, second-guessing whether or not he might be over-dressed for the occasion. Then he realized he was having the jitters of a schoolboy ready to embark on a first date. After all, this was only a dinner invitation and he had known quite a few women in his lifetime. Veronica Steinmann was the first to trigger this kind of emotion from the first time he saw her getting out of her car. Maybe, just maybe, he thought, this was the beginning of something entirely new.

"So where are you taking this lady tonight?" R.J. asked, wondering what woman had charmed this very attractive man, who, if a few years younger, she might make a run for herself.

"Actually, she's taking me," he confided. "A place called Alfred's Victorian for dinner."

"Now that's impressive," she retorted. "You'll get some of the finest Italian food to be found in this state. It's a bit pricey for most people, but we do go there for special occasions. It's cozy and can be very romantic. I think they must have quit counting the number of awards they've received. There have been so many. You'll like it, I'm sure."

"I don't think this lady's choice is romantic," he replied. "I think it's more due to the fact that she likes good food and knows where to find it. Do you know Veronica Steinmann?"

"Wow, now I am impressed," she said with a smile. "Everybody knows Ronnie. She is a knockout. I'd bet half the men of a certain age in Derry Township have tried to woo her, and the other half live with the regret that they never tried."

"And what might that certain age be?" he inquired.

"Now, Abe," she said. "You know you shouldn't inquire as to a woman's age once she turns twenty-one. Let's just say she's twenty-six and holding, but we won't tell you how long she has been holding."

Carlson simply grinned, took a last sip of his coffee and tucked money under the saucer.

"I'm glad to see such womanly loyalty on the important issues," he winked and headed toward the door.

Before he reached the etched glass door to the entrance lobby, it opened and a stunning Veronica Steinmann walked in. She wore a so-called simple black cocktail dress with spaghetti straps, a white shawl draped loosely over the shoulders. At the neck was a simple gold chain, with a small watch at her wrist to match. Her hair was pulled back tightly and formed a sleek bun to the rear, highlighting two diamond-studded earrings. She looked like she had just stepped out of a New York fashion magazine as she glided gracefully across the floor and offered Carlson her hand.

"My, you sure still do like to dress up, don't you Ronnie?" R.J. asked humorously. "Your sheer elegance has always had the fellows falling all over themselves. Please be sure to handle Abe gently. He's such a nice man."

"So long as the fellows merely fall all over themselves," Steinmann replied. "Any more than that and I'll slap them with a lawsuit so fast they won't even see it coming. As for Abe, R.J., I think he can pretty well take care of his own self. And doesn't he clean up well, though?"

Everyone had a chuckle, including Carlson, but he did redden a shade.

"I'll take that as a compliment," he said. "And I might add that you do very well in that department yourself. But, then I reckon you already were aware of that fact."

"Of course she does," R.J. broke in. "Still, a girl likes to hear that once in awhile, so long as it's said in a gentlemanly manner."

"I can assure you he's every inch a gentleman," she said. "What do you say, Sport, hungry for some great food and sterling conversation?"

"I've been looking forward to it since you first asked," he replied.

"See, R.J. He is a gentleman—as advertised," she said, taking his offered arm and walking away. When they came to her car, he confirmed his chivalrous intent by opening the driver's door for her before walking around to take the passenger seat.

It was a short drive of only four miles to Middletown, home of Three Mile Island—the famous nuclear power plant—and Alfred's Victorian Restaurant. Along the way they passed Indian Echo Caverns, a popular local tourist destination, particularly in the summer when the temperature underground in this limestone honeycombed area stayed in the upper fifty-degree zone.

Alfred's Victorian stood on Union Street like a grand old lady, a luxurious brownstone mansion built in 1888 by a wealthy merchant who lost his fortune and his house when the local bank foreclosed for the benefit of its creditors. Steinmann had reserved the corner turret window seat, a cozy and private nook with a beaded curtain. A bottle of white wine was already chilling in a bucket on the table when they arrived.

"You really know how to treat a guy," Carlson said as he slid into his seat.

"Actually, I know how to treat myself," she replied with a smile. "I spend what money I have on clothing and good food. I like to dress well and you already know about a healthy Pennsylvania appetite, so this can't be much of a surprise. I would suggest the Seafood Bisque, perfect to share for two, and the Shrimp Farcis, two delightful jumbo shrimp stuffed with crab imperial and encased in a puff pastry. Of course, I can vouch for most other dishes on the menu. The chef prepares and presents his selections perfectly."

Accepting her suggestion, they both ordered and the waitress poured two glasses of wine. The conversation turned to her professorship.

"Why teach and not practice," he asked.

"Oh, I do practice some on the side," she answered frankly. "My grandfather, whom I worshipped, was a Federal District Court Judge with an extensive library. He granted me full access to those hallowed volumes, not just law, but a range of classical literature. I developed a passion for reading early on and progressed from

Mark Twain to Shakespeare, to the law. Law seemed at first to be crisp and clear, logical and practical on the printed page. I entered law school with an idealistic mission—to become a determined defender of legal rights for any man, woman or child in the country."

"And you found things weren't so crisp and clear in the real world?" he interjected.

"Exactly," she admitted. "Contract Law I found fascinating because much of the Constitution is based upon protecting property rights, Criminal Law defends the accused, Civil Law defines acceptable behavior with our neighbors, and so on. It all stems from one source, the Constitution and the Bill of Rights. And we have a great source for determining the intentions of the Founding Fathers in the Federalist Papers and the State Constitutions drawn by such men as Madison and Jefferson."

The arrival of their meals interrupted the conversation. Both took a few bites and sipped the wine.

"When I got out into the real world," she continued, "I found the law to be a rather messy business, with lawyers arguing for suppression of vital information, and judges seemingly making up procedures on the spur of the moment—distorting fairness. Such cases would never make their way up through the appellate process because defendants didn't have the money or the courts were so backlogged there was no chance these cases would ever make it on the docket. And in my *pro bono* work for the Public Defender's Office, I all-too-often found myself negotiating a plea bargain for someone, when in fact, he deserved to be put away for the rest of his life just to protect society at large."

"It must have been frustrating," he commented.

"Yes it was," she answered. "I found myself at a juncture. Either I would continue in frustration and become cynical and jaded, or I would find the core to my fascination with the law and pursue that field. I decided it was the love for the intent of the Constitution to bring together the disparate interests of the states and the people that I so much admired. I wanted to be sure that the next generation of law students would be well grounded in the subject, long before they had a chance to bend the law in the interests of one client or another."

"And I'm sure you are pretty good at it," he said. "You do wax eloquent on the subject."

"As a matter of fact, I do," she said. "I like to think I can say that with confidence, without the vanity it might imply. The proof of what success I may have had is in the number of former students who continue to correspond after they have secured their positions in the world. Many tell me they find Constitutional questions in nearly every case they handle. That means I did the job right."

The rest of the meal was filled mostly with small talk about just how good the food really was; over pastry and coffee Carlson broached a new subject.

"Veronica," he asked boldly, "how has such a lovely lady as you avoided being entangled with a man? That's asking a bit bluntly and I trust I'm not being too personal, but I haven't been able get that question off my mind. I certainly don't want to offend."

"I'm not offended at all," she said with a hint of a smile and glint in her eye. "I really don't think I intimidate men, but I confess I can be formidable to fools. I have had several semi-serious relationships, but it simply has never been with any-one I want to spend the rest of my life. Perhaps it's the company I keep. As a whole, lawyers tend not to be my type and in academia most seem to be intellec-tually stimulating, but quite naïve about the world at large. I also share the bias of every single woman when I say that all the good ones already seem to be taken or are gay. But to be frank, I simply haven't met the right one. Now, why don't you answer the same question? You seem to be a likely prospect."

"I suppose I've had my chances," he said turning quietly serious. "It is just that I have always thought it wouldn't be fair to a marriage if I were away most of the time, tramping around the wilderness, or flying off to some other continent for weeks or even months at a time. To be quite honest, I want a partner who has her own professional career and doubt my absences would contribute much to the social obligations that incurs. I want to provide a much more stable marriage than that and marriage is something that takes some work if it is to last."

In the pause that followed, Steinmann looked at Carlson in a slightly different light. She could not remember ever meeting a man so deeply considerate and unabashedly honest, without equivocation. The strength of his convictions must have left women at a loss to know how to react. And she was convinced that any-one who would want to change him in that respect would not be the one he was likely to ask.

"So, how's the search coming?" she asked to lighten the atmosphere. "Did the uncle leave any traces?"

"Everyone leaves traces," he replied. "You just have to figure out which are true and which are false. A couple of new friends at the Brownstone Lodge are searching some records for me and I hope to hear from them soon."

"My grandfather, the judge, was a Mason," she said. "Thirty-second Degree Scottish Rite. He was very active and had all sorts of things around the house with the emblems on them. One day when I was eight or so, we were in his library and he took a small box out of his desk and showed me a small set of tools that looked as if they belonged in a doll's house. He told me they were the Tools of the Craft and tried to explain the significance of each. I remember one was a trowel and another a square, but can't really recall their significance. They all had something to do with living an honest life, improving yourself, being good to others and helping mankind to get along. Building a better world, he said."

"You understood properly," said Carlson. "I didn't take any advanced degrees above Master Mason, which is the Third Degree, but I always thought I was as much a Mason at that level as I'd ever be. The higher degrees are really only amplifications of the first three, fine-tuning the specifics. Did your father follow in the Judge's footsteps?"

"No," she said. "My mother was his daughter. My father was an active Catholic and a member of the Knights of Columbus. There was some sharp friction between the Catholic Church and Freemasonry over the centuries, but my father and the Judge got along just fine. Locally the two groups would pursue joint projects, such as co-hosting a breakfast to fund a program which brought two Irish lads—one Catholic and one Protestant—over here for a couple of months in the summer to live together and get to know each other. The idea is that if they cooperate here, perhaps they will promote peace at home once they return."

"That sounds like a worthwhile endeavor," he said.

"And because her father was a Mason," she continued, "my mother was eligible to apply for entrance to the Masonic Village in Elizabethtown, once she was a widow. When my father died five years ago, she sold the house and bought a cottage on the campus, and as time progresses she can move into assisted living, then to individual care at any level of need. She has a sense of humor, calling the facilities 'God's Waiting Room.' I didn't have the heart to tell her that the residents of every nursing home in the country use the same term. And, perhaps the best part is that if she ever runs out of money, they'll still care for her. They don't throw you out and even give you a little monthly spending money."

"And she also gets to keep her dignity," he observed.

"That's exactly it," she replied. "Dignity and self-worth can flee pretty quickly under other circumstances. The Masons do their very best to see that doesn't happen."

CHAPTER 9

▼

THE NEXT STEP

Abe Carlson did not awake in the morning until after ten o'clock—an unusually late hour for him—to a light breeze coming through the window, promising a simply beautiful day. He wondered if he had only dreamed of dinner with Veronica. He had not wanted the evening to end and had suggested an all-night diner where they spent hours in conversation over matters large and small. The diner napkin on which he had scrawled a few notes lay on his bedside table, testament to the reality of the experience. Still partially in the haze of sleep, he grabbed his shaving kit and headed to the bath, whistling quietly to himself.

As he fastened the last button on his shirt, his cell phone rang.

"Abe Carlson," he said into the mouthpiece.

"Abe, this is Bud," Hanover identified himself. "Doc Straussburger is back home and this morning I showed him the letter and the attached notes."

"Did he have any good news?" Carlson asked.

"Sure did. Just as we thought, the attached notes are a list of names of people and places throughout the area. A couple of the families have long died out or left the area. Three were men active in the Lodge at that time, veterans of the First World War who died of war-related injuries before the beginning of the Second World War. They appear in our records of the time. But the problem is that neither Doc nor our records have any clue as to the existence of Sheldon C. Slate or that he was a Mason. Doc does remember a bit of hubbub around town in those days, some rumored trouble among the Masons, but it was kept confined within the Masonic Community and finally just died away. People were more interested in another war shaping up in Europe and the old veterans hoped we could stay out of it this time."

"Did Doc say anything else worthwhile?" Carlson asked.

"Everything Doc says is worthwhile, if he sometimes seems a little vague and you think he takes too long to get to the point," Hanover said. "He is a walking encyclopedia on all things Hummelstown and Hershey. And he still vacuums up information like no one else. He just arrived home last night, but wanted to know how your date with the Professor went. I didn't have a clue you even knew her."

"We just met a couple of days ago," Carlson replied a little defensively. "And it wasn't really what you would call a date, merely two new friends getting to know each other. I wouldn't want people to get the wrong impression."

"Oh, nobody has the wrong impression," he stated. "There isn't a man or woman in this town who would begrudge anyone wanting to spend some time with her. She's beautiful, smart, witty and well liked. They also know that if you did anything out of line, they'd be hearing about how she shredded you on the spot."

"I promise to watch myself," Carlson vowed, a sober and serious look on his face.

"Glad to hear that. Now, Doc is going to be out and about catching up on things most of the afternoon, but asked me to invite you for a drink at his house at the usual appointed hour—five o'clock sharp. A few other fellows will be there with their wives, both Masons and non-Masons; it promises to be a nice casual affair."

"I gladly accept," Carlson agreed.

Hanover gave directions to the house and several suggestions from the list that showed some promise.

"By the way," Hanover said at last. "Doc says it would be nice if you asked the Professor to come with you. He said he'd like to have a look at the man who could catch her attention, but could make a better assessment if he saw you two together."

"Please thank him," Carlson replied. "I'll certainly try."

One quick call to Dickinson Law School sealed the matter. "Doc always refers to me as 'The Professor,' but I don't mind at all," Steinmann said. "When he gives you a title it is always out of respect and pretty soon everyone else addresses you that way, too. Of course, those who knew me in my formative years still usually call me 'Ronnie,' but I found I grew beyond my nickname after about age thirty. I recognize that I do have some vanity and perhaps as a senior citizen I'll want to go back to 'Ronnie' again, but for now I rather enjoy Doc's moniker."

Carlson thought that if anyone this bright and beautiful deserved to display a little vanity now and then, it was this remarkable woman. Yet, he very much doubted she had an ounce of it her entire life. She simply did not see herself as others do, remaining blissfully comfortable in who she was and just getting on with life.

Anticipating the evening's invitation, Carlson found himself at a point of distraction and embarked on his favorite activity for focusing concentration—he went for a walk. And for Carlson, a walk of ten to twenty miles was just a 'good stretch of the legs.' He remembered that phrase used in the old movie *The Quiet Man,* starring John Wayne and Maureen O'Hara and had adopted it as his own. He picked up his hat, went downstairs and out through the front door of The Wick, not donning the headwear until turning right on the sidewalk.

He walked at a steady gait down Main Street to the edge of town, then crossed over and came back, taking side streets and the alleys. He had discovered years ago that you could tell more about people by observing their backyards than how they presented the house from the front. He delighted in one such stroll through several neighborhoods in London, where he found, no matter the supposed class of the housing, if there were even a small patch of land available, it would be planted with flowers and a few vegetables. Even small children enjoyed gardening.

He passed the V.F.W. Post with its modest building set well back from the street, flags festooning the wide expanse of front lawn. When he arrived at the high school, students were taking advantage using the playing fields or picnicking among the shade of trees. The middle school was a mirror image, classmates staying with their age group and playing with the same. He was impressed with the large number of well-built and tended churches, some quite old and others more modern. Even the long cloth-covered awning of the funeral home looked as if it were occupying its proper space. Old and new, large and small, the homes and businesses were a delightful mixture that gave the town a homey, but vibrant feeling.

Having ambled back to the center of town, he took another direction at the square, walking through a railroad underpass while a freight train moved slowly overhead, finding an extensive array of typical suburban homes with neatly tended grounds and landscaping. Children and pets abounded and there was no shortage of people washing cars, trucks and boats and applying wax. A brace of

Labrador Retrievers, one black, the other chocolate, reminded him that the creeks and rivers in this part of the state provided good bird hunting.

Returning to The Wick for a quick shower and a change of clothing, he felt refreshed from his exertions and ready for whatever the next step provided.

Steinmann arrived as promised ten minutes before five o'clock and they drove less than five minutes up Main Street to the home of Harry Harrison Straussburger, M.D. The house proved to be a large brownstone, with ample lawn and shrubbery, set among several others of very similar construction.

"That's quite a big house," Carlson remarked as they parked in front.

"Not really," Steinmann replied. "It does appear somewhat daunting on first encounter, but remember that Doc had his office on most of the first floor and reared a passel of children on the other two. He had the basement and the attic mostly converted for use of children and young adults of parents who were hospitalized and had no relatives to care for them. Doc often says he sometimes felt as if he were running an Army billet and his wife, Fiona, ran the place with military efficiency. Those two took in every stray child or animal and many people down on their luck and in need of a job."

"It sounds as if the doctor is a real town institution," Carlson observed. "Is he still in practice?"

"Officially, no," she replied. "He's in his mid-nineties and supposedly retired twenty years ago. Let me tell you briefly what he means to this town."

His personality and sense of community were formed when he was still "Young Harry," constantly bringing injured animals of all kinds home, patching them up and finding new homes. He also visited with the elderly just to ease their loneliness and listened for hours to their tales of what their lives had been. Bright as a student, he helped his classmates with their homework and always took the younger ones under his wing.

As a doctor, he was literally the only general practitioner for many years, making house calls, delivering babies, referring patients to only the best surgeons, stitching up inevitable injuries from farm work or around the rail yard or the nearby Brownstone quarries. He always took middle-of-the-night calls for assistance, whether major or minor, and even found time to volunteer at the Hershey School for Boys or local school athletic events when possible.

People still stop in for medical advice, spiritual or what amounts to marriage counseling. Few people know it, but he still responds to middle-of-the-night calls, if only to lend comfort by his presence. People, who think it is sad that he gave up his right to prescribe medicines along with his license, do not realize that he wrote very few prescriptions and treated his patients with many natural substances and plain old common sense.

"This is one man I have to meet," Carlson said as they walked up to the front door.

"You are just about to," she replied. "Welcome to the link between what used to be and what is the present. If we are all very lucky, we'd like it to be the future for as long as possible. Doc is one of the steel threads running continuously through this town's existence."

As he rang the doorbell, Carlson noticed the original Victorian color scheme on the porch railings and latticework on the building and the meticulous detailing denoting a home in the finest repair. They were greeted by a small, ageless woman with white hair and dressed in a stylish skirt and blouse, ruffles on the cuffs and collar.

"Hello, Aunt Mattie," Steinmann said in introduction. "May I introduce Abe Carlson? He's visiting us from out west and will be here only a short time."

"Pleased to meet you Mr. Carlson," she said extending a hand of welcome. "You certainly have the grapevine buzzing. People have reported spotting you all over the area, or so they have told Dad. They are not trying to be rude, just curious in a harmless way."

"Mattie is Doc's eldest," Steinmann said in explanation. "Everyone calls her Aunt Mattie, whether related or not and I'm sure she will expect you to do the same.

"Fiona passed a few years ago and Mattie has since acted as hostess for Doc's impromptu social engagements."

"Very pleased to make your acquaintance, Aunt Mattie," Carlson said, briefly moving to tip his hat before he realized he wasn't wearing one.

"Good, now I can call you Abe," she replied, taking his arm in escort. "Dad's been anxious to meet you. I can tell because I had to re-tie his bowtie three times in the last half hour. That's always the signal. He has tied his own all his life and would allow Mother to re-tie it only as a way to sooth his anxiousness."

Steinmann nodded as the two started through the hallway, following behind as they ascended the stairs to the second floor. They found Dr. Straussburger in his library, with a sideboard of various bottles of spirits and wine, plus an array of snacks.

"So this is the famous adventurer," Straussburger called across the room. "Thanks for accepting my invitation."

"My pleasure, Dr. Straussburger," Carlson replied, shaking his hand. "I don't know how famous, but I do have some recognition in certain areas."

"This is a casual invitation, Abe. Please call me Doc like everyone else. It makes things easier. And famous you are, indeed. I don't confine my natural inquisitiveness to this area alone, you know. I have friends and colleagues all over the world and took the liberty of making a few calls this afternoon. You are well known and highly respected by more people than you might think."

"And that's a real seal of approval," Steinmann interrupted, striding over to give the Doctor a hug and peck on the cheek. "It's like having a sterling report from the F.B.I. Doc has a network to rival any in the world. If he says you're clean and upright, that's good enough for me."

"I would be prepared to wager fairly highly that you did something very similar, Professor," Straussburger replied. "I've known you to be a very thorough young lady. I seem to recall your asking my appraisal of several potential dates way back in high school."

"Must have been another young lady," she replied with a wink and a squeeze of his forearm. "You know we women have to have our secrets, never to be revealed. Are we early? I thought you always demanded promptness of your guests."

"Indeed, I do," he answered. "It was mostly Fiona who enforced that rule. I suppose Mattie does not present such a formidable front."

"Don't pay any mind to him on that score, Abe," Aunt Mattie broke in. "She was the most gentle and kind woman in the world. Guest showed up promptly so as not to offend her in any way. Besides, he knows full well the other guests were expected to be a little late so he could have a private shot at determining your intentions. He has been a particular champion of Veronica's since she was a child and beamed like a father over her many accomplishments. Plus, he wanted to see what prompted Veronica's interest in a man. Do I have everything about right, Dad?"

"Abe," he stated, looking to Carlson. "If you can help it, don't let so many women dominate your household. As you can readily see, even my daughter mothers me to no end. She speaks the truth, of course. You seem just fine. And I must add that you have very good taste."

"Does anyone not know I'm in the room?" Steinmann asked with a smile. "I'm not on auction here. Good Lord, Aunt Mattie, is there no longer any modern male with an open mind."

As they all chuckled, the other guests seemed to arrive all at once. The library and two other rooms were soon filled with people who had first paid their respects to the host and hostess, glanced unobtrusively at Carlson and Steinmann, then served themselves to bits of food and a drink. Doc watched approvingly when Carlson handed Steinmann a glass of wine, then poured himself a short portion of aged bourbon—sensing a man of taste and moderation. Aunt Mattie served her father from a pitcher of martinis. By unspoken custom, Doc preferred his guests limit themselves to one refill and noted Carlson only sipped and did not have another.

"Well, Doc," Bud Hanover said in the group surrounding Straussburger, "it looks as if you approve of Abe. You know why he's here. Why don't you give him a feel of what this town was like back in the 1930s?"

As many as were able took seats, while others lined the walls, he began his narrative. He remembered the days of his youth and the vibrancy of Hummelstown. To his eyes, this was not simply a sleepy farming town, but a thriving hive of activity. He witnessed the movement of goods on the railroad, the workers in the quarries, the busy shops and packed schools. Sure, there still were some local farmers who were eking the very last out of ancient steam farming equipment, but most were as up-to-date as possible and as the last horses faded from the scene, the Amish still carried on their livelihoods by horse and buggy. He also noted the rapid changes in automobiles, radio technology and scientific strides. His description of the evolution in medicine in his time was a wonderful tale, worthy of a book.

Doc recognized early that his deep interest in the lives of his neighbors and the affairs of the community was in reality a great zest for life in all its facets. This would be the cornerstone for the development of his character.

He related the swing and sway of society through wars, droughts and deaths, but also weddings, bumper crop years and births. He talked of families and businesses he had known, many of whom had descendents in this very room. For the latter, he was able to recall small antidotes about specific incidents relating to their relatives, mostly humorous, but more often displaying a reverence for religion, truth, honor or some other virtue.

For those unfamiliar with the details of Carlson's visit, Doc provided an outline of inquiry and purpose. He asked anyone who might contribute a fact, name or inquiry of a neighbor to lend assistance. Carlson immediately understood that Doc was quietly enlisting a veritable army for his cause and was both elated and humbled by the gift.

"One last thing," Straussburger reminded. "Sheldon C. Slate did not, as yet discovered, leave any mark on this town. However, I vaguely recall around that time a curious fashion. Perhaps as a result of World War I and what many in this largely German community saw as the gathering storm over Europe, those who had traveled more widely in the world tended to make slight changes to their names to make them less Germanic or adopt new names entirely. Please ask around and see if anyone remembers the fad and, more importantly, the names which may have been included."

In the next forty-five minutes of refills and mingling, everyone he had not met, who chatted briefly and promised to see how they could help, approached Carlson. "It isn't good to not have any family," one older woman said. "You must have a family with which to share life's triumphs and defeats," said another, "otherwise, what's the sense of it all?"

The affair dwindled as if right on cue; Carlson lingered to have a word with Straussburger.

"Doc," he said straightforwardly while shaking his hand, "I find it difficult to thank you enough for what you've done. That's quite a force you've marshaled on my behalf."

"They are all good people," Straussburger replied. "And they come from solid stock. It has been my experience that when you ask for help in this community, everyone is naturally glad to provide whatever assistance is within their power. There is also a portion of ethos at work here, a sense of reinforcing one's personal integrity by giving in the spirit that the request was made. We are just passing out of a period of great difficulty for the last two decades. People were shocked and saddened that our revered form of governance has chipped away at basic liberties, become intolerant of diversity, and sought to restrict the society and the world as a whole to a narrow, often discredited, set of ideals. Corruption of the system is not easily corrected, and will take some time to achieve, but we all recognize that it has to begin here, at the community level. If we are able to reinstate civility in debate and acceptance of views other than our own, we might have a fighting chance. I've dealt with these issues, in one form or another, all my life and know that change must be from the bottom up to be successful."

CHAPTER 10

▼

TRADITIONS

Steinmann made a brief telephone call on the way to her car, pausing to ask Carlson if he'd like to take a short drive to see the Masonic Village in Elizabethtown and meet her mother.

"That would be just fine," he replied. "Taking me home to meet the family, that's a good sign, isn't it?"

"Better rein in the buggy a bit, Sport," she replied with a smile, showing she appreciated the banter. "I thought you might like to see the beautiful campus and meet the woman who can put some historical perspective to your inquiry."

"Okay, Mother," she said into the phone. "We should be there in about a half hour. I'd like to give Abe a brief tour of the grounds and then we'll stop at your house."

Steinmann drove the back roads to Elizabethtown, knowing Carlson would appreciate the farms and houses along the way, rather than the more direct, but less scenic, Interstate 283. Glancing his way occasionally as she drove, she could tell she had made the right choice.

"You know one thing that continues to impress me?" he asked at last, not waiting for an answer. "People of the western states tend to think of the east coast as wall-to-wall people and tall buildings, concrete sealing the landscape. They don't think of the lushness of the land, the gentle spread of the valleys, or the dispersed population outside of the big cities. By and large, you still have quite a bit of elbow room in which to grow."

"And we in the eastern states think you have all the elbow room you could ever want," she replied. "We think of your huge ranches and local wars over water rights and barbed wire fencing."

"Some ranches are sizable," he explained. "But that is out of necessity. The range can be pretty sparse and it takes a lot of land to sustain a herd of any real size. As for water wars, they are true enough and will continue to be, far into the future. Anytime a life-sustaining commodity as basic as water is in short supply, people will fight furiously for their share, but most of the warfare is in the backrooms of government and corporations. As for wars over barbed wire, that's consigned to Hollywood movies that have no real idea of life in the latter years of the 19th and early part of the 20th Centuries. It ranks right up there with the myths such as the cowboy loses the girl in the end, but is satisfied to kiss his horse and ride off into the sunset."

"So, you've never kissed your horse?" she asked playfully.

"Now who is asking the personal questions?" he countered. "Yet, I can't plead the Fifth, as I understand you lawyers like to say. I may have kissed a horse or two in my time, but nothing I can recall of any lasting significance."

"And what about the wide-open spaces?" she asked. "Is that also a myth?"

"Oh, that's a reality, all right," he replied a little sadly. "As naturally beautiful as the landscape can be, it will not sustain a great deal of development. And where development has taken place, there is little room." Carlson explained the establishment of the once spacious valley that is home to Phoenix. For a variety of reasons, from the overwhelming federal vs. state and private land ownership to practical resources such as water, the population growth grew to fill the valley from east to west, north to south that all the surrounding towns were engulfed and overrun to such an extent that you could no longer tell which jurisdiction you were in unless you happed to see a sign. Closely packed suburbs sprang up right on the edge of ranches and small farms because people wanted a stylized view of nature, but then the residents suddenly objected to the natural smells of livestock. The ranchers finally sold out at inflated prices and moved further out, hoping to continue their way of life for at least their generation. They had little hope of a new generation of ranchers after that. "My point is," he said in conclusion, "we could have learned a lot about proper land development and integration of resources if we had paid more attention to how well people here have managed."

"Perhaps," she said. "But to be fair, we had one historic advantage you lacked. We had a whole empty continent as a place to vent excess population, talent and ambition. We had an open highway to everywhere. In that sense, much of the southwest was built on a cul-de-sac, nice to be there, but nowhere else to go, but back."

"I've never thought of it in those terms," Carlson admitted. "I think you may be perfectly right. No wonder you are a professor, and a good one at that."

"Don't give me too much credit," she replied. "I was taught to think under the tutorage of the best, my mother, who you are about to meet. She taught Civics and History for many years and is well versed in the Classics. She has a sharp, penetrating mind with an interest in everything, coupled with an easy manner and the countenance of a saint. She also knows more about Pennsylvania history than most college professors teaching the subject."

"I supposed most people see a lot of her in you, then," he commented.

"I hope so," she replied. "I really hope so. Of that, I would be very proud."

The Masonic Village was everything Carlson had expected and much, much more. Set on 1,400 acres of hilly farmland this continuing care retirement community included a children's home and community service organization.

"Very impressive," was all he could think to say as they slowly entered the tree-lined street, with substantial stone buildings overlooking broad expanses of lawn, formal gardens, picnic pavilions and walking paths.

"Yes, it is, isn't it?" came her reply. "Our Pennsylvania Masons can rightly boast of having the 'Jewel in the Crown' of such facilities scattered throughout the states. They built well, did not skimp on either materials or expertise and continue to expand to meet rising demand. They currently offer nursing services for up to about 450 residents, with dementia care a specialty, assisted living for over 125 people, about 330 retirement living apartments and more than 116 retirement living cottages. There is also a Residential Cottage, home to eight adults with mild to moderate mental retardation and up to 40 school-age youth live at the Masonic Children's Home. The retirement living cottages, one of which my mother has, are in an expansion mode to nearly double over a decade or so."

"That huge stone building overlooking the formal garden looks as if it would fit comfortably on any major college campus in the world," he said as he watched a shuttle bus disgorging a group of older people with walkers. As they ambled to the sidewalk and lined up facing the bus, the driver opened the baggage area and began handing out heavy round leather bags.

"That's the bowling team just back from the lanes," she explained, as they gathered their equipment and shuffled toward their building. "They're a feisty group and determined to go out kicking. A few years ago they had bowling shirts made with a quote on the back, which read: 'Do not go softly into that dark night.' That just about sums it up."

They slowly passed the Freemasons Cultural Center and Masonic Conference Center. Brossman ballroom, a multimedia center, museum, visitors center recreation areas, Masonic Lodge and dining area made the buildings ideal for requests made by the Fraternity and the community at large.

On top of one of the higher elevations, they saw a building used to vend the produce from the site's extensive orchards and gardens. Jams and jellies, related processed goods, candies and snacks were available over a range of foodstuffs.

Everywhere they turned, they saw only neatly manicured lawns, spectacular views and felt a sense of peace and quiet enhanced by a slight breeze and the sounds of nature. The word that came to mind for Carlson was 'idyllic.' He had felt this way on rare occasions in his life. It usually came when he was camping alone along a canyon stream, or high on some mountain at the close of the day, or watching from a distance the birth of a fawn. These enhancements by nature only added to our pleasure in life, if only we took the time to stop and observe.

Steinmann would have broken the silence, but their moods synchronized and she knew instinctively she was sharing the same sentiments. Not a word or gesture was needed. The momentary appreciation of Grace was complete.

The cottage was an attractive one-story duplex with a long sun porch to the back and walkout basement. Like everywhere else on this campus, the grounds were immaculate, with exteriors to match.

"Mother's place is even neater on the inside," Steinmann observed as she pulled into the driveway. "She is a fit sports enthusiast whose garage wall is covered with tennis rackets, skis—both water and snow—and other paraphernalia neatly hung, labeled and clean. I have never been able to keep up with her in that department. A dust bunny wouldn't dare enter her front door. It would die of fright at her cleanliness."

The full-paned storm door opened and out walked a slim woman of medium height, salt and pepper hair, dressed in neatly creased slacks, silk print blouse and casual shoes. Her earrings, necklace, bracelets and rings were not understated, but somehow complimented her outfit.

"Going on another cruise, Mother?" Steinmann offered in greeting, giving her an affectionate peck on the cheek.

"Now, Veronica," her mother replied in mock sternness, "You know very well that we don't cruise. We sail or motor, and at times paddle, but never cruise. So, who is this attractive specimen of a man you have brought to my doorstep?"

"Pay no attention to the attitude, Abe," Steinmann said, turning to him. "She knows perfectly well who you are and what you are about. She only puts on her 'queen act' when she wants to break ice with someone she wants to get to know. It's a compliment really."

"Of course I know who Abe Carlson is," her mother replied, taking Carlson's hand and giving it a firm shake. "She has talked of you often enough on the phone these past few days, Abe. If I weren't her mother, I'd say she was smitten. But then, I am her mother and mothers don't reveal their daughters' secrets, do they?"

"I'm not sure about that, Mrs. Steinmann," Abe said as Veronica rolled her eyes, "You see, I find women so mysterious that I never delve too deeply. It might shatter my myths and make you less intriguing."

"Veronica," she said, taking Carlson's arm, "you might have a keeper here. Don't throw this one back until you've looked him over very closely. They don't make them like this anymore. Come now, children, I've just brewed a fresh pot of coffee and Mrs. Keith next door brought over this week's baking—some sort of bread—that she insists I try. Bless her, she does like to bake and her husband does like to eat well."

The cottage was, indeed, immaculate, with everything perfectly positioned and polished, no stray item wandering out of its rightful place. As Veronica gave him the tour, Abe noticed that each room contained at least one bookcase, volumes neatly arranged by subject, size and even color. Multiple volume sets fit neatly on one shelf and if the set did not completely fill the width, stray volumes of appropriate height and width filled in the space. Only the guest room looked a little different, with two tall bookcases filled with antiquarian volumes, arranged in no particular order for size or depth, much like one might expect to find in a college professor's office.

"Mother's shrine to her dear Aunt Margaret," she said, watching him scan the titles. "She was a bit of an Anglophile, with a good dose of Francophile thrown in for good measure. She read voraciously anything she could find about Europe, with particular concentration on the 19th Century. She also had a peculiar interest in collective lectures by American theologians who were popular at the time. As a young girl, her mother had taken her to a few Chautauqua lectures and she was smitten with self-improvement through reading and study."

"She had an eclectic range of interests," he noted.

"Yes, and mother adored her," she replied. "She was a bit disheveled, didn't think much about house cleaning and was a very moderate cook—all opposites of my mother—but she was dearly loved and perfectly-groomed. Well-mannered ten-year-old Ruby was granted access to this library to her heart's content. It was Aunt Margaret who first taught her critical analysis, taking various subjects from a particular era—religion, governments, warring nations, individual occupations, national economies, etc.—and finding how they were related to the real world. Aunt Margaret had an extremely ordered intellect. This was the start of my mother's life-long interest in Civics."

Responding to a call from her mother, the two preceded to the sunroom, where a teacart had been placed loaded with coffee, cups and assorted baked goods. Apparently Mrs. Keith from next door had made quite a few gifts that were put in the freezer and brought out for special occasions.

"Okay, Mother," Veronica began after cups had been filled and plates passed. "You were always smarter than I."

"But, of course I am, dear," she interrupted, turning the Carlson. "You see, Abe, the trick is not to let them know it until they are adults. Don't want to bruise their self-esteem and all that." Everyone had a chuckle over that remark.

"Thank you for so graciously sparing mine, Mother," Veronica said with a smile. "Now, I've told Abe you are the best at putting his situation in historical context, so that perhaps he'll pick up some information he doesn't know he is looking for and be able to apply it."

"I'll see what I can do," she said. "Abe, I think the key to what you are looking for will be found in the context of what may be termed 'The Traditions of Pennsylvania.' They are the much-overlooked factors in what is occurring today."

She started with William Penn and his intentions for settling what was then known as Penn's Wood. To ensure prosperity and permanence, Penn invited hard-working farmers, merchants and artisans from Switzerland, Germany and other countries who were perceived as to fit the mold. More importantly, he insisted on his Colony being open to all religions. At the time, many Colonies excluded one group or another over religious prejudice. Penn was able to attract Quakers, Lutherans, Methodists, Baptists, Catholics, and every other mainstream Christians, plus held the door open for Jews, non-religionists and anyone else who cared to participate in his noble experiment. Tolerance was the key and civil discourse was the practice of the day. Penn held strong views on acceptance of differences and did all he could to impose this acceptance throughout this society.

"Can you see the atmosphere that allowed Freemasonry to take root and flourish so rapidly in Pennsylvania?" she asked. "My father stressed this fact throughout his lifetime, particularly when we faced periods of civic turmoil. William Penn was the shining example for building a strong and free society."

"Doc Straussburger seems to have a strong leaning in that direction," Carlson said. "In fact, most people I've met here seem to have that feeling to one extent or another. It gives a whole new perspective to the slogan 'You Have a Friend in Pennsylvania' which used to be on your license plates."

"Now you're getting the idea," Ruby replied. "We've got a bright pupil here, Veronica. I trust you noticed Aunt Margaret's books in the guest room, Abe?"

"I certainly did," he acknowledged. "And there are some fine volumes in the collection."

"That's true," she said. "What makes a book fine is not necessarily the cost of the binding. The thoughts on the page are the real gauge of its worth—the information successfully transferred to the reader. That collection appears at first as just a hodge-podge of random volumes for a particular era, but if you relate them to each other—including even the typical Victorian era novels—you get a pretty clear picture of life in its entirety during a certain period. What immediately becomes apparent is that since ancient times we all deal with the same situations, dramas, tragedies, triumphs, relationships and any number of aspects to just being alive. Generation after generation either successfully overcomes certain flaws in society at large or is doomed to perpetuate them."

"And in our all-too-brief time here on earth," he followed her train of thought, "we all only have few chances to correct human development. The real gratitude of mankind should go to those in our past who have stepped up and made a difference, no matter how incremental, and inspire us to follow their example."

"He's got it, Veronica," she declared. "By George, he's got it. I certainly would have enjoyed having you as my student, Abe."

"I'm not so sure I would have understood as much at that age to make any difference," he replied modestly. "It has taken years of living and observing life that has led to my current level of understanding and I like to think that I will always be open to influences which might alter that understanding for the better, refine my outlook right up until the end. Even then, I must admit that I doubt any of us can be perfect or we wouldn't be here. I admire the idea of reincarnation. It makes a lot of sense and I look forward heartily to the next number of times. It will be an adventure to my liking."

"How eloquently stated," Ruby remarked.

"He quotes Shakespeare accurately, too," Veronica said, "and some of the Greeks and Eastern philosophers, then mixes in Mark Twain, Bret Harte and, just as easily, the viewpoint of *The London Times.* He is remarkably deep and I have only scratched the surface, Mother. And now, knowing and loving you so well, I have to take Abe home. If not, you'll continue to quiz him far into the wee hours of the night and he won't be rested for tomorrow's labors."

"I would like to respond to that by saying you are an ungrateful daughter," she replied, "but I can't because you are, as always, truthful in your observations. I'd keep him as long as I could just to have someone intelligent to discuss matters."

"What about some of those elderly and distinguished looking men I see around the Village?" Veronica asked. "Surely they seem fairly intelligent."

"Oh my dear daughter, you have so much to learn," she replied with false dramatics. "Most of the good ones are married and here with their wives, many of whom are on the lookout that some other old lady such as I will snatch them up once they are widowers. I can't blame them. It can be a dog-eat-dog world out there when you're elderly. As for the rest of them who are unattached, they are in failing health and are just looking for a new wife to tend to them until the grave."

"So much for her tolerance, huh, Abe?" she probed.

"I don't think tolerance has anything to do with it," he replied. "It's the natural survival instinct. She has a right to her own pursuit of happiness, without the encumbrances others might wish her to endure. That is why this facility provides Assisted Living, Critical Care and all the rest."

"Veronica, take this man away immediately," she said. "I have this sudden urge to adopt him. Only, please promise you'll bring him back at least once before he leaves. And if it's not convenient, remember that I do have my own car, am out and about on a regular basis, and could meet you somewhere."

"My mother, always correct and always direct," she replied. "Come on, Abe, let's get you home."

"It has been a pleasure to meet you Mrs. Steinmann," he said in parting. "Thank you for your enlightenment."

"Let's drop the 'Mrs.,' Abe," she replied. "It's Ruby if you don't mind. It makes a woman my age feel so much younger and appreciated to be called by her first name."

"I'll be happy to oblige, Ruby," Abe said.

"Oh, Lord," Veronica stepped into the conversation. "You have turned my mother into a flirting schoolgirl, Abe. I can't say I've seen any man but my father have that effect. The funny thing is that I don't begrudge her at all."

With that said, the two headed for her car and waved goodbye to Ruby as she stood in the front doorway.

CHAPTER 11

▼

TRANSITION

Abe Carlson emerged from The Wick to a cool breeze and crystal clear air; his laptop was slung over one shoulder. He had dedicated this morning to some broad research in an effort to get a feel for what Hershey was like in the early 1900s and Veronica suggested that a good place to start would be the Derry Township Historical Society. He was just beginning to understand the levels of jurisdiction. There was a Hershey on the maps, but in a sense there was no Hershey, *per se,* with a government structure, only Derry Township, part of the huge Dauphin County. The Historical Society was located in a small museum and library near Hershey Park and nestled behind the always-popular Hershey Outlets.

He parked his Jeep well away from the entrance as a common courtesy. He planned to spend several hours feeding data into his computer, saving the closer spaces for those making shorter visits. As he walked across the parking lot, an elderly gentleman coming out of the building hailed him.

"If you are here to make a donation," the man said, pointing to the Jeep, "I don't think they'll take it. You might do better at the Antique Automobile Association across town."

"Not much chance of that happening," Carlson answered with a smile. "We've been together too long and I'd hate to part with it when it has so many more miles to go."

"Know what you mean," the man replied. "I've got a Ford Falcon at home that's still as reliable as the day I drove it off the lot. My wife prefers our Lincoln, of course, but she understands. Martha says that the day I want to trade the Ford in for a newer model, is the day she'll start worrying about what else I may want to update."

"Isn't love wonderful?" Carlson asked.

"It certainly is," the man replied. "You look like you're here for some serious business—through the door and take a left. The folks at the counter will take good care of you."

"Thank you, I will. And you have a great day," he said in parting, with a tip of his hat.

Approaching the counter inside, Carlson stated his interest in the history of Hershey about one hundred years ago. The two ladies sitting behind the front desk glanced at each other and winked.

"Would that be B.C. or A.C.?" asked the one whose nametag read Millie.

"I beg your pardon?" Carlson countered.

"That's either 'Before Chocolate' or 'After Chocolate'," the other woman said with a chuckle. "That's what passes as humor around here among us history buffs. We all can't be stuffy, you know."

"Actually, I think it's rather clever," Carlson said with a smile. "I'm interested in the period between 1900 and 1935. I was hoping you could recommend some books to read and a small out-of-the-way space so I could take some notes."

"We can do better than that," Millie said. "Does your machine run CDs?"

"It certainly does," he replied.

"To your left you'll see a rack of CDs on the counter. The one entitled *Our Town; A History of Derry Township* should be just what you're looking for. You'll note that the subtitle mentions before, during and after Milton S. Hershey. You will see the source of our B.C./A.C. humor and you have chosen the exact period of transition. That will be twelve dollars and sixty-seven cents, with tax, please."

Having paid for the disc, Millie led him to a back room with a small table against the wall, with a chair and table lamp. He thanked her, slid the disc into his computer and started reading.

Early in the 1700s, when the area was still frontier, the persecuted Scots left Ireland and emigrated to a village named Derry Church, followed by the hardy Germans. In the main, these two groups developed a rich dairy farmland. Swatara Creek and its tributaries provided much needed waterpower and by 1830-40 the area could boast of two gristmills, three saw mills, two tanneries and five distilleries.

By the mid to late 1880s there existed twenty limestone quarries and three brownstone quarries, the largest of which was the Hummelstown Brownstone Company which lasted until 1929. There were smaller quarries for marble, granite, slate and sandstone. The brownstone was of the finest quality, perfect for building large structures, bridges, canals and even tombstones. Eventually five brownstone quarries were cutting and shipping their product to New York, Florida and as far west as Missouri.

During the boom years of brownstone, large numbers of émigrés came to work the quarries. Many were Italian and a number of black Americans fleeing the south found work. It was hard and hazardous work, but paid well enough to establish families in the area. The peak of the industry was around the turn of the century as newer and more popular building materials were developed and brownstone made a rapid decline.

Born in Derry Church in a long line of Mennonites, Milton Snavely Hershey tried and failed in many businesses throughout his young adult life. Apprenticed to a candy maker, his venture into a business of his own as a candy-maker failed in Philadelphia; then after an odd adventure with his father to mine silver in Colorado, which also failed miserably, he took a job with a Colorado candy-maker, learning the importance of fresh milk in making the best candies. Another venture in candy making in New York City also ended in failure. After each failure he returned to Lancaster, Pennsylvania. This time, he started a caramel specialty factory, which was a great success and quickly made him quite wealthy. He toured the world to learn how candy was made elsewhere and married in 1898. Two years later, he sold his caramel business for one million dollars, with the understanding he would stay out of the caramel line. He used some of his money to buy back the old family homestead in Derry Church. In 1903 he embarked on another candy venture with chocolate, which was to become the largest chocolate manufacturer in the world and launch his legendary largesse to the community and the world at large and imprint the name Hershey on his birthplace.

"Interest you in a fresh cup of coffee?" Millie called from the doorway. "You've been at it for two hours straight and not a peep out of you."

"Sorry, I get wrapped up and don't know where the time goes," he said. "Coffee would be great, black, please."

She returned in a few minutes with a large coffee and a cinnamon bun.

"Can't have a coffee without a little nosh, now can you?" she asked.

"If I stay in Pennsylvania and follow your customs for too much longer," he replied, "I'll soon be too heavy to carry myself around. Have you got time for a few questions?"

"Sure, fire away, I'll do the best I can."

"First of all," he started, "I see why everything is pre- and post-chocolate. I can also see that he picked up what was soon to be a dying town and brought permanent prosperity. Everyone knows of all the great things he did—good jobs, housing, education, supporting churches and his famous school for orphans—all through the development of a chocolate empire. Yet there seems to be no feel for the lurching fortunes, both up and down, that must have accompanied such great changes in so short a period of time."

"You are right there," she conceded. "I suppose we think of history as a collection of events and trends. And we suppose our ancestors of a couple of generations removed to be rather plain, hard-working people, but without the passions and excitement we attribute to our own times. I do know, though, that my ancestors began in the quarries, which was very dangerous work. They moved on to the chocolate factories for better pay and more favorable working conditions. Also remember that Mr. Hershey's enterprise absorbed many other ancillary occupations such as stonemasons and other skilled workers in stone. As the quarries declined, he also hired mechanics and tool-and-die makers of all stripes. He was a great builder and as you can see by just driving through town the number of limestone buildings he erected. And don't forget a couple of his prime reasons for choosing this location—the number of dairy farms and an established railroad system for efficiently moving materials in and products out. The old saying about the tide raising all boats is literally true in this case. He also kept his employees working during the hard times of World Wars and the Great Depression."

"Your family made such a transition?" he asked.

"Yes," she replied. "Rossi was the name. My grandfather was a stonecutter who went to Mr. Hershey as a supervisor for new buildings, then to maintenance and repair. My father was a horticulturalist and from the very beginning Mrs. Hershey was very interested in beautiful landscaping and parks. They spared no expense on such things. The Rose Garden at the Hershey Hotel is first rate and world famous. I married Joe Campbell, a Scotsman to the core, as he'd let you know on first meeting. His family had a hand in the layout, building and care of the marvelous golf courses."

Carlson spent another two hours sipping coffee, nibbling at the bun and perusing the CD for information on various aspects of the development of Derry Township. Finally, he decided to take a break, go for a long walk and air out his thoughts. He thanked the staff for all their assistance and hospitality and went to a long walking path he had spotted on the way into town, near the Penn State Milton S. Hershey Medical Center at Route 322 and Bull Frog Valley Road.

The macadam path paralleled the roads, skirting fields of hay and winding up and down various grades. A steady breeze, little humidity and temperatures in the mid-seventies made for a perfect day for such activity. If he didn't have a good walk every couple of days he began to feel somehow sluggish and penned in. Besides, he did most of his best thinking when he was afoot.

His thoughts traveled back to the original inhabitants of the broad area in this part of the state, the Susquehannocks, who had thrived here for centuries before being nearly totally annihilated by the Iroquois about 1675. No other strong Indian Nation rose to replace them. The incursion of settlement by the Europeans a mere fifty years later might have been a bit harder than it was if the Iroquois had not so decimated the population. Still, the early settlers had to go everywhere, even into the fields to farm, fully armed to prevent Indian attack. The native population eventually accommodated the newcomers or melted back into the forests, mountains and streams of the wilderness.

Carlson also recognized the tie between William Penn's original goal of tolerance and acceptance between differing groups of people working together to establish a strong community with benefits to all with what Milton Hershey was able to accomplish in his lifetime and his legacy. Hershey was able to start a chocolate factory which would grow into a candy empire, erect affordable housing for his workers, establish cultural institutions in the community, promote a first-rate school system, parks and recreation, provide jobs even in the depths of the Depression and establish a school for orphan boys which would become one of the richest endowments in the world. Eventually the school would become coeducational, with state of the art facilities and high-tech appointments. When asked many times about his motivation for doing all these things, his answer was always to state his belief in the Golden Rule. To him it was a simple "Do Unto Others as You Would Have Them do Unto You."

Yet there was an even more important trend that his example inspired, even if unknowingly. Carlson noticed in his reading that in this short period of the first three decades of the 1900s a host of organizations sprang up. Fraternal organizations for the betterment of man were established. Civic groups of all types, relief societies, betterment guilds and social groups abounded. There was even an organization founded to gather farmers on a regular basis to learn new advances in agriculture and husbandry. Unfortunately, there was no indication that this latter group came to fruition. But the surge in the number and diversity of these groups all point to improvement for all.

The big questions for Carlson remained: where did Sheldon C. Slate fit into this dynamically changing community, was he really his father's half-brother, was he really a Mason and why would a Lutheran minister think he had been "Morganized?"

Carlson came upon the beautiful little Bull Frog Valley Park, with a nice pond and huge weeping willow tree, ducks paddling around in small groups, and a few people having picnics. Two small boys flanked a man who was showing them how to watch the bobbers on their fishing lines for a bite. By the looks on their faces, they must not have been having much luck. It was probably still too warm for the fish to rise and take the bait. He approached an older man leaning on the plank fence and smoking a pipe, just watching the ducks.

"What a nice little spot for a park," Carlson said, "very peaceful on a warm day."

"It's even nice in winter, if it's not too cold," the man replied. "I live just up the road and like to walk down on a daily basis. Since I retired, my wife thinks I'm under foot all the time. I've no interest in golf, and we can only travel so much, so I guess I'm not a very active retiree like you see in all the magazines."

"You look pretty active to me," Carlson said. "And what better exercise than a good walk? The boys don't seem to be having much luck with the fish."

"A bit too warm," the man said. "You should see it in May. The Kiwanis Club sponsors a fishing tournament for children. The Club stocks the pond with trout. In the middle of the week, it's a day of fishing for disabled children. You should see the delight on a child's face when they hook something from a wheelchair or on crutches or while simply sitting on the banks with braces on their legs. Of course, those with other birth defects add great joy just from their participation. It's like the Special Olympics, only on a smaller scale. At the end of the week the regular kids get their chance. A good time is had by all."

"Abe Carlson," he introduced himself and offering a hand.

"Justin Forks," the man replied, shaking his hand. "I retired from being publisher and editor of a little newspaper in the Reading area. We covered all the community news pretty thoroughly, I hope. But my great joy was venting my thoughts about the great national and international issues on the editorial page. Strictly non-partisan, you understand. I skewered the Republicans and Democrats alike, even made a run at an odd Libertarian or two. Conservatives and Liberals were my red meat when they stepped out of line. And, of course, given the demographics of my readership, I had to pay particular attention to European affairs—Germany in particular."

"So, why, may I ask, did you retire to Derry Township," Carlson inquired.

"We're both from here originally," Forks answered. "My father was a railroad man all his life. He was born in a house up in the Lehigh Valley, with train tracks running through both the back and front yards. He started at age fourteen with the Lehigh Valley Railroad, keeping the potbellied stove in the caboose going and generally cleaning up the car. He worked himself all the way up to be an engineer. He transferred to Hershey to make runs from Harrisburg to Philadelphia and New York. The parents of my wife, Mary, were both teachers in the local school system, so she and I grew up together. I was bitten by the journalism bug in high school and worked on my college newspaper as well, so when I had the opportunity to buy that small newspaper, I couldn't help myself."

"And how long did you own it?" he asked.

"Forty-seven years," Forks said. "Although I did make many good friends in those years, I also gathered more than my share of detractors. A rather large portion of my readership was, shall we say, rather Teutonic in view. After they discovered my Irish roots, they were always skeptical of my editorials. By the way, Abe, I notice by your belt buckle that you are a Mason."

"Yes, since I was a young man," he replied. "As a matter of fact, I'm here working with the Brownstone Lodge in search of a long lost relative from the early 1930s."

"That's a well thought of bunch over at Brownstone," Forks commented. "I'm sure they will be of all the help then can. If you ever want a real change of pace, visit the Teutonia Lodge in West Reading. The meetings are all held in German. The dress code includes Old World style jackets and ties. They also keep in close contact with Masons back in Germany, where you can only earn one degree a year, therefore taking you three years to become a Master Mason, rather than our more traditional three months."

"The Old World ties are that strong after all these years?" Carlson asked.

"You bet they are," he said. "They always have been. Did you know that at the outbreak of World War I, Wilhelm II, Emperor of Germany and King of Prussia, made a special plea to American émigrés who had served in either the Prussian Army or German forces to return and defend the Fatherland. Most refused, of course, saying that America was now their Fatherland, but a few did respond and were not thought any less of by their neighbors."

"And by the time of World War II?" Carlson asked.

"Another matter altogether. There had been some sympathy for the bankruptcy of the German economy and crippling inflation due to the severe war-reparations demanded by the Treaty of Versailles, but the rise of Hitler and his expansionist schemes turned the Americans of German descent against his government."

It was time for Forks to return home. His wife did like to have him out and about, he told Carlson, but she also expected him home at a reasonable hour for afternoon tea. With that, the two parted.

CHAPTER 12

▼

THE VISITOR

Abe Carlson arrived back at The Wick just ahead of a pouring rain that would continue off and on for the next few hours. A message had been left for him at the bar to please call Ben Noble with work and home numbers. The work number proved to belong to an insurance firm a few blocks away. He left a message on the answering machine and called the home number.

"Noble residence, how may I help you?" a feminine voice answered.

"Good evening. This is Abe Carlson returning a call from Ben Noble," he said. "Is he available?"

"So, you're the mystery man everyone in town is talking about," she said. "I'm Ben's wife, Josephine. He's out walking Munch, our cocker spaniel. He should be home directly."

"Would you like me to call back in a half hour or so?" Carlson asked.

"That would be fine, but make it fifteen minutes. Ben had been searching the Lodge records and could not find your Mr. Slate, who was supposed to be a member. He was a bit puzzled. So I asked him if he had looked over the visitors' log. He went back and sure enough he found something. But, wait, he just came in. I'll let him tell you."

"Hello, Abe," Ben said when he came to the phone. "I didn't have your number, so I left the call at The Wick. Dear Josephine was right. I don't know what I ever did without her. At her suggestion, I went back to the records and the visitors' log showed that one Sheldon Claude Slate was a frequent visitor over a six-month period, from November 1932 to April 1933. Something, unspecified, happened at that April meeting and the minutes reflect a unanimous motion to bar him from participation. There was no reason given, but by the unanimous vote, it must have been something clearly opposed by Freemasonry or personal behavior reflecting negatively on the Lodge."

"That sounds pretty serious," Carlson said. "I hope I'm not digging up some old family skeleton that would be better off left alone."

"Don't think about it in that light," Noble replied. "What family worth its salt doesn't have a blemish somewhere over the generations? Why, take my family for instance. Noble is a name that requires some extra effort to live up to expectations. We did fine in upholding the family name during the Civil War. Six or seven brothers fought in a Pennsylvania Regiment at Gettysburg and made it through the war with only one wounded. After the war, two headed out west to make their fortunes. One of those made it to Needles, California, where he was hanged as a horse-thief. We wouldn't have known about it except the surviving brother wrote home about it, saying he was hanged for cause."

"I suppose not knowing much about your family history does have some advantages," Carlson mused. "I simply wanted to discover if I have any surviving relatives. I hadn't given a thought to what type of people they might be."

"People are people, Abe," he replied. "Each individual is responsible for themselves. When we get married, whatever family comes with the spouse becomes our extended family, even if Crazy Uncle Earl makes a fool of himself by drinking too much every Christmas. He's still our Uncle Earl, who stays sober the rest of the year. It was ten years before I learned that Uncle Earl was jilted at the altar years before on December 23 and never married. He carried a torch for his bride-to-be for the rest of his life. The family never mentioned it out of respect for his privacy."

"Thanks for that thought, Ben," Carlson said. "I suppose I wouldn't mind if I uncover a couple of characters who are eccentric, at least they'll be family."

"I'll let you know when we find more," Noble said.

"I'd appreciate it," Carlson said. "And thank you for all you have done so far. Also, thank Josephine for her suggestion."

"Will do, and you take care," Noble said as he hung up the phone.

Carlson spent the rest of the evening in his room, going on-line to research U.S. immigration policies over the years and postings by genealogy buffs about what they found from their ancestor's experience. He was surprised how many of the latter were available. One thing he discovered was the frequency with which immigration officials would change people's names to fit their occupations, sometimes in their native language, others into English. That is why you find so many Coopers, Bookbinders and Sellers in the telephone book, much less Smiths— from blacksmiths to tinsmiths. In German, Steinmetz means stonemason. Also, many newcomers establishing themselves in their new country could change their names upon entry to something more Americanized. More than a few preferred Washington, Lincoln or Franklin. One genealogist reported that her ancestor with a particularly long Hungarian name tried Le Fayette, but when his wife followed two years later, she put a stop to such nonsense and chose instead a shortened version of the original, Conksey.

Another new insight he gained was his assumption that most of the first generation Americans would have a close affinity to their native lands due to relatives who had remained behind and the familiarity of language and social customs. He was intrigued to find how many of the first generation did carry these ties, but had no interest in returning to the old world whatsoever. They were becoming Americans now, and, besides, there were strong reasons they left their homelands in the first place. It usually seemed to take a few generations before interest in the old country sparked the imagination of those having never seen, only heard, of their roots.

In addition, the newcomers were eager to learn English and by the second generation were fluent in the dominant language of their new home. He wondered how a community could stay so tightly knit that even today a Masonic Lodge was still conducted entirely in German.

Carlson awoke early the next morning to a perfect July day, temperatures in the mid-sixties, a few high clouds passing overhead and a calm wind. This first stop was the newsstand for his usual papers, a quick stop for two cups of coffee, then on to find Isaac Porr at his usual station on the park bench.

"Good morning, Isaac," Carlson said in greeting. "How about a cup of coffee and a few questions?"

"I'll graciously accept the coffee," Porr replied, accepting the cup, "but you don't have to bring offerings to receive answers I may have. Since I retired, talking seems to be my major interest in life. Apolonia certainly appreciates her mornings with me out of the house. She says I'm a bit too chatty for her before noon. Actually, though, I think her real motivation is to send me out to get all the gossip so she can keep tabs on what is happening around town."

"I talked to a man named Forks yesterday," Carlson began. "He's a retired publisher who owned a local newspaper in Reading."

"That would be Justin," Porr interrupted. "We were in school together 'back in the day' as they say. I didn't know he was back in this area. In fact, I'm surprised he made it long enough to retire. He always held some pretty strong liberal opinions on just about everything and he wasn't averse to sharing his views with others. I always thought that someday he'd be ridden out of town on a rail, if they do such things these days."

"Well, I can assure you that he was very much alive and kicking yesterday," Carlson said, "although he did indicate there were some who seemed rather glad he retired and moved away. He apparently wrote some pretty hot editorials on controversial topics over the years."

"I'm certain he did," Porr replied. "No one here ever expected him to modify his views over time. I, for one, am glad to hear he didn't. That pot needs to be stirred every so often to keep the community on an even keel."

"As we were talking," Carlson continued, "he noticed my belt buckle and said I should visit a Lodge in that area which conducts all its meetings in German. It is the Teutonia Lodge in West Reading. Does that seem a little odd to you? Back in Arizona there is a radio station on the Navaho Reservation that broadcasts mostly in English. Many of the commercials are in Navaho, of course, and some call-in programs are conducted in both languages. It's a concerted effort to keep the Navaho language alive for the next generation. Even the Tribal Council meetings are mostly in English."

"I read a book once about the Navaho Code-Talkers in World War II," Porr said. "They were used in the Pacific Campaign so the Japanese couldn't translate radio traffic. They were very successful."

"Yes they were," Carlson commented. "I've met a few of those veterans and they were pleased for the recognition of their service, even if it was many years after the war was over."

"As for this German Lodge," Porr said, "I haven't heard of it, although it doesn't surprise me. Pennsylvania has many pockets of ethnicity on many levels. Take, for instance, the so-called Pennsylvania Dutch spoken mostly by the Amish. People say its use is dying out and a few years ago a professor at a local college instituted a course in order to preserve its significance. Among the rest of the German population as a whole, many families have kept the language, even if it's merely some words and phrases, but you'd be surprised at the number of people who still read newspapers, magazines and books in German. In my experience, I find German a very precise language. Some folks are thrown off stride by the length of some words, but the nuances of a particular word can convey a precise meaning. I mentioned this to old Mr. Joseph Strauss some years ago and he answered with some long sentence I couldn't even begin to decipher. When I asked for a translation, he said it was all one word, which meant something like 'the farm down the road across from the three oaks to the north and the rocky field to the west.' The joke was on me.

"Then there's the sentence structure. Children being educated in the English language have trouble translating German sentences into English. Like: 'Throw the horse over the fence some hay.' The structure seems off and often funny to them. But it's not just the Germans. Let me tell you about Steelton."

Porr had attended a funeral for a life-long friend in this town whose biggest industry was a long line of steel mills, now mostly abandoned, but with a few still working. In the heyday of steel, the mills offered employment to tens of thousands of people. To a casual visitor, Steelton had the feel of a dying town, the new generation having to look elsewhere for employment or a way out through higher education. Yet, with the long years of hard-working men and women leaving their imprint, there was still certain vibrancy in the populace. A large segment of those flocking to the mills were of Croatian descent.

The memorial service was held at the Prince of Peace Roman Catholic Church, or more properly the Prince of Peace—Assumption of the Blessed Virgin Mary Church, with an imposing large red brick edifice several stories tall with twin towers on the front and decorative white marble highlights. The interior was a Gothic Cathedral, on a smaller scale, with vaulted ceiling and tapering columns, large stained glass windows and colorful statues. Most impressive was the brightness of colors used. Rather than dark and shades of gray, this church exuded brightness and light.

Porr had attended many memorial services in recent years that claimed to be "a celebration of life," but in fact retained the sullenness of death to a great extent. This service, however, was a true celebration of life, with cheer for the departed and the wonderful journey we all experience since birth, the contributions we can make to our fellow travelers and continuing joy present even after the change we call death. Particularly moving and beautiful were the hymns, of which there were many. Much to his surprise, Porr heard the first hymn begin in what he thought a Slavic language, but not the harsh tones he had seen in the movies. He looked to his bulletin and realized what he was hearing was Croatian, lovely melodious tones conveying sincere happiness. He didn't have to know the words to experience the emotions. He also noticed a paragraph in the bulletin asking for prayers for peace and continuing prayers for those parishioners and relatives and friends who were actively serving in the U.S. military. He counted names, ranging in rank from private to colonel, one officer serving as Chaplin. As the service ended, he found he had, indeed, attained a certain amount of peace in his own life.

"It is an extremely active church," Porr said at last. "They have programs for just about any phase of life you can think of, along with at least one Mass a week conducted entirely in Croatian. I'm not Catholic, of course, but someday I want to take Apolonia and experience that Croatian service."

"The way you relate the story, it must have been a very moving experience," Carlson said.

"It certainly was," Porr replied. "After the service we were all invited to eat at the local Croatian Club. You see, every small or large town in this area has its own ethnic social club, sometimes several. The Italian Club is a big one in the Hershey area and years ago these served as gathering places for new immigrants to become acclimated to a new life in familiar surroundings.

"There was one big difference, though. Honoring heritage and traditions are wonderful things and to be respected, but if there is a strong element of exclusivity, it will wither and die. These clubs and organizations are very inclusive. Why, more non-Italians eat at the Italian Club than Italians on any given night.

"From what I know of Freemasonry, it has been kept alive by its very inclusiveness. You don't discriminate by race, religion or ethnic background. So if that Lodge conducts its meetings in German, I'm sure it's not in an exclusive manner. There is probably a large enough German speaking population to support such a Lodge. I'd bet there are probably several other Lodges in the same area that dropped that preference. For that's all it really is, a preference of the Lodge members to conduct business in the language of their forefathers."

"I think you're right," Carlson said. "Otherwise, the Grand Lodge would have withdrawn its sanction and revoked its charter."

Carlson could not help but think he was being overwhelmed by more information than he could sort through very quickly. He realized that most of his life was spent in a less populated, tri-cultural atmosphere. The big divisions in Arizona were between three basic groups: Caucasians, Indians and Hispanics. He had easily spanned the gaps of interest with all three and worked seamlessly between cultures, plus spent countless days on his own.

When he was called upon to track a man or an animal anywhere in the world, there were always discernable signs he could follow or behavioral patterns he could suppose.

This particular enterprise, he discovered, was complicated by the proliferation of groups and interests somehow living and cooperating with each other and accepting differences easily. Just the number of churches and denominations in any given small Pennsylvania town seemed formidable. The number of fraternal, social and civic organizations was mind-boggling. Veterans organizations were numerous, hale and hardy thanks to the proclivity of the federal government to wage war around the world every decade or so, both small and large. Then there were the neighborhood groups, women's clubs, book clubs and the Red Hats having tea and lunch on a regular basis.

This was, obviously, a culture of joiners, people seeking ways to improve the lives of many and explore the extent of human relationships. Intolerance was being banished block by block and civil discourse was becoming the rule of the day. So, with all the chaos and conflict in the world, perhaps this was what Doc Straussburger meant when he said change had to begin at the bottom and bubble upwards. That is, after all, the basis for a workable democracy. And that is also why democracy has to come from within a society and cannot be imposed from without.

Somewhere in all this confusion, Sheldon C. Slate must have left more footprints than just the one of having his name on the visitors' log at Brownstone Lodge. Where to look next was the most important question.

"Thanks for the conversation," Carlson said. "You've helped clear some lingering questions. I think I can get back on the right path now."

"Anytime, Abe," Porr said. "I'll be here at my post on most mornings. Stop by anytime and I'll do my best to be of assistance."

Carlson walked a few blocks to a little park tucked alongside the road to read his newspapers and think about what tasks he might accomplish that day. A picture of a centuries old barn that was falling into disrepair prompted his first inquiry.

CHAPTER 13

▼

LEGENDS: TRUE AND OTHERWISE

Carlson had been impressed in his ramblings with the size and intricacy of many of the barns dotting the countryside. Some he had noticed sported a decorative so-called hex sign on the gable end. He had heard local people refer to these devices as efforts by the original Pennsylvania Dutch to ward off evil and they called the fading ones "ghosts."

The barn in the newspaper article had one of these ghosts barely discernable and covered with layers of cheap white paint, but still detectable.

He drove through the countryside on back roads for only a few miles when he spotted a substantial wooden barn with a brightly painted hex sign, yellows and greens dominant in a six-pointed star arrangement. Placed high on the gable end, he judged the sign to be a full five feet in diameter. As he drove up into the barn's shadow, Carlson saw a man, perhaps thirty-five years of age, making adjustments to a tractor. He rolled to a stop and in alighting from his Jeep, introduced himself.

"Hello," he called. "I'm Abe Carlson and am looking for some information. I thought you might be able to help me."

"Dieter, Dieter Wolfson," the man answered, shaking his hand and glancing at the vehicle. "Arizona, huh? You're a far way from home, Abe."

"I am at that," Carlson replied. "May I ask you about the hex sign on the barn and what it signifies?"

"Sure," Wolfson said, laying aside his tools and wiping his hands on a rag. "Do you want the tourist version or something closer to the truth?"

"Both, if you have the time," he replied.

"Let's have a seat on the bench over here," Wolfson gestured, pointing to the seat. "It's about time for my morning break."

They both sat down and Wolfson pulled out a short pipe and lit it slowly, taking a few puffs. He offered his tobacco pouch to Carlson, who declined. He had often shared tobacco with his Indian acquaintances, a social courtesy common in the west, but did not have a pipe with him at the time. The pleasant aroma of licorice, with a trace of apple wafted his way.

"That's a nice blend," he said. "May I ask which it is?"

"Make it myself," Wolfson answered. "I'm sixth generation and we've always grown enough tobacco for our own needs. We cure it, slice or cube it, then blend in the family recipe of licorice base and anything we may have on hand. This is apple, but I also do peach and cherry. My grandfather preferred berry combinations, but everybody else in the family thought that a little too biting. Besides, his strawberry blend was just awful. Are you a pipe man?"

"On occasion," he replied. "I pick up a basic gold burley blend over the counter and eight ounces can last me a year or so."

"Very Spartan," Wolfson said with a grin. "Now about the hex signs. You may have noticed there is a cottage industry in this area for selling these signs to tourists or to locals who just want to decorate their houses—sort of like Early American on the outside, I guess. Some people with older ones on the barn don't have them repainted because those who do that for a living will charge three hundred dollars or more per sign.

"A legend had grown that the original intent was to ward off evil, protect the livestock, bring good luck and insure plentiful harvests. The yellow and green colors were supposed to symbolize fertility; a circle represented unity; and various stylized flowers denoted strength or fidelity, or some other cardinal virtue. Actually that's a lot of hooey, made to order by a sign painter about fifty years ago to increase sales and build a tourist business.

"I think the original purpose a couple of hundred years ago is simpler. The barn played a central part in the family's life. What better building was there to decorate? Star patterns were popular, whether with five, six or even twelve points. Bright colors reflected the joy of life, the geometric patterns bringing together the various functions that kept the family together.

"Of course, that sign painter wasn't the first to build a legend about those signs. My great aunt took me out to her barn when I was about five years old for a lesson in religion. She had me look at the sign on her barn and explained that the star's twelve points stood for the Twelve Apostles and the red dot in the middle was reminiscent of Christ's blood, shed for us all. So, take your pick. Creating a legend is not necessarily a bad thing and if it can be used for education, probably a good thing after all. I hope I haven't punctured your sense of the magical."

"Not at all," Carlson said. "Magical symbols are fine. How they are interpreted for good or bad is the real heart of the matter. Joseph Campbell, the college professor and prolific author spent his entire life probing myths and legends throughout history. Best known for his book and lecture series entitled *The Power of Myth,* and the PBS series on the subject with Bill Moyers, he also wrote *Where the Two Came to Their Father: A Navaho War Ceremonial.* Many friends who are Navaho tell me that Campbell understood their symbols in relation to life far more than any non-Indian ever had, or even most Indians for that matter, because he stressed proper interpretation. You see, to them the magic is all in the interpretation. It is the same with legends. What we gain from them is up to us."

"I remember seeing parts of that PBS series," Wolfson said. "The real fan in the family was my grandmother. She never missed a minute. And afterwards, she would, in her words, *sitzen stundenlang* in contemplation. It kept her mind sharp right up 'til the end."

"I apologize for my lack of German," Carlson said. "What was it she would do?"

"I should apologize for slipping into the German," he answered. "When I think of my grandmother, it is always in terms of our everyday conversations. We'd mix English and German together without a thought because we all knew both languages. It means that she would sit for hours thinking about what she had seen and heard. A few days later she would share her conclusions with the family, using her own experiences in life to illustrate the matter. She was a very deep thinker, always encouraging us to be open to new ideas, while respecting the old. Grandfather always said that during the Depression, she was the easiest touch in the whole county for a free meal and a night in the barn for every wayward soul. Word got around quickly and they had more than their share of drop-ins. The only payment she would accept was an hour or so of conversation about their families, where they had been, what they had seen and how were people in other parts getting along with their lives and their neighbors. Whether they had any religious affiliation or not, she sent them off in the morning with a good breakfast and a prayer for their safety."

"She sounds like a remarkable woman," Carlson said in compliment.

"That she was," Wolfson replied. "She was also keen on politics. She didn't care who we voted for, but she insisted we all vote at every opportunity. Although she had no party affiliation—a true independent who voted for the man or woman she thought most qualified—she was fond of quoting Will Rogers whom she had listened to on the radio as a girl. 'I don't belong to any organized Party,' she'd quote him as saying, 'I'm a Democrat.' Although, she didn't approve of such sayings as 'all I know is what I read in the newspapers.' She thought if that were the case, too many regular people would have to wallow in ignorance. She also used to say that she could forgive a politician a moral indiscretion, if he sincerely repented, or an ignorant one, if he were open to discussion, but she could never abide one that was just plain stupid, because he would be at the mercy of the whims of those with whom he surrounded himself."

The two men chatted for another ten minutes, Carlson stating his reason for coming to Pennsylvania and Wolfson about his family and the neighboring farms, with the prospects for good crops this year.

As Carlson was leaving, Wolfson asked him to wait a minute while he went into the barn, returning with three plastic bags, each containing a few ounces of tobacco. One was marked "apple," another labeled "peach" and a third "cherry."

"Thought you might like a few samples," Wolfson said, passing the bags. "You might have one of the occasions you mentioned and these may come in handy."

"Thank you very much, Dieter," Carlson said sincerely. "And I'd like to give you a little something." Carlson opened the passenger door to the Jeep and reached into the glove compartment.

"Peridot," Carlson said, handing him a small yellowish-green transparent olivine stone. "I carry a few around for good luck. Some tribes believe that if you carry one on your person when planting, you are more than assured of a good crop. It may be true and it may not. Symbolism, as you know, is in the eye and belief of the beholder."

"Well, thank you, Abe," he said. "I'm open to anything. I'll give it a try."

"You make your grandmother proud," Carlson said in parting. "Keep that open mind."

As he left the Wolfson driveway and turned left, Carlson could not help but think that if the many city dwellers who looked down on the rural people as uninformed locals could visit a farm like this one, they'd be quite surprised to find a very sophisticated society well up on current events, perhaps more so than the city dwellers themselves.

By the time he arrived back at The Wick, he realized his appetite was more acute than normal. He took a seat at the bar just minutes before the luncheon rush, ordering a Black Angus burger, fries and a large iced tea. Finishing within a mere twenty minutes, he was out on the road again toward Hershey.

He easily found what he was looking for, a small specialty tobacconist shop he had seen in passing. As expected he walked into the shop to the tantalizing aromas of rich mixtures; the man behind the counter was mixing a blend, a still smoking pipe in a holder on the counter beside him.

"I take it that's the aroma of the blend in progress?" Carlson asked.

"I see you know the tricks of the trade," the man said. "Best advertising in the world. What can I do for you?"

"Do you by chance carry refurbished pipes?" Carlson inquired. "I left mine at home and am looking for a spare."

"I'm Bill," the man nodded while continuing to toss the mixture. "A man of experience, I see. You look as if you could afford a new pipe, but will spring for a more expensive used model. I have a few. Do you know what you're looking for in particular?"

"Yes," Carlson replied. "A briar, medium sized. Irish or Italian, I think. English would be an extravagance for as little as I will use it, and not too fancy. It's just that I don't look forward to breaking in a new pipe, too time-consuming and a number of harsh smokes before it mellows out. I'm Abe, by the way."

"Ah, the bane of all pipe smokers, Abe," Bill said, "breaking in a new one is the price we have to pay up front for future pleasure. I've got a nice light Peterson's Kildare model, bent stem, or a heavier Molina straight and bent stem set, metal bowl protectors on both the Molinas."

"I trust the Molina's will travel better?" he asked. "I travel a lot into some pretty remote areas and breakage could be a problem."

"That would be your better bet," Bill said. "What do you travel with now, if I may ask?"

"Stone," he answered. "Red Stone to be exact. It was a gift from some friends."

"I'm impressed," Bill said in wonder. "I've heard about those pipes, but have never seen one in person. I assume these friends are Native Americans?"

"Yes, two Indians, one Navaho and the other Mojave and the pipe is several hundred years old."

"Tell you what I'll do," Bill said as he stopped mixing and wiped his hands. "I'll sell you the Molina set for the price of a single, if you'll let me take your picture and hang it on the wall as a conversation piece. I could get quite a bit of mileage out of having sold a pipe to a man who owned an authentic Red Stone."

"That's a discount I can't refuse," he agreed.

Carlson paid cash, then posed for a couple of digital pictures in various parts of the shop, holding first one pipe then the other. As he started the engine and pulled away from the curb, he could only shake his head at what some considered celebrity status. He supposed it wouldn't take Bill very long to start his own legend in Hershey about the man who owned a Red Stone. Of such minor things legends are born.

He drove to Bull Frog Valley Park where he had met with Justin Forks, the newspaper publisher, only to find it serenely empty of people. The ducks still paddled across the water or dozed in the grass and squirrels scurried about searching for a meal, while the weeping willow branches swayed gently back and forth. Filling the bowl of the bent stem Molina, he went to a bench and slowly enjoyed his first taste of the licorice and apple blend.

Carlson remembered reading that European writers from the Elizabethan Age onward found inspiration in smoking a pipe and that Mark Twain was infamous for the number and supposed cheapness of the cigars he smoked. His own experience with the Indians was an occasional practice, either for ceremonial reasons or a friendly smoke at the end of the day. Many did smoke cigarettes profusely, of course, just as some drank themselves into oblivion any time they had enough money in their pockets. But his was more of the English drawing room experience, as a nice aid to conversation and comradery.

His thoughts turned to Milton Hershey and his legacy. If there ever were a man who could be said to have been a living legend in his own time, Hershey fit completely. He was the larger-than-life type legend. It could not have been his reportedly short stature that prevented people from calling him by that term, Carlson thought—look at the other larger-than-life, but very short, legends like the Apache Geronimo or Billy the Kid, names that lived on in dime novels and western lore. Milton Hershey was either set apart from being a legend, or set himself apart, perhaps unwittingly.

It finally dawned on Carlson that Milton Hershey was correctly thought of as a legacy, much more importantly than any legend could. It wasn't just the legacy he left to the Hershey School, or the chocolate making empire he established, or even his famous concern for the welfare and happiness of his workers. Some of the most noted "Legendary Robber Barons" of the gilded age of the Industrial Revolution turned philanthropists towards the ends of their lives and left legacies in the form of libraries, museums and organizations. Hershey was a living legacy from the beginning. He passed on his heart-felt "Do Unto Others" example, created a community with a set of values that included civic and moral improvement, consensus, tolerance, acceptance of differences and civil discourse. Whatever was to become of this legacy, Hershey got it off to a solid start. Perhaps the people of Hershey, the town, already inherently knew all this and that he as an outsider had merely stumbled upon the fact. Carlson certainly hoped this to be true.

Carlson had been so deep in thought that he hadn't noticed his pipe was out and had grown cold in his hand. He tapped out the ashes into his palm and once assured there were no remaining embers, dropped the remains into the sand-filled bucket reserved for cigarettes.

CHAPTER 14

▼

MISSING

Abe Carlson was at the Square in Hummelstown waiting for the light to turn when his phone rang.

"Abe Carlson," he answered, pulling to the curb as the traffic began to move.

"Abe, this is Bud, we've got a problem and need your help."

"Sure, Bud, whatever help I can be. What do you need?"

"We've got a missing camper," Bud Hanover said with some urgency. "It's my grandson Henry. Twelve years old. The family is camping down along Swatara Creek and he wandered off somewhere just after breakfast. He spends a lot of time in the woods, so my daughter, Janet, and son-in-law, Frank Cunningham, didn't begin to worry until he didn't show up for lunch. They combed the area all afternoon, along with some fellow campers and just called in the police because it will be dark in a few hours."

"I'll be right there," Carlson interrupted. "Where do I go?"

"I'm at Doc Straussburger's house. If you're anywhere near, pick me up and I'll show you the way."

"I'm just down the street," he said. "Be there in less than three minutes."

That said, Carlson made a u-turn at the square and headed down Main Street. He knew that was probably an illegal maneuver, but there were no cars near the intersection and it was the quickest route. Hanover was waiting at the curb as he pulled up, Doc waving from the front porch.

"Take the next right," Hanover said, swinging into the passenger seat and then closing the door. "I know all the shortcuts."

The shortcut was a series of zigzags through narrow streets and alleys, ending at the road to Middletown. They turned left and tried to keep within five miles over the thirty-five mile speed limit. As they passed the entrance to Indian Echo Caverns, the second time he had noticed, Carlson made a mental note to visit the attraction before leaving town. The road had many open fields on one side and a series of new developments on the other.

"The road will widen to two lanes on each side," Hanover said. "You'll see a newer development on the right, Stone Creek. At the light, take a right on Swatara Creek Road. That will take you to the creek."

As they reached the creek, the road followed the meandering waterway along the bank. One low spot had evidence of recent flooding where the water had crested, leaving mud and debris covering the road. The Jeep had no problem skirting around the obstacles until they were on clean pavement again. A variety of tents and small campers emerged between the road and creek, spotting the bank at intervals. One glance at the water told Carlson the current was still running fairly strong. Not very good fishing conditions, Carlson thought, and he had not seen the expected small boats in the water.

Without having to be told, he pulled over next to a County Sheriff's car parked near a new green Volkswagen camper.

"They just bought it," Hanover said in explanation. "This is the first break-in trip."

Hasty introductions were made to the parents and Deputy Ralph Jackson, who looked as if he could have been a professional line-backer, which he may have been after playing that position at Penn State. But Jackson had a different plan: five years experience at the county level, then on to the State Police Academy.

"Abe is a professional tracker," Hanover said in introduction. "We are lucky he was handy."

"We can use all the professional help we can get," Jackson said. "Here's what we have so far: the chief concern is the creek, Henry is a good swimmer, but that current is pretty strong. A group of around a dozen people, including Frank and Janet, of course, have been searching up and down the bank all afternoon, probably obliterating any trace of Henry's passing."

Janet joined her hands and looked at her feet.

"Which is what they should have done," Jackson said, noticing the gesture. "You couldn't tell his footprint apart anyway. Henry is a fast-growing boy, with a size ten shoe. The feet grow first, to support the developing frame. He's going to be a good-sized man one day."

"Any brothers or sisters?" Carlson asked.

"Not yet," Frank said, "but we hope he will someday. Why do you ask?"

"Siblings usually know more about habits and tastes than the parents," Carlson said. "It could be of help. What about a cell phone? I see a lot of kids his age with a cell phone these days."

"That's the first thing we thought of," Janet volunteered. "We've been trying all day, but no answer. We keep leaving messages, for all the good that has done. We don't even know if he has it turned on. He's always good about preserving battery power."

"Does it have all the bells and whistles, text messaging, camera, perhaps a video player?"

"Hardly," Frank said. "We didn't want him to have a toy, just a stripped down basic model so he could keep in touch."

"Is it GPS equipped?" Deputy Jackson asked.

"I don't know," Frank answered slowly. "It is a newer model. No more than six months old."

"I don't know if we could triangulate the signal anyway," Jackson said, "if the phone isn't even on or he's not trying to make a call."

"Not necessarily," Carlson said, going to his Jeep and rummaging around behind the back seat. He pulled out a black rectangular object that looked like the so-called laptop computers of ten years ago, weighing thirty pounds or more. When he placed it on the hood of his Jeep and opened it up, it did look like such a device.

"Where'd you get that dinosaur?" Jackson asked. "That looks like the one I had in high school. I built up my arms just lugging it around."

"It's the same case, but different technology," Carlson said. He explained that he had sent the case to a friend in Germany, who was a wiz with electronics. When out tracking lost hikers or skiers, the device could often pick up a weak GPS signal on a cell phone or other equipment within a two-mile radius, often with pinpoint accuracy. The technology implanted in phones to trace 911 emergency calls had so advanced that the newer models emitted a slight signal even if the battery had run completely down.

Carlson pushed the power button and let the machine warm up for half a minute. He typed in a few commands on the keyboard and within seconds a map appeared, with a white blinking dot at the center. Terrain features slowly emerged until the onlookers began to recognize the topography within twenty miles, with the white blinking dot showing their location.

"Well, what do you know," Jackson said quietly under his breath. "We sure could use something like this."

"I don't even know if it's legal," Carlson whispered quietly. "I somehow forgot to ask."

Blue dots began to appear at various places on the map, then yellow, some moving and others stationary. "Those are people making and receiving calls," Carlson explained. "Blue is outgoing, yellow incoming."

"This can't be legal," Jackson said. "Too much room for abuse. What if someone wanted to hook up a recording device with this thing, or eavesdrop on conversations? The courts would have a fit."

"Which is why you never witnessed any of this," Carlson replied. "It is also why those in the know encrypt their communications and randomly change the encryption on a regular basis."

Carlson looked up and noted the sky was beginning to cloud over. It was going to be a very dark night. He scanned his surroundings.

"Frank," Carlson summoned, "how about crossing the road and climbing to the top of that rise. When you are set, give Henry another call. Keep the line open even if you have to leave a recording."

Frank did as he was asked and when in position dialed the number. It seemed forever until he heard the ring on the other end.

Carlson zoomed in to a five-mile radius, then quickly to two. An almost imperceptible red glow faintly pulsated on the screen. As he zoomed in even closer, the red glow was on the move, headed right towards them.

"We got a hit, Frank," Jackson shouted excitedly up the hill. "Keep it open and we'll track him in."

Within a minute a man emerged from the tree line at the next bend in the road. He had a faded Red Man Chewing Tobacco baseball cap on his head and a hammer in his belt. An open blue work shirt, with a white undershirt, plus worn jeans and work boots completed his ensemble. He walked along at a steady pace, neither hurrying nor tarrying, and approached Deputy Jackson. The white blinking light on the screen turned to pink.

"What's all the fuss?" he asked the Deputy.

"A boy gone missing," Jackson reported. "Aren't you Mel Perkins?"

"That's me," Perkins acknowledged. "I've been posting 'No Hunting' signs on this side of my property. Boy, they're making it hard on hunters these days. I used to let just about anybody hunt my land if they asked permission. Now the courts can hold the landowner liable for accidents and such. I hated to do it, but hunting season will be here before you know it and I wanted to give fair warning."

"Have you seen anything of a twelve year old boy today?" Jackson asked.

"No," Perkins answered, pulling a cell phone from his shirt pocket. "But I did find this in my woods. These summer campers are always leaving something on my property and it isn't always trash. I've found the oddest things at times. I brought this over to see if it belonged to somebody."

"It belongs to our son," Janet said with a glitch in her throat, clutching at the phone.

"Will you show us where you found it, Mr. Perkins?" Carlson asked.

"Sure, sure," Perkins replied. "Sorry about your boy, ma'am, I'm sure he'll turn up just fine. Probably lost his way, but there are plenty of cabins and farmhouses in this area. He'll get hungry and stumble onto one of them. Even if it gets dark, you can see the lights in the windows for a far piece."

As people gathered around, Carlson went to the back of his Jeep again and retrieved a medium-sized backpack, containing all the equipments he would need. Erring on the side of caution, he always had one on hand for just such emergencies. He also typed in a new set of commands on his tracking device. The blue and yellow dots faded into nothingness as Jackson watched over his shoulder. The white blinking dot remained.

"Jackson, do you think you can operate this device that does not exist?" Carlson asked. "If so, I'll give you a few more pointers. There should be enough battery life until morning. I better do this one alone. We don't need a group of people stumbling around in the dark and stamping out sign. You can check on my progress from here and I'll be calling in on a regular basis. Bud has the number if you need to get in touch. My phone will show up as a green dot. I programmed out the civilian traffic and you can't get it back without the right code. I didn't want to leave an upstanding officer of the law such as you with such a temptation to snoop. Not much light left, so we need to get going."

After a few more last minute preparations and arrangements, Carlson and Perkins headed back down the road at a brisk pace, entering the tree line just as a light rain began to fall. As many people as could took positions in the Cunningham's camper or sat under the awning suspended on the side. Other campers who had gathered went back to their own campsite to await developments. Janet put on a fresh pot of coffee and made some sandwiches with the materials at hand. Deputy Jackson called in a status report and gave his location.

Arriving at the site where Perkins had found the cell phone, Carlson immediately detected the spot where the boy had fallen, presumably losing the phone, and the direction he had gone. Within twenty feet, he saw signs that a doe and two fawns had been startled and ran. It looked like Henry decided to follow on their trail.

Another hundred yards through the darkening woods and he saw the tracks diverge, the deer taking an abrupt left turn uphill, Henry continuing on in a straight line down a ravine. He stopped to make a call.

"Jackson here," he answered. "I've got you on the speaker so everyone can hear."

"Have you got me on the screen?" Carlson asked.

"Sure do, green and blinking large as life."

"Looks as if Henry scared up a doe and two fawns when he tripped on Perkins place. He followed the deer. As you can see by your map, I'm at the mouth of a ravine. The deer took off in a different direction, but Henry proceeded straight ahead. The tracks must be from this morning, judging by the number of other animals who have crossed over them. Does this ravine lead to the creek?"

"No," Jackson answered. "It goes for perhaps eighty yards then intersects with another, following the natural fall of the land away from the creek. If he took that for another one hundred and fifty yards, he'd come out to natural farmland. That is if he came out. Those ravines are pretty rough, boulders and thick underbrush in some places. There are plenty of places for small animals and snakes to hide and breed."

The mention of snakes in the deep woods and the thought of her son being lost out there somewhere made Janet Cunningham turn a whiter shade than normal. She knew that copperheads and timber rattlesnakes could be found all over this part of the state, especially near creeks and rivers. She glanced at her husband and saw he also had paled. No one said a word.

"I'm going in," Carlson announced calmly in the now-pitch-black darkness. At least the light rain had eased for the moment. He switched on a low-beam flashlight, because high beams washed out the subtle shadows needed in tracking, and stepped forward. "Check with you later."

For two hours the watchers saw the green dot slowly move forward as Carlson followed the trail, finding evidence of Henry's passing in small signs such as broken twigs, the occasional footprint, and disturbances in the moss on rocks. At one point, an owl swooped down from above to a spot not far in front of him, clutched a small animal in its talons and flew back up the ridge with only a flap or two of its wings. He also had to sidestep several snakes. Finally arriving at the juncture of the two ravines he found where Henry had apparently rested on a rock and chewed a piece of gum for some time before putting the wad in its wrapper and placing it close by. That was long enough ago for the ants to have discovered it as they swarmed over the paper trying to get inside.

The trail had seemingly come to an end. Carlson very carefully circled the resting place at two-foot intervals, looking for any disturbance. On his fourth pass he found what he was looking for. "Way to go, Henry," he whispered to himself, "you're one bright boy."

The watchers at the camp saw the still green dot suddenly move more rapidly, up the steep side of the ravine to the ridge on top, then turn and follow the ridge along the intersecting ravine. Frank Cunningham was the first to speak.

"That's our boy," he said as he smiled hopefully to his wife. "I'm glad I took him hunting with me the last couple of seasons. He remembered that if you get lost, take to the high ground to get your bearings, walk along the ridges until you spot something familiar, like civilization."

At four o'clock in the morning, Carlson emerged from the woods to find he was at the far end of a pasture on a dairy farm. Following the trail now, he crossed over the pasture to discover an odd arrangement of livestock browsing around a particular spot. The cows only raised their heads slightly as he approached, then resumed their browse.

The clouds had cleared away and there was more light from the stars and half-moon to see. A dark patch, near the center of the loose herd, that Carlson had first assumed was an animal at rest, flattened out as he approached. It turned out to be a hole, perhaps seven feet by five. As he peered down over the edge with his flashlight, he found a sleeping Henry about ten feet down.

Within minutes Jackson's phone rang.

"Jackson, here," he barked.

"I've got Henry," Carlson reported. "He has a couple of sprained ankles and some bruises, but he'll be fine. He was walking across the pasture when the ground gave way. It's a sinkhole he says, common around here. Henry, why don't you talk to your parents?"

"Mom, Dad, I'm okay," Henry's voice came out of the speaker. "I tried to do the right thing."

"You did just fine, Son," his father said. "We're real proud of you. Put Abe back on the phone."

"Nothing wrong with his appetite," Carlson said when he returned on the line. "He's gone through three bottles of water and consumed half my supply of beef jerky. The lights just went on in the barn. It's a couple of hundred yards away. I'll carry him there."

"That's Jove Linden's place," Jackson said. "He must be getting ready for the morning milking. Tell him I sent you. He'll take good care of you both."

"Abe Carlson," Janet Cunningham broke in, "I don't know how we're ever going to be able to thank you enough for finding our son."

"No need," Carlson answered. "If you want to thank anyone, it should be these cows. Henry says they milled around and kept him company until it was time for their evening milking. The girls are curious animals and they returned to keep him company through the night. Not a Lassie, among them, though. Not one ran back to the house to bark that Timmy had fallen in a well and couldn't get out."

"We should be there within a half-hour," Jackson said.

"Bud," Carlson replied. "How about shutting down our little device and stowing it behind the back seat. Then drive my Jeep over. I don't want to tempt our Deputy Jackson anymore."

On the long trek carrying Henry up to the barn, Carlson tried as well as he could to explain just who Lassie and Timmy were and other characters from his childhood.

CHAPTER 15

▼

AFTERMATH

The sun was well up when Abe Carlson awoke and rolled over to look at his watch on the table next to his bed. It read a few minutes after nine, but he was surprised to see the date, which showed he had been asleep for over twenty-four hours. When he arrived back at The Wick, it was all he could do to take a quick shower before flopping into bed. Running his hand over his jaw only served to prove he had a two-day's growth of beard. The hotel was unusually quiet as he arose, shaved, dressed and went in search of coffee. As he descended the last flight of stairs, Rachel, a.k.a R.J., met him in the narrow entrance.

"I thought I heard you stirring," R.J. said. "Some people would like you to join them for breakfast out on the side porch."

"You don't serve breakfast," Carlson said stifling a yawn and scratching the back of his neck.

"Only on rare occasions," she replied. "You're a genuine celebrity around town, Abe. We were inundated with media all day yesterday, but no one in town would tell where you are staying. Doc Straussburger spread the word and every-one just clammed up. The group on the porch has been trading shifts, keeping vigil on you in case anyone wanted to bother your sleep. The boss even turned down a week's rent on the other rooms to give you your privacy. Come on, let me get you some coffee."

He walked out onto the porch and was greeted by the sight of Bud Hanover and Will Youst from the Lodge, Isaac Porr, his morning information provider, and the welcome smiling duo of Ruby and Veronica Steinmann.

"Good morning, Abe," they all said in unison, as R.J. set a hot cup of coffee at his place.

"Good morning, all," Carlson responded. "You'll have to give me time to have a couple of cups of this before I can do twenty questions. What's all the fuss, anyhow?"

"All of the fuss is over the fact that I, well known to be frugal," Bud Hanover explained, "offered to treat one-and-all to steak and eggs for whenever you ceased your slumber. I was sure you'd be hungry."

"You will notice," Bill Youst said, "that our benevolent host defines 'one-and-all' to encompass a mere six people, including himself. But, bless Brother Bud, his heart's in the right place."

"Don't be too harsh on Brother Bud," Carlson warned as the food was served. "By the size of these t-bone steaks we should all be eternally grateful."

"You are, indeed, a man of uncommon keen eyesight and discriminating analysis," Hanover said to a table of smiling faces, "and I thank you for appreciating my largess."

Barely a word was exchanged as the hungry group made quick work of their sumptuous meal, washed down with cup after cup of coffee and tea, depending on personal preference.

Over a light dessert of mixed fruit, Hanover informed of events. The group from the campground was already at the barn when Carlson arrived with Henry, along with an awaiting ambulance, which Carlson recalled, but later events were a little blurry.

Doc Straussburger had taken control of the operation. After a quick examination, the Doctor had Henry and his parents bundled off to his clinic and put them up for the duration. Henry would need a couple of day's bed rest before returning to his normal routine.

There was still a broad use of radio scanners among the populace, both as a hobby and as an aid to all the citizens in volunteer fire departments and police auxiliaries. Their channels were monitored regularly. The calls had started coming in to the police after Jackson's first report to the station. The sheriff wanted to hold off on a large volunteer search until the situation was further determined. Of course, local reporters listened to the same broadcasts and wanted a story. The sheriff had begged off with the promise of a morning press conference, should something newsworthy occur. He then called Deputy Jackson and instructed him to report in only by telephone. The press began to get suspicious when they picked up only normal radio traffic through the night. Several enterprising reporters headed for the campsite along Swatara Creek but arrived just after the group had left for the Linden farm.

"Doc took charge just in time," Hanover concluded. "We heard later that Old Jove had some fun with a reporter when one finally showed up at his place later in the morning. When asked about sinkhole accidents, Jove rubbed his chin and replied that, yes he'd had some problems in the past. 'Lost a prime bull back in '92,' he told the reporter. 'He was about his usual servicing chores at the time, just with a little too much enthusiasm. The cow was okay, but the bull ended up in the freezer. Yes, those sinkholes can be a nasty business.' He said it with such a sincere face the reporter believed him and just went away."

"It seems that an enthusiastic Deputy Jackson immediately told Doc about your interesting little tracking device," Veronica Steinmann offered. "Doc sensed some big problems ahead and swore everyone to secrecy, followed by a call to the sheriff, the only person outside the group to have heard of it. Then he called me. He thought you might be in need of some legal representation."

"And then my wonderful daughter called me," Ruby Steinmann said. "I still have contacts in all the right circles that might come in handy. Besides, I haven't had this much excitement in years."

"Doc put the word out around town that everyone was to keep your where-abouts from the press," Youst added. "No one questioned why, they just did whatever Doc asked. The official position was that you are shy of publicity and like to work low-keyed. He also told everyone to go about their business as usual and perhaps the whole thing would blow over quickly."

"The TV people began to show up about ten in the morning," Bud contin-ued. "Doc had them corralled in front of his house, had them served coffee, soda and donuts while they waited, and offered a half-hour photo opportunity on the front porch. After a little coaching, the group assembled on the porch included Doc, the parents, me as the grandparent and the sheriff. Deputy Jackson was on call at the other end of the county. It all went very quietly: grateful parents, an appreciative grandparent who had called on you for assistance, and the sheriff who said his department was just doing the routine job expected by the citizens. Henry, of course was mending nicely and asleep at present."

"I was posted on a special errand," Youst added. "Doc had to send me to the library to scour the shelves for any books on Lassie and Timmy. Henry simply wouldn't settle down until he had some reading material on the subject. Doc wouldn't divulge who it was, but apparently somebody mentioned it and it made quite an impression on young Henry."

Carlson thanked everyone for their concern and their protection. He was curious about sinkholes, however, and asked if the sign he had seen for Indian Echo Caverns was indicative of the local geological formation. He had heard of the sinkholes in Florida, but it was his understanding that many of those were caused by projects to reclaim suitable land for building by draining the swamps and channeling the water elsewhere, leaving falling groundwater tables.

"Exactly," Bud offered, explaining that the entire area was honeycombed with limestone, hence the large limestone quarries. Particularly after a heavy rain, the water rushing underground eroded the soil and the sinkholes appeared, quite commonly in the Palmyra area. Sometimes they were small, as in the case of the Linden farm. On other occasions they could be quite large and deep. They could be a bit of a nuisance as old farmland was developed into residential complexes or strip malls. Disturbing the land by digging basements and constructing runoff basins would often uncover the problem, but they were common enough that they were routinely filled with gravel and concrete, with a layer of soil covering the scene. The important thing was to detect them early and take corrective action, before they could spread.

"I think one of the problems which needs to be addressed," Bud said in conclusion, "is that the developers need to change at least one common practice. They will typically purchase a farm and immediately strip off a foot or more of rich topsoil, for which there is a ready market. I'm no engineer, but I can't help but think that does not bode well for the stability of the land."

"By the way, Sport," Veronica said as they were finishing, "Doc would like you to drop by when you can. He has a few questions and young Henry is asking to see his 'new best buddy.' The outside media had cleared out and moved on to the next news cycle. Doc has assured the local newspapers that if there were anything newsworthy, he'll call them first. I'd like to accompany you."

"And I," Ruby chimed in. "I'm curious to see how this episode ends."

"Your Jeep is out of the way in Doc's garage," Youst informed him. "It's too recognizable while the media is crawling all over town, so I jump-started it and hid it there. No damage done. If you can jump a tractor, you can surely do the same with a vehicle that old and simple."

"Thanks," Carlson said as they all stood. "If you don't mind, I'll meet you there. I stayed in bed much longer than usual and I need to stretch out some of the kinks."

As he walked up the sidewalk and crossed the square, Carlson noticed the rise in humidity and felt the temperature headed in the same direction. There was no wind. Even what clouds there were in the sky seemed to remain stationary, as if movement might disturb the scene. He let the warmth and moisture seep into his muscles, soothing his aches as they gradually diminished.

As he strolled along, other pedestrians would nod in recognition and store-owners would wave through the front windows as he passed. There was an occasional light toot from passing vehicles and several children would pause in their play to wordlessly watch as he went by. When Carlson smiled and offered a small wave, the children would return the courtesy. Apparently everyone in town recognized him by now and he was thankful that these kind people showed such great respect for his privacy, leaving him to his own thoughts and musings as he made his way.

He was deep in thought about where to go from here to solve the major questions of why he had come to Hummelstown. Sheldon C. Slate was now an established human being, leaving his mark on the visitors' log at Brownstone Lodge, but what happened to him so suddenly in 1933? And were there any descendents at all still in the area? The name was not common in any of the phone books or people's recollections. Since he was a visitor to the Lodge, he had come from somewhere else. How far would he have to cast his net? Did this also mean that his father was from another area, too? He did not seem to be related to any of the Carlsons in this part of the state, but there were so many of them. The search for Henry Cunningham had been a welcome diversion, but only a diversion after all. Where did he go from here? It was time to begin poking at the shadows again.

As if to confirm his last thought, half-way up the block a large dog stirred from the shadows of the front porch and stood in the middle of the sidewalk, staring carefully at Carlson. It was a dog of indeterminate origin, a mixture of several breeds, what people usually referred to as a 'mutt.' It was a mutt, but a very large one. The dog stood quite still, but as Carlson approached, the tail was raised and ever so slowly began to wag. Carlson reached down and scratched the huge head behind the ears. Satisfied, the animal sniffed his hand, licked the palm and returned to his spot on the porch. Carlson took the incident as a hopeful sign.

As he arrived at the house, Carlson could see Aunt Mattie holding court on one side of the front porch, engaged in conversation with a handful of people, while children sat on the steps and frolicked in the yard. Doc Straussburger occupied the far end of the wrap-around porch at the corner. He was standing in lonely vigil, smoking a cigar and staring off into the distance. Carlson quietly approached.

"Hello, Doc, mind if I join you?" Carlson asked.

"Not at all, Abe," Straussburger replied. "Don't mind the cigar. I gave them up years ago and many times since. I'm a doctor and know they can't be good for me, but I have one anyway about twice a year. Mattie doesn't approve, of course, but when I do indulge, she just looks the other way as if she doesn't see me. When a daughter gets to be a certain age, a father suddenly finds he has two women telling him what to do. You have to treat them kindly, say 'Yes, Dear,' then go about whatever you wanted to do in the first place. It makes them think they've made a contribution to your welfare."

"I thank you for covering my back, Doc," Carlson said sincerely. "You diagnosed the situation well and took the proper steps to alleviate the patient. I was able to get some much-needed and uninterrupted sleep. As for my little tracking aid, it may or may not be illegal in this country. All I know is that it does come in handy."

"Well," Doc said, exhaling through his nose, "I may not be up on the technology involved, but I do recall vividly that ruckus not too far back when it was revealed that the F.B.I. was monitoring the conversations and planting bugs in the cell phones of the bad guys."

"Yes, I know," Carlson acknowledged. "They used the same over-the-air technology used for updating cell phones and getting new ring tones to place a permanent GPS tracking system, and some reports said an operating hidden microphone to pick up conversations even when the devices were not in use."

"The Civil Libertarians had a field day," Doc said. "The A.C.L.U. was up in arms. Of course, the people in charge at the time had been playing pretty loose and fancy free with the Constitution on several fronts for some time. The state of violence in international affairs seemed to muddy the waters and make domestic affairs take a back seat. I think the related cases are still winding their way through the courts. I wouldn't want you to get caught up in that for a number of years, especially when you are so useful to the community at large just by doing what you do best. Henry may owe you his life and the community owes you its gratitude."

"Oh, I think Henry would have eventually made it all right," Carlson said. "As for the community, I'll always owe more to it that it ever will to me. I only make my contributions as I can. We're all in this life together and we might as well make the best of it for the most people. I'm only a factor in their lives in passing, giving a hand here and there."

"I do believe you are a man of true humility," Doc said, turning to look into his eyes. "I have met a few in my time, but to stumble onto yet another is always a refreshing experience. Now, why don't you go in and see Henry? He has been waiting so patiently."

Carlson went into Henry's room to find he already had Veronica and Ruby Steinmann as company. Henry was tucked in neatly, propped up with pillows.

"You certainly do seem to draw the ladies, Henry," Carlson said. "First the girls yesterday and last night, now the belles of society. I hope you'll tell me your secret."

Henry laughed and blushed. He was at that age when a boy started to notice something special about girls and it confused him. He knew it had to be a good thing, but simply could not figure out what it was, exactly.

"I didn't get a chance to thank you properly, Abe," Henry said quietly, reaching out his hand.

Carlson took the proffered hand and gave it a long, warm shake. "The best thanks I can receive," he said looking into the young, kind eyes, "is you passing it on to others in need. Everyone needs help now and again, Henry, and if you can be there for them, do so willingly. And if they want to thank you for it, tell them exactly what I just told you."

That thought struck a cord deep within Henry and he pondered for a moment. In an instant, he was in full stride telling Carlson all that he had learned about Lassie and Timmy and their adventures. He said he felt closeness with Timmy, as he survived falling into wells, trapped in caves, stuck in trees or in a log. He was going to ask his parents for a Collie for his next birthday.

"And are you going to name her 'Lassie?'" Ruby asked.

"No," Henry replied. "He's going to be a boy and I'm going to name him just plain 'Abe.' Is that okay with you, Abe?"

"Why, I'd be honored," Carlson said. "I've never had a dog named after me, as far as I know, and I rather like the idea. Of course, you'll take good care of him, brush him when he needs it and give him a lot of love, won't you?'

"You bet. He'll be the best cared for dog in the world," Henry replied with finality.

After the visit was over and he was walking back to the front porch, Carlson leaned over to the two women.

"I trust you appreciate my upholding your dignity in there," he said quietly to both.

"And, why pray do you mean by that?" Veronica said, looking at him quizzically out of the corner of her eye.

"The big secret that all the boys my age learned long after the TV series and movies were history. Lassie was actually played by a succession of males."

Veronica gave him a quick playful punch to the shoulder and smiled.

CHAPTER 16

▼

BIGLERVILLE

When he returned to the front porch, Abe Carlson was signaled to join Doc Straussburger at the other end. Doc was talking to a young man of perhaps twenty years, neatly dressed, with a straw boater in his one hand, the type fashionable nearly one hundred years ago, but a rare find these days.

"Abe, meet Daniel Kennedy," Doc said in introduction as the two men shook hands. "Dan is a management trainee at a local bank who hopes to be the president of that venerable institution one day. His dress reflects the fact that he also sings tenor in the barbershop quartet put together by the Elks Club. They will be performing for an event at the Hershey Senior Center this afternoon. He has a credible voice, but it is really his youthful enthusiasm that carries the performance."

"Nice to meet you Daniel," Carlson said. "I admire anyone who can carry a tune. I don't even like myself in the shower. I can whistle a bit, though. Pretty good at bird calls."

"Like everyone else in town," Kennedy said, "I've heard a lot about you and your particular mission. My grandfather on my mother's side is now ninety-eight and living over in Biglerville, near Gettysburg. He worked for the Hershey Chocolate Company for twenty years as a translator and held several management positions in the import/export section during the time in which you are interested. He may be of some help to you."

"I'd appreciate that very much," Carlson said. "Where may I find him?"

"First let me give you some background on the man who has become well known as 'The Crank of Biglerville,' and you can take that title seriously," Kennedy answered.

Kennedy's grandfather had a rather lengthy and haughty name when he emigrated from Spain. Though from a very small village in the rural area of his home country, his name gave him a sense of pride far above his humble beginnings. He was personally wounded when he came through Ellis Island and was processed simply as Francisco Pedro Seville, grafter by profession. He considered himself the best grafter anywhere, one who outshone all others in the styles of cleft, splice, whip or saddle cuts. This perceived slight to his ego only increased the intensity of his pride. He invented a heritage of Castilian nobility that he repeated so often, that he came to believe it was true and his humble village actually vanished from his memory.

Seville found plenty of work grafting, mostly grapes and a wide variety of fruit trees that grew in Central Pennsylvania, and developed a reputation that brought higher wages from the big producers. His vanities were many and his prejudices well vented, so those who wished to purchase his services had to contend with his haughtiness. He was the living embodiment of the saying that "if you were a cranky old man, you were a cranky young man." He would never lower himself to what he considered manual labor, planting a tree or picking the fruit. Grafting he did not consider as labor, but as an art and he was an artisan.

His big break in life came when the Hershey Company began scouring the world for key ingredients and securing supplies in sufficient abundance—the most important being cocoa—and thus needed his fluency in Spanish, English, Portuguese, Italian and French, plus a smattering of obscure South American dialects. Like Mr. Hershey, he had very little formal schooling, but was a student of the world and very much self-taught.

"He is now a bitter old man," Kennedy said, sadly. "He had three wives and twelve children, all of whom he outlived. He has plenty of money because he never spent very lavishly for anything but his own personal wants and needs. His children were put to work in the fields or elsewhere at an early age and he never paid one cent for their higher education. His attitude was that he had made his fortune, now let the children make their own; it built character. So now he sits in a little square cracker box of a house just outside Biglerville that belonged to his youngest and poorest son, chain smoking cigars he imports from Spain, drinking wine that comes only from vineyards he grafted, listening to the radio news stations—he wouldn't even allow a TV in the house—and railing at the world."

"That sounds like a pretty surly existence to me," Carlson said. "Yet, you still seem to love him."

"Yes, I guess I do," Kennedy said. "Mother was the only one in the family who would still talk to him and when she died five years ago, he had no one. I'm all he has left and he is my grandfather."

"And you think he can provide me with information I can't find elsewhere?" Carlson asked.

"I hope so," Kennedy replied. "Like many old people, he can't seem to remember much about current events, but yet remembers every detail about what happened many years ago. And, to be honest, I hope that if you can get him to tell you about the years of his prime, perhaps it will give him some respite from his miseries. There have to be some good memories in there somewhere that will give him some solace at the end of his years. I thought perhaps you might coax some of those forward."

"I'd be happy to try, Dan," Carlson said, putting his hand on the young man's shoulder. "I'm fairly good with most people, even the surly ones. Just give me directions and I'll see what I can do."

Veronica Steinmann volunteered to accompany him. She knew the area quite well. Ruby Steinmann flatly declined. "I said I liked the excitement," she said, "but I'm very familiar with that sour old fraud, Francisco. I taught a few of his children. I did not approve of his treatment of his children or his wives. Of the latter, people say he worked them to an early grave, waiting on him hand and foot. At my age, I avoid unpleasant moments as often as possible. My time is too valuable to waste."

When Carlson announced he wanted to take his Jeep, Steinmann hesitated briefly. She was wearing white designer slacks, with white shoes, a light-blue pastel sleeveless top and carrying a large white leather purse. Carlson always considered it one of the mysteries of the gender that they seemed to always carry almost everything they might need in their purses. At least he had considered it a mystery until he made such a remark to a woman friend on a ranch in Montana. The woman merely pointed to a horse at the hitching rail and asked what the saddlebags were for and did that make men somehow mysterious?

"Don't fret, Veronica," he said. "I assure you I keep the inside of the Jeep very clean and should we encounter puddles or mud, I will carry your Ladyship swiftly and safely across."

"My, aren't you the gallant one," she replied with a smile. "If this Mr. Seville harbors such chivalrous thoughts about his own behavior, you two should get along just fine."

"Where I was reared," Carlson said as he opened the passenger door and assisted her with the high step, "we take our manners towards women quite seriously. You never know just whose mother or sister you might be talking to and respect is always offered up front." As she buckled her seatbelt, Steinmann found the interior of the Jeep to be immaculate. This certainly was not what she expected from such an outdoorsman. But then, Carlson was not what she expected to find in most men in more ways than one. She found him more interesting by the day.

Following her directions, Carlson drove south on Middletown Road, took Interstate 283 to the Pennsylvania Turnpike and exited at Route 15 South. Although the backwash from the big rigs on the Turnpike rocked the flat-sided Jeep as they sped by over the posted speed limit, this route skirted much of the traffic and a series of traffic lights. Steinmann even found the experience to be slightly invigorating.

Pulling off at the Biglerville exit, they had a pleasant drive along back roads with little traffic in either direction. Many parts of the roads had long stretches of shade, provided by leafy arbors of mature trees meeting overhead. After first doubting the veracity of a fading painted sign announcing Biglerville as "The Apple Capital of the World," Carlson saw acre after acre of fruit trees filling the valleys, climbing up over the one side of the hills and down the other side, only to spread out over the next valley. He noted large warehouses and processing plants, with the biggest fruit crates he had ever seen stacked twenty feet or more and boxcars sitting on the rails around buildings bearing the names of internationally know brands.

"This could, indeed, be the apple capital of the world," he finally said.

"And we've only scratched the surface," she said. "There are many more thousands of acres in fruit trees expanding for miles in each direction. You don't see many people about this time of year, but come harvest in a few months, you'd think you had entered a beehive."

Carlson passed through Biglerville and traveled a few miles to Arendtsville before turning around. For miles in the distance he could see nothing but orchards, the landscape broken only here and there with single houses or buildings dotting the scene. He was truly awed by the land's fertility.

"Pretty impressive, no?" Steinmann asked.

"Very impressive, yes," Carlson answered. "I've always heard of the famous Washington State apple industry, but Pennsylvania can more than hold its own on that score."

"Oh, we do," she confirmed. "We're just a little more modest than some. We don't have to do a lot of advertising. The people who dominate the industry know we're here and we have big exports. There will not be much wastage by the end of the season and even that will go towards feeding the livestock."

Carlson pulled into a gravel lane as instructed and followed the winding path through the woods until spotting the small, four-room house, really no more than a shack, in desperate need of paint. He parked next to a twenty year old Lincoln that had seen its better days. They both got out and Carlson rapped on the front screen door.

A small aged man, stooped by curvature of the spine, sauntered to the door.

"I'm Abe Carlson," the tracker started to introduce himself, but was abruptly cut off.

"Carlson," the stooped figure barked from the shadows. "That a Jew name or a Kraut? Or if you're here to spout Bible verses, you've got the wrong place. I'm Catholic."

"I'm neither Jewish nor of German ancestry," Carlson said. "I'm here with Miss Veronica, ah, Lake, whose father was Catholic."

"Lake, like the movie star?" the man asked, taking a cigar from between his teeth. "Well, she is sort of pretty, if a tad too skinny."

"We are in search of the distinguished Spanish gentleman, Senor Francisco Pedro Seville (pronouncing it as SA-Vee-Ya, in the Spanish manner), noted for his service with the Hershey Company," Carlson said. "Can you be of assistance? We want to know what society was like in Hershey during the 1920s and 1930s."

With that, the man seemed to stand a little straighter and square his shoulders.

"I am he," Seville. "Would you care to enter?"

"Very much so, Sir," Carlson said, opening the door and ushering Veronica through the entrance. As she passed through, she whispered in his ear: "Nice save, Sport, on both counts."

Seville produced a rather regal-looking humidor and offered Carlson a cigar. "Only the finest from Spain," he explained. "Only Spanish cigars are of the best quality. Don't believe what you hear about Cuban or Dominican or some other West Indian island cigars. As for the much-touted Cuban seed tobacco, pure lies. Spain imports only the best leaf from high in the Andes for filler and uses only leaves from the lower elevations as a wrapper. True quality cannot be faked. The expert will always detect the fraud."

"Thank you, but no thank you, Sir," Carlson replied. "I've never been blessed to develop a taste for a truly fine cigar and you would be wasting one such cigar on the likes of me."

"That's all right," Seville said, taking three cigars out of the humidor and putting them into Carlson's breast pocket. "Take a few along. You may encounter someone who will savor them and thus, gain a place in his heart for your kind gift."

"Many thanks," was all Carlson could say.

"Perhaps a small wine for you and the Senorita?" Seville asked, as if dispensing hospitality from the veranda of his estate in the old country. "I see that Miss Lake does not have a chaperone, but I don't seem to be able to keep up on modern customs."

"That's okay, Senor Seville," Steinmann answered. "I'm his attorney, just here to keep him out of legal trouble. It's a little early in the day, but I'd love to have a glass of wine."

"Red only, of course," Seville said. "The whites aren't fit for polite company, unless you are trying to cover the taste of a particularly bad seafood dish. Our neighbors the Portuguese have developed some very good whites, but then again, they are big fishermen and they do live on the same blessed peninsula."

Having filled three glasses and serving his guests he offered them a seat on a worn cloth sofa whose springs had sagged terribly years before. Seville seemed oblivious to the reality of his surroundings. His mind was stayed on better times and more prosperous living conditions, whether real or imagined.

"Ah, my beloved *Espana*," Seville said as he took his seat in a tattered leather winged-back chair with inexpensive rusting brads. "I had such a grand childhood, growing up on my father's estates—he owned several, you know—and riding the fields and mountains. But, then, for any boy to become a man, he must strike out on his own and make a name for himself, not just bask in the glow of his ancestor's accomplishments."

"You seem justly proud of your roots, Mr. Seville," Veronica commented.

"But of course," he answered. "There is a great pride in having Spanish blood coursing through your veins. Once Spain, under the heaven-sent hand of Glorious Queen Isabella, had cleansed itself of those evil Moors, it turned to the problem of the Jews. They either converted to the One True Church or were deported. If they did neither, they were eliminated. And you never could trust a Jewish convert. They had no spine and demonstrated no honor. They just acquiesced. Better to have died or left the country than to face such disgrace."

"About your days with Hershey," Carlson interrupted, sensing the anger rising in Steinmann, "how were things in those days?"

"Well," Seville said, taking a puff on his cigar, then leaning back to exhale one long stream, "when Mr. Hershey personally summoned me for my services, I was rather flattered to be asked to take on such heavy responsibility."

Seville rambled on for a full half-hour about the heady days of establishing the Hershey Chocolate Company into an empire, always placing himself as a wise counselor when key decisions were made. Both Carlson and Steinmann began to wonder if this old man had finally crossed some invisible line between fantasy and madness.

"I saw the trouble coming before anyone else," Seville said, suddenly darkening the conversation. "Mr. Hershey had a fatal flaw. He was too tolerant, too indulgent to his workers and too acceptant of traitors in his midst."

As Seville remembered the story, it all began with Hershey's accepting Jews, not just as bankers or tailors, but also as factory workers and allowing them to build synagogues. Germans were already a big population in place, but they were joined by large numbers of Italians. When Kaiser Wilhelm called veterans back to the homeland on the brink of World War I, some of those who answered the call held key positions on the production line, but left with Hershey's well wishes. None of them returned after Germany had been soundly defeated, at the cost of many American lives. Germany then broke many of the items of agreement of the peace treaty, mostly by rebuilding its armed forces under the fascists. Fascism gained a hold in Germany and Italy, and then spread to Spain.

The bloody Spanish Civil War of 1936-39 was a conflict between the democratically elected liberal government, called the Republicans, and the conservative rebels, called the Nationalists. The Nationalists were backed by the emerging fascists governments of Germany and Italy, who used the war as a testing ground for newly developed weapons of war. The result was hundreds of thousands of dead Spaniards, and the beginning of thirty-five years of brutal dictatorship under the butcher Franco.

"My family lost everything," Seville said at last, deep in his imagined world of legitimacy, "lands, titles, everything."

Carlson and Steinmann could only sit in silence as Seville paused to take a couple of long draws on yet another cigar.

"I could see World War II coming by 1930," Seville eventually said. "I was a thirty-second degree Knights of Columbus, defender of the church and His Holiness the Pope. The sons of those who deserted Mr. Hershey for service to Germany in the First World War began to take jobs in town. Some of them were from over around Reading, a hotbed of Freemasonry, just as much as Lancaster or Lebanon. I was always very wary of the Masons. Several Papal Bulls had been issued over the years condemning the organization and its purposes, you know. A few of those German zealots applied for jobs in town and I did my best to keep an eye on them."

"Do you recall any of the names?" Carlson asked hopefully.

"Let me see," Seville said, taking another puff and thinking for some seconds. "I think Fleischer was one. Unger and Kanalzinburger come to mind. But Steinmetz is definitely one I recall very clearly. Wolfgang Steinmetz was most assuredly one of them. He was the Devil incarnate, a real fire-eater for all things German. He just disappeared one day and the entire town should have been thankful."

The first few miles on the ride back were uneventful and in silence. Both Carlson and Steinmann were left to their own thoughts. It was Steinmann who finally broke the silence.

"That confused old man probably doesn't know that Steinmetz means stone mason in German," she said. "He certainly doesn't know that Fleischer means butcher in the same tongue. He would have had a field day with that one."

"He's just living in his own world," Carlson commented quietly. "If a man has lived beyond the Biblically prescribed span of years, who are we to say what is his reality, or to judge him? He seems confused, yes. But perhaps we share in his confusion."

"Well, I can assure you of one thing," she said, taking one of the cigars out of his breast pocket and holding it in full view, "this isn't a fine Spanish cigar. Did you in the west ever hear of the Conestoga wagons which pulled the population westwards?"

"Sure," Carlson answered. "Everyone knows those wagons, romanticized as 'Ships of the Prairie,' or something like that."

"Well, let me enlighten you," she said. "Conestoga wagons are of local manufacture. The wagoneers were a very rough and poor bunch. They acquired the nickname of 'Stogies' and smoked the cheapest cigars available. The name passed on to their smokes and this, my friend, is a stogie. Why they haven't killed that old man by now is a mystery to me. Let's just hope he goes out still in his dream world."

"As Mark Twain, the prodigious smoker of lesser quality cigars, is widely quoted as saying, 'it's easy to give up smoking, I've done it hundreds of times,'" Carlson concluded. "And let's hope that Seville recalled some real names."

"One more thing," Steinmann said. "His delusions of grandeur are really too much. My father was in the Knights of Columbus and he was fourth degree, the highest degree attainable. There is no thirty-second degree in that organization, ever."

CHAPTER 17

▼

SHAKING THE TREE

Doc Straussburger's brownstone had become the unofficial headquarters for people to gather and trade information. And as Aunt Mattie told everyone, her father reveled in the activity. The usual crowd had gathered for the cocktail hour when Carlson and Steinmann arrived. Henry Cunningham had been placed on the leather Chesterfield sofa in the library, because he was not only the center of attention, but also Doc thought he had earned the right to join in discussions about his rescuer and new best friend, Abe.

Carlson and Steinmann reported on their visit to Biglerville and gave the thumbnail sketch of what Seville had to say.

"Well, Professor," Doc said when they had concluded, "I notice your choice today is brandy. I thought you were rather loyal to wine."

"Not today, Doc," she answered. "I have just been an eye witness to a very ugly past, and if Seville is telling anywhere near the truth, that is not a society in which I would choose to participate. It is beyond bias and prejudice. It is unbridled hatred. I earned this brandy today."

"Keep your perspective, Professor," Doc counseled. "Remember that Seville has been a bit delusional his entire life. He lived half in and half out of the real world. As he aged, the fantasy turned to reality and, I imagine by this time, he is passing into a phase of senility. It may seem that Fate has been cruel to let him live this long, but many prefer to think he is reaping a just reward. I, myself, cannot stand in judgment. I leave that task to God."

"How do you remember those days, Doc?" Bud Hanover asked. "You were always in the middle of everything."

As Doc related his memories of those times it became quickly clear that he had always maintained a philosophical view of the world. He remembered the hustle and bustle of a rapidly changing world around him. Nearby Harrisburg being the state capital was a city on the move, but the little towns on the fringe like Hershey, Hummelstown and Middletown, or further out like Palmyra and Annville were also changing. Lancaster and Lebanon were becoming their own small hubs of commerce and Reading seemed to be the railroad king of the area.

Milton Hershey had placed a chocolate factory in the middle of a cornfield and built a community around it in a very few short years. Doc did not have to learn about the Industrial Revolution in school. He was witnessing it from his front porch, a smaller scale version of what was taking place around the world.

Doc remembered being keenly aware that he was living in a global environment of his times. Events in Europe had a direct effect on his life. Evidence was revealed at every level of his existence. The Russian Revolution obliterated the centuries-old monarchy of the Czars and handed the reins of government to the people. World War I completely changed the face of Europe, followed by turmoil in Spain and elsewhere. The rise of fascism in Italy and Germany sent tens of thousands of people flocking to foreign shores. He even read stories in newspapers from New York and Philadelphia about Japanese militarism on the other side of the world.

The large organized groups within the area—whether Italian, German, Irish clubs or Lutheran, Catholic, Methodist churches—kept up with events around the world through their publications and their churches. The amalgamation of these diverse interests into a functioning, pulsating community was leavened by acceptance of differences, cooperative effort and civil discourse.

Even during the Depression, the Hershey area was blessed with the bounty of the land and secure employment based on the success of the chocolate factory. When jobs were scarce or non-existent, Hershey built and expanded. People came from all over the mid-state to earn an honest dollar.

Doc was also aware of the seamier side of humanity—the drunks and the wastrels, the con-artists and snake-oil salesmen, the frauds and the phonies. He was also aware of the illegal sex industry just below the surface. Yet, by-and-large, he experienced a fine community moving forward and progressing together. There would always be a darker side to human endeavor, but the trick was not to let that impede progress.

"In those days, Francisco Seville provided some amusement," Straussburger said. "We had plenty of people who had eccentricities and quirks, but we didn't think any less of them. Old Mrs. McNaughton took in laundry, for instance. She'd hang up shirts on the line to dry, strictly according to color and size. We used to say she had the most regimented laundry in town.

"And then there was Bill Jackson, a barber by trade. He seemed normal enough, but every Sunday afternoon, weather permitting, he'd go to different spots on the Susquehanna River to mine coal. There was an awful lot of loose coal that washed down from upstream in those days and if you could find the spots where it finally settled, you could literally get free coal. Bill wasn't that tight with a nickel, but claimed the coal burned much cleaner having been so thoroughly washed. It was the only kind he'd burn in his house or his shop."

"What about Mr. Tanner, Doc?" Joe Weiser asked. "My dad used to talk about him."

"I don't recall what his real name was," Doc said. "We just all called him Mr. Tanner because he had a tannery on a creek a few miles from town. On Saturdays he'd bring in hides to the shoemaker's shop on Second Street, Mr. Baumgartner. Tanner had a mule that was blind in his left eye. He would only make right-hand turns. It was quite a sight to see his wagon in town. He'd come to an intersection that was barely big enough for the maneuver, make three right turns in order to accomplish a left, hoping the wagon would fit. Tanner really loved that mule."

"But those were just colorful characters with different traits," Bud Hanover said. "Where did Seville fit in the scheme of things?"

"Seville was always a case apart," Doc answered. "You knew right away that his great flaw was excessive vanity, which when combined with a certain amount of delusion could mean trouble. Most of his traits were harmless enough to anyone aside from himself.

"Take his Spanish cigar affectation, for instance. When you saw him coming down the sidewalk on a Friday night, with a silver tipped walking stick and more than the usual amount of aristocratic air, you knew his shipment of cigars had arrived. He dealt exclusively with one tobacconist who was a Dutchman, from Holland. He always reminded people he would not take his trade to a German or a Jew outside of the workplace. The cigars were shipped in a small crate, covered in rubberized burlap, twenty boxes to the crate. The tobacconist would uncrate the boxes, crack the seal to check for damaged goods, and place them in a canvas tote bag. If you hadn't seen Seville coming down the street, but spotted the canvas tote on his way back, it was a dead giveaway.

"To make a long story short, the Dutchman eventually married a nice Jewish girl who happened also to be German. He began to chafe at Seville's anti-Semitic remarks. One day he opened the boxes and replaced the expensive Spanish cigars with bunches of seconds he'd picked up on the local open market—that's seconds of stogies. Seville never knew the difference."

Other stories of Seville's quirks began to be told around the room, but Doc soon put a stop to that. "Please, people," he said. "Let's not malign a man who already has one foot in the grave. Not one of us is perfect. At least I can say that of myself. You must be the judge of your own behavior. Let's allow our fellow man to live in peace"

The conversation drifted to Henry Cunningham and his health. His bruises were fading and his ankles were on the mend, but he still couldn't walk without pain. He was at that awkward age where he felt uncomfortable being carried back and forth to the bathroom, so Aunt Mattie discretely tucked a bedpan and urinal into the bedside table.

"Henry has had a slew of visitors today," Doc announced. "Nearly all his baseball teammates came by and three of the cutest young girls from school. He's quite a celebrity right now."

Henry reddened a little at the mention of the girls. They were one year ahead of him in school and all three had brothers on his team. They had dropped in to cheer him as best they could, but he was still shy in their presence. If they noticed his shyness, it did not show. They just chatted on and on about his adventure. His teammates presented a homemade get-well card, with a picture of his head peeking out of a hole and cows licking his face. Everyone had a laugh, including Henry.

"About those names Seville gave you," Doc said, turning to Carlson and Steinmann, "Bud will make inquiries among the Lodges within a hundred miles to see if we can find a match. They are fairly common names for Pennsylvania, but odds are that if they were all Masons belonging to the same Lodge, we may be able to trace them. And what about you Professor?"

"I'm a step ahead of you there, Doc," Steinmann said. "I called my sister, Gloria, in L.A. She's the family historian. I asked her to shake the family tree and e-mail the results. We've got more than a few Steinmetzes way back there somewhere in the family. Let's see if this fellow is one of them. Mother's going to contact her many archivist friends and ask them to comb their records."

"So your mother's back in the hunt?" Doc asked.

"You bet," she answered. "I think she carries a little guilt about not informing me beforehand just what a curmudgeon Seville really is and leaving me to face the music alone."

"I very much doubt there is anyone who could intimidate you," Doc said with confidence. "And you had this strapping outdoor fellow as your backup."

"That's true," she said, "but you know how protective mothers can be and, sadly, I simply could not resist trying to play the 'guilt card.' It's one of my worst character flaws from childhood that I can't seem to break."

"If that's your worst flaw, we can all live with that," Doc replied.

The cocktail hour being over, everyone was summoned to the kitchen where they saw a massive amount of food spread over the counter and table. You could take your choice of building your own sandwich from an array of sliced meats and cheeses, or filling your plate with pork and sauerkraut, selecting sausages in a variety of shapes and sizes, and having your pick of pies, cakes and cookies. Coffee, tea, soda and cider were on hand to wash it down.

"It's always this way," Steinmann told Carlson. "Whenever there is a birth, a death, or any event where numbers of people will congregate, everyone brings food. When Mr. Simpson, a life-long bachelor, broke his leg last year, neighbors up and down the street packed his larder with more food than he could eat in a year. A couple of men even cleaned his house until he could get back on his feet. By the end of the week, the usually bashful Mr. Simpson, who never socialized much, had to give a big party just to whittle down his stores. That's just what people around here have always done."

"It's a nice custom," Carlson commented. "It's heartening to see such expression of community."

As they took a seat on the front porch, balancing plates on their laps, a large, rosy-cheeked woman with broad shoulders and surprisingly small feet came up the walk. Her blazing red hair would have made her easy to spot in a crowd, Carlson thought as she approached. He had seen her earlier in the library.

"Abe Carlson, I'm Mary Grant," she said. "Don't bother getting up, you'll just spill your food. I see you have a piece of Katherine Fitzpatrick's bundt cake. Good choice."

"Mary is retired from the Hershey Company," Steinmann explained. "If she has some information, you can rest assured it's accurate."

"Nice to meet you, Mary," Carlson nodded.

"I heard what you said about your meeting with that old run-off-at-the-mouth Seville," Mary said. "As usual, he is full of beans. I've just come from the company library. In the late 1950s, during the Big Red Scare, the government requested information we might have on people aiding and abetting our enemies. I was assigned the task and went through our personnel records since the founding of the company."

"Unearth any closet Commies?" Steinmann asked.

"Of course not," she answered. "But I did find some interesting things about the First World War era. We had exactly twenty-three veterans of the Prussian Army employed then. They all told the Kaiser to stick it in his helmet, they were Americans now and if there was any fighting to do, they'd do it for their new Fatherland."

"That's the spirit," Steinmann said. "Loyal Americans of German decent. Makes me proud of my heritage. So far, so good, Mary. Why do I get the feeling you're about to drop a bombshell?"

"Because you know me too well," Mary answered. "Abe, this girl always had a lot of sass. You'd better take that into consideration before getting serious. I was just building up to the climax and she interrupts. She ruins good story telling on purpose."

"Pay her no mind," Steinmann said to Carlson. "Her son, Bobby, and I were seeing each other in our senior year of high school. His plans for the future were to get married and have children soon, while taking a job at Hershey. I, obviously, had other plans and we drifted apart. So the following September he married my good friend and classmate Darlene Higgins and they provided Mary with a whole slew of grandchildren. Those two were both some lookers and produced many beautiful children. How many are there now, Mary?"

"Nine, five boys and four girls," Mary beamed proudly. "I always liked you a lot, Ronnie, and hoped it would be you. But then again, I'm not sure you'd have made a dutiful daughter-in-law."

"You're better off with Darlene," Steinmann said, "but I assure you that if that were what I wanted to do, I'd have been all peaches and cream. Now, what's the bombshell?"

"Well," Mary continued, "at the time of my study I did come across one peculiar file. It was of a twenty-four year old man, a machinist, with a wife and two children, one girl and one boy. He was a recent émigré with the rest of his family still back in Germany. He quit his position and went back there, but whether it was to fight or to see after his relatives is unclear. He left his wife and children here. There was an old faded obituary in his file. Apparently he was drafted as a private in the Kaiser's forces and died in battle soon afterwards, buried somewhere in France."

"Lord how I hate wars," Steinmann said soberly. "All the waste and all that carnage. Why can't the world somehow get together and talk about their differences without resorting to armed conflict?"

"Solve that one and you'll be awarded the Nobel Prize for Peace," Mary said. "Then they'll retire the prize. But the story doesn't end there. The man's name was William Ransom Steinmetz. In 1932, the company hired one Wolfgang William Steinmetz, a machinist by trade. The latter was the son."

CHAPTER 18

▼

SOME ANSWERS

Very early the next morning Abe Carlson had just stepped on the landing to the second floor when his phone rang.

"Abe Carlson," he answered.

"Hey, Sport," Steinmann said, "Sun's almost up. Why don't you join me for breakfast?"

"I'd be glad to, Veronica," he answered. "Where should I meet you, if there's any place open this early?"

"Most eateries around here start serving at half past five," she said, "but this morning I'm cooking."

"But I don't even know where you live," he said. "You never volunteered that information and I didn't think to ask."

"That's one of your endearing traits," she said. "You give a girl her privacy. Nevertheless, the question is moot. I'm at Mother's cottage. I stayed here last night, as I do on occasion. We were up until the wee hours working on your behalf and I have a voracious appetite."

"I'll be there as soon as I can," Carlson said and closed the phone.

The sun was in his eyes on most of the trip east to Elizabethtown, distorted by the pitting of his flat windshield. The blowing sands of the desert had exacted a toll on the glass over the years. Yet, Carlson felt lighthearted at the prospect of this breakfast, and the cooling breeze blowing through his open windows seemed to promise a wonderful day. He wondered if he was getting in a little over his head with thoughts of Veronica. She had her own professional career and he did not know if there was a place for him in her life. Also, there was the age factor, although he did not know her exact age, he reckoned the difference to be at least ten years.

As he reached to ring the doorbell, the door opened and a radiant Ruby greeted him.

"Good morning, Abe and welcome," she said. "Veronica is in the kitchen cooking enough food to feed an army. She tends to do that when she's in the mood. I'll be feeding the neighbors with leftovers."

"Well, it certainly smells good," Carlson said as he walked through the living room. Veronica emerged from the kitchen with two large platters as she headed for the sun porch.

"Have a seat, Abe," she said. "It's time to *fressen*."

"Come now, Veronica," Ruby said. "I've reared you to be a lady, not a farm-hand."

They bowed their heads and gave a short silent prayer of thanks. The platters were covered with meats, sausages, fried red potatoes, eggs Benedict, eggs over and omelets, plus a large stack of whole wheat toast, slathered in butter and sprinkled with cinnamon.

"Sometimes I think she just does that to irritate me, Abe," Ruby resumed as they began to eat. "How is your German?"

"Not very good at all," he confessed, "mostly a few words I looked up in a German-English dictionary. Quite a few I have no clue to pronunciation."

"It's a very nice language, really," Ruby said. "Some words are very expressive and exact in their meaning. When used out of context, they can be seen as crude, or a funny play on meaning. I think Veronica's frequent use of certain words is an attempt at humor, but I can never be certain."

"What Mother is trying to convey with this lecture," Veronica said to Abe, "is that she does not want me to offend the older generation Germans who may lack a sense of humor. *Fressen,* you see, means 'to eat,' but it is applied only to animals and their less-than-desirable table manners. I learned it as a child from a boy down the street named George Klintz, who used to hoot and howl every time he used it. When he grew up, he changed his last name to Clinton and has built a nice career doing stand-up comedy up in the Poconos."

"I had him in class one year," Ruby volunteered. "He was always considered the 'class clown,' but he did very well in Civics. Many of us thought he might become a politician one day, but he always said that he couldn't compete with the level of humor of that group, never seeing the laugh ability of their own actions."

"George liked to say if he couldn't laugh at them, he'd have to cry," Veronica ventured. "He even learned a list of Yiddish phrases to get ready to go out on the circuit, but by the time he reached there, the Yiddish Theatre had all but vanished. His punch lines didn't have the same effect when translated into English, so he had to write his own material. Actually, he once told me that most comics steal each other's jokes like crazy and the only reason he was still in the business was that he had some credible impressions."

As Carlson reached for a pitcher to refill his coffee, Ruby thought she caught a glimpse of sadness around his eyes.

"Something wrong, Abe?" Ruby gently asked. He thought a moment before replying.

"Not really," he said. "I was just thinking about what it would have been like to grow up in this type of atmosphere. There is so much family and so many neighbors who have been around for generations, tightly knit communities and neighborhoods built, so that if you wanted to summon the guy next door, all you had to do was open a window or call across a fence.

"I've got no complaints, you understand. I really appreciated my boyhood. The mostly solitary existence suited my personality and has stood me well through the years. The land and the animals were plenty to stave off any loneliness that may have crept in at times, but the fact is that I never felt lonely. I always had many friends and acquaintances, although the population is very sparse compared to here, and I'm beginning to question this sudden urge to find some traces of my family's history.

"My father never said much about his life back here. I think he loved my mother so much that it pained him to remember their days of courtship and marriage before moving west. And he did suffer from loneliness after she was gone and he had only a child to come home to at the end of the day. I could often see it in his posture, or the way he would stand in silence looking out the window, not at some distant object, but more like he was searching for a memory he could no longer grasp. At times like those, I'd go over and give him a hug around the leg and pretty soon everything would be okay.

"My life has been full so far, no holes I can think of, but it could have been different under other circumstances."

A quiet few moments followed as Carlson poured more coffee and refreshed the ladies' cups.

"I guess I shouldn't ask why you just don't find a good woman and settle down?" Ruby commented.

"No, you are right Mother," Veronica said, "you shouldn't ask. That would be rude."

"Not at all," Abe said with a chuckle. "I don't think a fifty-one year old with a solitary profession, requiring so much time on the road is much of a catch. But if you would like to adopt me, I might reconsider."

"I'm too young to be snaring a 'boy toy,' Abe, and too old to be adopting anybody," she replied with a smile. "As to age, why Veronica, here, is already …"

"Twenty-six and holding," Veronica abruptly interrupted. "Now let's tell Abe what we've been up to nearly all night. I'm full and ready to get back to work."

What they had been up to was Ruby perusing various databases on-line, everything from Census, Immigration, Federal, State and local jurisdictions, to libraries, museums and organizations. Veronica meanwhile combed through the data her sister, Gloria, had sent, crosschecking with her mother now and then.

The first good news was to eliminate William Ransom Steinmetz from the Steinmann family tree. There was over a hundred years difference between the two immigrations and William was from an entirely different region of Germany. The son, Wolfgang, disappeared in 1933, the same time as Sheldon C. Slate. Of the other names mentioned by Seville, they found a Joseph Kanalzinburger who retired from Hershey Chocolate in the 1950s, an apparent bachelor who moved to Florida, and Boris Unger, who eventually joined the Merchant Marine and died in the Pacific Theatre in World War II. He was buried with military honors in a small cemetery in Palmyra. A granddaughter of Unger's named Sophia never married and still owned a used bookstore in Palmyra. There was no record of a Fleisher in the right place at the right time, but that might have been just a figment of Seville's imagination. Before retiring for a two-hour nap at three o'clock in the morning, Ruby e-mailed her findings to Bud Hanover and Aunt Mattie. Doc Straussburger still resisted learning to use a computer, but had allowed his daughter to set one up in his office for emergencies.

The house telephone rang and Ruby picked up the remote unit on the sun porch.

"Steinmann residence, Ruby speaking," she said.

"Good morning, Ruby, it's Bud," Hanover said. "Thanks for forwarding the research. It made things a lot easier. The entire bunch, excepting Slate, was part of a heavily German Lodge near Pittsburgh. That Lodge closed two weeks after Pearl Harbor. The Grand Lodge received the charter it had granted along with a letter saying the Brothers, to a man, were going into our Armed Forces and no one expected to come back. They did ask permission for the charter to be reissued if sufficient numbers did return. No reissue request was ever made."

"The entire Lodge?" Ruby asked. "Surely there were members too old or unfit for duty who couldn't possibly serve."

"The letter addressed that too," Bud replied. "In a gesture of solidarity with their Brothers, those who had to remain behind demitted their membership, became Masons-at-Large and petitioned for membership in other Lodges, only to be reunited after the veterans returned."

"Now, there's a patriotic group if there ever was one," Ruby said. "I'm sure there are hundreds of such stories in any war, but they get swallowed up by the bigger issues of actually fighting and are long forgotten by all but those directly involved."

"And that list of names and places Abe discovered at the Bindnagle Church," Hanover continued, "Youst has been tracking it down and it appears to have been a roster of places and people the Reverend consulted on Slate's disappearance. All the speculation seemed to lead back to Brownstone Lodge. I have to call Abe and give him the information."

"Don't bother," Ruby said, "he's here. I'll pass it along."

"Is Veronica there, too?" he asked.

"Why, yes," she answered. "Why do you ask?"

"Well, those two seem made for each other," Bud said. "A lot of us were hoping there might be something developing, if you know what I mean."

"You men do seem to like your gossip," she said, lowering her voice. "All I can say is 'from your mouth to God's ear,' if you know what *I* mean."

Twenty minutes later the kitchen counter was filled with plates of food neatly covered with tin foil. Ruby was dividing them and putting each share in separate bags for distribution.

"Why don't you two get along," she said. "Go see what Sophia might have to say."

"I only know her to see her," Veronica said. "Sometimes I'd go to church with Dad at Saint Joan of Arc and I'd see her there. She is a few years younger than I and attended Catholic schools, while I stayed in the public school system and went mostly to the Church of the Brethren."

"You'll find her quite a bit more worldly than you might expect," Ruby said.

"What do you know, Mother?" Veronica asked in mock disgust. "What have you been holding out?"

"There are some things one hears that a mother doesn't necessarily pass on to an impressionable daughter," Ruby replied, raising an eyebrow.

"Tell me, dear Mother," she said. "I'm older now and I can take it."

"Well if you insist," Ruby replied, dropping the pretense. "What I heard is that she was well on her way to becoming a 'Bride of Christ,' mastering Spanish and Portuguese so she could join some order of missionary nuns and take off for the wilds of South America and minister to the needs of the peasantry."

"What happened to that?" Veronica asked. "It sounds like she had a pretty good plan."

"Two words," Ruby replied. "Christopher Weeks. The summer after she graduated from high school she suddenly discovered boys and hormones at the same time. She took off with Christopher Weeks the night she turned eighteen to join the Peace Corps. He was also fluent in Spanish. They were going to conquer South America together.

"Instead, the Peace Corps had a better use for them in the Ukraine. After six years of trying to teach English to sixth grade Ukrainian children, she returned home alone, her ardor cooled and a bit wiser. The last anyone heard of Christopher Weeks he was serving a long sentence in a Turkish prison for dealing drugs."

"Wow, I'm impressed," Veronica said. "Who would have thought little Sophia Unger had it in her? I mean, she really put it all out there in one fell swoop."

"Yes she did," Ruby confirmed. "As did many so-called 'liberated women' of that era. I have always been grateful that you have been so sensible in your rebellions, Veronica. But, then again, you've always had me as your model."

"And such a perfect one you continue to be, Mother," she replied.

As all three were packing Ruby's trunk with the bags of food, she took a moment when Veronica had gone back into the house for another load to lean over and whisper in Carlson's ear: "Forty-six, if you are interested."

Carlson returned a wink and a smile of thanks.

Ruby returned inside to load the last bag and retrieve her purse. The trunk closed with a solid thud. She slid into the driver's seat, buckled up and put the keys into the ignition.

"Now, you two children play nicely today," she said through the open window. "If you're still in Palmyra for lunch, Abe, have Veronica treat you to Funck's Restaurant. They have the best fried chicken around and everything else on the menu won't fail to please, trust me. And, if you don't mind, there are a few dishes still in the sink."

"You wash, I'll dry," Veronica said, and the two raced for the door like a couple of children.

"Now, there's a nice little domestic scene I'd like to witness," Ruby thought as she pulled away. Hope springs eternal.

CHAPTER 19

▼

GROSS NACHMACHENS

As Veronica Steinmann switched back and forth on the back roads, Abe Carlson was beginning to regret eating such a big breakfast. The temperature and humidity were rising rapidly and it promised to be a very warm day. Despite an extra cup of coffee and a good night's sleep, he was beginning to doze off. Steinmann, on the other hand, with only a couple of hour's sleep and a bigger breakfast, was full of energy and ready to go.

He was jolted wide-awake as she bounced across the railroad tracks at too high a speed. Glancing at the driver, he saw a smile on her face and a twinkle of mischief in her eye.

"Sorry, Sport," she said. "When you started to snore, I lost my concentration."

"I'm the one who should apologize," he said. "That was rude. It might leave the mistaken impression that I'm not thoroughly enraptured by your sterling company. I assure you nothing could be further from the truth."

"My, but you do know how to turn a girl's head," she countered. "If I thought that was a line, I'd drop you off on the side of the road. Somehow you manage to sound sincere, so I'll grant you a reprieve."

"I appreciate the depth of your mercy," he said. "Where are we?"

"About eight miles from Palmyra," she answered. "See that house on the hill over to the left, the blue one with the crumbling barn to the rear?"

"The one with all the Christmas decorations still on in the middle of summer?"

"That's the one. The lights are on a sensor and go on and off every night of the year. The first great crush of my life lives there," she explained.

Carlson was silent, wondering where this conversation was going.

"Bobby Singer," she continued. "He was the prettiest man I had ever seen. I was a freshman in high school. Bobby was a senior. He had great grades, lettered in three sports, dated only the most beautiful and richest girls in school, plus he ran the youth group at church. He had it all."

"And what's the rest of the story?" Abe asked. "As you alluded to Mary Grant, I'm waiting for the other shoe to drop, though I doubt it's a bombshell."

"The rest of the story," she said, "is not what I expected. Instead of accepting a full athletic scholarship to any number of colleges, Penn State included, Bobby chose another path. After graduation, he couldn't get to New York fast enough. He became a hair stylist of some note, returned ten years later after his parents died, but this time as Roberta Singer. He was an only child and his favorite season, obviously, is Christmas. I'm not sure if Roberta has had the medical alterations, but I do see her around town once in a while and I can tell you she has a wonderful Escada collection in her closet. If she were more my size, I might strike up a friendship just to borrow her clothing."

"And what have you learned from the experience?" Abe asked.

"Never to trust the really pretty ones," she said.

"I sure am glad I'm not one of those pretty ones," Carlson said.

"You've got that right, Sport," she countered. "Perhaps that's why I'm getting to like you."

"I'll take that as a compliment," he said.

"By the way, it's Hershey," she said, quietly reeling off her street address. "That's where I live. See how much I'm beginning to trust you?"

Carlson did not know how to respond, so he remained silent. He suddenly did not feel at all sleepy and realized it was not the outside temperature that made him feel so warm. This was a complicated, wonderful woman he was getting to know and he did not want his quest ending so soon.

The rest of the trip was uneventful as they left each other to their own thoughts. As Steinmann pulled into a side street in Palmyra, the Sophia's Bookshop sign was immediately recognizable for its lavender and black lettering echoing the lavender façade. There was a large picture window in front and the row house type building was old enough to have been through many incarnations of businesses.

An array of three bells tinkled as they entered the front door. The stacks of books were all arranged neatly throughout the store and browsing the titles reflected an eclectic taste. There was a cozy little corner behind the counter furnished with a small settee, one chair and a coffee table for customers to rest and peruse their books before purchasing. The small counter had a stack of bookmarks and other trinkets related to the business, such as a cup holding pens with the shop's address and telephone number. There was an aroma of freshly brewed coffee in the air.

One of the cutest, small women Carlson had ever seen emerged from the curtained back room, curly blonde hair falling to her waist in a braid and reading glasses on her head, with a chain around her neck to prevent them falling.

"Ronnie Steinmann," the woman called out in a deep, pleasant voice, "one of the prettiest girls to grace our fair land. What brings you in? Does this handsome fellow belong to you?"

"Not by a long shot, Sophia," Steinmann said. "I see you've grown perkier since high school. You were always such a quiet little thing, like a church mouse."

"I never caught one worth pulling in either," Sophia said. "As far as perky is concerned, my father thought of me more as mouthy when I first came home. But he was a convert to the faith when he married my mother and you know how straight-laced those converts can be—more Catholic than the Pope. God rest his soul, we did reconcile a long time before he died and his last years were of close family ties. Life is too wonderful to regret past indiscretions."

"How is business?" Carlson asked by way of inserting himself into the conversation.

"Tolerable," Sophia said. "I get a little foot traffic now and then, but I do most of my trade over the Internet. My stock is mostly a mix of out-of-prints and remainders, with a few older family libraries thrown into the mix. I have some older theology works that do well and I pick up some classics at library sales. I pretty much keep the place open so I have somewhere to go on a daily basis."

"We're not really here looking for a book," Veronica confessed.

"I didn't think you were," Sophia replied. "But it's nice to see you anyhow. Now, what can I do for you?"

"It's about your grandfather," Veronica said. "We're looking for information about Hershey in the 1930s. Your grandfather's name keeps popping up, along with the names Kanalzinburger, Steinmetz and possibly Fleisher."

"Now, that's a great group of characters you've picked there," Sophia remarked. "My father referred to them as a 'rogue's gallery if there ever was one.' Grandpa, whom I never knew, was apparently quite a character and my father always said his eccentricities skipped a generation to me. Dad was big on his genetic theories and totally supported Darwin, no matter what the Catholic

Church had to say. I dug out a raft of letters between my grandparents during the time Grandpa came to work as a machinist at Hershey and when my grandmother finally joined him in the late 1930s. He was quite a candid correspondent."

"Did he ever mention the name Sheldon C. Slate in any of those letters?" Abe asked, hopefully.

"I don't recall that name off-hand, nor do I recall a Fleisher," she said, "but he certainly wrote quite a bit about Kanalzinburger and Steinmetz."

Sophia's grandfather had painted a vivid picture of his early days in Hershey. The three men, all Lodge Brothers, seized the opportunity for steady employment when such work was becoming scarce in the Pittsburgh area. The big plants there were laying off workers on a seniority basis in an effort to keep costs down. With little seniority, they decided to strike out on their own. Hershey Chocolate was one of the few enterprises in the mid-state to be expanding and hiring skilled workers.

They had taken residence in a boarding house of sorts, a bachelor suite of three rooms above a tavern on the edge of town. They sent most of their earnings home, but did keep enough to meet their simple needs for light entertainment. Food came with the price of the rooms. When they started to miss their fraternal activity, they were not inclined to petition for membership in the Brownstone Lodge because they favored meetings conducted in German.

Instead, they established an informal little group in the corner of the tavern below and invited other German speakers to join the club. Membership dues were pegged at a round of beer per meeting, held twice a month. They adopted the title *Gross Nachmachens*.

"What does that mean?" Abe interrupted.

"Loosely translated," Sophia explained, "it was meant to convey the idea of Great Imitators. You have to remember that this was a group of lively young men who sought amusement wherever it could be found. The first Masonic Lodges in this country held their meetings in taverns, where food and refreshment were readily at hand and they thought this leant a nice touch of irony to their endeavor."

As Sophia understood the situation, the members of this new club would take turns amusing each other with imitations or caricatures of people they knew, or those in the news. One of her grandfather's favorites was "Uncle Wolfie" Steinmetz's recurring impression of an old German Mayor named Fritz explaining world events to his constituents sitting around a potbellied stove in a general store. It was presented in broken German dialect that often brought peels of laughter to his listeners.

But as the months wore on, the club was loosing much of its gaiety as somber news about life in Germany started to creep into the meetings. Germany was bankrupt from having to pay the huge war reparations dictated by the Treaty of Versailles. Inflation was rampant and the government kept printing unsecured banknotes with a face value of millions of dollars, but worthless. Allied occupation of the Rhineland only worsened the problems. Middle-class savings were wiped out. By the mid-1920s the economy finally resumed expansion, aided by U.S. loans, but it took years for the benefits to filter through society. A new sophisticated and innovative culture emerged by the end of the decade, but the normally conservative public thought it decadent.

The worldwide financial panic and economic depression resulting from the 1929 crash of the U.S. stock market was followed by the 1931 failure of the Austrian Credit-Anstalt. By 1932, there were twelve million jobless in the U.S., five and a half million in Germany. Years of agitation by violent extremists were coming to a head, with the Nazi leader Adolph Hitler on the rise. He soon found ways around the partial demilitarization plan imposed by the Treaty of Versailles.

The mood surrounding club meetings became so gloomy, its founders imposed a new ironclad rule adopted from Freemasonry: no discussion of politics or religion; maintaining the peace of the club was paramount. But a pall had descended on the group and even the usually joyful "Uncle Wolfie" became morose and withdrawn. *Gross Nachmachens* faded into oblivion.

"Grandpa was very disturbed about that," Sophia said. "He wrote one of his longest and saddest letters to his wife at the time. From then on, his prose lost some of its youthful exuberance. It is as if the reality of life has suddenly removed any frivolity he had. He had job security when many others had none and he still applied himself as always, but the spark was now missing."

"Did it ever return?" Veronica asked, stirred by the real life story as told through the letters of so long ago.

"I don't know," Sophia replied a little sadly. "It was another three years before he was financially secure enough for my grandmother to join him. I like to think he did. His last letter, enclosing train tickets for his wife and children to join him, seemed to indicate a renewed hope for a brighter future. He did go home for a week at Christmas every year, though. My father used to say that explains why he and his three brothers were all born in September."

"Why did he decide to join the Merchant Marine?" Carlson wanted to know. "He probably wasn't going to be drafted."

"No one else would let him join," Sophia said. "He tried all the services, but he was considered essential to wartime industry. Even chocolate was classified as essential to the war effort. But he had his mind set. What my grandmother considered 'foolishness,' my grandfather thought of as patriotism. This was going to be the event of his lifetime and he wasn't going to miss it. Because of his skill as a machinist, the Merchant Marine just looked the other way, I guess. With war once again raging in Europe, he knew we would get into it sooner or later. He was right. When the sneak attack on Pearl Harbor was launched, my grandfather was out on the high seas, headed for Borneo or some other exotic location. My father says that's where I got my urge to travel to foreign lands."

"Whatever happened to 'Uncle Wolfie?" Abe asked.

"His name simply dropped out of the correspondence after a few months," she said. "Mr. Kanalzinburger, the third leg of the stool, kept in touch with the family and visited often. He had no immediate family of his own, so the Unger's became the next best thing. My father said he was there for Sunday dinner like clockwork.

"One warm summer evening in the 1950s, around the time Mr. Kanalzinburger was to retire, everyone had gathered on the front porch and my father often overheard my grandmother and Mr. Kanalzinburger talking over old times."

According to this version, Wolfgang Steinmetz became more and more despondent. He gradually drifted away from the group, going for long walks late into the night and not returning to their rooms until well past midnight. Where he was going and what he was doing he would not say, so his friends stopped asking. He would have these seeming bouts of depression, but always after working hours. He was healthy as could be and never missed a day at the factory. Sometimes he would snap out of it for a few days and be almost his old self, but whatever was bothering him would always return.

Finally, one payday he returned to the rooms, paid his share for the next month's rent, packed up his few belongings and left a note saying he was going to live with a distant cousin who had recently moved to town. On Monday morning, he didn't show for work and no one had seen nor heard from him again.

"Do you by any chance know what time of the year that was?" Abe asked.

"Not the slightest," she said. "What difference does it make?"

"Most likely no difference whatsoever," he said. "By the way, since you own a book shop, would you happen to have a World Almanac I can buy?"

"I certainly do. That's one book always in demand and one of the few I buy new."

His purchase made and thanks given for all her help, Sophia waved and the two strolled out the door, Abe with his World Almanac nestled casually under his arm.

"What do you say to my buying you lunch at that Funck's place," he said as Veronica turned the key. "I'm suddenly hungry for some good fried chicken."

"You really know your way to a woman's heart, Abe," she replied. "'Let's do lunch, I'm paying,' will peak my interest every time."

In the few minutes it took for them to reach the restaurant, Abe flipped to the index of the book, scanned until he found what he needed and opened to the proper page. He repeated this procedure twice more before the car came to a stop.

"I'll tell you over lunch," he said to Veronica as he exited the passenger side and walked to the other side of the car to open her door. She was so surprised at this action that she failed for a snappy comeback, so kept her peace.

Carlson ordered the fried chicken and Steinmann the liver and onions—needed the iron she said. When the waitress left to place the order, she put both elbows on the table and leaned forward to within a foot of his face, eyes sparkling.

"Okay, Sport," she cooed softly, "you've got something and I want to know what it is, so out with it. Don't keep a lady waiting."

"Oh, I love it when beautiful woman make demands," he whispered with a grin. "It makes me enjoy giving in to the demands so much more readily. All right, here's what I was thinking."

Carlson began sketching a few facts. Sheldon C. Slate shows up as a visitor to the Brownstone Lodge in November of 1932. He attends every monthly stated meeting for the next five months. The sixth month he is barred, in April of 1933, for Masonic reasons. In June of 1933, the Pastor from the Palmyra church writes a letter concerning his disappearance. Wolfgang Steinmetz turned up missing "about the same time," they were told.

Carlson opened the Almanac to a certain page, turned it sideways and shoved the two-page layout in front of Steinmetz, guiding his thoughts with his finger.

"This is a Perpetual Calendar table," he said. "The calendar for 1933 is the same as for 2006. The Brownstone Lodge holds their monthly stated meeting on the second Tuesday of the month. That would make April's meeting on the 11th, confirmed by Bud as the date Slate was barred. If the Monday Steinmetz failed to show up for work falls between, say mid-April and probably mid-May I think they may have been up to something together."

"But what do you think they were up to?" she asked.

"It's a little far fetched at this point," he answered quietly. "I'd like to keep it from the others until we get more information, but I'll share it with you."

"Oh, good," she said with delight. "Cross my heart and hope to die. Or do you require one of those deep Masonic oaths with all the dreadful consequences that are rumored about?"

"I think I can settle for a woman's word," he said seriously. "We'll make an agreement and shake on it. That's good enough for me."

"You've got a deal," she answered, sticking out her hand and giving him a firm handshake. "Now, what are you thinking?"

"I'm thinking that there are many historical consequences that are merely that, consequences. Those with conspiracy theories have a field day with them, twisting and turning events around until they fit. There is one historical fact here that is unavoidable. In January 1933, Hitler was named Chancellor and by March the Reichstag had conferred wide-ranging dictatorial powers on the madman. I'm not sure where it fits, but I have a feeling it's in there somewhere."

CHAPTER 20

▼

RECONCILIATION

At Carlson's request, a small group was gathered in Doc Straussburger's library when the tracker and Steinmann arrived. In addition to the first three, it included Bud Hanover, Will Youst, Ruby Steinmann, Mary Grant, the last minute addition of Tom Rogers from the Bindnagle Church, and the curious observer, Henry Cunningham.

Due to the heat of the day, the tall windows were open to catch any breeze that may come and Aunt Mattie brought a tray with iced tea and lemonade.

"Thanks for coming on such short notice, Tom," Carlson said, getting right to the point.

"It's not a problem," Rogers replied. "I was coming here to pick up some church bulletins from the printer anyway. Besides, I've been curious about how you were making out in your search, and you did say you'd let me know the results."

"All this was started by a letter from your Rev. L.W. Kleinfelter, dated June 12, 1933 and posted to my father in Arizona," Carlson said. "Can you tell me anything else about that letter."

"Well," he answered, impishly, "I took the liberty of having one of our older congregants, who is fluent in German, translate the letter for me, along with some other papers Kleinfelter had kept. Not just out of curiosity, you understand, although it is my duty to admit to some of that. If this involved the church, we had to be prepared for any repercussions. We found some interesting things."

What Rogers reported was that Reverend Kleinfelter unlocked the church one morning, and then went to his office on a brief errand. When he returned, he discovered a young man sitting in the second pew, leaning forward, head bowed and deep in prayer. Leaving him to his meditations, the Reverend busied himself by dusting the organ. Finally, the man cleared his throat. The Reverend walked over and asked if he could be of assistance. Thus began several months of on and off counseling sessions.

The man identified himself as Sheldon C. Slate and he was deeply troubled. He came from a home of abuse and neglect, motherless since age five, gaining a cherished stepmother at fifteen. With her encouragement, he went out on his own at age seventeen and never looked back. When he was ready, he sought out Freemasonry for the sense of family and brotherhood the organization provided, accepted on his own merits and not judged on the faults of his father.

What troubled him most deeply was what his future would hold, as the chaos of the world around him, seemed to worsen by the day.

Kleinfelter repeatedly urged him to shy away from the Masons, come join his congregation and seek solace in this church. He did not have a problem with Freemasonry; in fact, he admired many of the Masons with whom he had contact. He also understood that it was not a secret society, as some people thought, but a society with secrets. His sole objection was the taking of oaths in secret. He was a firm believer that all oaths should be taken in the openness of the church or a courtroom.

Slate never revealed where he had come from, but did tell the Reverend about a half-brother, the son of his stepmother by a previous marriage, who was preaching the Gospel to the Indians in Arizona. His greatest obsession in later sessions was the gathering clouds of war in Europe, Germany in particular.

When Slate suddenly stopped coming to see him, the Reverend made some inquiries and found there had been some commotion at the Brownstone Lodge. Having been born and reared in the area of Batavia, N.Y., he was well aware of the unproven fate of William Morgan. After Slate was nowhere to be found for a couple of weeks, the Reverend thought it best to write the letter.

"I wouldn't be surprised if Slate had been naturally drawn to Freemasonry," Hanover volunteered. "I know a number of the Fellows came in that way. We usually draw them through the affiliated youth organizations like DeMolay. We get a lot of troubled or just confused youth coming to that program, but, of course, not all end up becoming Masons."

"Mary," Abe asked next, "can you go back in the Hershey archives and retrieve some personnel information?"

"Whoa, there cowboy," she answered. "There are laws protecting employee privacy you know. I can't just go rummaging around in personnel files."

"I was thinking more of payroll," he explained. "All I want to know is the date on the last payroll check to Wolfgang Steinmetz in early 1933."

"What do you think Professor?" Mary asked Veronica.

"I think that it would be legal," Veronica answered. "All he wants is a date. I wouldn't ask the corporate lawyers, though. Their standard answer to everything is 'no.' And if there's a problem with that later on, you can always plead extenuating circumstances—you know, heat of the chase and all that."

"Better yet, how about free representation by you?" Mary bargained.

"It's a deal," she answered. "Want to shake on it? That's good enough for Sport, here."

"I'll do it anyway," Mary answered as she and everyone else in the room wondered what the reference to Sport was all about.

As Grant went on her assignment, Carlson and Steinmann gave a detailed account of what Sophia Unger had to say about her grandfather, with particular discussion of the *Gross Nachmachens.*

"It sounds as if that shy little girl grew up to be a mighty spunky woman," Aunt Mattie commented.

"You bet," Veronica said. "The harsh realities of the world will either make you or break you. She survived very well."

Carlson next turned to the two Masons in the room.

"Okay, Bud and Will," he said. "You are the two experts on all things Masonic. Why do you think Slate was barred from the Lodge?"

"The most likely reason seems very clear to me," Youst said first, looking to Hanover, who nodded for him to go ahead.

"It's simple, really," he continued. "What you said about the fading away of the original purpose of the amusement club, *Gross Nachmachens,* because of dissention in the ranks. They tried to keep politics and religion out too late. Because of his growing compulsion with events in Germany, I would expect Slate to bring his troubles to the Lodge, the only family he felt he had. Kleinfelter couldn't come between him and his family. The Lodge probably gave him a few warnings, but the rules were clear. Sowing dissention disrupts the peace and harmony of the Lodge. It was its duty to bar him."

"He must have been crushed by that," Veronica said. "Rejected by the family, he may have done something rash."

"Or impulsive," Carlson said to himself.

Mary Grant returned and made a great show of slowly reaching into her purse, retrieving a small notepad and clearing her throat to silence the room.

"And the winner is," she called dramatically, "April 29, 1933. In those days, you were paid every other week, on Saturday because you worked five and a half days. April was unusual that year, which saw three paydays because the 1st fell on a Saturday."

"Thank you for your usual thoroughness, Mary," Doc said, turning to Carlson.

"Okay, Sleuth, where are you going with this?"

"Just this," he said, producing his new World Almanac. "I was looking at the Perpetual Calendar section and calculated the days of the week for 1933. Slate is barred from the Lodge on Tuesday, April 12. Steinmetz, who has been brooding for months and taking long walks in the evening, draws his last paycheck on Saturday, April 29, and doesn't show for work on Monday, May 1. Six weeks later, to the day, Kleinfelter writes a letter on June 12."

"So, what do you make of that timeline?" Bud asked.

"Suppose these two men met each other?" Abe said. "It doesn't matter how. It could have been on one of those mysterious walks or in a corner bar somewhere. These two had very much in common: single, Masons, German, obsessive about events in the Old Country. Who knows, they may even have been brooding buddies. In that state of mind, how many ways you reckon they could devise to end their miseries?"

"Are you suggesting a suicide pact of some kind?" Doc asked, skeptically.

"Not as you understand it," Abe replied. "Slate was too close to God and the church not to think that would bring eternal damnation. There wasn't much of a fuss around town, except for grumbles about the Brownstone Lodge, and if a couple of stray bodies showed up everyone would have certainly known about it."

"They could have easily left town and headed for Harrisburg," Aunt Mattie said to no one in particular. "There have always been several nice high bridges over the Susquehanna and people have been known to jump now and then."

"Left town, yes," Abe replied, deep in thought, "but I think they had another destination in mind. I need a good stretch of the legs to think about this."

"Like a little company, Sport?" Veronica asked.

"I may not be much company for you," he answered. "I do my best thinking in the quiet of my thoughts, but I'd be pleased to have you along."

As they stepped from the porch, Carlson stopped to fill his pipe and light it. He noticed Veronica looking at the procedure out of the corner of her eye.

"You disapprove?" he asked.

"Not at all," she said. "It's just that I didn't know you smoked."

"Only rarely," he replied. "I read somewhere that there was a theory that the proliferation of fine writing of the Elizabethan era was a direct result of the introduction of tobacco into the court."

"At least yours smells pretty good," she commented as they stepped forward.

They had not walked fifty yards before the sun beating down made him begin to sweat. He stopped and looked up at the sky, shading his eyes with his hand.

"Only mad dogs and Englishmen ..." she began.

"Go out in the noonday sun," he finished. "What's with your metabolism? You don't seem to feel the heat. No sweat."

"Horses sweat, men perspire and women glow," she answered. "And I've been known to slip on long underwear in August. You said you wouldn't do much talking, just thinking, so let's get this show on the road."

They were off again, steering a route through tree-shaded streets where possible and strolling through parks with running water. As they passed under a railroad trestle, Carlson slowed in the shade to ask a question.

"I don't suppose Ruby knows any politician with enough clout to get us a peek at passport records?" he mused.

"Twenty years to life," she said. "I believe that is the federal minimum. Even POTUS would have a hard time and need a very good reason."

"Ah, yes, the President of the United States," he said. "I'd say there is good reason to keep his nose out of things."

They walked on for several more long blocks before he stopped again. His pipe had gone out some time ago and he refilled it.

"Wouldn't happen to have any shipping rosters from, say, May of 1933 about the place, would you?" he asked, while lighting his pipe.

In reply, Veronica merely rolled her eyes and resumed their walk.

Carlson went into a deep, silent concentration as he proceeded. She could almost sense the synapses firing inside his skull at an alarming rate, while outside was all calm and collected. She thought it odd that he now had no perspiration at all on his face or neck.

As they turned down a quiet street that Carlson recognized from previous walks, the same big dog stepped off his porch and stood on the sidewalk, only this time wagging his tail more heartily, as if he were glad to see Abe again. Abe patted his head, scratched behind the ears and accepted the lick to his hand. Satisfied, the dog returned to his regular place on the porch. Carlson then had a sense of *déjà vu*, recalling the last time he petted the dog he was thinking about probing in the shadows.

"Got you now," he nearly shouted, startling his companion.

"What have you got?" she asked, catching his excitement.

"I may have the key to where they went. Let's get back quickly. Do you happen to know what type of computer equipment Doc has?"

"Only the latest and greatest," she said. "Aunt Mattie's son sells them and she provided her father with all the bells and whistles, plus fiber optic cable. Now if she can only get him to go near it."

As the two rushed up the stairs, Carlson called ahead: "Aunt Mattie, how about cranking up that nice new computer?"

As they came into the library, the screen was already beginning to glow.

"I'll tell you all about it in a minute," he told the group. "I need to get an e-mail off as soon as possible. I don't think the time change will make much difference."

Everyone looked to Veronica for some clue, but she could only shrug her shoulders and roll her eyes, indicating she had no idea either.

They were all amazed at the speed with which Carlson played the keyboard as if it were a piano, pausing only briefly as he thought of a new addition. After four short minutes, he hit the 'send' button, but didn't take his eyes off the screen until the confirmation box popped up. He pressed the OK button and sat back in the chair, looking satisfied.

"What now, Abe?" Doc asked.

"Now we wait, Doc. Now we wait," he said. "Aunt Mattie, would you still have some of that iced tea on hand? Unlike my companion, here, I do tend to perspire in this heat and humidity."

When he was served and refreshed, they all sat around awaiting an explanation.

"Sorry to be rude," Carlson began, "I got a little excited there, but I had to act quickly. On our walk, I started out thinking of where Slate and Steinmetz might be going, if they, indeed, did get together and strike out on their own. I had only a speck of an idea where they might be going, but then I realized the more important question is how they would get there. If I could somehow follow that trail, I'd know for sure."

"That's why you mentioned passports and shipping rosters," Veronica said.

"Yes," he confirmed. "But I knew there was no way I could access that material even if an electronic database had been built around such old material.

Veronica had mentioned something earlier about 'mad dogs and Englishmen' that stuck in the back of my mind.

"I have a friend in London with the terribly English name of Trevor Oswald, who wears expertly tailored three-piece suits, with a gold watch and chain in the vest pockets. He loves being the caricature of the English gentleman. I've even seen him walk down the streets of London in spats, with a gold-tipped walking stick. You'd never know it to look at him, but he grew up in one of the worst neighborhoods of Liverpool, down along the docks.

"The important thing is that I came to know him through his employment as head of the Fraud Department at Lloyds of London. He'd say that his early years suited him perfectly to catch rascals up to mischief. I was called in on a matter under his jurisdiction and saved the firm a great deal of money. They wanted to give me an outlandish bonus, but I told them they were already paying me so lavishly that I found it embarrassing. We've been good friends ever since.

"I was thinking about the number of ships that must have sailed around the world between the First and Second World Wars. The big insurance companies, such as Lloyds, keep meticulous records going back hundreds of years. They have to, obviously, and it's all in computer banks. And I think Lloyds is probably one of the largest when it comes to shipping."

"Way to go, Sport," Veronica said. "What did I tell you Mother? This guy can track by land or by sea."

"You never said that," Ruby protested.

"No, but I should have," she replied. "It would have made me look so clever at this particular juncture."

A bell rang three times on the computer and a green light automatically showed on the printer, which spit out one page of text and turned off.

Carlson picked up the paper, stood in the middle of the room and began to read. The others gathered around and read as best they could. It was a piece of stationery with an elaborate Lloyds of London letterhead, the contents hand-written in beautiful script.

"Dearest Abraham,

I'm so glad you finally asked me to be of service, though hardly a challenging one. I will not bother you with tonnage and rates since you only inquired of the passenger list.

The Copenhagen Diamond sailed from the port of Baltimore May 8, 1933, destination Oslo, with stops in London, Amsterdam and Hamburg. The two passengers of your particular interest, Sheldon C. Slate and Wolfgang Steinmetz, embarked in Baltimore and disembarked in Hamburg.

I trust this information meets your needs. It was a pleasure to be of assistance in this regard and please do not hesitate to contact me if I can be of any further assistance.

With fondest regards,

Trevor Oswald

"Mystery solved," Doc said. "Thank you, Abe, for letting all of us be a part of it. And although I realize the sun is not yet over the yardarm, I think this calls for drinks all around."

As the sun was sinking lower in the evening sky, Carlson and Steinmann were standing on the front porch, just watching the slight breeze grace the leaves.

"Penny for your thoughts, Abe," she said. "You don't seem to be as pleased as you should. You found the long-lost Uncle and you've cleared the Brownstone Lodge of any hint of scandal. And you've managed to become a hero to young Henry along the way. You have the respect of everyone in town and you'll be sincerely missed."

"Things are not quite settled yet to my satisfaction," he admitted. "There will still be a question of whether those two idealistic young men went to Germany to prevent what was happening, although I doubt there was much they could do, or to become part of the reviving war machine."

"Sometimes we can't get all the answers, Sport," she said, quietly. "We need to settle for the answers that do come our way and get on with life."

CHAPTER 21

▼

THE RECKONING

Ruby Steinmann and Doc Straussburger had been fast friends for more years than either cared to remember. Doc had always had a knack for making new acquaintances into fast friends, even with people he saw only once every few years. His had an endearing quality Ruby appreciated. It was mid-morning and they were sipping coffee in Doc's library, reminiscing about previous days and decades.

"You know, Doc," Ruby said, "as I age, events seem to speed by at an alarming rate. As I think back, decades that used to seem so unending now appear in a blur, yet I can remember every detail."

"Trick of the mind," Doc assured her. "When we are young, it is hard to believe adults talking about friends of twenty or thirty years. I can only speak for myself, but about age thirty-five, two things happened. I was a practicing physician for a few years, of course, but there was certain credibility subtly granted to me that I had not experienced. Then when I passed sixty-five, I knew I was much wiser for the life-experience, and couldn't quite grasp why the younger generations thought they had all the answers. That's just human nature, I suppose. Each generation has to rediscover their own truth they think applies solely to them. At least they may be immune from what the community at large thinks. That would probably be a good thing."

"Ah, the community at large," Ruby chuckled. "At times, the community at large can be a great guide. Though at other times, differences in outlook can have comical consequences. I was thinking about the obituaries for General Lew Wallace, the great U.S. soldier and diplomat. He was also the author of *Ben Hur*. He died just after the turn of the 20th Century. One newspaper called his death 'at the early age of seventy-eight' another example of 'the deadly cigarette habit. But for the filthy weed,' they claimed, 'he might have lived to an even hundred.'

"Another publication, *The Primitive Christian*, as I recall, said that Wallace, 'who posed as a Christian, died at seventy-eight, having prolonged his life beyond the Scriptural three-score and ten by the use of those devilish drugs—cigarettes and coffee. God made seventy the sacred limit of our years, and those who violate it by employing drugs will surely suffer.'"

"Why is it that you remember that so clearly?" Doc asked.

"I used it as an example in my civics classes for over twenty years," she replied. "It was relevant to the students from the 1970s on and is still relevant today. They learned how society is so intermeshed, the differing interests and concerns involved, how we deal with conflicts over important questions, how passionate feelings from all quarters vie for the upper hand. It delves deeply into the murky area of how to define individual rights, on all sides, and to know how does a constitutional democracy settle its differences. They are responsible for their own future and how to deal with the mistakes of the past, while crafting that future. My only hope is that I provided them with some tools to resolve these issues through civil discourse and less-impassioned bias against other views."

"You are a remarkable teacher, Ruby," Doc said. "Judging from what I have seen from a number of your former students, you've done a fine job. Now, just what is it you are planning to do with Abe and the Professor today?"

"Late last night," she said, "I discovered just how quickly word can spread through the Masonic Village. Everyone there suddenly knew at least something about Abe Carlson and his inquiry. One woman in Assisted Living, Karla Simpson, asked me to drop in because she might have information we could use. It was fairly late, but I did as she wished and was glad I did. When she was a little girl, she lived right next door to Carlson's grandmother, during the period of her second marriage. I called Veronica and asked her to bring Abe by this morning. I have to leave my car at the shop and wanted those two to have lunch in Elizabethtown so Abe could discover more detail about a family member."

"Do you have any idea when Abe's planning to leave?" Doc asked.

"Not a clue and no one wants to ask," she answered, "least of all Veronica. I can tell it in her voice. She's scared to death it might be today. I trust you can still keep a secret? I can usually keep my own counsel, Doc, but I discovered something that I can't share with Veronica at this moment, but I feel the need to unburden myself."

"Have you ever known me to betray a confidence?" Doc asked. "Why, I'm the soul of discretion."

"I know, dear Doc," she said, patting his hand, "I just needed to hear it from you. You see, last night I couldn't sleep, so I thought I'd do a little research on Abe Carlson. I'll admit that this new relationship of Veronica's may not pan out, but I want to be ready just in case."

"And what did you find?" Doc asked. "I trust we haven't been harboring a fugitive from justice is our midst. He doesn't have a wife and a host of children he hasn't told us about, has he?"

"Come now, Doc," she said. "We're both better judges of character than that. What I found is that he is exactly what he presents himself to be, but then some."

"Details, Ruby, details," Doc said in mock demand. "Name names."

"There are plenty of names you would recognize," Ruby said, "but precious little detail. He works very discretely. What is very impressive, though, is running a few financials. I find it hard to believe the number of real estate, straight investment funds, charities and personal improvement programs he has invested in over the years. Sometimes the amounts are almost staggering. Doc, my little girl, now a grown woman, of course, has no idea she is running around town with a multi-multi-millionaire. And I'm talking multiples of tens of millions of dollars, all over the world. He could have retired years ago."

"Not the type," Doc said, flatly. "What fun would life hold if he did that? Let me guess, you're worried about the old saying marrying for money, you will earn every dollar."

"Perhaps a little," she admitted.

"Then, Ruby, you are severely underestimating your daughter," he said.

Carlson and Steinmann finally arrived, looking a bit worse for the wear, and both asked for a cup of coffee.

"You look a little peaked this morning, my dear," Ruby said to Veronica.

"It's been a hard night," Veronica answered. "We spent the night together at my house," she said, pausing for effect, "I was on my computer and Abe on his."

"I had one more source I wanted to explore," Abe explained. "It was a shot in the dark, but I reckoned that if I could access some data bank, like Simon Wiesenthal's famous Nazi hunter group, we might get a lead. The Germans were so noted for keeping meticulous records, I thought we might pick up some clue."

"Most records were from much later in the war," Veronica said. "The major emphasis, of course, is centered on the six million Jews lost to the extermination camps in every territory the Nazis conquered. Another six million or so others are estimated to have been murdered in like fashion. The numbers become overwhelming. Did you know that between 1933 and 1945 the Nazis established about 20,000 camps to imprison millions of victims? There were many levels of camps, from detention to elimination and everything in between. I started to feel like I'd been crawling through a sewer. At just the right moment, Abe raised another possibility, so I stayed in the hunt."

"I remembered the establishment of the United States Holocaust Memorial Museum in Washington, D.C.," Abe said. "Its aim was to cover the entire Holocaust, from start to finish, in whatever country it occurred. Coming into power in 1933, the Nazis immediately began construction of detention facilities to imprison and eliminate so-called 'enemies of the state.' The first to be gathered were German Communists, Socialists, Social Democrats, the Gypsies, known as Roma, Jehovah's Witnesses, homosexuals, and on and on and on."

"I took the main site," Veronica said, "Abe took the linked sites—there were literally thousands of them, from official reports to personal histories, to commentaries."

"Strictly adhering to 1933," Abe continued, "because I didn't think our pair would last very long in that atmosphere, I stumbled across the record of a newspaper editor in Germany who also happened to be a Fellow in Freemasonry. The Masons knew it was only a matter of time before the Nazis banned them altogether and drove them underground. In a letter of warning to his Brothers in the surrounding Lodges, he warned of repercussions from a local incident. Two men, fluent in German and carrying American passports, were shot dead when they attempted to assassinate Chancellor Adolph Hitler. Three bodyguards were killed in the melee and a search uncovered Masonic dues cards on their persons. The Nazis were canvassing all Lodges in the area for anyone who had had any contact with Wolfgang Steinmetz or Sheldon C. Slate."

"They came that close," Doc said. "I wonder what the world would have been like if they succeeded. But that is of little consequence. They obviously had some idea of what may lie ahead. I most sincerely hope they were not aware of the fullness of the horror we were to experience. I see what you meant, Abe, about perhaps it was not a suicide pact in the traditional sense."

"I had a notion," Abe replied, deep in thought. "In a way, I wanted to be wrong, but you can't choose for another how they depart this life. It's the lucky ones who have the opportunity to make a clear choice. It meant enough to them, so in that I salute their honor. May we all be afforded the choice?"

In the silence that ensued, Ruby arose and refilled their cups. All were left to their own thoughts for a few minutes.

"All right, Sport," Veronica finally said, getting to her feet. "Mother has found a woman who knew another woman in your life. Let's go see what we can scare up. You're sparse on personal history. Let us help you fill in the blanks."

Veronica and Abe sat in the Brossman Cultural Center, Three Loaves Café, at the Masonic Village in Elizabethtown, making small talk, as they awaited Ruby to retrieve Karla Simpson from Assisted Living.

"You seem a little anxious, Abe," she said. "Not sure about the name of this café?"

"I read the legend," he replied. "It's named after an incident in the life of Benjamin Franklin, the gentleman whose statue at the hand-printing press stands on the grounds. History says he arrived in town with only a couple of pennies in his pocket and purchased three loaves of bread as his food source. He ate one, but encountered a widow and her child who had none, so he gave them his extra two for their survival."

"Close enough," she said.

"Veronica," he replied with some feeling. "Yes, it is a new experience to find a person who knew my grandmother, someone I never met. I want to get to know more about her, of course—it's just that I'm getting into uncharted territory here. First you make me feel like a seventeen year old, then I confront another specter."

"Cheer up, Sport," she said. "I'll be here to hold your hand."

Ruby appeared pushing a little blue-haired lady in a wheelchair. Carlson rose at her approach and came forward.

"Mrs. Simpson," he said in greeting, "it's so nice to meet you. I understand you knew my grandmother. I never did and would appreciate whatever you can tell me about what you remember of her."

"So, this is the tracker we've all been hearing about," Simpson said to no one in particular. "I've read of your efforts with our young Henry. Good job. Now, tell me, Mr. Abe Carlson, what do you think of little old ladies with blue hair."

"As you can see, Mrs. Simpson," Abe said, "I'm a bit salt and pepper myself. I once had the occasion to use a sample rinse I picked up in a motel. The gray turned to blue and I had the devil of a time washing it out. Since then, I've have had nothing but the deepest of respect for ladies with blue hair."

"You pass with me, Abe," she replied. "What do you say we all go over to the east corner there, so we can have a more private conversation? We older people do like our gossip, you know, and I don't want the word to get around before I can spread it at my leisure."

As she wheeled Mrs. Simpson over to the requested corner, Ruby gave both Abe and Veronica a wink and a smile.

As Karla Simpson remembered her neighbors, no one on the block could ever fathom why Ellie Carlson ever consented to marry the widower Schmidt. In the end, they concluded it must have been for the sake of his son, Elmer. She loved the child as if he were her own, nurtured and groomed him for a life under better circumstances. Although she did not like to speak ill of the dead, Peter Schmidt was one of the most unpleasant men she ever hoped to meet.

Ellie always did her best to protect Elmer from his abusive father; at one point she threw Schmidt off the back porch to sleep off a drunken spree. When he awoke, he found he had slept under the porch with a mangy dog.

It was she who encouraged Elmer to change his name, as was the fashion among young men of the day, and strike off on his own. She told him how proud she was of her own son, who had dedicated himself to God and went to the wilds, with one hand on the Bible and the other on his heart, to fulfill his mission.

For a model, she has suggested Claude Swartzbaugh, or perhaps Sheldon K. Hoover, two men of integrity she had known and admired in her lifetime. Elmer decided to combine these two names and, therefore, reap the benefit of both.

Slate came from the stonemason heritage of Free and Accepted Masonry. Many others had chosen that path.

"What ever happened to my grandmother," Carlson asked.

"Oh, she survived," Simpson said. "The really good ones usually do, you know. Died peacefully in her sleep shortly after receiving a letter from her first-born son."

Her second husband was another matter all together. Peter Schmidt was a roustabout for the railroad, non-educated and able to perform only the most menial tasks; he was an alcoholic to boot. One winter night he was assigned as a switchman's apprentice, requiring him to sit in a little shack by the tracks and keep ice from forming at the switch or movable track. Unfortunately, he was drunk and fell asleep. The fire in a small heater died and he froze to death.

When Carlson informed her of the eventual fate of Elmer, all she could say was: "Ellie would have been so proud."

Two hours later Ruby and Doc were once again sitting in his library and awaiting the arrival of Veronica and Abe. Ruby had picked up her car, but lingered.

Veronica finally breezed in, alone, looking full of life and content with her world.

"Where's Abe?" Ruby asked with as much calm as was possible.

"Off to North Africa or the Steppes of Russia," she replied. "I couldn't be sure which because I had no idea of the place he indicated. He said I could look it up."

"Veronica Rosemary Steinmann," her mother declared.

"Calm yourself, Mother," Veronica replied. "He left a small parting gift, very nice really. It won't snag my hose."

With that, she produced her left hand, showing a platinum ring with a deeply embedded diamond.

"He said he needed to earn the money for the ring," she said. "I hope it didn't set him back too much. Mother, your eldest daughter is finally engaged."

EPILOGUE

▼ ————————————

Five days later, Veronica received e-mail from Abe, then located along the Ob River, near a town called Tomsk deep into the Russian Federation. As for what he was doing exactly, he merely alluded to the fact that the big multi-national corporations do not take kindly to having senior personnel suddenly disappear. In many parts of the world, kidnapping for ransom had become a lucrative trade and the corporations preferred to keep these incidents out of the public eye, dealing with them in-house. The skyrocketing insurance premiums to cover such occurrences were getting out of hand and the insurance companies themselves simply refused coverage in certain areas of the globe. She surmised that Abe was called in on one of these occasions, but knew she would never question him on the subject.

She double-clicked on the attachment bar and downloaded his first "My Dearest Veronica" letter.

He had stopped in London to have dinner with Trevor Oswald to thank him for his assistance. Abe related to Oswald some of the details of his foray into Pennsylvania and mentioned the beautiful Croatian service Isaac Porr had described attending in Steelton. This prompted his host to call over a diner two tables from them. Oswald introduced Jeff Edwards, a mining engineer and practicing Catholic who was reared in Steelton. His father had been an accountant for one of the big steel mills and suggested his son look elsewhere for work, predicting what he saw as the inevitable demise of American steel.

Against the backdrop of the Catholic experience in Steelton and surrounding areas, the Milton Hershey legacy gained a whole new layer of importance for its time—building a cooperative and inclusive community while others were mired in ethnic and class exclusiveness.

Making steel was a tough and demanding business and the hard-working immigrants brought with them the customs and mores of the Old World, as reflected in the number of separate Catholic churches in Steelton established in the late 1800s. Each ethnic group wanted their own parish, kicked in their nickels and dimes to erect large churches with accompanying schools, rectories and convents. St. James was Irish; St. Peter's, Slovenian; St. John's, German; St. Ann's identified itself as proudly Italian and St. Mary's, which was to become Prince of Peace, Croatian. Likewise, the ethnic clubs sprang up with an exclusiveness all their own. People kept apart and mixed with other groups to a minimum. "That's just the way life was in those days" and each succeeding generation merely continued the tradition. None-the-less, everyone still got along well in Steelton.

By the time Edwards attended high school in the 1950s, the closest Catholic school was Bishop McDevitt in Harrisburg. His grade school experience had been at St. James, the noted Irish parish in Steelton. The parishes in the city and close-in suburbs were a mixture of nationalities and races. Edwards recalled learning that St. Margaret Mary's Grade School in Penbrook was built in 1949 on ground once popular with the cross burning activities of the Ku Klux Klan. The legendary Father Francis A. Kirchner erased that blot of hate and erected a lasting monument to progressive education. The neighborhoods from which his pupils sprang were multi-cultural and followers of all the various religions, or not, as they chose. Edwards' high school years opened his eyes to the diversity contained under the umbrella of Catholicism.

Long after Edwards had gone off into the world, a move of cataclysmic proportions hit the settled pattern of Steelton Catholicism. The Bishop mandated in the early 1990s that Steelton would unite around one parish, St. Mary's, and it was to be called Prince of Peace. The other churches, though solvent, would be closed and the properties sold. The people were still chaffing, if not out-right rebelling against that church edict.

Ironically, the Islamic Society of Greater Harrisburg now owned the entire city block that contained the old St. James Church, school, rectory and convent. The church, now a mosque, still has a cornerstone reading: "1878 A.D. 1909" designating when the first church was first built and it's successor thirty-one years later, with pews, statues, etc. removed. Limestone blocks on the school's façade containing the names of saints had been painted over in white, while those of prominent Pennsylvanians such as William Penn were left undisturbed. Architectural medallions above doors were painted over and now had Arabic inscriptions, while others near the roofline still maintained the various papal and church-related castings. Presumably, this was still a work in progress and the buildings would eventually be stripped of all outward signs of the previous incarnation. There was a small, modern Mennonite church within two blocks of the Islamic Center and several businesses sported signs in Arabic as well as English.

In the question posed at the end of his letter, Abe said he was not sure whether this was an indication of more acceptance of Islam and civil discourse or an irritant to community relations. That was the dilemma facing many communities throughout the country and the world. How it was resolved would form the character of the future. Would history repeat itself or could we find another way?

ABE'S RETURN

CHAPTER 1

▼

THE PRELUDE

Veronica Steinmann stood before her office window at the Dickinson School of Law, looking across the brown grass landscape of late December and pondering her future. She was secure in her tenure as Professor of Constitutional Law, and related Constitutional Law and Religion, plus a course entitled: First Amendment—Free Speech. Her neatly arranged office was as ordered as her mind and as straight-forward as her life had been. Nearly five months before she had committed her first really rash act and since that time her existence was complicated with emotional ups and downs, illogical twists and turns, at times a sense of befuddlement, at others genuine happiness beyond her dreams. In short, at age forty-six, she had fallen in love with a mysterious man and become engaged on the spur of the moment. She did not think of him as mysterious in the two brief whirlwind weeks leading up to their engagement. He was the most forthright, honest, well-mannered and kindest man she had ever encountered—a gentle man with enormous inner strength who treated her with respect as an equal in all ways. He also had always been very deferential and considerate that he not put her in a position that would in any way compromise her reputation. She admired and adored him in more ways than she could count.

The object of her musings was Abe Carlson, a tracker from Arizona who had slipped into town one hot July day in search of his roots and for an answer to the question of what became of a relative he had not known existed until later on in life. His had been an outdoors upbringing in the southwest, primarily among the

Mojave and Pueblo Indians and the usual hard-working ranch life indigenous to the area. His education was well grounded in the liberal arts tradition, but he continued to be self-educated all through his adult life—delving deeply into the classics and many esoteric fields. In his younger days he tried a variety of pursuits, from placer mining, to ranch hand, to hunting guide, but he excelled as a tracker and through the years he had gained a worldwide reputation, whether it be animal or human. At age fifty-one he was looking to settle down in central Pennsylvania to be with the woman he loved. He had planned to finish one last contract in the Russian Federation in one month to six weeks, but two other crises in Europe had intervened and he had been gone five months. He was now ready for semi-retirement to see if this engagement could lead to a stable marriage.

The long distance relationship had been conducted via daily e-mails and telephone calls, with a steady stream of more intimate letters protected by the privacy of the postal services. Both Steinmann and Carlson were more than eager to move on to the next phase.

The ringing of the telephone on her desk shook Steinmann out of her reverie. The caller ID function displayed a familiar cell phone number. "What's up, Sport," she asked picking up the receiver, "and how is the weather, wherever you are?"

"Let's just say that global warming has not yet become evident in Europe this winter," Carlson responded. "However, it's cool, but no snow here in New York. I will be there around noon tomorrow."

"Great," she replied. "Why don't you see if you can catch 'The Nutcracker' at Radio City Music Hall tonight?"

"I'd love to," he said with a low chuckle, "but my date is stuck in her office and can't make it. Besides, I'm not in that part of the state. I'm cleaning up a few details on the way home so I can stay put for a while. I'm thinking of retirement, or perhaps semi-retirement. In any event, I'm not accepting anything less than dire circumstances for the next six months, at least."

"Right," she said, knowing better than to inquire about what he was doing at the moment. "Yet, I can't think of what you've ever done in the last few years that doesn't qualify as a dire circumstance. Come to my place and I'll give you the full Pennsylvania treatment. Mother will be disappointed, of course. (Ruby Steinmann had become the queen of her social circles at the Masonic Village and in Hummelstown, regaling people with hints of the man behind the mask of her soon-to-be son-in-law.) She wanted to give you a big welcome-home dinner and invite everyone who ever met you when you were last here. But, I've got news for you, Sport. I get first dibs. That's just the way it's going to be."

"I love it when you get so protective," he said. "You give me goose bumps. I tell you what, why don't you soften the blow by saying I'm hoping to solicit her assistance—as a backup to yours, of course—on a matter close to my heart. I've bought a place in a new development and would like you to decorate it. You have fine taste and I'm sure you wouldn't mind having your mother assist you. It could be a fun daughter-mother kind of project."

"You do know how to keep peace in the family," she commented. "What did you have in mind—southwestern chic in the Pennsylvania farm country?"

"Not at all, Veronica," he said seriously. "I'll rely on you to bring me up-to-date and pick something appropriate to the area and to your taste. I'm sure anything you choose will be just right."

"You keep that up, Abe," she said. "I'm getting to like you more all the time. Soothing words are a plus with me. And, Love, it's so nice you're finally coming home. I've missed you."

"Not as much as I've missed you," he replied. "I'll be there as soon as I can."

Steinmann locked the door to her office and walked down the hall with a renewed lightness in her step. As she turned a corner and headed for the front door a third year student of hers noticed a radiant glow and asked if Santa was going to be particularly generous this year.

"He already has, my dear," she replied to the girl, "he already has."

As she drove from the Carlisle campus to her mother's cottage on the grounds of the Masonic Village in Elizabethtown, Steinmann had to admire Carlson's choice of setting his new home in a new mixed single family and duplex development near Hershey—still within the sought-after Derry Township, with its good schools, proximity to the Hershey Medical Center and its promise to retain value. It was a sound investment. She was not bothered by not having been consulted in the selection. Carlson had said he had been used to making all such decisions himself, a habit he was still working to correct in their new relationship, and hoped he had not offended her. She knew there were many things they were going to learn about each other in the coming years and that taking things slowly and naturally was the right way to proceed. She also realized that part of his natural motivation was to protect her reputation in the community—a bit old fashioned, perhaps, but she deeply appreciated his consideration. In fact, she thought she would have been surprised—even a little disappointed—if he had suggested any other living arrangement.

As she drove through the county-side, she began to notice the trees, shorn of their leaves, and the fields, lying fallow until spring plowing, were not as barren to the eye as they had seemed in recent months. When Carlson had left in July, the land was in full productive green growth. The wide acres of corn were tall and tasseled, promising a bumper crop in the weeks to come. Vegetables of every sort were spilling over the bins at roadside markets and the fruit trees were sagging under the weight of ripening loads. She had kept him apprised of the changing of the seasons—the abundant harvest and the full pallet of fall colors—and abreast of all the local happenings. Both had discovered they were pretty well attuned politically, although she was a shade further to the left and he very much centrist. He, in return, could not convey much about his work for private clients, but was eager for news of south-central Pennsylvania. She never pressed him for details.

Ruby Steinmann was standing in her front doorway behind the full-glass storm door as her daughter arrived. She knew from the tone of Veronica's voice on the telephone that Abe must be coming home.

"How's the bride-to-be?" Ruby asked as she ushered her daughter through the door. "Perhaps you could put on a few pounds, look a little healthier for Abe's return. You know, where he has been in the wilds of Russia, or wherever, the women tend to have more heft, more muscle. He may have gotten to like that in his absence."

"Mother, please," Veronica replied. "I don't plan on pulling the plow if the mule gets sick. Nevertheless, I know the only time you try to bait me is when you are nervous and want to cover up your jitters. To put you at ease, I'll tell you up front that Abe will be home tomorrow."

"My, but you young lovers certainly get sensitive at times," Ruby countered. "Of course Abe's coming home tomorrow. I already knew that. Mothers have a nose for these things, you know."

"Oh, Mother," Veronica sighed. "Why are we both acting so edgy? It's not like either of us to do so."

"Perhaps because we're both in love with the same man," Ruby answered. "Not in the same way, of course, but I'm finding it difficult to wait for such a promising son-in-law. I've tried to give you two all the space you need and abstain from asking too many personal questions, but I'm not getting any younger, you know."

"Right," Veronica said with a sly smile. "You're healthy as a horse and will probably outlive all of us, Mother, so that dog won't hunt."

"What's with you and all these feed store colloquialisms?" Ruby asked. "You were reared to be a lady, didn't hang out behind the barn with a bunch of farm hands and hunters, plus I think that particular usage of the dog not hunting is more Texan or at least western in origin. Surely Abe hasn't succumbed to rude language."

"Of course, he hasn't," the daughter replied. "I'm just a bit edgy. I must be watching too many late night westerns, or perhaps reading about the last batch of Texas politicians swapping seats in Washington. To tell you the truth, I have no idea where that came from. Now, let me tell you what is going on."

Ruby quietly admired Veronica when told of having Abe to herself on his first day back and began to plan her community welcome for the next day. It brought tears to her eyes when Veronica invited her to participate, at Abe's request, in decorating his new house. She knew then that Abe Carlson wanted very much for her to be part of their new life together and she would do all she could to make his new house a home.

"So he doesn't want a ranch house theme at all?" Ruby asked at last.

"No," Veronica said. "He already has a ranch with, apparently, sufficient acreage to raise a nice herd of cattle and horses. He doesn't work it much these days, but keeps it open as a home for his two long-time caretakers, Julio and Maria Martinez and their children. Abe built them a large caretaker's house—because they have seven children—which he deeded over a few years ago to them so they'd have a permanent home. It will probably end up being our winter vacation destination, Abe says. The two brilliant decorative minds that we are, we'll just have to come up with something suitable. How could we go wrong?"

Ruby Steinmann merely rolled her eyes.

The winter had been unseasonably above average, but this was about to change as an Alberta Clipper came roaring down from Canada and producing lake-effect snow to upstate New York and parts of northern Pennsylvania. Since Veronica Steinmann had left the campus for her mother's cottage, the temperatures had dropped ten degrees—nipping at the mid-thirties and the wind was gusting upwards toward thirty miles per hour. Donning a borrowed coat, the two women decided to take a look at Abe's new home and assess what work needed to be done.

As many developments in this part of the state, Abe's new community had long been a farm, though a hilly one, tucked into the southern end of Derry Township. His unit was the larger of two models of duplexes situated on top of a hill. As they drove into the driveway, the cooling towers of the Three Mile Island Nuclear Power Plant could clearly be seen spewing steam skyward.

"I wonder what Abe will think about being this close to Three Mile Island," Ruby said, watching the steam rise.

"Oh, it won't bother him," Veronica replied. "In fact, he says that since the near fatal accident this is probably the safest nuclear plant in the world. He also says the close proximity is a plus. If another minor accident should occur, the fallout will be blown a good ten miles before coming back to earth. When I asked about a complete meltdown, he only said something about not having any cares in this world."

"How did he arrange to purchase this property without our hearing about it?" Ruby asked out of curiosity.

"He said something about his attorney in New York," Veronica answered. "There's a lot I don't know about him, Mother. That's one of the reasons I'm probably looking forward to a long engagement."

Ruby did not have a reply. She had long taught civics and knew how to work Internet databases for information. On pure impulse, she had done some research on Abe Carlson when he was in town last July and discovered he was a multi-millionaire several times over. Only local Doc Straussburger and herself were aware of Carlson's substantial wealth and neither wanted to tip the scales of Veronica's relationship by revealing that knowledge. They respected Carlson's privacy and knew he would tell Veronica only when he felt the time was right.

Retrieving the key from its hiding place Abe had told her about, Veronica opened the front door and entered. They were immediately impressed with Carlson's choice. The unit was built on a slab—no basement with all its attendant problems. The unit had two thousand and seven hundred square feet on the first floor, arranged for convenient one-floor living. An open dining room was to the left, a den with double French doors to the right. Beyond was the cathedral ceiling living room with built-in bookcase and fireplace. The spacious kitchen was off to the right of the living room, with light cabinets, stainless steel refrigerator/freezer, and Cambria counters and surfaces. A raised open bar surface opened to a modest breakfast room. To the left of the living room was a guest suite, with bedroom and full bath, two closets and a pocket door for privacy. To the rear of the living room was another set of French doors, sided by glass panels and transom windows above, leading to a lower cathedral ceiling of a spacious atrium with plenty of windows on all three exterior walls. Off the atrium they found a glassed-in all weather porch with all weather ceramic tile flooring. Along the adjoining wall with the next duplex unit was the master bedroom—again with a cathedral ceiling—elongated bath with a large tub to one side, double sinks and mirrored wall. A second section contained a large shower and commode, with a large walk-in closet to the rear. Down the hall from the master bedroom, walking toward the front of the unit was a laundry room and a door leading to the two-car garage abutting the front.

"What a great floor plan," Ruby remarked. "This could be ideal for just two people, with plenty of room."

"And there's a bonus room up the stairs above the garage," Veronica said. "There are another nine hundred square feet and the plumbing is roughed in if Abe ever needs to expand. Right now he plans to use it for storage."

"One of the touches I really like is the hardwood floors throughout," Ruby said. "The only carpet I've seen is in the walk-in closet and the steps leading to the bonus room. Abe has taste and he's right, this is not going to look like a ranch house."

"Okay, Mother," Veronica said, taking out a pen and pad of paper. "Let's take some notes. The first thing I see is that we need to get some color on these walls. Men always seem to think everything goes with white, but we need to educate them a little."

"And I see multiple area rugs to enhance these gorgeous floors," Ruby added. "What kind of budget are we working with here?"

"Take a look for yourself," Veronica answered, writing a figure on her pad and turning it toward her mother.

"My, his extended stay must have been very financially rewarding," Ruby commented. "He certainly seems to have more than covered that engagement ring he said he had to earn the money for. That should be sufficient for some very nice furnishings, too."

"At least this should keep you busy for a few days," Veronica said. "I already have a good idea of the colors I'd like to use, but I think we should steer away from wallpaper for the moment. If we do this just right, I believe we can do it all with paint. We want to preserve a masculine touch and if the right wallpaper comes along at a later date, it can easily be incorporated. Think flow, Mother, think flow. I haven't been this excited about decorating since I was thirteen and you let me select the colors for my bedroom."

"Don't remind me of that hideous project," Ruby replied. "You seemed to enjoy the color contrasts, but we couldn't let your little cousin, Jimmy, anywhere near that room because the only time he saw it he got dizzy and vomited on the hall rug."

"Little cousin Jimmy shouldn't have been allowed in a teenage girl's room in the first place," Veronica countered. "Besides what kind of taste did that kid ever have? Remember he married that Mary Sue Plum, the big-haired, gum-chewing waitress whose favorite patterns were leopard skin and zebra, even on the upholstery of her convertible? She used to say she liked the contrast with her pet pattern of dress—polka dots."

"I concede the argument," Ruby replied. "Now, get me home. I have many phone calls I need to make and you need to hurry home yourself to be ready for Abe's arrival. Have you got enough food for him?"

"I've had enough food for the occasion packed away for months," Veronica said. "I could choke a horse with all I have, but I'll mete it out in proper proportions. I don't think I'd like a portly man at the beginning. Maybe some years afterward—when he develops his prosperity, we'll have to wait and see."

CHAPTER 2

▼

THE ARRIVAL

Abe Carlson had finished his latest business in Pultneyville, New York, a small town on Lake Ontario, and headed south just after midnight. Although cold and windy, temperatures were in the low teens due to a front barreling in from Canada, remnants of previous snows here and there, but nothing active on this particular night. He was not concerned about getting through any weather. His 1973 Jeep Commando, canvas topped with an AM radio as the only amenity, had taken him through sand storms, snow storms and rain storms without a hitch. Because it was top heavy, he had to drive carefully going around corners, particularly on a downhill grade, as the flat, square sides were prone to the wind effects, but it was a real workhorse.

He passed through Manchester, a former railroad hub whose roundhouse had fallen into ruin years ago and famous among Mormons as the site where Joseph Smith received instructions from God through the Angel Moroni. He was aware of the deep history of this Finger Lakes region and recalled when he reached Canandaigua at the northern end of the lake baring the same name that this was the county seat that arrested Susan B. Anthony, the famous suffragette, after she dared to cast a vote before the passage of the Nineteenth Amendment to the Constitution in 1920.

As he traveled the length of the lake he could tell from the signs and the extensive vineyards now in their winter dormant stage why this area was so famous for its wines. A weathered sign on a closed-for-the-winter roadside stand announced the availability of grape pie in season. He wondered just what grape pie might taste like and decided it would probably be more like jelly than preserves and that he would take a pass should the occasion arise.

He pulled off the highway at a town called Painted Post and found an all-night diner. The only other patron in the place was a long-haul truck driver whose rig he saw parked along the side of the building. Taking a stool at the counter and ordering coffee and a piece of apple pie, he glanced at the truck driver three stools over and nodded.

"Lakota?" Carlson asked the man.

"Yes," the man replied, studying Carlson's features and dress carefully. "You know my people?"

"I do," Carlson said, mentioning several times he had been on the Lakota Reservation and a few of the people he knew.

"You must be the great tracker, the one they call Abe Carlson," the man commented. "You are well known among the Lakota. The Antelope Runner you mentioned is my cousin. I'm Two Sticks Johnson. I'm headed back home. Just delivered some horses to an upstate farm."

The man at the counter placed the slice of pie and a steaming mug of coffee before Carlson, who nodded his thanks.

"What's up with this Painted Post?" Carlson asked.

"Just the usual," Johnson replied. "The white settler won, so he got to write the history, no matter how far from the truth that history may be."

As Johnson told the tale, legend had it that when the explorers and early settlers arrived at the confluence of the Conhocton and Tioga Rivers, where they met to form the Chemung River in the 1780s, they discovered a wooden post painted with twenty-eight figures of captives, painted red. The area became known as the Lands of the Painted Post. A town sprang up called Painted Post. No one knew what the figures really meant, but there was no end to speculation over the years. Whatever the case, the post was removed, according to one tradition, around 1800 and successive posts were erected, and a series of sheet iron weathervanes adorned the top, followed by a cast figure of a famous local white man in 1894, which was blown down and shattered in a severe storm in 1948.

In 1950 a bronze Indian figure created by a local former art teacher was erected and placed in the middle of an intersection—a warrior, bow in hand, arm raised in greeting, standing before a representation of the original post. Johnson was a bit amused, however, when he first saw the statue, now moved from the intersection to a small park when the business district was upgraded. The artist had taken some liberties and the Lakota thought he could detect at least four different tribes depicted in the details. But what did he know? Maybe the artist wanted to create a composite from the beginning and failed to mention it at the time.

"They tell me the white tourists coming through town used to play a game with the children in the car," Johnson concluded. "They'd tell the kids to duck down behind the seat when they came to the intersection, so the Indian wouldn't shoot an arrow at them."

"Does that bother you?" Carlson asked.

"No, not at all," Johnson answered with a chuckle. "We do the same with our kids whenever we come up on a statue of Custer. I was in North Carolina one time and another driver, a Cherokee, told me the Yankees do the same thing coming through there. It seems every small town has a statue of a Rebel soldier with his hat in his hand, facing south so his back is to the north. So you see, it's a cross-cultural thing."

"I wonder how they'd react walking down Monument Avenue in Richmond?" Carlson mused half under his breath.

"Richmond, Virginia?" Johnson asked. "The Capital of the Confederacy. Why do you say that?"

"Monument Avenue is block upon block of Civil War monuments," Carlson explained. "Canons, rearing steeds, swords drawn for battle, all that sort of thing. I wonder how the northern folks would react to that?"

"Don't know," Johnson conceded. "But, man would I like to be there to see it."

Back on the road and heading toward the Pennsylvania border, Carlson wondered about the Finger Lake region of New York. He had become a Freemason in Arizona, raised to the third degree of Master Mason and only recently become aware of the chaotic outburst of anti-Masonry which was part of the formation of the Anti-Masonic Party of the United States which tried to throw out any Masons in public office and nearly ended the political climb of Martin Van Buren, a Freemason, in the election of 1830. Perhaps it was the aura of secrecy surrounding the Masonic Lodges that bred distrust among some in the general public, although what secrecy there was, pertained only to purely Masonic business within the Lodge. The Masonic goals for the individual and the community at large were always clearly stated in public literature—improving the individual, the community, bringing aid to those who lacked the wherewithal and needed a helping hand; they promoted a variety of charities over a broad spectrum of need and the inclusion of every variety of religious belief so long as there was a belief in a Supreme Being, by whatever name.

After passing through Williamsport, Pennsylvania, his thoughts turned to the pleasant subject of what awaited him in Hershey. It was still as if he had only dreamed of getting engaged to the most beautiful woman he had ever seen in a short span of two weeks.

It had been love at first sight when Carlson had first seen Veronica Steinmann stepping from her Mercedes on Main Street in Hummelstown. She was a vision of grace, covering the half block in long strides, to where he was standing. She wore a perfectly tailored pinstriped charcoal suit, hemline just below the knee, medium high-heels, delicate blue silk blouse rolled at the neck. A black lizard purse, which matched her shoes, was slung from the right shoulder and had perfectly manicured nails with clear polish. Yet, most stunning of all were her hazel eyes, ash brown hair framing the face, delicate jaw line and beautiful opaque skin that promised never to show age. What little makeup she wore was perfectly placed.

She had been introduced to him as "Ronnie" and on their first firm handshake he noticed her long slender fingers enveloping his rough square palms and the absence of a wedding ring. His first words had been along the lines of: "May I call you Veronica? It seems more fitting to a woman of your appearance." Although awkward, it seemed to please her and it was not long before she bestowed on him the term of endearment "Sport."

Approaching Hershey with plenty of time to spare, Carlson pulled off the main road and stopped to refresh himself in the parking lot of the Bullfrog Valley Park, with its small pond and ducks wintering on the shoreline. After a quick cold-water shave from a shallow basin he kept in the Jeep, a change of shirt and a swift buff of his western walking boots, he was ready to see his beloved Veronica.

Having stayed just ahead of the incoming weather front for the entire trip, both the front and Carlson pulled to a stop in front of Veronica's house at two minutes before noon. Temperatures were in the upper twenties, with a gusty wind blowing snow flurries in every direction. Carlson stamped his feet as he reached for his shearling-lined coat and Virginia Gentleman hat, shaking the stiffness out of his legs.

As he strode up the walk, Veronica stepped onto the porch, dressed—much to his surprise and pleasure—exactly as she had been when he first saw her on the hot July day.

"Wanted to be sure you recognized me, Sport," she called out, crossing her arms and experiencing a slight shiver in the wind.

"I'd recognize you in a flour sack," he replied, opening his coat and enveloping her in the warm shearling as they exchanged their first, long passionate kiss and embrace right there on the porch in broad daylight.

"That's Janis Miller in the window next door," she said, burying her head in his chest. "And if you look on the other side, that will be Ben and Bernice Williams. I won't enumerate the people watching from across the street."

"I guess they don't see many public displays of affection on this street," he answered.

"That's correct," she replied, "particularly from this woman. But that's okay. Everyone has been anxiously awaiting your arrival and it's acceptable behavior since I'm a certified engaged woman."

"Let's get you out of this cold," he said, escorting her through the door. "Something certainly smells good and I'm suddenly starving."

After many months of eating mostly boiled food, the meal was everything Carlson could have hoped for. T-bone steak, home fries, sausage and ham, biscuits and strawberry preserves, mugs of piping hot coffee and strudel for dessert were just what he needed.

"I was great amusement for the children in the neighborhood today," she said. "Word got around that the 'Professor Lady' was firing up the grill in the back yard just three days before Christmas and I counted eleven boys and girls gathered around by the time the steak was medium-rare. They dispersed in all directions, like the old town criers, spreading the word hither and yon: Abe's coming home today."

"Well, for what it's worth, you have one very appreciative and satisfied husband-to-be. I love you, Veronica," he said, taking her hand, "and this is a perfect first day of what I want our life together to be."

"Me, too, Abe," she said, rising and giving him a peck on the cheek. "Now, you clean up and I'm going to change into something more practical and warm. And by the way, I love you, too."

Carlson quickly adapted to the domestic chores. There were few food scraps, the bone from the steak and a half slice of bread, which he ate as the water in the sink was warming. He was pleasantly surprised to see that Steinmann cooked the same way he did, washing the pots and pans as he went along so there were fewer to deal with after the meal. He was putting the last two cups in the dishwasher and wondered where she kept the cleaning powder.

"Under the sink on the left hand side," Veronica boomed from the bedroom.

"I'm certainly going to be sure I have only pure thoughts from now on," he replied, filling the soap reservoir and closing the door. "If you're going to be reading my mind like that, I won't be able to keep any secrets."

"You've got that right, Sport," she said, coming into the kitchen dressed in slacks and a heavy turtleneck sweater that set off her figure handsomely. "I don't let my students get away with anything. That's going to go double for my husband."

"You're so cute when you get assertive," he responded, pulling her to him and giving her a kiss in an easy and natural manner, as if they had been married for many years. "Haven't you yet discovered what a good Boy Scout I am?"

"I'll tell you one thing," she whispered with a smile. "If I hadn't, you wouldn't be standing here in this kitchen right now."

The next few hours were spent in the living room catching up on events. Although they had corresponded and called each other almost every day, there were a number of little things that can only be imparted face-to-face. She told him how much she liked his selection for his new home and her plans for decorating.

"About all that," he interrupted, "I have to give you an apology right in the beginning. I have been so used to doing things on my own, I didn't think to consult with you until after the purchase had been made. I got to thinking about that and the fact I arranged a room with Doc Straussburger for a few days without telling you. I promise to try harder. It's no excuse, but I've been on my own pretty much all my life and this is my first engagement. I need to share more with you."

"I understand, Abe," she said softly. "I'm no different in my own experience, so I feel the same way. You just continue to be 'Mister Warm and Wonderful' and I'll be your female equivalent partner—things should work out for the best."

"You have a deal," he responded, reaching out his hand.

She grabbed the hand and gave it one good shake.

"As an attorney, do you want me to sign a contract or something to that effect?" he asked with a bit of humor.

"As an attorney," she replied, "I know that no contract is worth the paper it's written on unless the intentions of the signers are to uphold its contents. In the real world, your word is your bond."

As she continued to inform him of events that happened in his absence, she brought up the case of Henry Cunningham, a twelve-year-old boy who had wandered off from his family campsite and whom Abe had tracked through the night and discovered in a sinkhole on a dairy farm. Abe had been his hero ever since.

"You've really made an impression on little Henry," she said. "Although he is growing so fast that we won't be able to call him little for long. He must have grown four inches in the past five months and there is a hint of whiskers on his chin."

"I trust it was a good influence," Abe ventured.

"It depends on your viewpoint," she replied. "Ever since your little adventure together, Henry has taken up a new hobby. He started tracking all the pets in the neighborhood, dogs roaming around in violation of the leash laws, then cats on their nightly hunt for birds or something else to amuse their instincts. He progressed to the point where he could tell the town pets from those on the farm—even identify individual animals. Word got around and soon kids were coming to Henry to find their stray animals. The Methodist minister's cat was missing for a few days and Henry was able to track it to an abandoned feed warehouse where it had gone to have a litter. He also discovered the male who was the father—an old Tom who had wandered into town from who-knew-where. There is a happy ending, though. The Minister adopted the old Tom and now the family has a cozy little residence next to the church. Henry has become a bit of a celebrity among his classmates."

"I hope it hasn't gone to his head," Abe said seriously.

"None whatsoever," she answered. "His parents were a bit afraid it might, but their fears were allayed when Henry told them he wouldn't let that happen. He was going to handle these things the way Abe would. So now you're a real role model, my friend. Don't let Henry down."

"I hope to not let anyone down," Abe smiled. "Starting with you."

CHAPTER 3

▼

DOVER

Harry Harrison Straussburger, M.D., known affectionately by all as Doc, was a town institution in Hummelstown and the Hershey area in general. In his mid-nineties and supposedly retired for some years, he was still an active presence and organizer of community efforts in many endeavors. As a widower still living in his large brownstone house—which contained his office and where he brought many patients to stay during recovery—he continued to hold frequent cocktail hours, with his daughter, fondly referred to as Aunt Mattie, serving as hostess. Doc had gotten to know Abe Carlson well during his last visit and he had organized the community in the tracker's quest for his roots, as well as serving the needs of Henry Cunningham with his medical care after Carlson had rescued him from an unfortunate sinkhole accident. When Carlson had called asking for a place to stay for a few days, Doc was more than happy to have his company.

Carlson arose just before sunrise and was shaving when he caught the unmistakable aroma of premium coffee being brewed downstairs in the kitchen, soon followed by the scent of bacon and onions being fried. Donning a fresh shirt and sweater, checking the weather through the window and running a comb one last time through his hair, he was off to breakfast with high expectations.

"Good morning, Abe," Doc hailed him as he entered the kitchen. "Slept well, I trust?" Doc was just taking a frying pan of eggs off the stovetop and scooping them onto two plates at the kitchen table. Steam was rising from the newly poured coffee at three seats.

"Just fine, thanks, Doc," he replied. "I expected to see Aunt Mattie. You're up early, aren't you?"

"Just arrived home a short while ago," Doc replied. "Josephine Briggs was having a rough time of it last night—recovering from a gall bladder infection—and her husband, Clark, needed to be spelled for a few hours sleep. Josephine was a Hanson. I delivered her myself right there in that house more decades ago than I wish to recall. Delivered her first-born, too. Harry Briggs was the loudest infant I've ever coaxed into this world. I guess that's why she named him after me. Anyway, have a seat. Mattie will be here in a few minutes."

As if on cue, Mattie arrived just as the two men were taking their first bite of food. "Thanks for the coffee, Dad," she said as she reached for the cup and an apron simultaneously. "And thank you for getting our guest his breakfast. We wouldn't want to be accused of slighting a returning celebrity. He might question our upbringing."

"Not as your guest, Aunt Mattie," Carlson replied. "Remember, I'm marrying into this community. So I'm claiming a place in the family—and family ought to be able to scare up their own meals. As for celebrity, please spare me. I've got enough to be humble about, believe me."

Doc just smiled and sipped his coffee. "That's good enough for me," Doc said. "So when you're finished, you can start pulling your weight by cleaning up the dishes. I have to go get a few hours sleep. I'm not getting any younger."

"Not by a long shot, Dad," Aunt Mattie said. "He wouldn't want to take my job, now would he? Besides, someone who thinks Abe is a celebrity is on his way over. Everyone knows Abe is back in town and where he's staying. Henry Cunningham can't wait to see him. I passed him and Cassy Spease on my way over. They should be here in a matter of minutes."

"Has the Professor told you of Henry's new interest?" Doc asked using the term of endearment he had bestowed upon Veronica when she first began teaching law.

"She has about tracking," Abe replied. "She didn't say anything about his having a girlfriend."

"A friend who is a girl," Aunt Mattie corrected. "They are the same age and live two houses apart. They've always gone through school together. She's probably the biggest tomboy we have around here. Her mother has always had the devil of a time getting her to wear a dress to church. Henry has grown a few inches since you've been away. They are now the same height and will both be teenagers in February."

"She is a very pretty young thing," Doc added. "It will be interesting to watch what happens with those two in the next couple of years. Cassy asked Henry to teach her about tracking and he obliged a life-long friend. But Henry is just coming out of that awkward age as far as girls are concerned. I understand that one of his friends teased him about spending so much time with a girl lately and Henry stopped all such conversation dead by merely pointing out that his friend, Abe, was engaged to be married. So the test of manliness has been met."

Carlson could only smile inwardly. He had never been aware that he might be seen as a role model for some young boy. Now that he had apparently become one, he felt rather flattered, rather than discouraged that he was not up to the task. Having never had a child of his own, he was beginning to think of Henry as a nephew. That was just the right fit, he decided. He would be an uncle figure. He was very happy five minutes later when Henry and Cassy rang the doorbell, then rushed into the front hall.

"Uncle Abe, you're back," Henry yelled, announcing that he had already decided what the relationship would be. It was like Aunt Mattie. Doc called his daughter Mattie, but the rest of the town just naturally adopted the Aunt Mattie reference. "I've got a friend I want you to meet," he continued on into the kitchen.

"Nice to see you again, Henry," Abe said, standing and shaking the boy's hand.

"This is Cassy," Henry said in introduction as the girl reached out and gave Abe a firm, but gentler handshake than his first. "Please settle a question for us."

"I'll try," Abe replied, noticing the beautiful young woman this girl was about to become. At the same time, he also noticed that Henry was quickly loosing his boyishness to the first signs of manhood. Abe was painfully aware that he did not have a clue as to these changes as he went through them in his own life and was grateful for being left in ignorance.

"I can't wait for the first real snow," Cassy explained. "I think it will make tracking more exciting, but Henry isn't so sure. He's concerned it might make things too easy. What do you think?"

"Well, let me think about that a little," Abe answered, putting his hand over his chin as if pondering the question, but in reality stalling for time while he thought of an answer. "Every season has its challenges," he finally said. "Terrain and climate are the biggest factors, of course, but ground cover—like leaves on the ground in the fall—can obliterate some signs very quickly. At first you think of snow as leaving an easy track, but that may be misleading. You have to take into account the wind factor and the type of snow. Sure, relatively dry, gusting snow will obliterate a track in minutes. On the other hand, a track left in an icy crust can remain very clear for a couple of weeks, no matter what the wind conditions may be. In the latter case, you have no idea how old the sign may be. Always remember that we've been able to rediscover dinosaur tracks millions of years after they've passed this way. Those are usually found in fossilized mud turned to stone, of course, but you have to be open to all possibilities."

"So, we're both right," Henry said. "We just need to be open to the possibilities."

"Are you really going to marry the Professor?" Cassy suddenly blurted out.

"That is my intention," Abe replied soberly.

"Cool," she replied. "Let's go, Henry. Some critter has been after Mr. O'Malley's ducks again and he needs our help."

With a nod of thanks to all, the two youngsters were off.

"Good answer," Aunt Mattie said. "But wasn't the dinosaur reference a little over the top?"

"It's just a way of putting everything in perspective," Doc said. "I don't think Abe was trying to paper over confusion. I believe he was injecting a seed for thought about time and how short our individual stay really is; so, get as much out of life as you can."

When Doc retired to his bedroom upstairs to get a few hours sleep, Carlson helped Aunt Mattie clear the table and wash the few dishes. As they sat at the kitchen table for a last cup of coffee, she asked about his plans for the day.

"Veronica's finishing some end-of-the-term papers this morning and working on a series of lectures for the new term," he said. "She has a particular interest in a school board case from Dover, Pennsylvania."

"Dad followed that case closely," Aunt Mattie replied. "A small town misstep turned into national criticism is the way he puts it. He has a whole file of clippings in the library if you're interested. The school board in Dover wanted to add 'Intelligent Design' to the science curriculum to counter Darwin's *On the Origin of Species* and what became known as the Theory of Evolution. Dover is a very conservative community, but even the majority of citizens recognized the move as a very thin cover for the teaching of 'Creationism.' Not that the parents minded the concept being offered in some other class, just keep it out of the hard science department as a counter to Darwin. When the case came to court, the national and international media had a field day, painting Dover's actions as a retrial of the Scopes Monkey Trial—descent from the apes and all that sort of nonsense. The judge in the case had some pretty harsh words for the school board and when the election rolled around, the voters cleaned out the school board and replaced it with people opposed to the idea."

Carlson's mother had died within hours of his birth and his father, a circuit riding Calvinist preacher ministering mostly to the Mojave Indians in Arizona, passed when Abe was ten years old. The father and son had many discussions late into the night about religion and life in general. The Reverend Carlson had expressed his opinion on several occasions that he saw no conflict between the teachings of the Bible and the Theory of Evolution. The Reverend had actually read *On the Origin of Species* and the accounts of the deliberations before The British Association in 1860.

Darwin had published his little green-covered book in 1859, laying out the facts as an unequivocal endorsement of survival of the fittest by natural selection in the struggle for existence. Zoologists were amazed, the Church aghast and the common man reduced to falsely thinking of Darwin's theory as a charge that we all descended from a monkey. At the 1860 British Association discussion of the matter, the Bishop of Oxford, Samuel Wilberforce, denigrated Darwin as the Antichrist. In Darwin's defense, the President of the Royal Society, Thomas Henry Huxley, rose to speak clearly and incisively, with tremendous effect. It was reported that a lady fainted and had to be carried out. Another great supporter of Darwin was Oliver Wendell Holmes, the popular professor of anatomy and physiology, as well as noted for his contributions to literature. Darwin's observations from his famous five-year voyage on the *Beagle*, as a medically trained naturalist were vindicated and accepted by the scientific community.

The Reverend Carlson had urged his son to be open to different views on man's origins. He had found in his ministry that the so-called myths held by the Indian tribes—with images of man living on the back of a giant turtle or that man emerged from under the earth to populate the surface, or that the snake led man out of darkness—were all an earnest attempt to explain the unknowable. He discovered that the Indians did not immediately reject Genesis and the story of Adam and Eve. They merely accepted it as the white man's way of explaining the same unknowable.

"I think I'll take a look at that file Doc has in the library," Carlson said to Aunt Mattie. "If Veronica is preparing a series of lectures on the Dover school board case, I'd like to have some idea of what she's talking about."

"Welcome to the rest of your life," Aunt Mattie replied. "You're going to have a lot of catching up to that woman, with as many interests she has going at any given time."

"I know," he said with a smile. "And isn't it wonderful?"

Doc Straussburger's library contained several thousand volumes, with medical subjects well represented, but with a surprising range of works from classic literature, to novels spanning a few hundred years, to multi-volume references, plus fiction and non-fiction from several eras. A small bookcase tucked into a corner held two full shelves of manila folders, with colored tabs sticking out—just like Carlson had seen in a doctor's office with shelves of patient records. However, in this case, he noticed the folders, labeled by subject, contained newspaper and magazine clippings on whatever had gained the doctor's attention. He selected one labeled "Dover—J.J./P.I." and began to read.

Several hours elapsed before Carlson looked up to see Doc entering the library with a tray and two cups of coffee, with a small pot for refills.

"I thought you might need some refreshment," Doc said as he placed the tray on the library table. "I see you had no trouble tracking down the file."

"You did say your library was open for inquiry," he replied. "May I ask about this unusual section of clippings?"

"It's nothing unusual at all," Doc replied, taking a sip of coffee. "The explanation is quite simple. I keep up on affairs of the community and the world. I need to know what outside developments might have a bearing on the health of my neighbors. Of course, I am nosey to begin with. I'll admit to that. I never gave much thought to the fact I might live this long and I retain most of what is contained in those files. They are my back-up in case my memory begins to fade and I wouldn't know what the people around me may be talking about."

"I understand," Abe said with a chuckle. "There is an old Navaho named Peter on the reservation in Arizona. Nobody knows his age for sure, but many say he's over one-hundred-years old. With a solid college education behind him, he taught school on the reservation for many years and lived in a nice clapboard house. When he finally retired, he chose a more traditional life, building a hogan for himself and his wife to live in. He is very wise and I have been lucky enough to have talked to him at length many times. Anyway, although very literate, he keeps a record of current events on the walls of his hogan in the form of pictographs—just as in ancient times. He says it's in his genes. What he forgets in the form of English, he always remembers in the form of pictographs. 'A trick of the mind,' he says, 'for which there is no logical explanation.'"

"Well, good for Peter," Doc commented. "We older folks need to exercise our wiles to fend off you younger people."

"I'm curious about the initial you put on this Dover file," Abe said. "What does 'J.J./P.I.' signify?"

"Junk Journalism and Public Ignorance," Doc explained. "When a so-called journalist writes about a subject he or she has so little personal knowledge about, the writer passes on his or her own ignorance and further enforces public prejudice."

"And you think that's the case here?" Abe asked.

"Absolutely," Doc replied. "Most show a glaring ignorance of what Darwin was all about in the first place, very little knowledge of the Scopes case in the 1920s and not a clue about the present day setting of the community of Dover. They blatantly misconstrued what actually happened. Now that you've read these clippings, what do you think happened in Dover?"

"I see a perhaps well-meaning group of activists trying to counter something they may not want their children to be exposed to," Carlson began. "The courts ruled long ago on the propriety of Darwin's theory being taught in biology class as having a scientific basis. The Creationist theory, even in the watered-down version of Intelligent Design, is speculation of the supernatural sort, as pointed out by the federal judge who ruled in the Dover case. Neither the judge, nor the parents of the children who brought the suit, nor the newly elected members that replaced the old school board, questioned the veracity or validity of Creationism. They even support it being taught in some other venue, but not in the hard sciences. Teach it at church, in the home, in a religion or philosophy class, even on the street corner, but keep it out of the biology class."

"That's a pretty good description of what happened," Doc said. "You know, Abe, it never ceases to amaze me to the extent that individuals, communities, and entire countries—not to mention ethnic groups—can harbor such prejudice against anything unlike themselves. History is replete with examples, perhaps not ever more so as in the field of religion. I know many good people who pride themselves in being upright Christian citizens and true believers in the literal interpretation of the Bible. They know the Old Testament and the New Testament by heart and can cite Scripture for every human endeavor. They even claim to understand that the harsh and vengeful God of the Old is tempered by the loving God of the New, as embodied by the example of Jesus. Yet, they don't seem to take the literal truth of such statements about 'casting the first stone' or allowing only God to stand in judgment as in the Parable of 'the wheat and the weeds.' And if they ever really properly parsed the Sermon on the Mount, they'd be in for a really big surprise. That's the end of my sermon for the day. How about a refill?"

CHAPTER 4

▼

BEGINNING ROOTS

Late morning and early afternoon Abe Carlson set about putting down his first roots in his new home state. He discovered that PennDot was an efficient system for obtaining a Pennsylvania drivers license and a single plate for the back of his Jeep. Since he always kept his vehicle in top shape, the inspection process also went smoothly, although he did attract attention from the inspectors who had not seen a vehicle as old as his 1973 Commando in many years. Registering to vote was a simple task, but he found the structure of local government to be more than a little daunting.

From paperwork sent to him by his lawyer in New York—only one of several firms he had on retainer throughout the country and in Europe—he found it to be a bit confusing that his new home was in Hershey, but that there was no government entity by that name. He lived in Derry Township, which included Hershey, but he would receive his mail from the Hummelstown Post Office because it was closer than the one in Hershey.

The lawyer had also explained that the state of Pennsylvania had 2,015 authorities, 501 school districts, 1,548 townships, 961 boroughs, 56 cities, 67 counties and one incorporated town. Why at least some of these 5,149 jurisdictions could not be combined for greater efficiency and fewer layers of bureaucracy, no one he asked seemed to know. He was not the first to raise the question. In that morning's *Patriot-News*, which billed itself as "Pennsylvania Newspaper of the Year" above its masthead, a letter to the editor from a man in Mechanicsburg asked the same question. The writer pointed out that in Cumberland County, there were 28 separate boroughs and townships serving 223,000 people in 550 square miles. He compared that with Jacksonville, Florida, which consolidated with its county in 1968 and serves 780,000 people in 758 square miles. "I can only imagine," the writer said, "how much money could be saved by having only one each of an administration building, street department, law enforcement agency, recreation department, etc., rather than 28 of each."

Carlson had found that just reading the morning newspaper was going to be a challenge. The few weeks he had been in the area on his last visit he merely perused the pages of local news, but now that he was going to be here permanently, he needed to decipher the locations of stories grouped under the banner of the various townships, rather than the nearest town.

On his way back to Doc Straussburger's house, he swung by his new home. He was surprised to find a number of cars and trucks in his driveway and along the street. He recognized several of the vehicles, including that owned by Ruby Steinmann. As he stepped through the front door, he spotted Ruby standing in the middle of the living room directing what seemed to be a small army of painters and others swarming over the ceilings, walls and floors.

"You don't waste any time do you?" Carlson said to Ruby in greeting.

"Time is something I never waste," Ruby replied. "I think you know most of the people here. Do you see any faces that might be familiar?"

As Carlson looked around he suddenly realized that Ruby had marshaled many of the people he had met at Doc's house on various occasions, or that he had met on his own during his last visit. Several were his brothers in Freemasonry from the Brownstone Lodge in Hershey, like Bud Hanover and Will Youst, retired fix-it shop owner Isaac Porr, several younger people from The Warwick Hotel where he had stayed previously, and a number of people he only knew in passing. All acknowledged his presence and continued to work.

"This is quite a workforce you've been able to put together in a short period of time," Carlson remarked. "Do you happen to have another paint brush?"

"There was no problem gathering these people," Ruby answered. "When they heard you were coming home and had purchased this house, my phone was ringing off the hook with volunteers. It's two days before Christmas and they all wanted to give up a day of last minute shopping just to be a part of this. That just shows what an impression you made and the kind of community that is embracing you. As for an extra paintbrush, not on your life. You'd hurt everyone's feelings. This is their housewarming gift to you. Now, let me show you the colors your intended has selected."

Veronica had decided that the usual ceiling white was too stark a contrast for the cathedral ceilings, so she toned it down to a light cream, the same as those walls not getting more color. The main theme was a color called Mandalay Bay, a blue-green flat paint that dried to a rich, soft hue. She had wrapped the color around the dining room, living room, library, hallways, atrium and kitchen, accented by off-white paint on the molding, chair rail, doors and the single pillar to the open dining room. With the cream colored walls in the middle of the house as a contrast, the effect was to draw everything into an even flow, setting off the richness of the hardwood floors. The guest room was painted in a complimentary sea foam green, while the master bedroom was done in a soft lime shade.

"Absolutely beautiful," was all Carlson could say. "This is starting to look like a builder's model."

"Better than that," Ruby replied. "Wait until you see what she has in mind for your furnishings. You are to have a variety of area rugs, in different sizes, textures and designs. The furnishings will be an eclectic mix of contemporary, oriental and a few antiques. Window treatments will be woven woods inset into the casements. I discovered immediately that you were smart enough to have Vista film put on all the windows. You are on top of a hill with little mature vegetation to filter the bright summer sun."

"Being reared in Arizona," Carlson commented, "we know all about the intensity of light and how hard it can be to live with. I plan to spend most of my time in the atrium/office, facing east with all that glass, so I thought it would be a good idea."

As he entered the laundry room, he saw a familiar figure washing paint brushes at the sink. Even from the back, Carlson recognized Tom Rogers, caretaker and Sexton of the Bindnagle Evangelical Lutheran Church in Palmyra. Rogers has been extremely helpful with his search of church records in the past.

"Hello, Tom," Carlson said, placing a hand on the man's shoulder. "It's good to see you again."

"Nice to see you again, too," Rogers replied. "I'd shake your hand, but, as you can see, I'm up to my elbows right now. I've got to get back to the church. There's still a lot to do getting ready for our Christmas Eve candlelight service. You're welcome to stop in, Abe. It's quite a service and our biggest draw of the year. End your year on a high note."

"I'd like that very much," Carlson said. "I'll see what I can do. I just got in yesterday and I don't know what Veronica has in mind."

"Belated congratulations on that score," Rogers answered. "You've become a legend in this town as the only man to finally live up to Veronica's high standards. You must be living right."

"Thank you," Carlson said modestly. "Let's just say that the Lord smiled down on an undeserving man. It will always be a miracle in my book."

As he walked through the kitchen, Carlson saw platters of well-stuffed sandwiches, hot coffee and tea, sodas and even a pitcher of iced tea. He had learned that whenever two or more Pennsylvanians gathered together, there was sure to be plenty of food.

"Try the corned beef," suggested Joyce Hanover, wife of Bud. "Bud prides himself in the spices he uses to process the meat. He keeps the exact ingredients a secret, but just between you and me, it's more or less the same combination he uses in most everything he makes—only adjusted in amounts. You men are so vain when it comes to things you cook—worse than any old woman."

"It is particularly good," Carlson said after taking a bite and washing it down with coffee. "He should be proud."

"The men at the Lodge do most of their own cooking," Joyce continued. "And it's not just throwing a steak on the grill or frying eggs. Actually, some of them really do surpass their wives in the intricacies of some recipes, but we don't acknowledge it. It's sort of retaliation because we can't get them to do so at home very often."

"Your secret is safe with me," he answered.

"That's the only reason I told you," Joyce smiled. "For a Mason, you don't seem to gossip as much as the rest of the Fellows."

"Well, we do have our secrets, you know," he whispered with a glint in his eyes.

"Oh yes, you do," she said. "How many times have I heard Bud say: 'We are not a secret society, but a society with secrets?' All I really care about is that the Lodge members are some of the most upstanding men in the area and you do so well for the community. And I do believe in your contention that you take good men and make them better. I see evidence of that everyday."

"That has been my experience," he confirmed. "I have visited Lodges in many parts of the world and although their traditions may vary somewhat, Freemasonry is very inclusive. The first requirement is to have a belief in a Supreme Being, by whatever name you wish to use. Religious preference has no meaning. As I understand it, the British brought Freemasonry to India, but for years did not allow Hindus to become members because it was thought they had a pantheon of gods. Once the British figured out that each so-called god was merely a revelation of a certain facet of one God, a Supreme Being, Hindus were encouraged to join."

"We have an example right here," Bud Hanover said, walking into the kitchen and pouring a cup of hot tea. "We accepted a new member from Pakistan, a Muslim who works over at the Hershey Medical Center. He took his oath on the Qur'an—no problem. With more South Asian Muslims coming into this area, I expect we'll have a lot more of the same. I haven't had much contact with Middle Eastern Muslims, mostly Arabs, so I can't say if they'd be interested, but they would be welcomed to apply just the same."

"I've encountered Masons in the upper northwest who are followers of Wicca traditions, but I have no idea what book, or even object, they may have taken their oaths on," Carlson added. "By the way, Bud, I'd like to petition Brownstone for membership. I understand that dual membership is now possible in Pennsylvania. I don't ever want to drop my affiliation with my Arizona Lodge."

"I'll be glad to sponsor you, Abe," Bud replied. "We'll get Will Youst as a second, scare up a visiting committee and have a vote. It should be little more than a formality. Now, I have to get back to work or Joyce will charge me with malingering. I'll see you tonight at Doc's Christmas party. I understand he's expanding it to include your welcome home."

At that moment, Veronica Steinmann arrived with a look of relief on her face. She had obviously finished grading papers for the term and was well on her way with the lecture series.

"It looks as if you've had a nice settling effect on Abe, here," Bud said to Veronica. "He is petitioning for dual membership in the Brownstone Lodge. I guess he's going to be around for awhile."

"Way to go, Sport," Veronica said to Abe, with a playful punch in the arm. "I spotted the new plates on your Jeep on the way in. You're on the fast track to becoming a real Pennsylvanian."

"I simply did not want to be taken as an illegal alien," Abe replied with mock solemnity. "I saw in the newspaper that a mayor of a town in this area wants to drive the illegal workers out of town, fine landlords who rent to them, and the businesses who have hired them. He seems to be zeroing in on the Hispanic Community. We have our own problems in the southwest on that subject, but that mayor seems a bit more narrow-minded than most. Is what he is trying to do even legal, Professor?"

"Of dubious merit, I'd say," Veronica replied. "I see any number of Constitutional problems. It will probably work itself out in the long run, but if you are going to be surprised at intolerance and arrogance among politicians, please don't even go near our state legislature. It will make your hair stand on end."

Carlson could only smile. He had followed the activities of the Pennsylvania legislature for some months and found some of the members' actions painfully embarrassing: huge pay raises in the wee hours of the morning, resisting taxpayer objections, elections lost because of the issue, exorbitant bonuses to staffers and a host of other actions that would be laughable in a B-movie script satire, but increasingly shameful in the light of everyday life. He had followed politicos on all levels most of his life and had seen some pretty bizarre cases, but Pennsylvania was in the process of setting itself as a peculiar instance without peer.

"Veronica, what do you say we take a walk around the neighborhood and introduce ourselves?" Carlson asked. "Ruby won't let me do anything here today. She said it will upset the natives. There is a nice walking and biking path skirting the end of the development—corn fields extending from the path to the main road—and we might find some people enjoying the unseasonable weather. It's a bit cold, but we're not about to have a white Christmas, I'm afraid."

"You're on," she answered, grabbing her coat. "I actually did some checking and know a few people here. I'll be your guide."

Carlson knew it was likely to be like this indefinitely, Veronica staying one step ahead of him in anticipation and he returning the favor. He was certainly warming to the prospect of having such a lovely partner.

As they strolled through the neighborhood, she explained it contained a blend of mostly professional people: some were doctors, both active and retired, others business people, academics, attorneys, government employees reflective of a wide range of ages and ethnic backgrounds. The single-family homes usually contained a number of children; the duplexes were a few retirees or those who would soon be approaching retirement and wanted to reduce the size of their residence—willing to pay a home owner's association to take care of most of the outside chores and needed repairs.

"Have you met your neighbor in the abutting unit?" she asked as they turned the corner approaching his home.

"Not yet," he replied. "I do know that his name is Nagy, a writer of some sort, and his mother lives with him."

"John Nagy," she clarified. "I managed to meet him a few years ago when he was drumming up support for a youth educational initiative to get at-risk kids to stay in school. I think you'll like him. He retired as a high school teacher in a number of subjects—inter-city schools in East St. Louis—and is in his mid-sixties. His mother, Beatrice, is a dear soul who is one of the best cooks I've ever had the pleasure to meet. She says she has to be because if left to his own devices, her son, John, would have starved to death years ago."

"Do you know if he ever married?" he asked.

"He never did," she said with a tinge of sadness. "From what I've learned, he is absolutely brilliant in a number of subjects. He has taught English, History, Math, several sciences and Civics, like my mother. He is also highly knowledge-able in just about any competitive sport you can think of, both at the college and professional level. I've also heard that he can listen to any classical jazz recording and tell you by ear who is playing each instrument and the history of the piece. Like many men his age, though, his life was profoundly altered by the major event of his generation—Vietnam."

"Does he talk about it much?" he asked further.

"No, not at all," she said. "He just gets real quiet when the subject arises. However, there is a Political Science professor of my acquaintance at Gettysburg College who served with him as a Military Policeman in Vietnam. John Nagy was one of those who simply fell through the bureaucratic cracks. He was teaching school when he was drafted at age twenty-six—over the limits at the time. He fol-lowed the advice of his Draft Board and simply filed for exemption, but went into the Army until the paperwork could be completed. Then he was ordered to Vietnam, although he was classified as 'Sole Surviving Son'—his father had been dead for some years and he had no other siblings. It was a repeat of the draft—file the paperwork and it will catch up to you."

"And he was an upstanding American citizen who wanted to do everything by the book, assured the government would do the right thing in the end," Abe commented.

"That's exactly it," she said. "His company commander tried to keep him on town patrol and assign him to headquarters until his paperwork could catch up, but shortage of manpower forced his assignment to dangerous convoy duty. The Professor who told me the tale of Nagy's first convoy, where he found himself safely tucked into the least vulnerable position. On some impulse, Nagy darted out of line and raced ahead of the scout jeep, exploding a land mine and saving most of his buddies."

"How did he manage to survive?" he asked.

"Apparently, that wasn't supposed to be possible," she said. "He was the driver, sitting right on top of the gas tank. He was blown clear of the vehicle and his two companions were severely injured. Ironically, his machine gunner in the back was a professional jazz drummer. He lost both arms up to the elbow. John was unconscious and suffering from severe burns when he was taken to a field hospital. Two weeks later his honorable discharge finally caught up to him."

"I think I'm going to like my new neighbor," he declared. The world would have been a little lesser place without the likes of John Nagy, I believe."

"That, it would have," she agreed. "Let's go get ready for Doc's party."

CHAPTER 5

▼

STEELTON

For as long as anyone could remember, Doc Straussburger's Christmas party had been the event of the season—an open house where all were invited, that traditionally drew several hundred people. Food contributions by the carload began to arrive shortly after noon and by five o'clock every available surface in the kitchen, dining room and library was festooned with every imaginable variety of food and drink. There was added interest this particular year because word had spread about Abe Carlson being back in town and now engaged to their own Veronica Steinmann. This was truly a family affair for the community and Doc's office and examining rooms were converted into a nursery to accommodate all the infants. As the guests arrived, they paid their respects first to their host and then gravitated to the happy couple. Veronica introduced each well-wisher to Abe, remembering the names of all the children and who was a cousin to whom. Carlson thought she had a gift of memory that would make any politician proud.

Through the crowd, Carlson noticed a tall, reserved man crossing the room with a tiny older lady in tow. The man had a familiar air about him, as if Carlson had known him from somewhere, but could not recall where or when.

"Hello, neighbor," the man said shaking his hand, "I'm John Nagy, the other half of your duplex, and this is my mother, Beatrice Nagy. We just returned from some last minute shopping in New York only to find your place swarming with painters."

"Abe Carlson, Mrs. Nagy," he replied, shaking her hand while nodding to Nagy.

"Please call me Bea," the woman said, displaying the spunk that only older people seem to be able to muster. "We're neighbors and we ought to be friends, so formality is not necessary. And this lovely young lady must be Veronica, your intended. I've heard so much about you, Veronica; I feel I already know you. Your mother, Ruby, and I had a nice long chat this afternoon. She's such a smart and energetic lady, plus one heck of a taskmaster when it comes to getting things done."

"Just as you are, Mother," Nagy said. "That's why you get along so well."

"My son thinks I'm pushy," she said. "But then, your children rarely recognize when you are merely providing proper guidance, do they?"

"Speaking only for myself," Carlson replied, "I plan to be saying 'Yes, Dear' quite a bit over the coming years."

"Yeah, right, Sport," Veronica commented.

"He does seem to be starting with the right attitude," Bea said. "Just don't let him fool you, Veronica. It has been my experience that when men say 'yes, dear,' they just turn around and do as they blessed well please."

"And we wouldn't want to change them, even if we could," Veronica stated.

"Right you are," Bea answered. "Things would be so dull otherwise."

Aunt Mattie worked the rooms like a seasoned caterer, making sure everyone had enough to eat and always a full glass or cup. Although there was no snow on the ground, it was still cold enough that the preferred beverage seemed to be something hot, with cider topping the list. Doc was holding court in the library, nursing a short brandy that would last the entire party. Abe and Veronica stayed together as they went from room to room accepting congratulations and spreading season's greetings.

"How do you like our town so far?" Veronica asked Abe in a low whisper.

"It's beginning to feel a lot like home," he answered. "Look at the cute couple over at the sideboard."

Veronica turned to find Henry Cunningham wearing a sweater vest and tie with a wolf's head print, standing next to Cassy Spease in a velvet dress and looking comfortably feminine. Both looked to be several years older then they actually were.

"I had the impression she didn't like dresses," Abe said. "She doesn't seem at all bothered by that one."

"Just another example of how little you men understand women," she said. "Even at that age, we know when we look nice and enjoy the effect we have on others. We all have at least a bit of vanity and it helps boost our confidence."

As the party progressed, John Nagy gravitated to the library, admiring the breadth of subjects Doc had been interested in over the years. He was pleased to discover a first edition of *The Wound Dresser*, by Walt Whitman, a series of letters written from the hospitals in Washington, D.C. during the Civil War and published posthumously by his friend and literary executor, Doctor Richard Maurice Bucke.

"Interesting selection," Doc Straussburger said over Nagy's shoulder. "Did you know that Bucke was only one of a number of Whitman's literary executors? He was the only one who thought those letters worthy of publishing. And they nearly didn't get published at all. Yet, the book became widely popular and is still read by many over a hundred years later."

"I've always had the impression that Bucke must have been a very compassionate physician," Nagy replied. "I was always struck by Whitman's little courtesies that meant so much to the wounded soldiers. He haunted the wards, writing letters home for some of the men, and just reading to others; he also handed out small rations of tobacco, oranges and whatever else he could afford from his own meager funds. Added to that, Whitman changed dressings, helped clean the wounded and saw to physical tasks, as they were needed. Bucke must have observed Whitman at times and knew what a boost good bedside manners could do for the healing process."

"I've always had the same impression," Doc said. "I guess, as a physician, I wanted that to be the case. Thank you for accepting my invitation today, John. I've taken a particular shine to Abe Carlson and think that as neighbors you may do each other many kindnesses. I'm not sure what those kindnesses may be, but you are both well-traveled and well-read. He may provide you with some insight into areas you may know little about—such as his deep knowledge of Indian culture—and you, in return, can share your knowledge of sports and music. I understand you are a walking encyclopedia on those subjects and more."

"More of a repository of minutia," he answered. "I seem to be one of those people who come across bits of information and naturally file them away somewhere in my mind. When the occasion arises, the information simply pops up."

"I also understand that you tutor children and adults for little or no remuneration—the same with piano lessons," Doc noted. "There's a piano in the side parlor. It hasn't been played since my dear wife died. It just sits there gathering dust—at least it would gather dust if Mattie wasn't the meticulous housekeeper that she is. What do you say? Care to enliven and entertain our guests?"

"It would be my privilege," Nagy answered.

Nagy began with traditional carols suited to the season, rendered with a rather jazzy arrangement. Within the next hour and a half, he had covered the gambit of the modern musical eras from the late 1800s through the 1920s, on to the Swing Era and the Big Band sound. He also covered the crooners and the shakers of Rock and Roll, some country tunes, the break-out formats of the 1960s through the 1990s, sprinkling so-called Easy Listening music in between. Each generation in the house gathered around and sang the words to their favorite songs.

Beatrice Nagy brought a scotch and water and placed it on a coaster off to one side of the piano. "How about an intermission?" she asked. "You play so well and sing with such enthusiasm, but you are beginning to get somewhat hoarse."

"All that and you teach classical piano to your students," Doc said as Nagy took a sip of his drink. "Is there anything you don't do in the musical sphere?"

"I can answer that," Beatrice volunteered. "He doesn't do Rap. He says it may be Rap, but it's not music to him. Beat's okay, lyrics leave much to be desired."

Abe and Veronica joined the conversation as people milled around refilling plates and glasses. Henry and Cassy were over in one corner deep into a discussion of what it might be like to track a cougar.

"So, what type of tutoring do you do, John?" Carlson asked, wanting to get to know his new neighbor.

"Some of just about everything," Nagy answered. "I have many students preparing for the SATs, particularly among Koreans and other Asian groups. They're very keen on education for their children. I also teach English as a second language, European culture and history to second and third generation Americans, and coach immigrants preparing for their citizenship examinations. I find the latter particularly appealing and I haven't had one fail the exam to date."

"He also doesn't charge that group," Bea said. "Nor does he charge anyone else who can't afford his services, as low as his rates may be. You can take the teacher out of the classroom, but you can't take teaching out of the teacher—at least not in my son's case."

"Most of my work is in Steelton," Nagy said. "It has an interesting and diverse history, both ethnically and commercially, with smaller business supporting what had essentially been a one purpose town—the making of steel."

"I've heard some interesting things about the Catholic Church in that town," Carlson ventured. "What can you tell me about that?"

"Catholics have a grand history in Steelton," Nagy began, "and their story reflects the growth, decline, and search for economic diversity of many such towns."

Nagy explained that the small town of Baldwin, which eventually became Steelton, was but a resting place for traffic on the Pennsylvania Canal System that carried barge commerce all through this part of the state. A chief inducement was the availability of the nearby Cornwall ore deposit. A close neighbor, Highspire, developed as a Susquehanna River town, for lumber passing down the river and used the waterpower for various types of mills. It was not until the Pennsylvania Steel Company moved to Baldwin just after the Civil War, that the business of making steel became paramount. Being the first plant of its kind in the United States made Steelton the appropriate new name for the town.

Making steel was a tough and demanding business. Hard-working immigrants up to the challenge brought with them the customs and mores of the Old World, as reflected in the number of separate Catholic churches established in the late 1800s. As these ethnic groups poured in, their large numbers overwhelmed St. James, the mother church, and new parishes were opened along ethnic lines; the parishioners donated their hard-earned nickels and dimes to erect large churches with accompanying schools, rectories and convents. St. James remained staunchly Irish; St. Peter's, Slovenian; St. John's, German; St. Ann's proudly identified as Italian and St. Mary's, which was to become Prince of Peace after consolidation, Croatian. Each group had its own ethnic club, but the people all got along well, even as they continued their Old World traditions.

The rapid demise of American steel in the 1970s had a cataclysmic effect on the settled patterns of Steelton Catholicism. In the mid-1990s, under the Bishop's mandate, the five parishes, though solvent, were condensed into one parish. St. Mary's became Prince of Peace. The school facilities were combined at St. Ann's. To insure that the three other properties were kept in use for their original purposes, rather than become some commercial property as a restaurant or nightclub, St. John's and St. Peter's were sold to Black Baptist Churches. St. James was sold to the Islamic Society of Greater Harrisburg and the church converted into a mosque.

"I talked to a man in London recently who was from Steelton," Carlson said. "He knew all about the conversion of St. James into a mosque and all the changes made to the building and the fact that signs in Arabic were beginning to appear on Front Street. How is the Society assimilating with the rest of the town? I don't mean just with the other religious entities—I understand there is a small modern

Mennonite church within two blocks and various other churches all over town—but assimilating socially?"

"That's an interesting question you pose," Nagy said thoughtfully. "Quite frankly, I have no idea. I suppose there are some people who will have a knee-jerk reaction about 'terrorists in our midst,' but I simply don't know. I would hope, though, that they may become more quickly assimilated into Steelton's multi-ethnic society than the ugly realities for Blacks—racism, segregated into separate neighborhoods, with equally separate institutions, including schools. The success of the Black community in Steelton is one of the most remarkable tales that can be told, even more so because of the enormous hardships that had to be endured while turning a very negative burden into an extremely positive force."

Nagy related what he knew of the development and success of the Black Hygienic School, named so because it was built in a section known as Hygienic Hill. In the post-Civil War years, the Pennsylvania Railroad had an insatiable need for steel rails with which to expand. The Pennsylvania Steel Company stepped in with the revolutionary Bessemer process to establish the booming steelworks. The ever-expanding need for steel workers starting in the late 1800s compelled Pennsylvania Steel and its successor, Bethlehem Steel Corporation in 1916, to recruit heavily in the South. Nearly six hundred southern Blacks poured in to work the modernized plants during World War I alone, housed in corporate-built barracks. Overflow workers lived in shanties all along the Pennsylvania Canal and Adams Street.

Beginning in the late 1880s, Peter Sullivan Blackwell, owner of the *Steelton Press,* took up the cause of quality education for the Black community and over the years was able to marshal support for the all Black Hygienic School. As required by law, students were educated through the eighth grade. Few of the graduates were able to survive in the nearly all-white high school until Charles Howard graduated from Steelton High in 1885 and was appointed principal of the Hygienic School the next year. Thus began his remarkable fifty years career at the school. Howard inaugurated a tradition of excellence in education and scholarly inquiry that lasted until the 1960s when the Supreme Court mandated the integration of public schools.

"I've talked to a few of the people who had attended the Hygienic School," Nagy concluded. "To a person, they remarked on the close relationship between students and teachers, declaring their belief that their education was equal to, if not better than, that received by the better equipped and funded white schools. Judging from the careers of its graduates, that may very well be true."

"The racial divide was not as severe in Arizona," Carlson said. "I can't claim that we were any more progressive than the other states, but we had already integrated our public schools just before *Brown v. The Board of Education, Topeka, Kansas.*"

"Way to go, Sport," Veronica said. "Not many people outside of the legal community think to add the 'Topeka, Kansas.' Perhaps we should enroll you at Dickinson. I won't be your professor, though—conflict of interest, nepotism and few other prohibitions come to mind. The Law School also frowns upon fraternization between faculty and students."

"Perhaps I should apply to Yale, then," he countered with a smile. "In a more serious vein, I am starting to be concerned about the growing 'Islamophobia'— for lack of a better term—that I notice everywhere I go these days. I witnessed quite a bit of it in Europe recently. Due to its previous colonial ambitions, France has a large Muslim population that has not generally assimilated into the general populous—for many reasons, some of which the French government is responsible."

"And you are concerned that the American public is even more ignorant, in the non-pejorative sense of the term, about Islam," Nagy suggested. "I've given that some thought and at first saw some hope in what we Americans like to consider ourselves to be: a somehow uniquely polyglot nation that will cope better than others, just because of our ignorance."

"A hope that we'll make fewer mistakes along the way?" Veronica asked.

"Something like that," he admitted. "There is a certain innocence to our ignorance and at times it seems to do us no harm. Then I look at the election of 2006. Do you remember the controversy surrounding the freshman member of the House of Representatives from Minnesota?"

"Certainly," Veronica answered. "A Black American convert to Islam named Ellison, who wanted to be sworn in to office on the Qur'an. He overcame objections from a senior Virginia congressman that he had to use the Bible by requesting the Library of Congress allow him to use the two-volume Qur'an owned by Thomas Jefferson, a man he described as a visionary who believed he could glean wisdom from the book. Ironically, the Virginia congressman represented the district of Jefferson's Monticello and the University of Virginia that the former president helped to found. And, the Library of Congress provided the copy. The swearing in went smoothly and a footnote to history had been accomplished."

"Did you notice another irony to the situation?" Nagy inquired. "I was thinking of the ignorance of history by the media covering this historic event."

"I see your point," Carlson replied. "The reporters included the fact that Jefferson had sold several thousand volumes of his personal library to replace those burned by the British during the War of 1812. The library was at the time housed in the Capitol Building, set to the torch and gutted. What they failed to mention is that Jefferson very likely was studying one of the first English translations of the Qur'an as a way of understanding the enemy. North African pirates were devastating American shipping along the Barbary Coast, holding goods for ransom and selling off the crews into slavery. The previous administration of John Adams had already dealt with France capturing American shipping and expecting bribes to settle matters. On that occasion, Pickney gave Talleyrand his famous rebuke of 'millions for defense, but not one cent for tribute.' Jefferson sent gunboats and Marines to put an end to the practice and free crew members in Tripoli."

"Exactly," Nagy replied. "'From the Halls of Montezuma to the shores of Tripoli,' just as in the song. One would hope the media could provide more balanced and informative coverage."

"And as before the bar," Veronica said, "ignorance is no excuse."

CHAPTER 6

▼

DISCOVERING DIVERSITY

Christmas Eve Day dawned bright and clear, with only a few scattered clouds drifting in the sky and the temperatures in the unseasonably balmy fifties. As usual Abe Carlson was up before the sun crested the horizon and sat in Doc Straussburger's kitchen sipping coffee and chatting with Aunt Mattie. He was looking forward to a day of leisurely activities with his intended, Veronica Steinmann.

"So what's on your agenda today, Abe?" Aunt Mattie asked. "Last minute Christmas shopping or one of your famous 'good stretch of the legs?'"

"You know I lifted that phrase from *The Quiet Man,* starring John Wayne," Abe replied. "It was a great line of dialogue and seems so appropriate for my wanderings."

"I'm not saying it isn't perfectly appropriate to you," Aunt Mattie countered. "It is a nice fit. I trust you haven't been using other movie lines, such as 'Here's looking at you kid,' to woo Veronica."

"If I were to venture a guess," he said with a chuckle, "I would have been out of the picture long ago if I ever tried something like that. Veronica is not one to play games, even verbal ones, nor am I. It's one of her endearing charms that made me fall in love with her. As for last minute shopping, I put a few small gifts under the tree for you and Doc, brought a little something for Henry from Germany, and I think I have Veronica covered."

"You had Veronica covered just by coming home," Aunt Mattie said sincerely. "I must admit that I do enjoy seeing new love blossom, at whatever age. Everyone can see that in you two and, believe me, no community could be more pleased to see that than this one."

"I'm very aware of that fact, Aunt Mattie," he said quietly, "and am appreciative. I don't think there is another place I'd rather call home than right here. Everyone makes me feel part of the family."

"I noticed Henry called you Uncle Abe yesterday," she said. "Expect more of that from others, particularly the young. That's how I became everyone's Aunt Mattie. I take it as a compliment."

"I take it the same way," he answered. "Veronica will be here shortly to begin my education about Harrisburg and the surrounding area. I have a lot to learn."

"And she's just the one to teach you," she answered. "She's a good professor of law, but I'd bet she's also an excellent teacher of anything else she puts her mind to."

"I'm counting on that," Carlson said as he rinsed out his coffee cup in the sink.

The day's education began within the hour on the Front Street walking path along the Susquehanna in downtown Harrisburg. Several bridges spanning the river to the west shore stood out in the bright sunshine, which also highlighted the slow current in the channels. The bare trees on small islands in the river still drew avian visitors, but City Island, home to a large multi-use park and the local baseball stadium were deserted. Yet the pleasant weather did bring its share of walkers, joggers and bicyclists. They spotted several couples sitting together, steeped in pleasant conversation, gazing out over the river. In a fitting natural gesture, Carlson and Steinmann joined hands as they strolled north.

"A number of festivals and other entertainment are held along this stretch," Veronica explained. "The arts, music and sometimes just the seasonal changes are celebrated. They bring people out from all over the city and countryside, not to mention the many out-of-towners who come to enjoy the hometown atmosphere you wouldn't think you'd find in the middle of a major metropolitan center. People seem to just discover these events rather than otherwise, if you know what I mean."

"I can feel that sense," Abe replied. "Unlike some other cities I've visited, Harrisburg seems to have recognized the value of riverfront property for recreational use and prevented packed commercial development right up to the water's edge."

"There was a healthy dose of self-interest in the development, too," she continued. The Barons of Industry who saw to the growth as a railroad hub, coal center and state capital, were careful not to emulate the many other towns up and down the Susquehanna. Nearly every other town on the river is separated by railroad tracks near the water's edge. In Harrisburg, the political powers actually made the railroads snake further inland, skirting the riverbank. As you can see up ahead, the wealthier residents built huge residences, many mansions, along the east side of the street and have unobstructed river views."

"They don't look much like residences to me," he observed. "As far as I can see up Front Street, the handsome houses seem to have all been turned into office space, resplendent with large signs in the front yards offering their services. I notice quite a few law offices and varying associations."

"These days, it is like that all the way up to the Governor's Mansion," she said. "When we get that far, I'll tell you about a peculiar problem that has arisen near there, but let me point out that Second Street runs parallel to Front Street. Two large hotels, the Hilton and Crowne Plaza, anchor that street with such enterprises as big banks and the telephone company on the corners. It is also the site of City Hall, where the Mayor, who many referred to as 'Mayor For Life,' and the City Council have offices and conduct the business of the city. A big initiative of the Mayor has been the development of a restaurant row to draw young professionals and tourists to the inner city. He has been pretty successful with that one."

"Is that the same mayor who has been developing several museum projects, such as the Civil War Museum in Reservoir Park?" he asked. "I read somewhere that the Civil War Museum was a dramatic concept and very well done, but critics thought it should have been placed more aptly in Gettysburg. That article mentioned flagging attendance as the reason for rising criticism."

Veronica explained that the Mayor had been very good for the city over the years and that his penchant for museums was to draw more tourist trade. He used a discretionary budget to purchase artifacts for a planned Western Museum, which many people questioned. During one heated reelection campaign, one of his opponents suggested he 'sell Annie Oakley's underwear' to ease the city deficit. She thought he had actually purchased one of Oakley's signature pair of bloomers she wore for the Wild West Show performances. The museum is now a moot point. The accumulated artifacts had to be auctioned to make up for a city deficit. Another museum in the planning stage would honor African-Americans, but it had barely left the talking phase. The Mayor's other big push was to boost Harrisburg as a friendly, small town atmosphere where young professional couples could rear their families in a neighborhood setting.

The pair stopped to sit on a bench and enjoy the river. Veronica retrieved a thermos of coffee and two cheese rolls out of her cavernous purse and poured them each a cup.

"What else could you possibly be carrying in there?" he asked.

"None of your business," she answered with a smile. "That's one of the reasons women remain so mysterious, remember? Aside from which, as an attorney, need I remind you about the 'expectation of privacy?'"

He merely smiled in response and they sat for some time with their own thoughts.

"Abe," she said at last, "I need to ask you something. It's a subject we need to discuss. How do you feel about children?"

"I love children," he replied truthfully. "I always have and always will. But if you are asking whether I'd expect children with you, I find myself neutral. Please don't misunderstand me. I don't have any pressing needs in that direction, but if you want a child, I'd love and care for ours with all my being. It's you I want to marry, you who comes first in my life, and I pledge to support you in whatever you choose to do. Only, always remember that you are my priority."

"Thank you for that," she said in a tone barely above a whisper. "I guess you should know that among my insecurities is the fact that as I grow older, I wonder why I haven't felt the way some other women do. For instance, here I am at my age and have never experienced my so-called 'biological clock' ticking away. And do you know what? I can't even feel guilty."

"First of all," he noted, "there is nothing to feel guilty about. Second, you are not other women. You are Veronica Steinmann and the only one I wish to spend the rest of my life with. And thirdly ..." he came to a pause.

"You've done very well so far," she finally said. "What's the thirdly?"

"And thirdly," he continued, with a touch of mischief in his voice, "you're almost forty-seven. Aren't you a little old to be worrying about how other people feel?"

"Mother!" she spat out in mock anger. "Ruby told you how old I am. Well, I'll tell you a little secret about my mother. She's been lying about her age for years. She is three years older than it says on her driver's license and I could have her license revoked if the authorities became aware."

"I just discovered you have a mean streak," he answered in feigned surprise, as he leaned over and kissed her.

This time as they continued their walk, it was arm-in-arm, leaning into each other for comfort and support. A milestone had been passed and the future seemed more secure.

"You can see one of the major problems the city has always had along here," she said. "And I don't know that anyone has found a solution."

"Periodic flooding?" he asked.

"Floods along the river are not only periodic, but can be devastating," she replied. "For instance, Hurricane Agnes in 1972 brought water rushing over the banks, filling up the basements and rising to eight feet on the first floor along this particular stretch. In lower areas, entire sections of the city were inundated. There is a limit to how many times the citizenry can clean up, rebuild and make a valiant effort to get on with life. Some of the less affluent areas of the city are the most vulnerable, where people simply can't afford the cost of recovery."

"What about some sort of flood containment system?" he asked. "Surely other river towns have installed some precautionary structures."

"Oh, they have," she answered. "Many of the towns up-river had built flood walls, levees and other precautions, but that is costly and many critics think they are eyesores and ruin the view. It has been a long battle in some of those efforts, if only because more affluent residents with mansions above the flood plain don't care to look down upon a flood wall or levee of any sort."

"There are always certain unavoidable hazards living on a major waterway," he commented. "You'd think the people would demand cutting the risks wherever then can."

"One would think so," she said. "Perhaps we'll find a solution eventually. One thing is for sure though, not every risk is avoidable. We're having an unseasonably warm winter so far, but in some years the river freezes over to a reasonable depth and if at the end of the cold spell the temperatures rise too rapidly, the cracking ice sounds like cannons going off. One year, the ice jams were so bad they took out a major bridge."

As she continued her narrative, Steinmann described the usual problems of any mid-sized city in promoting and controlling growth, developing abandoned lots with an eye to economic enhancement, and the all-too-prevalent political battles between competing interests. Apparently the ever-colorful Mayor was nearly always at loggerheads with a strong and determined City Council. Some of the City Council sessions became so spirited that they ended up with assault charges being filed against bickering members.

"Ah," Abe said, "you've got to love a passionate City Council."

They had reached the intersection of Front and Division Streets.

"Come with me, Sport," she replied. "I'll show you a crime of passion."

With that, Veronica took his arm and led him a couple of blocks to a city park named Italian Lake, a beautiful park designed as a miniature version of an existing park in Italy. Water was the chief feature and in the middle of the lake stood a fountain sculpture featuring three nude nymphs.

"How do you like the fountain?" she asked. "It has a colorful history."

"Beautiful," he responded. "A graceful classic design complementing the intended use as a fountain. I can only imagine what it is like when the water is running."

Veronica related how the chocolate maker Milton S. Hershey had commissioned a fountain for his Hershey mansion in the early 1900s. Mr. Hershey, it seems, had a Mennonite background and was reputed to be rather close with a dollar at home, but less frugal on his many trips abroad. The commission went to Giuseppe Donato, a Philadelphia sculptor who supposedly agreed to a $3,100.00 price and accepted a $2,000.00 advance. When the sculpture was delivered, it had an accompanying $31,000.00 bill—ten times the original agreement.

Whether due to Mr. Hershey's frugality or to his conservative religious nature, he was aghast and refused to pay. Taking Mr. Hershey to court, Donato finally won a $24,000.00 judgment and the fountain remained crated at the Hershey railroad station until 1920 when it was donated to the Harrisburg City's Reservoir Park, where it remained for 18 years. Moved to a rose garden on the grounds of the Polyclinic Hospital, it became a ritual for the seniors of the School of Nursing to clothe the nymphs in lingerie the night before graduation. In 1971, the rose garden was paved over for a parking lot and the fountain once again was moved, to Italian Lake.

"I have the feeling that there's more to this story," Carlson said.

"Of course there is, dear," Veronica replied. "It all has to do with the model for the piece, a local small town girl from north of Harrisburg, born in the late 1800s, who changed her name to Madeline Stokes when she moved to Philadelphia and went on the vaudeville stage. She was a much sought-after model into her thirties, making the covers of many magazines, a model for an Alexander Caldwell sundial in Philadelphia's Fairmount Park, and for a mural for the governor's reception room here in Harrisburg. And, it was rumored that she had danced nude in a New York City night club."

"Interesting career," he replied. "It must have been a hot topic in its day."

"That it was," she said. "Now comes the delicious part. A special guest at the unveiling here at Italian Lake was none other than Madeline Stokes herself. She met her unfortunate demise one year later, aged ninety-eight."

"Nice story," he said, gazing off in the distance at a large building across the street. Even at a distance, he could see the breadth and depth of the structure, with a Moorish architectural flavor and an extensive awning at the main entrance.

The prominently displayed 'ZEMBO' lettering identified this as the Masonic Shrine.

"Pretty impressive, isn't it?" Veronica said. "That belongs to some of your Masonic Brothers. My grandfather was part of the Scottish Rite Cathedral—the other impressive building right beyond—but never joined the Shrine."

"I'm afraid I don't know much about the Shrine," he replied. "But I do know that you have to be either a thirty-second degree Scottish Rite Mason or a Knights Templar Mason in the York Rite tradition to be eligible for membership. At least you did until a couple of years ago. I understand that you can now go from the Blue Lodge as a Third Degree Master Mason directly to the Shrine."

Veronica mentioned some unease had begun to arise in this neighborhood. One of her students had a grandmother living just a few blocks away, a deeply religious woman reared in a strict Catholic tradition in another state. She was taught since childhood to be wary of the Masons because at least two popes in the past had issued edicts denouncing them. With the heightened anxiety over terrorist threats from the Middle East over the last few years, the Shrine symbols were being interpreted much differently. Just as the variances between different Muslim traditions were not recognized, the symbols were misunderstood. When people like this grandmother saw a fez, a scimitar, or crescent, they could only link them to Islamic violence.

"I can only imagine what such people would think if they knew the official title," Abe said. "How do you think that grandmother would react to 'The Ancient Arabic Order of Nobles of the Mystic Shrine' and seeing a man in a fez with 'Mecca' ornately stitched in the front?

"The point is that in the past, as now, there has always been a great diversity here in Central Pennsylvania," she replied. "Just as the Germans, Italians, Irish or whomever immigrated in fair numbers in older times, so have the Hispanics, Vietnamese and others in more recent years. And now we have an influx of people coming in under the banner of Islam at a time when there has been tremendous heightened violence in the Middle East for years and the average person on the street hasn't a clue to their actual religious diversity. I only hope we can all educate ourselves about these newcomers and that they can come to understand us without severe personal consequences. And I have a certain faith that our Constitution can be the framework to make that possible."

"There goes that passion again," he said, taking her hand. "One thing for sure, our life together will never be boring."

CHAPTER 7

▼

CHRISTMAS EVE

Abe and Veronica spent a leisurely hour to get back to the car, strolling through neighborhoods near the river to admire the Christmas decorations, sidling back through the commercial district to see the numerous window displays and watching last minute shoppers darting in and out of the stores making final purchases. It was amusing to see cars with wreaths and garland on the front grill—some with trees strapped to their roofs as traditionalists prepared for the Christmas Eve decorating—while many shoppers wore shorts with light-weight jackets as they maneuvered through the crowds and traffic.

With the knowledge that they would be dining on seasonal fare through the holidays, they decided on Italian cuisine for a late lunch. When she discovered one of Abe's favorite dishes was shrimp Portofino, Veronica suggested The Macaroni Grill, located on the way back to Hummelstown, as one of her favorites.

"I know it's a franchise," she said, "with restaurants all up and down the east coast, but the food is authentic, with atmosphere to match."

"I trust your taste," he responded. "If there is one thing I've discovered, it's that you do know and appreciate good food."

The Macaroni Grill was one of two restaurants anchoring both ends of a popular u-shaped strip mall called The Shoppe's at Susquehanna Marketplace. Carlson had to smile at the quaintness of the 'Shoppe's' spelling, as if a modern, streamlined mall could capture some Old World charm with that version. It reminded him of some housing developments he had seen with the word 'mews' in the title, without the buyers being aware that in London, a mews normally connoted a dreary back alley mostly for horse stables, with very small apartments above. America had reinvented the term and now it meant cozy little streets of townhouses with an optional garage on the first floor.

As they entered the restaurant, he saw classic Italian American décor, down to the wine racks and little-too-loud music. The bar area had a distinctive elongated and polished granite bar surface, with a sunken gas-fired pit at its circular end.

"May I recommend to the gentleman the shrimp Portofino?" Veronica asked in her best hostess voice. "You will note from the menu, it is a dish of tender, sautéed shrimp with mushrooms, pine nuts and spinach in a tangy butter sauce, served with pasta. And for less than two dollars more you may add the special Caesar salad."

"I will certainly take that recommendation," Abe replied in mock formality, "but only if the Lady would be so gracious as to join me at my expense."

"At your expense, anytime," she accepted, "yet, I need to know your intentions."

"Absolutely honorable," he replied. "I just want to smother you with kindness and whisk you off to the preacher—only after a suitable term of engagement, of course."

After their server took the orders she picked up the bottle of extra virgin olive oil that was on the table, poured an amount into a small plate and added ground fresh pepper from a pepper mill. Their iced teas and a square loaf of warm fresh bread were brought within minutes. Veronica broke the loaf in half and they both dipped it into the olive oil and savored the result.

"You sure you're not part Italian?" he asked. "You perform that like a native."

"The way I was reared," she answered, "this was the only time, except when we had fried chicken, that my mother would allow us to handle the food. I always experienced a little rush as if I were getting away with something."

"Then how did you ever eat a cookie when you were a kid?" he asked factiously.

"Well, you know what I mean," she replied. "Now, about this term of engagement, is it for a set length or is it negotiable? I sincerely don't want to seem to be pushing about this; I merely need a ballpark figure so I can make some plans. I promise not to throw any legal obstacles in our way, like a thorough background check, a full physical or making you sign a tight prenuptial agreement."

"I thought we were just sort of making up the plans as we go along," he said with a smile. "A background check is okay with me, but like a physical, I'm sure I can easily pass. I'll sign any type of prenuptial agreement you may require. I will not be offering you the latter in return."

The meal was served and they both enjoyed every bite, the moments between filled with small talk, before resuming the more serious matters under consideration.

"Now, my dear Veronica, I think it is time to let you know our financial prospects," he began. "I expect you to keep all your assets and income for yourself to do with as you wish. I'm having my will changed to include you as a fifty-fifty partner. My accountants in Europe, who oversee our interests on that side of the Atlantic, in New York, who cover North America, and in Seattle, who cover the Pacific Rim holdings, will have reports to us by the first of the year. Here is a thumbnail sketch of our holdings."

Carlson quietly ran down a list of items to include his, now their, extensive and varied portfolio of stocks and bonds, and their extensive commercial and residential real estate around the world. A second category included precious metals, mining and oil interests. They had a number of trusts established for Indian schools, medical aid to third-world countries and a low-key lending institution that disbursed short-term, no-interest loans to individuals. All these entities were profitable and returns were plowed back into the ventures and then a small portion of the profits were contributed to a very quiet foundation that sought out opportunities to make anonymous contributions "to improve local individual or community well-being." This foundation did not accept applications for grants, but used its open-ended statement of purpose to assist others who would never be covered by the more formal grants.

"I really like that last one, Abe," she commented. "You don't have all those groups coming by with hat-in-hand. It does kind of put a kink in the professional fund-raiser's style, though."

"That was the point in setting it up that way in the first place," he replied. "And please remember it is 'ours,' unless something happens to me before I can sign the papers."

"You really know how to turn a girl's head," she countered. "I would have defended you with my life to begin with. Now, it has garnered a more mercenary aspect. This gets more exciting all the time."

"All right, Lady Rambo," he chuckled, "let's get this over with. Those assets pretty much take care of themselves. We have many good people making nice salaries and retainers to keep things running. Now to what the accountants like to refer to as ready assets, or what I think of as cash on hand, because we can write a check or walk into a bank and they'll put cash in our hands. We have an all-purpose checking/savings account of thirty million dollars, another checking/savings account of twenty million dollars and you have a checking account of ten million dollars, which at your discretion can be converted into savings also, which I might suggest is a good idea because it earns pretty nice interest."

"This is all a might overwhelming, Abe," she admitted. "I've never given much thought to being that financially secure or being able to do so much good in the world with the proper financial backing. But you know what, Sport? It's all Monopoly money to me. I'm marrying you for you and you're marrying me for me. I don't need a lavish lifestyle and neither do you. Perhaps we should keep this to ourselves. People can behave differently when they know you might be set financially."

"Our secret is safe with me," he replied with a wry smile.

When they arrived again at Doc Straussburger's house, Aunt Mattie was at the door, dressed for evening services at her church.

"My, don't you look splendid?" Abe said as they stepped into the hallway. "Are you taking Doc along with you?"

"Absolutely," Aunt Mattie replied. "I don't get him there as often as I would prefer, but he can't resist the candlelight service. He claims he likes all the pageantry and seeing people who only attend once or twice a year. If you ask me, what he really likes is all the gossip at the fellowship hour following the service."

"It seems to me to be a good source for that," Veronica replied. "I know how good Doc is at getting people to unburden themselves when they talk to him. Perhaps it's his Christmas gift to these people—you know, confession being good for the soul once in awhile."

"Please don't tell him that," Aunt Mattie said. "That's exactly the kind of justification he would love to use. Yet, I concede you may be right on that point, even if it is a subconscious trait of his. It would be just like him. How about you two, want to join us?"

"We'd like to," Veronica answered, "but we're already committed to the candlelight service at the Bindnagle Lutheran Church. Tom Rogers is so proud of his little church and would be disappointed if we did not attend."

"That's fine," she replied. "At least you are going to church somewhere. By the way, Henry Cunningham and his friend Cassy Spease are in the library with Father. Henry is apparently dealing with some sort of moral dilemma and he dropped in to talk to you about it, Abe. Actually, I think he wants to talk to both of you. He sees you as a couple, equals in a partnership. I know boys and I think he wants Cassy to see that it's nice to be a couple. Of course, Cassy is so far ahead of him at this point that she never gave such things a second thought. She's bid-ing her time, waiting for him to catch up."

The pair entered the library to find Doc sitting in his favorite wingback chair and the two young people on the leather Chesterfield sofa, deep in conversation.

"Just the people we were waiting for," Doc said to the newcomers. "I know a little about a lot of things, but I'm afraid I don't know much about the tracking business, Abe. And Veronica, I think you're qualified to rule on matters of ethics. Tell them the problem, Henry."

"Well, Uncle Abe," Henry said with a pause, "it's like this. We're getting pretty good at this tracking business and we've found a lot of animals for people. My friend Peter says we ought to start charging for our services. That way we could save up for equipment, or a bike, or maybe even a dog. Money would be nice, but I just don't feel right about it. What do you think?"

"Henry's afraid people will start calling him 'altruistic,'" Cassy interrupted. "That's a word I learned in school and it means 'unselfish regard for or devotion to the welfare of others.' Henry thinks it will make him soft and unprepared for the hard business decisions he will have to make in the future. He's trying out this 'strong, silent type' persona and he's not sure how it will fit this image."

All three adults in the room had a difficult time keeping their laughter con-trolled. These two serious young people were grappling with a difficult subject with little experience of their own to show them the way.

"Let me ask you one question, Henry," Abe said with a slightly furrowed brow to show his seriousness. "Why have you been doing this tracking for all these peo-ple?"

"For the experience, I guess," Henry answered. "I want to develop my skills, help the neighbors and protect the animals."

"Then the community is providing you a free education in this field and your friend Peter thinks you should charge them?" Abe asked further. "That would seem mighty ungrateful in my book. I think you should educate your friend Peter through your own example."

"Thanks, Uncle Abe, I will," Henry said with a sigh of relief.

"And altruism doesn't make you soft," Veronica answered. "As a matter of fact I think it's rather manly. Abe has it by the truckload. It's one of his virtues I so admire."

"Thanks to you too, Aunt Veronica," Cassy said. "Sometimes it just takes a woman's perspective to keep the man in line, don't you think?"

With that rhetorical question left floating in the air, Henry and Cassy were out the door, heading home.

"And so it starts," Doc said as he watched them depart. "Uncle and Aunt, you are now officially christened by the younger generation. Yet, I think I'll still call you Professor. I'm much older and have earned certain prerogatives."

As Veronica went home to change for church and Abe did the same in his room at Doc's house, both had time to reflect on their new status as a couple and how that was changing their lives and the perception of the community. This new feeling of closeness was warmly comforting and the undercurrent pleasurable in its own right. Each decided they truly liked the idea.

The last time Carlson had seen the Bindnagle Evangelical Lutheran Church in Palmyra, it had been on a scorching July morning in bright sunlight. The two hundred year old brick structure stood like a proud sentinel over the cemetery, where the remains of the many generations who had worshiped within its walls were interred. He had seen the nearly illegible gravestones of men who had fought in the Revolutionary War, including the founder of Palmyra who had been a surgeon during that war, along with his several wives.

Approaching the church on this Christmas Eve in darkness, the building shone brightly with a single candle in each of its many windows and a couple of strategically placed flood lights on either end. The parking lot was nearly full and a line of people was filing through the front entrance.

The historic church had been empty the last time he was here. The interior had the feeling of open space; high stiff-back, narrow-seated pews ran along three walls, with gallery seating above. It was designed in the form of a Greek cross, with an impressive wineglass pulpit towering from the far wall, accessed by a very narrow, steep staircase.

When they entered, the first available seats were in the back pew by the front door, so they accepted their programs and stepped sideways into the narrow space. The entire church was filling up quickly and they could see Tom Rogers, looking grand in his well-tailored suit, ushering people to the gallery. The church was tastefully decorated with appropriate garland and poinsettias along the gallery rail and scattered throughout the first level. A line of white lights adorned the two arched doors on either end.

"What do you think?" Abe asked as he leaned over and whispered near Veronica's ear. "I seem to detect as many as four generations of the same family in these pews."

"I feel the same," she whispered in return. "And you can feel the deep devotion of the people. Many may only attend sporadically, but you can sense a true, simple faith."

The service was uncomfortable and long, but they hardly noticed either as the program progressed. Many old bedrock hymns were sung and long devotional prayers were read, but the small choir, backed by two organs, and the participation of a handful of children made the time pass quickly. The lighting of the candles was particularly moving as each worshiper passed their good wishes along to one another.

"That was really very nice, Abe," Veronica said as they walked, arm-in-arm, to the car. "Just the two of us sharing our first Christmas Eve candlelight service."

"What do you say we do this again for the next, oh fifty years or so?" he asked.

"You're on," she replied, nuzzling her hair against his cheek. "And now we still have a long evening ahead of us."

"Doc's workshop?" he asked. "I've heard rumors to that effect."

"You bet, Sport," she replied. "It's a long tradition in Doc's household. Every year Santa needs a few extra elves, at least those handy with tools. Santa brings the parts, but sometimes there is 'some assembly required.' After the children are all snug in their beds, people with boxes begin showing up on Doc's doorstep. At times the procrastinators can keep this little workshop open until the wee hours."

"It sounds like a good tradition," he said. "I'd bet Doc stays up with them all."

"He does at that," she confirmed. "He says that abandoning the project before it's done shows a lack of resolve, a weakness of character, if you will. These last few years he takes a nap in the afternoon so he's ready for the night."

"God bless Doc," he said sincerely.

"God has done that," she replied. "And God has blessed this community by placing Doc in our midst."

CHAPTER 8

▼

CHRISTMAS DAY

At dawn on Christmas morning, the air was crisp and clear, the result of a weather front passing through during the night hours. Doc Straussburger's house resembled more of an encampment than a staid residence. Doc had outdone himself with his workshop this particular year, inviting several people who had no place in particular to go and stay overnight. Between the guest rooms, his office and examining rooms, plus couches in the library and throughout the house, there were accommodations for all. Doc and Aunt Mattie had hosted Abe and Veronica, Veronica's mother Ruby, John Nagy and his mother Beatrice, and the Grant brothers, Jan and Jon—identical twins who owned a bicycle shop in Cornwall and were handy to have on the workshop crew for obvious reasons. The Grants were older bachelors with no family in the area except each other and always looked forward to Doc's on Christmas Eve.

After getting properly dressed for the day—a house rule of Doc's—everyone gathered in the kitchen. Doc had prepared pancakes with a special maple syrup sent from a former patient in Canada. Abe and Veronica had teamed to provide eggs, sausage and ham. Aunt Mattie and Bea were in charge of biscuits and toast. Jan and Jon Grant cooked the potatoes and liver with onions. The task left to John Nagy was boiling water for tea and making coffee in the electric coffee maker.

"My otherwise brilliant son," Bea said, "is unfortunate in the kitchen. He doesn't seem to be able to grasp the essentials of making a decent meal."

"But I do what I do so well, Mother," John countered. "If we could all only live on coffee and tea."

"And how did you sleep, son," Bea asked.

"I rested well, thank you," he answered.

"You see how he so artfully avoids the question?" she asked no one in particular. "My usually quiet son stays up all night chatting with Abe like they were a couple of little girls having a sleep-over. I could hear them through the wall— including their laughter."

"I haven't bunked in with another person since I was in the Army," John said. "Abe and I drew the library couches and just hit it off splendidly. You can rest and talk at the same time, you know. But I think you may have a point—that was very uncharacteristic of me."

"Yes it was, my son," she replied. "And I thank God for Abe Carlson bringing you out a bit. I see you two are going to be fast friends. So what was all the laughter about?"

Carlson and Nagy looked at each other and both tried unsuccessfully to contain a closed-mouth chuckle.

"It was my doing," Abe confessed. "We were deep in conversation about something or other and I was studying John's face. He looked very familiar and I was trying to place where I had seen him before. I'm pretty good with faces and mannerisms, but I couldn't quite recall. All of a sudden, John says, in his best imitative voice: 'I'm Howard Cosell and this is Monday Night Football. The hairline's the same, only mine is real. And that's telling it like it is.'"

Both men started to laugh out loud anew while their antics brought smiles all around.

"Well," Veronica said, "at least I know that Abe has retained his boyish humor. I haven't seen this side of him yet, but I sort of like this new facet. A touch of innocence is good, I think."

The one other thing John Nagy was allowed to do was to clean up after the meal, with Abe and Veronica lending a hand. That done, a tray of coffee and tea was prepared and all retired to the living room to exchange gifts. Everyone was curious about a few presents in front of the tree, wrapped in identical floral scene paper, placed there by Carlson.

"Are you an admirer of the Impressionists, Abe?" Ruby asked as she selected one with her name neatly printed on the tag. "This is Monet, if I'm not mistaken."

"Yes it is," Abe answered. "When you're buying at the last minute, the selections are limited. I like to think of it as appropriate for all seasons and occasions—at least that's what the woman behind the counter said I should say."

A note on the present read: "There are always two sides to any story." Ruby carefully unwrapped the box to discover a two-volume set of leather-bound books entitled *The War Between the States* by Alexander H. Stephens, 1868.

"Oh my, Abe, how appropriate," Ruby said. "Stephens was Vice President of the Confederacy under President Jefferson Davis, you know. It will be interesting to see his side of the story—the old scoundrel. Thank you very much."

John and Beatrice were surprised when they were handed presents with their names on them. "How thoughtful of you, Abe," Beatrice said. "How did you know we were even going to be here?"

"Let's just say I have my sources," Abe replied.

Beatrice, an avid letter writer, received a beautiful woman's desk set with embossed writing paper and envelopes. John was presented a copy of *Goodbye Mr. Chips,* by James Hilton, the classic story of a teacher and head master at a fictional English boarding school.

Aunt Mattie opened her present and discovered a lead crystal bud vase. "How did you know, Abe?" she asked.

"I've seen you take a single flower in a little glass vase up to your room each night," Abe replied. "I assumed you could use this."

Doc Straussburger received *The Pennsylvania Pilgrim, And Other Poems,* by John Greenleaf Whittier, 1872. "I noticed you had several well-worn Whittier works in your library," Abe said. "I didn't see this particular set of poems."

"'To the tired grinder at the noisy wheel/Of labor, winding off from the memory's reel/A golden thread of music.' I've long admired that part," Doc said. "Thank you."

"I've always liked: 'The Indian trapper saw them, from the dim/Shade of the alders on the rivulet's rim,/Seek the Great Spirit's house to talk with Him.'" Abe replied. "And you are welcome."

"My word," Aunt Mattie said. "You two keep that up and we'll be having a poetry reading hour around here before you know it."

"I'm sorry I don't have anything for you two," Abe told the Grant brothers. "I didn't know you'd be here."

"No problem," Jan said. "Our present every year," Jon added, "is that when the youngsters crash their bikes, they come to us for repair."

The last present was a box with Veronica's name attached, with the note: "Something for your office—meant to inspire." Inside, she discovered a set of three framed prints. One was of Charles (Robert) Darwin. The other two were his great historic supporters, Oliver Wendell Holmes and Thomas Henry Huxley.

"Thank goodness I'm marrying a practical romantic," Veronica said, leaning over and giving Abe a kiss on the cheek. "Thank you, Sport. I know just where they will go on my office wall and who will be the first certain professor I'll invite to view them. They're sure to chafe his hide more than a little."

The next several hours were reserved for small talk, mostly about Christmases past and in different settings and different eras. All in the room were old enough to have stockpiled many memories. The most touching was a simple tale by John Nagy about spending his one and only Christmas in Vietnam. He was on his first and last convoy, pulled in to a holding area for the night on Christmas Eve. One of his fellow MPs had opened his package from home. His sister had sent a foot-tall artificial tree, fully trimmed, a box of Slim Jims and several Polaroid pictures of the family back home around their Christmas tree. A neighbor had included two boxes of cigars. They put the tree on the hood of a Jeep and the soldiers gathered to share in the spirit. The Slim Jims stretched as far as they could and everyone, even the usual non-smokers, received at least two cigars. They had a brief, peaceful pause out in the middle of nowhere in an active war zone, each thankful for just one more day. Nagy made no mention of the fact that two days later he nearly lost his life.

"John, Son," Beatrice said, her eyes welling up, "do you realize that is the first time you've ever mentioned anything about your time over there? All these years and never a peep."

"It's one of the few good memories I have about those days," John said in response. "Perhaps it's the company we're keeping here. All I know is that I told Abe that story last night during our long chat that you kept hearing through the walls. He had just finished telling me about the Indian philosophy of sharing your best memories with your people, but to take the worst with you to the grave. It just seemed right at the time."

Beatrice stood and gave her son a kiss on his forehead and a motherly hug. She then walked over to Abe, took both his hands in hers. "Abe Carlson," she said in a near whisper, "you have given us the best gift of all. Thank you. Thank you for helping John take his first step away from that darkness he has been holding inside."

A moment of silence descended on the group, broken only by a few sniffles and nose blowing. The ringing of the doorbell seemed much louder than it had ever been, suddenly bringing everyone back to reality.

"I'll get it," Aunt Mattie said, looking at her watch. "It's probably some children coming around to show Doc what they managed to get for Christmas, as they do every year. They're a little early this year, though."

Henry Cunningham and Cassy Spease came into the living room panting for breath. "Merry Christmas, everybody," they said in unison.

"Did you two run all the way over here?" Doc asked.

"Just the last two blocks," Cassy managed to say. "We had a race and I won, as usual. Henry needs to grow more. Once his legs get to where they're supposed to be, I don't think I'll be racing him again."

"I think you're a wise young lady," Doc said. "Did you get what you wanted for Christmas?"

"We sure did," Henry said with relish. They both pointed to camouflaged binoculars hanging from their necks. "They're plastic cushioned, waterproof, with 30x magnification. They come with a carrying case, but we wanted to try them out on the way over."

As if on cue, both produced identical small packages from under their coats. Henry presented his to Abe, Cassy to Veronica. "Merry Christmas," they said again, almost in unison this time—Cassy loosing this race by a fraction of a second.

"We made them ourselves," Cassy proudly boasted.

Each package contained an identical deer-hide pouch, hanging from a leather thong-cinch closure. The only difference was the letters "UA" on Abe's and "AV" on Veronica's. The leather was surprisingly soft and pliant.

"My dad got two deer this year," Henry explained. "We asked if we could have some of the hide to make things. We had a heck of a time getting the fur off, until Cassy called a cousin who does tanning and he gave us some solution to soak it in for a couple of days."

"The stretching, scraping and drying was a long and hard process," Cassy broke in. "Did you know that you can't let it get bone dry or it will crack and fall apart in the process?"

"I think I've heard that somewhere," Abe conceded.

"Well, we made each other one of those," Cassy continued. "Henry used his wood-burning gun to burn our initials so they'd look like a brand. We figured they should come in handy for carrying special things, particularly when we're out tracking. We saw in some books that the Indians carried things around in pouches just like it, tied around their necks."

"We thought that since you two will be tracking together a lot now, these will come in handy. The letters are for Uncle Abe and Aunt Veronica so you won't get them mixed up."

"They're very distinctive," Veronica said. "They're quite beautifully worked and we thank you for your thoughtfulness. We will treasure them, right Uncle Abe?"

"Absolutely," Abe replied. "We'd better keep them out of sight from some of the Arizona leather workers I know, though. It might make them feel inadequate. Give me a minute to get something I think we need."

Carlson went to his room upstairs and returned within a few minutes. He took two small, oblong, smooth green stones and put one in each of the pouches. The other two he handed to Henry and Cassy.

"This is peridot," Abe said as he presented them. "It is sacred to the Mojave. They carry it for any number of reasons. Some say it is good luck. Others that it provides safety to travelers or insures good crops if you carry one while planting. It can be a symbol for whatever you choose. Veronica and I hope you will carry these in your pouch as a reminder of our friendship."

Henry and Cassy looked at each other, visibly moved and unable to say anything but a simple thank you.

"And here is another thing you will want to carry on your belts when tracking," Abe said, handing them each a box. "Sorry that I didn't have time to wrap them yet."

Each box contained a rectangular black leather snap-pouch with a belt loop in the back. Opening the snaps, they discovered a burnished-chrome device with a large compass on its face.

"I had a friend in Germany make those," Abe explained. "The instructions are in the bottom of the pouch. As you can see, it is primarily a compass with a lighted dial so you can see at night. It has a piano hinge on the left side, so push the little button on the right and open it up. Good. See the switch at the top? You turn it to 'S' for short distance communication. It's like a walkie-talkie on a special frequency so you can talk only to each other in case you get separated. The range is only about two miles. Turn the switch to the 'L' position and you have a cell phone, using the power switch and keyboard. You talk into the little slit at the bottom. The small rectangular screen is a GPS display I understand will work to a depth of one hundred feet underground. It comes on automatically when you have the power on. The internal GPS feature is on all the time and the battery is still under development, but is estimated to have a ten-year life, maybe more. It doesn't have a camera or play music, nor can it be used for text messaging. This is not a toy. It's a professional survival device. It is entirely waterproof and will withstand a blow from a sledge hammer."

"Do you two have a set of these?" Cassy asked in awe.

"We will," Abe answered. "Ours are on order."

After many heartfelt thanks and hugs from the two for both Abe and Veronica, Henry and Cassy were off to show their family and friends what they had received.

"How did you manage to pull out that string of pearls this time, Abe?" Veronica asked out of the side of her mouth. "You had no idea about Cassy while you were in Germany.

"Sheer luck," he answered honestly. "I had one for Henry, but ordered a backup in case something happened to the first. And I didn't tell a fib, either. I do have a set on order for us. I'll bet you'll look real cute out tracking with me, a super device on your hip and that pouch strung around your neck. It gives me a thrill just to think about that image."

"I'll tell you one thing for sure, Sport," she answered. "We won't need that short distance communication. I'll be riding along in your back pocket."

"Mother," Nagy said. "I think it's about time we should be getting along."

"Not so fast, John Nagy," Aunt Mattie said. "People will be coming in and out all day and they'll expect a little something to eat. You may not be able to cook, but you can help put the food on platters and plug in the coffee maker. As a matter of fact, wash your hands. I'm going to teach you how to make a proper sandwich. You'll be making quite a number today."

"Mattie doesn't mother everyone," Doc said to Bea after John had left to wash his hands, "just selected people. And you know you are a special case to be taken under her protective wing when she asks you to wash your hands."

CHAPTER 9

▼

REFLECTION

Abe Carlson awoke to a silenced household at his usual hour of dawn. As he looked out his window, the landscape was shrouded in a thick fog, hugging the ground in its misty embrace, yet gently creeping in a slight breeze around trees and buildings—vague gray specters against the whiteness. Although he had stood witness to this remarkable scene on many occasions, the experience was still singular in its ability to move his emotions each time.

The aroma of coffee drew him to the kitchen where he found a fresh pot, with a small tray of clean cups and mugs to one side. Filling a mug, he strolled through the quiet house, noting the telltale remnants of a busy Christmas day. Unwrapped gifts were placed back under the tree, clearly displaying the joy they had given those who had received them. He smiled when he spied the bright gilt titles contrasted against the deep blue spines of his gift from Veronica—a two-volume set entitled *The History of Pennsylvania Freemasonry*. It was a subtle touch to ease his way in establishing some Pennsylvania roots and greatly appreciated.

He wandered into the library to find Doc sitting quietly in his wingback chair, perusing a large folio of maps. As he stepped back to leave the man to his privacy, Doc looked up and smiled.

"Please come in, Abe," Doc said. "I see you found the coffee. This is one of the mornings of the year that I insist Mattie sleep in late. She gets so few of them, what with all the pampering she does to see to my comforts."

"I didn't mean to disturb you," Abe said. "Are you contemplating some travel? I notice you're checking some maps."

"Travel?" Doc answered with his own question. "Yes, that's as good a way as any to describe it, but in the opposite direction. You see, ever since I officially retired, I take a couple of days between Christmas and the New Year for reflection. I always begin with this book of maps. I've already reminded myself what a relatively tiny speck of solar dust Earth is. I use these maps to remind myself how small this community is in relation to the rest of this planet. Then I journey inward and reminisce about what I've done or failed to do to make this span of years a contribution to the welfare of my neighbors. It may be one of my many eccentricities, but it seems to work for me."

"That doesn't sound so eccentric to me," Abe replied. "Many people from many cultures take similar stock of their lives at the end of any given period. I always thought that was behind the practice of New Year's resolutions. In Arizona, I have Indian friends who simply get up and wander off into the desert or the mountains and think about things for a few days. And this is any time of the year. When troubled about something, they have sense enough to do something about it. No one ever questions the comings and goings. I meditate every few days to keep myself balanced."

"Good for you," Doc said. "There are quite a few people in this world who ought to meditate every so often, unfortunately, they're the ones most likely not to even consider it. Anyway, once I get myself centered, I think about the state of the world and how we frail humans keep making the same mistakes over and over throughout history. But I balance that with all the great strides we've managed to make as a species. It occurs to me that our periods of greatest progress have been when we share information, talk to one another, learn from the best what others have to offer and work out our conflicts across the table rather than on the battlefield."

"We could use someone like you at the United Nations, Doc," Abe commented.

"That's exactly my point," Doc countered. "When people finally come to understand that each of us, individually, is a mini-member of the U.N. and carry the responsibility to get along with each other, this world will be much-improved."

"How about a refill on that coffee, Doc," Abe asked, noticing the empty mug on the small side table.

"Yes, thank you," Doc answered. "Just a refill, though. Leave the pot so Mattie finds it when she gets up."

Carlson collected the mug and went to the kitchen. When he returned, he found Doc leafing through one of his file folders of clippings and miscellaneous information.

"Thank you," Doc said when Abe placed his coffee on the table. "I didn't mean to sound so negative earlier. I'm not one of those old men who decry the challenges of the world and feel bitter that they won't be around to see the change. I've been fortunate to live through times when rapid change passes so quickly that most people don't take time to notice. I remain optimistic that even the worst situations seem to yield some good."

"Like wars resulting in medical advances?" Abe asked. "I've read about leaps in medical knowledge coming from the carnage of the battlefield."

"Or the ultimate personal tragedy of hanging," Doc answered, "providing many of the first opportunities for dissection. I'm also thinking of vast social changes. I wasn't old enough to remember women getting the vote for the first time, but between the two world wars, I did see women freed from strictly domestic duties and the opening of educational and professional pursuits, regardless of gender."

"Not to mention the battle for civil rights," Abe added.

"Yes, I've seen a step in the right direction there," Doc conceded. "But we still have a long way to go on that one, along with such questions as gender preference, religious choice and personal privacy protection. Science and technology developments are far ahead of most individual experience and it will be decades before we know just what effect they will have on the long-term survival of mankind."

Aunt Mattie appeared at the library door with a tray carrying the coffee pot and some sweet rolls. "Is this a strictly bastion of male prominence today, or can a lady venture in without intrusion?"

"You know you're always welcome to join, Mattie," Doc said. "We were just solving all the woes of the world, but we certainly value your opinions."

"That's what John Adams said to his wife Abigail as she pushed for women's rights protection under the Constitution," she countered. "And look where that got her."

"Surely we males have become more enlightened these days," Doc replied.

"Perhaps the men in this room," Aunt Mattie said, "but the jury is still out on quite a few men I know. By the way, I just called Veronica and she's on her way over."

Veronica arrived dressed in a lime cashmere sweater and matching slacks, as if she just stepped out of a fashion magazine.

"How do you manage to always look so perfect the first thing in the morning?" Doc asked.

"That's a woman's secret," Aunt Mattie answered for her. "See what you have to look forward to, Abe? This is as bad as it gets with Veronica."

"It's nice of you to say so," Veronica replied. "Now, I could sure use a cup of that coffee. I'm a little grumpy this morning." She poured herself a cup and took a few sips. "I'll have to get another unlisted number. Former students keep calling me at all hours of the day and night. What can they be thinking?"

"Perhaps that they appreciate how much you know about the law," Abe suggested. "And that you can resolve a particular point of law they've run into."

"Not this time," Veronica said. "I received a call at the crack of dawn from a former student, Charlie Snavely—great name for a lawyer, don't you think? Charlie barely made the grade in a couple of my classes, which he thought wouldn't make much difference because he was going to use his degree to work for his car-dealership father, mostly filling out owner transfer papers and hiding questionable unnecessary finance charges in the small print."

"I don't remember anything in the Constitution covering that," Doc ventured.

"Neither do I," Veronica answered. "How Charlie ever passed the bar exam is anyone's guess. Perhaps North Carolina has lower standards. In any event, a cousin of his came calling for legal representation that was out of Charlie's field of expertise."

As Veronica related the telephone conversation, Charlie's cousin, also a Snavely, taught ninth-grade world history at the local public high school. He got the bright idea of asking a friend to come and talk to his class. The friend was a representative of the Kamil International Ministries Organization, based in Raleigh, whose declared mission was to "raise an awareness of the danger of Islam." The anti-Muslim lecture had many references to Jesus and literature was passed out to the class, including a pamphlet entitled: "Do Not Marry a Muslim Man." The father of an offended Muslim student reported the incident to the Council on American-Islamic Relations in Washington, D.C., which promptly protested the incident.

"So, Charlie conveniently remembers my course in The First Amendment—Free Speech," Veronica continued. "Charlie thought he could get his cousin off the hook with the Board of Education by arguing the free speech clause of the First Amendment, but he was a little troubled about what might happen if it got to the court system—particularly if it rose all the way to the Supreme Court."

"And what answer did you provide?" Abe asked with feigned bated-breath.

"I told him he should have paid more attention in class," Veronica said. "Then I suggested he go back and re-read the entire Constitution to see if that will clear his thinking. After that, I told him to get his cousin a real lawyer who might just be able to save some remnants of his shattered career. As far as I know, admitting to being stupid is not a plea allowable in court."

"That's my brilliant wife-to-be," Abe announced. "She's quick on her feet, isn't she? But this isn't really a laughing matter. I hate to imagine how many variations on this same theme could be taking place across the country on any given day."

"And not just in this country," Doc added. "Look at all the anti-Islamic feelings popping up all over Europe and elsewhere. It is a reaction based on ignorance and stark fear—fear that, unfortunately, is stoked by governments to obtain their own objectives. Fanning those fears always leads to war."

"And the first casualty of war is truth," Abe said quietly. "And so we have the state of the world today. Such talk puts a bit of a damper on the joyous season, doesn't it? Maybe we should leave that alone for at least the rest of the day."

"Agreed," Doc confirmed. "Let's turn to the more pleasant subject of how the beautiful Professor is going to arrange your new masculine manor."

Veronica had an entire list of items she had already been able to locate. Nine area rugs, mostly oriental or North African in design, were in a local warehouse ready to be picked up. Abe's office would have campaign-style furniture and a Chesterfield sofa, plus a small desk in the corner for Veronica's use. Walnut bookshelves would line three walls of the library, with a library table in one corner and another Chesterfield sofa in the middle of the room, with a long, low chinoiserie coffee table in front. The rest of the furniture would be an eclectic mix of contemporary style and antiques. The lamps and other accent pieces would be a similar mixture of styles. She had taken extra care to keep the furnishings in proper scale to the rooms, to keep an open flow to the home.

"And I hope you don't mind, Abe," she said, "but I have a plumber coming tomorrow to replace the commodes. I know men probably don't think much about bathrooms, but I dislike those newer 'children's toilets' that make you feel like you're sitting on the floor. I'm putting in a higher, pressure-assisted model that will make you think you're on an airplane or a train every time you flush. They take a little getting used to, but promise to be a conversation starter when you have guests."

"Sounds like it could be fun," Abe said with a smile. "I trust your judgment entirely."

"And one more thing, Sport," she said. "I trust you aren't in the habit of wearing spurs around the house, are you?"

"Only on the ranch," he answered. "And then only in the bunkhouse, never in the big house, except into the mud room."

"Good," she said. "I don't want you to ruin those gorgeous wood floors."

"I think you will find Abe to be quite considerate," Aunt Mattie said with a wink. "He's always neat and clean. I don't think he's the type to be tossing his clothes in a pile on the floor."

"I broke myself of that habit years ago," Abe winked back. "Piles of clothes on the floor draw snakes, you know. Things can get a bit nasty."

"Okay, you two, I get the picture," Veronica laughed. "I should also mention that Mother has been on the phone and e-mailing people since early today. She's a real tigress when it comes to organizing things. She knows everybody who is somebody—and everybody is somebody to her, regardless of social station—to collect and deliver everything Abe may need. She has claimed the dishware as her special provenance, but leaves the cookware to me. I've ordered an extensive set of Calphalon, the best I've ever cooked with. If she has her way, Mother will have you fully-furnished and ready to go in a couple of days."

"What's the rush?" Doc answered. "I've gotten to like Abe's company and he's a pretty good conversationalist. He is no inconvenience at all and can stay as long as he likes."

"Father," Aunt Mattie commented, "you know what it's like when you bring a child into the world. When it finally comes, it's out and gone. Just think of this as Abe's rebirth. After all, he has a romance to conduct and we just might be cramping his style."

Carlson looked out the window and noticed the fog had lifted and the sun was shining. He had been so deep in conversation with Doc that he had not realized the passing hours.

"Well, it's noon," Doc announced, as if reading his thoughts. "What do you say we all go to the kitchen and see if we can scare up an old crust of bread? I do so enjoy leftovers."

As Carlson had expected, Doc's characterization of "an old crust of bread" proved entirely facetious. He counted at least five major items in all the food groups, seven side dishes and numerous desserts to choose from. Wondering how these hearty souls would ever find themselves without plenty in the larder, he selected a single slice of bread and wrapped it around two slices of ham, washed down with a glass of iced tea.

"Not feeling well, Sport?" Veronica asked. "Lose you appetite?"

"My dear Veronica," Abe replied, "maybe you should know right now that I can't possibly keep up with all this food—particularly when I'm not out burning off all the calories. I can eat well and often, but I only have a certain capacity at any particular sitting. The food is great, but I need to pace myself."

"Fair enough, Abe," she responded. "I tell you what. When we've finished this little repast, what do you say to a 'good stretch of the legs?' We'll walk down to the square and browse the wares. You like to pick up the big national newspapers and might like some of our quaint little shops. I promise not to ask you to stop and buy me an ice cream."

"You're on," he replied. "I might even buy you that ice cream, if I can work up an appetite, but I'll have only one scoop."

Their walk to the square was pleasant and many people waved in recognition. Schools were closed until the first of the year, so children were out riding new bicycles, scooters and skateboards. They saw one boy of about ten years old pulling a wagon with a huge golden retriever in tow. A little girl was sitting sadly on her front porch with her new sled, as if her power of concentration would make it snow.

They stopped at the newsstand Carlson had frequented when he was staying at the Warwick Hotel and purchased issues of *The New York Times, Washington Post* and a couple of local weeklies. The proprietor, an East Indian man Abe had come to know by his Americanized name of Frank, was busy behind the counter talking rapidly on the telephone with someone about a loan.

"It is a loan for six months, only," they overheard Frank say. "The prospects for success are good. I checked them out myself. They are willing to pay any interest rate within reason. Well, okay then, thank you for your time and consideration."

Frank seemed downhearted when he put down the phone.

"What are you supposed to do?" Frank asked of no one in particular, shrugging his shoulders and splaying both hands.

"Having a problem, Frank?" Abe asked, putting money on the counter for his papers.

"Oh, hello, Abe," Frank answered. "I heard you'd come back. I'm only having some problem lining up a loan for my parents. They have green cards and will become citizens next year, but no one seems to want to lend them any money—at whatever rate."

"A business venture?" Abe asked.

"Yes," Frank replied. "Both my parents were teachers back in India, but now they are too old to find work here. They want to open a little bookshop here to give them something to do and to tide them over in their waning years. Investors aren't interested because of the number of big mega-bookstores in the area, but my parents don't want to compete with them. They want to sell old books, not just used, but old, do you understand?"

"You mean antiquarian books?" Abe asked.

"Yes, that's it exactly," Frank replied. "There's an abandoned space just three doors down from here, used to be a fix-it shop. It would do nicely."

"That would be Isaac Porr's old space," Abe said.

"Yes," Frank said. "Do you know Isaac?"

"I certainly do," he replied. "What does Isaac think of the idea?"

"He likes it, I think," Frank answered. "When I talked to him about it, he said he would let the space, free, for six months. That would give my parents a chance to see if they could make a go of it. If that worked out, he said he would sell at a very reasonable price."

"You know what, Frank?" Abe asked. "I may know someone who would be interested in backing such a venture. May I use your telephone?"

"Sure, sure," Frank replied. "If it's long-distance, use my cell phone here."

Carlson dialed a number and asked for Jack. When Jack came on the line, Abe said: "I've got an opportunity here that I think may be of interest to you, Jack. I'll put Frank on the line and you two can work out the details."

Carlson handed the telephone back to Frank and waved as he turned and went out the door.

"Is that the foundation you were telling me about?" Veronica asked when they were standing outside on the sidewalk.

"As a matter of fact it is," he answered. "Now, how about that ice cream?"

CHAPTER 10

▼

IMMIGRATION

Carlson and Steinmann took a leisurely walk around town in the warming afternoon sun. People would see them coming, arm-in-arm, deep in conversation and apparently oblivious to their surroundings. Individuals would wave or nod in passing, but the citizens of Hummelstown showed a quiet respect for their privacy and did not interrupt. When they arrived at a small park tucked away on a back street, they sat at a picnic table to peruse the newspapers.

"Tell me about immigration over the past few decades," Carlson said, flattening out his *Washington Post,* while handing her *The New York Times.* "I'm well versed in the repeated waves of immigrants from the late 1800s, up through the end of World War II and its aftermath. This area seems remarkable in its ability to absorb people from just about anywhere on the globe. I'm sure it has been harder with some groups than others, but all-in-all it did appear rather less raucous than it could have been."

"You may be giving us a little too much credit," Steinmann answered. "At times it has been rough, both on the immigrants and the locals themselves. Yet I see your point. One of the reasons may be that most groups followed where their countrymen had already led. Europeans found Europeans, without regard to religion. By that I mean that even large groups following the Jewish faith fit in right along with the Lutherans, Methodists, Catholics, what-have-you. And the much-quoted 'Protestant work ethic' we were taught in school I think is more accurately defined as the 'immigrant work ethic.' As for the other grand claims of

America being the 'great melting pot,' all I can say is that many groups don't melt very quickly."

"Most of the Indian tribes have a wry sense of humor on both those concepts," Abe commented.

"And with every right," Veronica added. "Now, under the auspices of the Catholic Church, many Vietnamese resettled in the Harrisburg area in the era of the so-called 'Boat People.' A large segment of these Vietnamese is Catholic, of course, but even the Buddhists were able to make the transition fairly easily because of the Vietnamese culture. The same is probably true for others from that area of the world, Cambodia and Laos, but they came in much smaller numbers."

"Then why the sudden interest in illegal aliens," he asked, "particularly the Hispanic population?"

"Just following the national trend, I suppose," she answered. "I know the people in the southwest have been dealing with this issue for a couple of hundred years, but we've come to a point in this part of the country that is a highly volatile mixture of events that have our citizens confused and fearful. As Doc said, ignorance can be our worst enemy at times. Play the terrorist card every chance you get, throw in the growing globalization of the marketplace where people see an increasing number of jobs going overseas, repeatedly press home the idea that whoever is not one-hundred percent with us is against us, foster a culture where individuals feel so inadequate to deal with any of these problems that some well-intentioned patriotic citizen thinks all he can do in his own small way is to post a sign in his carry-out window that all orders must be in English only, and what do you have but chaos?"

As they both pondered what had been said, Abe produced his pipe for a rare smoke, something he did when he wanted to think things over. Veronica liked the aroma of his tobacco blend. It reminded her of college days when her roommate would burn incense while studying late at night as an aid to concentration. She wondered if perhaps pipe smokers were like that, too.

"A penny for your thoughts," she said finally as he reached the bottom of the bowl and set the pipe aside to cool.

"I was just thinking of my own ignorance," he answered. "I know so little about Islam. Some of my new neighbors are Muslim. There is a relatively new mosque in Steelton, in what was once a Catholic church. There is your student whose grandmother is fearful of passing the Zembo Temple because what she sees as Arab symbolism used by the Shriners. Then I started to think about what Doc says about democracy and that change at the top has to begin with an effort from the bottom, at the community level. I can't help but wonder if we are successful in how we adapt to these new circumstances, that we might be able to spread it around to other communities and prevent the world from blowing up once again."

"You certainly don't have any small thoughts, do you?" she asked.

"Of course I do," he answered quietly. "It's the small thoughts that often lead to the key for resolution of the larger thoughts, if we can only follow the right path. Remember, that's what I do for a living. When people see a woman with a certain headscarf on the street, they think of the Middle East and Arab terrorists. But I read somewhere recently that something like twenty percent of Muslims are Arab. The country with the largest Muslim population is Indonesia. I also noticed on the web site for the Islamic Society of Greater Harrisburg that due to so-called 'cultural differences,' the Muslims from the Middle East have broken away from those from south Asia to form their own organization. I wonder what that's all about and where it may fit in to the bigger picture."

"You may have another advantage in your perspective," she said thoughtfully. "The Middle East developed out of a tribal heritage, with many of the tribal dynamics still in play. It may be quite a difference, of course, but you are very familiar with tribal structure, culture and mores."

"I hadn't really thought of that, Professor," he answered. "I like the way you think ahead and fill in the gaps. We're going to make quite a couple."

"Don't look now, Sport," she replied with a warm smile, "but we already are—even the community recognizes us as such."

They spend the next hour immersed in their respective newspapers with only an occasional comment on what they were reading.

"Here's one you'd be interested in, Abe," Veronica said. "Authorities have spotted a beaver building his home on the Bronx River in New York City. A congressman managed to get a fifteen million dollar project to clean up that river a few years ago. It had been a dumping ground for old cars and tires, too polluted for most wildlife. There hasn't been a beaver sighted there in over two hundred years. They've named this one Jose after the first name of the congressman who provided the funds. What do you think, are beavers going to take back their home ground?"

"I hardly think so," Abe answered. "Beavers need a lot of trees, preferably young ones and saplings, to establish a colony. There's too much concrete and asphalt there to sustain much. It's probably a young male that came down from up-river someplace doing what comes naturally—building a home to attract a female."

"He reminds me of someone I know," she chided. "Do beavers have a lot in common with humans?"

"I remind you, my dear Veronica," he replied, "that I had already attracted a certain female. I didn't have to build a home to impress her. Besides, I don't think she'd have fallen for that at all."

"I don't know about that," she said with mirth in her voice. "If you come bearing the right kind of gift on the first date, there's no telling what a girl might do."

"I know what one particular girl would have done," he countered. "Right now I'd be sitting at the ranch, counting cattle and horses and waiting to be discovered."

They continued to read in peace until Carlson put his paper down with a rustle.

"Here's one you're not going to like," he said. "It's an AP story datelined Alexandria, Egypt. A young twenty-two year old blogger, a former student at Egypt's Al-Azhar University with ties to a pro-democracy reform movement, is going to prison. So much for free speech on the Internet. A judge sentenced him to three years in prison for insulting Islam and the Prophet Muhammad and inciting sectarian strife. The judge added another year for insulting the President of Egypt. Apparently, the insult to the Prophet had to do with the young man saying that Muhammad was 'great' but that his teachings on warfare and other issues should be viewed as a product of their times, the Seventh Century. I would assume four years in an Egyptian prison for these crimes will not be a pleasant experience."

"That university is known as one of the most prominent religious centers in Sunni Islam," she said. "Many of the students who rebelled against that school call it 'the university of terrorism' and say it promotes extremism."

A single file of twelve children came ambling into the park, holding on to a string, with an adult woman at each end of the file. Abe and Veronica watched as the children dropped the string and produced small paper bags filled with breadcrumbs and seeds, which they scattered on the ground. One little boy tugged on the lead woman's skirt and whispered something into her ear as he pointed toward the picnic table. She nodded and told the boy to stay where he was.

Approaching the table, the woman was all smiles.

"Excuse, me, my name is Christa Moore and these little charges are the daycare," she said gesturing back to the group. "Little Mark wants to know if you might be the famous Uncle Abe we've all been hearing about."

"He is indeed," Veronica offered, warming to the opportunity to make something happen. "Would Mark like to meet him?"

"All the children would," Moore replied, turning back to the group. "Okay children, come gather around me here."

The bright-eyed group of five to eight year olds gathered on command and stood looking inquiringly at Abe. One little girl suddenly turned to Veronica.

"Are you Aunt Veronica?" she asked.

"I certainly am," she answered in mock surprise. "How did you know?"

"My sister says you are going to get married," she said seriously, "but you're not going to go live with the Indians. You're going to stay right here and Uncle Abe will just have to get a real job—not like that blow-hard brother-in-law up the street who just sits around all day."

"Your sister is smart," Veronica replied with a chuckle. "See, Abe, we're a real couple and you're just going to have to find yourself a real job."

"I promise to do so beginning tomorrow," Abe pledged with his hand over his heart. "I wouldn't want to be known around town as a blow-hard."

With that said, Carlson introduced himself and Veronica, shaking each child's hand and then the adults. He learned the children were on their daily outing to feed the birds that came to the park and that this was particularly important in the winter months because there was less food available. The children clamored for a story from Abe and he was at a loss to think of one.

"I know a good one he can tell you," Veronica prompted with a wink to Abe. "Make it up as you go along, Sport," she whispered out of the corner of her mouth. "Let's see if you're up to the challenge.

"Have him tell you about Jose, the Bronx Beaver," she said, turning to the children. "It's a story of hardship and great endeavor that pays off in the end with its just rewards."

Carlson started slowly with the coming of age of Little Jose leaving his loving family deep in the wilds of the mountains in search of his destiny. He took to the river as his instincts told him and was carried down by the currents. Along the way, he met his first humans, a group of boys and girls, just like the ones here, and they were kind—feeding him pieces of apples and bread and wishing him well. His long journey was fraught with many perils and with each triumph against adversity he grew more confident and able to take care of himself. The kindness he learned from the children he passed on to other creatures, like the time he allowed a family of turtles to ride on his broad tail as he ferried them across the raging river one-by-one to safety. As he neared the city, he learned to be careful around boats as they motored along, propellers often too close for comfort for a growing beaver. When he first encountered the Bronx River, from which he was to take his nickname, he was at first very scared of the concrete and tall buildings—taller than any tree he had ever encountered in the wilderness. He was at the point of despair when he rounded a bend and discovered just the right growth of trees on the bank to make his home. By the end of the story, he had built his home, found a wife and they had twelve little beavers, just like the day-care group. The beavers taught their little ones to be kind and polite to all they encountered, but to look out for boats with propellers.

It was a gleeful group of children who marched back to daycare that day, chatting and singing and making plans to form their own Jose, the Bronx Beaver Club.

"Wow," Veronica said as she watched the children retreat in such spirits, "you are an inspiration—just enough adventure for the boys, an equal amount of kindness and love for the girls. I nearly cried at the image of those turtles being ferried through the waves on the beaver tail. I'll bet if you had more time, you'd have had the beaver family going on a swimming vacation to Staten Island."

"No, too commercial," he replied. "I would have made it Liberty Island—much more patriotic, you know."

The rest of the afternoon was used to walk through neighborhoods, window shop, and watch young adults playing sports on the fields and courts around town. They had stopped for coffee and a piece of pie at Bill's Restaurant on the square, learning from an overheard conversation at the next table that things were looking up for business. Word was spreading up and down Main Street that a new business was opening next month in an empty building where Isaac Porr's fix-it shop used to be. It was going to be an antiquarian bookshop, not just a used bookstore, with real classic literature and professional texts. Frank at the newsstand was ecstatic. His parents were the new merchants coming to town. Several patrons of Bill's were already pledging to support the new enterprise, ordering any books they might want through the new store, all in support of the local economy. The news brought a quiet smile to the faces of Abe and Veronica as they finished their pie and left a twenty-percent tip.

By the time they arrived back at Doc's house the sun was fading and the temperature dropping quickly. They found Doc and Aunt Mattie in the library. Doc was just hanging up the telephone.

"I don't think we can let you two go out alone together again any too soon," Doc said in greeting. "We seem to have created an uncontrollable duo here, Mattie. What do you think we should do with them?"

"Leave them to their own devices," Aunt Mattie replied. "They're doing a lot of good from where I sit."

"Okay, Doc," Veronica ventured. "Whatever our transgressions, we'll plead and throw ourselves on the mercy of the court."

"The only charge that can be brought as far as I'm concerned," Doc said with a wide smile, "is that of disturbing the peace and tranquility of this little town. My telephone has been ringing off the hook this afternoon and people keep dropping by. It seems that a couple, who shall remain nameless, has been regaling our young people with a saga of mythical proportions, one that grows in the telling from young imaginations embellishing the original story."

"Does this saga have a protagonist?" Abe asked.

"Well, I should say so," Doc answered. "In fact it has many champions. There's the hero of the tale, a coming of age beaver. Then there are a number of children who have shown him kindness and good will, which the beaver passed on to his own children. It's a cycle, you see. When you receive a kindness, you have a duty to pass it on to others. It also seems that if you are mannerly and polite, plus modest in your efforts, you get extra points."

"It's starting to jostle my memory," Abe admitted. "How about you, Veronica?"

"It's becoming more familiar by the moment," Veronica replied.

"The calls I have been getting are for a copy of the book that contains the story," Doc continued. "No book dealers seem to be able to trace the title. Children all over town want to start a club based on the lessons of the tale—passing on kindness."

"I admit to all," Abe said seriously. "I tell you what, Doc, don't you think it would be better if the children got together with their older brothers and sisters to write out the tale to their specifications? It would be a great exercise, like writing their own constitution. I'll pay to have it illustrated and published. The club can sell copies through the new bookstore we hear is opening up on Main Street next month."

"I think that's a great idea," Veronica agreed. "Just think of all the lessons that can be learned through such a hands-on process. Even the youngest would learn new lessons for life."

"They've already learned one new lesson," Doc replied. "I'm so proud of you two. You have started something that the children in town will carry with them and pass on to innumerable others during their lives. They've already learned something from their first major decision. Since the champion's name is Jose, the Bronx Beaver, it has been decided that they will ask the Hernandez boy, Ricardo, to be the first president of their club. They think Jose may be a cousin or some relation to Ricardo. They know how many cousins they have in their own extended families and think Jose is probably a Spanish name."

CHAPTER 11

▼

DAN BUTLER

Abe Carlson sat at the kitchen table reading *The New York Times* and drinking his second cup of coffee. It was yesterday's edition of the newspaper, but he hadn't had a chance to read it. Aunt Mattie, standing at the counter preparing a fruit medley heard a low sigh and turned to see Carlson staring out the window at darkening clouds.

"Father does that some times," Aunt Mattie said aloud. "I usually tell him that perhaps he's had enough news for the day and suggest he pick up a good book instead."

"I guess I just get exasperated sometimes at the stupidity of my fellow man," Carlson said quietly.

He explained to Aunt Mattie that he had just read an editorial under the headline: "Game With No Winner." The editors were waxing nostalgic for practices such as streaking and sitting on flagpoles of the old college days rather than a trend sweeping campuses which had finally made it to the grounds of New York University. An intern for the College Republican National Committee decided it would be a good idea to come up with some new recruitment gimmicks, which led to her being fired—but not before a couple of new games she had invented had taken hold and spread to other campuses via the Young Americans for Freedom and the Young Republicans, considered right-wing politically. One game, "Catch an Illegal Immigrant," was an updated version of hide-and-seek played by children all over the country. One player poses as the immigrant, at times dressed in ethnic garb, and the other players try to find him. "There's a prize, usually $200 or less," the editors say, "but enough to celebrate the cheap exploitation of a fellow man." Another game is called "Fun With Guns," which invites young Republicans to fire BB guns or paint balls at cardboard cutouts of Democratic leaders. Republican Party leaders had done little or nothing to stem these practices and the school administrators are tepid, striving to walk that thin line between free speech and offensive behavior.

"College students may be considered more educated," Aunt Mattie observed, "but that doesn't mean that a certain ignorance to the point of stupidity is impossible. All that youthful energy is simply wasted with nonsense like that. It is demeaning to the school and they are demeaning themselves personally. They just aren't bright enough to see their own weakness."

"Perhaps the next generation will be different," Doc said as he walked into the kitchen and poured a cup of coffee. "I couldn't help but overhear your conversation. If you start them young enough, with programs like Abe's Jose the Bronx Beaver Club, they may be more open minded by the time they get to college."

"It looks like we have some ugly weather coming in," Aunt Mattie said to change the subject. "If you're going out today, Father, please dress accordingly. The temperatures are not expected to climb out of the mid-thirties, but with the wind and the rain we might be in for some discomfort."

"I don't have any plans of going out today," Doc answered. "It's not as if I'm called upon for medical emergencies these days. I admit that I do miss that sometimes, though. It gives one a sense of being needed."

When the telephone rang, Aunt Mattie answered and had a brief, mostly one-sided conversation dominated by the caller. "Okay, Cissy, I'll tell him," she said at last. "Keep us informed and if you need anything you know where to call."

"Cissy Butler?" Doc asked as she placed the phone back on the receiver.

"Yes," Aunt Mattie replied. "Dan's missing. He went out to do his usual chores this morning and didn't come back for breakfast. Frank went to fetch him, but he wasn't anywhere around the barns, so Frank's canvassing the rest of the property. Frank wanted you to know."

"Frank and Cissy Butler have a farm near here," Doc said to Abe by way of explanation. "It is mostly dairy and corn, with a few head of beef and a couple of pigs. They also took in an old swayback horse that someone was abusing, but I don't know if they still have it. Their son, Dan, an only child, is a bit of a sad medical case."

As Doc described the case, Dan Butler was a fifty-five year old male, never married, who worked the family farm all his life. He was a star athlete in high school who turned down several scholarships to stay on the farm. It was all he ever wanted to do in life—carry on the family tradition. And he was good at farming. Five years ago, his parents started noticing some behavioral changes that caused them concern and came to ask Doc to have a talk with Dan.

"It started with the beard," Aunt Mattie said. "Cissy began to notice that Dan had quit shaving altogether, not just every few days or so. It was in mid-June and he was always scratching his whiskered jaw like it was irritating him. After a few weeks of that, she noticed Dan wouldn't look at himself when he passed the hall mirror. When she asked about it, Dan wasn't forthcoming. He wasn't sullen or anything of that order. He simply shrugged off the question."

"Dan started to forget what day of the week it was," Doc continued. "Work on a farm, particularly a dairy farm, is pretty routine. The same chores seven days a week, fifty-two weeks out of the year. It's easy to loose track of the days. But then he began to forget other things, such as recent events and when this happened over a span of years, they brought him to see me."

Although not technically in the position of a patient-physician relationship, Doc did not feel it appropriate to reveal the content of his discussions with Dan Butler. In several sessions of an hour or more conducted over a two-week period, Dan slowly unraveled a string of memories that led to a preliminary diagnosis. Simply put, Dan awoke one morning and began to shave when he suddenly did not recognize the face staring back at him from the mirror. He was startled at first, but not fearful. When it appeared again on the second morning, he decided to give up shaving for a while to see how things progressed. Passing by the mirror in the hall one day, he discovered the same stranger peering back at him, so he gave up on mirrors altogether. Over time he began to forget other things and have no recollection of many past events he thought he should know; his parents would have to remind him of past holidays and passing relatives. It seemed to make them happy, so Dan just kept allowing them to remind him of such times. He eventually found himself in his mind as he was as a senior in high school. There the memory loss stopped. He could recall his childhood up to that point very vividly, but other than that, he was stuck in neutral. His work on the farm had not diminished at all, but he did have to be reminded how to use machinery improvements over the past few decades. Thankfully, the Butlers had kept their old rotary telephones so that Dan was not mystified about how to use touchtone dialing. He seemed to have lost the ability to learn new things.

"The most important aspect of his digression," Doc said, "was the relatively painless process. Dan did not suffer all the pangs of regret we would associate with our own frustration at seeing this occur. Because he was unafraid and accepting so long as his daily routine continued, he was satisfied to retreat into a bygone world where he felt comfortable and capable."

"Is he suffering from Alzheimer's disease?" Abe asked. "I usually associate that with older people."

"That's a common misconception," Doc answered. "Alzheimer's can strike at any age and that could certainly be the case here, but I don't yet think so. Alzheimer's can be mild at first, but since it is a degenerative condition of the central nervous system, it can progress rather rapidly. Dan has been stable for the past five years. I rather think his condition is more along the lines of early senility with some type of dementia. He doesn't seem to pose a threat to others or himself and is productive. The Butlers did have to take away his driver's license, of course, but they now fear what might happen to him after their own passing. What if some social worker decided he couldn't survive on his own and forced him into some kind of home, with the sale of the farm to pay for the care?"

"Do you think he could be suffering some sort of blackout and just wandered off?" Aunt Mattie asked. "Could it be that sudden?"

"Anything's possible, I suppose," Doc answered. "There is little that modern medicine knows about cases like this, no matter how many physicians like you to think otherwise. We don't have all the answers in a lot of other instances either. But I wouldn't think so here. Dan has been steady on a certain plane and relatively free of stress, I would think. To me, a sudden blackout is a rather small probability."

All three were left to their own thoughts for a few minutes as they refilled coffee cups and sampled Aunt Mattie's fruit medley.

"I have a question," Abe said at last. "I'm no medical expert by a long shot, but I have had some experience in observing human and animal behavior. There is usually some reason for and logic to changes in normal patterns. What if just the opposite of a blackout occurred?"

"What are you getting at?" Aunt Mattie asked.

"A momentary stimulus of some sort," Abe answered, "something that could prick an idea and strike a certain emotion or urge immediate response."

"That's an interesting approach," Doc admitted. "You'd have made a promising clinician, Abe. Approach the problem from all angles and you soon find opposing approaches will result in opposite results."

When the phone rang this time, it was Doc who picked up the receiver.

"Doc, this is Cissy," the voice came over the line so loudly that Doc held the receiver a few inches from his ear so the others could listen. "Frank says to tell you he's checked the entire property, favorite fishing holes, picnic glades and the like, and can't find hide nor hair of him. On the way back in he checked the far storage shed and found the farm truck is gone. Poor Dan probably doesn't remember we took his license and that old truck is for farm use only, no plates and dangerous out on the road. We've notified the authorities and the neighbors to be on the lookout. He should be easy to spot. Frank's going out now to look for himself."

"While I have you on the line, Cissy," Doc asked in his most calming bedside manner, "any excitement out your way lately?"

"I don't know what that's got to do with the price of milk at a time like this," Cissy answered even more loudly. "Let me think. No new calves that I've heard of, but Patsy Swartz did have her third boy—only that was two months ago. Things are pretty quiet here as usual."

"What about exciting gossip?" Doc pressed the question.

"Who's got time for gossip on a working farm? And why would you think I'd be telling tales out of school?" Cissy countered.

"Of course I wouldn't think of you spreading tales," Doc answered soothingly. "But one does hear things."

"Well, what comes to mind is that the Leonard girl came home for Christmas and managed to get engaged to Burt Small, the John Deere dealership boy over in Cornwall. Some say he's quite a catch, but I don't even know the boy."

"From what I hear, he's a decent sort," Doc chatted. "Your friend Miriam Geiger told me he sings in the choir at her church and leads the children's Bible Study."

"Must be okay, then," Cissy said and paused. "Oh, one other thing, Doc. You remember Grace Lawson from next door? That's her maiden name. She was Grace Schneider for some years, but she's now a widow and has taken back her maiden name."

"How could I forget Grace?" Doc answered. "I delivered her way back when. I did hear that the farm has been empty since her parents passed a few years ago."

"Well, the farm is officially occupied since yesterday. Grace has returned and will make it a working farm again. Her husband left her quite well off and she wants to come back to the land."

"Does Dan know about that?" Doc asked with excitement rising in his voice. "I seem to recall that Dan and Grace were some item back in their high school days."

"That was a long time ago, Doc," Cissy answered. "We told Dan when she called last night, but it didn't seem to register. And he has the attention span of about a minute. Forgets that fast—in one ear and out the other, God bless him."

"Cissy, if Frank hasn't gone yet, tell him to check Dan's old favorite spots when he was in high school," Doc commanded. "Just do it and I'll explain later."

"I'll catch him in the yard," Cissy nearly yelled as she slammed down the phone.

"Well, Abe, you were right," Doc said. "We have your stimulus, I believe."

"Does Cissy always shout like that over the phone?" Abe asked.

"Her parents went deaf in their declining years," Aunt Mattie explained. "She got into the habit of talking loudly. Since Father is much older than her parents, she thinks he must be going at least a little deaf by now himself. In fact, I think Cissy may be loosing some hearing capacity herself, but doesn't want to admit it."

The telephone rang once again.

"This is Doc Straussburger's residence," Doc answered rather formally.

"Doc, Cissy again," the voice boomed through the receiver. "Something extraordinary just happened. Grace Lawson just dropped in for a social call. She was still in her housecoat in the kitchen early this morning when Dan knocked on her door and welcomed her home. She didn't recognize him at first with all that beard, but when he flashed that big smile, she knew who he was."

"Get that word to Frank," Doc reacted to the news. "He'll know what to do with it. And keep us abreast of developments."

The phone rang regularly throughout the morning as town people called with questions or information, under the correct impression that, as usual, Doc's house would become communications central during any community crisis. A powerful thunderstorm was strafing the countryside, impeding visibility and making movement more difficult.

Veronica Steinmann arrived for lunch, dripping wet, with an update on how things were progressing with Abe's new home. She reported that Ruby had gotten bookshelves assembled just in time for the arrival of two crates of books Abe had forwarded, but was concerned that two entire bookcases would be empty.

"I suggested we wait until next month," Veronica said. "I understand there will be a new antiquarian bookshop opening on Main Street and you'd probably want to give them some business, Abe."

"Good idea," Abe said. "I always like to help new businesses get established."

"How's the search for Dan going?" Veronica asked.

"He's covering a lot of territory in a rather small area pretty quickly," Doc answered. "There have been plenty of sightings, but often conflicting and they nearly caught up to him at least once."

"The closest they've gotten yet was at the suggestion of Doc," Abe said. "He reckoned that each local generation doesn't really change drastically in its habits, particularly among the young and spirited. With limited choices, they tend to frequent the same spots year after year. Armed with his vast knowledge on the subject, he suggested three popular locations for amorous encounters."

"I'm merely a good listener when my patients tell me something," Doc pointed out.

"Schuler's barn I think was the location mentioned," Abe continued with a grin. "They missed him by minutes. The fresh tire tracks weren't quite filled with water. They reckoned it was Dan because of the baldness of the treads."

The phone rang again and Doc engaged in a muffled conversation with the sheriff that lasted several minutes. "I'll get right on it," he said ending the conversation.

Doc looked to Abe. "We require your assistance yet once again, Abe," Doc said. "They found the truck along Route 322 near the high school and Dan was reported to be seen nearby, walking down the road toward Indian Echo Caverns."

"If he's just getting out of the rain, that shouldn't be a problem," Veronica said. "I've been there many times since I was a small girl and it is nearly impossible to get lost in there."

"Under normal circumstances, you'd be right," Doc said. "However, Jerry Prince called this afternoon. Cave-ins last night have closed the place. It can't be fully secured."

CHAPTER 12

▼

THE CAVERNS

The caverns had been a curiosity to the settlers since they began pushing into William Penn's Woods in the early 1700s. Originally designated as being part of the Cave Farm on a 1754 deed, visitors mentioned details of their findings in correspondence from the latter part of that century and throughout the next. Unheeding the damage they were inflicting, many people chipped off stalactites and stalagmites to have as souvenirs of their visit. The smoky torches used in their explorations blackened the interior of the caverns to an appreciable degree. In the 1880s the press designated the site as Echo Cave. The first commercial development into a tourist attraction began with much fanfare when the Indian Echo Caverns were opened in 1929, but the early success faltered during the ensuing depression and its prospects did not brighten until a new owner bought the property in 1942. The new owner made much-needed improvements and added features over the years and managed to survive the vagaries of the market to keep his venture profitable and a local institution.

Carlson and Steinmann rushed to his Jeep and drove as fast as the conditions allowed, heavy raindrops splattering on the flat windshield with the short, light wipers having a hard time keeping up. Winds buffeted the vehicle's flat side and rattled its canvas top. It was only about a mile to the caverns, but the headlights penetrated a mere ten feet into the gloom. The ambient daylight did help, but was of little consequence.

"As you know, this entire area sits on honeycombed limestone," Steinmann began as she related what information she knew, "the caverns are just the most visible proof of that. Situated on the east bank of the Swatara Creek, they have been flooded on occasion, most notably in 1972 as Hurricane Agnes passed through. You may remember seeing the barns and fenced fields from the main road. That is the working portion of the farm for livestock and hay operations."

"You said it was nearly impossible to get lost in there," he said. "Why is that?"

"It's essentially no more than four so-called 'rooms,' connected by corridor-like walkways. If you get separated from a tour, you can meander around and still be walking in a circle, back to the entrance."

"And this report of cave-ins?" he asked.

"That may be a relative term," she replied, "at times a bit of debris may fall onto the floor, or a chunk become dislodged and become an impediment. There are some holes in the ceiling leading to small cavities and at times these holes may widen from the constant drip of moisture that forms the stalactites and stalagmites. I've been told that such occurrences are more of a nuisance than a danger."

"What do you think would be the worst case?" he asked.

"I'm afraid it could be catastrophic," she answered sadly. "If a large portion of the ceiling were to give way, perhaps caused from a sinkhole from above, that would be bad. This rain would only make things worse. The alternative, a wall or walls opening up to reveal new, undiscovered caverns wouldn't be much better. I don't even want to think of the possibilities if a portion of the floor gave way. Obviously the lighting system has failed and anyone in there stumbling around in the dark could just step off into oblivion."

Carlson turned into the long drive leading to the gift shop and carefully made his way ahead at a slightly higher speed. He came to a screeching halt only to see a huge longhorn steer staring at him from five feet away.

"Kind of cute, don't you think, Sport?" Veronica asked lightly, grasping at the chance to break the tension. "On a visit to Texas about fifteen years ago, the owner of the caverns liked the look of these animals and had a half-dozen shipped to the farm. They are an attraction here in the east."

"I've seen longhorn before," Carlson said as the steer turned and walked off into the rain, "but never that big. What is he feeding these animals?"

"Only the best Pennsylvania hay," she replied. "Like Wonder Bread, it helps build strong bodies twelve ways."

Carlson drove the last yards to the gift shop carefully and pulled in alongside the sheriff's car.

Inside the gift shop was expansive, chock full of any souvenir imaginable, from plastic bow and arrow sets and appliqué "authentic" Indian tattoos for the children, to expensive books, tapes, glassware and other products for the adults. Three men were bent over the long counter studying a layout of the caverns. Sheriff Bert Tate looked up and greeted the two newcomers.

"Hello, Abe," the sheriff said. "Good to see you again. By the way, belated congratulations on your engagement. The Professor is one of the best you're apt to find, second only to my Thelma, so consider yourself a lucky man, indeed."

"Thank you, Sheriff," Abe responded. "I'm very aware of how lucky I am. How do things look?"

"Pretty bad and getting worse," the sheriff answered and nodded to a second man. "Jeff here had just closed up for the evening yesterday when he heard a rumbling sound coming from the entrance to the caverns. He went to investigate and found part of the gating had collapsed and large stones partially blocking the entry. He boarded up as well as he could and locked the entries to the property. Then he reported to the owner, who is in Florida at the moment, and in turn he called us. Contractors and inspectors are to be here tomorrow to assess the damage and see what can be done."

"What about Dan Butler?" Veronica asked.

"I was straightening inventory a couple of hours ago," the man named Jeff replied. "I saw a man fitting his description heading toward the main entrance to the caverns. The front gate out by the road was locked, but he was on foot. He didn't even stop here to buy a ticket. Anyway, it was raining pretty heavily and I went out to stop him, but he had slipped into the caverns through an opening on the right side. I heard some noises that made me think there was a new slide of some kind going on, so I erred on the side of safety and came back to call the sheriff."

"I've got two deputies at the entrance now," the sheriff said. "Half a dozen volunteers are carefully probing the grounds over the caverns and within fifty yards to see if anything has fallen through. This weather certainly isn't making things any easier. We've had at least two more episodes of deep rumblings coming out of the caverns. I can't send anyone in there under these circumstances. The electricity was cut with the first slide, so it's pitch black in there. We'll have to wait until the situation stabilizes. That's about all we can do. In case some opportunity opens up suddenly, I thought your expertise might advise us how to proceed."

"There's fresh coffee and donuts in the back," Jeff said. "Help yourselves."

The pair accepted the offer and went into the back, which proved to be the business offices and partial storage area. They settled in on one side of a desk with coffee and donut in hand to think things through. Abe could tell that Veronica had something to say, but was keeping it to herself.

"Okay, my love," he finally said, "let's not hold things back from one another. What's on your mind?"

"Concern," she began, hesitantly, but honestly. "Neither one of us could stand a marriage where things were 'allowed' or 'not allowed' by one or the other. I hope to heaven that I never turn into one of those wives who blurt out that they won't allow their husbands to do something. And I expect the same in return."

"I'm your man on that score," he agreed lightly. "And I'll respect any choices you make, whether I happen to agree with them or not. As far as I'm humanly capable, there will also be no judgment in this marriage. Things just are as they are."

"I also know we both don't want to change each other," she continued. "All that leads to in a few years down the road is that one decides that 'this isn't the person I fell in love with and married.' That's when the lawyers start being consulted."

"I'm happy to be reminded of that," he replied with a smile. "If that were to occur, I'm afraid my lawyers would out-lawyer yours and there would be such hard feelings."

"Okay, Sport," she answered. "I know you're just trying to make this easier on me by injecting levity, so I'll simply express my concern. Unless you really feel you need to, I would prefer you not squeeze through that front entrance under the current circumstances."

"You think I'm crazy?" he asked with a comical gasp of incredulity. "Of course I won't—at least I don't think I will. Or perhaps it's a possibility with a very small probability."

"You'd make a poor politician, Abe Carlson," she said. "You don't lie well and are terrible at trying to skirt the issue. So, give me a straight answer."

"The straight answer," he said in suddenly sobering tones, "is that I don't really know."

She had gotten his honest answer, knew it was pure truth and could say nothing in response. Abe stood up and paced the room to think. He picked up a small gray pamphlet from a stack on a side table. The title read: "Life of Amos Wilson, the 'PENNSYLVANIA HERMIT' Who Lived in a Cave near Harrisburg, Pa., for Nineteen Years."

"What's this all about?" he asked, showing the pamphlet to Veronica.

"It's one of the legends connected with the caverns," she replied, "and a pretty weak one, if you ask me. I never gave it much credence. It's a fanciful morality tale that reads like a 'Perils of Pauline' melodrama. Virtuous, innocent young girl falls in with a cad, surrenders her most precious gift to promises of marriage. The cad takes off because he's already married. Girl gives birth and hides infant in the woods to cover her shame. Strangers find infant, girl is tried and sentenced to be hanged. Even more virtuous older brother takes up her cause and finally through an impassioned plea is granted a pardon from the Governor. Brother races back but is delayed by swollen rivers and only arrives to see her hanging from the gallows. Girl leaves long confessional letter to warn other girls not to tempt her fate. Brother hides out from the world in the caverns, with little outside contact, except, of course the writer of the story, and dies leaving a manuscript of his own praising the goodness of God's mercy, our only true anchor in times of travail. All this was supposed to have taken place around 1800 or so. Mothers of the Elizabethan Age lapped it up and made it required reading for all their young daughters, I suppose."

"It could happen, I guess," Abe said as Veronica merely rolled her eyes in response. "The point is did someone really live in the cave for nineteen years?"

"Jeff," he called after the pair walked back to the main room, "any substance to this Amos Wilson tale?"

"I couldn't honestly say," Jeff replied. "The legend came with the ownership papers."

"I saw in another pamphlet that it was a group of successful businessmen who opened this place to the public in 1929. Surely they had some survey documents and schematics somewhere. Do you know if there are any side elevations?"

"Let me check the old safe," Jeff answered as he scurried off.

"What are you thinking, Abe?" the sheriff asked.

"I was just thinking about someone living in a cave the size of the caverns," Abe answered. "What improvements might he make for his own comfort and survivability?"

"We've received a report from the volunteers," the sheriff said. "The ground on the topside looks clear—no sinkholes. So maybe the ceiling is sound."

Jeff returned with a fat roll of blueprints that he put on the counter in front of Abe, who rolled them out and started to flip through the pages, stopping at a clear horizontal elevation of the caverns dated 1928. He ran his finger across the elevation slowly and carefully until he stopped at a smudged vertical line with a footnote number at the top. He bent to read the small-print footnotes at the bottom of the page, apparently made by the on-site engineer.

"I think we have an in," he announced calmly. "Someone, whether Amos Wilson or not, dug an air shaft for better ventilation. During the readiness phase of the 1929 opening, the engineer capped the shaft because too much rain was coming in that way. If we can find that cap, maybe I can drop down and take a gander. I've got a hundred-foot braided nylon rope in the Jeep and this shaft looks to be only about sixty feet."

Abe looked at Veronica and smiled. She smiled back and nodded her approval.

"Another thing," Abe said. "Jeff, is that your blue Chevy pickup out front with the electric cable winch on the front? I noticed it on the way in."

"It's a company vehicle," Jeff answered. "We use it to winch out fallen timber around the farm and pulling the tourists out of ditches when necessary."

"How about seeing how close you can get that to the shaft head?" Abe asked. "It could make things much easier."

"You bet," Jeff replied as he ran to the truck and turned the key.

"Thanks for that," the sheriff said. "That will go a long way in the eyes of the owner when he finds out his employee and his equipment had a big part in this."

"Purely self-interest," Abe answered with a wink. "I'm getting too old to be climbing ropes like I used to."

As the rain began to abate, the other preparations went quickly. Abe grabbed an emergency pack out of the back of his Jeep, pulled a canvas saddle harness from under a seat, lifted a rolled nylon rope to his shoulder and cinched leather gloves at his wrists. The cap was already removed from the shaft when he arrived. Within minutes he was in his harness, attached to the winch and being lowered into the four-foot wide shaft.

As soon as he felt the open cavern air hit his face, Carlson switched on a powerful flashlight to find he was still twenty feet from a broad ledge beneath. When he reached the ledge, the slack in the rope was the signal for the winch to stop. The beam made a slow survey of his surroundings. There were some signs of damage, but this particular chamber appeared to have little. He stepped out of his harness, got his bearings and started his search. After a half-hour of navigating around boulders and pieces of broken stalactites scattered among the upright stalagmites, he found Dan sitting in a niche in the wall, his knees bent toward his chest, arms crossing his knees and his head on his arms. His slow breathing told the tracker that Butler was asleep.

Placing the flashlight on a rock so both men would be illuminated and the awakening man would not be alarmed, Abe gently shook his arm until he raised his head.

"Hello, Dan," he began quietly. "I'm Abe Carlson and I've come to take you home."

"Did you know Grace is back?" Dan asked immediately.

"So I heard," Abe answered. "What are you doing here in the first place?"

"Just thinking," Dan replied, "thinking real hard. I've been having snapshots of memories I didn't know I had. I'm trying to figure out how things fit together."

"Are you having any luck?" Abe asked.

"Some I think, Abe," he answered. "That's what you said your name was, Abe, right? I didn't used to remember things like that."

"Abe it is, Dan," he replied. "Your memory is correct. What else have you remembered?"

"It all started when I was about my morning chores," Dan explained. "I thought I remembered my mom saying the night before that Grace was home. We were sweethearts in school, you know. I went over to her house to check and, sure enough, there was Grace, looking a lot older, of course, but I'd know her anywhere. Then I just wanted to see some places that were important to me. When I got near the high school, I ran out of gas. Than I remembered I didn't have a driver's license anymore. It was raining pretty hard and I spotted the Indian Echo Caverns sign and remembered what a great place it was to sit and think like I used to do. I also wanted to get out of the rain."

Dan fell silent for a few moments.

"You know what, Abe?" he asked at last, putting his hand to his chin and scratching his beard, "I'm beginning to think that that man in the mirror was no stranger. I think I'm that man. I just forgot. I also think I need a shave."

"Well, come with me then, Dan," Abe said taking his arm and lifting him upright, "Let's see what we can do about getting you that shave."

CHAPTER 13

▼

INTOLERANCE

Abe Carlson stood under the hottest shower he could tolerate for over fifteen minutes, turning slowly and massaging his aching muscles all over his body. Maybe he was getting too old for this kind of rigor, he thought. The cable winch had been a blessing, but he still felt like he had been rolled down a hill in a barrel. After he dried himself, he applied a heat salve Aunt Mattie had brought from Doc's medical offices. By the time he was dressed and clean-shaven, he felt almost normal again. Perhaps he wasn't getting as old as he thought, but he marked the experience as nature's way of telling him not to push so hard. A heavy gust of wind rattled the windows in his bedroom and splattered rain hard against the panes. He knew it was that last gasp of a dying storm and that the night would bring clearing skies.

"How's Dan?" he asked Aunt Mattie, whom he met at the bottom of the stairway.

"He's in good shape," she answered. "Father gave him a thorough check-up, persuaded him to shower and we found some dry clothes that fit fairly well. Cissy and Frank came to take him home, but he wanted to stay until he could thank you again for finding him. That's a sign that his short-term memory may be coming back. His parents persuaded him that he could take care of that later and offered to help him shave once he returned home. They told him he had to look his best because Grace Lawson was coming for dinner. That brought a big smile to his face and he asked me to thank you for him. He bolted out of the door so fast he almost toppled his mother."

"He already thanked me," Abe said, "and that was plenty. What else do you expect when a neighbor is in trouble? You know what I'd really like now, Aunt Mattie? How about a few cups of your great coffee and permission to raid the larder? I'm suddenly hungry enough to eat a half-a-side of that longhorn I met this afternoon."

"You are a guest in this house, Mr. Carlson," she answered. "You don't need to ask permission to raid the larder. This is Pennsylvania, where we would be offended if you didn't. All we ask is that when you leave, you don't take the linens and silverware with you."

"I believe my own linens and silverware are on order, Ms. Mattie," he replied with a grin.

"Anyway, you won't have to," she countered. "In anticipation of your wishes, Veronica and Father are in the kitchen laying out a nice spread for you."

Carlson walked into the kitchen to find Doc arranging platters of food at the counter and Veronica at the stove, frying a thick steak. She had on an apron and her hair was pulled back, but a few stray strands had escaped and were dangling from one side. Abe had to smile at this homey domestic scene.

"We're rustling up some grub," Veronica said as she noticed his approach. "Doc doesn't have a grill, but assures me that pan-fried suits any hungry man."

"Doc's right as usual," Abe replied, bending over and giving her a peck on the back of the head and enjoying the clean scent of her hair. "I must say you smell great," he whispered in her ear.

"You smell pretty clean yourself, Sport," she replied. "I do love that hint of horse liniment you're wearing. It brings out your rugged masculinity, while revealing a certain vulnerability to aching muscles and joints. I do have one warning for the future, though. Don't expect to be seeing me do this over a campfire. This is tricky enough as it is and I dislike ruining a good piece of meat."

"Don't be concerned about that," he replied. "I've got campfire cooking covered. I'm hungry, Doc, but I trust you don't expect me to eat all that."

"You can eat as much as you like," Doc said. "Most of this is for the visitors I expected to be dropping in as soon as the storm eases. A few hardy souls braved the weather this afternoon and came by to hold a sort of vigil—I think that's the right word. When there's a disruption in the community, folks always gather here because we provide the headquarters for information. The majority of those drop-ins provide a dish or two because they know people will get hungry. Your

Masonic Brothers are looking out for you. Bud Hanover made a special trip to drop off that steak Veronica's trying her utmost not to ruin."

The next hour was spent at the kitchen table where they ate their fill, engaging in small talk about everything except the major news of the day. There promised to be numerous retellings of the tale throughout the evening and everyone wanted to give Abe a little breathing room before the onslaught. At the end of the meal, Abe and Veronica volunteered to do the dishes—a chance for them to have some quiet time to themselves as well as a desire to help.

"Thank you for figuring out a better approach today," she said quietly as she dried the dishes he was washing. "I thought the other way was going to be too risky."

"There's always some risk in a situation like that," he replied. "I always try to err on the side of caution, not make any rash moves. Minimizing the risks is always my first thought. And now that I've found you, that will be my second and third thoughts, too. I'm just honest enough to admit that I have a selfish streak. I want as many great years with you as God will allow. I want to be very careful not to do something foolish and shorten that span."

The storm had passed and the bright setting sun was hovering just above the horizon when a delegation of thirteen children, led by Ricardo Hernandez and escorted by Ricardo's parents, arrived on the front porch and rang the doorbell. Aunt Mattie led the solemn procession into the library where the others were gathered. The children formed a semi-circle in front of Abe and Veronica, the parents to the rear and Aunt Mattie to one side.

"Abe and Veronica, will you please rise?" Aunt Mattie announced in her best judicial tone of voice, with a wink to Doc to show she was in on this show. "The Jose, the Bronx Beaver Club, Number One wishes to make a formal presentation."

Abe and Veronica stood as Ricardo stepped forward with a cloth-covered object in his hands. "On behalf of my fellow club members," Ricardo began, "we wish to present this first official desk plaque award for all the kindnesses you have passed on to this community."

Two young girls stepped forward and unveiled the award. It had the walnut base of a desk nameplate with the club's motto across the front: "Due Unto Others." Mounted on the base was a depiction of a beaver's splayed tail, nearly black in color. Atop the tail sat a nicely painted box turtle with multi-colored blotches that made the shell appear quite realistic. On the other side were the words: "Uncle Abe and Aunt Veronica, We Salute You."

"You honor us with this gift," Abe replied, accepting the award and handing it to Veronica. "May we wish you every success with all your endeavors. Whatever the future holds, always remember that we are proud of each and every one of you. We thank you."

Ricardo turned around and led his group through three cheers of "Hip, Hip, Hurrah!"

The formalities ended, the children rushed to Abe and Veronica in a cacophony of voices telling them what part they had played, whether it was helping to choose the colors for the "multi-racial" theme on the turtle's shell or the selection of the "We Salute You" tribute. The cheer was Ricardo's idea. He had seen it in an old movie once and thought it added just the right touch. A few minutes of congratulations all around and the Hernandez couple corralled the children and took them home.

"That's quite an honor," Aunt Mattie said after the children had left. "Do you mind if I put this on the mantle for the evening? It will ensure the conversation never flags." Permission granted. The award was placed on the mantle. "Don't let this go to your heads. The first secret ballot taken by the club wasn't unanimous, you know. Six-year old Horace Weisner thought the first award should go to Santa because he passes on more gifts than anyone. He didn't like to think what next Christmas might be like if Santa took offense. It took the others some time to explain things and bring the effort back on course."

"That Horace has a quick mind," Abe commented. "I know I sure wouldn't want to offend Santa. You sure seem to know quite a bit about what that group is doing, Aunt Mattie."

"When they drafted me for my part this evening, I asked some questions," Aunt Mattie replied. "They have some very ambitious plans. Once the book is finalized and printed, they plan to give a certain number to children who cannot afford to buy it and sell the rest. The profits will be invested back into the organization for plaque awards—Ricardo's father owns a trophy shop and made yours up in his workshop—to be presented to people the children see passing on kindness to others. This will all be done very quietly and the hope is that once words gets around town, that everyone will want one and start passing on kindness more than ever. They may never know when a child might be watching them."

"And the children shall lead them," Veronica said rather wistfully.

"The best part is that the children will never know they're leading," Abe added.

"Perhaps more people will begin to see what I'm always saying," Doc said with a philosophical lilt, "change for the good nearly always starts at the bottom and works its way to the top."

A number of people did drop by throughout the evening to get a first-hand account of the afternoon's adventure, have something substantial to eat and to exchange pleasantries. Henry Cunningham and Cissy Spease were proud of Abe and Veronica's success and went to work as co-hosts, passing around trays of snacks and refilling glasses. They even went so far as to emulate their heroes by keeping a steady line of dishes washed and dried, just as they heard Abe and Veronica had done.

When the conversation turned to the Bronx Beaver Club and the children's efforts, it naturally led to the subject of acceptance and tolerance. Everyone agreed that these were two separate concepts and that the latter was being inter- preted far differently these days in a way that was a significant departure from its historical meaning and usage. The advocates for "English-only" education and instruction were seen by many as being basically intolerant, but since that word was rapidly changing in meaning, perhaps we should agree on the English words actually conveyed before making them mandatory for all.

"I've seen some very well-intentioned programs in the school system go south," Louise Thompson, an experienced schoolteacher, said. "As the programs evolve, unintended and unforeseen consequences can occur."

"Why Louise," Doc said playfully, "I didn't think you were allowed evolution of any sort in the schools these days."

"We won the Dover case, Doc," Louise replied. "The Neanderthals are back in their caves, never again to be allowed to evolve—at least until the next election cycle. What I'm talking about is the 'zero-tolerance' title we've placed on too many policies with common-sense safeguards. Most people agree with zero-toler- ance policies in our schools for drugs, weapons and even smoking—although the last has seen some resistance from the faculty. Most even support community efforts to keep convicted child molesters from living within a certain distance of our schools, although that's a community decision and not really the responsibil- ity of the schools. But, lately zero-tolerance is reaching into areas where we might be wiser not to go."

"Do I hear a lecture on political correctness coming?" Doc asked. "I know that is one of your favorite subjects, Louise."

"Then you heard me loud and clear, Doc," Louise answered. "Parents are demanding more and more that the schools handle behavioral problems that are better resolved in the home. One of the new politically correct causes is bullying.

I'm not talking the old-fashioned beating someone up in the schoolyard or fighting in general. We've always had policies to deal with that kind of problem, including suspension or even dismissal. The term has been expanded to include verbal bullying, although no one seems to be able to define that term."

"Are we getting to a certain case that occurred at a California middle school?" Doc asked.

"I realize you are not interrupting just to be rude," Louise said, "but to rile my indignation and make the story more colorful. That is the case."

She continued her tale with a case that occurred about five years ago, when a middle school girl, who happened to be Mormon, was teased in the hallway by a group of girls who asked if it were true she had ten mothers. The girl's retort was: 'That's so gay.' The poor girl was hauled off to the principal's office, reprimanded and an admonishment put in her school record. The school claimed it was only enforcing a zero-tolerance policy.

"The girl probably didn't even know what she had said," Louise continued. "The slang used by her age group of the time was a popular way of saying something was so stupid. Her parents have filed suit to have her record expunged and the school punished. Although their argument for the abridgment of free speech may not stand up in court, the school is certainly going to have a difficult time explaining why the original taunt about having ten mothers wasn't considered religious stereotyping at the same time and why the other girls received no punishment."

"Good going, Louise," Doc said. "You're really quite the advocate once you get your dander up. Does this mean you are considering early retirement?"

"Not on you life, buster," Louise replied with a laugh. "I'm hanging in there for the sake of the students. I may even be able to protect some of the idiots—pardon me, that's a pejorative term and, therefore, not allowed. Let me change that to 'the less enlightened people' whom I may be able to protect from themselves."

"I wouldn't be too sure about not being able to win on the free speech argument," Veronica volunteered. "Stranger things have been known to happen in court. Of course, a judgment in favor of the Mormon girl might not survive the appeals process, but you never know. The definition of free speech used to be much clearer."

"That's your field of expertise, Professor," Doc said. "What little bedevilment are you cooking up for your students in the next term? I hear you can pose some very thorny legal problems for our budding attorneys."

"Merely a simple problem," she replied with a glint of mischief in her eyes. "The classic citation made for the limitations on free speech is: 'You can't yell fire in a crowded theatre.' What I will pose to my class is to write a paper on the legal and social ramifications if someone were to yell 'crusaders' in the middle of a crowded fundamentalist Arab mosque. That should get their little gray cells working, don't you think?"

"Professor, did anyone ever point out to you that you can be cruelly instigative?" Doc asked. "Abe, have you seen this side of her before?"

"I don't think of her as cruel at all," Abe answered. "I do know that she has several Arab and non-Arab Muslim students in that class. I'd be quite interested in the results of their deliberations. It might tell us a lot about what the immediate future may hold for us in this country."

"Well said," Doc replied. "Well said. Come to think of it, I'd be interested in the results myself."

CHAPTER 14

▼

MOVING DAY

The morning broke bright and clear. Although cool and windy, with a slight frost noticeable on the ground, temperatures were still above normal for the season, a sign that the warming trend would continue. When Abe Carlson spotted an eagle sitting on a limb of a barren oak tree through his window, he knew this was a propitious day to move to his new home. He gathered his few belongings in a small duffle, had a cup of coffee with Doc and Aunt Mattie in the kitchen and thanked them for their hospitality. He tried to appear as if he were not in a rush, but his hosts understood he was anxious and did not impede his progress.

When he picked up Veronica Steinmann, she was radiant and as anxious as he.

"Just like a second Christmas, isn't it, Sport?" she said and gave him a warm kiss that lasted a full ten seconds.

"All the Christmas I'll ever need is sitting right here beside me," he replied after their lips parted.

"It's nice to see you still have your priorities straight," she said. "Now, let's go see how well the Steinmann ladies have fulfilled your expectations."

When they arrived, he stopped on the front porch and unzipped his duffle to retrieve a leather pouch. Opening the pouch, he took out a small handful of tobacco mixed with other herbs and sprinkled the ground around the doorway and the air at the four cardinal points. He then reached into his pocket and brought out a small piece of peridot and using his thumb, pushed it deep into the flowerbed to the right. During the entire process, he chanted lowly in some Indian dialect she did not understand.

"That's something I learned from the Sioux," he explained. "It's an offering to the Great Spirit to protect this lodge, provide a good wife and bring many horses."

"I think that last one isn't allowed by the covenants," she said thoughtfully, "but I know a good lawyer who is willing to represent you on that score. What about the peridot in the flowerbed?"

"That's Mojave," he answered. "It's not very specific. You can wish for whatever you want and have the stone symbolic of that wish."

"Do you have another one of those?" she asked. When he provided her with one, she used her thumb to push it deep into the flowerbed to the left of the door.

"And what did you wish for?" he asked.

"Oh, no you don't," she answered with a smile. "It's like wishing on a wishbone and getting the bigger half. If you tell, your wish won't come true."

She dug into her purse and presented him with a ring of six large keys.

"Have I got that many locks in this modest house?" he asked.

"The locks are all keyed to one key," she explained. "You merely have multiple copies. You know, if you wanted to give one to a neighbor for extra protection or to a special friend who may want to drop by."

He took one key off the ring, unlocked the door and handed it back to her. "For a special friend," he said.

The efforts of Veronica and Ruby surpassed any expectations one could have. The interior accomplished the look of a designer model, while still capturing the comfortable feel of a home made for living. As they toured the rooms, she pointed out specific pieces of furniture, where they had come from and the reason each was chosen. The pantry closet was filled with canned goods and utility items. The kitchen was fully appointed, the side-by-side refrigerator and freezer was stocked and a second freezer in the laundry room was full. Abe was surprised that the dressers in the master bedroom where full of neatly arranged clothes, from underwear and socks to sweaters and vests. In the walk-in closet, he found a wide array of shirts and pants, dress and casual, and several new suits.

"You can't keep a secret in this small town," Veronica explained. "We got your sizes from Maloney's Men's Shop where you bought some new clothes last July. He was only too happy to sell us anything we wanted. What he didn't carry, we easily picked up elsewhere. You'll notice that the only void you need to fill is footwear and headwear—we thought you might be a bit particular about your boots and hats."

"I'm a bit overwhelmed," he said. "You've thought of everything."

"And we left the best part for last," she replied. "Believe it or not, we couldn't seem to spend the entire budget. Mother has a hefty amount of Pennsylvania thriftiness and refuses to pay too much. The caterers for tonight's open house have already been paid, including a nice tip and you still have a nice tidy refund coming."

"Why don't you take that refund and spread it around anonymously to the various church programs to feed the hungry," he said. "You'll need the practice if you're going to keep up with our other contributions."

When they came to his new office in the atrium, he sat at his desk and looked through the drawers. It too was well stocked with pens, pencils, pads and file folders—everything one would expect to find.

"I don't know," he said sorting through the last drawer, "something still isn't right. I get this nagging feeling that we're missing something important here."

"If you mean the remote control," she said, "it's in the clip on the right side of the television."

"No, it's not the remote," he replied, pondering a moment and swiveling in his chair toward her. "You're the lawyer. Do you think the courthouse is open today?"

"It certainly is," she beamed. "And I have the private number of a certain judge. She's a popular marrying jurist—keeps things short, sweet and legal."

"What are we waiting for?" he asked.

At the stroke of two o'clock in the afternoon, Mr. and Mrs. Abraham Carlson emerged from the courthouse as the newest married couple in town. They would hold that title for a total of thirty minutes, when the next such couple would emerge. They walked to the Jeep arm-in-arm.

"You know, darling," she said looking at the sun glancing off her new gold band, "the Mojave are right about the powers of wishing on peridot. I can tell you now that my wish has been granted."

"Well, you know, my love," he answered looking at his own gold band, "my wish of this morning has also been granted."

Veronica's cell phone rang. "Hello," she answered in a cheery voice.

"Congratulations," her mother said. "I was hoping you two were going to come to your senses soon."

"Mother," Veronica answered loudly, "can't I get away with anything without you finding out? How did you know so quickly?"

"It's no big secret, my dear," Ruby replied. "You're not the only one who knows people at the courthouse, you know. My friend Marge from the archive section happened to be passing through the office when you were getting your marriage license. So, of course, she called me immediately. She thought I needed to know."

"That Marge is such a gossip," Veronica said with a lilt in her voice.

"Daughter, that's not gossip," Ruby replied with the same lilt to her tone. "Marge is in the archive section, remember. She was merely passing along information, in an official capacity, of course. So, how is that new son-in-law of mine?"

"Well, Mother," she answered. "He was just telling me how you have been hounding him for days to take me off your hands. Something about the burden being too much on an aging lady."

"Oh, Veronica," Ruby said. "I know Abe never would say any such thing. As a matter of fact, I would go so far as to bet that he admires our new relationship so much that he'll leave the room the minute anyone tries to tell a mother-in-law joke."

"That's one of your most endearing traits," Veronica replied, "your total lack of vanity."

"Would you like me to bring a wedding cake for tonight's open house?" Ruby asked"

"That's very thoughtful, really," Veronica answered sincerely, "but, no, I don't think so. I know I've only been married for a few minutes, but somehow I feel like it has been months. I'd rather just keep tonight as our open house. Besides, all a cake would do is announce our wedding and if I know this town—present company excepted, of course—no one will arrive who won't know already."

"Okay, dear," Ruby replied. "Now, if you don't mind, present company excepted needs to make a few dozen telephone calls. I can assure you there will be many broken hearts among your prospective suitors by nightfall. See you tonight."

"You'd better give Doc a call," Veronica said to Abe. "I'm sure he'd like to hear it from you first."

Abe did call Doc Straussburger, only to discover he knew even before Ruby Steinmann. A security guard at the courthouse had seen the couple heading for the marriage license office and thought Doc should know.

"And I thought word spread fast on the Reservation," Abe said after he hung up.

"Welcome to small town America," Veronica replied. "These are really well-meaning people who are simply happy for us. They will respect our privacy,

I can assure you. They just like to share in the joy of good news. It reinforces community bonds."

"It's easy for you to be so gracious," he responded with a forced frown. "Think about me for a second. I'm the one who has to go out and get a real job, so I don't turn out like that blow-hard brother-in-law."

"Don't worry on my account," she replied. "I won't tell a soul if you don't find work and in most cases wives can't be forced to testify against their husbands. If push comes to shove, I'm a lawyer who can either plead attorney-client confidentiality or the Fifth Amendment."

"Let's stop by your house and pick up as many of your things we can carry," he suggested. "We can get the rest later."

"It will be a short stop," she admitted. "I've had my bags packed and lined up along the bedroom wall for a couple of days, just in case. A girl needs to be prepared for anything, you know."

"Mrs. Carlson," he said. "I love you."

By the time the caterers arrived at four o'clock, Veronica had all her clothes hung in the closet or neatly tucked into dresser drawers. A model of efficiency she had even carefully organized the cabinets on her side of the double-sink bathroom with all the things women find necessary. It was all a mystery to Abe. He only had to shave and change into a suit, but his new wife somehow managed to get things organized and was dressed beautifully before he was able to finally put on his tie. He stopped half-way through the tie knotting process to glance in the mirror at Veronica just putting the final touches to her jewelry—simple gold earrings on the small lobes of her perfectly shaped ears. The same two words kept coming to him: simply stunning. The elegant lines of her long velvet skirt and the flashing folds of her deep blue silk blouse were nearly enough to take his breath away. Although he did not know how it would be possible, he was certain he was going to love her more every day of their lives.

The caterers literally took over the two-car garage. Trays of food on racks were rolled off the truck. Linens, dishes and silverware were brought in sturdy plastic tubs by the helpers. There were even cleaning supplies and two vacuum cleaners. Every item that was needed was provided for and when the party was over, the house would be cleaned and not even a spoon to be washed would be left behind. Any trash generated by the affair would also be hauled away.

Five minutes before the appointed hour of five o'clock, John and Beatrice Nagy arrived to offer assistance. They presented the couple with a small vase of flowers in honor of their marriage. "You two are an inspiration," Bea said. "Perhaps sharing a common wall in this duplex will rub off on John. I'd like to see him find a nice woman and settle down."

"Don't let her kid you," John said in his own defense. "George Staples, a widower down the block, has taken some interest in mother and she thinks having a grown man already around the house might be intimidating to suitors."

"George is just a friend," Bea said. "Why, that old boy is so afraid of the widows around here he gets nervous and has the hiccups. He's deathly afraid they want to snatch him as a husband. I'm not interested in any of that, so I'm no threat."

"We could use a little help," Abe said. "I'd appreciate it, John, if you'd sort of look after the people in the library—keep the conversation going."

"And I'll protect poor George," Bea volunteered. "I'll keep him away from all the little old ladies. But, come to think of it, I'm a little old lady myself," she laughed.

The guests began to arrive promptly at five o'clock, most bearing gifts of flowers, with children carrying a single stem. Word of their nuptials had, indeed, spread quickly.

Abe and Veronica worked the rooms as a pair, like pros, accepting congratulations graciously and ensuring their guests had everything they needed or wanted. Ruby arrived and took charge of the growing number of flower offerings. She had foreseen this onslaught and had called the caterer to order a case of small vases delivered. Soon the vases were spread everywhere around the house and the excess flowers were stored in buckets in the garage when the rooms were filled to capacity. Between flower runs to the garage, Ruby brought a seemingly endless procession of Veronica's relatives to be introduced in twos or threes—some Veronica was familiar with, but when it came to third or fourth cousins once removed, most she had never met.

The Masonic Fellows from the Brownstone Lodge were well represented and pledged their support for Abe's dual membership. The contingent from the Dickinson School of Law was larger than expected, with many wanting to meet the man who was finally able to win Veronica's hand. Henry Cunningham and his new side-kick Cassy Spease made themselves self-appointed guardians of the children, keeping them entertained and out of the way when possible. The now-twenty-five-strong Jose, the Bronx Beaver Club arrived early and stayed only a short time, managing to stay a cohesive group under the light-handed leadership of its president, Ricardo Hernandez.

Surprisingly, the number of people passing in and out made for some crowding, but always remained sufficiently fluid as people, feeling they had sufficiently expressed their congratulations and appreciation to their hosts, made room for others who wanted to come in.

Particularly gratifying to the hosts was the number of new neighbors the Nagys were able to invite. The neighborhood was a blend of ethnic, racial, religious and professional groups found in few other places. There was a good representation of both medical and administrative professionals connected to the Milton S. Hershey Medical Center and related facilities. There were a number of retired medical doctors from several specialties. The director of the regional Veteran's Administration Hospital nearby was a neighbor, as was a former Lt. Governor of Pennsylvania. A number of people worked in the high-tech fields of computers, audio-visuals and financial banking. A few were in insurance or real estate and a number in higher education were represented. There were also a number of practicing lawyers in several specialties.

The open house passed quickly. As abruptly as it had begun, it ended as quickly at eight o'clock. Save for one large arrangement on the kitchen bar, Ruby had loaded up the flowers to be distributed around the Masonic Village at Elizabethtown. By half-past eight the house was cleaned and vacated by all but its two residents.

Abe and Veronica sat in front of the lit gas fireplace with a glass of wine.

"To us," Abe toasted and their glasses touched. "Thank you for becoming my wife."

"Thank you for asking, my love," she replied, taking a sip. "You know, this really does feel like home to me. Perhaps some of that is due to having a hand in the decorating and furnishing, but I think it has more to do with the comfort and ease I feel when we're together. I don't know if most couples are best friends, but I appreciate that aspect of our relationship. I am really going to love the experience of going through life with you."

"All I can say is that I flat love you," he replied.

CHAPTER 15

▼

MARRIED

Veronica Carlson awoke her first morning as a married woman to the smell of coffee. Abe, her husband of less than a day, had placed a steaming cup of that brew on her bedside table, along with a small bowl of fruit medley. If this was any indication of what married life was going to be like, she thought she could get used to it very easily. The little touches of consideration on a daily basis were much more important than any grand gestures on given occasions. Fifteen minutes later she had dressed, brushed her teeth and combed her hair—ready for the day.

She found Abe in the atrium/office working at his computer, a tray with a fresh pot of coffee and two mugs sitting on the credenza.

"Good morning, Sport," she said, putting her arms around his neck from behind and giving him a hug. "Thank you for the coffee. You really know how to spoil a girl. I won't mind if you make a habit of it."

"That's exactly what I plan to do," Abe replied. "And as you can see, when I have the time I like to read the newspaper and then go on-line to check the state of the world first thing in the morning. Some people might think I'm a news junkie, but I must tell you that I'm really just basically nosey, with a keen interest in international affairs."

"And how are things going in the world this morning?" she asked.

"About the same as yesterday," he answered. "The Middle East is a violent mess, war rages in several spots, anti-American protests continue unabated and the French still don't like us any better. Oh, and the UN diplomats still refuse to pay several hundred thousand dollars in parking fines. Religious differences continue to split regions, countries and communities at an alarming rate."

"How are we doing on the domestic front?" she asked, hoping for some good news for a change.

"There's an interesting new book out," he replied. "It's about religious literacy in this country. Did you know the United States is the most religious nation in the developed world, but also the most religiously ignorant?"

"That really doesn't come as any surprise," she said. "I have read that fewer than half of Americans can identify the book of Genesis as the first in the Bible and only one third know the Sermon on the Mount was delivered by Jesus. That's probably the same third who can name at least one of the rights guaranteed by the First Amendment."

"It gets even better," he continued. "More than ten percent think Noah's wife was Joan of Arc, many believe it was Thomas Edison who said, 'Let there be light,' and only half can name even one of the four Gospels. Fully three-quarters of the population live under the mistaken impression that the Bible teaches that 'God helps those who help themselves.' How much do you think these people know about Islam, Hinduism, Confucianism or Buddhism, not to mention Judaism? People probably know more about Wicca than any of the world's major religions."

"Do you really want to start your day pondering the ills of the world?" she asked half-jokingly.

"Just some days," he answered. "Along with a couple of cups of coffee, it gets the blood going. Speaking of which, I'll pour us some."

"You poured the first," she said going to the tray, "let me pour the second. I'd like to spoil you a little too, you know. What are your plans for fun today?"

"Well, I'll never surpass yesterday," he answered. "So lets have a good breakfast and catch a train in Middletown. I'd like to walk around New York City and see all the decorations and window displays for the season. We could even get a little shopping done."

"You just said the magic phrase," she said. "That ranks right behind, 'Let's go to lunch,' but still third to 'I love you.' That last one is still the best. And I have a great place to eat. The Brownstone Café in Middletown is right on the way."

The Brownstone Café was housed in a stately building on a North Union Street corner lot, in the Richardson Romanesque Style popular in the Victorian Era. Opened in 1893 as the National Bank of Middletown, it served as a succession of banks for almost a century. In 1998, new owners turned it into a café, but kept the large bank vault, several smaller safes, along with the etched-glass teller windows intact. Safe deposit boxes in various configurations were used to accessorize the eating areas.

At Veronica's suggestion, they both ordered a four-egg omelet, hash browns, bacon and whole-wheat toast with strawberry preserves, along with hot tea with honey. Abe walked to the train station feeling a little sluggish, but food seemed to energize Veronica.

"Now aren't you glad I suggested we park at the station?" she asked. "This way you can walk off some of that breakfast."

"I'd have to walk all the way to New York for that to happen," he replied.

"You'd better do some walking once we get there," she said. "I know of a little deli tucked down a side street that makes the biggest sandwiches you've ever seen. Hot pastrami and cream soda are not to be missed on any trip. If you're not hungry, I'll let you watch me eat."

"I'd love just to watch you do anything," he said. "I particularly like to hear your low hum when you are enjoying your meal."

"You're easy to please, Sport," she said. "Now that we're married, just give me the signal and I'll hum in your ear all you want."

Abe was partial to train travel, particularly on the European lines. He was saddened when Amtrak kept reducing service over the years in order to help financial viability, but still rode the line often, so long as he was not on a tight deadline—Amtrak had a well-earned reputation for being notoriously behind schedule.

Two obvious businessmen seated on opposite sides of the aisle a few rows ahead were engaged in a lively discussion, comparing horror stories of mishaps on the trains they had used. One continuing problem for one man was finding an opportunity to smoke, especially on overnight routes. The longer the route, the longer the delay in arrival and that was particularly hard on smokers. The other man's chief complaint, aside from what he considered shoddy service overall, was having to ride in packed trains with what he called "swarthy looking types," young men of dark Middle Eastern complexion who inevitably wore backpacks. It was obvious to him that Amtrak was ignoring what happened in Spain with terrorist bombs on trains and he would get off the train, no matter where it stopped, if he saw anyone fitting the description. The first man admitted that he took similar precautions before boarding airplanes.

Veronica leaned over to Abe and said in a low voice: "Maybe those two ought to put themselves in the path of real danger by getting in their cars and driving the highways."

"They're not the type we need on the highway," Abe answered. "They would probably cause some accidents by talking on their cell phone while speeding. However, I am concerned about this growing fear, even among supposedly educated and well-traveled people such as those two. When I was in Europe recently, I detected a silent undercurrent of changing attitudes, a distrust of foreign influences even among the so-called cosmopolitan classes. Even their own homegrown problems, like hooliganism at sporting events, are blamed on outside influences—whether another European neighbor or the situation in the Middle East. Britain is even concerned about hooligans spoiling cricket matches. Can you imagine that?"

"That is hard to imagine," she agreed. "I had a visiting colleague from Oxford, a man who has lectured at every major law school in six different countries, tell me last year that people in Europe are looking to this country to find a way out of our current global problems. After all, he told me, if this great polyglot country settled by immigrants and a constitution favorable to a wide range of freedoms is unable to deal with globalization, immigration and a host of other matters, what chance has Europe?"

"My Indian friends always like to point out that we immigrated to their country and we just pushed them aside," he said. "We had no intention of living peacefully alongside the Indian Nations. Our overwhelming numbers meant we could take what we wished and demand the Indian assimilate into our society. I'm afraid some of the tribes have assimilated too well. They've picked up several questionable habits from us."

"You'll have to enlighten me on what you mean," she said.

Abe explained that historically, most tribes had ways of assimilating members of other tribes into their own. Sometimes it was an individual who had struck out on his own into new territory or a small band that was the last of their numbers dwindling into extinction. At other times, it would be captives, either Indians or Whites. It was a proud heritage for many hundreds of years—inclusion instead of exclusion. All that had changed in recent years.

One instance was the sovereign Seminole Nation, whose origins were of questionable context to historians. Seminoles did not exist when Europeans colonized the United States. Anthropologists argue they are really an Afro-Indian tribe, formed when refugees from other tribes joined runaway slaves in the Florida wilderness. The word Seminole itself is translated as "runaway," "separatist" or "pioneer." General Thomas Sidney Jesup called the Seminole Wars "a Negro war ... not an Indian war." Along with the other tribes of the southeast, the Seminoles ended up at the other end of the Trail Of Tears in Indian Territory, now Oklahoma. The distinction of "freedman" as opposed to "blood Indian" used among the differing Oklahoma tribes never applied to the Seminoles, who were multiracial from the beginning.

In 2000, a reactionary group within the Seminole Nation forced a vote to cast some 1,500 freedmen descendents out of the tribe, some say because they were floating a gambling initiative and wanted to narrow the number of beneficiaries of that enterprise. The United States would not recognize the election and ultimately cut off most federal programs. The government also determined that since the Seminoles no longer enjoyed the proper relationship with the United States, they were not authorized to conduct gambling. The freedmen were eventually allowed back into the tribe, but the damage to the Seminole Nation's reputation had already been done.

"That's a sad commentary on events," Veronica said when he was finished. "Aren't things hard enough on the Indians as it is?"

"They most assuredly are," Abe replied. "A more recent example is even worse."

The Cherokee Nation, Abe explained, owned slaves. When the Cherokee joined the other tribes in Oklahoma, a treaty of 1866 agreed that the freed slaves were adopted into the tribe. In the 1890s a federal government commission planted a sleeping bomb when it created a definitive roll by tribal membership, but with two separate lists: a blood list of non-black Cherokees and a freedman's list of blacks regardless of significant Cherokee ancestry. By a vote of seventy-six percent, the Cherokee Nation's constitution was amended, stripping 2,800 freedmen descendants from the tribal rolls. How many of the latter will still be able to take advantage of tribal-provided services such as medical care are now very much in doubt.

"As a sovereign nation, the Cherokee argue they are immune to federal oversight on purely tribal affairs, is that it?" Veronica asked.

"As far as they are concerned, U.S. civil rights, *per se,* do not apply," he answered as the train pulled into New York City.

As much time as he had spent on the wide open plains or vast wilderness expanses around the world, Abe Carlson had always enjoyed walking for hours on the streets of New York. He always found a certain energy in the air, the bustle of the crowded sidewalks where you could still turn a corner and suddenly find a small oasis of quiet in a little park or side street. Many people found the tall buildings whose tops were out of visual range to be confining, but he thought of the many steep-walled canyons he had experienced and found them refreshing.

Veronica had always thoroughly enjoyed the city, also. She felt the same energy and bustle, which she always thought of as the hum of some huge engine churning away on the societal path of progress. She also loved the people of the city because they were helpful, friendly and only too pleased to give directions to out-of-towners. To show Abe what she meant about asking for directions, she gave a practical demonstration.

Stopping at the corner of a major intersection, he asked an elderly couple for directions to Saks Fifth Avenue, by the quickest and safest route for a pair of walkers. The man was only too happy to oblige, giving a lengthy detailed description of the route and what landmarks they would see on the way—"You couldn't possibly get lost," he ended. The woman, on the other hand, gave her opinion on a much shorter route where Veronica could find some real bargains in out-of-the-way shops where she personally took her trade—"Just tell the owners that Sara G. sent you, they'll fix you right up," was her conclusion. Fortified with this information, they thanked the couple and walked away arm-in-arm.

An hour later, laden with a few purchases in a large shopping bag, they easily found the deli Veronica had mentioned earlier. They both ordered the biggest hot pastrami sandwich Abe had ever seen, munching on a large bowl of pickles and pickled tomatoes as an appetizer and two cream sodas each.

"You certainly do know the best places to eat," Abe said after they finished. "Do you frequent the city often? You seem to know your way around."

"There are many things you will learn about me, dear," Veronica replied with a smile and a wink. "It will help fill in those awkward gaps over the years."

"Why do I get the impression there will be so very few of those?" he asked, returning her smile.

"Lunch is on me," she said, picking up the bill. "I'll let you pay the next time. Now, Sport, we have another stop to make."

Veronica led the way through a maze of side streets until she came to a small bookstore in the middle of a residential block, with the simple weathered sign that read: "Sam's." The store's owner was named Bernie, but when he purchased the establishment, he kept the original name, thinking that the good will factor gave an added worth.

The three-bell chime tinkled as they opened the door to find Bernie sitting on a stool behind the counter reading a Florida newspaper.

"Hello, Mr. Shultz," Veronica called as she approached. "Are you still keeping up on your parents? Has your father had any more letters to the editor printed?"

"Well, hello, Miss Steinmann," he replied, putting down the newspaper on the counter and removing his reading glasses. "Yes, I'm still trying to keep informed about my parents. My father only had that one letter published, but he insists I continue looking since I missed the first one. He is not above wedging a little guilt in there where possible. Oh my, excuse me. I just noticed the wedding band. Is this the fortunate gentleman?"

"I am he, Abe Carlson," he answered, shaking the man's hand. "Pleased to meet you."

"Then, you would now be Mrs. Carlson?" Bernie asked. "Or are you too liberated to take another man's name?"

"Of course, I've taken his name," Veronica replied. "To do otherwise would show a lack of commitment. Besides, we women have been shackled to a man's name for centuries. We either carry the name of our fathers or of our husbands. I could file for a name change to something else, of course, but I don't think Nancy Drew would strike the right amount of fear in my students."

"I understand," Bernie said in a deadpan manner. "There's always that, of course. Now is there anything I can do for you today?"

"There certainly is," she replied. "Have you been able to find any more of those remainders on Fanny Holtzman?"

"I was lucky there," he said. "Two weeks ago I found twelve copies at a going-out-of-business sale over on the east side. Shall I send them along as usual?"

"Yes, please," she answered, pulling out a credit card and writing down her new address. "And, of course, if any more come your way, I'm interested. That book is getting more scarce every day."

"Well, my congratulation to you both," Bernie said, handing the credit card receipt to be signed. "I wish you all the best in all your endeavors."

As they walked back to the train station, Abe asked about the book.

"It's a tradition I started a few years ago," Veronica said. "Each of my female students who earn an 'A' in my class, and there are unfortunately not many of them, receive a copy of the book on the life of Fanny Holtzman."

"And she being?" he asked.

"She being an inspiration to all women attorneys," she replied. "It's the story of a young woman of a bygone era right here in New York City, who defied convention and her father's wishes to become an attorney, just like her older brother. When no firm would hire a woman, she set up a small office near the theatre district in the Vaudeville Era. At first she would read letters from home for actors who were illiterate, usually for free or a pittance. Word got around and she received small commissions for legal documents of various types. Eventually the actors would bring their contracts around for her to take a look at and she would point out egregious clauses. That grew into her becoming the legal agent for what would later become the biggest and highest paid stars in the profession. She became quite wealthy, eventually got married, and paved the way for any number of women."

"Now, there's a book I'd like to read," he said.

"As soon as the shipment arrives," she answered. "I presented my last copy at the end of term."

The train ride back to Middletown was comfortable and pleasant as they discovered more about each other and found they could keep a simple conversation going for hours. Time passed quickly and before they realized it, they were detraining. As they drove out of the station parking lot, she leaned over and hummed into his ear.

"Okay, Sport," she whispered. "I'm ready to go home."

CHAPTER 16

▼

DISTINCTIONS

Abe Carlson began to adapt to a domestic routine by picking up the morning newspaper from the short driveway and placing outgoing mail in the curbside mailbox, raising the flag to signal a pick up. As he turned back toward the house, his neighbor John Nagy came out of his duplex unit on the same errand.

"Good morning, Abe," John said as he picked up his newspaper. "You sure seem organized. It must be nice to move into a new home where everything is already in its proper place—not like me, who always seems to do those things piece meal."

"All the credit goes to Veronica and Ruby," Abe replied. "I've been blessed with not only a wonderful wife, but also a great mother-in-law. So far I'm batting one thousand on the home front."

"If you're still interested in the Islamic Society of Greater Harrisburg in Steelton," John said, "I've gathered some material and talked to a few people about their efforts to assimilate. Since you've inspired me to look into the subject, I've gathered some clippings that shed more light on the situation. Perhaps we can share materials and both become educated together. I'll drop a folder by later today, if you don't mind."

"That's great," Abe answered. "I appreciate your thoughtfulness. We might be on to something here that will help the community."

"You'll find at least one clipping that is disturbing," John added. "It is about a Muslim scholar from Saudi Arabia who is redefining the rise of that country under the sway of an 18th Century preacher named Muhammad ibn Abd al-Wahhab. I think we'll have to pay close attention right from the beginning to draw distinctions between differing Muslim groups. I foresee a bumpy road ahead. And, by the way, what you said about your appreciation for Ruby as a mother-in-law, my mother has dropped many not-so-subtle hints over the years that she would be a model in the same role, whomever I may wish to marry."

"Good for her, John," he replied. "May you be as fortunate in that area as I."

When he reentered the house, Abe found Veronica in the kitchen, pouring a second cup of coffee and toasting English muffins for the two of them.

"Thanks for the coffee on the nightstand again this morning," she said. "I trust that's going to be a habit. Your little considerations are greatly appreciated and I'll try to return them in kind."

"I know they are appreciated," he replied. "You just keep humming in my ear and we'll call it even."

They took the tray of coffee and muffins to the all-season porch to greet the early morning sun streaming through the large windows. The special windows reduced the glare, but allowed the warmth of the sun to make the temperature quite comfortable. Several types of birds were pecking around in the grass of the backyard and the common area looking for food. Abe complimented Veronica on her eye for detail. She had had the forethought to place several bird feeders with varying sizes of seeds around the house and the spillage on the ground fed other birds and squirrels alike.

They sat at the large round glass table Veronica had selected, with a line of ferns and other small plants along the two walls, watching the birds and enjoying the evergreen trees and the unusual magnolia that kept its leaves throughout the year. This was an ideal setting in a home that met all their needs for comfort and peaceful living. Neither bothered to reach for the newspaper and they simply enjoyed each other's company. He told her of his encounter with John Nagy and she discussed her plans to pose the question of yelling 'crusaders' in a conservative mosque to her First Amendment class. For her Constitutional Law class, she had plans for an in-depth examination of the restrictive so-called Patriot Act and its questionable enforcement that had led to widespread government abuse.

Their light breakfast over, they jointly cleaned the few dishes and retired to the office to read the newspaper—passing sections back and forth.

"Here's an interesting article along the lines of what John was saying to you about diversity and distinction," Veronica said. "A Buddhist Center is opening on North Second Street in Harrisburg. 'We're passing along pure Buddhist teaching from more than 2,500 years ago that is about reaching out to develop compassion, kindness and selflessness,' says a teacher and center spokeswoman. 'We learn to solve all our human problems.' It goes on to say that this is a form of Buddhism designed for the Western world, with other forms more suited to areas throughout Asia. She ends by saying: 'Western people living in this culture learn how to approach and be helpful to individuals. We always adapt to the culture of the group who we are studying, following and practicing.'"

"That must be a branch of the Buddhist Center in Baltimore," Abe said. "That was started by a Brit meditation master, teacher and author. If I recall correctly, he has established somewhere near five hundred such centers in thirty-six countries. I heard about him in London, but never had the opportunity to meet him personally. He does sound like an interesting man, though."

"People receive Buddhists in their midst readily enough," she countered. "That's because they are perceived as peaceful and benign—no threat to our mainstream Christianity."

"Buddhists may be no threat to other religions," Abe replied, "but to political tyranny they can be a rather big bane. I can remember years ago Buddhist monks burning themselves alive in protest on the street of Saigon. The worldwide attention they focused led to a toppling of the regime."

"I was thinking more along the lines of non-acceptance of the Wiccans," she said. "A student submitted a paper last year on the subject of legally denying a Wiccan symbol on grave markers under the jurisdiction of the U.S. Department of Veterans Affairs. The Wiccans sued."

The suit she referred to had been filed on behalf of a Wisconsin group that claimed a membership of 400,000 nationwide, although other estimates were closer to 100,000. They wanted the pentacle, the five-pointed star representing earth, air, fire, water and spirit, to be allowed on Wiccan veterans' gravestones. They cited three qualifying veterans, one each from conflicts in Korea, Vietnam and Afghanistan. The suit also pointed out that since the Army Chaplain handbook had listed ways to accommodate Wiccans since 1978 and that an estimated 1,800 active duty service members identified themselves as Wiccans, denial of the symbol was outright discrimination and a violation of the Constitution.

"And how was the case decided?" Abe asked.

"No pun intended," Veronica replied, "but the jury is still out and it could be in appeals for some years to come, no matter which way the court rules. I imagine the Armed Services will okay the move before it ever gets through the courts."

Veronica's telephone, placed in its recharge/speaker attachment on her desk, began to ring and she looked down at the caller ID and refused to answer. Abe looked up from his newspaper quizzically. After the fourth ring, she punched the speaker button.

"Mother, I hope you're dying or won the lottery," Veronica said. "On second thought, only the first qualifies as acceptable and you have another daughter, Gloria to call. I'm on my honeymoon and was just beginning to really enjoy myself. Please don't tell me my honeymoon is over. I have you on the speaker and you will break Abe's heart."

"Don't be silly," Ruby replied. "Haven't I always counseled you that in a really good marriage, the honeymoon is never over, just hums along through all the years? Anyway I just need a few minutes of your time. Is Abe listening?"

"He's stretched out on the couch in pure exhaustion," she replied, "but I think he may be able to hear."

"That's nice dear," Ruby said ignoring the sarcasm. "Now, here's what I need. Doc received a call from Henry and Cassy asking permission to look in his library for a book on something called the Shadow Wolves. Doc knew he didn't have any books he remembered along those lines, so he called me. Of course, I own nothing like that, I'm sure. I would have remembered it. I went on-line to book-stores, and found plenty of books on wolves, but none that seemed to fit the shadow designation."

"You're not likely to find a book like that either," Abe interrupted. "Much of what they do these days would be classified, but they have been an open secret for more than thirty years and you could probably find some old magazine or news-paper articles fairly easily. I know because I was a Shadow Wolf for a time and had occasion to revisit over the years."

"Oh my," was all Ruby could reply at first. "I didn't know. Am I about to step on government toes here?"

"The Shadow Wolves are a group of trackers centered on the land of the Tohono O'odham Nation which straddles the Arizona-Mexico border," he explained. "The U.S. Customs Service and the Border Patrol have used these Indian trackers—really a contingent made up of seven tribes—mostly for drug interdiction."

"Would you two be amenable to a single hour for tea this afternoon at Doc's?" she asked. "You do know that you have inspired another little club in town dedi-cated to tracking matters and you could explain about those efforts to half a dozen or so young people. Besides, we all miss you terribly and are lacking for want of your company."

"Perfect, Mother," Veronica replied. "Guilt and sympathy, the old one-two punches."

"Why, whatever can you mean, my dear?" Ruby answered in feigned innocence.

"I'll make a bargain with you, Mother," Veronica said, looking to Abe for approval, to which he nodded, "we'll graciously spare the hour if you'll loan me that cashmere scarf for the rest of the winter. I understand it's going to be a mighty cold February."

"Not the green one that goes so well with my emerald earrings?" Ruby pleaded. "It would mar my appearances at the club."

"That's the very one," Veronica said with a smile. "Take it or leave it."

"If you insist, my dear," Ruby replied. "You know I can spare no sacrifice for my daughters. See you at Doc's, four o'clock sharp. I'll bring the scarf."

"You two are a real piece of work," Abe chuckled after they had hung up. "You do seem to enjoy playfully prodding each other, but I can tell you that I hope never to have to spar with either one of you."

"Then, you are a man wise beyond your years," she replied.

"I trust this doesn't really mean the honeymoon's over," he stated.

"Not by a long shot, Sport," she answered. "I'll keep up my end if you'll keep up yours."

"That's what I signed up for to begin with," he said and gave her a kiss.

An hour later John Nagy phoned to see if it was all right for him drop off the information he had mentioned earlier. Veronica suggested he bring his mother, Beatrice, along so they could all get to better know one another. Beatrice was pleased to be invited because her son had not been very sociable over the years and she had too little social contact outside the home for her taste. They gathered in the library with hot tea and finger sandwiches. A small bowl of fresh fruit was poised on the end of the library table in the corner.

"So, John, what caught your interest about the Saudi historian?" Abe asked.

"Well," John began, "as you probably know, Saudi Arabia is reasserting its commanding presence in the Arab world after some years of neglecting the leadership role. It has always been a conservative, tightly run country, with little tolerance for internal criticism or not toeing strictly to the official line, which includes the account of its founding."

"It seems to me they experience a tightening or loosening of control of their own citizens on a recurring economic cycle," Abe observed. "The price of oil goes down, unrest begets murmured demands for reform to cede more power to the people. The price of oil goes up, the kingdom hands out more cash and talk of reform fades back into the woodwork."

"The price of oil is rising again, with record profits in the hundreds of billions of dollars range," John replied. "The Saudis are in a new cycle of cracking down on dissidents, both at home and abroad. As an intellectual and professor named Dakhil, who had done research and a doctoral thesis on the history of the Wahhabi movement, may have uncovered a simple answer to a perplexing question about the founding of the country, but it's not the answer the clerics or the royal family want to hear. Take a look at this newspaper clipping from *The Washington Post.*"

The article said that when Dakhil was growing up in Saudi Arabia, clergymen strictly ruled the day-to-day lives of all citizens, taking attendance at morning prayers, preventing smoking in public or listening to music because it was sinful; stick-wielding clerics were forcing men to pray. The clerics were following the teachings of Muhammad ibn Abd al-Wahhab, an 18th Century religious leader whose ideology inspired Islamic extremism and pervasive religiosity in everyday life. Dakhil was looking for the answer to the question of how these clerics gained such power.

The answer was that the Wahhabis allied themselves with the House of Saud over dozens of contenders vying for power over central Arabia. The clerics invoked jihad, or holy war, to rally the people to the side of Saud. Saud was the victor and named Saudi Arabia after himself. The alliance paid off for the Wahhabis as they freehandedly eliminated all other doctrines but their own, took charge of education and enforced their strict brand of Islam in mosques and schools throughout the country to this day. The Wahhabi movement had always claimed it was bringing religion to people who lacked religious commitment. Dakhil found that the political aspects were overwhelming and pointed out that there was no lack of religious commitment at the time, but the lack that was the backing for the Wahhabi version.

"Islamic divisions in the Arab world are deep and probably permanent," Abe said. "The violence between the Sunni, Shiite and Kurd, and each sect against anyone not supportive to their particular view of the world seems never-ending. The fight over oil resources is the base of the problem, of course, but there isn't much we, as individuals, can do on that score. What bothers me is the fact that Arabs are only twenty-percent of the Islamic world. What about the other eighty percent? How are people supposed to make a distinction if they know so little about what they feel is an alien religion?"

"I see where you're going," Veronica interrupted. "Can the United States, with its strong Constitution, be inclusive to the free practice of Islamic traditions within our borders and still provide the personal protection to all guaranteed under that Constitution?"

"Your context is much better than mine," Abe answered. "But then, you're better at open debate than I'm ever likely to be. I look about this neighborhood and some of the doctors, academics, lawyers and other professionals are Muslim. They fit well in their chosen professions and their religious beliefs are not an impediment. But what happens when a physical presence like a mosque comes into the picture—particularly if the mosque replaces an ethnically-oriented Catholic property, strips the building of Catholic ornamentation and replaces it with words in Arabic that the great majority of our citizens cannot read?"

"A deeper suspicion of what may be going on inside," Beatrice said as her first comment in this conversation. "Unfortunately, that fosters distrust and the negative rumors begin to grow and take on embellishment from fertile imaginations."

"You see?" John asked to no one in particular. "My mother is a very smart woman with good common sense. I must say that I always strive to be her best student. I'll leave the file with you two so you can see what other materials I continue to collect."

John and Bea stayed for another half-hour of polite conversation and less weighty matters. By the time they departed, new friendships had been cemented all around.

Abe asked Veronica to their office to show her something. He turned on his computer and within a minute the screen showed a picture of a worn and tattered building sitting alone on a bleak scrub landscape. There appeared to be no visible human activity at all. A quick command typed on the keyboard and the camera zoomed in to show a long slate blackboard with chalk markings—unintelligible to Veronica.

"What you're looking at is grass-roots economic progress at its finest," he said. "This is a rural area of a not-to-be-named African country. And that's a produce warehouse. The blackboard posts the price the broker is paying for various products on any given day. Note the time stamp down in the corner. That indicates the image was taken yesterday at the opening of business."

"Let me guess," she said. "This is another one of the programs undertaken by our foundation."

"Smart girl. You catch on quickly," he replied. "It's a simple idea really. Most good ideas are. We picked up a number of cell phones in the aftermarket and performed various minor modifications. These we distributed free-of-charge to a number of local farmers who can find out on a daily basis what the market is for their produce in distant cities. They call each other and know when the broker's profits are exorbitant in relation to the price he was paying on the local level. Armed with this knowledge, they can negotiate with the broker. It doesn't hurt that there is another broker just a few miles distant that they can sell to with a little more effort and expense. Neither broker knows of the existence of the cell phones, so now has to compete on a more level field."

"And how is it working out for the farmers?" she asked.

"Very nicely, thank you," he replied. "They are getting better prices in line with the market, but not enough to endanger the broker's profits. Of course, if the market price goes down, the farmers accept less without complaint. The brokers are freed of the headaches when that happens. Everyone has found a happy medium they can live with."

"And the picture?" she asked.

"We have a man with a camera phone who walks by each morning, then uploads the picture via satellite," he said. "So far, so good."

CHAPTER 17

▼

LEGAL MATTERS

Since school was out until after the New Year, Doc Straussburger was able to assemble a number of the loose-knit tracker's club in his library for the four o'clock tea arranged by Aunt Mattie. The tea was plentiful, but the snacks were light because Aunt Mattie did not want to ruin young appetites for their dinner.

When the Carlson's arrived at the appointed time Aunt Mattie suggested they go right to the library and save Doc because the children were looking politely bored as he related how to track infectious diseases throughout a population. Ruby Steinmann was sitting quietly in an out-of-the-way corner with a green cashmere scarf neatly folded in her lap.

"Are you warming up the crowd, Doc?" Abe asked as he walked into the room.

"I've been trying to," Doc answered, "but this is a pretty tough crowd. I don't believe anyone at the Center for Disease Control in Atlanta ever thought to call themselves anything as exotic as Shadow Wolves, so they've a hard time coming up with a title that would grab the imagination of a group like this."

"I don't know about that," Veronica replied. "I think we have the potential for a couple of doctors or law enforcement officials in this gang. They may need to know that in the future."

"And perhaps a law professor, too?" Doc asked.

"Perhaps," she said. "I'm not real concerned about the competition, though. By the time one of these is ready to take my job, I'll be retired and living in a sunny clime somewhere, resting on my laurels."

"You have to talk funny like that to be a big professor," a voice from one of the younger children whispered.

"Now to the subject at hand," Abe said by way of introduction and gave a brief outline of who the Shadow Wolves are and what they do. "The land of the Tohono O'odham Nation shares a seventy-six mile border with Mexico. Anyone or anything crossing over into the United States faces the daunting task of crossing forty miles of very rough terrain, blazing hot in summer and bitterly cold in winter. It is so forbidding that most guides smuggling in illegal immigrants try to avoid this section entirely."

A hand shot up like a student in school asking permission to speak. "Are the guides the ones they call 'coyotes'? I read that in a book."

"Good point," Abe replied. "They name them that because the coyote is considered a trickster, a wily creature who uses stealth to avoid his enemies. Many people have died making that attempt."

"What about the drug smugglers?" Cassy Spease asked.

"That's a different story," Abe answered. "They like the remoteness and are motivated by large amounts of money. In fact, one of the reasons the Shadow Wolves were organized in the first place was that too many of the young men in the tribe were being hired or bribed and were straying from traditional tribal values. They are a strong, tight and proud group. One requirement to join is that you have a certain amount of Indian blood or you are not qualified."

"But you were one," Henry Cunningham said.

"Yes I was one of the few exceptions asked to join," Abe replied. "I know it will make me sound like an old man to you, but it was thirty years ago, when I was a young man of some experience who had already been adopted as an honorary member of several tribes."

"Do you remember your first time?" Henry asked.

"You never forget the first time," Abe replied. "It may be a trite phrase, but I truthfully remember every minute of the experience like it was today."

On Abe's first track with the Shadow Wolves, the oldest in the group picked up the track of drug smugglers at three o'clock in the morning and followed the trail for twelve hours until they spotted the trackers; then the smugglers dropped their loads and ran, only to be picked up by another team sitting in wait. At the time, marijuana warehouses in Mexico were full but this periodic crackdown from the Mexican authorities, bowing to pressure from the United States, was about to make a token sweep. Shifting as much product across the border was a salvage attempt and the Indian lands the best bet for moving large amounts in record time. Using little traveled wagon-rutted trails or out of the way animal migration routes, chances were good that most shipments would make it across.

"How did you know they were smugglers?" Cassy asked.

"By the sign," Abe responded. "When we first struck the trail, the boot prints were deep and unnaturally spread apart. This human-mule way of smuggling marijuana requires irregular burlap bales of sixty pounds or more strapped to a man's back. The smugglers travel in groups, take frequent rests, stay within any cover they can find and are sloppy in discarding food wrappers and water containers at rest stops along the way. Even the more careful can be tracked. Fibers from clothing get snagged on thorny underbrush, the heavy loads may glance off a canyon wall leaving a smudge, and dust covering rocky areas may be disturbed. When they think they are being careful by stepping down into an arroyo to keep a low profile on the landscape it leaves more sign than you can imagine."

"How do you tell if the trail is hot or cold?" a boy in the second row asked.

"There are several ways," Abe replied. "It helps if you are familiar with the territory and the movement of animals and insects. If you find a clear track that no other animal or insect has crossed, that's an indication it may be fresh. If there is a slight wind and the track is filling in with dust or soil, you can guess by the fill-in rate how long the track has been there. Remember that my first track was in the American southwest. Here in the east you have an abundance of terrain that can give you more sign, but there may be so much sign that things could get confusing. You have to know the patterns of weather and the habits of animals. After you've mastered all that, you face knowing about human behavior. That last one I'm still working on."

His audience was so intent on what Abe had to say that they neglected their tea, which was now cold in their cups. Aunt Mattie and Veronica topped off their beverages with hot tea.

"Are the Shadow Wolves still active?" Henry asked at last.

"They certainly are," Abe answered. "In fact, they have become so well known in background work that they are training other border officers and even a few select military personnel in the art of tracking. I understand that men and women who have gone through this training are now using those skills around the world in many different ways. Much of what they do outside of the Nation lands is classified."

"We can't use Shadow Wolves as a club name," Henry said to no one in particular. "I suggest we call ourselves Abe's Wolves. What do you think?"

"Come into this century, buster," Cassy answered. "In case you haven't noticed, there are now three girls who want to contribute to this club. If you want Abe's Wolves and Wolvettes, you may have a deal."

Abe looked to his wife and could only see that she was stifling a laugh so hard that it brought tears to her eyes. Doc sat silent as the Sphinx, as if he were hearing a patient relate a personal medical history.

Their hour having expired, the young people thanked Abe for his explanation and headed home to dinner, chatting among themselves all the way down the block.

"Shades of Abigail Adams, Sport," Veronica said to Abe quietly. "We will be heard and proffered proper consideration."

"Thus it has been since the beginning of time," Abe answered. "Most men simply didn't recognize that fact until relatively recent times. Ancient philosophers knew it, but failed to write about it for fear of masculine retaliation. Now, I think we should be going. I have another surprise for you that I want to show you at home."

"Does it have anything to do with humming in your ear?" she asked.

"That would be nice, of course," he replied, "but you may want to wait until the installers leave. We have two steamer trunks of equipment arriving that are going into the bonus room space above the garage that will make our lives a little easier."

Once Ruby had made her stolid presentation of the green scarf, they made their excuses and departed.

As Veronica drove her Mercedes into the garage and turned off the engine, a plain white van pulled into the driveway. In her rear view mirror, she watched as three men emerged from the van and walked toward the back. Abe asked her to open the front door and proceeded to help with the unloading. Each trunk required the strength of all four men to carry one at a time up the stairs to the bonus room space. That done, Abe introduced the three men to Veronica and left them to set up the equipment, saying he would put on a pot of coffee.

"I noticed those trunks had stickers from several countries," Veronica said as the coffee began to percolate.

"That's one of the quirks of Miguel, our electronics wizard in Germany," Abe answered. "He likes to remind himself just how many countries he has sent his projects to and allow his customers to know how big his market really is. He's also a bit decal happy. Wait until you see his lab. There are decals on just about everything."

"Is Miguel German?" she asked. "I don't think of that as a German name."

"He's German, all right, Miguel Swartzbaugh," he replied. "His mother discovered shortly before she gave birth to Miguel that she had some Mexican heritage somewhere in her family tree and named him that in honor of her ancestry. The entire family is quite colorful. You'll meet them one of these days."

"And what sort of equipment is in those trunks that will make our lives easier?" she inquired.

"The simple answer is very high-tech computer equipment," he said. "It is custom designed to fit our exact needs. One trunk has coded and encrypted devices that will keep us in touch with various projects around the world and access to various databases from different countries. The other trunk is mostly for you. Also coded and encrypted, it will give you quick access to court records and case proceedings from most countries, down to the municipal level. All inquiries will be answered in the language of the questions submitted. Depending on how the question is phrased, the answer will be very specific or very broad, incorporating a summary of multiple views. It also gives you access to a wide range of law libraries."

"That sounds fantastic," she said. "I can't wait to give that a trial run. How soon can we start?"

"It shouldn't be long," he answered. "They just need to get us wired in. For security reasons, I stay away from wireless when I can. You never know who's listening in and even my personal communications I like to keep to myself."

"You intrigue me more every day," she said. "I had no idea that a tracker would be so high-tech. Is everything that complex?"

"Everything in the world runs on information," he replied. "I need to know all I can about a situation before I step into it. I try to take full use of technology where it applies, but it's not always applicable. You can have all the high-tech sensors and unmanned drones you can get to keep an eye on our borders, but you can't beat boots-on-the-ground tracking to find people or things."

"Let's make some sandwiches for the men upstairs," she said. "We can have a quick bite and get to work as soon as they're gone. By the way, I hope that system doesn't search around and vacuum up proprietary or classified information. That would be against the law, you know."

"Not at all," he assured her. "Miguel will not let a system out of his lab unless it has a series of filters to protect against just that. He is very ethical, which is one of the reasons I've used him for years."

Veronica noticed that Abe washed his hands before helping to prepare lunch, but was impressed that the three men did the same before coming to the table.

They had eaten and were back on the road in fifteen minutes. Abe rinsed the dishes and put them into the dishwasher.

"Why don't you go ahead and boot up your computer?" he said, reading her thoughts. "I'll pour us more coffee and be in shortly."

"Thanks, Sport," she replied. "I do appreciate all your little considerations, really I do. It makes you so easy to live with."

By the time he had placed the fresh cup on her desk, Veronica was already into the proper program, which was asking her to submit a question.

"Please give me a one item summary of proposed reforms to the Patriot Act," she typed, then pushed the enter key. Less than one second later, an editorial from the *New York Times* appeared on the screen.

Entitled "The Must-Do List," the editorial was a laundry list of changes Congress needed to make to the Patriot Act and the policies that resulted. The first item was a call for the restoration of *habeas corpus,* the ancient right to challenge individual imprisonment in court that had been denied to anyone the government chose to label an "illegal enemy combatant." The second item was to put a stop to illegal spying on the American public by intercepting international calls and e-mail messages without first obtaining the required warrant of a court. The third item was to "ban torture, really," in compliance with the Geneva Conventions and to reduce the risk of a captured American soldier enduring the same.

The rest of the list was extensive, but not exhaustive. This included: closing secret C.I.A. prisons, accounting for so-called "Ghost Prisoners," banning extraordinary rendition, tightening the definition of combatant, screening prisoners fairly and effectively, banning tainted evidence and secret evidence, better defining "classified" evidence and respecting the right to counsel.

The editorial also called on Congress to put a halt to the federal government's "race to classify documents to avoid public scrutiny" and a United States apology to "a Canadian citizen and a German citizen, both innocent, who were kidnapped and tortured by American agents."

Almost as an afterthought, the editorial concluded: "Oh yes, and it is time to close the Guantanamo camp. It is a despicable symbol of the abuses committed by this administration (with Congress's complicity) in the name of fighting terrorism."

"I'd have to say the *New York Times* has just about covered that subject," Abe said, standing behind and reading over her shoulder.

"Just the highlights," Veronica commented. "Each one of these items spawned perhaps hundreds of others and thousands of abuses done under the cover of these protections."

"How do you rate the computer's ability to provide the information you requested," Abe asked.

"It's almost scary," she answered. "It's like the program was reading my mind. Normally I'd have needed another ten questions to get to that exact point. Does this program have a name and is it commercially available? The law school could certainly use one like this."

"Miguel calls the program Francis," he said. "It's not commercially available, but designed especially for you."

"Why Francis," she asked.

"He wanted to name it Wilbur," he explained. "You know, after the owner of Mr. Ed, the talking horse. Miguel is a fan of old potboiler detective novels and likes the ring to the phrase, describing defense attorneys as a 'mouthpiece for the mob.' Unfortunately the company that owns the rights to Mr. Ed said they'd sue. So, he decided to create an inside attorney joke and was delighted when another copyright holder leased him the rights for one dollar. The program is named after Francis, the talking mule."

"He doesn't think much of the legal profession, does he?" she asked.

"Sure he does," he replied. "He's a member of the bar himself. It is just the majority of his colleagues he holds in distain. He's also a fan of old movies and named my program Dudley in honor of the angel character in *The Bishop's Wife*, starring Cary Grant and Loretta Young. That he thinks of me as an angel, I take as a high compliment."

CHAPTER 18

▼

DIVERSITY

If the forecasters were correct, by late afternoon the area would receive its first winter blast, rapidly falling temperatures, high winds and a hard frost overnight. With these conditions in mind, Abe and Veronica decided to take advantage of the last mild morning to go for a long walk through their new community and surrounding fields and woods. Abe carried a small pack with a thermos, sandwiches and other provisions just in case they were gone longer than expected.

They started at the end of a street where an asphalt walking path wound up, down and around between the houses and cornfields. The corn had been harvested late in the season and all that was left were short, spiked stalks, standing as small sentinels, row on row in flowing lines, guarding the soil until plowed under for spring planting. The landscape was a series of browns and grays, dotted here and there by the whites of houses and farm buildings or the reds and blues of barns and silos off in the distance. To Abe, the fields were not dead, just sleeping and dreaming of the promises to come in other seasons.

They walked hand-in-hand in solitude along the bank of Swatara Creek as it snaked its way through low-lying areas and they climbed a knoll to sit and watch the dairy cows engage in their early-morning browse at a farm across the creek.

"This is rich, fertile country," Abe said at last, quietly. "There's little wonder why the native people fought so hard against loosing all this to the coming wave of white Christians who wanted not only their lands, but also their souls. Although my father, the Reverend, died when I was only ten, I used to watch closely as he ministered to the needs of the Indians. People would probably think of him as the last in a line of preachers out to convert, and thus save, the savage. We've certainly had our share of those down through history. As I remember him, though, he seemed to be atoning for the abuses of others, showing Christianity only by his own example, not trying to force it on others."

"I don't recall reading in my Pennsylvania history anything about a great conversion rate in this part of the country," Veronica said. "I always thought that was due to the highly developed culture and religion among the tribes."

"I agree with you there," he replied. "In fact, if they had paid more attention to one Indian orator in particular, they might have discovered how differing cultures and separate religious beliefs could live side by side in harmony."

Abe related the story of Red Jacket, the famous Seneca chief who earned his red coat by fighting alongside the British during the American Revolution. The occasion was in 1805 when a white missionary had just finished speaking to a council of the Iroquois Confederation about the benefits of Christianity. Red Jacket asked the missionary why he said there is only one way to worship and serve the Great Spirit. If there is only one religion, why do whites differ so much? If they all read the same book, why such fierce disagreement? The forefathers of the whites and the natives handed down their religion to their sons and daughters. Indians were taught to be thankful for all the favors they received, to love each other, and to be united. They never quarreled about religion, did not want to destroy any other religion, wanting only to be left to enjoy their own.

After pointing out that he had seen money collected at Christian services, Red Jacket suggested perhaps the Christians just wanted some Indian money too. He concluded by saying that the white people in the area were receiving the same sermons and the Indians would wait a little while longer and see what effect the preaching had upon these neighbors. "If we find it does them good," he said, "makes them honest, and less disposed to cheat Indians, we will then consider again of what you have said."

"There is much to be said for Red Jacket's view of diversity," she commented when the narration was finished. "I always teach my students that there is a good reason for the First Amendment to the Constitution being placed in that position. I also remind them that it is an extensive group of rights covered, with particular use of the semi-colon which makes all the difference in legal interpretation: 'Congress shall make no law respecting an establishment of religion, or prohibiting the free exercise thereof; or abridging the freedom of speech, or of the press, or the right of the people peaceably to assemble, and to petition the Government for redress of grievances.'"

Their sandwiches eaten and thermos empty, the couple leisurely made their way home. Other neighbors had emerged from their houses to enjoy the last of the warm weather, waving and exchanging greeting with each other and the Carlson's. Veronica was thankful that Abe had chosen this neighborhood because it represented a mini-UN and spanned all age groups. Children abounded and health-conscious seniors were everywhere, walking, talking and biking. Even the large number of dogs being walked ran the range of breeds, with no two alike.

"I'd like to show you a real monument to diversity, Abe," Veronica said. "Milton and Catherine Hershey, who were without any children of their own, took in four orphan boys and schooled them at no cost. Today that school is expanding to two thousand coed students. Children aged four to fifteen from low income or limited resources and social need may apply. Founders Hall at the Milton Hershey School proves what can be done with a simple idea and solid financial backing."

"Fine by me," he said. "You drive, though. I'd like to get a closer look at things and you like to drive."

Even at a distance, Founders Hall was, indeed, an impressive sight. The white cylindrical Rotunda rose an impressive one-hundred-thirty-seven feet high on the exterior, seventy-four feet on the interior and was built of one-thousand-five-hundred tons of marble. The acoustics were so refined that you could stand on the Italian marble mosaic medallion in the center of the floor, speak in a normal voice, and be amplified across the entire expanse. At the base of the dome was a canopy of state flags representing the geographical diversity of the student body, with six state flags on the floor representing the states from which the majority of students were enrolled.

The original Hershey Industrial School for orphan boys was opened in 1910 and in 1918 Milton Hershey dedicated all of his personal fortune to the school in the form of a trust. By 1934, the Junior-Senior High School was added, followed in 1966 by the Catherine Hall Middle School. A modification to the trust in 1976 permitted the enrollment of girls and eliminated the requirement that students be orphans. The students lived in group-homes and the school provided all services free of charge, including housing, education, clothing, meals, medical, dental, religious, and psychological services.

"Backed by the now multi-billion dollar trust," Veronica explained, "this school is more up-to-date than many colleges and the facilities are equally as impressive. How did you like that medallion on the floor of the Rotunda—the one depicting twelve important aspects of Milton Hershey's life?"

"Very nice," Abe answered. "The circle read like a biography in pictures, although I may have missed some of the significance of the symbolism. I know he was reared in the Mennonite Church, but that section with the depiction of the Ten Commandments eluded me. Why were there only four commandments on the left tablet and six on the right?"

"Good eye, Sport," she answered. "Most people don't pick that up and very few ever ask. Hershey insisted that the children have some mandatory exposure to religion, although he made sure it was always in a nonsectarian service. After Chapel on Sunday morning, the children who request it will be transported to any church, synagogue, or even mosque of their choosing. As for the tablets depicted in the mosaic, he always wanted the children to learn that the first four commandments dealt with one's relationship to God, the other six our relations to one another. It provided a good basis for how one should conduct oneself."

On their way off the grounds, Abe noticed a sign for transitional housing and wondered what that might mean.

"That's for seniors," Veronica said as if reading his mind. "This school, that does so much for the students, doesn't want the graduates to go out and face the real world unprepared. The transitional housing is where they live and learn to cook for themselves, do their own laundry and all the other skills it takes to be self-sufficient."

They drove around different parts of Hershey and Veronica pointed out the usual sites and showed him some out-of-the-way spots she had discovered on her own. She pointed out once thriving residential areas that were now slowly going to seed and empty or boarded up small businesses.

"The price of progress?" he asked.

"A shift in demographics," she answered. "The Penn State Milton S. Hershey Medical Center was a great boon to this town; its expansion of facilities, like the first building for the new Cancer Research Center, to eventually consist of twelve new buildings, has changed the character of Hershey."

"Changed the character for better or worse?" he asked.

"That would depend on whom you ask," she replied. "While it has certainly enhanced the prestige in people's perception of the town, some point to the erosion of the former paternal partnership between Hershey Chocolate and employees. After several generations of close personal ties, the so-called Hershey Family is watching the relationships deteriorating, with nothing short of divorce in the end."

"Do you mean the loss of jobs and building new factories in places like Mexico?" he asked.

"That's just the latest bump in the road," she said. "The Hershey corporate structure had a long tradition of giving back to the community through different kinds of sponsorship—usually little monetary support that reaped great rewards in public good will. Things began to change over the past number of years as the corporate giving has dried up, employees have found it more difficult to negotiate favorable contracts, the out-sourcing of entire units within the corporate structure and the constant blame put on global competition as the major reason for the changes."

"Things always seem to get strained first in any family unit," he observed.

"Often true," she conceded. "But I'm afraid this particular family is on the brink of becoming dysfunctional. And, I really dislike watching the deterioration of the relationships."

Veronica drove home by back roads and short cuts she had discovered over the years. She did like to drive, of course, but she seldom went anywhere and returned the same way. If asked, she herself could not say if it was her sense of adventure or to relieve boredom. Her only reply would be: "Now, what fun would that be?"

There was an abrupt change in the weather as winds gusted and temperatures dropped quickly. Loose plastic bags and light debris skipped across the road and tumbled through the open fields. As they rounded a bend in the road, a man and woman were struggling mightily to bring in laundry that had been drying on the line—pants, shirts and sheets blowing parallel to the ground. Their dog was fiercely barking at the offending wind from the safety of the front porch.

"I've seen weather change this quickly on a few occasions," Abe observed, "but that was on the high northern plains."

"We get it like this once in awhile," Veronica explained. "When the conditions are just right, the ground winds funnel through the mountains and the gaps in the lower hills. They pick up speed and cause quite a fuss, but they don't last long. As long as you're not on a bridge or out on the water in a sailboat, you're pretty safe."

Once home, retrieving the mail from the box at the curb was a challenge, but Abe managed it well, although he did have a close call when two large trashcans rolled and bounced down the street, nearly clipping his heels.

Knowing that Veronica wanted to get her computer files in order and switched over to the new system, Abe offered to make an early dinner. She headed for the atrium and he to the kitchen. Putting a pan of water on the quick-boil stove burner, he rummaged through the refrigerator for needed ingredients and began chopping. In one hour he called his wife to a dinner of chicken over a bed of rice, with finely chopped green pepper, onion, celery and delicately seasoned cream sauce. The salad of simple baby spinach leaves, shaved carrots and sliced radishes with wine vinaigrette dressing and sprinkled with a few slices of almonds was an attractive dish as well as low in calories. A glass of chilled white wine complimented the meal.

"Where did you learn to cook like this?" she asked as they ate. "This is delicious and looks very complicated."

"As you say of yourself, I like to eat," he answered. "As for being complicated, you'd be surprised what you can do to dress up one can of cream of celery and one can of cream of mushroom soup."

"When it's that easy you shouldn't tell," she said. "It takes all the magic out of the experience."

"Did you get your files integrated okay," he asked.

"Yes," she answered. "It was a snap with the new programming. I was done in fifteen minutes. Then I made a few inquiries with the Francis program and there is an ugly legal trend brewing that will keep lawyers in business for some years to come. That program is so sophisticated that it puts more cross-checked information together in a single package than any ten separate packages I used to be able to assemble."

"Miguel will be so pleased," he said. "We should send him some flowers or something and tell him what a genius he is. He really likes compliments. So, what's this legal trend that's bothering you?"

"A significant number of Muslims from all over the world have immigrated to this country," she began, "particularly since the 1970s. Many are highly educated professionals, with American citizenship. They established Islamic Centers around the country, and made every effort to assimilate. Some groups call themselves progressive and have altered some traditional practices, such as dividing the men and women with a curtain during worship, or not requiring women to wear headscarves in the mosque."

"I've seen men named Mohammad come to the United States who start introducing themselves as Moe," he said, "So I know what you mean about assimilation."

"Everything changed after September 11, 2001," she continued. "The wide use of such terms as 'Islamo-facism' and 'Islamic terrorists' put an ugly label on all Muslims. The general public didn't know any better and the panic that ensued remains with us today."

"And what did Francis come up with?" he asked.

"Thousands of clear violations of the Fourth and Fifth Amendments, to begin with," she said. "The Fourth Amendment: 'The right of the people to be secure in their persons, houses, papers, and effects, against unreasonable searches and seizures, shall not be violated, and no Warrants shall issue, but upon probable cause, supported by Oath or affirmation, and particularly describing the place to be searched, and the persons or things to be seized.' How many times do you think our politicized Department of Justice has violated that amendment since then, all in the name of fighting terrorism?"

"I doubt I can count that high," he replied. "And the Fifth Amendment?"

"That's a multiple choice question," she said. "'No person shall be held to answer for a capital, or otherwise infamous crime, unless on a presentment or indictment of a Grand Jury ... nor shall any person be subject for the same offence to be twice put in jeopardy of life or limb ... be compelled in any criminal case to be a witness against himself, nor be deprived of life, liberty, or property, without due process of law ...' How well do you think we're doing on that score?"

"Don't shoot the messenger," he interrupted. "Francis is just giving you the facts."

"What Francis is giving me is worse than that," she said. "Francis points out that in desperation to not offend the authorities, many Muslims have begun to seek advice from the entirely Afro-American Nation of Islam on how to protect themselves."

"That could be a helpful sign," he said.

"Let me spell it out for you, Sport," she said somberly. "A group of innocent people already under scrutiny for their religion alone hooks up with another group of people of the same religion, but who recruit heavily in the African-American population of our prisons. The second group is already under close watch by federal, state and local authorities. Throw in the use and abuse of the Patriot Act and you get a huge spike in violations of the First, Fourth and Fifth Amendments to our Constitution. Francis put this together very neatly."

"I see what you mean," he answered. "That's not a pretty picture. What do you propose we do about it?"

"If I had the answer to that one, I'd be the first female President of the United States," she answered. "That is, if I wanted to be, which I don't. I can assure you of one thing, though, I'm going to find a million little ways to help this country save itself from itself."

"And you're going to have a partner right at your side helping," he promised.

CHAPTER 19

▼

CRUSADES

Abe awoke to discover the first snowfall of the season had begun overnight and promised to accumulate twelve to eighteen inches over the next two days. Two inches of snow were already on the ground when he retrieved the newspaper from the driveway with winds swirling flakes in every direction, creating mini-drifts that promised to grow much larger as the slow-moving weather system progressed. He stood at the large windows in the atrium, coffee mug in hand, to watch the silent snow blanket the grass and quiet the neighborhood. Little seemed to be stirring and the wild creatures were all snug in their shelters.

"Good morning, my love," Veronica said, coming into the office carrying her own coffee. "What a beautiful snow. With the schools closed, I'll bet this neighborhood will be swarming with children."

"And good morning to you too, love," he answered. "Did you know how great you look even first thing in the morning?"

"You're easy on the eyes yourself, Sport," she replied. "I want you to know that I do appreciate your courtesy in shaving and being decently dressed before coming out for the day. Added to placing coffee on my nightstand every morning, I'd say you're batting a thousand, so far."

"That's one of your most endearing characteristics," he noted. "A woman who is so easy to please. As for the snow, I have the feeling that young Henry and Cassy will be putting their snow-tracking theories to the test. Anything in particular on your agenda for the day?"

"If you're asking if I'll come outside and play in the snow with you, I'm game," she replied. "I'd like it to be later this afternoon, though. On a day like today I get hungry for my version of French onion soup, with croutons and topped with singed mozzarella. With a toasted cheese and sliced tomato sandwich on the side, you have a great lunch."

"Sounds great to me," he said. "Anything I can do to help?"

"Sure," she answered. "I'll get the stock going and you can slice the onions and sauté them. We'll let it simmer for an hour on low heat. I'd like to get real close to my new friend Francis to see what else he can do. What about you?"

"I need to do some research of my own," he said. "Let's get to those onions."

Abe began his research delving into the particular character of America's fear of all things Islamic. The root cause on the surface was ignorance and simplicity in the "Islamo-facism" and "with us or with them" knee-jerk reaction to the destruction of the World Trade Center towers. This was the beginning of a long chain of events that unnecessarily pitted nations against nations and ordained perpetual war under the banner of fighting terrorism. The Islamic world was deemed to be a monolithic set of groups and nations posing an immediate threat to every non-Islamic nation, rather than the diverse and divided groups and nations who had strong disagreements on any number of fundamental issues for centuries. The distorted view of Islam as being either "radical" or "moderate" is ludicrous. The very real divisions in the Middle East alone include at least: religious-secular, Sunni-Shia and Arab-non-Arab. Muslims in the rest of the world reflect even more diversity.

Unfortunately for America and Europe in particular, much of the Islamic world sees Christianity in exactly the same mistaken simplistic form. Many Americans would be surprised to hear that there are no real differences in various Christian churches, including the Catholic Church, which is important because they historically have every reason to loathe and fear the Church of Rome. America as a whole has no idea of the Crusades, much less how they were conducted. The European nations that launched the Crusades fare only slightly better in that department. In the Arab portion of the Islamic world, the Crusades are bitterly ingrained in memory as fresh as yesterday, which is why the very word sparks hair-trigger hatred even today.

"How is it coming, dear?" Veronica asked as she placed a tray with cups and a pot of tea on the credenza. "I thought we could both use a break."

"That's thoughtful, thank you," he replied. "How much do you remember about the Crusades?"

"More than I used to see in the movies," she answered. "I was doing a paper on international property rights under English law some years ago and somehow, I don't remember why, I was sidetracked into the Crusades. It wasn't a pretty picture. I remember one historian characterizing it as an invasion of barbarians into a much more highly cultured and sophisticated world. There was rape, plunder and murder on a massive scale, by both sides, and the relatively few Europeans who made it home did institute some social graces they had learned while in enemy territory. How am I doing so far?"

"You have the general idea," he commented. "Although no single event ever sparks another as vast, unless many other factors are in place, the abuse of a single pilgrimage to holy places is generally accredited to have begun a two hundred year series of Crusades which ended as it had started—utter failure for the Crusaders."

In the 11th Century, pilgrimages from Europe to Palestine were very popular among those who could afford the costs. A group of seven thousand individuals was common, and certain token levies were exacted along the way, but when the Turks took possession of Jerusalem in 1076 they began to plunder the rich pilgrims and abuse the poor. Since pilgrimages were religious, as well as commercial enterprises, this was a blow to both. Religious fervor in Europe, fanned by Pope Urban II, sent up the call for an attempt to conquer Palestine. It became a sacred duty "to deliver the tomb of Christ from the hands of the Infidels." A series of Crusades between 1094 and 1299 all failed in that effort.

"Perhaps the worst of the attempts was the so-called Children's Crusade of 1212," Abe explained. "Two obviously insane priests, under the delusion that the innocence of children would conquer where the avarice of adults had failed, marched through France and Germany, gathering unarmed children without provisions, promising miracles and food from grateful Christians as aid. An estimated fifty thousand boys and girls joined. They split into two groups, one going through Germany, across the Alps to Genoa. They were robbed, abused, sickened and died in great numbers. Seven thousand finally made it to Genoa, were disheartened when the promised parting of the Mediterranean did not occur and dispersed to their various fates. Very few returned home."

"Why am I so reluctant to ask about the other group?" Veronica asked.

"Because you are an intelligent woman," Abe answered. "None in the other group made it home. The French went to Marseilles, where two worthy merchants named Iron Hugh and Pig William offered free passage in seven ships, all for the love of religion and out of pure kindness. What the group of children did not know was that these merchants were in the lucrative business of kidnapping

Christian children for the slave market in Alexandria. On the journey, two ships were lost in a storm, but the other five arrived safely and the cargo sold—the Sultan of Cairo buying forty boys for the amusement of his best soldiers, the most attractive girls ended up in harems far and wide, and only God knows the sufferings of the rest."

"You're right, I probably didn't want to know all of that," she said sadly. "On the subject of property rights, I do know about the proclivity of some of the nobles and knights capturing towns and territories, setting themselves up in these new fiefdoms and wishing the armies well in their quest for Jerusalem. None controlled these new fiefdoms for long. Many others, who had pledged their lands in England to fund their Crusade, never made it home again, or came back without the requisite treasure and lost their property."

"So, what do you suppose the people of the Middle East think of the latest western forays into their region?" he asked.

"Oh Lord," she answered, "I see what you mean. We're there for the oil and this time we're demanding democracy for people who don't want it, forcing western ways down their throats and we're carrying the baggage of Christianity. It's the Crusades all over again and we're uniting disparate elements against the common foe—us."

"Let's have lunch," Abe said at last. "We can eat in the all-season room and enjoy the snow."

Lunch was peaceful and quiet. The snow continued and was predicted to accumulate fourteen to eighteen inches before finally ending during the night. A sanding truck came through the neighborhood, but very few cars were on the roads. The telephone had not rung all day and they cherished their moments in their own private little corner of the world. Veronica shared her childhood memories of snowfalls and playing outside with other children, while Abe recalled the beauty of snows in the Rocky Mountains or on the plains of Montana and Wyoming.

"So, how are you and Francis getting along?" he asked as they cleared and rinsed the dishes. "You seemed as glued to your computer as I was to mine."

"Francis is amazing," she said. "He's a whole lot smarter than I am. As I worked, I began to get the feeling he was building file on my methods and tastes so as to more accurately anticipate where I might want to go. I tested him—I know it's an inanimate object, but I've personalized it—with subtle changes in word usage and he picked it up immediately, even to the point of congratulating me for doing so. How can you not personalize a guy like him? And a guy created him, you know, because a woman's perspective is in the subtle nuances, which he seems to lack. Yet, he's allowing me to teach him."

"You see," he replied, "and women always say that a man never stops to ask for directions. We're much more sensitive then we're given credit."

"You and Miguel I can vouch for," she said with a smile, patting the back of his hand. "The rest of the males will have to prove themselves one at a time."

"What else have you discovered about Francis?" he prodded.

"He, or at least Miguel who created him, has a proclivity toward conspiracies," she replied. "He looks for patterns in the data he mines and lines up all the facts to suggest there might be a conspiracy involved. I ask him to examine each fact and weigh it, pro and con, to see how much validity it may have to the whole. He does that well and quickly, giving me a mathematical probability scale. When I ask for his conclusions, he hesitates, and then rearranges the pattern to point out different possible conclusions. He does not judge which may be most accurate."

"Now, there's a smart man," Abe commented.

"Here's the interesting part," she continued. "When I ask for possible motivations behind the facts he stumbles and tells me that requires emotional analysis, which is beyond his capabilities. He even asked if I would teach him how to do that."

"And what did you answer?" he asked.

"I told him I hoped technology never progressed to that point," she said, "because this world would be in very grave danger of destroying itself. And do you know what Francis said to that? He said it would open the doors to widespread abuse and that it would be all for the better if we never reached that point."

"It sounds to me like Miguel may have unwittingly given Francis a conscience," he replied. "I get to like Francis more all the time."

Two hours later, they had both been at work on their computers and were taking a break over fruit and an afternoon coffee.

"Francis is about to make me the most dreaded professor in the country," Veronica said, pealing an orange. "Just on a whim, I inserted a disc with last year's term papers that were filed and stored electronically. I asked him to double-check citations, punctuation, grammar, etc. and to see if he could find any cases of plagiarism. I had him do that on a background program so I could continue to work."

"And did you find multiple problems?" he asked.

"No, not really," she answered, "just a few small details I missed. Plagiarism in the electronic age is the bane of every school in the world, even trickling down to the elementary level in this day and age. It has spread like the plague through colleges, but it has been my experience, limited to Dickinson, that by the time the student gets to law school, that habit has been broken. Of course law students are as likely as any other person their age to see nothing wrong with downloading free music from the Internet in spite of the obvious copyright infringements. It's the same with pirated CDs and DVDs."

"So what did Francis find?" he asked.

"Well, at first I thought we had a situation to deal with," she answered. Francis seemed a little over-eager in the grammar department. Legalese bothered his sensibilities from the beginning, but the butchering of legalese as practiced today seemed to make the hair on the back of his neck, so to speak, stand on end. He even tried to suggest editing improvements to several amendments to the Constitution and the Constitution itself. He said my objection was noted, but he'd add a footnote stating his position. He's starting to sound like a legal expert himself. I was going to exclude that area from the search, but thought I might find some interesting things, so I left it in and I'm certainly glad I did."

"How so?" he asked.

"Francis uncovered a massive fraud," she answered. "I'm very disappointed that one of my star students who was supposed to graduate with honors in the spring will be tossed out on her ear the first week of next term."

Veronica explained how Francis put together a possible conspiracy at several of the best and largest law schools in the country. Some of the most successful and well-known lawyers provided their children pursuing a career in law every one of their own law school papers and tests. Some had junior members of their firms write some of the papers for the students. One simple mistake was the key—consistency in wrong answers or faulty analysis. Mistakes were preserved so a perfect paper would not raise suspicions. It was an easy trail to follow through separate databases. Veronica knew that the report she was to submit to the dean would have ramifications throughout a large number of law schools and when the methods applied were spread through the law school community, it promised permanent change.

"Well, it is a shame," Abe said, "but at least you uncovered one for the good side."

"I've discovered something much larger and more important," she said with some excitement creeping into her voice. "With the powers of Francis, I've been able to identify a multitude of firms, interest groups, societies and associations working on various aspects of the Patriot Act and ways to fight the abuses or abolish it altogether."

"That sounds like an effective group if they can harness the effort into a single broad cause," he replied. "Of course, I suppose there will be more than a few stumbling blocks in the way."

"Let me count the ways," she answered factiously. "Actually, when I think about it, there are many basic parallels to your concerns about the diversity within Christianity and Islam. The profession of law really comprises a subset of groups, much misunderstood and easily despised by many. Prosecutors are at odds with defense attorneys, trial lawyers are abhorred by corporate entities pleading tort reform, the judiciary must toe a fine line between staying above the fray and sorting out squabbling interests without having their judgments overturned on appeal on a technical question and we academics like to think of ourselves as purists interested only in the intellectual properties of law. Of course, the general public has a never-ending list of lawyer jokes involving sharks and bottom-feeders."

"That's a pretty good list of generalities," he said, "but what about inside the institution itself?"

"That's a good question," she replied. "Inability or unwillingness to share information is a huge problem. An attorney or firm representing a client must keep most information close to the vest, in the interest of the client and for the protection of the firm. The subject of legal ethics is decided on a case-by-case basis. It is an adversarial process from top to bottom with everyone looking for that slight advantage which will benefit its side. And those who are successful tend to be very well paid—quite an incentive in itself."

"You make it all sound so glamorous," he said with a grin.

"There is a saying in law circles that every once in awhile, just as in Congress, justice will be done," she said. "That's what most really strive for—simple justice."

"I can tell you one thing—actually several things," he said. "First of all, I love you and what you stand for. Second, I'm sure that you will soon be in there stirring the pot just to see what happens, come Hell or high water."

"You're on a roll, Sport," she said. "Keep going."

"I have also come to realize something," he said in all seriousness. "We're working together on the same problem, but from different angles and on alternate levels. You want to insure that the Constitutional system of government remains intact and I want to insure its tenets apply to all those who come to our shores. I think we make one heck of a dynamic duo. Who can resist such a lovely couple?"

"And I can tell you that I love you, first of all," she answered. "I also think your analysis of the situation is correct. We are working in the same field. After all, it seems to be the cause of the hour—a complex one, to be sure. Who knows, we might even be able to make a difference?"

CHAPTER 20

▼

WINTER PLAY

A glorious winter morn greeted Abe as he stepped into the atrium, beckoning him to leave his inside chores and come enjoy this rare gift of nature. The snow had stopped during the night, the bright blue sky was graced with puffy clouds racing the strong surface winds to the horizon and the sun reflecting off the snow lit up the landscape. Ten minutes later, Veronica joined him with a tray for their morning coffee ritual, setting the contents on the credenza and wordlessly linking arms to share the view.

"It sure does feel like we've been married a lot longer than we have," he said quietly. "We've already developed a nice morning routine."

"I like this routine," she replied. "I'm going to miss it when the term begins. I'm afraid this leisurely hour or so will not fit the schedule."

"Then what do you say we declare a holiday and go out for a winter's play?" he asked. "I wouldn't want Francis to monopolize your time."

"That's fine with me, Sport," she said with a chuckle. "I'll simply feed the beast a couple of difficult problems to chew over all day. It will give him something to do and keep those canines sharp."

"That means we don't have to get a dog just now," he replied with his own low chuckle. "Also, Francis doesn't require all that cleaning up after. Another plus is that he can get all the exercise he needs just sitting there on your desk."

The doorbell rang and they both went to answer the call. They opened the door to find Frank Butler, hat-in-hand and swaddled against the elements.

"Good morning to you and the missus," Butler said. "I'm sorry not to call first, but my telephone went out with a heavy tree branch of snow."

"Please step in, Mr. Butler," Veronica invited. "What can we do for you?"

"It's Frank, Professor," he answered, stepping into the foyer. "I don't mean to be disturbing newlyweds such as yourselves, but I've come at the behest of Dan. He's usually so quiet, but for two days he's been chattering away. At first he kept going over and over everything that has happened since you found him in the caverns—as if he were afraid he was going to lose the memory if he didn't keep repeating it. Once he became comfortable that wasn't going to happen, he started recalling little incidents—just bits and pieces at first, then asking us if he remembered real events or was it his imagination. Cissy was up half the night with tears of joy and I must admit I did my share of the same."

"We're so happy for you," Veronica said. "I'm sure he'll be improving more quickly now."

"He's in God's hands," Frank replied. "We'll trust in His judgment. This morning, Dan connected a memory from boyhood with one from his adult years: his enjoyment of going for a sleigh ride in the first suitable snow. So on behalf of the Butler family, we'd like to offer you a sleigh ride of your own as our wedding present."

"We'd be honored," Abe said. "Please join us for coffee and we'll bundle ourselves properly against the cold. We were looking for an excuse to play hooky anyway and the universe sent us you."

"Thank you, but no," Frank replied. "I need to go harness Jasmine to the sleigh. She's a spirited girl, but you know how to handle horses, I presume? You take your time. Cissy would like to give you a good breakfast. She insists and she'll be packing you a nice lunch and a thermos, so just bring yourselves."

"We'll need sunglasses," Abe said after Butler had gone. "The sun will be intense glaring off the snow. I think we should take the Jeep. Do you want to drive?"

"I thought you'd never ask," she replied. "Let's go get that breakfast."

The main roads were clear and fairly dry as they left the neighborhood, but Veronica wanted to take the back roads so she could try her hand at the four-wheel drive. She was a careful driver, always on the lookout for slippery spots and making only slow gradual turns and using the lower gears on downhill grades. The smaller side roads had hard-packed snow and they spotted several people on skis out enjoying themselves and even a few hikers with snowshoes and ski poles crossing the fields. It struck Abe that these people really knew how to take advantage of the opportunities, whatever the season.

"How are you at those sports?" he asked Veronica.

"I can hold my own with the skis," she answered, "but I'm just plain clumsy on snowshoes. I don't so much walk in them as plow with them—that is when I can move at all."

"I find that hard to believe," he replied. "Maybe you just need more practice. Perhaps I'll buy you a pair for your birthday."

"Do as you wish," she said with a smile. "There won't be any snow on the ground then, but I doubt we'll be able to find them when the season rolls around again."

As they drove up the lane to the Butler farm, Jasmine was in harness and feeding from a bucket of oats. Abe knew horses and he judged this one to be beautiful and well muscled. She was jet-black with a silky mane and tail, with a graceful curve to her lines that spoke of some Arabian heritage. Abe was drawn immediately to the horse and went to introduce himself—stroking her neck and talking softly into her ear. Jasmine responded with a shake of her head.

The breakfast was sumptuous and the company charming.

"This is all part of what we call the 'farmers' diet," Cissy explained. "My two men keep fit and need the fuel to work this farm. Of course, if you look at some of the waistlines around town, you'll see some people still on that diet, but without the farming—if you know what I mean."

"Dan went over to Grace Lawson's place next door to clear her drive," Frank said. "He asked if you would mind dropping by on your ride so he can see how you look. She has been spending a lot of her time over here, but we don't mind. She's real good for Dan and even helps with his chores."

"Now you two had better get on your way," Cissy said, packing the last few items into a large picnic basket on the counter. "I see Jasmine's getting restless and is ready for some exercise. You'll find two lap robes stowed in the back locker and some oats."

"Don't bother clearing the table," Frank instructed. "I'll help with that. We're all friendly around here, so go anywhere you like, but if you get as far as the Harvey place—he has the big yellow silo painted like an ear of corn—you'd better stick to the road. His arthritis gives him no comfort in this weather and he's apt to be real cranky."

As they walked to the sleigh, the wind that had been blowing hard and drifting snow against any stationary object in its path began to subside. Still, the air had a bite to it and they were glad to have the lap robes for cover.

"You want to drive?" Abe asked.

"Not this time, Sport," Veronica answered. "This is more along the line of your expertise. I'll just sit an enjoy the scenery."

A short flick of the reins was all Jasmine required—she was off in a slow trot down the lane. Their first stop was to see Dan and Grace and thank them for the present. Grace proved to be a kind, diminutive woman who barely reached to Dan's chest and wore the glow of a schoolgirl when she laughed. After a short visit, they were on the way again.

The countryside was like a Currier and Ives print: splotches of snow clung to the branches of fir trees, breath steamed out of the nostrils of meandering live-stock and smoke curled from chimneys of the farm houses. They slowed to watch a group of children sledding on a locally favorite hill and returned waves from people shoveling porches and steps or going about the seemingly never-ending chores of farm life. Abe stopped briefly at the crest of a hill just to admire the wintry scene stretching the entire length of the valley. There were a number of horse-drawn vehicles to see—not only the Amish buggies, but also aged sleighs that had been waiting patiently in barns and sheds for just such a day to arrive.

Abe guided Jasmine into a widely spaced stand of trees along a creek so that the horse could drink and the passengers could eat lunch. They were pleasantly surprised to find Cissy had packed fried chicken, hot German potato salad in an insulated container and apple pie for dessert. One small thermos contained hot cider and a larger one coffee. The brisk air had given them both an appetite, which made the meal all the more satisfying. Jasmine was fed her oats by hand.

"This is the kind of day I don't want to end," Veronica said softly. "This is so much better than a carriage ride through Central Park. I haven't been in a sleigh since I was a little girl in pigtails."

"And I'll bet you were a cute little thing even then," Abe replied. "Sleighs are still pretty common in Montana and a few countries I've been to in Europe, but I never gave much thought to the possibilities in Pennsylvania."

"Since the advent of the automobile, you don't find them in many towns," she replied, "but farms have the space and the storage, so you do see them here. Just a few years ago, I saw an old bearded man coming out of his woods, double-edged axe over his shoulder, with a team of oxen pulling a sledge piled high with fire-wood. It was a scene quite in keeping with colonial America. People here are practical and use the tools at hand."

"Sometimes the simplest ways are best," he commented. "It's like that on a cattle ranch—which is farming, but the only digging you do is for a well or fence posts."

It was a leisurely ride back to the Butler farm. The Harvey silo painted to resemble an ear of corn could be seen easily from a distance and Abe made sure they stayed to the road in passing. Once in the barn, Abe showed Veronica how to properly curry and brush Jasmine. He did one side while she did the other. It was their way of thanking her for a splendid day. As they emerged from the barn their hosts were walking from the house.

"I'm sure she liked that," Frank said. "Just like a woman, she likes to be fussed over. Don't spoil her though."

"Just like a man, you mean," Cissy replied. "I fuss over you and you get all mushy inside." Her husband merely smiled in return.

"The phone is working again," Dan said. "We just had a call. Henry Cunningham and something he called the Wolves and Wolvettes—whoever they are—need your advice. You should be on your way. They're on the road a mile east of the Planner place."

"I know the way," Veronica said. "Thank you again for the wonderful wedding present. This was a day we'll always remember. And please thank Dan again for us."

Henry Cunningham, Cassy Spease and their group were easily found at the spot indicated. Veronica pulled over to the side of the road out of the traffic lane.

"What do you need, Henry?" Abe asked and he stepped from the Jeep.

"Would you please give us a hand, Uncle Abe and Aunt Veronica?" Henry replied, a plea in his voice. "We're not sure what to think. We've got tracks here of a pickup truck and what is probably a horse trailer. You can see a man's boot tracks where he unloaded an animal and let it out into the field, but they aren't like any horse tracks we've seen. The animal must be sick or injured by the way it seems to have staggered across the field. Who would just dump an injured animal like that in somebody else's field and drive away? He'd have to be a pretty sorry individual to be that cruel, if you ask me."

Abe examined the scene carefully for a full five minutes, squatting ever so often and picking at the imprints. He finally stood and looked in the direction the animal had gone.

"Henry, you're going to have to learn not be so judgmental or jump to conclusions before you have all the facts," Abe said quietly, but kindly. "You need to closely read the story tracks have to tell. Let's start with the truck. If you look closely, you'll see the front tires are nearly bald and way out of alignment. The back tires aren't much better. The driver must be desperate to take that truck out in these icy conditions. Now, what can you tell me about the trailer tracks?"

"They look okay to me," Henry said, squatting and taking a closer look. "The tires aren't new, but there's good tread and they are deep enough to pick stones lodged in the one on the left."

"And what does that tell you?" Abe asked.

"That he either borrowed it or it hasn't had much use," Cassy Spease answered.

"I think she's right," Henry admitted without any embarrassment. "It's only logical. And Cassy's pretty observant."

"And the man's boots?" Abe prompted.

"They're old and worn," Henry replied after careful examination. "They're down at the heel and the soles are worn mighty thin. You can see holes opening up on both."

"And now to the horse," Abe said, "and it is a horse in pretty bad shape. It's unshod and the hooves haven't been tended to for far too long. The ragged and turned edges mean they are curling up and fracturing. That horse is severely lame and the only reason it is still on its feet is that it is also undernourished. What story fits the facts?"

"Well," Henry replied, looking off in the distance to where the horse had gone, "most people who own horses love the animals. This man seems to be down on his luck and probably can't afford to feed it, much less give it proper care. He could have just killed it and buried the carcass somewhere, but wanted to give it another chance to live rather than just waste away like that. So he leaves it in farm country, far from his home because somebody might recognize the horse as his; here however, there is every chance someone will find it and take it in."

"Right you are," Abe said. "What do you and your group think you should do about it?"

"I think we should split up into two groups," Henry said authoritatively. "Being that lame, the horse probably didn't get that far. Cassy, you take one group and get the sheriff and line up some medical assistance. I'll take the other group and we'll find it. I'll call you to tell you where we are. Then we'll have to find someone to take it in."

"If I may make a suggestion on your last point," Veronica said, "I think you should contact the Butlers. They have a horse and a couple of extra stalls. And, I think Dan and his neighbor would like nursing it back to health."

The group scattered to their separate chores and the adults climbed back into the Jeep.

"Do you think we should stay and help?" Veronica asked before turning on the ignition.

"As a matter of fact I don't," Abe replied. "I think we should step aside at this point and let them earn the responsibility. I'm sure they can handle the situation and they should get the credit. It will be an important step in their journey to maturity. Their shoulders may be small right now, but their spirits are broad and convictions run deep."

"You're right of course," she answered. "Besides, if they get into a situation where they need help, I'm sure they won't be shy. Keep your cell phone charged, Sport. Uncle Abe and Aunt Veronica are officially on standby."

When they arrived in their neighborhood, they found plenty of activity. Families were out building snow sculptures—men, women, animals and one rather fanciful rendition of a troll. In the common area behind their house, two short snow walls had been built thirty feet apart and a snowball fight was in progress. Invigorated rather than spent by their day out of doors, they asked to join the fray and were immediately accepted, each taking a different side. Abe heard a young boy on his side make a scoffing remark that Veronica on the other side probably was no threat because she would throw like a girl. With her first toss, Veronica had knocked the boy's hat off his head and led her side to victory. All the boy could say to Veronica as the sides shook hands in a show of good sportsmanship was that she had an "awesome" arm. She had gained a new respect among the boys and girls alike.

Abe and Veronica invited all the participants into their all-season room, with it's tiled floor, for hot chocolate and petit fours left over from the Christmas holidays. By the time the young people left for home—there was the promise of a rematch the next time it snowed—Abe and Veronica had a new set of friends.

"You know," Abe said after their guests had gone, "you do have an awesome arm. Where did you learn to throw like that?"

"It was simple," she answered. "I was a tomboy when I was younger and competed against all the neighborhood boys whenever I could. I developed a good pitch for pickup baseball games. Wait until you see me on the basketball court. I've got a mean hook shot."

"No doubt," he said. "How about football?"

"My mother wouldn't let me compete there," she replied. "She drew the line there, saying it wasn't very lady-like."

"How about a rodeo event?" he asked.

"I'm competitive," she answered, "not crazy. A girl could get hurt in that type activity and I'd end up suing a bull or something."

CHAPTER 21

▼

BEGINNINGS

When Veronica opened the shade on the master bedroom window, she was surprised to see Abe standing on the back patio smoking his pipe and watching the sunrise over the distant mountain. This was a sure sign that he was deep in thought, mulling over some problem in his mind, so she left him to his solitude and went to the kitchen to fix breakfast. He did not seem to notice as she put place settings on the table in the all-season room where they ate most of their meals. It was not until she had brought the food and filled two cups of coffee that he looked up and smiled through the window. She smiled in return as she waved for him to come to the table.

"Good morning, love," he said as he came through the door and divested his jacket, hanging it over the back of his chair. "Thank you for yesterday and every other day. In fact, thank you in advance for this day and all the others to come."

"You're welcome," she said warmly. "And I return the thanks. Who would have thought marriage would be so wonderful? You make my life complete."

"That's just what I've been thinking," he said, kissing her good morning. "I thought I'd let you sleep in or I would have made breakfast."

"Six months ago, I would have," she responded. "These days I don't want to sleep in. There seems to be so much extra to enjoy in life that I don't want to miss one minute."

They ate slowly, watching the snow melt as patches of grass peeked through. A warm weather front has passed through during the night and the day promised to be above the normal temperature.

"So, what's on your agenda for today," he asked when they had finished eating.

"I thought I'd start with Francis," she answered. "It should be interesting to see how he did with the little projects I submitted yesterday and go from there. And you?"

"I need to check on a few projects overseas," he said. "Later this morning I'll check on Henry and Cassy's progress with the horse and I want to talk to John Nagy about heading up a new foundation idea that has occurred to me. There will be a healthy stipend attached and his mother could be included. I also want to look into doing something to assist our newly returned veterans, particularly the Reserve and National Guard forces."

"Please assure me that you're not thinking of going somewhere and putting yourself in harm's way," she said. "I'm getting to like this marriage arrangement quite well. Besides, I don't look well in black widow's weeds."

"You look great in anything, especially black," he chided. "No, I'm not thinking of putting myself in harm's way. The only injury I'm likely to suffer will be eye strain from too much time in front of the computer monitor, unless, of course, I hurt my back showering you with love and kindness."

"You do have a silver tongue, Sport," she said. "Do you want me to hum in your ear?"

"Maybe later, dear," he replied. "We've both have work to do first."

They both worked at their computers throughout the morning, with Veronica sliding recording discs in and out of her machine every so often. By long habit, she always backed up her work just in case she had a computer crash or a power surge, not to mention a power outage. That happened often enough at the law school. She knew that Abe had a whole-house surge protector installed and that the odds of her new computer crashing were next to nil. She also had a five-hour battery backup, but didn't want to get in the habit of not making copies at school.

"How are you and Francis getting along today?" he asked over the large hoagies she had made for lunch.

"Splendid," she answered. "He had quite a time yesterday while we were at play. He scoured the country for cases and law firms working on First, Fourth and Fifth Amendment issues related to the Patriot Act. He set up a nice, thorough database to network e-mails to all those found. I sent out an inquiry to see if there is any interest in sharing what they are doing with others through a central location in return for a look at what others are doing, free of charge. I reckoned that the big firms with active clients are already being paid, as are those on retainer. They can't afford not to join, if only to be sure they haven't missed something that would jeopardize their winning in court. And the little firms would have access to the thinking of the big boys, along with a great deal of research at their fingertips."

"Won't some of the big firms be concerned that such a system might cut down on their number of billable hours?" he asked.

"Not at all," she replied. "It's no secret that some of those firms keep their billable hours at the maximum level by charging just for thinking about a case or a client. It is no stretch of the truth to say I personally know of one partner of a big Philadelphia firm who went on a golfing vacation for an entire two weeks. Every night in a bar he chatted with another big-time attorney from California over certain points of law. When he returned to his office, he billed each of his clients who had anything pending on the subjects discussed, both for his time and the expenses on his bar bill."

"So there really are lawyers who are as bad as the jokes?" he asked.

"Oh, he's not the worst," she said. "Would you believe the California attorney sent the Philadelphia attorney a bill for his time and expenses? It may have been in jest, because there is no way it will be paid, but this California wizard of the law will probably use the loss as a deduction on his taxes. Welcome to the wonderful world of legal ethics, or lack thereof."

"The firms I use—make that we use—are on retainer," he said. "Each attorney was a friend first and I had done work either for them personally or one of their clients. I think we're pretty well covered on that front."

"I trust your judgment," she replied. "You had the common sense to ask me to marry you, didn't you? Oh, by the way Francis has his first pen pal. He stumbled upon a political science student burning the midnight oil in the law library of the University of Virginia. His name is Morris and Francis saw he'd never accessed the material he was looking for, so Francis gave the kid some suggestions on how to go about it properly. They had a friendly keyboard conversation for over one-half hour and Francis wanted to know if it was okay to contact Morris in the future."

"I trust you said yes," he said earnestly. "Francis probably gets a little lonely out there on the road at night."

"Oh, brother. Don't tell me you're beginning to think he's human," she laughed. "So, what have you and Dudley been doing with yourselves all morning?"

"Just guy things," he shrugged. "You know, hanging around the pool hall in cyberspace and talking about football."

"My, you're full of yourself today," she smiled. "What makes you so giddy?"

"You, my love," he said. "You make me feel like I'm seventeen again."

"I bet you weren't giddy at seventeen," she replied. "In fact, you were probably very serious at that age."

"You're right, of course," he admitted. "I suppose you gave me a second chance at capturing my young manhood. Actually, I did have a prosperous day so far."

Abe listed a number of projects they were involved with overseas, their joint real estate holdings and an anonymous contribution they had made to pay off the mortgage on a private small community hospital in upstate New York that was about to go into foreclosure. Unburdened by the mortgage, the hospital could now restructure its debt in a more manageable package and remain open for at least a few more years.

"You've just given me an idea," she said when he had finished. "You know that generous account you set up for me? You told me to spend it any way I chose and a girl can only buy so many pairs of shoes. If I get the kind of response that I expect from my blanket inquiry this morning, I'd like to spend some of those funds to endow a chair at Dickinson and open a center for compiling and distributing information on cases dealing with the preservation of the Constitution. Do you think Miguel could build us a computer system that would handle so much information in a timely and efficient manner?"

"I'm sure he'd be delighted," he answered. "You work up the specifics of your needs and I'll donate the system. That way, we can make this a joint project."

"You're on," she said, hurrying to her computer.

Abe made a few telephone calls and e-mails. Veronica made only one telephone call. It was to her mother to offer a place in the new center at the law school, topping off the pitch by observing that Ruby would be in the right place to hear all the gossip and do the right thing for the country at the same time. It was an offer Ruby could not refuse.

"Our trust in Henry and Cassy was well placed," Abe said after Veronica had finished her conversation. "Frank Butler said that the sheriff came to his place yesterday with Cassy Spease in tow. Frank could hardly contain himself as Cassy gave him her plea and says she 'used all her feminine wiles in the name of humanity.' Frank was predisposed to take the horse, but let her complete her entire argument before agreeing. Once the deal was made and they shook hands on it, Cassy whispered to Frank that she was going to nominate him for a Jose, the Bronx Beaver award, but not to tell anybody."

"She's my kind of girl," Veronica said. "Perhaps I can interest her in law school in a few years."

"Meanwhile, Henry was at the top of his form," he continued. "He found the horse only fifty feet from a barn full of hay. The animal just couldn't take another step. He had his team members haul a bale out to the horse, along with a pail of water, called in his find and stroked the animal to keep it calm until help arrived. When the owner of the barn came to see what all the commotion was about, Henry tried to give him six dollars—all he had on him at the time—to pay for the feed, but the man insisted on making it his contribution. He also managed to find some oats, but cautioned not to over-feed or allow too much water, which would do more harm than good."

"What great young people," she said. "When they get back in class, the teachers are going to wonder how they matured so quickly over such a short break."

"John Nagy will be over shortly," Abe said. "Why don't you sit with us in the library while I hash over some ideas with him? I asked him to bring his mother. There could be a place for her in this too."

By the time John and Bea arrived, a pot of hot tea and a few snacks were on the table in the library.

"I've read all the material you gave me on the Islamic Society of Greater Harrisburg," Abe began, "and with your background in education, I have a proposal that might interest you."

"I'm open," John said, "and Mother is interested in doing anything she can to help."

"I went to the website of the Islamic Society" he continued, "and I was impressed that one of its efforts is intriguing. It conducts an outreach program to all the other churches in the area to let them know what they are about and invites them to participate in inter-faith activities. As the same time there is an education program for their members making them aware of the different churches and what they stand for, differences in religious practices and things of that sort. I'd like to supplement these efforts with the citizenry at large. From some of the comments we've heard lately, there certainly is a need."

"I know what you mean," John said. "Either many people don't remember the civil rights movement or they seem to think the anti-discrimination laws don't apply to Muslims."

"What I'm thinking about is creating a non-profit entity to foster a community relations speaker's bureau with a twist," Abe said.

As he described what he had in mind, he outlined a non-rigid organization open to any number of approaches, but starting with a speaker's bureau. The Islamic Society would be approached for assistance in selecting volunteer speakers who were not necessarily clerics, well versed in the diversity of the Muslim world and the variety of cultures included under the banner of Islam. Luncheon or dinner speakers would address various fraternal and civic groups such as the Masons, Rotary, Lions and Kiwanis. Another idea, still in its infancy, would be to rent a large room at the Hotel Hershey—a four-star operation—offering an extensive buffet dinner, free of charge. Groups of perhaps fifty to one hundred people from a series of neighborhoods would be invited to hear a talk and it might be a good idea to have at least a few Muslim professionals sprinkled around the room so that the neighbors could have a face-to-face conversation, even if there were no Muslims in their particular neighborhood.

"That could get a little expensive," John said.

"Perhaps, and perhaps not," Abe replied. "What I hope may happen is that if we are successful in the first few months, those most interested may want to sponsor their own dinners. These may take a different form, such as a get-together in a community center or an open house to accommodate fewer people. I'd like to reach our academics—a group that appears to be woefully short in the knowledge department on this particular subject. If they can attain a new perspective, this will be passed on to the students, at least to some extent."

Abe mentioned a healthy stipend if John would take on such a project and that he would provide all the computer equipment he might need if he wanted to start this from his home. If he preferred office space and staff, there would be sufficient funds to cover these expenses as well. He would have complete freedom to pursue any other avenues he wished to test theories and follow opportunities that came his way. The non-profit would have a generous budget and not accept contributions for the first eighteen months, a sufficient period to see if such a project were needed or purposeful. Abe wanted to avoid people making charitable contributions to a cause until it had proven its validity.

"You really are an admirer of Whittier, aren't you?" John commented rather than questioned.

"What makes you say that?" Veronica asked.

"His Christmas gift to Doc," John answered. "It was an original edition of *The Pennsylvania Pilgrim and Other Poems* by John Greenleaf Whittier. As I recall, both Abe and Doc were able to quote passages from the titled poem. I was curious and looked in my own library to reread the story. There is a section with a description of how much the pilgrim enjoys just sitting around with a diverse group of people, discussing their views on a wide range of topics, with no subject taboo. 'To touch all themes of thought, nor weakly stop/For doubt of truth, but let the buckets drop/Deep down and bring the hidden waters up./For there was freedom in that wakening time/Of tender souls; to differ was not crime;/The varying bells made up the perfect chime.' Is that what you're after, Abe, insuring the varying bells are heard?"

"That's exactly it," Abe admitted.

"Then, I'm your man," John said.

"And I'm your woman," Bea said. "I'll be an unpaid volunteer and jack-of-all-trades. I'd like to stir things up in this country—shine some light into those dark corners where too many people are cowering."

"Mother, welcome to the cause," John said as he gave her a kiss on the cheek. "Let's go get organized and give these newlyweds some time to enjoy the school break."

"Abe," Veronica said when they were alone once more, "I really do admire you more each day. I like your 'hand up, not a hand out' approach to things. You put your money into worthy causes, and then fade back into the shadows. You work behind-the-scenes and shun the limelight. Your ego doesn't need the boost and you are naturally suited to that role. How am I doing so far?"

"I'd say you are a fair judge of character," he answered, taking her by the hand with a grin. "You just keep on those rose colored glasses and we can make a go of it, quite nicely, thank you."

"You, too, Sport," she cooed. "Now, we need to make some decisions about New Year's Eve. 'The date is fast upon us,' as someone famous once said."

"Unless you have something else in mind," he replied, "I like to stick close to home. I'd rather just have a quiet celebration here. There are always too many amateur celebrants on the road. Maybe we should invite John and Bea over. Ruby, too—we have the guest room and she wouldn't have to be out on the highway either."

"That suits me just fine," she agreed. "It would be a pleasant way to usher out the old and welcome all the possibilities for the new. My, how our lives have changed in a brief six months."

EPILOGUE

▼

The first month of the New Year was a flurry of activity in the Carlson household as plans for the new ventures took form. As expected, Veronica received widespread interest in her information exchange center for Constitutional Law—so much interest, in fact, that she had to revise her predictions upward. The Dickinson School of Law was delighted to allow her to endow a chair and welcomed the idea of a new center with enthusiasm. Not only would these enhance the prestige of the school, but also all of the expense would be borne by the contributors. She had won a new level of respect from the administration, not to mention the governing board, but only a begrudging recognition from some of the faculty. She was learning lessons about the consequences of philanthropy, both pro and con. Ruby and her hard as nails approach proved a saving grace as did her long experience in dealing with school bureaucracy. To its credit, the administration had handled the cheating incident quietly and efficiently. When confronted with Veronica's report, the one student involved quietly withdrew from the school. There would be reverberations at the other schools involved and every law school in the country would be revising their policies now that they knew where to look.

Abe split his available time between Veronica's efforts and John's start-up project with the Islamic Society of Greater Harrisburg. The Society was only too happy to join in the effort and spread the word throughout Muslim circles. There was some excited discussion about making this a national program, but Nagy cautioned a gradual approach to see if the idea was workable on a local scale first. To no one's surprise, Bea proved to have a natural knack of raising volunteer interest across all age groups. She quickly became a grandmother figure to the younger set and charmed her own generation, gently prodding when the situation warranted. It was John who had christened this new enterprise "The Whittier Center for Constructive Comparison," a title he thought sufficiently vague as to be accepted without comment from those of bureaucratic mind. The Center had scheduled fifteen speakers in various venues for the month of February and the expectation of many requests as a result.

At the first stated meeting of the year at the Brownstone Masonic Lodge, Abe's petition for dual membership was granted and he became involved in the Lodge's projects. He had always felt most comfortable at the Blue Lodge level because that was where Masons were made and he felt closest to the community. He had a particular interest in a new project still in its infancy to be of assistance to Masonic members of the Armed Forces who were returning to civilian life after service in war. Wives and family members were urged to join in the effort and Abe knew this was another level of opportunity in which he and Veronica could participate.

On the last day of January, Veronica was walking across campus when a student from the mailroom hailed her and presented a thick special delivery envelope. Its contents could mean a career changing experience. The cover letter congratulated her on the establishment of the new center at Dickinson and carried an official invitation to become part of a new group being formed on an international basis. The importance of her participation was stressed because she would fill a gap with her unique center. Enclosed was a fifty-page report on the effort and her potential influence should she accept. The package was from Georgetown University's School of Law, the center for international legal studies. The rallying point of this new group was entitled: "Human Rights in Time of Terror." Her developing work on the domestic front, with real cases winding their way through the court system would be a natural fit, like being on the street end of the process, she thought. In return, the amount of information on the international level she could pass back through the center and out into the country would be invaluable. She rushed home to tell Abe first and he was as elated as she. Only then did she inform the school administration.

The first day of February, it seemed half the residents of Hummelstown attended an all-day open house for its newest enterprise: "The New Antiquarian Bookshop; You Ask, We'll Find." The parents of Frank, the East Indian newsstand owner, were open for business. Even with the remodeling, the shop was small, so in an act of inventive adaptation, several bookshelves to the rear were cleared of volumes for the day and plates of Indian delicacies and other foods were placed on the shelves. The new owners had received a warm welcome by the community. In typical fashion, nearly every family that attended the open house brought something to eat, thus lessening the burden on the owners. Frank and his parents stood by the door welcoming each guest personally. A couple of neighboring businesses volunteered to supervise the food and drink.

Abe and Veronica found an out-of-the-way corner near the front of the store with view of the street, watching people come and go. Abe had been studying a woman across the street. She had a pronounced limp as she slowly and sadly passed up the street, with a gaze far ahead that could only indicate one thing— she had the intense look of a recently returned war veteran lost in her own thoughts. When he turned to Veronica, he saw she had been watching him and the woman. As if reading his thoughts, she merely nodded. All he said was: "I think I have my next project. We own a nice condominium in the Washington area. It's about to get some use."

NEW VENTURES

CHAPTER 1

▼

HOMECOMING

It was an overcast March morning, with the remnants of the season's last snowfall still tucked away in small corners of the landscape and slowly melting, that Sgt. Bradley Lucius Trimbel, aged twenty-one, was laid to rest in a small cemetery on the outskirts of Hummelstown, Pennsylvania. His flag-draped coffin stood testament to where he had been, how he had died and why he was joining the growing list of the freshly fallen to lay side-by-side into eternity. This cemetery contained the remains of veterans dating back as far as the Revolutionary War, with every major conflict this country had engaged in since. This was the recurring cycle that mankind had never been able to break since the beginning of time. Wars were fought for whatever reason and those who carried the burden on the battlefield who were lucky enough to return home, did so in a box, as walking wounded, or as simply changed forever.

Among those attending the funeral were the American Legion, the Veterans of Foreign Wars and a respectable contingent from the Brownstone Lodge, Free and Accepted Masons. Sgt. Trimbel had become a Master Mason just prior to shipping out and would have joined one or both of the other two organizations upon his return.

The memorial service at the funeral home included the brief, but impressive, Masonic funeral service, with its pure message of farewell to a worthy brother moving on—they would meet again on the other side. Four officers of the Lodge—Master, Senior and Junior Wardens, and Chaplain—clad in formal tuxedos, white gloves, lambskin aprons, and collars from which were suspended the jewels of their office, conducted the simple rites accompanied by dark-suited members of the Lodge. This was the only formal rite in Freemasonry witnessed by the general public and gave insight into the depth of feeling within the brotherhood. A pedestal next to the flag-draped coffin held a picture of Sgt. Trimbel in uniform and his Masonic apron. With few words, the officers placed there a scroll inscribed with his name and Masonic record, then three sprigs of evergreen as emblems of faith in the immortality of the soul. Each Mason stepped before the coffin to silently say "Farewell, my Brother," then passed quietly from the room.

At the graveside, the service took on a more military bearing, with cause. Merely one month hence, Trimbel's younger sister, Rebecca, would be deployed to a combat zone, carrying on the family tradition. A final volley was fired and taps played from a tape recorder—the military no longer provided a bugler—then the mourners quietly dispersed.

Two older women walking from the graveyard were Ruby Steinmann, a retired civics teacher from Elizabethtown's Masonic Village, and Mary Stevens, a retired operating room nurse from Steelton.

"It seems I attend too many funerals these days," Ruby said. "At our age, our friends and family are expected to go sometime, but with the young, all I can think about is what a future they may have had. I taught Brad's father in school and remember how proud he was of both his children. I attended his funeral too, when he and his wife were killed in that accident two years ago. Now three of the four slots in the family plot are filled. I just hope it is many, many years before Rebecca joins them."

"Yes, it's been hard on Becky," Mary replied. "I sometimes think that she joined the service directly out of high school so she could be near her brother. They were always very close and he was so protective of her. I believe she thought that somehow she could return the protection."

"I've been watching men come home in a coffin since Korea," Ruby said, "far too many as far as I'm concerned. Now they are being joined by an increasing number of women. Honor the soldier, but despise the war—any war."

"On a more pleasant subject," Mary said, "how are the newlyweds doing?"

"Splendidly, I'm happy to report," Ruby answered with a sudden lilt in her voice. "You'll see for yourself. I invited us to lunch today."

Ruby's daughter, Veronica, was a professor of constitutional law at the Dickinson School of Law. At the age of forty-six, Ruby didn't think Veronica would ever get married. Although very successful and quite a beauty, Veronica simply never met a man that was up to her standards. Everything changed last July when

Abe Carlson, a fifty-one year old tracker from Arizona, with an international clientele, walked into her life. He had never married either and had no such designs because he thought his frequent and protracted trips around the world would not bode well for such a relationship. Nevertheless, in the couple of short weeks he was in town, they were engaged. When he returned from an overseas trip five months later, he moved into a new house that Veronica and Ruby had furnished and decorated, well within his generous budget. On the day he moved, between Christmas and New Year's, Abe told Veronica that she was the only thing missing, so they went to the courthouse and were married by a judge Veronica knew well.

"I hear they're both wonderful with children," Mary said.

"With children and adults alike," Ruby corrected. "For the younger ones, Abe made up a story to go with an actual newspaper item about Jose, the Bronx Beaver, turning it into a lesson in kindness to others. The children liked it so well that they formed a club and, with the help of some older teenagers, wrote and published the story in book form. They sold some copies and gave others away to children who could not afford them. With the money earned above production costs, they have award plaques made, and present them to people around town they see showing kindness and giving aid to others."

"Is that where that thing got started?" Mary asked. "I've heard of a similar project just starting in Steelton, but I didn't know Veronica and Abe were involved."

"They like to do things from behind the scenes," Ruby said. "After Abe tracked the lost Cunningham boy through the night and pulled him out of a sinkhole, young Henry and his friend Cassy Spease started their own group of trackers. With a little help from Abe and Veronica, the group tracked a very sick, dying and severely lame horse and brought it to safety. It is now recovering under the auspices of Dan Butler and his neighbor, Grace Lawson."

"My, those two are a busy pair," Mary remarked. "What are they up to lately?"

"Abe was pretty well heeled when he came into the marriage," Ruby said in a confidential tone. "Veronica was able to open the Exchange Center for Constitutional Law, where, as you know, I've been working. She's also part of a much larger project in conjunction with the Georgetown University's School of Law. We have a computer system designed by that German, Miguel, who designed Veronica's Francis system and Abe's Dudley system. Miguel Swartzbaugh may be a bit quirky when it comes to naming his systems, but he's an engineering genius. Abe's Whittier Center for Constructive Comparison is up and running very well, educating Americans on the great diversity within the Muslim world and the cultures that have shaped the great varieties of Islam to be found around the globe."

"I've heard only good things about Abe's efforts in Steelton," Mary said. "His work with the Islamic Society of Greater Harrisburg has made great inroads in our town."

"The Whittier Center is in the very capable hands of their neighbor, John Nagy and his mother, Bea," Ruby replied. "I think Abe is fishing around for a new project—as if he doesn't have enough on his plate."

It was a short drive through the countryside to the Carlson's new home. As was increasingly the case, their new development of mixed single family and duplex homes was built on former farmland. Located near the southern edge of Derry Township, which included Hershey, it was close to major roadways and surrounded by working farms and timbered acres, with views of the surrounding hills. Situated on the top of a hill, the residents of the development could see the steam rising from the cooling towers of the Three Mile Island Nuclear Power Plant.

The Carlson home was a large duplex unit built on a slab, with ample room for one-floor living and the option of finishing a bonus room above the garage. They spent most of their time in the well-lighted atrium and all-season room built to the rear of the home, with views of the common area and the mountains in the distance. It was a change from Abe's long view of wide-open spaces from his ranch house in Arizona, but he welcomed the change as fostering the intimacy of his recent marriage. They were close enough to Carlisle so it was an easy commute for Veronica to the Dickinson School of Law and Abe did most of his work through his computer in their office. The state capital of Harrisburg was within a few miles and there was easy access to southern routes to the nation's capital of Washington, D.C. Both Veronica and Abe found their professional lives being drawn to the south.

As Ruby drove up their street, Abe and Veronica were just returning from a late morning walk. They made a handsome couple. Abe was a man of medium height, with a trim muscular frame and weathered look of an outdoorsman. In his lightweight jacket and casual slacks, there was little to distinguish him from any man on the street, but his low-heeled western walking boots gave some indication of his regional roots. Veronica, her tall slim figure clad in a wool rolled-neck sweater and wool pants, was radiant as always with her long ash brown hair pulled back into a ponytail, with just the right touch of makeup.

"It looks as if marriage has been very good for both of them," Mary remarked as Ruby pulled into the driveway and parked in front of the two-car garage.

"He seems to have shaven five years off his age," Ruby agreed, "and she has developed a mature contentment that is very becoming. That just goes to show: love at any age can make life a joy. Those two have been loners most of their lives, but as a couple, they are complementary. And that, dear friend, can only improve and deepen with time."

Luncheon was served at a large round glass table in the all-season room, with ferns and other plants that were indoors for the winter ready for the first warm days of spring. Veronica had made a quiche-like savory summer pie for the occasion and Abe improvised a Mediterranean salad from a mysterious mix of ingredients on hand.

"Tell Mary how Miguel comes up with those interesting names for his computer systems," Ruby suggested as they began their dessert of chocolate mousse.

"Miguel has an interesting sense of humor," Abe began. "He is a big fan of vintage movies and television shows. The system he designed for me he named Dudley. That is after the angel character in the movie *The Bishop's Wife,* originally played by Cary Grant against Loretta Young's character as his wife."

"Of course, Abe can't hold a candle to Cary in the looks department," Veronica interrupted, "but then again, Cary can't begin to fill Abe's other fine points. I'll take Abe anytime."

"Thank you, my dear," Abe replied. "I happen to be of the opinion that you outclass Loretta in all departments, so there is no comparison."

"Gee, Sport," Veronica answered, "You really do know how to turn a girl's head. Now, to get on with the story, Miguel originally wanted to name my personal system Wilbur, after the owner of Mr. Ed, the talking horse on television, but ran into copyright infringement problems. Miguel, it seems, took a shine to the defense attorney in the movies being called 'a mouthpiece for the mob.' So he went to another copyright holder and obtained an even better name, free of charge. Francis is dubbed for Francis, the talking mule. Fitting for the profession, don't you think?"

"Perfectly apt in your case," Ruby replied with a smile. "Of course, as a mother I try never to judge my children, one way or the other. I can only hold myself to 'always be all that I can be' and trust my children will wish to emulate such behavior."

"That was a slogan used by the Army for recruitment purposes, Mother," Veronica sighed. "You, in reality, are such a paragon of virtue that no daughter could ever hope to match."

"Just keep trying, dear, for my sake," Ruby said, patting her hand and giving her a wink.

"And what name has he given to the system at the law center?" Mary asked.

"That's an interesting and complicated question," Abe answered. "Miguel is a man of far-reaching intellectual gifts with a flare for classical imagery. What can you say about someone who reads Sanskrit for fun and Egyptian hieroglyphics for relaxation? Greek mythology is another area of interest to him. He named the new system Prometheus."

"The Greek god who brought fire from heaven as a gift to mankind?" Mary asked. "As I remember the story, Zeus punished him for that act by having him chained to a boulder and had an eagle or a vulture eat out his liver everyday, while healing him overnight. Since Prometheus was immortal, it was a perpetual torture to last into eternity."

"That's the one," Veronica answered, "but it's much more than that. "I've had to delve deeper into Greek mythology to try to understand a suggested file system Miguel set up, should we choose to use it. Miguel found Zeus to be a flawed god, to say the least, who fought for and gained the top rank of the Throne of Eternity. After gaining the throne, Zeus had big plans for reshaping creation. He had no interest in the mere mortal race of men and intended that race to live as primitives until they all simply died off, so he ordered Prometheus not to interfere with his plans. In my research, I discovered a book entitled *Greek Mythology: From the Iliad to the Fall of the Last Tyrant* by Michael Stewart. It is clearly written, full of the intricate political maneuverings and revengeful acts between the ruling gods that makes the machinations of Machiavelli look elementary by comparison. Stewart paints a rather gruesome picture of Olympian gods creating such entities as Pandora, just for spite, to undermine the gifts Prometheus brought to mere mortals."

"Keep in mind the purpose of this system," Ruby said to Mary. "The Exchange Center for Constitutional Law is the clearing house for information linking federal government actions of dubious constitutional nature and the legal community throughout the country questioning those actions, either through direct litigation or on behalf of individual clients."

"Miguel designated the file name Zeus to the federal government," Veronica explained. "A large number of files dedicated to Prometheus cover the wide range of gifts he brought to the mere mortals, not just fire. Other gifts included: brickwork, woodworking, seasonal changes indicated by the stars, the alphabet, yoked oxen, ships, sails and saddles. Along with all art, he also gave the mining of precious metals, healing drugs, signs in the sky, the craft of the seer and animal sacrifice. Miguel does not have a high opinion of attorneys as a group, but he is gracious enough to give them the designation of the mere mortals of Greek mythology."

"Anyone hacking into your system would have to be well versed in Greek mythology to find anything worthwhile," Mary said. "It's like another layer of security—so simple, yet so effective."

"I told you he was a genius," Ruby said.

"What's of interest to you these days, Abe?" Mary inquired. "I mean aside from your new bride, of course. Ruby has told me of the early success of the Whittier Center project and I want you to know that my hometown of Steelton is already a beneficiary of the Islamic Society of Greater Harrisburg. Under the auspices of their members, we will soon have a decent local grocery for the first time in about fifteen years. Except for a few mom-and-pop stores and convenience stores we have to go out of town to one of the chains for full supermarket services. We have a large aging population—many people no longer drive—and the ability to walk to a full-service store is a godsend."

"That's good to hear," Abe said appreciatively. "The Whittier Center wants to foster actions along those lines to help us all be good neighbors."

What Abe did not mention was a problem he had been mulling over for nearly two months. While attending the opening of a new antiquarian bookshop on Main Street in Hummelstown on the first day of February, he had glanced out the front window to see a very lonely young woman walking down the sidewalk on the other side of the street. Making a series of discrete inquiries, he discovered the young woman was a recently discharged wounded veteran. She had experienced all the military programs the services had to offer for the National Guard and Reserves, with all the bureaucratic nightmares involved, and returned home to care for her aging grandmother. She had found no solace with the usual service organizations in town, such as the American Legion or the Veterans of Foreign Wars. There was also no comfort in rejoining in the activities of the church where she was reared. Her childhood friends were grown and getting along with their civilian lives, having no idea how separate her experience had been or how to communicate with a wounded veteran. In short, she had fallen through the cracks of organized society and her future looked bleak. Abe was worried about her and all the veterans who found themselves at the end of the road. He had to discover a way to help these people find the path all the way home. That was the big question: how?

CHAPTER 2

▼

INTERPRETATIONS

The profession of law is, of necessity, an adversarial process. Perhaps the most remarkable tribute to the U.S. Constitution is its relative strength. Since ratification in 1788, members of congress have proposed over ten-thousand amendments, of which only thirty-three have been formalized and sent to the states for ratification, and a mere twenty-seven have been adopted. Ten of those twenty-seven were the first ten amendments to the Constitution known as the Bill of Rights, adopted three years after ratification in 1791. What would seem to the layman as a relatively stable body of law with little need for change, has, in fact, been the hotbed of controversy when it comes to application and interpretation of the nuances of law for well over two hundred years. Rather than a weakness, disputes over the application and interpretation attest to the flexibility inherent in the Constitution that allows for growth and the evolution of the law to serve in changing times and circumstances.

On the first warm and sunny Saturday of the year, Abe and Veronica took their early morning routine of coffee, mixed fruit and muffin out to the patio. The signs of spring were everywhere, from the full-throated chirps of various birds seeking food or new nesting sites to the newly-evident buds on the trees and plants poking their first green shoots above the ground. As usual, Abe had risen first and placed a cup of coffee at Veronica's bedside—a ritual he had begun their first day of marriage that had continued to endure. Veronica had gratefully accepted this small consideration, always fresh as that first day.

"It looks as if there are some big things happening at the law school these days," Abe said, reading from an article in the newspaper. "Contributions are up and the school is adding a number of new professors across all departments. What's behind all that?"

"The administration is giving me the credit for starting the process," Veronica answered. "I'll try to accept that without undue modesty, but it is really the inspiration of the student body, with the help of the alumni. The program was announced at a faculty meeting yesterday."

"How did you start the process?" he asked.

"By my teaching methods," she answered. "I begin with the first year Constitutional Law students. The first day of class I use as an introduction, refreshing their memories about what they should already have learned about the forming of the document and the motivation behind that—including the politics involved. From the second day onward, I relate the Constitution in terms of what is happening in their everyday lives. It may be a discussion of a case that made it all the way to the Supreme Court because some knuckleheaded high school senior thought it would be cool to be seen on television holding a fourteen-foot banner reading 'Bong Hits for Jesus,' then pleading his school suspension was unconstitutional under the First Amendment right of free speech. Or it might be an examination of the personal dilemma for a so-called 'enemy combatant' being held by the federal government. This person is claiming U.S. citizenship under the Fourteenth Amendment because he happened to be born here during a brief assignment by his parents to a diplomatic post—neither of whom are citizens. I often throw in the consequences of a federal court ruling against the Washington, D.C. handgun ban as unconstitutional under the terms of the Second Amendment. This opened up a real can of worms with the judge's opinion. He wrote that the argument used by the anti-gun advocates about the right to bear arms was linked to service in a state militia is null and void. In his opinion, the right is assigned to the individual gun owner, period."

"I assume you end up with some deep thinking students," he replied. "I can only imagine what they must be thinking after you guide them through the permeations and permutations of those issues."

"The end result," she said, "is a group of students who discover the Constitution is a living, breathing body of law that has a direct effect on whatever specialty they pursue, from corporate law to family law. I'm afraid I've made life a little more difficult for some of my faculty colleagues with the barrage of questions they've gotten over the constitutional aspects of their specialties."

"I would think that would make them better professors," Abe replied. "That, in turn, should make for a better law school."

"It does," she admitted. "The students have been exerting pressure on the school for the last few years to add a professor in each department with a particular talent for the constitutional aspects of his or her field. Some of the larger law firms who are participating in the Exchange Center caught wind of the idea and gathered funds to contribute to the new slots, with their promise that they would be looking to recruit from departments, which have this added depth. It's an investment for them. They would be able to recruit one new attorney instead of a half-dozen otherwise."

"Well done, my dear," he said, cheerfully. "Hope takes form—that's quite an accomplishment."

"More like luck of the draw, Sport," she replied. "Now, please hand me that section of the newspaper so I can see how much of it is correct."

"I want to discuss a few observations I've made," he said after she had finished the article, "to see if I'm on the right track."

He began with the subject of the seeming proliferation of outdoor advertising along the major roads in central Pennsylvania. He had noticed an old red barn along the Pennsylvania Turnpike that had one entire side facing the road that carried a faded, but still discernable image of an advertisement for Mail Pouch chewing tobacco. That once popular form of advertising was replaced by a huge number of lighted billboards. Apparently, Lady Bird Johnson's highway beautification program of the 1960s had bypassed Pennsylvania when other states were limiting or lessening the number of such structures as unnecessary eyesores. Some billboards carried clever messages such as one leased by a woman divorce attorney that depicted a Pennsylvania license plate bearing the words "Was His." Others were selling every product and service imaginable. A few touted community concerns such as a newly renovated Catholic Charities or a series of six billboards leased by a wealthy businessman who was an immigrant himself depicting a waving American flag with the message superimposed on the background: "To Succeed in America Learn English."

"I know that woman attorney," Veronica said. "That billboard reflects exactly what she is so good at achieving for her clients. She does very well among the upper tiers of the wealthy. As for the learning English signs, it's unfortunate that the great majority of people viewing that billboard don't notice that it is not grammatically correct. It should have a comma between 'America' and 'Learn.' The latter billboard is an offshoot of our great political debate over illegal aliens—mostly Hispanic in this part of the country. It's simply one of the issues that is responsible for the current assault on the Constitution."

"I was thinking more along the lines of the assault on the sense of community," he replied. He cited the long traditions established by people like Milton Hershey and H.B. Reese; both candy makers, who instilled a sense of community in all their business endeavors. They established their companies with close employee relationships, both on and off the worksite, which saw them through both the good and the bad times—always forging a strong sense of community and integrating the waves of immigrants into the society. Abe knew of the legendary efforts of Hershey, but only recently read about how Reese was a dairy farmer who went to work for Hershey running an experimental dairy farm for the chocolate maker. When Reese wanted to start his own candy factory to produce the now-famous Reese's Peanut Butter Cup, it was Hershey who supplied the milk chocolate. In the early lean years, Reese's employees would delay cashing their paychecks until enough money was in the bank to cover the payroll. The Hershey Company finally bought the Reese brand in 1963, preserving the same paternal relationship.

"So, you're wondering if the community traditions will survive the recent globalization trend that has meant the loss of jobs here for plants being established in Mexico and parts of Asia?" she asked.

"There is a sense of disappointment," he replied, "not to mention a bit of betrayal, over the loss of jobs. It's affecting the whole community and all the small businesses that rely on their regular customers. The seasonal tourist trade will not be enough to sustain many and people will have to move elsewhere in search of suitable employment. The character of the community will change perceptively."

The radical changes at the core of the Hershey Chocolate Empire came quickly. Few local citizens really kept up on the global nature of the business or the fact that over the years twenty plants had spread to Canada and South America. Sale of the company had been averted a few years prior when the majority stockholder, the Hershey Trust, vetoed the idea. Corporate restructuring that contributed to the rapidly rising profits included a new plant in Mexico, the purchase of a huge share of an Indian candy conglomerate and a presence in Singapore, as the platform for contesting the huge opening market in China and other parts of Asia. The days when the top corporate offices were filled from within the company's ranks were long gone and in the view of the outsiders who took over management, cutting jobs in Hershey and shipping them overseas made sound business sense. The Hershey legacy of the Milton S. Hershey School was financially sound in perpetuity and the Penn State Milton S. Hershey Medical Center brought added prestige, which would only be enhanced by the coming Cancer Research Center now under construction.

"I think you may not be giving enough credit to the people," Veronica said. "Local mores may change over the span of several generations, but with close community ties to such institutions as churches and civic groups, along with the strong cooperative efforts at the local level, you may be surprised. Sure, those companies fostered the spirit of acceptance and civility, but the people took these into their individual moral code. It will take much more than the corporate decisions of a few companies to pry that away. It has become a permanent part of one's makeup."

"What would you say to an early lunch at The Wick?" Abe asked, looking at his watch. "I'm suddenly in the mood for the Greek salad—just the right mix of olive oil and ingredients for my taste."

"If you're buying, I'll eat anywhere," she said with a smile. "I've become partial to the tuna on rye toast, along with a cup of one of their great soups."

The Wick was the Warwick Hotel on Main Street in Hummelstown. Over two hundred years in operation, it was not so much a hotel as a spacious bar with dining areas scattered throughout the first floor. Abe had stayed there on his recent trip back east—in a little room on the third floor no bigger than most walk-in closets—and had appreciated the extensive menu. His preferred table was on the glassed-in sun porch with the view of the garden.

They had parked on the street a half block down from the hotel and when they approached the front door, they spotted a tall man in a three-piece suit surrounded by Henry Cunningham, Cassy Spease and a contingent from the budding trackers club, peppering the man with questions.

"Hello, Henry and Cassy," Abe called as they came near. "You seem to have treed a critter."

"It's Mr. Stiles, Uncle Abe," Henry replied. "He's new in town and is a full-blooded Indian. We're looking for some tracking and trapping tips."

"I'm Abe Carlson, Mr. Stiles," he said offering his hand, "and this is my wife Veronica. Are you giving any good advice to these budding wanderers?"

"Jim Stiles," he answered, shaking Abe's hand and nodding to Veronica. "I'm afraid I don't have any advice to give. I'm a city boy through and through. I was trying to tell this nice group how few animal tracks are left on concrete and asphalt. Why, I probably couldn't track a squirrel across a city park if I had to."

"Iroquois?" Abe asked, noting the classic features of that tribe.

"It's that obvious, huh?" Stiles replied. "My father always said the bloodlines showed. I'm an accountant by profession and recently opened an office just off the square. And, please call me Jim."

Veronica invited the entire group for lunch. Stiles accepted gladly, but Cunningham and his group were on their way to help a neighbor. "It's the Smithe place," Henry said. "Mrs. Smithe's little dog has been missing for two days now and there are some tracks of a much bigger dog in the alley. We were asked to investigate."

After they were seated on the sun porch and the food was ordered, the trio began to get acquainted.

"I was reared in Rochester, New York," Jim began. "We lived just off Lake Avenue across from Kodak Park. It was an older Irish block that was in transition when my father and two uncles moved into a big four story house. There was plenty of space for all the families."

"What did your father do?" Veronica asked.

"High steel," he answered. "My father called it the biggest run on the Anglo since Manhattan was sold by a tribe that didn't even own rights to it. You see, it's difficult constructing a steel-framed building and the degree of difficulty rises with each floor. A couple of generations of Iroquois and a few Senecas convinced the steel contractors that they had no natural fear of heights; they climbed around on the high steel as if they were on the ground. They were able to sew up a nice little niche in the labor market for themselves—and demand higher wages, too."

"I take it, then, that it wasn't entirely true?" Abe asked with a wry smile.

"Of course it wasn't true," he replied. "They were all scared when they first started, but eventually got used to it—they just didn't let anyone know they were scared. One of my uncles couldn't quite pull it off because he'd get a nosebleed above the second floor. So the rest convinced the construction company that their team needed a 'ground spotter' to insure correct alignment and safety. It was 'the Indian way,' they said. How they got away with that I'll never know, but that's the way it still is today."

"You didn't want to follow in that profession?" Abe asked.

"It is hard and dangerous work," Jim answered. "My father was a far seeing man who wanted the best education for all his children. He likened it to a sort of 'reverse immigration.' We were here first when the immigrants came into our land, but these immigrants didn't want to assimilate into our culture. So, if we wanted to get along in this changing world, we'd have to assimilate into their culture—thus reverse immigration. My father is very wise, so I became an accountant."

The rest of the meal was a comfortable conversation with Veronica telling Jim what she could about being reared in the area and Abe imparting his background and current interests.

They were finishing an after lunch cup of coffee when Henry and the group looked in through the window, then tapped on the glass, motioning them to stop on their way out.

"What are your conclusions?" Abe asked once they met the group on the sidewalk.

"Don't jump to conclusions until you understand all the sign," Henry answered. "That's what you taught us with the horse last year. We think that Buster, Mrs. Smithe's dog was doing his business at the edge of the lawn and didn't hear the other animal's approach. The two animals had a tussle and only one set of tracks led away. There's something unusual about that trail, though. It isn't like any set of dog tracks I've ever seen. At this point we can only cautiously assume that the other animal carried Mrs. Smithe's dog away in its mouth."

"Good, very good, Henry," Abe said. "Always err on the side of caution and don't judge what you don't know. Tell me about the trail."

"If it were a dog, the paws were smaller than I expected and it was light in weight, judging from the shallow prints. It went down the alley along one side, close to the fences. It crossed the road and went in a straight line off toward the hills. There was no loping in the gait, like a dog will do in an open field, just a straight line of closely spaced tracks, as if it were at a steady trot."

"One more question," Abe said. "You say the paws were smaller than you expected. What do you mean by that?"

"Well," Henry answered, thinking back to his study of the track, "I suppose a more correct description would be that the pads on the paws seemed extremely small, as if the clawed toes were too large in proportion."

"There's your answer, Henry," Abe said. "It must be a coyote and this probably happened in the dark. A coyote is what's called 'digitigrade,' which means it walks mostly on its toes, with just enough pad to provide balance. If the ground were sufficiently muddy or had an inch or so of snow, you may have detected another anomaly. The coyote has a dewclaw—a remnant of a fifth digit—on the forefeet, while the hindfeet have only four digits."

"A coyote?" Henry questioned. "I've never heard of coyotes around here."

"They're everywhere," Abe assured him. "The coyote's range has been spreading for decades. They are now found in the middle of major metropolitan areas such as New York City and Chicago. They've even been seen trotting down the middle of the Mall in downtown Washington, D.C."

"Wow," said Cassy Spease, talking for the first time. "What about this being after dark?"

"The coyote has a well-earned reputation for being wily," Abe answered. "You can safely assume it was browsing for opportunities in the garbage cans in that alley. He's also lazy and will take advantage of easy pickings. I also think you are right about his element of surprise with poor Buster. The trail pattern is classic, too. The coyote used the fence line as cover, staying in the shadows. By the time it came to the open field, it would have stayed along the fence or tree line if it had been in the daylight. With the cover of darkness, it beat a hasty retreat directly toward the hills. I'm afraid you're not going to see Buster again unless you discover his bones somewhere in the woods or some makeshift den."

"We'd better go break the news to Mrs. Smithe," Cassy said. "I know she'd like to know what to expect. Thanks, Uncle Abe."

As the group trudged down the sidewalk, Stiles asked if Abe were their uncle.

"If you stay around long enough and the children take a liking to you," Veronica answered, "you'll be Uncle Jim. The children have a way of adopting adults. To them, we're Uncle Abe and Aunt Veronica. We're all part of an extended community family."

CHAPTER 3

▼

PANDORA

On their way back to their home office, Abe and Veronica stopped at Papa's Printing and Engraving to order a new supply of personal stationery. With the sophisticated computing power on hand, they could have done the job as easily at home, but they both felt strongly about supporting local business whenever possible and still wanted the face-to-face contact missing from electronic commerce transactions. The owner of the firm, Marvin Kaplan, was a third generation printer and a Masonic Brother of Abe's from the Brownstone Lodge.

"Greetings, you two," Kaplan said from behind the counter as they entered. "Sara will be disappointed that she missed your visit. She's on an errand to Annville and won't be back for another hour or so. What can I do for you today?"

"We'd like to reorder our personal stationery," Veronica said. "I have no idea how we managed to go through our supply so quickly, so you'd better double the order."

"You could have picked up the phone and called that in," Kaplan said, "but then, I would have been deprived of seeing the second most beautiful woman in the world—Sara being the first, of course."

"You're always so pleasant in your compliments," Veronica replied. "You don't have to be, you know. Sara's no longer my student. Remember, she graduated with honors and passed the bar in short order—all through her own efforts."

"That's very true," Kaplan said. "My father always taught me to tell the truth, though. Not only do you and Sara have all the looks, you're both smarter than I."

"And Sara chose you," Veronica replied with a smile, "so, don't start questioning her taste now. I haven't seen much of her in the last year or so. Please have her give me a call and we'll catch up on all the news over lunch next week."

"She'd like that," Kaplan replied, "but that may not be possible for some time. We're very short-handed and will be working overtime for the foreseeable future."

Kaplan explained that two of his five full-time employees were in the National Guard and on their second deployment overseas in the last two and one-half years. The law required all public and private employers to reinstate veterans to their former positions or the equivalent within a specified time. He would have done so in any case of course, but felt it would have been unfair to hire replacements for so short a period of time. With the whole-hearted support of the other three employees, plus he and Sara, the additional work was shared equally.

"We just got word of Nancy Anderson this morning," Kaplan continued. "Sara's in Annville consoling her husband and her parents. She was hit by the shockwave of a powerful roadside bomb—you know, the ones that are called 'improvised explosive devices'—and has suffered an undetermined amount of brain damage. Not another mark on her otherwise, we understand, but she's likely to lose her eyesight, speech or hearing—perhaps all three. Whatever disability she may finally have to live with, we're going to alter our schedules and modify the premises to accommodate her. Sara's assuring the family that she has a place right here and we're expecting her to come back."

Abe Carlson was familiar with the federal Uniformed Services Employment and Reemployment Rights Act, as well as the Employer Support of the Guard and Reserve and all the layers of potential assistance, such as the more than two hundred Veterans Affairs Vet Centers located across the country. Yet, he also knew from experience among veterans over the years that after returning from a combat zone, most just want to get on with their lives, are reluctant to seek assistance for counseling of any type and just want to be left alone generally to deal with their feelings personally. Not many would aspire to putting on their field jacket, pumping gas and telling war stories. Unfortunately, too many would get into the habit of celebrating their survival by living life to the hilt in bars, clubs and at parties for so long that the habit became a barrel of vice with no discernable bottom. Eventually, marriages and relationships buckle under the strain and all these veterans have left is their own bitterness to stew in. Some veterans come home from the combat experience as true loners, unable to share their experience with those who would not or could not understand, forever locked in the cell of their own minds. While there was much truth in the saying that there are no atheists in foxholes, there is an equal amount of truth in the fact that many returning veterans begin to seriously question whether there really is a God who could forsake their war.

When they returned to their office, the third light on a panel beside Veronica's computer was blinking red.

"I see that Francis doesn't believe in taking the weekend off," Abe said. "Isn't that the line connected to the Prometheus program at the law school?"

"That's the one," Veronica confirmed. "I gave Francis an access code to use Prometheus as a backup source and to monitor any interesting cases that might be of interest. Let's see what he's found."

What Francis had uncovered was a new set of files Miguel had created under the title of "Pandora." Francis had searched the Michael Stewart excerpts from his book *Greek Mythology* for the references to Pandora. The ever-scheming Zeus had given the earthly mortals a gift to undo all the good Prometheus had done as one of the Titans, the pantheon of gods, and already had punished Prometheus, an immortal, with never-ending suffering chained to a boulder high in the mountains where an eagle would eviscerate him on a daily basis, heal him overnight, only to start the process all over again come morning. Zeus "fashioned a hateful thing in the shape of a young girl and called her Pandora," according to Stewart. Her name meant "giver of all" or "all endowed." Athena gave her dexterity and inventiveness, while Aphrodite (the goddess of Love) endowed her with a spell of enchantment. The god Hermes added the depth of pettiness to her tiny brain.

Zeus gave Pandora to the brother of Prometheus, Ephemetheus, as a gift, although Prometheus had warned him never to accept gifts from the gods, especially Zeus. Ephemetheus was immediately smitten and accepted the gift, which when "opened" released evil and despair into the world. Mistrust and disease were spread across the mortal world and Pandora emptied her gift of curses. All that was left in what others called "Pandora's box" was hope. But, according to Stewart it was "unreasonable, groundless Hope that makes the curse of life into a blessing."

"Now, that's a pretty grim assessment of the state of the world," Abe said after Veronica told him about Miguel's scheme. "What kind of files did he have in mind?"

"Legally loaded cases," Veronica answered. "Miguel set up files by subject matter, constitutional issues, and looked at the progression of the law. It's a simple scheme, really. Take the case of the Supreme Court's Dred Scott Decision of 1857, with Chief Justice Roger Brooke Taney writing for the majority that Scott was not a citizen of the United States, merely property, and therefore not afforded the protection of citizenship. Blacks were property and not U.S. citizens, therefore not competent to sue in federal courts. Just because Scott's owner moved to a free state, Scott, as property, was still a slave."

"And the matter was not settled until after the Civil War?" Abe asked.

"Exactly," Veronica answered. "The Fourteenth and Fifteenth Amendments to the Constitution from 1868 and 1870 remedied the situation of citizenship for freed blacks, but contained a phrase that has complicated the law. The Fourteenth says: 'All persons born or naturalized in the United States *and subject to the jurisdiction thereof,* are citizens of the United States and of the State wherein they reside.' In the practice of the law in the days since, an amendment which sought to protect the rights of former slaves has been used by aliens, legal and otherwise, to claim citizenship by right of birth."

"So these are troublesome constitutional issues that are resolved over time," Abe replied. "Stewart's 'unreasonable, groundless' hope isn't always true. There is genuine hope for the law to evolve into something more appropriate to the times."

"I'd call it more of a precarious hope," she said. "Many of these issues are more sensitive to the makeup of the court than one might wish to acknowledge. The court has the power to change the direction of the country for generations to come, just with a mere majority forming an opinion. Conservative, liberal or mainstream, the effect can be tremendous."

"So, what kind of cases is Prometheus inserting into the Pandora files?" he asked.

"For openers," she replied, "First Amendment cases on free speech and press, Second Amendment cases on the right to bear arms, Fourth and Fifth Amendment cases apply to citizenship and voting rights, plus a number of other cases dealing with the powers of the several branches of the federal government. The question of invoking executive privilege for non-national security reasons alone could bring about a constitutional crisis of unknown proportions. Remember, the last time that was invoked, President Richard Nixon was trying to keep the secret tapes away from Congress. Justice Lewis Powell, one of the most conservative justices at the time, hoisted the White House on its own petard on that one. Barely two weeks after the oral argument before the Supreme Court, the justices unanimously ordered the President to turn over the tapes. Nixon felt compelled to resign."

"It sounds to me as if we're working toward full employment of attorneys here, my dear," Abe commented. "Somehow, I don't particularly like the sound of that."

"Neither do I," she replied.

"Why the designation as Pandora files?" he asked. "Are these cases so volatile?"

"Take one of the so-called minor ones," she replied. "In an effort to stem violent crime committed with handguns some years ago, Washington, D.C. banned the in home ownership of unregistered handguns. A federal court said that was a violation of the Constitution because the critics who claimed the Second Amendment was geared to state militias were incorrect. The judge's decision clearly supported the gun lobby argument that the right to bear arms was an individual right, protected by the Constitution, without any connection to militias. The mayor of Washington was aghast, as was the police department. He threatened to appeal the decision all the way to the Supreme Court, if necessary. The trouble for the mayor was the current conservative makeup of the court. What happens to other gun control measures throughout the United States if the Supreme Court sets the judge's opinion in concrete? The ensuing calamity would be of Pandoran dimensions, don't you think?"

Veronica spent the next two hours going over the various case references classified as Pandora files, while Abe perused his Dudley system of all his local and global interests. One pleasing item of interest was the development of parallel efforts to his Whittier Center for Constructive Comparison to educate Americans on the subject of Islamic diversity and cultures. Several Muslim-backed Internet websites had interactive efforts printed in both English and Arabic, outlining programs for Muslims to bridge the knowledge gap—educating Muslim members on how to reach out to the Christian and Jewish communities to join in cooperative efforts. The Whittier Center effort was a perfect complement on the strictly local level. Although John Nagy, the director of the center, lived just on the other side of his duplex, Abe filed an e-mail report with all the details and footnotes. He also suggested to Nagy that if he could use the services of an accountant, he might like to contact Jim Stiles, the new man in town that was just building his business.

Another item of interest he found amusing. The Dudley program contained a highly sophisticated and redundant security system, sufficiently attractive to be envied by most countries around the world. When Miguel had designed the Francis and Prometheus programs for Veronica, he had inserted a program in both to test Dudley's security for flaws. Both of the newer programs had probed Dudley's vulnerability on a number of occasions, but could not put even one dent in the first wall of security, much less penetrate to the file level. When the joint number of probes had reached fifty, Dudley was programmed to communicate a record of the failures to Prometheus and Francis, automatically uninstalling that feature in both programs.

"How about a break, Sport?" Veronica asked, bringing a tray with two cups of coffee and a slice of pound cake for each. "You seem deeply entranced about something. Care to share your thoughts? Perhaps I can help."

"Thank you for the coffee," Abe answered. "I guess I was concentrating so hard that I didn't even hear you get up. And, yes, I am puzzled about how best to serve our returning veterans. Some of the Fellows at the Lodge are starting a new effort to be of whatever assistance they can be to returning Masons and their families. So far, it's just a general plan, doing things like taking them to the VA for medical appointments if the spouse is working and the children are in school, but the veteran is unable to transport him or herself for some reason. There are also any number of errands that may need to be done—small things, really, but helpful. Most importantly, they will just be there to help the veteran make the transition back into the community. Most of the Fellows who volunteered are veterans themselves, so they understand the stumbling blocks and can help guide people back to 'normalcy,' if there is such a thing."

"That sounds like a worthy effort to me," she commented. "It's a nice community effort that supplements all the other formal programs that currently assist veterans."

"It is worthy," he said, "and understated, just the type of low-key behind-the-scenes work the Masons do so well. The veteran finds a friend, one that isn't going to preach some particular line of religion or social program, nor judge the decisions the veteran may make on particular issues. And this assistance extends to the families. The Fellows are involving their own wives and children in the effort, so it's family-to-family."

As Abe explained the situation, his concern centered on where this effort might lead, how it could expand, if it could and would be replicated in other lodges and if a similar effort could be started in the community at large. He was troubled by the number of National Guard and Reserve forces who were repeatedly deployed overseas and the effect that had on their civilian employment and the strains on the family. They were returning with a strong set of leadership skills and cooperative achievement with their comrades in arms, yet, in many cases, found themselves behind their civilian colleagues in career advancement for whatever number of years they had been in service.

As Veronica sipped her coffee and nibbled at her pound cake, she listened quietly, knowing that Abe still held the image of the woman walking down Main Street in Hummelstown—obviously a wounded veteran, with the look of the loneliest person in the world. It was an image she, herself, had not been able to shake.

"When I was in college," she said when Abe paused, "I had a professor who was a Vietnam veteran. He was part of an effort called the Vietnam Veterans Leadership Program, a group of vets who came together to change the mistaken public image of those who fought that war and to assist the unemployed or under-employed veteran—those who were playing catch-up because of the gap that applied to current returnees. One of their posters showed the hand of a man hanging his uniform up in a closet full of civilian attire, with the motto: 'What do you do with experience like this? Put it to work.' Is that what you have in mind?"

"That's the basic start of the idea," he replied, "but that was an effort the veterans themselves conducted—one that I would hope current veterans are anticipating. What I'm thinking about is a community-based panel, with veterans participating and advising, that could match up existing job opportunities with veterans qualified to fill those positions. The panel could also work with schools for training or re-training and higher education that would boost the veteran's marketable skills. The panel would need a couple of well-qualified personnel directors to pay close attention to the needs of women veterans—an entirely new classification in the resource field."

"I also see the need for someone knowledgeable in the entire arena of veterans' assistance," Veronica interjected. "That would be someone who knew where to refer veterans with particular needs that could be covered under existing programs."

"You've got it, my dear," Abe said. "That's just the type of program I have in mind. With a little seed money to start, I think that if this works it could be self-sustaining in the near future."

CHAPTER 4

▼

ABE'S SQUAD

Monday morning dawned bright and unseasonably warm—the type of day that was always a gift from Mother Nature, with the promise of spring just around the corner, which was sure to frustrate the predictions of the various 'official' ground-hogs predicting six more weeks of either winter or spring, depending on whether they saw their shadows. Most Pennsylvanians found such predictions harmless fun, while others found the tradition quaint, but useless.

Since she had no classes for the day, Veronica called in for a 'mental health' adjustment day and wanted to spend the time with Abe. They decided it was too nice not to take advantage of the break in the weather

Their first stop was to Frank's newsstand in Hummelstown to pick up copies of the *New York Times* and *The Washington Post* newspapers, along with several local journals.

"How are your parents doing with their New Antiquarian Bookshop?" Abe asked as he paid for the publications.

"Much better than we had hoped, Abe," Frank said. "That referral you gave me did the trick. We were able to float a loan at a very low interest rate to carry the venture through six months, to see if it would work. My parents paid the loan in a remarkable three months and are now in negotiation to buy the building from Isaac Porr, with promised funding from the original source at rates far below what we could get from the bank."

"That's great, Frank," Veronica said. "May all the merchants be as prosperous. The town deserves it."

"I also have some amusing gossip for you," he said, "and you are both responsible for this turn of events."

"Oh no," Veronica said in mock surprise. "What have we done now?"

"It's that group of young trackers inspired by Abe," Frank said with a grin.

"Surely I can't be held responsible for my husband's actions before we were married," Veronica said in feigned protest. "That would never hold up in a court of law."

"You should have thought of that before you accepted," Abe retorted. "Sorry, kid, but you know how marriage is—sink or swim, we're in this together now. What are young Henry and Cassy up to now, Frank?"

The first thing Frank had to report was that the group had undergone a name change. Cassy Spease had originally suggested the group who called itself Abe's Shadow Wolves and Wolvettes because it was less sexist. Now approaching her thirteenth birthday, she wanted a name that was neutral and equal. Although the boys in the group weren't quite certain what all the fuss was, they were amenable to anything, so long as it sounded cool and elusive. Henry, the developing diplomat, settled the question by suggesting the arrangement made in an old television program, The Mod Squad, which had two male and one female major characters. Henry argued that this would cover any new areas they may want to branch out into, although he did not specify any particular project. So for now, the group entitled itself Abe's Squad, rededicating itself to serving the needs of the community, protecting the unprotected and the pursuit of truth and justice. No one really knew what the motto meant, but it certainly had a great ring.

"So, we have a budding feminine activist on our hands," Veronica noted with a smile. "Things could be worse, you know."

"Well, guess who is the new project of Abe's Squad?" Frank asked, then answered his own question. "Poor Jim Stiles, the new accountant in town, has been singled out for tutoring. In a completely innocent and not-intrusive way, the Squad thinks that he needs to acquire some of the traditions of his Iroquois heritage so they will not be lost to future generations. They've given Jim a book called *Forest Lore,* which was used by scouting troops and has been out of print since the 1930s. They wanted to ease him into the subject, but did say there would be a test in a couple of weeks."

"I feel for Jim," Abe said. "How's he taking all this?"

"With a great sense of humor," Frank replied. "He says too much of his youth was wasted in pool halls and pin-ball arcades, when any true Indian should have been out in the woods learning the craft of the wilderness. He said he did spend some time watching the squirrels in a city park, but that didn't count. The Squad seemed pleased that Jim asked for some tracking tips once he has digested the book. Everyone thinks the relationship will be equitable."

Lunch was a sandwich at a sidewalk café, with iced tea and an ice cream for dessert, followed by carryout coffee. Afterward, they strolled through town and stopped at a picnic table in a small park to read the newspapers. An hour later, Abe put down his newspaper and lit his occasional pipe, an indication that he was deep in thought over some complex problem. Veronica left him to his thoughts until he finished his pipe, cleaned it, and returned the bowl to his pocket.

"Don't look now, Sport," she said, looking over his shoulder, "but the children must have had a half-day at school and there is a delegation from the Squad coming down the street. I think we're about to have visitors."

Abe turned to see a group of eight young people coming into the park, Henry Cunningham and Cassy Spease in the lead, with walking sticks and small packs as if they were on their way to follow some animal's track.

"Hello, Squad," Abe called as they approached. "You seemed to be prepared for business."

"We are, Uncle Abe. Hello, Aunt Veronica," Cassy said in greeting. "We promised Mrs. Smithe and her neighbors we'd keep an eye on their neighborhood for any signs that the coyote might be prowling around."

"Will you please tell us a little more about coyotes, Uncle Abe?" Henry asked. "People we've asked around here don't have much experience with them. They do have experience with foxes, though, and say from what they've heard of the wily coyote, the fox is just a smaller version."

"And people out west call the coyote a 'little wolf," Abe answered.

Abe started with the original home territory of his native southwest portion of the United States. He explained the four basic groups within the genus: the Gray wolf, in the one hundred to one hundred seventy-five pound range whose diet included deer, elk and larger animals, hunting in packs; the smaller Mexican wolf, also a pack hunter with a similar diet; the coyote and the fox.

"The coyote comes in two basic sizes," Abe explained. "The desert coyote weighs about twenty pounds. The larger mountain coyote can be twice the size and weigh fifty pounds. Coyotes, like the fox, will eat just about anything, but its regular diet includes mice, rabbits, ground squirrels and other small rodents. It also eats fish, insects, fruits and berries, plus reptiles. A coyote is very smart, adaptable and will pounce on any opportunity for food. Although historically extremely shy of humans, continued contact with expanding population into its territory has left the coyote less fearful. In some cases, people who don't know any better have been feeding them, not realizing they are truly a wild animal, best left alone."

The wholesale eradication of the gray wolf over the past two hundred years in the American west removed the only real check on coyote predators. Today, the gray wolf is generally confined to Alaska and Canada, with a small population in Minnesota still wild. Reintroduction of the species programs around Yellowstone National Park and other experiments are still too young to be able to claim success. The Mexican wolf is considered extinct in the wild. The coyote, on the other hand, has increased its range exponentially over the past two hundred years to encompass the enormous area from Alaska to Mexico and Central America as far as Panama. It now includes all across the continental U.S. to Florida and northward to Nova Scotia, then back west over most of the habitable land of Canada.

"We've been searching the Internet," Cassy volunteered. "There have been many sightings of coyotes in urban areas in the last few years. We've found stories in downtown Chicago, New York, and one in New Jersey where a coyote tried to snatch an infant playing in his yard with his older brother. Now we have one right here in our hometown. That's scary."

"And I found a story from the state of Washington," Henry added. "There was a scientific program to add pigmy rabbits back into the wild at a wildlife reserve. The rabbits are on the endangered species list and a couple of dozen were released. The coyotes wiped them out very quickly and the scientists were only able to rescue two males. They are trying to figure out what to do now."

"I trust you're not blaming the coyote in that case," Abe cautioned. "Perhaps the scientists might re-evaluate their methods. The coyote was just doing what comes naturally. Perhaps I can help you put this into perspective."

Abe related the story of a friend who as a boy visited his grandparents on their farm in southern California for the summer. It was his first experience hearing coyotes howling at night. His grandfather taught him that coyotes howl to communicate with others in the area, marking territory or soliciting a mate. Yelping is reserved for play among young pups or a celebration or criticism with a small group. Barking, from which the coyote gets its scientific name, *canis latrans* or 'barking dog,' is thought to be a threat display when protecting a kill or a den. Huffing behavior is used to call pups without making a great deal of noise. That summer, a neighboring farmer decided to eradicate the coyote population in the area. In a week's time, my friend and his grandfather counted thirty-five coyote carcasses nailed to a fencepost along the road. Shortly thereafter, the entire valley was inundated with thousands of rodents in a population explosion. Crops and feed storage were ruined and it took several years to recover.

"Like all God's creatures, the coyote has a rightful place," Abe concluded. "It is up to all of us to balance nature as well as we can. Unfortunately, previous generations haven't done such a great job in many areas. It is up to your generation to improve our record."

"What do the Indians of the southwest think of the coyote?" Henry suddenly asked. "They must have had thousands of years experience with them."

"The tribes I'm familiar with have a love-hate relationship with coyote," Abe replied, slipping into the Indian vernacular as he dropped the article. "Among the Pueblo people, he is a clown or a buffoon used in teaching Pueblo children the risks of not being true to community, family, tradition and self. He is accused of excess whining over his own folly and undue vanity that only leads to harm of his person and his family. For the Chiricahua Apaches, coyote proves the consequences of foolish behavior, but also serves a positive role in Indian traditions, plus mocks the gullibility and greed of the white man. One heroic tale among the Apaches tells of coyote stealing fire from the birds and bringing it to the people to make their lives more comfortable, while singing his tale, leaving a black spot on the tip. To the Navajos, coyote is a complex mixture of cultural hero, wise counselor and the greatest troublemaker on four legs."

"What can we do in Buster's memory to help his neighborhood?" Cassy asked with serious conviction.

"Well," Abe replied, "the first thing you need to understand is that to coyote, cats and small dogs are like candy. He is fast, with a speed of nearly forty miles per hour, he leaps eight foot fences with ease and has been witnessed climbing over a fourteen foot cyclone fence. The bigger breeds of dogs will send coyote packing in a heartbeat. In Arizona, suburbia is ever expanding into the desert, the stronghold of coyote. Several people I know who live there tell me that when they first moved, they liked to walk their small dogs early in the morning and towards sunset. They had to walk their dogs on a leash because coyote would trot alongside waiting for the opportunity to snatch the pet for a snack. By the way, there wasn't an outdoor cat in the neighborhood that survived more than a few days. There was no problem with the bigger breeds because they'd chase coyote away. Coyotes were too wily to be caught, but would not face down the larger animal. On my ranch, cattle and horses were under no threat, but we still kept new foals under watch until they were big enough to take care of themselves. Sheep were more vulnerable, I understand, but we didn't have many around, except among the Navajo. What would be your suggestion for protecting that neighborhood?"

The group retreated to a picnic table across the park to have an animated conversation for a good fifteen minutes before returning to Abe and Veronica.

"Okay, here's what we think," Henry said as the chief spokesperson for the group. "We do more research and come up with a pamphlet. We include all we can learn about coyote, the legends, the scientific behavioral studies and recent sightings in this part of the country, along with the experiences you've mentioned about how people in Arizona are coping."

"Then we add a list of dos and don'ts," Cassy said. "We add a cautionary list for protecting pets and say that people might want to increase their protections like keeping foxes out of the henhouse, only sturdier. Never leave small children unsupervised in the yard; and tell children of all ages never to approach a wild animal that might wander into the neighborhood because it's dangerous."

"And we include common sense precautions," another of the group interjected. "Things like keeping a tight seal on trash cans, not leaving food and water outside for pets, emptying backyard children's pools and placing wire mesh over in-ground water features."

The Squad did their share of brainstorming that day, with Abe and Veronica participating only to bring an idea that got too far off the track back to the subject at hand.

"So, what do you think, Uncle Abe and Aunt Veronica," Henry finally asked. "Do you think we have a plan? We could distribute the pamphlets free of charge, beginning with the Smithe neighborhood, and merely ask if the people would like to contribute to the cost of printing them so we can produce more. I'll bet we could make this project pay for itself."

"I think you have a sound business proposition here," Abe said. "I'll tell you what, you know Marvin Kaplan, the owner of Papa's Printing and Engraving, don't you?"

"Sure, everyone knows Mr. Kaplan," Henry replied.

"You go see Mr. Kaplan tomorrow," Abe said. "We'll stop by his store on the way home today and tell him to bill the costs of printing to our account. He can help you with layout and graphics and I understand Mrs. Kaplan has an eye for good illustrations. You tell him I think we'll need an initial run of one thousand copies. If this works out as well as I think it can, he'll be printing many more. You may end up blanketing Central Pennsylvania before you are finished."

An invigorated Abe's Squad left the park to perform their promised surveillance of the Smithe neighborhood and to talk over their new printing venture. Abe and Veronica proceeded to the Papa's Printing to have a talk with Marvin. "Do you know what an inspiration you are?" Veronica asked as they gathered the newspapers. "You seem to hit just the right chord with everyone. You quietly nudge the ball to get it rolling and then trust people's innate talent to be up to the task, whether they've ever had this experience or not."

"In the first place, it's we doing this work," Abe corrected. "And this is a very capable group of young people who don't know they can't do something if it is for the right reasons, so they inevitably succeed. And even if this doesn't succeed, the purity of effort will be its own reward. They will unwittingly be helping themselves and the development of their character just by trying. If it does succeed, it won't go to their heads because they never doubted this was the right course to help the community. This, my dear, is the proverbial win-win situation."

"I do have one question, though," Veronica said. "Why the wry smile when that youngster suggested emptying children's pools and covering water features with wire mesh?"

"Simple," he replied. "I think that all the talk about Indians on the southwest most likely transported him there, if only in his imagination. His suggestion makes absolute sense in that arid region for depriving coyote of a water source. There are so many rivers, creeks and streams in this area, not to mention troughs for the cows and horses, that water is not a problem. However, standing water is a sure draw for mosquitoes, which may carry the West Nile virus or some other nasty disease such as malaria, so it's a good preventative measure in that sense."

"Do the coyotes themselves carry any particular diseases?" she asked.

"No more than any wild creature," he answered. "Rabies is one, but the most unsightly is an ugly form of mange, where huge chunks of fur simply drop off. That is a common occurrence, but as far as I know, it doesn't pose any threat of being passed on to humans. Its fur can be rather highly prized. Desert coyotes are light gray or tan with a black tip on the tail. Mountain coyotes inhabiting higher elevations are darker, have thick, long fur and often sport a white tip on the tail. The belly fur can be nearly white and in winter when the fur can grow long and silky, trappers hunt them for their coats."

"I'm not partial to fur coats of any kind," she replied. "So please don't bother to buy me one made of coyote skins."

"I wouldn't ever think of it," he said with a sly grin. "Besides, I rather think you would look even more beautiful in buffalo—at least that would keep you warmer during the cold Pennsylvania winter, that is if you're not really interested in being a fashion plate."

CHAPTER 5

▼

TURKEY WRANGLING

Veronica returned home from a long day of classes and checking on the Exchange Center for Constitutional Law. The chair she had endowed for the Center's Director would not be filled until the fall term and she wanted everything running flawlessly by then. Although physically tired, she found an internal exhilaration from bandying about meaningful issues and having stimulating conversations with people all over the United States. She knew that the next day would be as challenging because she would be immersing herself in the same basic issues, but at the international level. As she walked into the house, the rich aroma of Irish stew wafted through the air, causing her salivary glands to perk up. She found Abe in the kitchen preparing their evening meal.

"You are a gift from God," she said. "How can one not love a man who knows his way around the kitchen? You've even set the table and I see the wine is breathing. It will take me only a few minutes to change into something more comfortable."

"Take your time, my dear," he replied, giving her a kiss on the cheek while keeping his hands working on a salad. "Dinner won't be served for another twenty minutes to a half hour. I've drawn you a nice hot bath that should be just about the right temperature by now and I thought you might need some luxury time to soak. Pamper yourself a little. You deserve it."

"You're so perfect for me," she said, wrapping her arms around his waist and putting her head on his shoulder, "both psychic and considerate at the same time. I certainly accept your offer with gratitude."

The meal was delicious and the wine just the right complement when sipped at intervals. The meat in the stew was as flavorful as any Veronica could remember.

"It's buffalo," Abe said when asked. "We received a big box today from a friend in Wyoming. Buffalo being much leaner than beef, it needs to be tenderized before cooking or it will be too dense and chewy for a good stew."

"Who is this friend of yours who I have yet to meet?" she asked, thinking of all the interesting people Abe must know and looking forward to meeting them.

"John Colter from Cody, Wyoming," he replied. "You will be meeting him sooner rather than later, I would expect. He's a real native-born son of Wyoming, named after the first American known to have traversed the Yellowstone area of the state in the very early 1800s, although he doesn't claim any kinship. His profession is that of a very successful trial lawyer, specializing in equal rights. That's the state's motto, 'Equal Rights,' and it takes some effort to get to the top of your field in Wyoming."

"He sounds interesting," she said. "We could have some enlightening conversations."

"At the time of the first European contact," he continued, "the area was home to at least five different peoples: Cheyenne, Ogallala Sioux, Shoshone, Crow and Arapaho. I have some acquaintances among the Sioux and Crow tribes. The Territorial Legislature granted the right of women suffrage and to hold office just four years after the Civil War, in 1869. John Colter is very proud of the fact that he is carrying on the first traditions of the state."

"Were all the western men more enlightened than their counterparts in the east in those days," she asked semi-seriously, "or was there something in the air or water?"

"Actually, I don't think it had much to do with enlightenment," he replied. "It was probably more the sharing of the perils of survival as equals. It took iron-willed women as well as men to make a living."

"How long have you known John?" she asked. "Did he do some legal business for you?"

"Not legal business, *per se,*" he answered. "John also pursues his first love—breeding fine quarter-horses on several thousand acres. He has always seen the practice of law as more of a hobby than anything else. When he first started ranching, I helped him gather his first breeders and we own a small stake in his operation. That's how he first discovered we were married—when our lawyers filed for adding your name to the deeds."

"Well, you certainly make life a journey," she replied. "I guess I'll have to do some independent research to determine what the quarter-horse business is all about."

"It won't take you long to understand it, believe me," he said. "John sent a letter along with the package, saying he is contributing cases to your Exchange Center and receiving valuable information in return. He knew I was settling in here and made the connection with your new name at the law school. He sends us congratulations on our marriage and wishes you all the best with what he sees as a vital service you are performing. He says you must be a very strong woman to dare to go where no other lawyer had dared to venture before. He also wants you to become the nation's top turkey wrangler."

"You lost me on that last one," she said. "What is a turkey wrangler?"

"It's an inside joke," he replied. "It's also a long story. Let's clear the table and do the dishes, and then have some coffee in the atrium. I'll give you all the details."

As Abe related the tale, the events took place about thirty years ago, when John Colter was starting his breeding operation. The two of them had gone to a small college town in the upper western corner of Missouri to pick up a pair of quarter-horses belonging to the town's sole doctor. Being the only general practitioner for miles, the doctor also served as the town's veterinarian, was a deacon of his church and had a small side business buying and selling quarter-horses. He was also a colorful character even by western standards who was the team doctor to the college's football and basketball programs.

The deal completed and the horses loaded, the doctor told them that there wasn't much amusement in the area, but if they wanted to see something that would lighten their day, they should stop by a certain farm on their way out of town. A local farmer had been to the college campus recruiting some football players to do a job he couldn't get the local farm boys anywhere near—at any cost. All the young football players were city boys who did not know any better.

Abe and John found the farm in question and pulled to the side of the road near an open field. A large pen had been erected in the field using snow fencing. The pen was crammed shoulder to shoulder with several hundred turkeys, calmly awaiting their fate. A semi-tractor trailer was backed to a spot along one side with its rear doors open. Inside the trailer, they could just perceive chicken wire spread over a flimsy wooden frame, with an open gate in the middle. When the farmer arrived in his pickup truck carrying eight football players, Abe and John simply looked at each other in awe. They knew they were about to witness a disaster.

The farmer placed three of the young lads inside the rear of the trailer and motioned for the five others to climb into the pen. Having given his instructions, the farmer climbed into his truck and went about his chores elsewhere on the property. Apparently, the plan was to have those in the pen grab the birds and toss them to their friends in the trailer, who would, in turn, toss them through the gate and into the confines of the chicken wire.

The first few tosses seemed promising, with only a few scratches and peck marks, but as the turkeys gained more maneuvering room, chaos broke loose. Squawking turkeys, yelling and bleeding college students, feathers flying everywhere and the sight of the birds taking short flights in and out of the trailer and pen was a scene which no intended farce could have matched.

The struggle raged for an hour before the boys finally sat down exhausted to rest and gather enough strength for the next siege. About half the turkeys were in the trailer and the other half were evenly divided between cowering at the far side of the pen or milling around outside the arena. Many of the birds simply sat in the grass near the others and seemed to be taking a nap.

"Still no sign of the farmer coming back," Abe said during the lull.

"He probably thinks that college boys must be smart enough to figure things out for themselves," John replied. "Perhaps we should lend a hand. I do hate to see those dumb birds being terrorized so."

The unspoken plan was simple. Abe and John saddled the two quarter-horses and slowly walked them to the site of the trailer so as not to excite the birds further. They pulled up sections of the snow fence and doubled it over several times. Using more fencing as under support and for the sides, they managed to form a crude ramp and chute from the ground to the gate inside the trailer. They motioned the athletes to one side and mounted the horses.

"A quarter-horse has two valuable talents," Abe explained to Veronica so she would understand the story. "It is an expert at cutting a steer from the herd for branding. It is also a pro at corralling strays back into the herd on the trail."

Abe and John slowly walked their horses in circles around the turkeys and nudged them toward the ramp. Any bird that tried to bolt from the group was quickly cut off by the horse and moved back with the others. Within fifteen minutes the turkeys were calmly climbing the ramp and in another ten minutes, the rear doors of the trailer were closed.

When Abe and John had re-loaded the horses and were pulling back onto the road, they could see the grateful college boys dismantling the ramp and making a neat stack of the fencing.

"That must have been one surprised farmer when he returned," Veronica said.

"We didn't stay around to see," Abe replied.

"So I guess John thinks of all these cases out there as so many turkeys," Veronica said. "My efforts to shepherd them through in some orderly fashion to make a whole body of cases would make me a turkey wrangler. I may need to enlist two worthy steeds to act as my cutting horses, though."

"You already have them," Abe commented. "In fact you may have two pair to keep things in the chute: Prometheus and Francis as one span, the Exchange Center and Georgetown School of Law as the second. With you holding the reins, I'd say that's a pretty formidable force."

"Thanks for the moral booster," she said. "I've always operated on the premise that if I don't know something can't be done, I might just be able to accomplish the task. And when people tell me something can't be done, I take that as a challenge and get it done just to show them they are wrong. Mother has always told me that wasn't a character flaw, but a sign of strength of character. Now, how is your project going?"

"Promising," he answered. "I'm pleasantly surprised at the number of young human resource people in this area—the majority being professional women, by the way—who want to volunteer to set up a program along the lines we want. I'm finding that the so-called 'old boy' network can't hold a candle to these up-and-comers. On a related matter, let me tell you what John Nagy and his mother Beatrice are doing in their spare time from the Whittier Center."

As a wounded Vietnam veteran, John Nagy had returned to his civilian profession as a school teacher and gotten on with his life, but always kept his war experiences bottled up inside. It had only been in the last nine months, since he had met Abe Carlson that he began mentioning Vietnam at all, even to his mother. He knew first-hand what these newer veterans were facing. Encouraged by her son's new openness, Bea, who was a volunteer at the Center, suggested he have a talk with a certain young woman she had encountered on the street in Hummelstown. This was the same woman Abe and Veronica had noticed on the day the New Antiquarian Bookshop held its grand opening.

Nagy, reading a newspaper, had positioned himself on a bench in front of Maloney's Men's Store along the woman's usual route. With a veteran's innate ability to recognize a fellow veteran, he was able to engage her in conversation. Her name was Margaret Cullman and she lived with her aging grandmother who was unable to take care of herself, but wanted to die at home. Between the grand-mother's Social Security and Margaret's small medical retirement from leaving most of one knee on foreign soil, they managed. Several days later a second conversation with Nagy revealed that Margaret entered the service right out of high school and the only marketable talent she possessed was as a self-taught graphic artist. Nagy had arranged for her to work part-time for a small interior design firm—working alone at her drawing board at home producing interior layouts on a per-piece basis.

"Through her experiences with her own son," Abe said, "Bea can identify likely candidates on the street, she relays the information to John and he takes things from there. I understand he has found useful employment for two others, including a severely injured former medic now employed as a pharmacy assistant in a local drug store."

"It's like you have always maintained, Abe," Veronica answered seriously, "the most effective help is on a local basis, particularly with cases like these. At least it has given a few a new start."

"It's more than that, my dear," Abe replied. "I can foresee a time when these people can move on into our new effort for higher education, retraining or new employment opportunities. Better than that, John is taking a bold new step to overcome what he feels has been one of his personal shortcomings—an unfounded and unidentified bias, if you will."

"I can't imagine John Nagy having a biased bone in his body," she said. "He's too well educated and well-rounded."

"Not being a veteran myself, I can't fully appreciate the depth of the feeling," he explained, "but I think it may have its roots in the military practices of his time. These days, entire groups are deployed, brought home and re-deployed as a unit. As casualties occur, troop strength is regained through integrating new individuals into the ranks, but movements are always as a cohesive unit."

"And that wasn't the practice in Vietnam?" she asked.

"Not entirely," he replied. "Units were deployed as units in the beginning, of course, but as the war wore on, it became a system of individual replacement. You went over on your own, plugged into a slot and served your mandatory number of days. You came home by that same calendar, but again as an individual."

John Nagy felt quite alone when he returned and was not a "joiner" in the first place. He shunned the American Legion and the Veterans of Foreign Wars as social halls where people drank beer and told war stories—stories he did not wish to recount. He now thought he had been wrong in that assessment. On behalf of these new returning veterans—those who held the same attitude as he had—Nagy now would go to these organizations and seek their assistance in helping those who were falling through the cracks of the system. He may have made a mistake some years ago, but he hoped he could prevent an entirely new generation of veterans from making such judgments without first giving it a try. He felt fortunate that he had a profession already established in which to return. He wanted this new group to avail itself of the opportunities.

"You have to admire him for his willingness to change after all these years," Veronica said. "No one can doubt the strength of his character."

CHAPTER 6

▼

LAW AND REMEMBRANCE

A strong nor'easter pounding the east coast did not provide for the most pleasant drive, but Veronica and Abe had two appointments in Washington, D.C. The first was to the Georgetown University Law Center near Union Station and the second a commemorative service at the National Presbyterian Church on Nebraska Avenue, N.W. Still, a few hours' journey through the rural countryside past Gettysburg in southern Pennsylvania and Mount Saint Mary's University in Maryland was scenic, even in the often driving-rain. And the cloud-shrouded Catoctin Mountain range, home of the famous Camp David presidential retreat, held its own charm.

Veronica always preferred to drive, which suited Abe because he was never bored with new landscapes to explore. Some fields had been plowed, awaiting just this type of rain to soak the soil before spring planting. There were signs everywhere that the farmers were preparing for the coming season and a few oddities to catch one's attention. In one small corral, Abe counted three aging horses, two donkeys, one goat and an emu. The last he thought must have been a remnant of the fad decades ago to raise the exotic bird for meat, feathers and hide. One imaginative farmer had a large silo painted in the likeness of an ear of corn, with bright yellow and orange kernels standing out from the deep green husk.

The further south they proceeded, the more vegetation was in bloom. Daffodils and tulips were in evidence everywhere and many trees were in blossom. Light spring green was coming into the wooded areas. The drive along the Potomac River on the George Washington Parkway was the prettiest stretch of road, where the greening backdrop showed off the blooming redbuds to dramatic effect.

As they approached the city, Veronica called Abe's attention to the high spires of the venerable Georgetown University campus on a hill across the river in northwest Washington. She explained that the Law Center was several miles away from the main campus, very close to the Capitol, the Supreme Court and the various institutions at the east end of the Mall bounded by Constitution and Independence Avenues.

The drive down the Mall was engaging, with all the massive monuments and impressive buildings; the aura of importance could be felt everywhere. Every major city had its own peculiar atmosphere, whether it was the bustling commerce of New York and Chicago, the wealthy display of Dallas and Houston, or Los Angeles being whatever it felt like being on any given day. Abe had visited all of those places and many major cities around the world, but in Washington he always encountered an uncommon blend of ambition and power found nowhere else.

"Impressive, isn't it?" Veronica asked. "I always experience a sense of understated excitement knowing this is the seat of the Congress that makes the laws, the Executive that enforces the laws and the Supreme Court that interprets those laws. This is the physical manifestation of the Constitution and the image we reflect to the rest of the world. Once you look beyond the veneer, of course, you start finding the flaws and fissures that could throw the entire system out of balance."

"The system can be flexible, though," Abe replied. "Look at all the crises the system has managed to survive since the beginning. I've always taken some comfort that this is such a transient town. With new blood, there's always the hope for an improved herd."

"The next time our congressional seat changes," she said, "I'll have to tell our new representative your thoughts. It is sure to be comforting."

The Law Center was a complex of modern up-to-date buildings. Chiseled in stone on the façade of the Edward Bennett Williams Law Library was the motto: "Law is but the means—justice is the end." Veronica pulled to the curb in front of the new Eric E. Hotung International Law building that housed the John Wolff International and Comparative Law Library, her destination.

"The buildings all have distinguished names," Abe commented. "They are all named after noted alumni, I suppose?"

"As far as I know," she replied. "This will take a few hours, at least. Why don't you drive the car and take in the sights, or otherwise amuse yourself. I know there are a few places you wanted to visit. I'll call when it looks as if we're about to finish. We have to be at the church by three o'clock."

There were several Masonic landmarks Abe wanted to see. The rain had ceased and one look at the sky promised a respite of a few hours.

His first stop was the House of the Temple on 16th Street. Modeled on one of the Seven Wonders of the Ancient World, the Mausoleum at Halicarnassus, the temple was home to the Supreme Council Thirty-second Degree Ancient and Accepted Scottish Rite of Freemasonry. Two large sphinxes guarding the door spoke of the building's grandeur; a labyrinth of rooms dedicated to the memory of famous American Masons detailed Masonic contributions to the founding and continuation of this democracy.

His second stop was 3rd and D Streets, N.W. to see the huge statue erected to the memory of Albert Pike, who rewrote Scottish Rite rituals in their entirety and in his eighty-one years of life was an editor, poet, author, lawyer, judge and a Confederate general in the Civil War. He is the only such general to be so honored in the nation's capital. A towering six feet, four inches and weighing three hundred pounds in the flesh, Pike's larger-than-life statue proclaims his prominence in Freemasonry.

His third stop necessitated a short trip across the Potomac to Alexandria, Virginia, the site of the George Washington Masonic National Memorial. Three hundred and thirty-three feet tall, the memorial houses a three-story bronze statue of America's first president in full Masonic regalia, standing on a pedestal. One room is a re-creation of Washington's former lodge room, Alexandria No. 22, while other rooms were dedicated to other aspects of Masonic history and legend.

Washington, D.C. and surrounding area are a treasure trove of Masonic symbolism, which is why so many conspiracy theorists with a Masonic bent have their plots running through the city. Just the nature of the nation's capital as the seat of government is a gold mine for conspiracy theories of all kinds, both national and international.

Having returned to the Law Center campus, Abe wandered around the grounds and read notices posted on various bulletin boards. One notice in particular caught his attention. It was an announcement of a symposium for Muslim-Christian Understanding entitled "What it means to be Muslim in America," a panel discussion of how practicing Islam supports or contradicts the American way of life. He made a mental note to inform John Nagy of the symposium to see if he could use some of the ideas presented.

Reading a basic pamphlet on the Law Center, he learned that it had begun in 1870 as the first law school established in the United States by a Jesuit institution of higher learning. Although he knew of the Jesuit reputation for sound academics and the long history of Jesuits serving in the diplomatic arena, he wondered if anti-Catholic feeling among many Americans of the time presented many obstacles from the beginning.

He also pondered, with an inward smile, whether a group as thorough as the Jesuits would place so-called Indian Law in the domestic side of the curriculum or in the international school where it belonged. His telephone rang before he could find the answer.

"Okay, Sport," Veronica said, "I'm ready to go and I'm hungry. Let's catch a bite to eat on the way to the church."

Abe was amazed once again that just as in New York, Veronica seemed to know just the right out-of-the-way places to have great food. This time, she introduced him to an authentic New York-style deli in the middle of a northwest Washington residential district. The pastrami was piled high on the sandwiches, the rye bread was thick-sliced and the dill pickles crunchy.

"So, how did your meeting go?" Abe asked as they finished their meal.

"Splendid," she replied. "At least that's what Dr. Cavanaugh said. Of course, she's from England and everything is splendid or top cricket to her. She's a short, petite woman with enormous energy and a towering intellect. And, as the saying goes, you can tell right away that she doesn't suffer fools gladly. I wouldn't want to oppose her in a court of law."

"Don't sell yourself short, my dear," he said. "I'd still put my money on you against any attorney in the world."

"I know you would," she replied, patting the back of his hand. "You're that sweet, but just out of curiosity, what would be the odds you'd demand?"

"Pretty high, I have to admit," he said with a wink. "Not because I thought you'd lose, but as punishment that anyone would think you could possibly fail. Why, I'd be protecting our family honor."

"Your charm has once again saved your hide," she replied. "When in doubt, say flattering things. Now let's get to the church."

Robert Thomas held a very special place in Veronica's life and in her heart. He played a central role as the loving brother she never had. He was always larger than life, in stature as well as in the eyes of the community. They had grown up together and were part of a large group that always participated in the same activities, in school and out. When they were in high school, he was a star tackle on the football team. Veronica was always the first one there for him on the sidelines to congratulate a win or console a loss. Bob was very protective of Veronica and never failed to intervene when he thought someone was being too forward, even though she did not need the assistance. When Bob would end a relationship with a girl, Veronica was a shoulder to cry on or simply a friend to talk to. After attending separate colleges, Veronica and Bob became close again in law school. While Veronica chose a career in the Public Defender's Office before turning to her professorship in constitutional law, Bob went to Washington for a slot at the Department of Justice. Neither had married over the years and always stayed in touch. When in Washington, he would take her to lunch or dinner. When he came home to visit, she reciprocated.

It had been three years since Bob died of a sudden heart attack. He was an organ and tissue donor who was then cremated and interred in his native state. Every year since, Veronica attended a gathering hosted by the Washington Regional Transplant Consortium at the National Presbyterian Church in Washington. This was an annual event for donor families to honor and remember those who had died and so generously given the gift of life.

The church complex was vast, with mostly interconnected structures several stories high. In the corridor outside the main sanctuary, a series of quilts were on display.

"That is a major theme," Veronica explained. "Each quilt includes ten by ten inch patches submitted by donor families to remember their loved ones. As you can see, some include favorite photos or themes important to the donor. These are displayed at various functions to make more people aware of the program and hopefully to give them an opportunity to become donors themselves. Bob's patch is over here. It was the proudest day of his life—law school graduation. Those are his parents on either side. They tried to attend the first donor gathering after his death, but it was too emotional. So, I've been coming as their representative."

"You can feel the heightened emotions of the people passing here," Abe replied. "Yet is seems to be more of joy than sadness."

"I'll tell the organizers what you said," she replied. "That is the goal they strive to reach."

As they walked into the sanctuary and took seats to one side, Abe noticed that all the pews had small personal tissue packages placed along the seating. As he relaxed in his place and listened to the fifteen minutes of music played in prelude to the program, he began to take in sensations he often felt in Indian blessing ceremonies over the years. The vaulted ceiling of the sanctuary, with narrow stained glass panels reaching several stories high gave the impression of opening up to the heavens. The beautiful uplifting notes of the organ echoed from the walls, beginning in the front, seeming to gently caress the pews all the way to the rear, then bestow a quieter, softer blessing on their return. This gathering of donor families, living donors, recipients and friends were silently bonded in an unseen, yet tangible way.

Those gathered, as was the case in the community at large, reflected the heritage of all the nations of the world. Where else but perhaps the United Nations could one find among a gathering of a few hundred people the ethnic, racial and social mix here today, Abe thought. At Indian blessing ceremonies, the vision was often raised of the brotherhood of all the native nations, no matter the tribe. Here he found the more profound image of the brotherhood of man.

The program itself was a low-key, dignified affair with prayers, remarks by the organizers and two people who were recipients, along with the presentation of the year's blank quilt and the gift of a plant and candle to each donor family in attendance. One highlight was two choral offering by the eighty-member Choral Arts Society of Washington, with a piece by Johannes Brahms and a favorite hymn of Dr. Martin Luther King entitled: "If I Can Help Somebody." The touching ending was a candle lighting ceremony which included the lyrics from "Light a Candle" by Paul Alexander, a prayer to a loved one who became a donor. By the end of the program, they saw the wisdom in placing tissues all along the pews.

"That certainly makes me glad that I had that green organ donor printed on my new Pennsylvania driver's license," Abe said as they walked to the car. "More people need to make this decision long before it is necessary and let their families know their wishes."

"That's what programs like this are all about," Veronica said. "Bob made his wishes known back in high school, expressing his desire to have his body donated to science. He was one of the first to sign up for the donor program designation when that became available. That's only one of the reasons I will always love him."

The rain started again before they reached the Maryland state line and the wind began to gust. They stopped for a cup of coffee at Thurmont, which billed itself as the gateway to Camp David. By the time they crossed the Mason Dixon line into Pennsylvania the rain ceased, but when they were ten miles from home, the western sky portended a rough night. The nor'easter was going to last another day or so with even stronger winds before finally blowing itself out.

Shortly after dark, the rains came again, stronger than before, with gale-force winds using the drops to play a tattoo, a rapid rhythmic rapping against the windows. Nestled safely on the couch in their office, Abe and Veronica simply shared personal reflections on the day.

"What did you receive from your Masonic wanderings today?" Veronica asked at length. "I wasn't sure if you were making a pilgrimage of sorts or if you were searching for some pieces to a puzzle you are trying to solve."

"As usual, you put you finger on the issue, my love," he answered with conviction. "I'm in search of the pieces of the puzzle."

Abe reiterated his thoughts on the Blue Lodge, which all Masons had to pass through to reach the Third Degree of Master Mason, with all the rights and privileges bestowed—the steppingstone to advancement to the higher degrees. To him, the Scottish Rite and the York Rite degrees were merely delving into the finer points of the first three degrees and the Thirty-second Degree signified that one had explored the deeper meaning of Freemasonry.

Various people and groups over the years had tried to use the inherent secrecy of Freemasonry to concoct a looming menace that had to be eradicated or at least reined in for the betterment of the society at large. He saw the truth in the simple statement attributed to Benjamin Franklin, very much a Mason himself, that the real secret of Masonry is that there is no secret. Recent writers had used the Masonic movement and its history as a backdrop to fanciful tales of intrigue and conspiracy that were entertaining, but missed the core values at the heart and purpose of the fraternity.

"What were the founding fathers and people like Albert Pike doing that made so many people suspicious?" he asked. "Why such a backlash of dissent throughout the centuries against the movement? How could political and governmental leaders from presidents of the United States to the director of the F.B.I., to the movers and shakers of governments around the world affiliate themselves with the organization unless it had the best interests of the people and its members as its foremost concern? As I understand it, Freemasonry is partly to blame in its efforts to attract aristocratic members into its speculative ranks as it made the transition from operative, or working Masons, to the accepted Mason status, but once exported to other countries and cultures, why did they become suspect? Of course, if I could answer any one of those questions, I might be elevated to whatever Masonic rank is the equivalent of the Nobel Prize. I say this last in jest. I really do believe that the heart and soul of Freemasonry is in its simple unvarnished truth. I would like to have more people understand that concept. The movement can trace its roots to the Enlightenment, but it is relevant to any age. The challenge is to make that case clear to the general public."

CHAPTER 7

▼

HABEAS CORPUS

The nor'easter that had returned with a vengeance during the night was still very much in evidence as Abe followed his early morning routine. Much of the northeast had been inundated with heavy rain or snow and the wind was responsible for power outages all up and down the east coast. Tornadoes spawned by the storm were responsible for extensive damage to some areas. Central Pennsylvania remained relatively unscathed, with the exception of local flooding, but driving continued to be hazardous in some places. The overcast sky still held its menace as Abe looked out his office windows, watching trees and bushes sway before the winds. He had retrieved a large volume from the library and was sitting at his desk drinking coffee when Veronica appeared.

"No newspaper this morning?" Veronica asked, noticing the publication was not in its usual place on the credenza.

"I'm afraid not," Abe answered. "I went out to put some mail in the mailbox this morning and I didn't see newspapers on this block at all. I did detect the telltale orange plastic bag in evidence a block or so up the street, but I expect the fierce winds carried ours off into a cornfield somewhere. I'll just go on-line later this morning and get what news I need from the Internet. It's ironic that in this electronic age we're still in the habit of getting our news in pulp form and don't really seem to mind when it's not here."

"Speak for yourself, Sport," she replied. "I miss the ads. What if someone is having a big sale and I don't know about the splendid opportunity such an event presents?"

"With your shopping instincts," he said, "I doubt they'd be able to pass under your radar."

"Point taken," she agreed. "What are you reading there?"

"With all the legal issues you're dealing with these days," he explained, "I thought I'd refresh my memory and hopefully educate myself on some points of law. I'd like to hold up my end of the conversation. I'm starting with *habeas corpus*—you should have the body."

"You sure don't start with the easy ones," she replied. "That is the central question. By the way, the full phrase is *habeas corpus ad subjiciendum*—you should have the body for submitting, a writ for inquiring into the lawfulness of the restraint of a person who is imprisoned or detained in another's custody."

"A small town attorney in Montana once gave me an interesting definition," Abe said. "He said it meant 'produce the body, Jack, tell me the charges so I can either hang him or let him go free.' I'm not sure he used that phrase in court, though."

"One would hope not," she commented. "That would be sure to offend the court's sensibilities. I must admit that he's pretty close to the mark."

"Well," Abe continued, "I keep reading about challenges to the Patriot Act and the so-called unprecedented nature of the law and the consequences to constitutional rights, not to mention the effect on international law and agreements. One would think that the statutes and international agreements that brought an end to the British and French impressments of American seamen would have settled these issues centuries ago."

"I can assure you many lawyers are combing over those cases right now," Veronica stated. "No one wants to see cases go before a military tribunal of questionable legality and merit. We need to get these questions before a proper federal court."

"I don't pretend to know much about the law," he asserted, "but as an outside observer, my common sense tells me that these great law minds are overlooking a huge body of established decisions dealing with many of the same entities we have now. What about the federal government's legal dealings with the sovereign Indian nations? There were some interesting arguments and rulings to be found there, particularly between the Civil War and the turn of that century."

"I have to plead that I don't know much about that phase of the law," she admitted. "What do you think is a representative example?"

"Try Standing Bear v. Crook, 1879," he answered. "That should provide most of the precedents you need to begin your pursuit. Keep that date in mind because although this land belonged to the Indians for thousands of years before the white men came, they were not classified as citizens of the United States. It took one world war and the establishment of a woman's right to vote before Congress reluctantly granted the Indians citizenship in 1924."

As Abe related the tale, he talked of the latter decades of the 19th Century as a time of turbulence in U.S.-Indian relations. The Ponca tribe was peaceful and by the 1859 treaty with the U.S. was granted a tract of land in the Dakota Territory as their permanent home. The Ponca lived in peace and often intermarried with the neighboring Omaha tribe. As a result of later treaties with the Sioux and without being consulted, the government relocated the Ponca to another designated Indian Territory in Oklahoma. Standing Bear and five hundred and eighty-one Indians went to Oklahoma. Within a year or so, one hundred and fifty-eight had died and a great number of the others were sick or disabled. To help insure survival of his family, the fifty-year-old Standing Bear and sixty-six of his followers left Oklahoma and resettled with the Omaha tribe; there they were given land to cultivate and employment.

On orders from the federal government, Army General George Crook was sent to arrest the Ponca Chief and his followers and return them to Oklahoma. Imprisoned by General Crook, Standing Bear sued for a writ of *habeas corpus* with the Federal District Court, the first time any Indian had done so. District Judge Elmer S. Dundy presided.

"In his lengthy ruling," Abe said, "Dundy set many precedents counter to the government's arguments. Among others, he pointed out that the law governing such writs used the terms 'persons' or 'parties,' that the term 'citizen' was purposefully omitted and therefore citizenship was not in any way or place made a qualification for suing for such a writ. He was also the first federal judge to define an Indian as a 'person' included under the law by reading the definition provided in Webster's dictionary. He also noted in his opinion that this was not the tribunal of choice for the Indians, but the only one into which they could go for deliverance."

"Dundy sounds like my kind of judge," Veronica said. "What did he conclude?"

"Five points," Abe answered, going to the last page on the case. "First, that an Indian is a person within the meaning of the law. Second, General Crook had custody of the Indians, under color and authority of the United States, and in violation of the laws thereof. Third, no rightful authority exists for the removal by force of any of the tribe as the General had been directed to do. Fourth, that the Indians possess the inherent right of expatriation, as well as the more fortunate white race, and have the inalienable right to 'life, liberty, and the pursuit of happiness.' Fifth, and most importantly, that being restrained of liberty under color of authority of the United States, and in violation of the laws thereof, the Indians must be discharged from custody and that it was so ordered."

"So Judge Dundy ruled in the Indians' favor and invoked the basic constitutional protection against imprisonment without due cause," she said. "Why doesn't that seem to make you very pleased?"

"Because the Commissioner of Indian Affairs," Abe said, "immediately declared that Judge Dundy's ruling had no bearing on other tribes. The Ponca were given a reservation on their former homeland in northern Nebraska eventually, but there was no gain for all the other tribes going through similar dislocation."

"Okay, Sport, out with it," Veronica said. "I can tell you're holding something else here. I'm ready for the other shoe to drop."

"There is one sentence in this lengthy opinion that isn't going to make the current state of affairs less complicated," he said. "Here, read it yourself."

Abe handed her the book and pointed to the sentence which read: "Every nation exercised the right to arrest and detain an alien enemy during the existence of a war, and all subjects or citizens of the hostile nations are subject to be dealt with under this rule."

"Taken out of context," Abe observed, "what does that mean to people held for years without charge who find themselves in legal limbo?"

Veronica did not dally to answer, but went to her computer and started a bulletin to those firms across the country to look into federal case law with the Indian nations. Abe must be right, she thought. This could be a gold mine for the cause.

The nor'easter gradually blew itself out over the next few days and the sun finally reappeared, bringing more seasonable temperatures. Toward the end of the week, Dan Butler called, asking Abe and Veronica to stop by for lunch on Saturday, if they could. Dan wanted Abe's opinion on something, although he was vague on what that something might be. Dan also mentioned he had invited Henry Cunningham and Cassy Spease. Since he wanted to check on the progress of the abandoned horse under Dan's care, Abe readily agreed. Veronica shared his interest and speculated what the Butlers might be serving for lunch.

"That's an interesting guest list," Veronica mused to Abe. "I wonder what Dan has up his sleeve. Mysterious doings are afoot, my friend, believe me."

"We don't rush to judgment in these things, remember?" Abe said with a grin. "We're open to whatever will be presented. That makes life so much easier and freer of stress, don't you think?"

Before retiring for the evening on Friday, Veronica checked with Prometheus for a week's end report. She was both amused and gratified by what she found. The response to her inquiry about exploring Indian law had unexpected consequences. As a profession, the practice of law is always in anticipation of opportunity, but the opportunities being discovered in the fields of property, tax and even international law were phenomenal. Abe's simple suggestion was spawning a new industry of inquiry and, naturally, likely additional billable hours.

After a leisurely Saturday morning, Abe and Veronica had made arrangements to gather Henry and Cassy for their mid-day luncheon at the Butler farm. Cassy had consulted Veronica on which outfit would be appropriate and the professor was pleased to see Cassy walking toward the car in a matched slacks and turtleneck sweater combination, with sensible casual shoes rather than her usual hiking boots.

"It looks as if we have a budding fashion plate," Abe said quietly to Veronica. "Is that what happens to girls her age?"

"That would be revealing trade secrets," Veronica responded. "Henry doesn't seem to notice any difference."

"Oh, he notices the difference," Abe responded. "Look at the way he is hesitant to walk too near and keeps his hands deep in his pockets. There are a lot of thoughts going through his mind right now and he's trying to sort his emotions. It is she who doesn't appear to know what effect she is having."

"For someone who doesn't claim to know much about the opposite sex, you're very perceptive," she observed. "Cassy is probably so self-conscious about her budding femininity that she isn't seeing Henry's reaction."

The short ride to the farm was pleasant and full of small talk about the amount of moisture still making exposed soil muddy and the first signs of a warming trend heralding the arrival of spring.

"Can we ask a question, Uncle Abe?" Henry finally said. "Do you think we'd be jumping to conclusions if we asked what you thought about this arranged lunch? Dan Butler is nice and we appreciate being invited—particularly since we want to see how Hope is doing, but Cassy and I have been talking things over and we're just curious."

"Hope?" Veronica asked as she turned into the lane leading to the house. "Is that what Dan named the horse?"

"He let us name the horse," Cassy volunteered. "The day we brought her to the barn, Dan Butler asked what name he thought he should put on the stall. We discussed it among ourselves and came to the conclusion that 'Hope' was about all we had going for us, so we decided it would have to do."

"Good choice," Abe said. "In answer to your question, Henry, I might suggest we all simply relax and see how events unfold. People have their own way of asking for help and they need to present things at their own pace and in their own way. We have been asked as friends and we are obligated as friends to respect our host's judgment."

They were warmly welcomed to the Butler household and were presented with a variety of foods, from sliced meats and vegetables to breads and pasta. Some of the remains of last year's canning were evident, along with freshly baked desserts. The conversation centered on the coming season and plans for crop rotation, new seed and weather predictions. Dan's friend and newly returned neighbor Grace Lawson, who had taken a large part in the saving of Hope and Dan's recovery of his memory, was very much in the thick of things and a gracious complement to the gathering. With the dessert finished and the dishes washed and dried, everyone participating, the time came for action.

"Why don't we all go to the barn and see how Hope has recovered?" Dan asked.

As they all walked up the gravel walkway to the barn, anticipation was building between Henry and Cassy as they caught each other's eyes and smiled as if sharing some private secret.

As the group entered the barn they were greeted with the usual aromas found on working farms, the blend of fresh hay, horse manure, oil and lubricants for the machinery, plus the smell of livestock. Abe could detect the slight addition of the scent left behind of brooding birds in the rafters. To people used to this environment, it was a pleasant and comforting experience.

Along one side of the building were five stalls, only two of which were occupied. Jasmine, the fine mare native to the place was in the first stall. Her name was elegantly emblazoned in red letters on the gate. Jasmine herself stood silently with her head over the gate watching the visitors. The gate of the second stall had the name Hope painted in similar lettering, only in green.

"Jasmine has been a great help," Dan said. "She has been a source of companionship and comfort for Hope these few months and a source of gentle encouragement. Abe, why don't you lead Jasmine out into the yard? Henry and Cassy, you follow with Hope. It will be her first view of the outside."

Abe did as was requested, leading the mare slowly out of her stall. She hesitated for a moment, looking back toward her companion as if questioning her fate. Abe soothed her neck and proceeded outside.

Henry and Cassy opened the gate to Hope's stall and found her standing still against the far wall, quivering in anticipation. The two young people gently caressed her sides and inched her out of her stall.

Once outside, it was clear to everyone there that Hope had put on needed pounds, her well-curried coat showed marked improvement in regaining its natural luster and that her properly trimmed and shod hooves were healed. Even her mane and tail were showing signs of their former health.

When the hands holding the bridles were released, the two horses wandered off to one corner of the enclosure at a slow pace and stood shoulder-to-shoulder looking back at the group.

"You don't need my evaluation, Dan," Abe said quietly. "You've done a magnificent job. The odds that Hope would survive were mighty slim from the beginning. Whatever you've been doing has saved her life. I offer my sincerest congratulations."

"Thank you, Abe," Dan said. "I accept your compliment in the spirit in which it is given. But that is not what I needed your advice on. Come back into the barn. I want you to see something else."

Dan led them to a small enclosure at the far end of the barn where Abe immediately spotted the dilemma. On a thick bed of fresh hay was a Labrador-Collie-mix suckling nine newborn puppies. The shape of the newborn's muzzles and distinctive coloring, even at this young age, were telling.

"She came in last week, probably seeking refuge from the storm," Dan said. "She looked pretty pathetic and obviously ready to drop her offspring. I fixed her up with this spot and put water and food next to her. She ignored the nourishment and just lay down on her side. I sat down on the floor and put her head in my lap, rubbing her gently. I suppose you could say that we had these nine little rascals together. What do you think?"

Abe squatted to examine the puppies for a full five minutes before venturing an answer.

"Collies and labs are gentle breeds," Abe said at length. "The muzzle shape and length could be the dominant feature either way. The coloring is distinctive and the paws, even this early, may tell a different story. I'd say the tails are the answer. They will be long and bushy as these youngsters grow. I assume you want to know what to expect?"

"That's what I'm looking for," Dan admitted. "If this is what I think it is, I'd like your advice on how to handle the situation."

No one had any idea what the two men were talking about. Dan and Abe were having a private discussion about something no one else was privy to and they awaited a conclusion.

"It's a common enough occurrence in the west," Abe said. "The Indians have dealt with the situation for as long as they can remember. Domesticated breeds get together with their wilder cousins. Coyote will breed with domestics. They call them 'coy-dogs.' How they turn out seems to be all a matter of raising and training. Coyote learn to hunt from their mother. Domestic breeds feed from bowls and other man-provided systems. I would suggest you keep a close eye on their development. They could grow up to be fine farm dogs. I think you should give them a chance."

CHAPTER 8

▼

CONSPIRACY

When the Carlson's arrived home, John Nagy and his mother, Bea, were sitting on their front porch, enjoying the first pleasant weather of the new spring season. The afternoon sun bathing its warmth across the front of the duplex allowed for light jackets and thoughts of new plants and mulch in the garden. Bea waved the couple over and offered iced tea, which they readily accepted.

"John has some good news," Bea said. "We may have worked ourselves out of a job and we couldn't be happier."

"So give us the details," Abe replied. "You sound happy for someone who has eliminated their current position. I know you are a volunteer, Bea, but won't you miss the busier pace?"

"The point is that we probably aren't needed anymore," John said. "Your idea for the Whittier Center was sound. We just didn't know it was going to work so quickly. It has taken off and the groups involved have taken the blueprint, adapting it to their efforts in unique ways. You were right that the Muslim community and their friends in the community would want to pick up the costs and organize their own events. They are working closely with other groups running Internet websites to build bridges between communities and explore avenues of understanding. We can keep the doors open for awhile, just to give referrals and advice, of course, but I'd say the main purpose has been fulfilled."

"That's great news, John," Abe said. "Perhaps you might consider continuing your services in a slightly different way. I understand Bea has been alerting you to veterans in need, one at a time."

"I tag them, John bags them," Bea said in her best dramatic voice.

"Mother, please," John commented with a wry smile. "You have to excuse her, she's been watching far too many re-runs of the detective genre on the cable channels these days. Her success has given her a new lease on life and added a spring to her step. If we're lucky, she'll never be the same."

"Veronica, I merely find your mother, Ruby, an inspiration," Bea said. "She has been showing me the ropes around computers and how to tap into various databases. You'd be surprised what you can do with a computer these days, believe me."

"My mother, the cyber-chick," John said with a mock sigh, shrugging his shoulders and raising the palm of his hands. "I'm thinking of activating the parental control buttons so she doesn't stray too far off base."

"Parental controls, my foot," Bea replied. "With Ruby's help, I'll bypass those in a few seconds. I might remind you, my son, that I've always told you that a family is not a democracy, but a benevolent dictatorship, so keep yourself in line. Now, Abe, what's this little diversion you have in mind?"

"An extension of your tag and bag efforts," Veronica said. "Abe's convinced he can gather some talent to help our veterans gain the necessary training, education, or whatever, to return to a productive and enhanced working environment. He has already identified several resources that are willing to participate—many of them veterans—who could make the concept a reality. People want to help. They just need an organizational outlet to funnel their enthusiasm."

"I'm willing," Bea said quietly. "What do you think, John, or is it still too early for a step that big?"

"The question isn't if it's too early," John answered soberly. "The question is whether it's too late. I don't think it is. We're in."

Bea had adapted to computers with the enthusiasm of a dedicated convert, spending countless hours discovering the many wonders of cyberspace. John, on the other hand, appreciated the utility, but was somewhat wary of how easily a book-length document could be erased in the blink of an eye, or a surge in electric current. From his many years of teaching, he was more comfortable with the solid printed page in his hands. The one feature that finally sparked his interest was the ease with which he could start up his search engine, type in a remembered phrase or scrap of poetry, push a button and be presented with at times hundreds or thousands of references. The memories he had of seeing someone walk across a school campus or down the hall in a major business carrying a tall stack of computer punch cards made him feel like a fossil. He made the firm decision that he wasn't yet ready to be fossilized.

"How about a nice stretch of the legs?" Abe asked Veronica as he picked up his pipe and filled the bowl—a sure sign he had some deep thinking to do.

"That would be lovely," she replied. "Just give me a minute to change shoes. That was a grand luncheon and I still eat as if I were a college girl, but I'm not quite that age anymore. I wouldn't want to wake up one morning and see that I'd become all lumpy, if you know what I mean."

"I doubt that will ever happen," he replied with a grin. "If it does, I'll just have more to love about you—lumps and all. I do know what you mean, however. One of the Fellows at the Lodge was surveying the other members as they filed in for the meeting. Noticing the ample girth on some of the men, he remarked that the Brothers were still on the Pennsylvania farmer's diet, but they weren't doing the farm work anymore."

They decided on a walk along the Swatara Creek as it wound through their part of the township. Early signs of spring were everywhere. Forsythia and weeping willow trees were in early color, the lower shrubs were greening along the bank and buds were appearing on the younger trees. They stopped to rest on a rock projecting into the stream and observed the dairy cows milling about in a field across the creek. Abe lit his pipe and began to share his thoughts.

"That was an interesting trip to Washington," he said after a few puffs. "I visited a little known Masonic landmark not far from the Georgetown Law campus, at Third and D Streets, N.W., in fact. It is a larger-than-life statue erected to the memory of Albert Pike, the only former Confederate general to have an outdoor statue in the District of Columbia. He was quite famous in his day for his Masonic work. He led the Supreme Council of the Scottish Rite, Southern Jurisdiction for thirty-two years, was a prolific writer who edited several newspapers in his time and re-wrote the ritual degrees from the Fourth to the Thirty-second which make up that rite."

"I don't believe I've ever known much about him," Veronica replied. "I do have a vague memory having to do with a group backing an obscure political candidate and a call for the statue to be removed. I was researching the right of assembly and it was in the footnotes somewhere."

"I don't believe the candidate would have liked being labeled as 'obscure,' not by a long shot," Abe said. "He was the very conservative Lyndon LaRouche."

LaRouche was always considered by many to be a minor fringe candidate in his perennial run for the office of president.

In life, Pike was a large man, standing six feet four inches and weighing around three hundred pounds. Then years after his death in 1891, the Scottish Rite Masons applied to Congress for permission to pay for and erect this memorial in his honor. Pike is depicted in full Masonic regalia, standing larger than life-size on a pedestal, at the base of which sits a bronze lady in Greek dress holding the banner of the Scottish Rite. With his long hair and flowing beard, Pike could easily be mistaken for a modern-day Moses. LaRouche and his followers claimed Pike was a Grand Wizard of the Arkansas Ku Klux Klan, involved in keeping the southern states in slavery. Failing that, LaRouche claimed that the entire legal system in the United States was controlled by the Scottish Rite and it was this Masonic conspiracy that was responsible for his being imprisoned on credit card fraud charges. After all, Pike was a noted jurist in his day, along with being an author, philanthropist, philosopher and scholar.

One year later, a city council member from the District of Columbia proposed legislation titled "Albert Pike, Ku Klux Klan Memorial Statue, Removal Resolution," a request to have the President of the United States remove the statue.

"Further inquiry found the Klan connection baseless," Abe concluded. "So there the Pike memorial stands today. On the eight corners of its base are carved the words: Author, Poet, Scholar, Soldier, Philanthropist Philosopher, Jurist, Orator. The front carries the inscription *Vixit Laborum Ejus Super Strites Sunt Fructus,* which means 'He has lived. The fruits of his labors live after him.' People tend to forget the outcome, so even today Pike carries the taint of conspiracy and Klan membership."

"Pike hardly seems like a man to draw such animosity one hundred years after his death," Veronica said.

"He wouldn't have been such a man," Abe replied, tapping out the deadened tobacco from his pipe, "if it hadn't been for one of the worst hoaxes ever perpetrated on the Masonic movement and the Catholic Church, the outrageous brainchild of a Frenchman by the name of Leo Taxil. Come walk with me and I'll tell you what I know."

Taxil was the pen name of Gabriel Jogand-Pages, born in 1854 and Jesuit educated. That experience embittered him to the church and he became a so-called "free-thinker" of his day, even joining Freemasonry. His Masonic career did not last as early on he was expelled as a result of wrongdoing. Some sources suggest he may have been a pornographer. He decided to have his revenge on both the Catholic Church and Freemasonry by concocting a fantasy tale about Albert Pike, leader of the Scottish Rite in the U.S., heading a secret Masonic order called the Palladium which practiced murder, worshipped the devil, Satan, in a form called Baphomet. The book included a now-famous supposed quote from Pike who goes to great length to justify his so-called Luciferian Doctrine, with its God of Light and God of Good being Lucifer himself. Taxil included the fictitious Diana Vaughn into the mix as a one-time disciple committing sexual rites within the confines of Pike's rituals.

"For uncovering the 'true nature of the evil Masonic practices,' Taxil became the darling of all Europe among the Catholic Church and anti-Masonic groups," Abe said. "I forget the exact details, but at some gathering held under the auspices of the Church, Taxil finally unveiled his hoax, thus revealing the religious zeal of the anti-Masonic forces to be both gullible and rather naïve."

"Let me guess," Veronica remarked, "confession and recantation once again failed to impress many people."

"Exactly," Abe answered. "In the early 1900s, the hoax prompted the anti-Masons to begin filing specious charges at Pike such as his possible Klan activities and worse. Several well-known television evangelists to this day still make charges against Freemasonry based on the Taxil hoax. As for conspiracy theories, Freemasonry has always been a favorite target and with the Internet, the proliferation of conspiracies are astounding."

"All I know is that they are sure grist for the modern best seller yarns," she said. "I must admit that they do add spice to some good books which have entertained my imagination in the past few years. It deepens the plot and urges me on to see how things will work out in the end. Such books are a welcome escape from the all-too-negative realities of the world today."

"I agree wholeheartedly," he replied. "I simply hope most people don't take some of the literature too literally. There's a fine line between enjoying a plot and hatching one."

As they followed a bend in the creek, they were surprised to see Indian Echo Caverns just a short distance away. Abe had helped rescue a trapped man in the Caverns when an abundance of water had eroded some of the supports which led to partial cave-ins, but they were now pleased to see so many workers cleaning up debris, providing needed repairs and improvements, and getting ready to reopen as soon as possible. The establishment was not a seasonal business, but a year-around one and the faster they could be reopened, the better. A man at the top of the rise waved to the couple and they both waved in return. They recognized the man as Jeff, the employee who had scrambled to get his winch to the airshaft so Abe could descend into the cavern and retrieve Dan Butler.

On their return home, Abe decided on another path, an animal trail more removed from the creek waters, but running in a generally parallel direction. He spotted numbers of deer tracks and signs of other woodland creatures, as expected, but when they came upon a small soil and rockslide, an unusual shape caught his attention. As he crouched to examine the shape, Veronica crouched beside him.

"What are we looking for, Sport," she asked in a whisper.

"Why are you whispering?" he asked in a normal tone of voice.

"I don't know," she whispered honestly. "I thought perhaps you found some shy little creature and I didn't want to scare it away."

"This one won't scare so easily," he replied, pointing to a rock partially covered by leaves and dirt. "Gently brush the leaves away and then the dirt. We may have found something interesting and very old."

Veronica took his directions to heart and slowly removed the debris to uncover an odd-shaped rock half embedded in the soil. She could not tell exactly what it might be, but it did seem to have signs of being shaped by human hands.

"What do you know about the Ice Age and Pennsylvania?" Abe queried.

"As a matter of fact, I took a great interest in that subject when I was in grade school," she answered, finally speaking in her normal tone while continuing to brush soil away a little at a time. "The glaciers halted about fifty miles north of here so the topography wasn't affected, except for the runoff from the melting ice. There were reports that a farmer not too far from here found the jawbone of some gigantic animal while digging a limestone quarry around 1850 or so. The farmer kept it as a curiosity and some years later showed it to a writer who described the teeth measured something like three and one half by seven and one half inches. These turned out to be the molars of a mastodon and I think they now reside in a state museum somewhere."

"You can stop now," Abe said, taking out his pocketknife and prying the large stone loose without filling the cavity impression with dirt or leaves. "Welcome to an artifact from the ancient world, my dear. You may have unearthed a spearhead circa 10,000-8,000 B.C., the Paleo Period of Indian pre-history. These early spearheads were invariably made of flint and fluted, just as we have here."

"What do you mean when you say that I unearthed this relic from the past?" Veronica asked. "You first spotted it and we unearthed the thing."

"Ah, but yours was the hand to first touch it," Abe said with a gentle smile. "To the first to touch belongs the glory."

"I know you just made that up out of thin air, Sport," she said. "I'm not buying it. Do you have some fanciful tale on the tip of your tongue about old Indian customs or western ways that will convince me otherwise?"

"Not at all, my love," he said sincerely, "although the honor in counting coup on one's enemy might be stretched a bit, but that's a matter for another time. I merely liked the sound of the 'Veronica Carlson spearhead' on the card placed before the artifact in a museum case."

"So you think this is museum quality?" she asked. "Okay, this marriage is a fifty-fifty proposition. Make that Veronica and Abe Carlson on the card and I'll go along."

"I like your attitude," he replied. "You're not only beautiful but very loyal too. And fierce, too, I might add. That's a wonderful characteristic to find in a spouse."

"Another good save, Sport," she said. "Now, should we just leave this thing in the ground and cover it back up before we call in the archaeologists?"

"I don't know that it's all that important," he replied. "I think we should probably take it with us, but not clean it up. We'll show them the exact spot where we found it and let them decide it they want to excavate anymore of the site. You can get into a heap of trouble in Arizona for disturbing Indian artifacts, but in this case, it's pre-Indian in classification."

CHAPTER 9

▼

GIFTS

As Abe Carlson stood in his office, morning coffee in hand, he looked out over the common area and the hills beyond and knew that spring had arrived overnight. The buds on the pear, cherry and dogwood trees that had been slowly teasing their petals for nearly a week were suddenly in full bloom. The young red maples had popped into full leaf and the forsythia gained full color. The crystal clear skies shone as magnificent blue, with the only evidence of cloud being a faint paling along the horizon. He had to admire the determination of one young boy in the distance trying with all his might to launch a kite in the stillness of the air. Most days for the past month had their fair share of strong winds, but this day provided only a slight stirring that never approached the breeze stage. Neighbors appeared on the sidewalks for an early morning stroll, jacketless, with some wearing shorts, displaying the grace of a pleasant amble.

"God's in His heaven and all's right with the world," Veronica announced in arrival. "The seasons can change at the drop of a hat here on occasion. It's one of those nice little surprises Mother Nature likes to impart to her charges, an unexpected gift of kindness."

"My, you're waxing lyrically this morning," Abe replied. "Of course this is the kind of weather that brings out poetic thoughts in us all."

"Yes it does," she agreed. "I've been so happy in marriage and so utterly busy that I had almost missed the significance of a single day. What would you say to a holiday? This is too nice a day to be penned inside, even though our work is important. Let's get out and enjoy the simple pleasures in the community, talk to people and just be best buddies."

"Now, there's a plateful I can't refuse," he replied with a broad smile. "I've never had a best buddy to hang around with—you know, pool halls, bars, shooting hoops and all those guy things. What does a man do when his best buddy is a girl?"

"Just trust in me," she said with a commanding glint in her eye, "I'll show you the ropes—which might even include shooting some hoops—but, I can assure you, I'll do my best to steer us clear of the bars and pool halls."

They spent the morning walking around their own neighborhood, greeting other neighbors on a similar walk and introducing themselves to the ones they had yet to meet. Many of those they had not met before seemed to know quite a bit about their locally noted presence—not as gossip they would say, just information passed along the grapevine. Abe put them at ease with his understated charm and forthright manner.

When they decided to go window-shopping in Hummelstown, Abe suggested they take his '73 Jeep Commando, rolling up the sides and back of the canvas top so they looked more like a vehicle on an African safari than the usual off-road vehicle cruising small town Pennsylvania. Surprisingly, Veronica declined his offer to let her drive. He seemed a natural at the wheel and she wanted to enjoy the scenery.

They saw more than the usual number of people busily about their various errands along Main Street. Shop doors were propped open and those smaller cafes with the means, set up tables with umbrellas for outdoor dining. Clothing stores placed some items on racks outside and a local art gallery moved some displays to the sidewalk.

All the local merchants were experiencing a brisk business. Of particular interest to Abe and Veronica was the New Antiquarian Bookshop, where the East Indian owners were busy filling orders and passing out free candy to the children and adults alike. Despite the presence of a modern computerized register, the wife was using an ancient crank cash register just because she liked to hear the music it made as the chimes announced every sale.

One gratifying sight were two racks of literature displayed on the checkout counter. The first rack contained multiple copies of *Jose, the Bronx Beaver*, the second, a row of pamphlets entitled *Coyote Facts: How to Live With Your New Neighbor*. The latter publication was marked as free of charge, but they noticed the large donation jar by the side was nearly full.

They encountered Jim Stiles, the new accountant in town and full-blooded Iroquois, coming out of his office.

"Hello, Jim, how's business," Abe asked.

"Surprisingly well," Jim replied. "Thank you for all the referrals. People keep telling me you've passed my name along. In appreciation, I'd like to take you two to lunch. You picked up the tab the last time."

Despite the number of patrons at The Wick, they were able to secure a corner table on the sun porch overlooking the sidewalk and the garden at the same time.

Stiles gave an enthusiastic description of his establishing business and his friendly relationship with the merchants and professionals in town. He had been heartily welcomed by the townspeople and already felt he belonged. Near the end of the meal, Abe ventured an inquiry.

"How is the Squad treating you these days?" he asked. "The word around town is that you are being tutored."

"Finely tutored," he replied, "and with kid gloves, I thank you. Henry and Cassy are very patient with me. I'm proud to say that I rather think I've reached the point where I could identify a coyote track even in downtown Rochester, New York. Inspired to do outside reading on 'my Indian traditions' has been an eye-opener. I have found that my ancestors were probably more concerned with wolves than coyotes, but then, the wolves are gone and the coyotes are here. So, I feel blessed with my new knowledge, although I don't really see myself tramping around the forest and practicing woodland crafts anytime soon. I'm more of a 'room at the Hyatt with the window open' outdoorsman, if you know what I mean."

"I imagine they ask you a lot of questions," Veronica said. "Have you imparted any words of wisdom lately?"

"I don't think so, Veronica," Jim answered. "They seem interested, of course, and politely listen to what I may have to say, but how much wisdom can one impart as an urban Indian spending way too much time on the streets? All I can really tell them is how I managed to remain just this side of the line to becoming a juvenile delinquent."

"Then I'd say you have imparted some very worthwhile information," Veronica said. "A working knowledge of life on the city streets can be of assistance to anyone. These may not seem like 'mean streets' to you, but believe me, small town America is just as prone to have city problems like illegal drugs and alcohol abuse by under-age drinkers. How they deal with such temptations is the same everywhere. Young, dumb, risky and frisky remain the same no matter the size of the community."

"Henry asked me if I was planning to attend the annual pow-wow in Middletown this weekend," Stiles said. "What do you think? Will it add to my knowledge of my Indian roots?"

"Whoa!" Abe exclaimed loudly before stifling a full-fledged laugh. "That is likely to be as far from an authentic Indian pow-wow as you can get. In the west, a real pow-wow is a gathering of Indian people for several days of festivities, exchange of goods and gossip, punctuated by dances and entertainment in full traditional dress. It would most likely include foot and horse races, competitions in feats of strength and agility, plus religious ceremonies in celebration of life."

"That sounds as if it could be instructive," Stiles remarked.

"Jim, let me tell you something," Abe said, understandingly. "Some years ago, a pow-wow became a big tourist draw and the commercial aspects began to overshadow the original intent. The so-called Hippies and New Age Movement began to crave all things native and the proliferation of smaller, local craft fairs. Now, there's nothing wrong with these craft fairs, but I do have some problems with the billing as pow-wows. At best, it would be like a back-water carnival coming to town, with just as many ways of separating you from your wallet, through whatever means."

"I believe I'll take a pass on that one," Stiles replied. "I wouldn't like to pick up any misconceptions that would be proof of my ignorance."

As they continued their ramblings around town, Abe stopped to have a snack without being asked. Veronica was impressed that her husband was catching on to some of the more important subtleties for a happy marriage.

They passed several small parks where families were having picnics and children were playing in the grass, tossing balls and Frisbees, playing tag and just being themselves. Several young boys wearing the distinctive blue shirts and yellow bandanas of the Cub Scouts were trying to organize a pickup baseball game and were having trouble enlisting as many girls as they needed to flesh out two opposing teams. Veronica had a difficult time holding back her urge to join in with the girls, but after one glance at Abe reading her mind with a grin, she demurred.

On the way home, they decided to stop by the Indian Echo Caverns to check on their progress toward reopening as soon as possible. The wide entrance drive lined with mature trees now in bud promised a welcoming entry to this year's visitors. As they neared the entrance to the parking lot, they encountered the longhorn steers Abe had last seen in the middle of the night, glaring back at his headlights. Just behind a fence stood a magnificent bull feeding from a hayrack. He was a huge animal, the biggest longhorn Abe had ever seen, with his impressive horn-span adding to his regal composure. Four more females could be seen lying among the shade of the trees or further down in the grass. Near the hayrack were three new calves, basking in the sun.

"I wonder if your friend over there remembers you," Veronica mused. "It was just a brief encounter, but could have been so meaningful, I mean in a cowboy and steer kind of way."

"No cowboy in his right mind would try to have a meaningful relationship with a beast that large and potentially dangerous out on the open range," Abe said, seriously. "That bull may have been hand-raised and pampered, but common sense dictates you step around him very gingerly. You could be very seriously injured, even though the animal meant no harm."

The large parking lot in front of the gift shop showed a number of people were being employed to make the final repairs and touch-up for the proposed reopening of Indian Echo Caverns as a paying tourist destination. The sluice box, with its turning water wheel was receiving final adjustments so that visitors could engage in an "authentic mining experience." The pavilion had been repainted and the landscaping restored. A small pen enclosing three kid goats was clean and ready.

The man they knew only as Jeff was in the gift shop arranging products on the shelves.

"Hello, Jeff," Abe said by way of getting the man's attention. "Remember us? We thought we'd just drop by to see how you're doing with the repairs."

"Why sure," said Jeff a little nervously as he quickly approached and gave Abe a quick, moist handshake. "How could I forget Abe and Veronica? You saved my job and probably this business. We'll all be forever grateful. Have a look around all you want, but please stay out of the caverns. We have our final safety inspection in a few hours and we're not to let anyone inside until that's done."

"No problem, here," Abe said, trying to tell what was making Jeff so nervous.

"Just make yourselves at home," Jeff said, returning to his chores. "I need to get back to work."

Veronica had watched in bemusement the exchange between the two men and leisurely examined several items for sale. Abe did the same. After less than one minute, Veronica cleared her throat. Abe looked in her direction and noticed her eye-movement toward the counter.

Abe walked over to see a stack of booklets they had seen before, which described the legend of the hermit of the caverns and his tragic life. Next to that stack was another, this one entitled "RESCUE: The Mysterious Stranger and Winchman Wilson." Abe merely looked at Veronica and both smiled.

"Say Jeff," Abe called as they walked toward the door, "we've never been formally introduced. Is your last name Wilson, by any chance?"

"Yes it is, Abe," Jeff replied, hanging his head in shame. "Look, let me explain."

"Nothing to explain," Abe answered raising his hand, palm out. "Use the tale with my blessings. I won't tell a soul. I just hope you've written a rip-roaring account that will entertain the public and bring in more visitors."

"That was a very magnanimous gesture," Veronica said as they were driving out of the parking lot. "I hope he didn't write that thing in the 'Perils of Pauline' genre of the other legend."

"Oh, I don't know," Abe replied with a grin. "It would make a nice companion piece—sort of like matched bookends. People who find these tales interesting probably won't realize they are rediscovering the long-dead tradition of the dime novel. Where would be the legends of Ned Buntline, Bat Masterson, Wyatt Earp, Kit Carson, Jim Bridger and the rest be without the tried and true medium of the dime novel? It may not be great literature, but people enjoy it. That's just fine with me."

Abe and Veronica returned home to find a hand-written note taped to the garage door. It was from John Nagy, asking them to join him to meet some guests he was entertaining on his back patio.

"That's a rather buoyant note from the usually reserved John Nagy," Veronica said. "He must really be coming out of his shell."

They walked out their back door to discover John in full chef's apron standing over a grill. Seated at a table in the shade of an umbrella were Bea, Veronica's mother, Ruby and a middle-aged woman they did not know. All were engaged in an animated conversation and seemed to be having the time of their lives.

"We saw your note, John," Veronica said, eyeing her smiling mother with suspicion. "No pun intended, but what has my mother cooked up now?"

"No pun taken," John replied with the first broad smile they had ever seen. "I will have to correct you, though. My mother and your mother cooked up this little scheme together. Please let me introduce you to Julie Fry, the lovely lady who is our guest. Can you stay for dinner? We're having steak and Julie is teaching me to grill like her husband, now departed."

Once the formal introductions had been made and the two had agreed to stay for dinner, the no-nonsense Julie Fry got right to the point.

"I'm a neighbor of Ruby's at the Masonic Village," she explained. "Ben and I bought a cottage eight years ago, but he passed going on five years. Dear Ben may have had his faults, but he could grill a steak over the candles of a birthday cake if need be. Ruby thought I was still too young for the aging gentleman on the prowl at the Village, so she thought she'd match me up with someone more my age. That's where Bea and John come in."

"You make it sound so uncomplimentary, Julie," Ruby said. "I was only looking our for your welfare."

"Julie's an old warhorse," Bea interrupted. "She served as an Army nurse in Vietnam and her husband, Ben, was a chopper pilot. They met at a field hospital where she tended his wounds that lead to his medical retirement. Isn't that romantic?"

"If we could cut to the chase, as they say, please," John said with a smile. "Julie and I get along just fine. We have a common experience and she wants to volunteer her services for the Whittier Center's efforts on behalf of veterans. She's more than qualified on the medical aspects and, as you may have perceived, does not put up with a lot of nonsense from anyone."

"Life's always been too short for that," Julie interrupted.

"And although you would never guess once you've seen her," John continued, "this lovely lady and I are nearly the same age."

"You're right, Bea," Julie replied. "This educated son of yours really is a silver-tongued flatterer. I could get used to that very easily. Okay, John, let's throw on a couple of more steaks and show these fine people the real art of grilling."

"You lead the way, Julie," John said. "I've got your back."

"What can we do to contribute?" Abe asked. "Veronica keeps a well-stocked larder and our freezer has a range of complements."

"Not a thing," John answered. "Mother opened the refrigerator this evening and discovered a remarkable array of side dishes already prepared, with garnishes on the platters, nonetheless. She claims it must have been a miracle, but I doubt it. I quit believing in miracles at a very young age. However, now that I'm growing older, I might just once again trust in the impossible."

"A renewed faith in the possible is a good thing, my friend," Abe said, placing his hand on Nagy's shoulder. "All these friends are here for you now and we've all got your back."

The rest of the evening went well. This turned out to be the most pleasant gathering those involved had had in many years, if ever. John Nagy was gaining a new lease on life. Bea Nagy could not have been any happier—the glow of satisfaction on her face told the tale. Julie Fry had been jolted out of her complacency. Ruby Steinmann tried to hide the fact that she was pretty pleased with herself and Veronica was very happy for her mother's success. Abe and Veronica retired with the shared appreciation for the gifts of this day.

CHAPTER 10

▼

THE SUPREMES

Returning to her office between morning classes, Veronica stopped by the Exchange Center to check on progress. Her mother, Ruby, was so entranced in front of her computer monitor that Veronica's arrival seemed to go unnoticed. When Veronica glanced toward the ever-present coffee maker, Ruby suddenly spoke without taking her eyes off the monitor.

"I wouldn't if I were you," Ruby said. "That has to be the worst coffee on campus. George Tanner, our well-meaning intern and second year law student, doesn't drink anything but tea. He thinks he's being helpful when he puts on a pot, but has a problem with proportions. You'd have to cut that tar at least ten times to make it drinkable."

"How do you do that?" Veronica replied. "You're spooky sometimes, Mother. I often think you really do have eyes in the back of your head."

"It's instinctive," she said, matter-of-factly. "You don't teach as many years as I have and survive without developing that talent."

"What has riveted your attention so?" Veronica asked, walking up behind her and peering over her shoulder at the screen. "Has Prometheus found something interesting?"

"Very," she replied. "Ever since you put the suggestion out to the country that they might want to pay particular attention to Indian law, Prometheus has been asking questions about classification. He wanted to know how the constitutional protections of the American citizenry apply to the Indian nations, who are citizens, living on a reservation that is considered sovereign. Should this be international law or domestic law?"

"An interesting point of logic," Veronica said. "What did you tell him?"

"I asked for a representative case that was causing the confusion," she said. "So what does he supply? *City of Sherrill, New York v. Oneida Indian Nation of New York, et al.* He questions the court's jurisdiction, wants to know how it climbed all the way up to the Supreme Court and how 'The Supremes' could overturn previous rulings on such flimsy grounds as were present in the majority opinion. Prometheus thinks—in the loosest sense of the word—that the lone dissent by Justice Stevens would have been a more logical decision."

"Wait a minute," Veronica said. "The Supremes? Where did that come from?"

"Miguel's sense of humor I suppose," Ruby answered. "When he wrote the programs, some of his own biases and tastes were not spared. He apparently doesn't think that highly of our illustrious members of the Supreme Court, with all that pomp and sense of importance. I don't blame Miguel. That rarified attitude does lose some of its pretense of dignity when a Chief Justice redesigns his own robes to look like a Starfleet Captain."

"Are you denying those who have reached the august pinnacle of our justice system their little vanities?" Veronica asked.

"Only when they are that silly," Ruby answered. "Now, the point is that Prometheus had put that, and similar cases to the top of the list among Pandora files."

At first glance, the case in question looked like a long shot for the Oneida Nation.

By original treaty with the federal government, the Oneida were guaranteed sovereignty over a large tract of land, placed in reserve for their sole benefit, which could not be sold without the approval of the United States Congress. In a clear violation of the law, the State of New York purchased three hundred thousand acres is 1795 and moved the Oneida elsewhere. The land was then sold to settlers. Over two hundred years later, direct descendents of the tribe bought back some of the original acreage, claimed the land had never lost its treaty-protected aboriginal rights of possession and refused to pay property taxes. The Indian position was upheld at the federal district court and appeals levels, but the Supreme Court reversed those rulings. Even the filing of an *amicus curiae* brief by the powerful National Congress of American Indians, representing more than two hundred and fifty tribes, failed to sway the court.

"That was just a couple of years ago," Veronica said. "Some legal scholars thought it was one of the worst and weakest rulings of the Rehnquist court. It showed that both liberal and conservative courts were not immune to charges of 'activist judges' making, rather than just ruling on the law. The ruling carried a rather specious argument about the amount of time having passed without protest, as if there were a statute of limitations on violations of that magnitude."

"Why is Prometheus so keen on the lone dissenting opinion?" Ruby asked.

"I would imagine for two reasons," she answered. "His ability to link information and detect even subtle patterns points to the importance of dissent in the history of the court. What may be a minority opinion in one era could well turn into the majority view in the next. This has happened so many times with the major national issues that we have lost count. The Stevens dissent also raised the issue of whether the question should be before the federal court or the Congress, which has primary jurisdiction in Indian affairs."

Veronica knew this was likely just the first wave of cases involving Indian affairs that would come before the Supreme Court in the foreseeable future. She made a mental note to assign a few cases in Indian law to her students. Some would likely encounter these issues during their professional careers.

It was not until she turned to leave the room that Veronica noticed identical nameplates on the three working desks in the room.

"It was my idea," Ruby said without turning from her monitor. "It boosts morale and puts visitors at ease right from the beginning. It's a great conversation starter."

"You're getting a little creepy again, Mother," Veronica said. "Please cease reading my mind."

"It's sort of clever, though, don't you think?" she asked. "No one here minds being called a Turkey Wrangler, in fact they take some pride in the designation. Heaven knows many of the cases we're finding certainly deserve to be called turkeys. George calls us a lean, clean billing machine, whatever that's supposed to signify. When I don't know what the younger generation is talking about, I simply remain quiet. That way, I'm not perceived as being too old and un-hip and I can remain blissfully ignorant. They'll think I'm with it, if you know what I mean."

"I know exactly what you mean, dear Mother," she said with a warm smile. "I do have a bulletin for you, though. If you start throwing around terms like 'hip' and 'with it,' they'll know you are a dinosaur."

After her last morning class, Veronica was walking across campus in the warm sunshine wondering how long this unseasonably pleasant weather would last when she spotted the familiar sight of Abe's Jeep parked at the curb. He had been talking to a senior couple that had attended a lecture series the school held for the general public and they were half way down the block when she arrived.

"Recruiting a new class of students, Sport?" she asked. "I didn't know you were coming on campus today. What's the occasion?"

"That nice couple was telling me about the battle of Gettysburg," Abe replied. "Everyone here seems to be an expert on that subject. As for the occasion, I love you and I missed you, so I thought you might like my bringing lunch, while this weather lasts."

Abe retrieved a picnic basket from the Jeep and they walked hand-in-hand along a walkway until they found a bench under the shade of a tall hedge. He produced plates, utensils, cups and cloth napkins before opening a small cooler built into one side.

"Oh, wraps," she declared. "How thoughtful and how elegant."

"I certainly do get a kick out of people who have only recently been introduced to this particular cuisine to think it's elegant," he replied with a smile. "In the southwest, this would be considered a poor man's meal. Take a soft tortilla, fill it with whatever is at hand—beans, leftover meat or vegetables—and you have a sandwich. Call it a wrap and people think of it as something perhaps imported from Europe. I simply used ingredients I found in the refrigerator and added my own spices."

No matter what the ingredients in the food, Veronica found them delicious. She realized, of course, that Abe's thoughtfulness and saying he missed her, along with the tinges of spring in the air, whetted her appetite and added to her enjoyment. The conversation eventually came around to her questioning his thoughts on the Oneida decision.

"I don't think you'll find much justice in most Indian dealings with the government," Abe said wistfully. "Indians have found themselves to be on the short end of the stick too many times. In the important cases, there is always the element of money, big money. Whether it's the railroads, the timber interests, mineral deposits or simply land, the money interests usually come out the winners. To the Indian, provisions in a treaty are sacred pledges of honor. To many whites, they are simply suggestions."

"Are you getting to be cynical on the subject?" Veronica asked. "That doesn't seem quite like you."

"Not cynical," Abe replied, "only realistic. Mostly, I try not to judge these things. I recognize the reality of the situation and try to deal with whatever it is. The Indians I know have a remarkable way of toying with state and local governments that gives them moments of relief from the constant confrontation."

"Give me your perspective," she asked.

"I'll give you one small example from the same state as the Oneida case," he said.

The state of New York had one of the most oppressive records from the Indian point of view, he explained, but that was most likely because New York had a longer experience than those west of the Mississippi River. While the newspaper headlines were full of the controversy over whether the Indian lands should be allowed to establish casino gambling in competition to established gambling enterprises off the reservations, that wasn't a choice for most tribes. Either the lands were too remote, located too near successful enterprises, or too small—in either acreage or population—to be practical.

Many tribes had turned to small enterprise—specifically the sale of tobacco products and gasoline without the added state and federal taxes. Abe was familiar with a small Seneca spot of land near Niagara Falls, New York, which had been fighting the state for years over its refusal to tax their sales to the non-Indian population. In one instance when the governor of New York tried to prevent gasoline deliveries to the facility by stopping the tankers outside the Indian land, the Senecas took to the street and blocked a major highway. A large contingent of state police had to be called upon to restore order.

"The most humorous situation—from the Indian point of view—is the state pressure to have the Indians collect state taxes on cigarettes and other tobacco products. The state has probably the highest tax in the nation and has exerted enormous pressure on the Seneca. They started tightening the screws by persuading credit card companies to disallow tobacco sales. That move effectively cut off a burgeoning Internet and telephone sales business. So the Seneca sold only on-site or by check for mail orders. The state then put equal pressure on private delivery companies like United Parcel and FedEx, with the threat of the state's tax collectors stopping and inspecting packages for untaxed products."

"Can they legally do that?" she asked.

"Who knows?" he answered. "The point is that the threat was made. The Seneca weren't finished though. They switched exclusively to the United States Postal Service, where a warrant with probable cause is required to open each individual package—which proved as impractical as it was improbable. With the intensity of the anti-tobacco campaign increasing daily, there hasn't been much sympathy from the general public about the rights of the Indian to pursue this legal activity."

"Certainly this can't be a big drag on the local economy," Veronica said. "I assume there are local non-Indian citizens involved in these enterprises."

"Plenty," he answered. "These employees contribute their state and federal taxes just like everyone else. My concern is on a broader scale—what can happen on other Indian lands if other issues come to the fore."

"You're losing me there, Sport," she said. "Where are you headed with this?"

"Take a few elements that could change a situation into a disaster," Abe replied. "Illegal immigration is a hot-button political issue these days and will likely continue to be for some time. Eleven million, or twelve million illegal people are currently in the population and many communities are over-reacting. What if some of those sought refuge on sovereign Indian lands, employed by an Indian enterprise? I don't mean asylum, but refuge—an added protection from U.S. authorities. The local or state authorities, perhaps with the assistance of U.S. immigration people, raid an Indian factory and round up the illegal workers for deportation. Do we have an international incident or a more modest local confrontation of serious proportions? How is our legal system likely to respond?"

"Wow," Veronica responded. "You do have an imagination, but a perfectly plausible threat to public order. What frightens me is that just such a situation could naturally occur and the consequences are a totally unknown factor."

The rest of the luncheon was spent in quiet contemplation, with snippets of daily news and rumor. As with all academic institutions of higher learning, the Dickinson School of Law was rife with rumor, but delightfully peppered with sardonic legal interpretation and commentary.

"I heard from John Nagy this morning," Abe said as they walked to his Jeep. "He has come across an interesting program that might be of interest to this school."

"I trust we'll always be open to new ideas," Veronica replied. "What has John found?"

"Well," Abe said, "as I understand it, law schools across the country are stepping up efforts to help veterans—particularly those newly returned from combat zones. The University of Detroit Mercy Law School had a converted RV once used for efforts to bring *pro bono* assistance to seniors and the elderly. It was staffed by first and second year law students for hands-on experience in the field. This law-on-wheels approach is now being used to reach veterans of all conflicts—from World War II to the present—for assistance in getting disability benefits or Social Security, plus helping with the complexity of family law issues such as child support. Detroit has an advanced Veterans Center, a one hundred and four bed facility for the homeless veterans who could greatly benefit from this free legal service."

"That is the type of program best suited to Philadelphia, Pittsburgh or even Harrisburg," she said. "The potential client base would be much broader. Yet, I know your affinity for local efforts, no matter the number of people served."

"Who is serving the less populated areas of Central Pennsylvania without having to travel to Harrisburg or some regional center?" Abe replied. "There are small town veterans everywhere who could use a little assistance. Many are averse to traveling any distance to stand in a line and go through the bureaucratic process—opening themselves to public scrutiny and loss of personal privacy that helps them retain some semblance of dignity."

"As usual, I have to admire your concern for your fellow human beings," she commented quietly. "Every bureaucracy carries a non-humanizing element. It's the nature of the beast. Retaining your sense of personal dignity may be hard to maintain under the rigors of daily experience. How much harder must that be for veterans whose experience far exceeds what we civilians will ever achieve?"

"Would you be interested in making a proposal to the school?" Abe asked. "The Whittier Center will provide a converted van with a driver who is not only a retired attorney from the Judge Advocate General's Office, but also a successful attorney with his own firm, now retired from civilian practice, as one side of the service. Where John found him, I don't know, but I'll be willing to bet Julie Fry and her network of military contacts had something to do with it. Would the school be willing to provide the volunteer students with proper supervision to fill out the equation?"

"I have just the woman for the job," Veronica replied. "She is a professor of family law who lost her father in Vietnam and I'm sure she will jump at the chance. How soon could you put this together?"

"Just about as long as it takes to put gas in the van," he answered with a pleased smile. "I expect you'll need more time than that, so I'll just say that we're ready at any time."

Veronica found that parting was not so difficult on this particular day. She had a wonderful lunch with her husband and a new venture to pursue in their joint efforts. She could hardly believe her happiness and the day was only half finished. Unsure, really, of what she had expected life to be, she was personally nurtured by all that was now offered.

Abe had similar thoughts as he drove through the countryside toward home. Life appeared to be unfolding rather than speeding by, as it would have in other times of heightened activity. The more he became involved in community issues, the stronger the anchor of his marriage became. It was a feeling he had seen reflected in the eyes of a very few people he had met, but one that sustained a belief in possibility beyond one's expectation.

CHAPTER 11

▼

BASICS

For the Exchange Center on the campus of Dickinson School of Law, it was the busiest and most productive week to date. Veronica was grateful for Miguel Swartzbaugh's foresightedness in providing an enormous computing capacity with programming sufficiently sophisticated to handle the myriad tasks linking even obscure cases of simple law with more complex litigation involving local, state and federal law and bundling those issues with constitutional implications. Prometheus began to find certain patterns emerging and when sufficient data had been collected, often starting a sub-category linking a single aspect. One aspect right before everyone's eyes, but little noted—an instance of not being able to see the forest for the trees—was religious viewpoint or religion-related action or inaction.

Catholic Charities, a highly organized, effective and far-flung organization came to the fore on immigration, naturalization and resettlement cases. Catholic Charities had been instrumental in the resettlement of a large number of Vietnamese and other Southeast Asian people in the Harrisburg area. It was also instrumental in the influx of Buddhists that led to the vast boom in Buddhist temples in Fort Wayne, Indiana. The influx of Buddhists in the area were mostly Burmese or Sri Lankan. Because of the tendency to start small in suburban residences, a culture alien to the other residents disrupted entire neighborhoods.

There always seemed to be a controversy afoot over the teaching in schools of Darwin's theories on the origin of man and the survival of the fittest, as opposed to "creationism" or its cousin "intelligent design.". The overwhelming majority of American Christians had no idea how to perceive the internal debate in the Muslim community over whether to modernize or take Islam back to the 7th Century.

Rights to privacy and property were under attack on so many fronts, due mostly to international turmoil, that many organizations from the churches to the American Civil Liberties Union seemed to be joining the fray. The Federal Educational Rights and Privacy Act of 1974 forced schools to closely guard student information, even from parents, further compounding the problem and blurring the line between the so-called rights of the parents who were footing the bill and the newly created rights to privacy by the students.

It was all the Exchange Center could do to keep on top of the situation and insure the continuous flow of information in and out to the thousands of points where the information was being utilized.

Perhaps the change in the weather from warm spring sunshine to plummeting temperatures and four days of drizzle, punctuated by fairly heavy downpours made the hours examining data while juggling her class schedule seem even longer. When she arrived home early Friday evening, Veronica was more than ready for the change to beautiful weather predicted for the weekend.

When she walked in the door, she found Abe in the kitchen in the process of preparing a light evening meal. Without a word, she walked up behind him at the counter and put her arms around his waist and gave him a hug.

"I sure hope you're my wife," Abe said, leaning into the hug. "If not, I'm going to have a lot of explaining to do. You're also putting me in an awkward position of having to explain why I didn't resist, tooth and nail. Have you had a hard day, my love?"

"Not hard, Sport," she said, "just very busy. I need some time to step back, let all this information settle into the proper files in my brain and gird my loins for the next onslaught. It's not easy being a turkey wrangler, you know."

"That's the spirit," Abe said. "I think you'd look very cute in that outfit. Please let me see how you look before starting off to the arena. Just what does a modern day turkey wrangler wear anyway?"

By the time Veronica had changed her clothing and joined him for dinner, she was her normal refreshed self again.

"Why don't you let me help you regain some perspective," Abe suggested over after-dinner coffee. "I've been wanting to take a short trip, a small pilgrimage to Lititz. I want to see what has become of the great Moravian movement. I know you have roots there."

"Of course," she replied. "My father was Catholic, but my mother came from the Church of the Brethren tradition. I attended my father's church infrequently, but I was reared in my mother's church. However, I can give you quite a bit of history on the Moravians."

"I'm most interested in Count Zinzendorf from Saxony and his efforts to establish church communities on a global scale," he said.

"Count Nicholas Louis van Zinzendorf was his full name," Veronica stated. "He established the closed Moravian community and named it Lititz in 1756 and it remained closed for about one hundred years."

Zinzendorf was from the northwestern section of Germany called Saxony, Veronica recalled. He was ordained a Lutheran minister with a peculiar fervor to establish Moravian settlements, creating a religion within a religion to carry on that work. His zealousness was at odds with the Saxon Government support of Lutheran tradition of the times, which prosecuted his religious labors, forcing him to travel to Holland, England, the West Indies and America, planting branches of the Moravian body wherever he journeyed. The first American settlement was in the colony of Georgia in 1735. James Oglethorpe was populating his new colony with persecuted, but upright Protestants, which seemed to bode well for the Moravians. Trouble arose almost immediately, though. Oglethorpe was battling for control of the Georgia border with the Spanish occupying Florida and called every man in the colony to arms. The Moravians, refusing to forsake their principles of non-resistance and dependence on prayer, abandoned their lands and joined other brethren already established in Pennsylvania in 1740.

"The many churches you find throughout Pennsylvania are supposedly branches of the original Zinzendorf efforts," Veronica concluded. "To this day, they remain non-resistant and seek alternative service options in time of war. I believe I have a couple of uncles who were in alternative service during the Korean War. I'm sure the same holds true today."

"I've seen a brochure here and there on Lititz," Abe said. "It seems to have many historically significant buildings still in use today."

"Lititz is teaming with those," she replied. "One of the most prominent and famous is the Moravian *Gemeinhaus*, a combination church, parsonage and school erected in 1746. The name comes from the German meaning country congregation. If you're interested in a tour of the town, I'm familiar enough that I would be a great guide to all the significant sites, especially if you're interested in Wilbur Chocolate or the Sturgis Pretzel House—both have interesting tours and free samples. I can also introduce you to a number of shopping emporiums."

"I'm confident of your ability on all fronts," he said. "What if we just have lunch somewhere nice and see how it goes. You must know a good establishment for lunch."

"The 1764 Restaurant in the General Sutter Inn comes to mind," she replied without taking a single breath. "It is named for John Augustus Sutter, who carried the rank of general in the Mexican War of 1848, but better known for Sutter's Mill in the Sacramento Valley of California responsible for touching off the Gold Rush of 1849."

"That's where the term '49ers' comes from," Abe said. "He couldn't keep those gold-fevered maniacs from overrunning his land. They ruined his health and his wealth. As I recall, he was on the verge of bankruptcy when he was run out of town. I didn't know he ended up in Lititz."

"He came to town in hopes of restoring his health in the famous mineral springs," she said. "He spent the last two decades or so of his life there and is buried in the local Moravian cemetery. His restored house is just across the street from the inn."

Abe was still vague on the subject of why he was so interested in Lititz until they were in Veronica's Mercedes and on their way in the early morning sunshine. The promised change in the weather arrived just in time. As usual, Veronica drove on the back state roads because she knew of Abe's continuing interest in the landscape. If anyone doubted that this entire area of the state was farm country, rather than dominated by the big chocolate factories and others, a cruise through downtown Hershey proved agriculture was still very much in evidence and provided many first signs of spring labor. Along Route 322, the parking lot of the upscale Hershey Lodge and Convention Center was holding a large equipment exposition with new John Deere farm machinery, gleaming stainless steel sided dump trucks and a variety of vehicles suitable for farm and road work.

Emerging into the rolling hills of the valleys beyond the small town, the expansive fields that had lain fallow during the winter were plowed for crop rotation, awaiting a soaking rain before first planting. They drove by widely separated farms with corrals of new-shorn sheep and frisky kid goats nuzzling their mothers for breakfast. Dairy cows, hours past their morning milking, milled about enclosures attached to barns as if deciding what to do with the rest of the day. Horses grazing in the fields dotted the landscape.

Another sure sign they were in Central Pennsylvania was the number of ice cream stands, parlors and vendors open for the first weekend of their season. The ratio of "soft" ice cream outlets to "real" ice cream dispensers left no doubt of people's preference for the traditional, full-bodied type.

"Were you aware that Zinzendorf and his Moravians hold a place of honor in the memory of the Indian nations?" Abe suddenly asked in a quiet tone.

"I had no idea," she replied in surprise. "Did you get that from the Indian telegraph or grapevine that you've told me about—the one you said kept the western tribes aware of events since the Mayflower landed?"

"Since Jamestown was founded in Virginia," he corrected. "That was an earlier date. Yes, that's my source. Let me tell you what information was conveyed to the western regions."

According to Abe's information, Zinzendorf and his Moravians were ardent missionaries establishing their first mission among the Mohican Indians near the New York-Connecticut border in 1741. Bigoted whites and authorities forced the Moravians to take refuge in Lehigh, Pennsylvania so they established a new mission twenty miles above what is now Bethlehem, Pennsylvania and gave the mission the name of *Gnadenhutten* or Tents of Grace. The news of Mohican prosperity spread quickly among the other friendly tribes such as the Delaware and Shawanees. As the so-called Penn's people pushed further west, the tribes and their Moravian missionaries moved to the Susquehanna River then far up the Allegheny River and beyond into the wilderness, suffering incursions from unconverted warriors and hostile trappers alike. Despite the hardships, they were well established among the tribes by the 1760s and in the early 1770s they were invited to spread among the Wyandotte even further west in Ohio. By 1775, the number of Moravian Indians in a variety of villages reached four hundred and fourteen.

"During the Revolutionary war," Abe noted, "most of the villages were on that very dangerous line between Pittsburgh and Detroit, positioned directly between the opposing forces. The situation became impossible."

Then the beginning of the end came in 1781, Abe continued. By order of the British commander at Detroit, the villages were disbanded and the inhabitants robbed of all their possession, removing them to Sandusky, Ohio. The following February, a starving party of ninety-six returned to their ravaged homes in an effort to prevent complete starvation by gleaning the corn left standing in the fields. An American force from Ohio swooped in and massacred the lot of them.

"So the germ of the idea of how to deal with the so-called 'Indian problem' successfully, was scattered and gone," Abe concluded. "A few survivors who had not returned to their original villages managed to survive in Canada for years with their Moravian missionaries, and eventually returned to their land, but they were then totally surrounded by whites."

"The Moravian missionaries became martyrs to the western tribes?" she asked.

"Not in the sense that you use the term," Abe replied. "From the Indian perspective, the way the eastern nations were treated was a series of examples of how they would be dealt with when the inevitable migration west came to them. Some people think of the Indian as a fatalist, but nothing could be further from the truth. The Indian has a strong core belief and trust in the Great Spirit who decides all things.

"The Moravian missionaries, unlike those from other Christian sects, came among the Indians in peace and non-violence. Some missionaries intermarried and gained converts among the tribes, not insisting the entire people be converted. The missionaries and the Moravian Indians were welcomed openly to live among the tribal unit. The converts were seeking their own path to the Great Spirit and did not challenge the traditional Indian religious beliefs."

"So the Indians respected the Moravian missionaries?" she asked.

"That's the point exactly," he answered. "The missionaries showed respect for the Indian and won their respect in return—always through personal example. Yet, they also gave the Indian a very important gift—the gift of hope."

"Hope?" she asked.

"Yes, hope," he replied. "If the Moravians and their ways could be found among the whites, perhaps there was hope that other whites would come forward and deal honestly and openly with the Indian nations. Hope is an intangible, but very potent force in human relations."

"Thank you for sharing that knowledge," she returned quietly. "I've always appreciated the strong pioneer spirit of the people who settled this land, but think of how much braver and hardier those missionaries must have been—and committed—to go out into the wilderness and share the hardship, while retaining their devotion to principle."

"Not just the hardships, my dear," he replied, "but the triumphs, gladness and the accomplishments of the people as well. Life is always full of joy as well as sorrow. We need one to appreciate the another."

As they entered into Lititz, Veronica first drove slowly by the complex of buildings called the *Gemeinhaus,* with the church, parsonage and school standing firmly and boldly against the deep blue sky. These building seemed ready to withstand another few hundred years of wind, weather and the ravages of progress.

Since it was still too early for luncheon to be served, Veronica parked the car and they took a leisurely stroll around town window-shopping. There were a number of small quaint shops featuring colonial, Victorian and Americana selections of every stripe. Stopping before one store window, they spotted an elaborate Victorian dress and matching, exotic hat that looked as if it had come right out of the backstage dressing room of a production of "Hello, Dolly." Abe tried to picture what Veronica might look like in such a combination, but they caught each other's reflections in the glass and both simply laughed.

They spent a full hour walking through the Moravian cemetery, paying homage to those who had gone before. Then they quietly walked arm-in-arm to the inn.

The General Sutter Inn was originally built in 1764—hence the name of the restaurant—by the Moravian Church and named Zum Anker or Sign of the Anchor, considered one of the finest inns in Pennsylvania in its day. Major renovations took place in 1803 and 1848, with many improvements in the ensuing years. The interior décor was decidedly Victorian.

After they had been seated in the dining room and placed their orders, Abe opened a brochure he had picked up in the lobby. The inn had sixteen rooms and suites decorated in antique country and Victorian style, he discovered. Two restaurants, a full service tavern and a seasonal outdoor patio completed the list of main features.

"It says here that the Victorian bar is called Pearl's," Abe read aloud. "It says that Pearl is the inn's most famous resident and invites us to visit. Who is Pearl?"

"I've often wondered about that myself," Veronica answered, "but somehow have never thought it appropriate to inquire. I haven't really been here that often, but I've always had the feeling that it's some kind of inside joke only the locals are in on."

Their light lunch of a sandwich and salad were satisfying and they passed on the dessert in favor of another cup of coffee. On their way out, both stopped to freshen up and Abe emerged with a smug grin on his face.

"How about a pretzel?" Abe said, taking her arm once they reached the sidewalk. "My uncanny sense for mystery has solved the puzzle of Pearl. I just met her in the men's room and must say she possesses a flair for the dramatic."

Abe described his visit to the men's room, which was downstairs from the dining area and quite dated. When he opened the door, the facilities were to the left, but just ahead he found a wooden replica of a bathtub painted bright red, with the name "Pearl" in elaborate gold lettering on the side. Inside the tub he found a mannequin of a woman taking a bubble bath—heaps of cotton replicating the bubbles. Above the bath was a painted mirrored sign that read: "Pearl is here to make you smile and laugh. Please do not remove her from her bath!"

"Oh, those wacky Moravians," Veronica smiled. "You must admit they have a different sense of humor. It must be due to all those long, frigid winters before they had central heating."

"I don't know," Abe said. "I find it rather charming, in an innocent way. They prove themselves to be authentic flesh and blood people, not the staid portraits you see on ancient tin-types you find in grandpa's attic."

"You're right, Sport," Veronica replied. "I suppose we all have a difficult time picturing our grandparents and great grandparents having a little fun once in awhile. I also think much of the humor wasn't as tame as Pearl in the bathtub. I also believe I know what direction Prometheus is urging us to take. He wants us to get back to basics—basic law, basic issues and basic common sense."

C H A P T E R   12

▼

SOURCES

Abe was in the middle of reviewing the monthly report on one of his foundation efforts when he received a troubling call from Veronica.

"You remember Sue Daily, don't you?" Veronica asked. "She's the young artist who illustrated *Jose, the Bronx Beaver* for the children, free of charge."

"I don't remember if I've met her or not," Abe replied. "I can tell from her work that she is very talented, though. She has a promising career in the offing."

"She does unless someone cuts it very short," she said, "and she is feeling very threatened right now. I just got off the phone with her and she has a problem."

As Veronica related the conversation, Daily had received a call from a boy she knew in high school, Dennis Pratt, who was still vexed by the number of times his advances had been rebuffed by Sue in those years and was threatening revenge. Pratt was an aspiring journalist, a freelance writer working by the piece for small local newspapers. As yet, he had only managed to be a stringer for high schools sports, but had big plans to break into a real position in journalism with a scathing expose on a pending copyright infringement suit naming her as a co-defendant.

"How many ways can you draw a beaver for a children's book?" Abe asked. "Does this Pratt character think she copied someone else's work?"

"That's not the angle," Veronica said. "Pratt says he has an unimpeachable source who wrote the original story years ago, but was unable to find a publisher. This source supposedly has a typewritten copy on yellowing paper as proof, along with the original copyright form submitted to the Library of Congress. This so-called original is word for word as it appears in the children's version. Dennis 'The Red Menace' Pratt was an image he promoted in high school, but all the girls thought he was simply a jerk. He claimed his flaming red hair was due to his Viking heritage, while everyone knew he got it from his mother's Irish side of the family. I'd like to call him up and put the legal fear of God into him, but he'd probably use that to beef up his story."

"I imagine he hasn't named this mysterious source," Abe surmised. "The book sales have been a moderate success and the children are using the profits to refurbish the Day Care Center. As I understand it, they are about to sponsor two benches and six bird feeders for the park. This has all the earmarks of a shakedown."

"This would be a purely frivolous suit," Veronica said. "We'd clean their clocks in court and counter-sue for everything they have, which probably won't amount to much. After all, I was there at the creation and heard first-hand the oral version."

"What do you think the experience would do to the children?" he asked. "Perhaps Pratt, or whoever is behind this scheme is, counting on the fact that we don't want to subject them to a public forum. Pratt may be seeking revenge for perceived slights, but the source is most likely banking on a financial settlement out of court and is using the children as leverage. Sounds like a great guy."

"And people wonder why I left the courtroom for the halls of academia," she remarked. "What do you think we should do?"

"Maybe we can stop all this nonsense in its tracks," he replied. "Let me look around a little. I'll make a visit to the only person in town I know to be at least nearly as nosey as I am."

"And who might that be?" she asked.

"Couldn't tell you," he replied straightforwardly. "Confidential sources, you know, just like Pratt claims he has to protect."

"That won't hold up in court, my friend," she replied, "anymore than Pratt's claim to protection for journalistic confidentiality, much less to being a journalist. Besides, I'm your wife, remember? I can't be forced to testify against you in court."

"I thought that spousal exemption was only in criminal cases," he said. "Also, don't you have several obligations as being an officer of the court? I've been flipping through several law books you have around the house, you see."

"Don't simply scan law texts, dear," she replied. "If you are interested, read them all the way through. Or, better yet, go to law school and learn what's correct, rather than making specious arguments with so little knowledge."

"I concede your point, professor," Abe replied. "I'm going to see Frank at the newsstand."

Abe arrived at the newsstand during the mid-morning lull. People had already made their early morning purchases and business would pick up during the lunch hour. Frank was stocking magazines on the shelves to the rear.

"Hello, Frank," Abe called. "How's business?"

"I'm doing very well, thank you," Frank replied as he walked back to the front counter. "You have been good for business, you know. Thank you for the referrals. I've added three more major newspapers and at least six new magazines to my lists. I must also thank you for steering business to my parents at the New Antiquarian Book Shop. They are grateful. Now, what can I do for you today?"

"I need some information, Frank," he replied. "You seem to be a man who keeps a fairly good eye on what's happening in town."

"I do receive a lot of gossip and observe even more, but don't spread it around," Frank admitted. "I am at you disposal."

"Where do the local newspaper people hang out after working hours?" Abe asked. "Everywhere I've been, there seems to be a favorite watering hole."

"In the city I have seen this, yes" Frank said in his slightly accented English. "Small town Pennsylvania is a much different story. The newspaper staff tends to congregate in cafes to eat and drink coffee, then go home to their families. There are some exceptions, of course."

"Do you know Dennis Pratt and is he one of the exceptions?" Abe asked forthrightly.

"Everyone knows Dennis," Frank conceded. "Opinions vary, of course, but I don't think too highly of him or his habits, particularly in the past few months."

"Why is that?" Abe encouraged.

"It is only my personal opinion," Frank said, "but I have always regarded Dennis as a light-weight, and not a very knowledgeable one, at that. He seems to read nothing but high school sports stories. He has no interest in matters of the world—only what concerns the local community. Lately, though I see him on a downward slide. He drinks too much, even in the middle of the day. He is one of those people who should not drink."

"Where does he do his drinking?" Abe asked.

"No one is supposed to know, I guess," Frank said, "but everyone does anyway. There is a small seedy bar called Tinker's a couple of blocks off East Main. I hear he drinks away the day with another barfly named Brady. Brady has become the caricature of a town drunk, a washed-up local reporter who has been fired from every position he ever held in the local newspaper business. I'm told he was a fair reporter in his day, when he was sober. The trouble is that he hasn't been sober in years. I also hear he runs up quite a beer tab near the end of the month, just waiting for his Social Security check to arrive."

"I think you've just provided all the information I'm likely to need," Abe said. "If you'd kindly give me an address, I'll be on my way. I thank you for your help. By the way, is it okay if I leave my Jeep parked out front for an hour or so? I'd like to walk."

Tinker's bar would not have been an easy place to find if you did not know where to look. Tucked away down an alley a couple of blocks off Main Street, Abe found what seemed to be an old converted garage. Tinker's was hand painted on a pealing front door and a single brand of beer was advertised in a small dark window by a blinking neon light with several letters missing. Abe walked into a dark, smoke-filled room reeking of week-old cooking oil and stale spilled beer. As his eyes adjusted, he saw a short L-shaped bar and two tables set in dim corners, a slim door in between indicating a unisex water closet. He found it hard to believe that the liquor authorities would grant a license for such a dive, except that the tables indicated food service was available. The lone bartender, wearing a soiled tee shirt and filthy apron, showed that he served double duty as the cook. Even in the darkness, Abe could make out Pratt, with his head of red hair, sitting at a table with the only other patron in the place—a large brooding figure of a man with the bloodshot eyes of a severe alcoholic.

"Are you Brady?" Abe asked quietly as he approached the table.

"The one and only," Brady replied, releasing a loud burp, followed by a drunken chuckle shared by his companion. "Care to buy me a beer?"

"Not today, Brady," he replied. "I'm Abe Carlson, the author of the beaver story. You may have heard I moved to town."

Brady seemed to suddenly jolt out of his drunken haze for a moment and a look of recognition managed to seep out of his deep red eyes.

"I understand you used to be a fair reporter, Brady," Abe continued. "I'm sorry to see you in such reduced circumstances. Since you have been incapable— and your friend there had no interest—you would have known from reading the national news that the story is based upon a real beaver that appeared less than a year ago. I rather doubt whatever proof you think you may otherwise have will pass the legitimacy test. For all I know, you may have come to believe in your own version. Still, if charges were brought against you and you were found guilty, how well do you think you'd fare in an alcohol and smoke-free environment of jail? I've seen cold turkey withdrawal in my time and it's not a pretty sight, believe me."

Brady took a long draw on his beer, filled his lungs with cigarette smoke and glared back at Abe, but did not say a word.

"As for you, Pratt," Abe said, addressing the younger man, "I'd suggest you look up the legal ramifications of violating the laws dealing with verbal threats, slander, libel and stalking. You may be a friend of Brady, but do you think that friendship would last long if you had to share a cell?"

With that, Abe turned on his heels and left Tinker's, knowing that when he arrived home, he was going to need a long hot shower. Right now, he needed a brisk walk in the fresh air, so he steered a course toward the nearest park.

So much for journalistic sources, particularly unidentified ones, Abe thought as he began to walk. That was such an overused term in that field. He remembered a television reporter in a particular major city who overused the term to the point of sounding ludicrous. As if to lend authenticity or authority to his reporting, he remembered seeing the reporter doing the usual stand-up with a burning building in the background. "Sources say there's been a fire," he reported gravely. "Sources say it was a major fire. Sources say we may never know what caused the fire." He had seen this same reporter turn to the camera at the end of a so-called "exclusive" interview and say: "Sources tell me ..." Abe never could recall the man's name, but always thought of him as "Sources Say."

Abe came to the park, entered the tree line and followed a meandering creek. He thought about our sources of news and information. He wondered how many people received the majority of their information mostly from television, or newspapers, or magazines, or simply by word-of-mouth. He questioned the number and types of filters the information had to pass through before being presented to the public in a neat package. Was the massive amount of information available in the electronic age going to overwhelm even our most sophisticated computerized gathering systems? Was the truth of any particular matter going to be lost in this giant homogenized process? What of the institutional sources such as schools, churches, governments and, to a lesser extent, organizations?

Most of all, Abe began to think about the technological wizardry of the Internet, the primary source of information for the younger generation, which provides new breakthroughs in knowledge in the blink of an eye, and at our fingertips with a few keystrokes. The big problem with the Internet was, that as a basic source for all manner of information, it had become a dumping ground for bad information, misinformation and disinformation. Anyone with a personal cause, an axe to grind, a grudge to settle or a conspiracy theory to feed had free rein.

How was an ordinary citizen supposed to discriminate among the vast array of sources? He decided to conduct a few experiments along those lines.

When he turned to walk back into town, Abe used his cell phone to leave Veronica a message that she could reassure Sue Daily the matter was settled and she wouldn't be bothered in the future.

As he slipped behind the wheel of his Jeep, his phone rang. It was Veronica returning his call.

"I was in class, Abe," she said in greeting, "but then, I suppose you knew that. How did it go? Any fisticuffs involved? I wish I could have been there to see it."

"You've been watching too many old westerns," Abe replied blandly. "Nothing of the sort occurred. I merely tracked down Pratt and an unknown accomplice and explained to them that, like most plots hatched over a day of drinking, theirs contained several fatal flaws. I think I convinced them of the wisdom of withdrawing from the field, never to return. If I'm not mistaken, the concocted evidence involved will have been destroyed by nightfall and our sleepy little burg will return to harmony."

"You are a silver-tongued man when you want to be," Veronica said. "May I be privy to the name of the unidentified source?"

"A rather disheveled character named Brady," he replied. "Do you know the man in question?"

"I know that poor man well," she replied, "only, I didn't know he was still alive. I'll keep that nugget to myself. We don't need that being rumored about town. He has given his family enough grief. Let him take this latest shame to the grave."

After a long shower and a light lunch, Abe retired to his office with a fresh pot of coffee and a renewed attitude, ready for a few hours at his computer. Following the typical pattern for users, he went to his search engine and typed in one word: Freemasonry.

As expected, thousands of websites were listed, beginning with three sponsored sites selling Masonic merchandise. He immediately dismissed the site for "wikipedia, the free encyclopedia" listing, wondering who thought that venture was a good idea. The site was probably created with all the right intentions—to provide a comprehensive encyclopedia, by allowing readers to make any corrections, additions or subtractions they wished, to keep it accurate and up-to-date—but ended in disaster as people with their own point of view, or agenda or by plain mischief mutilated entries with outright falsehood, rumor and innuendo. At times, the changes were libelous and criminal.

A number of sites high on the list were legitimate Masonic endeavors, Abe found, but there was also a full range of hate sites pushing conspiracy theories, satanic connections and all manner of malicious innuendo. He was pleased to see that Freemasonry was fighting back against the misinformation being spread about the brotherhood with sites such as masonicinfo.com, a comprehensive set of linked pages dealing with nearly every aspect of the history and practice of Masonic life. The information was there for anyone making a serious inquiry about the subject, but he wondered how many of the curious would explore this site, resisting the other more sensational depictions of black hearts and black arts.

Abe had a sudden inspiration. Closing down this inquiry, he opened his personal communication program with Dudley, programmed by Miguel as a friendly and comfortable way for Abe to "talk" to his computer, much like the program designed for Veronica to "converse" with Francis.

"Hello there, Dudley," Abe typed on the keyboard. "I'd like you to run an errand for me."

"Hello to you, Abe," Dudley replied. "It's nice to hear from you again. How can I be of service today?"

"I think we can be of assistance to Veronica and Prometheus," Abe said. "I'll give you the parameters of the problem and ask that you find at least one instance where it may have occurred in real life."

"Type away, Abe. I'm ready to do your bidding."

Abe typed in the instructions and hit the enter key. In the little time it took for him to get up off his chair, walk to the credenza and pour a fresh cup of coffee, a bell sounded, indicating that Dudley had completed the assignment. Abe eased into his chair and began to peruse the results.

Dudley had easily found an instance where attorney A had argued a case against state government B. Attorney A had lost because the government had questioned the relevance of the case law which attorney A had cited in his argument. Attorney C argued a similar case against a county with the same argument used by attorney A, but failed to mention the failure of A's case. Attorney C received a ruling in his favor. A rash of similar cases erupted across the state with that attorney always citing the success of attorney C. Thus, bad law became entrenched in the system. Abe e-mailed this example to Veronica, cautioning her to have Prometheus run a similar link check on her cases, so as not to corrupt her system or perpetuate the error. "Always check the soundness of your sources," he ended.

Dudley, who had Miguel's sense of humor and irony, added another instance for Abe's enjoyment. Dudley cited a southern attorney, the son of a very old and prominent family, with political connections. This attorney was the son of a revered sitting judge. Whether through laziness or chicanery, the attorney would often make oral arguments citing cases and rulings that he made up on the spot out of thin air. Opposing attorneys would not point out that the citations were fiction for fear of gaining the wrath of his father, the sitting judge, in some future case. As a result, there was a gold mine of bad case law within the state system to this day.

Abe would tell Veronica about that after she arrived home.

CHAPTER 13

▼

JUSTICE

Veronica peered out her bedroom window on a still, warm morning to discover Abe sitting on the patio, his coffee getting cold and an unopened morning newspaper before him on the table. He was taking short, slow draws on his pipe and staring off into the distance at the mountains. Veronica dressed quickly and carried a tray with fresh coffee and mixed fruit out to her musing husband. She quietly warmed his half-filled cup and waited until he had set his pipe aside before she spoke.

"Deep thoughts, my love?" Veronica asked at last. "You seem to be pondering a question for which there is no clear answer—or at least an answer to your satisfaction."

"You're right on all counts," Abe answered. "When I was still in elementary school I spent many of my summers with friends on the Mojave reservation doing what boys do to fill up their hours—hunting, fishing, swimming and exploring the world within our reach. Every Saturday, towards evening, we would join one boy in our group on his weekly pilgrimage to his grandfather's house. I have no idea how old the grandfather was, but, to us, he seemed ancient, with his long white hair and deep wrinkles. His face always reminded me of the parched surface of a dry creek bed during the drought. He could neither read nor write, but had a thirst for knowledge that knew no bounds. We would all gather around on the floor while our friend read from the only book the grandfather owned—a gift given to him years before, that he had never been able to decipher."

"I trust the book was worthwhile," she said.

"It was to him," he replied, "and also to us. It was a collection of *Bartlett's Quotations*. A quotation would be read and the author cited. The grandfather would then think about what had been read and relate it to his own life experiences, encouraging the audience to say what they thought."

"So this served as a type of summer school for you boys," she said. "That sounds wonderful."

"It was magical to us," Abe said with reverence. "The grandfather was partial to the ancient Greek philosophers, particularly the tragic dramatists. He was convinced the Greeks were just another Indian nation from across the waters. They possessed too much wisdom to be otherwise."

"Did he have any particular favorites?" she asked.

"Yes," Abe replied. "He was partial to Aeschylus, particularly with his works on *Prometheus* and *Agamemnon*. Perhaps it was the name Prometheus and your computer program that has jogged my memory. First on his list was a fragment about an old Libyan fable: That once an eagle stricken with a dart, said, when he saw the fashion of the shaft, 'With our own feathers, not by other's hands, are we now smitten.'"

"That's timeless," she said. "It could apply as well to our society today. I remember one from law school about it not being 'the oath that makes us believe the man, but the man the oath.' I can't tell you how many witnesses have been coached because of that one."

"He also liked another from Agamemnon," Abe said. "'Exiles feed on hope.' So it was with the Indians after the white man came and so it will be through time. That, coupled with another attributed to Aeschylus gives me pause to think: 'In war, the first casualty is truth.' I'm very bothered by what is happening to our veterans these days, Veronica, and I'm bothered by what is happening to our democratic system at home and our reputation abroad. The question I need answered: 'Is Justice blindfolded or is Justice being blinded?' If the latter is the case, we're all in deep trouble."

Veronica was amazed once more at Abe's uncanny ability to analyze a complex set of circumstances over a broad range of fields, see the connections and pose the problems in a simple, easy-to-understand, yet profound way. Justice was not simply a matter for the courts, but a human need at all levels. The American people in general had an expectation that before the bar and a jury of their peers, they had a fighting chance of receiving justice. If their peers were frustrated in not receiving a fair amount of justice in their everyday lives, how could they be expected to bring a true feeling of justice into the jury box? There is a rarely invoked theory that those within the judicial system never want to see mentioned, much less applied. Still hotly debated behind closed doors, but as infrequently allowed by a public hearing, is the idea of "jury nullification"—finding a defendant not guilty by nullifying the law behind the charges as unconstitutional or severely flawed. If even one of the recent attempts to restore *habeas corpus* to unlawful arrests and detention were allowed to be brought before a federal court, hundreds, if not thousands, of cases would follow. In that event, the specter of such nullification would become reality. The tragic aftermath in cases from the Guantanamo detention camp in Cuba could expose a lengthy record of torture and abuse, of forced confessions which would not hold up in an impartial non-military court and of long campaigns to deny legal contact or representation. These would be more ugly scars exposed to the public. The *New York Times* would be applauded for its often repeated editorial stance that "this is a nation of laws, not the whims of men, and giving legal rights to the guilty as well as the innocent is the price of true justice."

"My love," Veronica said, "you may not know it, but you are a genius with words at times. Would you mind if I passed along the 'blindfolded or blinded' analogy to the Georgetown School of Law project or any number of other legal efforts in the works? If I'm not mistaken, that is exactly the type of title around which to build a popular movement."

"With my blessing," Abe replied. "Take it as your own or give it to anyone who can use it. I don't need attribution. Also remember that we're taking a break today. Uncle Abe and Aunt Veronica promised to take Henry and Cassy to brunch and a stage play. Neither has been to a performance of Theatre Harrisburg. An introduction to the local arts scene should be good for them both."

When Veronica parked her Mercedes in front of Cassy's house precisely at noon, Cassy and Henry were sitting on the porch, dressed in their Sunday best. Henry wore a beige summer suit with a light blue dress shirt. His tie was tastefully selected to pick up both the blue and beige, with a hint of white. There was a high shine to his shoes. Cassy's dress was a vision, shades of lavender with ruffles on the sleeves and hem. A simple string of pearls and matching lavender clutch purse and shoes completed her outfit.

"I certainly didn't have that fashion sense at her age," Veronica said. "She promises to be quite stunning in the next few years. I'm so used to seeing her in blue jeans and oversized shirts, she probably has no idea how lovely she looks."

"Well, the look is not lost on Henry," Abe replied. "He looks very nice himself, but is a little self-conscious being in her dressed-up presence. I feel like the uncle taking them on their first date."

"I'd say that's exactly what we're doing," Veronica commented. "I've never had the opportunity to serve in this role, so tell me if my nervousness is beginning to show."

Abe was not concerned on that account and Veronica, as expected, graciously guided the young couple through the day.

Brunch was at Raspberries, located in the Hilton Hotel on the corner of Second and Market Streets in Harrisburg, just a block away from the Whitaker Center where the play was being performed. Henry was obviously impressed with the extent of the buffet and the number of dishes served. Cassy introduced Henry to the wonders of the salad bar and Henry taught her the quickest way to peel steamed shrimp with a knife and fork. Henry proved methodical and selective as he consumed the breakfast fare, then luncheon items and sliced meats usually reserved for dinner. Cassy followed his lead, only in smaller portions. That the young couple had a strategy in mind became evident when it was time for the dessert course. Between them, they sampled nearly every dessert offering, choosing from a wide array.

The conversation during the entire brunch centered on food, with Abe being peppered with questions about what exotic meals he may have had in his travels. Abe answered with a list of unusual things he had eaten in various parts of the world and that he had found in many instances it was better not to ask a host what it might be before tasting the dish. He said that the only meat he simply could not tolerate was on his home ground of Arizona. The javelina, a particularly odorous wild pig, or peccary, found in abundance in the mountainous regions, tasted awful even to many Indians, who refused to feed it to their dogs. Cassy said she knew just what Abe meant. Her mother refused to do anything with the bay blue fish her father would bring home occasionally from his fishing trips to Delaware. It seemed nearly everyone living along the Chesapeake Bay had a special family recipe that made the fish edible, but her mother did not believe that.

"We still have some time before the play starts," Abe announced over after-brunch coffee. "Anyone up for a stroll around downtown to walk off some of this food?"

As they strolled the few blocks to the banks of the Susquehanna River, Abe removed his suit jacket and draped it over his shoulder. Wordlessly, Henry did the same. When Abe took Veronica's hand to cross Front Street to the walking path, Henry again followed his example. Unlike Abe, Henry dropped Cassy's hand after escorting her safely across the street because his palm was beginning to sweat, for some unknown reason.

Inside the Whitaker Center complex, Theatre Harrisburg used the Sunoco Performance Theater, an intimate venue with seating always within clear view of the stage. The play was "Steel Magnolias." Henry and Cassy had seen the Hollywood film, but the stage version, with one set and the six-women cast for the four-acts, would focus their attention on the full meaning of the dialogue and let their imaginations paint their own picture. Henry's attention was heightened when the man in the lobby taking the tickets cautioned that there would be gunfire.

"How can a man write a play on what goes on in a beauty parlor?" Henry wanted to know during the intermission. "We live in a small town, too, but I don't see any men dropping into the beauty parlor."

"That's pretty obvious," Cassy replied. "The writer certainly had a mother. He probably had at least a sister or two and many woman friends he could rely on for accuracy. I believe each and everyone of the characters because I can identify women in Hummelstown that are very much like them—only without the southern accent."

The second half of the play was more dramatic and touching, but was not without its sense of irony. Without the diverting images conjured for film purposes, the subtle movements of the actors and hesitations in the dialogue seemed to force the audience to delve deeply into their own emotions. The mother giving a kidney to her daughter, then the daughter passing away in spite of that gift, left more than a few tears—including Henry's. Cassy looked at her friend and companion with a renewed sense of respect that he could display his emotions without seeming somehow unmanly, as other boys might have felt. She merely placed a comforting arm on his shoulder and shared her tissues.

"So, how did you two like the stage production?" Veronica asked as they waited for the theater to empty after the final curtain call.

"I liked it very much," Cassy answered quickly. "I think it was much better than watching a movie. I guess that's why people call movies entertainment, because you just sit there and watch the action. One of my teachers called it 'sensory overload,' because there is so much happening at one time that you can't really catch it all in one sitting. A live play is different. It made me feel like the actors were inviting me on stage to be part of their story."

"Very well said, Cassy," Veronica remarked. "That's how I felt after my very first experience, but I couldn't have said that as well as you just have. And, what about you, Henry? You were very quiet most of the time."

"As I always say, Cassy is pretty smart," Henry answered after some hesitation. "I agree with her completely. It's like the difference between watching a nature program on television and being out there doing your own tracking. As my dad always says, it's like comparing apples and oranges. It just can't be done."

As they walked to the car, Henry followed Abe's lead once again and draped his jacket over his shoulder.

"Was that a true story, Uncle Abe?" he asked as they walked. "If it's just fiction, that's okay, because it probably could happen just that way. If it's based on a true happening, then I'd be a little sadder. I don't think it was quite fair for that woman to have to die and leave her new daughter to be raised by the father and grandparents. Her husband never appeared on stage, of course, but by the way they were talking about him, I don't think he was up to the job on his own. I watched an old black and white movie once that ended with a lady in a long dress standing at the edge of a cliff, her hair blowing out behind her from a heavy wind. She was yelling at the sky and saying something about there being no justice in the world. I'm starting to think I now know what she was saying."

"We've been talking a lot about justice ourselves today," Abe replied. "If we can ever come up with a good answer, you'll be the first to know. Now, Henry, what do you say that we buy a couple of ladies an ice cream?"

"Sure," Henry agreed. "Is that one of those things that's good to know about dealing with girls?"

"I certainly hope so, Henry," Abe said, giving a wink to Veronica and Cassy, "that's the only one I know and, so far, it seems to work well for me."

"Aunt Veronica," Cassy whispered so that the others couldn't hear, "are boys still a little silly when they grow to be men?"

"Only if we're lucky," Veronica whispered in reply, "only if we're lucky."

By the time the group was eating their ice cream, the sadness of the play was behind them and they talked about some of the funnier lines that had been delivered and the bright pink and blue paint as a theme for the set, along with the overstated costumes that reflected the personalities of the characters. Henry said he did not think much of pink, but he was very partial to lavender tones. Cassy reddened at her ears over that remark, and smiled politely.

When Veronica dropped the young people off at Cassy's house, they proffered their sincerest thanks for a wonderful day. Abe watched as Henry escorted Cassy to the door, then turned and waved, walking the short distance to his house two homes away.

"What do you think, Sport?" Veronica asked as she drove slowly down the street. "I believe we were quite successful as chaperones. Most importantly, they seemed to learn so much so quickly. It was as if they were two little sponges, soaking up every bit of information and squeezing it out as a finished product."

"They are a remarkable pair," Abe agreed. "I believe the majority of youngsters their age are equally as astute. It gives me much more confidence in the future knowing children like them are in the rising generation. I particularly admire the way they look at the big issues in the world and adapt them to their own experience."

"You are a very considerate man, Abe," she said quietly. "Thank you for the suggestion we take those two to brunch and the theater today. It was even more successful than I could have hoped. Also, thank you for sharing your life with me. It's fun doing things together."

"And I thank you for sharing your life with me," he replied. "I suppose it must be love."

CHAPTER 14

▼

KNOWLEDGE

Having discovered a very active form of Freemasonry in Pennsylvania, Abe was deciding whether to petition the Harrisburg Consistory of the Ancient Accepted Scottish Rite to enter the program to rise through the higher degrees. If so, he wanted to be prepared as thoroughly as possible to understand the degree work and the significance of the rituals involved. With that goal in mind, he knew he would have to immerse himself in the history of Freemasonry. Although he knew he could probably gather much of the information over the Internet, he had always found that there was a better way. He was going to spend many daylight hours in the library of his Brownstone Lodge reading books written by Masonic historians and scholars—some covering global Freemasonry, others devoted to its establishment and growth peculiar to Pennsylvania. He would take a volume or two home most evenings.

When Veronica left for the law school in the morning, Abe went to Brownstone Lodge with a thermos of coffee and sandwiches. There seemed to always be a few of the Fellows about on one lodge errand or another, but the library was very quiet and peaceful. Just before noon, as Abe was finishing one book and thinking about taking his lunch outside to a bench, Tom Chandler entered the library. Chandler was a Past Master of the lodge and had served as director of Masonic education for many years.

"Well, Brother Abe," Chandler said as he entered the room, "I'm pleased to see you taking seriously your first instructions upon becoming a Mason—

advance your knowledge in all fields and you will find yourself a more well-rounded individual and of better service to your Fellows. I'm sorry to say there are far too many who take that as a suggestion, rather than an injunction."

"I'm afraid I've been lax in this particular field, Tom," Abe replied and explained why he was doing this research.

"Very admirable," Tom replied. "I have a fair knowledge of the ins-and-outs of the symbols and rituals of the blue lodge. I should probably know more about the history and practice, plus the philosophy behind the scenes, but, to tell the truth, I sort of get bored reading the Old Charges from operative Masonry of the Middle Ages."

"I was reading several of those earlier this morning," Abe said. "Although the Old English phrases muddled things a bit, I found them to be a solid forerunner for what was to become contract law. When those men contracted to build a church or a cathedral, the charges not only set the building standards, but dictated the social manner in which the masons would conduct themselves during construction."

"Always honorably and don't dally with the local damsels?" Tom asked.

"That's it," Abe answered with a smile. "There are also several references to sobriety. I'll have to ask my dear Veronica what she thinks of my impression that this could have influenced today's contract laws. In fact, I will be discussing many of these things with her. As I recall, anything that is printed is permitted to be shared with non-Masons."

"Absolutely," Tom answered. "Many people think of us as being so secretive just because we don't share oral history and ritual outside the Brotherhood. If they only knew how little isn't shared. Yet, these same people won't bother to take the time to read the voluminous material that is in print."

"I was just going to sit outside and have a sandwich," Abe said. "I have an extra. Would you care to join me?"

"Thank you, but no," Tom replied. "Alicia is preparing a special lunch for just the two of us. It's a monthly tradition she started when the last child left home. I really appreciate and enjoy these moments. I wish you success in delving into the mysteries of our fraternity. If you uncover anything really exciting, please be sure to share it with me."

As he sat alone on a bench in the shade of a tree, Abe tried to digest his morning reading along with his sandwich. It was easy to see why the Masons followed the traditions connected to the working masons of old. There was a natural path back through the history of the building trades that led to the superlative example of the raising of Solomon's Temple. The tools of the craft lent themselves easily to the symbolic effort of Masons individually building themselves into better men, expressing certain virtues and, if necessary, modifying their own behavior to improve themselves and contribute to the community as a whole. This simple, worthy concept brought people together from all walks of life, social standings, religious beliefs and race. Abe began to understand the significance of the fact that Masons did not proselytize. The individual was required, of his own volition and free of outside coercion, to petition the lodge for membership. If he met the basic qualifications and was deemed to be of good character, the petition was usually granted.

Abe could see the roots of the great question of secrecy among the operative masons during the cathedral building era in Europe. It seemed to him that those masons formed separate organizations resembling unions more than fraternities. Out of economic necessity, they had to travel widely to practice their highly skilled craft, which took many years of apprenticeship to master. Certain closely held code words would be required for someone finishing one project to be able to join in another project and be recognized as sufficiently skilled. After the need for their highly specialized skills began to wane and their ranks were depleted, the working masons opened their membership to merchants, businessmen of all types and even members of the aristocracy just to survive. There was also an element of protection and assistance in traveling to a new country or city and seeking assistance from fellow members. To this day, one can approach major cities and even small towns and be greeted by a welcome sign displaying the symbols of local civic organizations such as the Lions, Rotary, Moose and Elk. In Pennsylvania, the square and compass symbol of Freemasonry will also be displayed.

"You're solving the troubles of the world, I trust," Bud Hanover said. "Pardon me for interrupting. You seem very distant in your thoughts."

"It's no problem, Bud," Abe replied, shaking his friend's hand. "I've been in the library all morning and was just putting my thoughts together."

"I saw Tom at the gas station not long ago," Bud said. "He told me about your project. You know how gossipy we Masons are—besides, it's difficult to keep things to yourself in a small town."

"I remind you that Masons are not prone to gossip," Abe corrected with feigned propriety. "We are observers of the human condition and purveyors of information for the good of all concerned."

"Okay, so we're just nosey," Bud countered. "How is the studying going?"

"Let me bounce an idea off you," Abe said. "You are a Past Master of the lodge. Tell me if you think I'm on the right track."

"Fire away," Bud replied. "To the best of my limited ability, I'll give you an honest answer."

"The so-called 'cloak of secrecy' aside," Abe said, "do you think the literalist view by those who misinterpret our symbolic traditions are actually complicating matters—and have been for hundreds of years?"

"I may be a retired English teacher," Bud replied, "but I don't know that I completely understand the question. Will you be more specific?"

"I was thinking about the use of the legend of Solomon's Temple," Abe said. "There is historical evidence that such a temple existed and that a legend grew out of that fact. We draw heavily on the symbolic significance of that temple. There are those who say Masons claim to be the direct descendents of those who built the temple—not the traditions of the builders, but the literal descendents. Now, take that literal interpretation and extrapolate it over the symbolism behind the Fourth through the Thirty-second degrees. Now we are said to claim direct descent status from such historical groups as the warrior-monks of the Knight's Templar and we even name our youth program after their martyred leader, DeMolay. There's little wonder the conspiracy theory enthusiasts and many modern writers use Masonic imagery as something secretly subversive by nature."

"You have a point there," Bud agreed. "I've personally felt that suspicion of Freemasonry was just ignorance and a little silly—after all, our aims and pro-grams are out there in the public arena for all to see. I also admit to taking some pleasure from the fact that some people find me a little mysterious because of what they may think of the fraternity."

"And how do you feel about the possible implication of a Masonic lodge being responsible for the dumping of tea in the Boston harbor?" Abe asked.

"You've got me again," Bud admitted. "I suppose since we were on the win-ning side—therefore being able to write the history—I choose to think those Fel-lows were patriots, even though that would not have been a strictly Masonic act. That's one of my perfectly human flaws I'm working on."

"We're all a work in progress, Bud," Abe said. "Otherwise, we wouldn't be here."

"What about your experience with the American Indians?" Bud asked. "From what little I know, there seems to be a heavy reliance on symbolism throughout entire societies."

"It's all in the difference of perception," Abe said. "The legends and symbols are understood as a way for the people to comprehend the lessons of life. All Indian nations have enough animal fables to put Aesop to shame, but the fables are looked to for the truths that lie behind the tales. The Indian can readily accept the Christian concept of Adam and Eve because it is not taken literally—it is as good an explanation as any about creation. The point taken is the truth behind the tale, which is that the Great Spirit is the Creator."

"Well, I'll leave you to your studies," Bud said. "I need to go work on my character flaws. Please give my best to Veronica."

Abe returned to the library, immersing himself in the legends and history of the Templars to find why they were selected by Freemasonry as worthy of emulation—if only in ritual form. The order was founded in 1118 with the selection of nine valiant knights, to wed the two characters of soldier and monk for the expressed purpose of providing protection to the pilgrims to the holy lands—Jerusalem in particular. They filled their ranks selectively with those proficient at arms and recruited heavily from the sons of the aristocracy, who pledged funds and lands to the cause. The order became enormously wealthy in lands and from its role as the precursor to international banking. They built castle fortresses all along the route, scattered throughout Arab territory, serving the pilgrims well until after the last crusade and the fall of Acre in 1291. The Templars abandoned their efforts as hopeless and resettled their headquarters in Cyprus. Many returned to their home countries and built temples. Their vast accumulated wealth was a cushion against secular authority and the chief cause that led to their downfall.

From the historical perspective, the fall of the Templars was easily predictable given the state of European society of their times. Their rumored wealth and the cash-starved monarchies were bound to clash eventually. The suddenness of the order's demise and the particulars surrounding that event caught Abe's attention. At least in France, he found eerie parallels to the Masonic experience.

The order in France was particularly strong and wealthy. This was the so-called Era of the Two Popes. Burdened by their vast land holdings, the Templars did not take the side of the church against the French sovereign, Philip IV, in the struggle for the Papacy. Philip's need for funds to back his continuing wars precluded his showing any gratitude for an order now isolated from Rome. Philip saw the powerful and secret society of the Templars as a danger to the safety of the state.

Dark rumors began to spread among the over-taxed and oppressed people, undoubtedly fanned by Philip's supporters. Imaginations soared with tales of blasphemy, horrible infidelity, debauchery, every dark vice and crime man could think of were hurled against the monks. Philip seized every Templar he could get his hands on and confiscated their wealth and property. The leaders were jailed, tortured into confessing heinous crimes and sins, and burned at the stake, despite recanting their confessions. England and other countries followed suit—taking the opportunity afforded—but they rarely put those seized to death.

As Abe was pouring the last remnants of coffee from his thermos, Tom Chandler walked into the library.

"Have you cracked any mysteries, yet?" Tom asked. "I thought I'd drop in and check on your progress."

"Not solving any mysteries," Abe replied, "but gaining some understanding, I hope. How was your lunch with Alicia?"

"Terrific," Tom beamed. "After all these years of marriage, life just keeps getting better. I wish the same for you and Veronica. Now, what are you reading?"

"I was reading about the destruction of the Knight's Templar," Abe said. "It wasn't a pretty picture."

"Those brave souls of long ago did not go out the easy way—that's for sure," Tom agreed. "Stalwart fellows who stayed true to their creed, showing their human side when broken on the rack or other devious tortures into confession, then recanting those falsehoods rather than being spared the stake for an easier execution. Grisly, to be sure, but the stuff of legends, nonetheless. Most of the Fellows don't want those details. They are satisfied with the tale's more potent example of staying true to one's God and to the moral principles displayed in life."

"I think about the number of new legends created," Abe said. "As the surviving Templars faded from the pages of history, new speculation arose about how much of their wealth they may have taken with them and where they may have gone. Holy artifacts, jewels, gold and silver, whatever items of value that were rumored to exist and were portable, became fair game for speculation. No wonder the conspiracy skeptics of today have tied Freemasonry to some grand nefarious scheme. We align ourselves with the virtues confirmed, while others see that as an act of conspiratorial collusion."

"The ignorant, malicious and malign will always be with us," Tom replied. "Look at all misinformation and spite you can find on the Internet. All we can do is to lay out our principles and follow our own course. I, for one, have neither the time nor the inclination to argue with those who will never willingly rise above their ignorance. I'm too busy improving myself, staying true to my family, trusting in the Supreme Being and building a strong community. My personal belief in the biblical parable of the wheat and the weeds, precludes me from judging others, no matter how wrong I might think them to be. I leave that to God."

Abe was silent for some moments, considering what he had read and what Tom had to say, before making a comment.

"Tom," Abe began, "what I'm beginning to understand is that as Masons, we select images from various places and eras to illustrate each step in the degree work—the values, lessons and even virtues involved. These are not all examples out of the ancient, murky past. Examples right up into the current time are used, when appropriate."

"Now you've got the right idea," Tom replied. "I am prepared to suggest that if we could somehow decipher an applicable moral point in the cave paintings of pre-history, we'd find a way to use that too. Of course, we'd gain some detractors if we did so, whether we were correct or not."

Abe placed most of the books he had been reading back on the shelves and carried only one, which explained the various Masonic symbols, home with him. By the time Veronica arrived home, he had a nice dinner ready to serve. He really enjoyed this part of domestic life, where he could contribute more than his so-called allotted half of the effort. When both partners have that same attitude—as was the case in his household—marriage could be a solid success.

They took a long evening's stroll along the walking path adjacent to their complex, noting the tulips in bloom and the trees approaching full leaf. A farmer had plowed a fresh field and was now planting hybrid corn as they watched from the hillside. Abe shared his activities of the day with Veronica and she returned the courtesy, with some of the gossip that was spreading around the campus that day. He was apologetic that he did not have much neighborhood news because he had spent so much time in the lodge library, but promised to improve in the future.

"You know what, my love," Abe finally said, "I may not need to tell you so often, but I must express once again how good life is living with you. When we're off to our own pursuits during the day, it's such a pleasure to look forward to coming home to be with you."

"You can never tell me that too often, my dear," Veronica replied. "I want to tell you the same thing just as often. Let's try real hard to keep it that way."

"There's no effort involved," he answered. "It just is."

CHAPTER 15

▼

MANIPULATION

An unseasonable Canadian cold front had dipped as far south as the Mason-Dixon Line along the Maryland border overnight. The overcast sky was dull gunmetal gray and a misty drizzle hung over the landscape, but Veronica's spirits remained high and her senses sharp. She spotted the figure of a student from fifty yards away, sitting on a low wall, too lightly dressed for the weather, with an umbrella covering most of her face. Still, Veronica identified the familiar figure as one of her star students who would be graduating at the end of the term. The young woman was obviously depressed about something—a solitary soul brooding in her loneliness. As Veronica neared, she confirmed the identity of Jane Matthews, from Belltown in rural Mifflin County—a quiet, but brilliant student who would make a solid attorney in any field of law she chose.

"Good morning, Jane," Veronica said in greeting. "You should have a sweater or jacket on in this weather. You've worked too long and too hard at your studies to be exposing yourself to disease this close to graduation."

"Good morning, Professor Carlson," Jane replied, wiping tears from her cheek. "The problem is that I don't think I'll be graduating at all. I'm thinking about dropping out of school."

"What on earth for?" she asked. "Come with me to my office and we'll talk about this. I have coffee and tea to take off the chill."

As they walked across campus, Veronica tried to remember what she knew about Jane Matthews. She herself had never been in Belltown, but Veronica had seen many of the small communities in the area, farming being the basic industry. From her application to law school, Veronica knew Jane had blossomed academically at Penn State, graduating with honors, a degree in Political Science. Veronica had found it interesting that Jane had also completed a full course in pre-medical studies. Perhaps at the time she was trying to decide between law and medicine. Whatever the case, a basic knowledge of medicine would only enhance her practice of law.

Taking her time preparing hot tea, allowing Jane to settle in a chair and compose her thoughts, Veronica thought about what she might know about her social life. Jane was attractive and presumably had dates in college. At Dickinson, she was often seen in the company of other students. She seemed popular with both men and women and Veronica recalled her dating an athletic young man who had graduated last year who had joined a prestigious law firm in Chicago.

"Okay, Jane," Veronica said, placing the tea before them on opposite sides of her desk, "what has prompted this crisis? I trust you're not thinking about giving up a promising career in law over some minor matter."

"I wouldn't call it a minor matter, Professor," Jane replied. "I'd say a basic flaw in the legal system and how that system operates in the real world is giving me some serious doubts as to whether this is the career for me."

Matthews said that her parents had a small mom-and-pop business in Belltown—a combination hardware store, fix-it shop and consignment outlet. In recent years, they had thought about dropping the consignment business due to a particularly litigious attorney in town who preferred to settle even minor disputes in a court of law. At first these were no more than a nuisance to local businesses, but as the years progressed, the cost of legal representation was becoming a burden on the defendants. One of the reasons she wanted a law degree was to specialize in small business law and tort reform to help her parents and business owners like them.

"I wasn't a naïve little country girl when I applied for law school," Jane asserted. "I understand that law is an adversarial system, the courts are about the business of settling disputes between opposing viewpoints and the advocates will argue the law best suited to their interests. From my studies here, though, I find so many cases, in every branch specialty, where advocacy has become blatant manipulation of the system, for monetary gain and/or punitive revenge."

"I understand your feelings," Veronica said. "Although if you want to get along out there in the tough world of litigation, I might suggest the more politically correct term of 'massaging the law,' not 'manipulating' it."

"Thank you for you efforts to lighten my mood with a bit of dark legal humor," Jane said, "but what I'm really seeking is some enlightenment. At the very least, I'd like some assurance that our system is not in the throes of a major melt-down."

"Do you think the situation is that serious?" Veronica asked.

"What I think is that we're going in the wrong direction—and fast," Jane said. "First we have our litigious citizenry bringing suit for their own rash actions, whether it is spilling hot coffee in their laps while driving a car or sitting in a bathtub misusing the hair dryer. Have you read some of the more ridiculous warning labels on products these days—merely to avoid a lawsuit? There are any number of fraudulent suits brought forth in the courts every year by attorneys who are willing to take them on for the billable hours and/or a percentage of the settlement in the off chance of success. Then you have the attorneys like my hometown crank bringing officers of the court under the same umbrella. When members of the bar start playing this game, it is more than sad, it is a blight on the profession. This was bound to get out of hand sooner or later. Well, sooner has come and the consequences are nothing less than tragic for some people."

"I'm glad you had the opportunity to vent some of your frustration," Veronica said with a knowing smile. "So, unless you've been merely practicing your closing argument, I believe you are about to reveal the instance which has tipped the balance."

"I'm sorry, Professor," Jane replied. "I do tend toward dramatics when my emotions have been stirred, but how would you react to a story about a federal judge who has filed a sixty-five million dollar action over a pair of pants? Judges are supposed to be the good guys and gals, aren't they?"

Matthews explained that she was working on the Internet late at night when she came across an AP item datelined Washington, D.C. A Korean family, realizing the American dream by owning a dry cleaning business in the nation's capital, was being sued by a federal administrative hearings judge—acting as his own counsel—over a pair of pants that were misplaced for a week. The event happened two years ago and was going to trial in one month. The judge refused a number of out of court settlements and made demands such as fifteen thousand dollars—the price of renting a car every weekend for ten years to take his cleaning to another business. The judge claimed fraud had been committed because of two signs previously displayed in the establishment: "Satisfaction Guaranteed" and "Same Day Service." Using a strict interpretation of the consumer protection law for the District of Colombia, which calls for fines of one thousand five hundred dollars a day for violators, the judge added up twelve violations over one thousand two hundred days, then multiplied that by three defendants—the older Korean couple and their son, who owned the business.

"A family has been ruined," Jane said. "They were so frustrated over our system of laws allowing such outright, malicious abuse to get as far as it has, that they wanted to return to Seoul, but cannot until the litigation is settled. Why can't our legal system protect such people and why should a federal judge, of all people, be allowed to manipulate the law so egregiously? I have to ask myself if I really want to spend the rest of my working life in such a corrupted field."

"My grandfather used to say there exists a wide gulf between the ideal and the real," Veronica said, "and nowhere is that more evident than in government or the law. You've just outlined the best argument for you to stay in the profession—because the law needs bright new blood to counteract such abuses. You also possess a working knowledge of basic medicine, which could be of enormous use in cleaning up one of the murkier areas of law—medical malpractice or incompetence. Why don't you wait until that federal judge has his day in court before making any final decisions?"

"Do you really think the judicial system will do the right thing here?" Jane asked with skepticism.

"I wouldn't be surprised," Veronica answered. "The law has been known to pull itself back from the precipice on more than one occasion. Let's wait to see what happens this time."

Jane reacted with a shake of her head, a wry smile and a low chuckle. "I served as a summer intern in a congressional office between my junior and senior years in college. It was just enough experience to see the truth in the old saying that there are two things you don't want to see being made, sausage and our nation's laws. That was one of the reasons I turned to law as a 'higher calling.' I suppose I thought that I'd have a better chance to correct some of the flawed legislation the congress has passed. I guess I'm still enough of an idealist to think I can still make a contribution. Thank you for your assistance, Professor. You've helped me get over a rough spot."

"That's one important reason I'm here," Veronica replied. "Stop in anytime you need to hash out the problems of the world. We may not come up with the answers, but we can go down fighting."

The wet, dank weather continued throughout the day. The mood on campus, usually quiet and sober during classroom hours, with spirits rising toward the late afternoon, remained almost somber—students and faculty alike. Veronica shortened her last lecture on constitutional law to second year students for a period of questions and answers, which usually loosened the tensions in the room.

"Okay, ladies and gentlemen," Veronica said, walking around to the front of her desk and crossing her arms, "there must be something on your minds other than the weather. Has something of monumental importance happened that has not yet come to my attention? I feel a sense of gloom usually reserved for exam week. What is going on in your lives today?"

When there was no response from any of the twenty students in the room, she turned her attention to a young man in the rear of the classroom.

"Mr. Jamison," she prompted, "you have a well-earned reputation for knowing everything that's happening on campus. You are also noted for your glib assessments. What's on your mind today?"

"The same three things that are on everyone else's mind, Professor," Jamison replied hesitantly. "Jack Fender, who dropped out before the fall term to serve his country, just came home in a box. The funeral is this Saturday in Lewistown."

"I'm very sorry to hear that," Veronica said. "I didn't get to know Mr. Fender very well, except to see him. I remember him as a bright, energetic young man."

"He wanted to be just like his father," Jamison continued. "He wanted to serve his hitch, come back and finish law school and one day become a federal judge. He had his entire life planned since he was five years old. Now he is reduced to an obituary and a name on a gravestone—soon to be forgotten."

"Word was all over campus this morning," another student added. "Those of us who knew him couldn't miss the irony in his passing."

"And what might that irony be, Miss Wilkins?" Veronica asked.

"He had aspirations of becoming a federal administrative law judge," Wilkins replied. "His father holds that appointed position and knows the '65 Million Dollar Judge.' Jack told us his father never could understand how that idiot was ever selected for appointment. Google that story on the Internet today and you'll find flaming commentary coming from students in every major law school in the country calling for his disbarment and his head—in no particular order."

Veronica conducted a controlled discussion of the legal matters involved for a full twenty minutes. Interestingly, most of her students were concentrating on the legal ethics of bringing such a case.

"Mr. Jamison," Veronica finally said, "you previously mentioned three things were on your mind. I see two. What was the third?"

"The Supremes, plain and simple," Jamison replied. "No one seems to know why the number of cases coming before the Supreme Court is declining so rapidly in recent years. We all know that the justices themselves select which cases they will hear. The Chief Justice recently gave a speech where he gave three reasons for the decline: the lack of any major legislation coming out of Congress in the last couple of decades, the lower courts interpreting statutes in a more uniform manner so the Supreme Court has fewer disputes to settle, and the ability of the circuit courts to locate previous legal decisions online in cases where they previously would have turned to the Supreme Court for guidance. Then the Chief Justice concluded that although the numbers are in decline, he thinks there is a higher percentage of significant cases being decided."

"So, you don't agree with the Chief Justice?" Veronica asked.

"The legislative branch of government passes sweeping legislation stripping citizens and non-citizens alike of an array of constitutional protections," Jamison began, "and the Chief Justice denies this is significant legislation. The legislation is signed into law by an executive with an annoying habit of appending his thoughts about which sections he will enforce and which he will ignore. In the name of national security, the executive branch sets up an unbelievable number of roadblocks to allow its actions to be judged in an American court of law and turns a deaf ear to international agreements such as the Geneva Conventions. This from a court that thinks it needs to decide who fills the office of the presidency, but the Patriot Act and attendant legislation is not significant."

"Jack Fender goes overseas to fight for his constitutional government and comes home in a flag-draped coffin," Wilkins added. "We are left wondering if it was worth it, while living with the knowledge that it was worth it to him. It's not just the returning veterans who experience survivor's guilt, you know. We are all affected one way or the other."

"You've just erased any lingering doubts you may be harboring," Veronica commented. "Take that passion, that verve, and pursue your career in whatever branch of the law you choose. You will represent the law for your generation and set the new standard for generations to follow. Set your goals high and keep them there. You may not reach those lofty goals, but I can promise you'll never regret the journey."

By the time Veronica arrived home, she was fatigued, but mentally stimulated. A long, leisurely bath reinvigorated her body and calmed her mind. She emerged into the hall from the master bedroom just as Abe was coming through the door to the garage with a large grocery bag. A wordless kiss of greeting and they strolled to the kitchen.

"A good day, my dear?" Abe asked as he placed the bag on the counter and emptied its contents.

"An excellent day, my love," she answered. "And how has yours been? I was hoping for a break in the weather, but it seems we'll have this rain through the night."

"I've had a productive day, thank you," Abe responded lightly. "The rain doesn't affect my mood as it seems to do with others. When you are reared in an arid climate, days of rain are few and far between. A good gentle soaking is a rare occurrence. I can only think of how this day will benefit the farmers. Anyway, I thought I'd make something a little different for us tonight. It is a concoction I learned from an old newspaper fellow who introduced me to it on just such a night as this. He called it 'western Hawaiian surprise,' swearing to its ability to raise one's spirits. Of course, he used liberal amounts of whiskey as a chaser, but I refrained and still enjoyed the meal."

"What are the ingredients?" she asked.

"As you heard me tell Henry, it's not always a good idea to ask before you've had a taste," he replied with a smile. "Should you not care for it, there's always pizza in the freezer."

"You certainly are full of yourself today," she said. "I don't want to even think about how cheery you must be during a hurricane."

"I'll be absolutely silly," he replied, beginning to prepare the meal. "So tell me about your school day."

Veronica told him in great detail about Jane Matthews' dilemma, the way word had spread so quickly around campus and her pride in the fact that her students were so caring and committed.

"You should have an Indian guest lecturer," Abe said. "If your students want to be exposed to manipulations of the law for larcenous purposes, that ought to do it."

Abe began with a soft tortilla that he brushed with extra virgin olive oil. On this he placed long green sections from spring onions, mincing the white sections and sprinkling these lightly. From the refrigerator, he removed a pan in which long spears of pineapple wrapped in two types of meat had been left to marinate. Sliced green and black olives and a few capers completed the filling. Once wrapped with the ends tucked in, Abe used more olive oil and fresh ground pepper as a topping. Several sections of Mandarin orange finished the presentation. Veronica found the dish to be delightful and refreshing.

"That was an interesting blend of flavors," she said. "Now, what's the secret?"

"It's the meat," Abe confirmed. "Both thinly sliced types are from the buffalo—pickled tongue and salted, mesquite smoked liver. That was what my friend happened to have in his refrigerator at the time. I brought the pineapple."

"Was he another of those colorful western characters I heard so much about?" she asked.

"Colorfully eccentric," Abe replied. "You two would have gotten along famously. He had been a professor of Latin here in the east—Virginia as I recall. It was one of the states that still allowed you to read for the law and pass the bar."

"Virginia is still one of those states," she confirmed.

"When he moved west, he found he was about a century late," Abe continued. "All he could scratch up were old mining claims for played out mines. So, naturally, he turned to publishing a local newspaper. I don't think he ever made much profit, but he loved to write blazing editorials against corruption in all its forms—particularly the 'political beast,' as he called it. I know exactly what he would say to your discussions with your students today."

"Something I can use as the basis of a lecture?" she asked. "I'll need something to address the questions which were raised today and I need a solid theme that will stand the test of close scrutiny."

"Then I have just the theme," Abe said with a flourish. "*Corruptio optimi pessima,* the corruption of the best is the worst of all."

CHAPTER 16

▼

BENT SPIRITS

The call came at three o'clock in the morning to a cell phone number Abe had reserved to be used only in emergencies. The conversation was short, with the caller doing most of the talking. Veronica knew from Abe's side of the conversation that he had a friend in trouble and they were going for a ride somewhere. She was up, dressed and brushing her hair when Abe came into the bathroom for a quick shave.

"Jimmy Brand," Abe said, applying shaving cream to his face. "He's my godson. He is the son of Domingo Brand. We grew up together and I was his best man at his wedding. He married the prettiest girl on the reservation, who also happened to be his best friend. I talked to Domingo about a year ago and he told me Jimmy was headed overseas for his third deployment. He is one of the best trackers the Army ever had. I should know. His father and I taught him well."

"Where is Jimmy and what kind of trouble is he in?" Veronica asked.

"He's in Washington, D.C., down by the wharf, under a bridge," he answered. "His spirit is bent and he needs help."

"His spirit is bent?" she asked. "What exactly does that mean?"

"That is a term the Mojaves use for those who come back from war very much troubled by the experience," he answered. "It is not shell shock, or post traumatic stress that you hear so much about. It's not even so-called combat fatigue or any other euphemism we've been able to come up with to try to disguise the symptoms. When Jimmy says he is a bent spirit, it means he can't go home and live among his people until he heals himself inside, regains his upright spirit."

"Then, let's go get Jimmy," she said as he toweled his face. "The Mercedes has a full tank. We can get coffee and something to eat on the road."

Except for the usual number of big trucks on the Pennsylvania Turnpike, there was little traffic on the road to Washington. The sky had finally cleared while they were sleeping, leaving the pavement nearly dry by this hour. Veronica had to watch her speed carefully to keep within the limits that changed often along Route 15 as they passed through settled areas. She knew that the vast majority of "driving under the influence" arrests were made between midnight and four o'clock in the morning. Excessive speed on the open road would make her an easy target.

As she drove through the darkness, Abe told her about life on the reservation and what it was like for Jimmy being reared Mojave. He included the high expectations the tribe had for those who joined the Armed Forces to retain their personal morals as honorable men and women.

"I'm worried about Jimmy," Abe said as they crossed the Mason-Dixon Line into Maryland. "He is somewhere deep inside himself and searching for a way out. He has reverted to old Indian phrasing, as if he were trying to communicate with his ancestors. For instance, he told me he had 'wintered at Walter Reed.' That's from the captain of his winning debate team in high school who joined the Army as a way to fund a college degree in English Literature. When he was in the eighth grade he became smitten with Shakespeare—that's the word he used at the time, smitten. All through high school, he used the bard's words to charm the girls."

"That's a new approach," Veronica said. "Did it work?"

"Only for laughs at first," Abe replied. "The girls at school knew Shakespeare when they heard it. Jimmy was so good natured, that he laughed at himself and soon the girls were offended if he didn't try that approach."

"Then perhaps you misunderstood his use of that phrase," Veronica said. "Perhaps he used 'wintered' in the sense those well off New Englanders say 'wintered in Palm Beach.'"

"Believe me, that's not the case," Abe replied. "When you are reared on the Mojave reservation there is no wintering in that sense at all. Jimmy's also very down to earth and would never harbor any pretensions of being upper class."

The sky began to lighten as they approached the city and Veronica was glad this was a Saturday morning. The usual rush hour traffic would have impeded her progress substantially. Knowing the city well allowed her to take a few shortcuts and ease onto the wharf road just as the sun broke the horizon. There were some men loitering around the doorways of several buildings, but only one lone silhouette of a large man showed under the bridge.

"If that's Jimmy, he is certainly larger than I had pictured him in my mind," Veronica said.

"Jimmy's the runt of the family," Abe replied. "His mother is a couple of inches taller and Domingo has six inches and forty pounds on his son. I'd better go get him alone."

Veronica watched as Abe walked slowly toward the bridge and stepped into the shadows. Jimmy gave Abe what looked like a bone-crushing bear hug as he lifted her husband off the ground. After a few moments of conversation, the two men walked toward the car. Veronica was struck by the long graceful strides of a man Jimmy's size and how easily he carried his belongings in a rolled blanket under his arm. She also noted his hair was longer than she had expected for someone just leaving the Army. It was not until they were formally introduced that she discovered he was missing two fingers on his right hand.

On the return trip, Abe kept the conversation light and on familiar grounds, allowing Jimmy as much time as he needed to tell them whatever he wanted. He had been medically discharged from the Army and the Walter Reed Medical Center six weeks prior. Whenever his disability checks would be issued, they would go to his home address. His family could use the extra income or simply save it until he returned home. He had taken up residence under the bridge to be near the water, which he had hoped would aid in his internal healing. So far, that had not worked. It was very easy for a man reared in the desert to live on the streets of a city. Populous areas were so wasteful in their habits. The dumpsters behind the best restaurants and hotels provided a wide array of fine food. You could pick up a few dollars now and then by helping unload trucks at warehouses or markets. Water from the Potomac River served many uses.

Jimmy said he was lucky his first week on the street when he met several other new veterans in the same circumstances who were being tutored by Vietnam veterans who had lived on the streets for years, if not decades. These homeless veterans tended not to swap war stories or tales of woe among themselves. They were all on the streets for one reason or another. That was the reality. Now they banded together in small groups to help each other survive. They stayed away from the public shelters because those could be very dangerous places. The drug addicts, alcoholics and violent mental cases could strike at any given moment. They and many other homeless people would steal what little you might have.

"There are many dangers, anyway," Jimmy said. "Last night I almost killed three people. That's why I finally called you. They came for my blankets."

During the silence that followed, Veronica thought even three people in a gang must have been pretty desperate or out of their minds to take on this man.

"But you didn't kill them," Abe said as a statement, not as a question. "How did you leave them?"

"Hurt some," Jimmy said matter-of-factly. "Not very good swimmers, though—too much splashing in the dark. I am a bent spirit. Maybe we all are. My heart must be whole before I can return to my people."

For the remainder of the ride, Jimmy Brand wrapped himself in silence, staring out over the countryside and thinking thoughts only he knew. He stayed in the car when they stopped for coffee, but nodded his thanks when presented with his own large cup, accompanied by two breakfast sandwiches. The coffee was sipped slowly over many miles. The sandwiches were left in the bag, uneaten and untouched.

When they returned home Jimmy was given a tour of the house and placed his bedroll in the guest room. He was shown the pocket door that would turn the guestroom, short hallway and bath into a private suite. Since there was still a damp chill in the air, Jimmy took one of his blankets and went outside to the back patio to sit in the sun and think, while Abe made a few telephone calls and Veronica made two pots of coffee. The first she put on a tray with a few snacks and placed it quietly on the patio table, where Jimmy sat with his blanket around his shoulders, eyes closed as if in meditation. The second she took into the office.

She had been working at her desk for two hours, glancing up occasionally to check on Jimmy, when Abe announced they were buying some new property.

"It's some acreage with a cabin and a few out-buildings," Abe said. "It's up on that mountain overlooking Big Valley, right near the place where you had the rocking chair made for your sister."

"How nice," Veronica replied. "I've always wanted a weekend cabin as a getaway, just like normal people."

"Well, now we have one," Abe said quietly. "I thought we could let Jimmy stay there for as long as needed. Going from a desert environment overseas back to the desert environment of his home is probably not the best remedy right now. I think he needs the lush greenery, thick forests and running creeks and streams to soothe his inner wounds. There is even a smoke house that Jimmy can turn into a sweat lodge for traditional purification."

"I've often wondered what the Swedish and Norwegian immigrants thought when they first encountered the Indians of the plains," Veronica said. "I would think they should have been well disposed to a people that already were civilized enough to have developed a sensible sauna culture."

"I hadn't thought of that," Abe said. "My guess is that the Indians wondered how their sweat lodge tradition reached all the way to Sweden and Norway."

"I have a question," she said. "I don't think Jimmy has moved so much as a muscle in the last two hours. Is he okay?"

"I'm sure he's perfectly fine," he replied. "He's able to do that for several days if need be—if the conditions are right."

The front doorbell, chiming a four-note pattern, interrupted their conversation. They opened the door to find Henry and Cassy on the front porch, walking stick in hand and carrying personal backpacks.

"To what do we owe this honor?" Veronica asked Cassy.

"We were at Indian Echo Caverns for the day," Cassy replied. "We hiked down to where you made your prehistoric find to watch the archeologists digging in the earth."

"We thought we'd hike over and see if you were home," Henry added. "It gets a little boring watching people using small brushes and trowels. It must take forever to uncover anything."

"I was just going to make some sandwiches for lunch," Veronica said. "Would you two care to join us?"

"That would be great, Aunt Veronica," Cassy said. "I was hungry and ate my lunch early."

"What kind of sandwiches are you going to make?" Henry asked out of boyish curiosity.

"Well," Veronica replied as she winked at Abe, "if we have the ingredients on hand, I was going to ask Uncle Abe to prepare his famous 'western Hawaiian surprise,' without the traditional chaser, of course. It's rather exotic for Pennsylvania, but I think you'll enjoy it and have a tale to tell your friends."

"I know what Uncle Abe says about not asking before tasting," Henry said seriously, "but if he's making it, I trust him."

"Good then," Abe said. "While we're making lunch, why don't you two place your packs and sticks here by the door and go out to the patio. We have a houseguest I believe you will find interesting. Go introduce yourselves."

"Do you think one of us should go with them?" Veronica asked quietly as the two walked through the house toward the back.

"This is a gift sent from the universe," Abe said. "I probably didn't mention it, but Jimmy absolutely adores children of all ages and they all love him. This may be just the boost he needs."

Henry and Cassy were surprised to see the big Indian, wrapped in a blanket, sleeping in a chair. They tiptoed around to stare at the man from the front.

"Do you think he's dead?" Cassy whispered. "I don't see him breathing."

"I think he's playing possum," Henry whispered in reply. "I've seen possums do that. They lay real still and you can't see them breathing either. This one sure does a good imitation."

The children jumped back a step, startled when this sleeping Indian suddenly snapped one eye open, slowly lowered the eyelid to a closed position, only to repeat the performance with the other eye. A slight grin appeared as he snapped both eyes wide open. He stared for a full two minutes without blinking before Cassy finally broke the spell.

"You can be very scary doing that," she admonished. "That's not very polite. I'm Cassy and he's Henry. Uncle Abe said we should introduce ourselves."

When Jimmy reached his big arm over and shook their hands, they didn't seem to notice his two missing fingers. "I'm Jimmy," he said in introduction, "full-blooded Mojave, master of my craft and the third greatest tracker in the world."

"A real Indian tracker," Cassy said, unable to contain her glee. "We're working in the same field, only we're just starting."

"You said you're the third greatest tracker," Henry said. "Who are the others better than you?"

"My father and your Uncle Abe," Jimmy said. "No one can tell who is the better of the two. I can only say my father is the best Indian and Uncle Abe the best non-Indian."

By the time luncheon was served, the three were chatting away like old friends. Cassy and Henry peppered Jimmy with questions about tracking and Indian ways, which he did his best to answer honestly, with some editing, in consideration for their ages. The questioning continued through lunch and when Abe told them at the conclusion what they had been eating, they nearly squealed in delight. Now they really had something to pass around the neighborhood.

"I'll bet you feel like you're home eating buffalo tongue and liver," Henry said to Jimmy.

"You'd lose on that one," Jimmy replied. "There's never been many buffalo that have made it to our desert neighborhood since the last Ice Age—maybe not even then. Some of my ancestors did think camel was pretty tasty, though. A long time ago, the Blue Coats thought that camels would be the best thing to fight a war in the desert, so they shipped some to our area. So many ran away that there could have been big wild camel herds before long, but my ancestors liked them better for breakfast. Camel jerky wasn't much—too flaky when dried, no matter what you tried to do."

Abe and Veronica knew that Jimmy was a big hit with the children when, as they were leaving, they asked if they could call him uncle.

Ruby Steinmann dropped by John and Bea Nagy's with some good news for the Whittier Center veterans' efforts. She called next door to see if it was okay to stop in unannounced.

"Really, Mother," Veronica said when she answered the door. "You don't need to call from next door if you're already here."

"I don't want to be a pushy mother-in-law," Ruby replied with as much dignity as she could muster. "I'm so pleased that you finally married. I wouldn't want to do anything that would upset your bliss."

"So, come into the office and give us your good news," Veronica answered, rolling her eyes.

"Abe, Mother is in one of her moods of high drama," Veronica said as they entered the office, "so be on your toes."

"Hello, Mother," Abe said in greeting, giving her a peck on the cheek. "How is my favorite mother-in-law feeling today?"

"Unappreciated by some parties who will remain unnamed," Ruby replied. "My important news is that Julie Fry has pulled off a real coup for us. Thank goodness that woman has more brass than you can find in most candlesticks. She has convinced a husband and wife team of psychiatrists to come out of retirement and volunteer their services to the cause."

"That's great," Abe said. "Have they done much work with veterans?"

"They certainly have," Ruby answered. "They had separate practices next door to one another in the same building. His specialty was returning Vietnam veterans. Her specialty may be the more important of the two, due to one of the ugly little secrets coming out of our recent conflicts. The number of mental problems among the troops increases as deployments become longer and the numbers skyrocket when there are several deployments involved. As we have lowered the standards to fill the ranks by giving waivers for levels of education, criminal records and the like, some pretty bad characters have made a bad situation worse on every level and in every way. We're discovering a devastating problem among the women coming out of the service—as if they needed another problem to deal with. Her specialty is the worst violation a woman can endure."

CHAPTER 17

▼

FREEDOM?

Veronica awoke on Sunday morning to hear Abe and Jimmy talking softly on the back patio outside her bedroom window. Their voices were so low that she could only recognize a few words—many seemed garbled, as if Jimmy were talking in an Indian language. She moved slowly in her usual morning preparations, allowing the men their privacy. She peeked into the guestroom in passing to see the bed showed no signs of having been slept in. Jimmy's bedroll was neatly wrapped and standing in the corner by the closet. In the kitchen, she found Abe had prepared a tray of mixed fruits and rye toast with honey. A half-pot of freshly brewed coffee was on the counter. She poured herself a cup, picked up the tray and walked to the patio.

"Thank you for the breakfast," she said, placing her tray on the table. "Where's Jimmy? I thought I heard you two talking."

"You'll have to thank Jimmy for the breakfast," Abe replied. "We told him to make himself at home and he complied. He had prepared one for each of us. Rye toast with honey is one of his favorites and he wanted to share his pleasure."

"How considerate," she remarked. "Where is he? I'd like to thank him. I noticed his bed looked as if it hadn't been slept in. I hope it wasn't too soft."

"He most likely slept on the floor," he replied. "As to his whereabouts, he went for a walk. He took some bread and cheese, so I don't imagine we'll see him until nightfall or perhaps tomorrow morning."

"I don't quite understand," she said. "Wouldn't he rather sit and talk things over with his godfather—or is he simply enjoying the gifts of freedom?"

"Our conversation this morning is likely to be all he can muster for now," he answered. "Also, he doesn't look at those so-called gifts of freedom as you and I do. His spirit is bent. He is in inner turmoil. There can be no real freedom on the outside if there is chaos on the inside. We can only imagine what he has been through. I think the first question he will need to answer is very deep and personal: has his moral compass also been bent? If he can rid himself of the turmoil and regain his internal peace, he will be free. Inner freedom means that even if you are behind bars, you retain personal freedom. Whether it's religious belief or any other anchor an individual may turn to for solace, that freedom cannot be taken away."

"So, your idea of the cabin as a healing refuge is perfect," she replied. "He'll take long walks, be soothed by the forest and the valley, getting back in touch with nature and therefore himself."

"That's a good way to put it," he answered. "I might add that the part about being soothed by the forest and the valley is true enough, but only because, to Jimmy, he will be admiring them as reflections of the Great Spirit."

Veronica ate her breakfast in silence, recalling the conversation.

Abe and Veronica spent a restful morning reading the newspapers and catching up on magazines they had received during the week. As was their habit, they set aside an hour or so each day for meditation, spiritual reading and reflection. They would attend services at various churches at times, but were able to fulfill their spiritual journeys in the quiet of their own home.

"What will life be like for Jimmy after he returns home?" Veronica asked over lunch. "Except for what you tell me, I—to my own embarrassment—know so little about Indians. I have read about the unemployment rates and the poverty, but have no idea what the Indian world is like."

"The so-called Indian world is just like every other society on earth," Abe replied. "They cope with the same problems we all deal with: alcohol abuse, drugs, rebellious children, paying the bills, keeping food on the table and a lack of good medical care. Many of the ills of the Indian society are a result of poverty and a shortage of educational opportunities, plain and simple. The perceptions the non-Indian communities have of the Indian have always been problematic from the start."

Abe pointed to the works of James Fennimore Cooper and his *Leather Stocking Tales,* so dear to the hearts of the Victorians, with their image of the noble savage. Cooper's stories, set in early colonial America, were actually thinly veiled

Christian morality plays. The radical position posed by Cooper was that, unlike most of his readership, he argued Indians had souls and he expected to be considered a heathen for taking that position.

From Cooper's time until the present, the perception about Indians had been reinvented by nearly ever generation, with the current version of them being such great environmentalists and preservationists. Of course, filmmakers and writers conjured their own myths and perpetuated them for a profit. Every time a Navajo friend of Abe's would view a particular public service ad on television showing an Indian protecting wildlife numbers, he would simply shake his head and wonder if no one had ever heard how a small group of Plains Indians would drive thousands of buffalo over a cliff just to secure their small needs in comparison to the waste.

"Of course, my Navajo friend was biased against the Sioux and the Northern Cheyenne who engaged in that practice in ancient times," Abe said, "long before the white man came on the scene. With so few people and so many millions of buffalo, the vast natural resources must have seemed inexhaustible. I try not to judge. For all I know, they could have been culling the herds so they didn't eventually increase in numbers that would have stripped the prairies bare.

"Like every other group of human beings, Indians are the same as everyone else. There will always be the good, bad and indifferent among us as part of the human race. I've heard pundits say that the Creator did a fair job in fashioning the human race, but why did He have to add free will into the mix? I point out to them that it allows us all the freedom to choose who and what we will become as individuals. That's the core of freedom to me. What organized society chooses may be another thing entirely."

"Sorry," Veronica said quietly. "I didn't mean to push one of your buttons there. I didn't know it was a sensitive spot."

"No, it's I who am sorry," Abe replied, apologetically. "I suppose it was seeing the shape Jimmy is in on returning home. Life can seem so harsh at times. I only wish I could spare him some of the hardships he must overcome. You've discovered another of my flaws, I'm afraid, my dear. I know perfectly well that I can't be the judge of another's path in life. All I can do is to be here if another needs assistance. Now, what was the question again?"

"About conditions on the reservation," she replied.

"I suppose that's a relative question," he said with some thought. "Consider two types of reservation life in the same area of the United States. On the one hand, consider the Navajo Nation occupying twenty-seven thousand acres across three states—Utah, Arizona and New Mexico. That's an area larger than ten of the fifty states. There are approximately two hundred and fifty thousand Navajo on that reservation.

"On the other hand, the Fort Mojave Reservation has some twenty-five thousand acres in agricultural development along the Colorado River, encompassing parts of three states—Arizona, California and Nevada. There are fewer than one thousand Mojave on that reservation."

"Let me guess," she offered. "The successes and the problems are relative to the sizes of the communities—all things being equal."

"That's a simple comparison, yes," Abe answered. "I don't think Jimmy will have any problem fitting in once he has settled his personal dilemma."

What Abe had said about personal freedom enabling us to choose what we want to be and how organized society may insure or restrict personal freedom gave Veronica an entirely different perspective as she pursued her work on constitutional law throughout the afternoon. She believed deeply that the constitutional safeguards of personal liberties must be defended at all costs. She also recognized the duty placed on the government by that document to form an orderly society and prevent abuse. Now as she was studying various aspects of the Second Amendment, she began to wonder if her own personal bias might be impeding her consideration of the viewpoints of others.

"Abe, my dear," Veronica said, swiveling her chair in his direction, "do you have a few minutes? I'd like to share a few thoughts with you and see what you think."

"Of course," Abe answered. "That's one of the privileges I gained when you had the wisdom to accept my proposal. Then again, I was wise enough to make that proposal in the first place; you gained the same privilege in return."

Veronica said that she had always considered herself on the more liberal side when it came to the constitution, which meant that she supported a broad interpretation of most amendments. Lately, she began to wonder if her narrower view, the collective "militia only" interpretation of the Second Amendment rather than "personal right" to bear arms, would need to be broadened in light of the changing views of scholars and recent judicial rulings.

"I was reared in a gun culture," Abe said. "I know most of the arguments on both sides of the question. I'm sure you remember the amendment verbatim, including the relevant punctuation."

"'A well regulated militia, being necessary to the security of a free state, the right of the people to keep and bear arms, shall not be infringed,'" Veronica answered.

"Correct," Abe replied. "Now, for the last couple of decades, the pro-gun lobby has consistently dropped the last comma in their arguments and deleted the first part entirely or say it is ambiguous. Hammer that home enough times and the man on the street begins to agree with their position, without bothering to read the amendment. Even legal scholars, yourself included, begin to doubt their previous position."

"You have that right," she admitted. "I've always kept in mind what former chief justice Warren Burger said about the argument for the right to have firearms. He called it 'one of the greatest pieces of fraud on the American public by special interest groups' that he had seen in his lifetime."

"That might stand as a simple difference of opinion," Abe continued, "if it hadn't been for what else the pro-gun crowd has done to gut the amendment and put in danger the society at large. Through their lobbying efforts, Congress has passed laws barring state and local police departments from getting access to information on illegal gun sales collected by federal inspectors. In the past, police forces have used that data to help trace and stop gun trafficking. That resource has now been taken away. Congress also passed a law allowing the sale of firearms to people on the federal watch lists of terrorist suspects. Did you know that in one six-month period, agents uncovered such sales to forty-four people on those watch lists? How is that for homeland security?"

"I'm sure you own some firearms yourself," she said.

"Of course I do," he acknowledged. "They are mostly rifles for hunting and I keep them locked in a gun safe on the ranch. But believe me, I see no reason for anyone to own an automatic assault rifle. Those are made for killing people, not hunting. I also see no justification for the number of handguns, both legal and illegal, out on the streets of our cities, large or small."

"What about the legends of the wild west, where everyone wore a holster with at least one pistol?" she asked.

"That's exactly what that is—a legend," he replied. "Most people armed themselves for a specific purpose. The rest of the time, side arms—if they even owned any—were left at home. I don't have a problem with owning a handgun to protect from home invasion. But did you know that in Virginia you are allowed to wear a gun on your hip into a restaurant that also sells liquor, as long as the gun remains visible? And what about Utah, where college kids can carry a gun on campus and into the classroom? That's a nightmare for law enforcement and an accident just waiting to happen. Little wonder Europeans think Americans are just plain gun-crazy."

Veronica went back to work trying to think why she had questioned her position in the first place. She knew that one of the hazards of being so intimately involved in the law was that you can be so involved with the legal interpretation of any given statute that you can lose sight of how that statute applies to the public at large—if only temporarily. She also realized how much she appreciated Abe's perspective on matters. He was a man of the world who constantly stood back and analyzed the situation and the possible implications. That was a necessary talent to be successful in his chosen profession. She was deep into reading a case on *habeas corpus* when she chanced to look up and glanced out the window.

"Abe, my dear," Veronica said, "we have an unannounced visitor in the common area."

As Abe looked out the window a large dairy cow bellowed a long low moo.

"Consider her announced," Abe said. "The Sullivans' large barn and farmhouse are just over the hill. I didn't know that farm still had any livestock. Since we're on the former farm acreage, perhaps she's been away and wanted to visit her old pastures."

"More likely, Mr. Sullivan is tending a friend's livestock," Veronica countered. "Someone must have left a gate open. We'd better get that girl home. She looks like she's ready to calve any minute."

The cow had a sweet disposition. Abe and Veronica each took hold of the bridle on each side of her head and ambled down the street. They did draw attention, however, and soon there was a small group of children who wanted to help—or at least to join this novel procession. Not many of these city-reared children had ever been this close to a live cow and delighted skipping alongside gently caressing the animal's flanks. Abe had to caution them not to get too close to the hooves because of the danger of being stepped on. A neighbor along the way waved and told Abe he really ought to get a smaller dog. He also heard one little girl tell another: "See, I told you he was a real cowboy."

As they came up the long lane to the farmhouse, Mrs. Sullivan walked out of the house and stood on the porch. When the group came within hailing distance, she waved and pointed toward the barn.

"You must be that Abe Carlson we've heard so much about," Mrs. Sullivan said. "And this must be the beautiful Veronica you wed."

"Yes ma'am, you're right on both counts," Abe replied. "This gal between us came visiting and we were just walking her home. The children thought she could use more company."

"Well, you're all welcome," Mrs. Sullivan said. "Cyrus is in the barn with her five sisters—that is if he hasn't lost another one. I told him he was too old to be hand milking, but Bob Knolls had to tend to his ailing mother over in Ohio for a week and Cyrus had no one else to turn to. Take her to Cyrus and I'll be along with some ice water and something to eat."

Cyrus Sullivan was a man in his early nineties, with little hair but a generous smile. He introduced himself and thanked the group for returning the cow, which he then led to a clean spacious stall. He told them he was the sixth generation to tend this farm, although lately his acreage was dwindling because he could not work it all and had no next generation to take over the place. They had lost three sons in two wars and their only daughter had died in a car accident when she was only twenty. Mrs. Sullivan arrived with pitchers of ice water and two plates of cookies for the children.

"I like to see growing children with healthy appetites," Mrs. Sullivan said. "Cyrus, you didn't lose any more, did you?"

"No, Martha, I didn't even lose that one," he answered.

"Your family tradition again?" Martha asked.

"I'm afraid so," Cyrus answered, turning to Abe and Veronica. "Back before the Civil War, this farm was a stop on the underground railroad. My ancestors fed and hid over three hundred of those poor souls on their way to Canada."

"That's an achievement to be proud of," Veronica remarked.

"We're very proud of our ancestors," Cyrus said. "When I was a boy, we had maybe twenty dairy cows at any given time. When it came time for them to give birth, they would often wander off to be by themselves. My father wouldn't allow me to go get them. He'd say they were off to Canada and deserved every little bit of freedom they could gain—if only for a short time."

CHAPTER 18

▼

SOLACE

It was mid-week before Abe awoke to the welcome aromas of coffee being brewed and bacon frying in the kitchen. Jimmy Brand had returned from his sojourn to the countryside. Daylight was a mere hint of gray on the horizon. Abe quickly dressed and shaved for the day as Veronica, awakened by the same smells, joined him. As they entered the kitchen together, Jimmy was using a spatula to lift omelets from the frying pan onto three plates. He nodded in recognition as Veronica wordlessly retrieved two trays from a cabinet. Abe poured the coffee and they went to the patio to eat. Jimmy ate very slowly, savoring every morsel. He did not break his silence until he reached for the pot to refresh his coffee.

"You keep a very full larder," Jimmy said to Veronica.

"I like to eat," Veronica replied. "When I'm hungry, I want real food, not some tasteless factory prepared meal that would serve better as a doorstop."

"My mother is like that," Jimmy conceded. "I am a big man, but my father is much bigger. My mother always prepares enough real food to fill us. There are few leftovers in our family. That's why our dog is not fat and lazy. My mother says she is happiest when she is cooking."

"I said I liked to eat," Veronica replied. "I didn't say I particularly like being in the kitchen all the time. When I do cook, I tend to prepare several meals and put them in the freezer."

Jimmy nodded his understanding.

"Did you find our countryside to your liking?" Abe asked.

"Yes," Jimmy said simply. "I have prepared myself for a visit to your cabin in the mountains. I would like to see the sunset over your Big Valley. I would like to walk the hills. I would like to use the sweat lodge."

"We can take you today," Abe said. "Veronica has no classes today and she knows the area much better than I. We could be there in less than two hours."

"That would be good," Jimmy replied. "Before we go, I need a pen and paper to leave something for Henry and Cassy."

"I have plenty of legal-sized tablets in the office," Veronica volunteered.

"That would be nice," Jimmy said. "Would you happen to have a set of colored pencils around too?"

"I sure do," she replied. "I have a small box of art supplies for just such occasions."

"You get Jimmy set up and I'll clear the table," Abe said to Veronica. "I'll make a few telephone calls to insure the cabin is properly provisioned. There's a pickup truck in the garage. I'll make sure it's in working order."

"I can take care of the truck," Jimmy said. "I do have a request about the provisions, though. Don't let them stock any surplus MREs, you know, Meals Ready to Eat. Believe me, in my opinion, they aren't real food."

Jimmy worked for over two hours at the desk in the library, making sketches, with accompanying narrative printed in neat, small letters. He proved to have a natural gift for art and a remarkable detailed memory. When he had finished, he brought a small stack of papers into the office for inspection.

What Jimmy had produced was a series of minutely detailed sketches of the local landscape so finely rendered that both Abe and Veronica recognized many of the locations immediately. Each page had an orderly legend at the top corner, indicating scale and the colors represented. Various trails used by a variety of wildlife—mammals, reptiles and birds—were color-coded for both day and night activity. Landmarks were clearly indicated and artfully rendered. Perhaps the most interesting sketch was the last one that told its own story. Not one, but two coyotes had staked claims to distinct territories. Both were male and they had located their dens on opposite ends of a mountain range. They respected each other's marked range, but Abe knew that could change should a female wander into the area.

"Wonderfully thorough," Veronica said.

"Thank you," Jimmy replied modestly. "Don't worry. I didn't include one-time movement—the cow you walked down the street, for instance. I saw that from the top of a hill."

"Henry, Cassy and the Squad will certainly appreciate this," Abe said. "Now, let's take a ride to the country."

On the first part of the ride, Veronica described the Big Valley area and what Jimmy could expect to find in the neighborhood. She relayed the local history, as she knew it, pointing out the number of Amish and Mennonite he was likely to encounter. She suddenly became silent as she approached a particularly narrow gap at the convergence of two mountains. The abundant foliage gave the illusion of a stage curtain and she could not readily see the opening in that drapery until she was literally there.

One glance in the rearview mirror told her the effect was not lost on Jimmy sitting in the back seat. The Mercedes seemed to zip through a portal in time, because within moments, a sharp turn in the road left the curtain once more quickly closing behind them. Jimmy sat as if transfixed on something in the distance. He was a man who had readied himself as best he could and was now embarking on a great personal expedition. There were no words to describe his experience, so he remained silent the remainder of the trip.

As they passed through this same gap a few hours later on the return trip, Veronica told Abe about her impression the first time through. She said she was uncertain how much she was influenced by her childhood fancy when watching western movies, or if it was the close proximity of a full-blooded Indian, but for the first time in her life she felt entering the mountains was akin to passing through a gateway to a place of refuge.

"I am very pleased it had that effect on you," Abe said. "That is the very same impression I received. Every tribe I know has some similar tradition, whether it be mountains, or intertwined canyons or some other topographical feature, they all have a place they consider sacred, a refuge, a hermitage or any other term we give to places of solitude."

"I suppose I was unconsciously thinking about the purpose of the trip," she commented. "Our new property in the mountains is, as you said, a place of solitude. It provides a respite from the busyness and cares of our fast-paced world. It is almost as if he is making a pilgrimage in Medieval Europe—seeking the peacefulness of a monastery."

"That's an apt description," Abe said. "I don't know for sure, but I've always felt that societies of all ages and all parts of the world have always done similar things. For people like Jimmy with his Indian heritage, it is a journey of necessity. From my outside perspective, I'd call it a 'Journey For Solace.' This journey has several stages. After his interim time on the streets of Washington, D.C., he took the first step in wandering the countryside near our home. He needed to find solace in his heart, to alleviate his grief and anxiety, in preparation for the second stage. The stage now is to grant solace to himself, purify his body through the sweat lodge and purify his mind by letting go of the demons he may have bottled up inside. The third stage will be to return home, to receive solace from his family and his people. Then he will no longer have a bent spirit. He will be whole again."

"Find, grant and receive solace," Veronica commented. "That is so simply, but beautifully put, my love. You'll have to give me some time to think that over. Right now, I'm hungry. Let's stop for something to eat."

When they arrived home, Veronica had a message on her computer from her mother, Ruby, asking to be called at home at the earliest convenient time. There was something strange happening with the Prometheus system at the Exchange Center and Ruby could not figure out exactly what was happening.

"Who does this Miguel Swartzbaugh think he is?" Ruby asked Veronica when she called. "As far as I'm concerned, he is one of those over-educated Germans who are not at all attractive when they get up on their high horse and flaunt their learning in an arrogant manner."

"Mother," Veronica replied. "Must I remind you that you are one of those over-educated Germans who on occasion gets on her high horse and flaunts her learning? As I recall, you are of Teutonic heritage on both sides of the family tree."

"Don't be impertinent, Veronica," her mother replied. "I am an educated teacher who merely enlightens her pupils to the wonders of the subject at hand. How was your day off, by the way? Some of us drones have been toiling in fields without cease."

"It has been a fine day, Mother, thank you," Veronica replied. "What has Miguel done now to disturb your day?"

"I tend to think of myself as fairly well educated," Ruby said. "However, I may not be as versed in Greek mythology as your dear Miguel."

"I understand he reads it in the original Greek and Latin, with a Chinese translation now and then to break up the monotony," Veronica replied. "What is it in Prometheus' programming that seems to be bothering you?"

"Okeanos and the River Daughters," Ruby said. "Prometheus seems to think we need a file cache by that name, filtering them into a select number under the file name of Io."

"You are perfectly right in your judgment, Mother," Veronica said. "Miguel is an arrogant Teutonic personality. How does he expect us to be so acquainted with Greek mythology as to follow such circuitous reasoning? Let me do some research and get back to you in the morning. I'll be in your office first thing and perhaps I'll have some answers by that time."

Veronica explained Ruby's dilemma to Abe, then consulted Michael Stewart's *Greek Mythology: From the Iliad to the Fall of the Last Tyrant*. She found Stewart only a little less arrogant.

Abe's father, the Calvinist preacher, had always been suspicious of the writings of the Greeks. When Paul spread Christianity among the Greeks and they translated the Old Testament into Greek, then Latin, his father had found a harshness not found in the New Testament. He was young when his father died, but Abe still remembered the impression. He would stand aside and let Veronica put her own intuition to the test.

According to Stewart, Prometheus was shackled to the boulder when Okeanos, the Ocean, and the river's daughters, who sympathized with his plight, visited him. They were shocked at the excesses of Zeus in exacting such punishment, but Prometheus warned them not to speak out because it would do no good and that, in any event, Zeus would soon fall from his throne.

Another visitor was Io, whom the vengeful Zeus had turned into a black and white heifer, doomed to wander the earth tormented by a gadfly, biting at her flesh as she went about her travels. Io was tormented, but was lucky. Prometheus was immortal and would suffer through eternity. Io, however, was mortal and would eventually cease her sufferings with death. Io was key to Prometheus' eventual release. She traveled to Egypt and was returned to her human form. Thirteen generations later, her direct line produced Heracles, who would climb the mountain, kill the eagle and free Prometheus from his shackles.

Veronica and Abe hashed out the possibilities of what Prometheus was doing in directing a growing number of files, culled from the Pandora and the Okeanos files under the new classification of Io.

"Perhaps it's the long-term possibilities of those particular cases," Abe said. "What do the selections by Prometheus mean to you? What are the legal implications?"

"Most seem, on the surface, to be rather small matters," Veronica said, thinking. "They involve constitutional matters, in a backdoor sort of way. They are all brought by individual, small-time attorneys or firms—usually on a *pro bono* basis. None are likely to garner the attention of the larger firms. No big headlines along the way. The only time a larger firm is likely to gain in reputation is if a case makes its way to consideration by the Supreme Court. The majority have little possibility of completing that arduous process. At that level, of course, an *amicus curiae* brief could be of assistance, but would be judged as a weak gesture after the fact, like riding on the coattails of a long-shot politician. I know of no attorney who is willing to wait thirteen generations for a case to come before the Supremes, no matter how confident of the outcome."

"Do any have the potential to make it through the process and make a difference in interpretation of the constitution?" Abe asked pointedly. "Is there any hope?"

Veronica pondered the questions for some moments without comment.

"My dear," Abe said at last, "do you know the Dieter Wolfson farm? I had a talk with him last summer concerning hex signs. He was kind enough to provide me with a bit of tobacco, which he grows solely for his own personal use. We've an hour or so of daylight to pay him a visit."

Veronica had no idea what her husband was contemplating, but she went along without saying a word. He was a man of only well-thought-out and usually correct actions and she wanted to see where this was going.

They arrived to a warm welcome on the Wolfson farm. Dieter gave them a tour, which ended in the tobacco-drying barn. Only a few leaves were left hanging on the poles, awaiting conversion into a twist or Dieter's favored cut processing. When Abe asked if any early planting had occurred, Dieter showed them a field behind the drying barn with a couple of acres of plowed land. If you look closely enough, you could just detect the green sprouting leaves breaking the surface.

"Would you mind if we just stayed here and looked over the farm for awhile?" Abe asked.

"Not at all," Dieter answered with question. "Honk when you pass by the house on your way out and don't be strangers. You're welcome to come back anytime. Nice to meet you Veronica, eh, Mrs. Carlson."

"It has been my pleasure to finally meet you too, Dieter," Veronica answered graciously. "Please call me Veronica. I feel we're friends already."

Abe led Veronica to a plank bench attached to the rear of the drying barn. As they sat looking over the emerging field, Abe pulled his pipe and tobacco pouch out of his pocket and filled the bowl. He mentioned that it was Dieter's apple blend as he motioned to a nearby field where a small apple orchard was in bloom.

"What do you know about growing tobacco?" Abe asked, taking a few puffs on his pipe.

"It's a dwindling industry around here," Veronica answered. "I've heard that it is now confined primarily to the Amish. They will not accept government buyouts of any type, so when the state of Maryland began paying tobacco farmers not to grow a crop, the Amish began filling the need. In my lifetime, it has always been considered a 'cash crop' for small farmers. It was the one crop that could mean the difference between a black profit and a red deficit in the checkbook at the end of the year."

"Aside from the political correctness involved with the subject of smoking these days," Abe said, "what do you know about the actual process?"

"I've seen tobacco in the fields," she answered. "Those little shoots in the field don't look like much now, but those will grow perhaps four or five feet tall, broad green leaves, turning a tan brown as it matures. The leaves are cropped and hung in drying barns with vertical vents, hung by the stem on poles to cure."

"What do you know about squeezing worms?" he asked.

"I don't have a clue what you're talking about," she answered.

"I knew a man once, from Virginia," Abe said. "He told me about squeezing worms from tobacco as it was growing in the field. It was a backbreaking affair— labor intensive. He would bend over all day, reaching under the leaves to snatch these little worms, which would feed on the leaves. They would be full of tobacco juice and he had to efficiently pull them off, squeeze them and drop the remains in the furrows between the plants. At the end of the day, he would have a sore back and hands stained so badly with tobacco juice sucked from the leaves that his skin had to grow out to finally get rid of the residue. Tobacco insured the survival of our first fragile colonies and sustained a new nation. The tobacco leaf is inscribed in the marble pillars of buildings all over Washington, D.C. This is part of our heritage and tradition."

"I can appreciate the imagery," Veronica said, "but I can't quite make the connection. What does all this have to do with the Io files?"

"If you want to have the constitution survive intact," Abe replied, "perhaps it's time to squeeze a couple of worms. It will be a nasty job, I'll grant you, but what is the alternative for the survival of the plant? If I'm not mistaken, some of those Io files are worthy of being advanced through the legal system. There must always be hope for the future."

"The ultimate solace," she answered, "the solace of hope. We have the ability to protect the system from eroding our rights. It may be mixing metaphors, but perhaps if we wrangle enough turkeys into the field, they'll eat the worms. Oh my, I'm becoming a Pennsylvania farm girl making comparisons such as that. What would my esteemed colleagues think of me?"

"That you may be a little quaint," Abe replied, "but you are absolutely correct."

CHAPTER 19

▼

PROBABILITY

Veronica awoke unexpectedly at three o'clock on Saturday morning to find an empty space beside her. The sheets were cold to the touch, so Abe must have been out of bed for some time. A clear sky, nearly full moon and the ambient glow of the streetlights allowed her to search the house without having to turn on any other illumination. Looking out the office window, she saw Abe's silhouette next to a tree in the common area—his hands in his pockets and seeming to study the sounds of the night. She found it easy to imagine his striking this identical pose many times in his life on the open spaces of the west. Not sure if he wanted to be disturbed, she leisurely started a pot of coffee and changed her nightgown and robe to slacks and a sweater. By the time she came back into the kitchen, the coffee had brewed. She checked to see if Abe was still next to the tree before turning on a light, pouring two mugs of coffee and joining him on the grass.

"Sorry to have awakened you, my love," he said as she approached. "I know you had a long week and hoped you'd be able to sleep in later than usual."

"I suppose it was your absence that awakened me," she replied, handing him coffee. "I was feeling lonesome there by myself and when I saw you standing out here, I thought you might enjoy some company. You can probably communicate fairly well with the creatures of the night, but I will say with confidence that I am a better conversationalist."

"I always enjoy your company, my dear," Abe replied. "As for your being a better conversationalist, I'd say you win hands down—and you're much more beautiful."

"Keep that up, Sport and I'll hum in your ear," she said with a smile. "May I ask the reason for your roaming around in the middle of the night?"

"I am pondering the question of probability," Abe replied. "More accurately, I'm thinking of chance events, which would be a simple coincidence, as opposed to the probability that something else had occurred."

"I don't know that I'm sufficiently awake to explore these deep mysteries," she said. "Come inside and we'll have another cup of coffee—and maybe a little snack—so I'll be able to focus my full attention."

After they had returned to the house, while Abe was preparing bits of ham, cheese, celery and crackers, Veronica noticed that he had not yet shaven. She then asked herself why someone who awoke in the middle of the night to go outside would take the time to shave. She really did need that second cup of coffee.

Once they were sufficiently fortified, Abe explained what had happened. He had awakened to a sound that shouldn't have been there, just as you often find lost people in the wilderness by spotting what was not part of the natural landscape. He had heard a very low rumble of a car with a modified exhaust system, the slight echo effect of vibration from the macadam indicating a low-rider vehicle slowly cruising the neighborhood. He certainly did not think a police vehicle would make that sound.

When he went outside and stood in the middle of the common area, Abe could follow the sound ebb and flow through the complex as the vehicle circled the streets. Once he glimpsed a dark brown low-rider between two houses as it passed under a streetlight. All the vehicle lights were dark, including the brake lights, indicating those lights had been taped. The first thought that came to mind was the appearance of drug activity. The local younger men he had observed preferred jacking up their pickup trucks and cars. Low-riders he identified with the Hispanic community, particularly Mexicans.

"There is a large Latino contingent in this area of Pennsylvania," he said. "They have enough people suspicious of their legal status and intentions without bringing in the criminal element. I also don't think the dealers would be so dumb as to cruise a neighborhood like ours—with all our doctors, lawyers and higher end professionals—looking for customers. To me, it is more probable they would be making a delivery."

"You said events, in the plural," Veronica said, proving she had been listening intently. "What else has occurred?"

"The other evening when we were coming home from Dieter's farm, we stopped by the side of the road to admire how well Jimmy had captured the view in one of his sketches. He even managed to include that weathered cabin through the trees where the foliage had not yet matured. I have a vague recollection of seeing a brown car parked at the side. It could have been the one I saw this morning. Do you know who owns that cabin?"

"I have no idea," she answered seriously. "It has been my impression that many small hunting cabins dot the area. They are only used during the hunting season and since they tend to be passed down from generation to generation, they often go vacant for decades. I'm sure we could find out easily enough."

"Another thing," Abe continued, "as we were about to get into the car, an older blue pickup truck with more than its share of rust came out of the dirt lane from the direction of the cabin and passed us quickly."

"I do remember that," she said. "It had a big wooden chest for a toolbox and was hauling several bales of hay. Two men were in the cab and both were smoking."

"Very observant," Abe said in compliment. "I caught a whiff of several odors in its wake. One was the distinctive aroma of marijuana, another was the particularly pungent odor I only recall from the Orient—opium."

"I find it hard to believe anyone would be peddling opium in this area," Veronica commented. "Pot and methamphetamine, perhaps, but opiates?"

"Charcoal opium to be exact," Abe answered. Here's what I do know. Meth has been moving into the rural areas very quickly in the last few years. At first it was manufactured with home recipes in someone's kitchen. Any idiot could make it—except those so inept that the mixture blew up in the process. Local manufacture was popular because it reeks while being made and with houses fewer and farther apart, there was less of a chance of being caught."

"I remember reading about the problem," Veronica interrupted. "Law enforcement cracked down hard and fast, putting those manufacturers out of business fairly quickly."

"That's one of the reasons, as I understand," Abe said, "that huge amounts of meth are being manufactured in Mexico. The United States is the biggest market."

"From a legal standpoint you're getting very close to probable cause," Veronica said.

"There was one more odor I detected," Abe replied. "That was mesquite. People in the southwest couldn't believe that a nuisance shrub we were always trying to eradicate, found a market in the east as woodchips for barbeque. Believe me, there was more than one rancher laughing all the way to the bank."

"I think hickory chips are more popular in the Hershey area," Veronica said. "Of course, any number of franchise restaurants with the word 'Texas' in their title have located here."

"A franchise restaurant, yes," Abe said, "but using mesquite out in the middle of farm country? So, if we add up all these elements, what do you think is the probability that a full-service drug business has come to town?"

"I think it's time we called Sheriff Bret Tate," Veronica said, firmly. "I also need to notify campus security to be on the lookout."

Sheriff Tate was only too happy to accept his invitation to breakfast with the Carlsons. His wife had been gone for the week to take care of her mother in Williamsport and would not return for another ten days. He acknowledged that his own cooking skills left a lot to be desired, but no matter how many times he related that to the Sheriff's Department staff, no one had risen to the bait with an invitation to dinner. After a breakfast that could be classified as nothing below sumptuous, he was not shy in accepting an offer of leftover strawberry pie Bea Nagy had provided the day before.

"So, what do you think, Sheriff?" Abe asked when they were finished.

"That's quite a string of circumstances you two have come up with," Tate replied. "I particularly like the idea of opium being involved. That's a pretty exotic drug for this area, to put it mildly. It would certainly establish an international link that would lead me to believe if there is meth involved, or even simple marijuana, it would be of foreign origin and not a local product—the guys involved in this type of operation like to keep it all in-house, offering a package of their own products. They also must have just arrived on the scene. I haven't seen or heard anything about a jump in drug use in the schools or on the streets. There is one particularly explosive issue here. Abe, go over your observations from early this morning again, please. Don't omit the smallest detail or impression."

Abe produced a street map of the complex that was part of his homeowner's booklet and traced the route of the sound. This time, he remembered the gaps, where the vehicle was too far away and the houses in between obstructed the sound. He concentrated on whether the gaps could account for an interruption to the steady cruising speed, indicating the opportunity to stop and make a delivery. The majority of the complex contained large single-family homes, the duplexes were fewer and tucked to one side. His finger came to rest at a short block at the northern end of community.

"That's what I was afraid of," Tate said suddenly, pointing to one particular house. "We're looking at a big problem."

This newly acquired residence was the home of a sitting state senator who was about to announce he would seek his party's nomination to become the next Supreme Court Justice for the Commonwealth of Pennsylvania. The nominee would be a shoo-in for election—a stepping-stone to his ultimate goal of a seat on the federal bench.

"I'll have to make a series of telephone calls," Tate said. "The senator is under investigation by several state and federal agencies for bribery, corruption, a number of felonies involving drug lords, trafficking in illegal firearms and his ties to organized crime. Thankfully, we can turn that end of things over to people who will be only too glad to step in."

Tate used the land-line telephone for security purposes—cell phone communications were too easily monitored. He laid out a scenario of making a delivery long after the bars had closed on Friday night, avoiding heavier police presence. The dealers were smart enough not to make delivery later in the day for a Saturday night party. Besides, a low-rider in that neighborhood would hardly go unnoticed. The senator's children would be home from college and there had been reports of previous drug parties with the adults taking part. This was probably the first delivery from this supplier, since they had to cruise around to find the address. Tate would take care of the supplier.

"Okay, you two," Tate said when he had placed the receiver into its cradle, "I'd like to have a look at those sketches."

They all retired to the library, which became the makeshift command center for the day. Tate was so impressed by the sketches that he requested several copies. He could think of any number of uses for his department.

"We'll have to keep this one close," Tate admonished. "Communication will be face-to-face or land-line only, on a need-to-know basis. Let's keep this as contained as possible until we know what we're dealing with and how we're going to handle the situation."

Veronica was in charge of procuring a warrant for probable cause to search the property, which had been deeded to a local church when the owner had died five years ago. She had easily tracked a friendly judge to a golf course and Tate dispatched a deputy to get a signature.

Abe studied the sketches of animal trails and natural obstacles and consulted topographical maps e-mailed from the Sheriff's Department. Sheriff Tate was taking inventory of the equipment he might need and assessing the manpower available. He was particularly concerned about the lethal firepower international dealers had been known to carry. The special unit from the state police would have the best equipment and training, plus access to helicopter backup. Because of the political ramifications sure to follow the federal end of the operation, the governor would have to be informed, but that notification would be delayed until after the assessment of evidence discovered under the warrant.

By lunchtime, two more deputies had joined the planning in the library and Veronica was amused when Abe directed everyone to wash their hands before helping themselves to a platter of sandwiches. Abe smiled when they dutifully obeyed.

"May I make a suggestion, Sheriff?" Abe asked as he put a sandwich on his plate.

"I'll take any suggestions you may have," Tate answered. "This may be getting out of hand."

"That's a point I've been considering," Abe replied. "Perhaps you should be thinking more along the lines of a minimal operation. Setting up in a rural location makes sense as a first step. Opium suggests to me there will also be cocaine and heroin—all of which are for a higher-end market. Meth and pot for the locals, but the major target has to be Harrisburg. One rich and connected suburbanite does not make a market. In fact that was probably a fluke—and a major mistake."

"Continue," Tate said. "You have my undivided attention."

"Here's the way I see the situation," Abe continued. "There are four people in this right now, five at the max. To establish yourself as the new supplier in town, you have two or three well-dressed members—one almost certainly a woman—handing out free samples, discreetly, in the clubs and hotels up and down Second Street on a Friday night. This also means there is another vehicle involved—a nice Lexus or Mercedes, perhaps even a sporty BMW. This part of the operation is living large in Harrisburg and only comes to the country for new supplies."

"So, in a desperate move to keep an important client happy, they dispatch a low-rider to this kind of neighborhood," Tate mused. "These guys are not rocket scientists."

"They never are," Abe said. "That means there are two people guarding the supplies at the cabin, one or both of whom indulge in their own products. I sure smelled them the other day. Tonight is Saturday night. The downtown contingent will be working the streets. The two at the cabin can't leave for a night on the town, but they certainly have the means at their disposal to have their own private party."

"Fewer officers tramping around a crime scene preserves the integrity of the evidence and forensics," Tate said. "Radio traffic will be the norm for a Saturday, with accidents and DUI incidents. We retain a very nice element of surprise."

"Another thing, Sheriff," Abe said. "If you're not familiar with the practice, an opium smoker will usually place himself on his side, either on a couch or a bed, perhaps even on the floor. He will place the stem of a long opium pipe in his mouth. The pipe rests on a coffee table or a chair so when he drifts off into oblivion he won't upset the works. His partner will place the opium in the bowl on the other end and light it. A few puffs and there is one less bad guy to worry about."

"You certainly make it sound like a walk in the park," Tate observed.

"On the other hand," Abe replied, "I could be completely off the mark. In that case, you'd better have plenty of backup."

A simple plan was devised based upon Abe's analysis. Sheriff Tate had several telephone conversations with the Harrisburg Chief of Police and the head of the city's anti-drug task force. A new Lexus with Nevada plates found in the garage of a posh hotel was registered to a couple that had booked a penthouse suite for two weeks. They were followed leaving the hotel and walking the short distance up Second Street to the restaurant and club row. At midnight, the Police Chief called the Sheriff to report the successful apprehension—very discreetly—of two suspects and a large amount of various narcotics seized from their persons, their rooms and their car.

"You missed your calling, Abe," Tate said after that call. "You should have gone into law enforcement."

"Never gave it a thought," Abe replied. "Too dangerous."

At one o'clock in the morning, a man stepped out of the cabin in the mountains, followed by a billow of dark gray smoke, to stretch and get a breath of fresh air. He was severely intoxicated and put up no resistance. Inside the cabin, a second suspect was found on the floor in an opium-induced stupor—acrid smoke choking the room. Authorities found an enormous number of automatic weapons of various manufacture and configuration—all lethal instruments of death. Under the floorboards and inside the chimney, they discovered what would finally be tallied as over eight million dollars, street value, of opium, cocaine, heroin, methamphetamine and marijuana. From the trunk of the low-rider car parked to the side of the cabin, they recovered many boxes of prescription medications.

As the last of the evidence was being loaded and the area sealed and taped, Sheriff Tate turned to one of his deputies at his side.

"Here we find ourselves because one man heard a sound in the night that shouldn't have been there," he said. "What do you think of the probability of that?"

CHAPTER 20

▼

ANALYSIS

Veronica had had difficulty falling asleep in the wee hours of Sunday morning. Sheriff Tate had called with his thanks and to report on the quick success, without a shot fired or any injuries on either side. The call came at two o'clock. Within fifteen minutes, Abe was sound asleep, but Veronica was still awake at five o'clock. Her mind was restless to the point that she arose, dressed and went into the office in search of a distraction. Abe found her there working at her computer at six-thirty.

"It's the adrenalin rush," Abe called from the kitchen as he prepared a pot of coffee. "The first time is the hardest. It can play havoc with your system."

Veronica emerged from the office and stood with her hands on her hips, looking at her husband in disbelief.

"Did I also mention that it can make you a little grumpy?" he asked with deadpan humor.

"I couldn't sleep," Veronica replied evenly. "I couldn't get my mind or my imagination from running amok. I kept thinking of 'what ifs.' What if the sheriff had asked you to go along? What if you had gone? What if the plan fell apart and turned ugly? What if something bad happened to you?"

"Please don't confuse risk-assessment with analysis, my love," Abe answered calmly. "I did my best to analyze the situation and tell the sheriff what I thought of the various factors that were coming together. It's part of his responsibility to assess the risks. Law enforcement has the job of going out into the field to protect the general public. Would I have put myself in that kind of danger if asked? Possibly, when I was still young, dumb and single. I'm glad to say I'm older and wiser now. You are the top priority in my life, period. I say that with all sincerity, finality and love that I can muster. Lest you think that to be a fine noble statement, I admit to an abundance of selfishness in the mix. I'm selfish enough to want to love and share life with you until we're so old that our idea of exercise is to sit on a park bench, holding hands, trying to figure out what day of the week it is."

Abe walked around the counter, embraced his wife and kissed her. They held to each other for a few moments.

"You are a wonderful man, Abe Carlson," Veronica whispered, breaking the embrace and wiping a tear from her eye. "Thank you for asking me to marry you."

"It's you I thank for saying yes," Abe replied. "Now, what do you say to another big Pennsylvania breakfast? You must be hungry. We'll take a long walk afterward so we can burn some of the calories."

"Breakfast first, Sport," Veronica said with a smile. "We'll discuss how to burn those calories later."

An hour later, as they were having coffee on the patio, the telephone rang.

"Does my beloved daughter have some news she needs to share with her adored mother this morning?" Ruby asked when Veronica answered the phone. "It's a good thing for other people to observe what a close mother-daughter relationship can do, you know."

"Why, Mother dear," Veronica replied sweetly, "whatever could you be referring to?"

"Don't be coy with your mother," Ruby said. "It's a bad habit to get into. The word is spreading like wildfire through the Masonic Village this morning. Julie Fry saw several vehicles from the Sheriff's Department come and go from your house all day yesterday. Then, there's the judge who was called off the sixteenth green at the golf course to sign some sort of warrant. Now the local news networks are breaking in on the morning television programs with bulletins about a big drug haul right in your backyard."

"I don't believe they call it a 'drug haul' anymore," Veronica corrected. "I think they refer to it as a 'drug bust.' That gets you more credibility on the street."

"I've taught inner city kids for years," Ruby countered. "So don't lecture me on 'street creds.' I learned the terminology when you were still in diapers. And don't avoid the question. What have you two been up to?"

"Well, since I wouldn't want to jeopardize your 'street creds' on the mean streets of the Masonic Village," Veronica said, "here's how it 'went down,' as you'd say."

Veronica related the story, omitting any reference to the senator, and lavishing praise on Jimmy Brand's artistic ability and attention to detail—giving a modest assessment of her and Abe's contributions. She knew that being in on the Jimmy Brand connection would put her mother on top of the information pyramid for weeks to come.

"That conversation ended a bit abruptly there at the end, didn't it?" Abe said with a grin.

"I imagine Mother had a few more calls to make and people to meet," Veronica replied. "She does like to liven things up at the Village, particularly on Sundays, when time seems to run so slowly."

"Frank's newsstand in Hummelstown will be opening in fifteen minutes," Abe said, looking at his watch. "We could pick up the usual out-of-town newspapers and head for the park as we like to do. I'd like to spend a nice, leisurely morning in this nice weather—perhaps lunch at a sidewalk table."

"As you well know, my dear," Veronica replied, "with me, lunch is never 'perhaps.' You pay for lunch and I'll pay for the dessert afterward."

When they stopped in to purchase the newspapers, Frank was as informative as ever. He said the reason for the nearly deserted Main Street this morning was due to many people going to watch the media circus in front of the sheriff's office or to drive by the scene of the crime. It was not the usual tendency of people to gawk at an accident, Frank thought. The media would have been appalled if they knew the people were coming to watch the antics of the reporters and watch traffic as it tried to get past inappropriately parked remote television vans, with their telescoping antennas rising many feet into the air. This was a form of entertainment to the local people simply because it was out of the ordinary pace of life in the community—it afforded novelty. Most families, of course, were still in church.

As they sat at their table in the park, Abe started with the *New York Times;* Veronica preferred *The Washington Post.* Abe began with the international news, followed by the national news, skipping the sports section entirely and savoring the book reviews—his favorite section. Veronica's approach to her newspaper was to first scan the pages for stories of legal actions, legislation and inside-the-beltway politics, with special emphasis on anything dealing with the court system.

"Would you believe there is a new book published on the art of graffiti?" Abe asked, looking up from his paper. "When did defacing public property on a grand scale become a form of art?"

"Since politically correct defense attorneys started arguing 'freedom of expression,'" Veronica answered, "linking it to 'freedom of speech.' They say that if a right is not specifically guaranteed by the constitution, then it is inferred. They use the Ninth Amendment: 'The enumeration of the Constitution of certain rights shall not be construed to deny or disparage others retained by the people.' This has been argued so often, that some courts are beginning to recognize it as credible defense."

"That's just dandy," Abe replied flatly. "Some kids spray paint slogans or symbols on the side of the Grand Canyon and now it's a protected form of art, and speech."

"Trying to stretch the legal definition of free speech is getting more popular every day," Veronica said.

She cited two cases that appeared in the day's newspaper she had been reading. Both had to do with the misuse of the Internet, by posting fictitious web pages under someone else's name. This was becoming a popular pastime for high school pranksters posting a page under a teacher's name without his or her knowledge.

"The Internet has opened up a whole new area of the law which we are just beginning to test," Veronica said. "At the same time the schools are trying to develop policies to prevent bullying, including on-line bullying done off campus using computers, they have to deal with the pranksters. One of today's cases was harmless enough. A student posted a web page under the name of one of his teachers and answered inquiries from other students in the school who thought they were communicating with that teacher. In fact, that's how the teacher found out about the site. Students were coming to him at school asking him about it. The web site was closed, the prankster found, and now the school has to decide what to do with him. Since the student didn't post anything malicious or harmful, his attorney is arguing 'no harm, no foul;' it's a clear case of freedom of speech."

"In this era of privacy rights and identity theft," Abe said, "you'd think someone would come up with some violation of the law."

"They have," Veronica replied. "The other case was worse. Three students, another male teacher under the same venue and this time the teacher supposedly admits to having alcohol in school and sexual relations with students. A similar outcome, but where does the victim go to restore his reputation or erase the doubts which will surely shorten his career, if not end it?"

"Has Prometheus uncovered many of these cases?" Abe asked.

"Far too many," Veronica replied, "but he's been weeding them out so they don't mistakenly end up as Io file possibilities. These caliber of cases are clogging the courts, making it more difficult for legitimate violations of the constitution to gain their just recognition."

"Separating the wheat from the chafe," Abe mused quietly, "but what do you do with the kernels once they're identified?"

They both went back to reading their newspapers in silence. One half hour later, Abe noticed Veronica seeming to lose her concentration due to lack of sleep. He quietly rose and went to purchase coffee. When he returned, Veronica was deeply in thought, staring off into the trees. He removed the lids from both cups and placed one before her.

"Help me think this through," she said suddenly, reaching for her coffee.

Abe's off-handed remark about what to do with the kernels sparked a new train of thought. There were many types and levels of analysis. Abe's entire career involved analyzing bits of information, calculating the possibilities, then factoring in the probability of any given scenario before coming to a conclusion. Most legal analysis tends to concentrate solely on the possibilities and taking a position in favor of the possible outcome that is favored.

"Although most in the legal profession would not acknowledge the fact," Veronica said, "it is common practice, where possible, to shop for a judge or a venue most favorable to the client. If funds are available, experts are brought in to help pick a jury. Since Prometheus is culling the chaos out there for the kernels, why not apply probability to the process. We have hardly begun to tap Prometheus' vast resources."

"I think you are about to lose me here," Abe said. "Where are you going with this?"

"It's very basic, really," she replied. "Look at case history in any given city or area. The jury pool will be composed of fairly like-minded individuals for the society in which they live. What has been the outcome of quality cases reflecting our interests? Determine which venues are favorably disposed to a successful outcome, then determine the probability on a scale of one hundred."

"Sounds to me more like an actuarial table for selling life insurance," Abe said.

"That's exactly what we'll call it," Veronica said excitedly. "The cases will no longer be considered a crap shoot where it's the luck of the throw, or a card game with the luck of the draw. It won't even be handicapping a horse race. It will be an actuarial table of strict probability."

"Do a lot of gambling, do you?" Abe asked. "You certainly know the terms."

"Don't get silly on me here, Sport," she rebuked, "particularly now that we're in the home stretch—here's another one for you. What I'm saying is that if you can go to the big law firms with all the resources and show them that a small case has an eighty or ninety percent chance of winning at the local level and will survive the appeals process all the way up to the Supreme Court, most are likely to want in on the ground floor. It is not only the prestige these firms are looking for, but also the amount of paying business that will result from their efforts. And what do you think would be the impact on some lone and unknown attorney getting a call from a huge, prestigious firm offering to serve as co-counsel? Everyone benefits, not the least being the law itself. And just as important, the issues could get to the Supreme Court in a matter of a few years rather than three decades."

Abe knew how excited and serious Veronica had become when she said she'd rather skip lunch to get home and start her work. On the drive home, she did agree to his suggestion of "fixing them a little something to get them through the day," so he knew she had not entirely lost touch with reality.

Veronica was typing away at the keyboard when Abe brought lunch and iced tea and placed it on her desk. She nodded her thanks and kept typing. When she finally paused to take a bite of the food and a sip of the tea, Abe was sitting at his desk finishing a newspaper.

"My buddy Francis here is developing his own personality," Veronica said to Abe. "I realize it is only some of the little quirks Miguel programmed into the system, but I would swear in court that Francis is taking some pleasure in conveying to the much larger Prometheus what I have in mind. He even signed off his last transmission by asking Prometheus to give his regards to Io and the girls."

"Well, I told you in the beginning that Miguel was somewhat eccentric," Abe replied, "but you have to admit that he's good."

"Very, very good," Veronica acknowledged. "He's Aces in my book—oops, there I go with the gambling metaphors again. My love, I do believe I'm getting a little punchy. I think I'll go take a nap after I eat. I'll check later to see what Francis and Prometheus have managed to agree on."

Veronica's nap turned into a well-deserved five-hour affair. She walked back into the office looking refreshed to find Abe deep into Stewart's Greek Mythology.

"I think age is beginning to catch up to me, my love," she said. "I've pulled all-nighters for years—one of the hazards of becoming an academic—and have never gotten that giddy."

"My dear," Abe replied, "anyone who can go through the hectic pace of the last couple of days and come out looking as ravishing as you do—as you always do—still has a few years before anything will catch up."

"Thank you as always, my dear," Veronica replied. "Bless you and your rose colored glasses. If I may venture just one more metaphor—this one from baseball, not gambling—I recently favored what Satchel Page said about not looking behind you for fear what may be gaining. With you, it's all looking forward."

A blinking red light on her computer told Veronica that Francis had some answers to her inquiry. She transferred to the indicated screen and discovered hundreds of pages of case listings, designated by venue, status, position in the system and any number of other categories before listing a probability percentage column at the far right side. Francis requested she approve the format, which she did. He then indicated she could push the start button and view the probability numbers in real time.

"You have to come see this, Sport," she said to Abe. "Let's launch this big girl and see what she'll do."

"Are you sure it's a girl?" Abe asked. "Francis and Prometheus are both male."

"I'm a girl," she replied. "I specified the program be a she, not a he. Francis liked the idea, just to ruffle the feathers of a certain unnamed computer program at the Dickinson School of Law."

Veronica pushed the start button and they watched the amazing speed with which the probability numbers changed as the cases were analyzed and compared to all the other cases in the system. They both felt this was going to be a complete success.

CHAPTER 21

▼

MAY

The first day of May has been an important date throughout recorded history for a variety of reasons. To farming communities it is a day of hope, marking the faith with which the fields were planted for a bountiful harvest in the months to come. The promise of that faith could be seen everywhere as the first shoots broke from the earth to bask in the sun. It was perhaps fitting that on the first day of May, Private First Class Rebecca "Becky" Trimbel, aged nineteen, was laid to rest beside her brother Sgt. Bradley Trimbel in a small cemetery on the outskirts of Hummelstown, Pennsylvania. At least that was what the presiding minister said when he officiated at the burial. Beloved Becky was being greeted by her brother at the gates of heaven, according to the cleric, where she would repose for eternity, free from pain and suffering. What was not mentioned was the fact that beloved Becky, one more casualty of war, was the last of her line. She filled the last grave in her family plot. There would be no more Trimbels buried there. With no member of her family to receive it, the flag from her coffin was presented to the funeral director. For those left behind, life would go on.

Hope could also be found in the bustling activity on Main Street, where many shops and houses were receiving a new coat of paint. Tables and chairs were placed on the sidewalk in front of restaurants under newly unfurled awnings, porches were swept and plants hung from the rafters and street lamps. There was a renewed confidence evident in the people of the community. It could be seen in the spring of a step or a polite tip of a hat. A friendly people by nature, they seemed particularly friendly this time of the year. Although there was still doubt about the economic effect of the number of jobs being lost in nearby Hershey, there was hope for the future in the new medical research facility being built.

The campus of the Dickinson School of Law seemed almost devoid of human activity as students stayed in their dorms or squirreled away in the library in preparation for the end of the term examinations. In the small offices of the Exchange Center for Constitutional Law, the atmosphere was serene on the surface, but a boiling cauldron underneath as Prometheus processed thousands of communications across the country.

"I think he's being somewhat smug today," Ruby said as Veronica walked into the room. "As you can see from the empty chairs in front of the terminals, our volunteer students are all studying. And there sits Prometheus, humming away as if they were superfluous to the system."

"What little surprises have you discovered today?" Veronica asked. "You know that Miguel has a rather wry sense of humor. When he programmed that system, he included some quirks to keep you on your toes so you wouldn't be bored."

"He keeps me on my toes, alright," Ruby said. "He'll never be accused of not having a healthy ego—I can tell you that much. Did you know that he's telling other computers that it was his idea to create a probability index? That takes a lot of nerve, if you ask me."

"Don't personalize him so," Veronica replied. "Miguel probably put things like that into the program just to get a rise out of you. Think about this rationally. Here you have one inanimate object talking to another inanimate object. Prometheus has a very highly sophisticated system. Most other systems aren't bright enough to understand the nuances of his statements. Now you've got me personalizing computers. Just trust me, Mother, it's harmless."

"You're right, of course," Ruby said. "Prometheus is really a remarkable piece of work. It's the snide asides he throws around once in a while that make him seem so human."

"I stopped by to let you know that I had to fend off the alumni association again," Veronica said with a sigh. "It's the same old story. They'll contribute millions of dollars to expand, amend the original charter to turn this operation into something resembling a big law firm, set enormous fees, then sit back and watch the money roll in."

"I should have flunked that Billy Rantz back in high school," Ruby said. "He always had some scheme up his sleeve. I heard he had a racket going selling term papers, but he never tried that in my class, so I couldn't catch him in the act."

"He wasn't any better when I had him," Veronica volunteered. "He was always looking for ways to bend the constitution for financial gain. Now that he has grown filthy rich in corporate law, he insists on being called William, and he likes to throw his weight around. He likes to think of himself as a great white shark, when he's only a big fat bottom feeder."

Veronica had little patience with the shortsightedness of some people. They may think of her as altruistic in setting up the charter as she had, but they could not see that it was exactly why the plan worked. She did not want a massed bureaucracy sure to break the plan apart. The beauty of the plan was its simplicity: one powerful computer system reaching out to other systems across the country, acting as the central point of exchange. There were no fees involved, although she did accept voluntary contributions. Her goal of keeping the service free was one of the mainstays of the program. If some greedy individual tried to charge for the service, it would kill the program. The information from law firms would come to an abrupt halt.

"Well, my dear," Ruby said, "don't let them bother you. Remember I've always said that most great philosophers go unrecognized in their own time."

"I don't need recognition," Veronica replied. "I just want the freedom to take a good idea and make it better, for the benefit of all."

As a civics teacher, the thought ran through Ruby's mind that many visionaries such as her daughter had ended life being assassinated, but she kept such thoughts to herself.

Now that the media interest in the big narcotics case had moved on with the story, Abe decided it would be a good time to visit Sheriff Tate. As he approached the office he could see an object placed on a pedestal in the front window. On closer examination, he saw it was a Jose, the Bronx Beaver award placed in a glass case.

"He's prouder of that award than any he has received in his life," a deputy manning the front desk said as Abe walked through the door. "And he has certainly gotten his share."

"Good morning, Deputy Simms," Abe said, looking at the woman's nametag. "I would certainly have liked to be here for the presentation."

"It was a real corker," Simms said. "A cute little delegation of twenty children came marching in two-by-two asking to see the sheriff. While I went in the back to get him, the children lined up in three rows, making a semi-circle. The entire staff came over to see the show. The sheriff was touched, seeing all those serious faces performing their practiced rituals of presentation."

"I've heard they're getting pretty good," Abe said. "They've continued adding rituals until it began to resemble a three ring circus. Some older teenagers helped them streamline the process, bringing order out of chaos, as the saying goes."

"They did a fine job of streamlining, I can tell you," Simms replied. "They've gained almost military precision. There was hardly a dry eye in the place when they all took one step back, in unison, and gave a salute. The sheriff accepted the award solemnly on behalf of the department and two little girls presented each member of the staff with a single rose. That was a week ago and you can still feel the boost in morale around here."

"Is the sheriff in right now?" Abe asked. "I'd like to give my regards."

"I'm afraid not," Simms answered. "He has stayed on the road as much as possible to avoid all the media attention. Even though they are now gone, it has become a habit. I'll call him on the radio. I know he wouldn't want to miss your visit."

As Simms made the call, Abe went to the water cooler, depositing the empty cup in the trashcan.

"He'll be here in five," Simms said. "Before he gets here, let me thank you on behalf of the entire department and the departments of the other organizations involved for your plan of operation. You probably saved a lot of lives that night, mine included. The sheriff gave us a full briefing, detail by detail, and the reasoning behind each piece. He used it as an educational tool for our benefit and as an example of not allowing the fact that someone is a civilian, get in the way of taking good advice."

"You're welcome," Abe said. "I was glad to help."

Abe and the sheriff had a full hour of conversation in his office. Tate gave his own version of the award presentation, in detail and with vigor, using hand-gestures to illustrate the high points. He also informed Abe that the federal government was closing in on the senator and that it would be only a matter of days until they were ready to move. The sheriff wanted Abe to know that everyone in town recognized his contributions to the community since his arrival the past July. It was amazing how many lives he had touched in such a short period of time. All that, and he also managed to wed the ideal lady, Veronica.

"That was a blessed gift from God," Abe said. "I won't claim to deserve it, but will humbly accept it without reservation."

"Which leads me to another matter," Tate said quietly. "Abe, you are one of the finest men I've ever had the opportunity to observe. I've never given any thought to Freemasonry until I found out you were a Mason. That made me think of other men in town who are Masons. They are unassuming men from every walk of life and social standing. They all seem to be good men, in word and in deed. And, like you, they live their lives by example. No one has ever tried to recruit me. How do I become a Mason?"

"The simple answer is that we don't recruit," Abe said. "If you want to know more about Freemasonry, there are a few pieces of literature we can give you. Then, if you decide you want to join, all you have to do is ask."

"Well, I'm asking," Tate said with conviction.

"Fine," Abe replied. "Why don't I get a couple of the Fellows from Brownstone to come over and have a talk with you? They can answer any questions you may have and they'll bring a petition for membership, explaining the procedures. You know Tom Chandler and Bud Hanover. I'll ask them to give you a call."

"I'd appreciate that," Tate said, shaking his hand. "I'll look forward to hearing from them."

As Tate was escorting Abe to the front door, another thought occurred to him.

"Those sketches of Jimmy's are proving invaluable," Tate said. "Henry Cunningham was kind enough to bring in the originals so we could make copies for several fire departments and other law enforcement offices, search and rescue, including at the state level."

"I'm sure Jimmy will be glad to hear that," Abe replied. "I'll be sure to tell him."

"They also provided Abe's Squad with a summer job, doing what they like to do and getting paid for the effort," Tate added. "Henry is very familiar with the ground and he pointed out a few things on the sketches I didn't fully understand. With parental permission, we've offered the Squad the job of doing similar surveys of other parts of the area. This could lead to more work over the years because we'll most likely need updates every now and then."

"I'm pleased to hear that the Squad is not only on solid financial grounds, but is turning a profit," Abe said with a laugh. "I bet Henry and Cassy will probably turn this project into a book, too."

"They are way ahead of you already," Tate remarked. "Henry has already filed for the copyright on the original sketches in Jimmy's name and intends to pay him a percentage of the net. The Squad will hold the copyright on any work it does for us."

"And people don't think trackers can have a good mind for business," Abe chuckled as he waved goodbye.

Abe stopped at the Brownstone Lodge to relay Sheriff Tate's request for membership and to tell Tom Chandler what Tate had to say about his admiration for the Masons as good men.

As he drove home, Abe realized that he had been wandering around looking for something to do, trying to decide on a new venture. The Squad was on its feet and running, with a bright future in the offing. John Nagy had the affairs of the Whittier Center well in hand and did not really need his assistance. Veronica had her hands full between teaching and the Exchange Center. He was not interested in even considering any offers for work that would take him away from home.

As he drove into his garage, John Nagy came from his unit with a message from Jimmy Brand. It was a thank you note saying that his spirit was now straight and his heart was whole. He had found his solace through a combination of hard physical work on Amish farms during the day and at night, with meditation and spiritual reflection. His weekends were spent wandering the mountains and getting in touch with the cycles of the earth. He had earned enough money to restock the cabin, make a few minor repairs and made sure everything was neat and clean. The truck needed a new carburetor, but he had taken care of that. With his remaining funds, he had purchased a plane ticket home. He knew Abe would understand.

Since she had no afternoon classes, Veronica came home to have lunch with her husband. Abe had a nice meal prepared when she breezed through the door.

"I have great news, my love," Veronica said excitedly, hardly able to contain herself. "I received a telephone call from Georgetown and a formal contract and proposal will be sent by overnight express. We have to make some decisions very quickly."

The telephone call from Georgetown was exciting. The new task force was to be up and running by the fall semester. They were aware of the phenomenal success of the Exchange Center for Constitutional Law and wanted to know if Veronica could replicate the effort on an international scale. She would have free rein, within certain guidelines, of course and the type of computer system required would make Miguel Swartzbaugh a very wealthy man. Of course, she would have to take a two-year sabbatical from Dickinson, which would be no problem.

"What do you think, my love," she asked, "or am I going too fast?"

"I think, my lovely bride," Abe answered, "that you have saved my life for a second time."

EPILOGUE

▼

Abe was very proud of Veronica's new once-in-a-lifetime opportunity to make another large contribution to her chosen profession. She had no problem whatsoever, of course, in being granted her two-year sabbatical, with fully reserved rights to return. The Dickinson School of Law was gaining prestige in leaps and bounds. The school had been inundated with applications for admittance from some of the best and brightest candidates in the last month—particularly from women. Abe also began to think of this new venture as a sabbatical of his own. The opportunities in Washington D.C. were many. He thought he might indulge his interests in any number of subjects, not the least of which was his curiosity about the history of Freemasonry and the marks it had left on the nation's capital.

Abe had owned a condominium in the Washington area for years, but that was an investment property he rented on a three-year lease. He wanted them to have a new place to live, one they would find together. He could have done the research himself, but the opportunities were so vast that he called a realtor he knew to cull the list to a manageable number.

The cabin in Big Valley had become useful to the Whittier Center, a place where veterans in need could choose to follow the example of Jimmy Brand in any fashion they wished. John Nagy had two volunteer counselors in the valley to visit the cabin on a regular basis and to be on-call. The first new residents were three women with common experiences who were helping each other work out their problems. Abe and Veronica had decided to keep their present home as their weekend getaway.

Miguel Swartzbaugh was delighted with his new challenge in designing a suitable system to meet Veronica's needs. She was not too sure what to make of his promise to leave little surprises in many different languages, but she asked him to please keep them within bounds of propriety.

Veronica began to get the feel of what work in Washington might entail when she began to find resumes in her mail—should she have staffing needs in her new position. She was not surprised that the students graduating from Dickinson would submit their resumes, but she was disconcerted at the number she received from other professors and school staff. She did take some solace in the action of one professor she never particularly cared for. Staying true to form, he stopped by her office and asked if he could have a couple of her bookcases and her coat rack.

The people of the community would be sorry to see them leave, but wished them well, comforted by the fact that they were keeping their home for periodic visits. Jim Stiles, the Iroquois, sent a thank you note to tell Abe and Veronica that he had finally passed his Abe's Squad's unofficial certification test. He said his ancestors would be so proud.

At the annual spring reunion of the Consistory, Scottish Rite Bodies, Valley of Harrisburg, Abe Carlson became a Thirty-second Degree Mason.

978-0-595-69627-7
0-595-69627-9

LaVergne, TN USA
24 March 2010
176959LV00002B/61/A